THE BIG ROCK CANDY MOUNTAIN

THE
BIG ROCK
CANDY
MOUNTAIN
Wallace Stegner

Doubleday & Company, Inc., Garden City, New York, 1973

THE BIG ROCK CANDY MOUNTAIN

I

The train was rocking through wide open country before Elsa was able to put off the misery of leaving and reach out for the freedom and release that were hers now. She tucked her handkerchief away, leaned her shoulder against the dirty pane and watched the telegraph wires dip, and dip, and dip from pole to pole, watched the trees and scattered farms, endless variations of white house, red barn, tufted cornfield, slide smoothly backward. Every mile meant that she was freer.

The car was hot; opened windows along the coach let in an acrid smell of smoke, and as the wind flawed, the trailing plume swept down past her eyes, fogging the trackside. Two men up ahead rose and took off their coats and came back toward the smoker. One of them wore flaming striped suspenders and stared at her. She turned her face to the window. The wires dipped, lifted, dipped, in swift curves like the flight of a swallow. She felt her stomach dipping and lifting with them. The tiny thick locket watch that had been her mother's said eleven o'clock. They must be about thirty miles from home. Except for one visit to relatives in Iowa she had never been so far from home in her life.

By eleven thirty the rocking of the car, the bite of the smoke-smell, had begun to make her sick. Forlornly she tried to brighten herself, sat straighter and stared harder, with a sick simulation of interest, at the country outside. But the wires dipped and lifted; her stomach lifted with every swoop of the wires, and she had to shut her eyes. Her face began to feel stiff, and there was a briny taste in her mouth. She swallowed.

A preliminary spasm made her stand up desperately, her throat locked against the surge of nausea. Staggering, clinging to the seats, she made her way back through the car, looking neither right nor left. There were toilets on trains, she knew, but she had no idea where. At the end of the car, seeing a man come out of a small side door, she made for it. Her hand was on the knob when she read the sign: MEN. Sick shame gripped her. There were separate toilets, then, and she had almost walked into the men's room. The women's must be at the other end. She would have to walk the whole way back past all those people. . . .

A lurch of the car threw her sideways, and her throat muscles locked. In desperate haste she went back between the plush seats, head down, burning with forlorn and miserable shame, the vomit in her very mouth. In the women's room she retched, rose, tidied herself shakily before the smeared mirror, started to go out, and returned to retch again. It was so hot in the little cubicle that perspiration burst through her skin and left her sticky all over. Bathing her face in cold water helped, but then she discovered that there was no towel except a blackened rag. Her handkerchief was back in the seat. All she could do was to wait till her wet face dried.

But the closet was too smothering. Instead of drying, she grew wetter. It was all she could do to stand. In a moment she was on her knees again, her lips wet with bitter gall.

In despair, fearing that at this rate she never would get back to her seat, she washed again and dried her face on the lifted edge of her petticoat. Then back to the middle of the car, past passengers who looked at her, she was sure, with disgust or lurking smiles, until she fell into her seat with a half sob and closed her eyes, feeling defiled and dirty and weak.

People the length of the car were eating. Papers rattled, tin tinkled, and into the stuffy heat came the strong smell of peanut butter. Elsa's stomach rolled, and she gritted her teeth. She was resolving to do a half dozen desperate things rather than go back in that women's room when the train began to slow, the wheels pounded in a gradually lessening tempo, and the conductor poked his head in the door. "Sioux Falls," he said.

Her lunch box under her arm and her telescope in her hand, Elsa followed the crowding passengers out to the step. Her stomach was still queasy, she felt that her face must be green with nausea, and the station platform was strange and busy, but she clinched her mind around the thought of a rest, a stop. On a bench up under the protecting eaves of the station she sat the full hour of the stop-over, letting her stomach gradually settle and her muscles relax. After a long time she opened her shoebox and tentatively nibbled a sandwich. It made her feel better, and she ate another, then a little square of cheese, then a piece of cake. By the time her train was ready she could face the prospect of another three hundred miles.

Afterward she found that the train no longer made her ill. Through the long hot afternoon she sat and watched the immediate trackside flowing straight as a river backward, the horizon revolving in a slow circle. There were few trees now. Somewhere, while she had been sick, they had come to some sort of dividing line. Farms were more scattered, the buildings unpainted, and either ramshackle or staringly new. There were no hills, only a wide bare green-gold plain, pasture and unthrifty-looking cornfields. Once in a while they came to creeks or rivers flowing turgidly in sandy beds between strips of dusty cottonwoods. Mile after mile, hour after hour, past sod shanties with weeds growing green on their roofs, past unpainted shacks and ragged sheds, past windmills and discouraged plantings of saplings, past fields of wheat still meadow-green in the heat, past flocks of crows that flapped heavily off the wires as the train roared by, past herds of nondescript cattle with cowbirds sitting on their hipbones.

The sun went down redly behind a ridge of scattered buttes, throwing into black relief the broken skyline and flushing a low range of hills beyond. Elsa ate from her lunch box, watching the light die and the dark come up out of the ground. When they stopped at a town the elevators loomed high and angular against the darkening sky, and the spout of a watertank outside the window was like the upraised trunk of a huge elephant. A little later, when it was black as a wall outside, the porter came in and lighted the kerosene lamps at the ends of the car. The girl leaned her head against the dark reflecting glass and watched the strange, unknown, lonely country flow past like a banner of darkness starred with tiny ephemeral lights. After a while she slept, and when she woke they were in Fargo.

There was a half hour stop, and she got up to walk on the platform. On her second round through the group of workmen and trucks and strolling passengers, a man lifted his straw hat and smiled, and she stopped in surprise, thinking he must be someone she knew. But he was a total stranger, and the half-bow he made, the uplifted hat, the smirk on his face, put her to flight. She went in and sat down in the station restaurant and ordered a cup of coffee.

After the momentary glad shock of thinking she had met an acquaintance the depression of utter strangeness was on her again, accentuated by the flaring yellow lamps, the tired movements of the waitress, the midnight lackluster actions of the people sitting there, the dusty last-year's calendar on the side wall telling her that it was December 24, 1904. She looked at the smoke-grimed hands and faces of the trainmen eating at the counter, the withered pies and bare hard stools, and through the door at the yellow benches of the waiting room, and the sense of being alone, friendless in a desolate land, rose in her like a sickness, so that she gulped her coffee and went out to the friendlier activity of the platform.

The oppressive darkness crowded in from the far side of the tracks, pushing against the platform lights and the clustered yellow panes of the town. When at last the train started again she sat for a long time staring blankly into the solid black outside, looking past her faintly-mirrored image and thinking of her father and Sarah and home. Her home seemed now very dear, her rebellion childish and petulant; oppressed by her own loneliness, she could understand Sarah's now.

Then she slept again, waking fitfully through an interminable drowsy discomfort until the world outside lightened into color, emerging in flat lines of cloud and horizon and field. At five thirty the conductor came through and shook her, thinking her still asleep. The next stop was Hardanger. She did not remember until she stepped off the train that she had entirely forgotten her uncle's instructions to wire him when she would arrive. And she had forgotten to tip the porter. Hurriedly she felt for her purse and started back, but the train was already moving. The conductor waved from the step and she was alone, with the helpless feeling that everything she had done in getting there had been done wrong.

The country about her was flat as a floor and absolutely treeless. On both sides of the tracks the town sprawled, new, temporary-looking, cut by rutted streets whose borders were a jungle of sweet clover and weeds. Across the roofs of two cottages Elsa could see the square high fronts of stores on what seemed to be the main street. Toward them she started, pulled off balance by the weight of her telescope. As she passed the first cottage a man in his undershirt threw open the door and stood in the sun yawning and stretching and staring at her.

The main street was a river of fine powder between the raised plank sidewalks. On both sides a row of hitching posts stood in vanishing perspective down to the end of the street, which trailed off weakly into open country. As she walked, looking for her uncle's store, Elsa saw with sick certitude that Hardanger was ugly. Frame buildings, false fronts, gaping vacant lots piled with old barrels, boxes, blowing newspapers, ashes. Dust-choked streets and sidewalks that were treacherous to walk on because sometimes the ends of the boards were loose. A general store whose windows were crammed with overalls, pitchforks, gloves, monkey wrenches, spools of barbed wire, guns, boxes of ammunition, ladies' hats. A butcher shop and bakery under the same roof, the windows of both opaque with fly specks. On the first corner a two-story frame hotel, its windows giving her a momentary glimpse of leather chairs and a disconsolate potted palm. A drug store across the street, its sides plastered with advertisements for medicines. Next to that a vacant lot, then a pensioned railroad car set end-to to the street and wearing on its front the legend "Furs bought for cash." Another vacant lot, a store labeled "Gents and Ladies Haberdashery," a billiard hall and bowling alley, and then her uncle's store: "Karl Norgaard, Plain and Fancy Groceries."

But the store was closed. It was only, Elsa discovered by a look at her watch, twenty minutes past six. There was not a soul in the street. She was standing on the sidewalk, clasping and unclasping her fingers to restore the circulation after the weight of the telescope, when a young man came out of the pool hall. He was tall, slim, but heavy in the shoulders. His black hair was parted in the middle and pomaded flat over a forehead dark as an Indian's from the sun. His sleeves were rolled up to expose powerful arms, thick in the wrists and roundly muscled.

"Hello!" he said, staring at her. Elsa flushed. The man had a merry and speculative glint in his eye; his stare bothered her as the smirk of the man at the station in Fargo had.

"You looking for somebody?"

Elsa stooped and picked up the telescope, some notion in her mind that that showed she was leaving in a minute. "I was looking for my uncle, Mr. Norgaard. You don't know where he lives, do you?"

"Sure. Just down around the next corner. You can see it from here." He came toward her with a slightly lurching stride, his shoulders swinging, and pointed to a gray frame house on the first cross street.

"Thank you," Elsa said, and started away.

He followed her. "You his niece? I could tell, though, by that hair."

Her hot, suspicious look made him laugh. "No need to get mad. We all been expecting you."

"I was supposed to wire him," she said. "He didn't know when. . . . Well, thank you for . . ."

"Can I lug that satchel for you?" He kept pace with her, watching her, talking with a hidden burble of laughter in his voice.

"No thanks. I can carry it."

She hurried faster, and he stopped, but all the way to her uncle's house she could feel him watching her, and her mind's eye could see him standing in his shirt sleeves on the sidewalk with the sun on his dark face. It irritated her. There was something fresh about him.

Karl Norgaard was not yet dressed when she knocked. After a moment his red head appeared in an upstairs window.

"Hello, Elsa! I thought you were going to wire me."

She tilted back her head to smile at him, feeling suddenly very tired and hungry and soiled. "I forgot, Uncle Karl. Can I come in anyway?"

"You bet you," he said. "Be down in a minute."

In a minute the door opened and he was grinning at her, his pink round face so full of welcome that she found herself laughing weakly aloud. *"Velkommen!"* he said. *"Velkommen,* Elsa."

Elsa unwound her scarf from her hat and said, "Thanks, Uncle Karl. It's nice to be here at last."

"You came in a hurry," Karl said. He stood in his felt pantofles and regarded her with shrewd eyes. "How's everybody at home?"

"Fine. Everybody's fine. But I had to come in a hurry, Uncle Karl. I couldn't stay there a minute longer."

Karl rubbed one apple cheek. "Well, you're young. *Herregud,* the fool things you do when you're young." He grabbed her by the arm. "Well, come in, come in. Come on upstairs. Want to wash your face? Take a bath? There's a tub in the cellarway. I'll heat some water."

"Let me get my breath first," she said. "Can I put this bag somewhere?"

He showed her her room, led her into the other two upstairs rooms, one his own bedroom, one his office. "You might as well learn right away to leave the office alone," he said. "I can't find anything as it is."

"How about your bedroom? Can you sleep if I take off those dirty old sheets and put some clean ones on?"

"It was changed two weeks ago," Karl said. "That's pretty good for an old batch." He frowned. "Maybe I made a mistake letting you come. You get so neat a man can't stand you and I'll send you home."

"I'll be good," she said. "I'll be as sloppy as you want, but don't send me home." She took off her hat and lifted her hair with her fingers to ease its weight. "You go get a fire going and I'll get your breakfast."

After breakfast he went off to the store. In spite of his instructions to go to bed, she tidied up, swept, changed the beds and laid out a washing for the next day, cleaned up the sardine cans and cracker boxes and cheese rinds from the kitchen. The curtains, she decided, had not been washed since the flood, and took them down to add them to the washing. Then she went up to her room and unpacked. By the time she had things put away, the telescope stuck into the attic, and the daguerreotype of her mother set up on the dresser, she began to feel settled and permanent. The mere fact of working in this house made it her own, her clothes hanging in the wardrobe gave her proprietorship.

But when she sat on the bed and looked at the dark, thin-faced woman who had been her mother, she felt herself go slowly, weakly sick with the old anger. Staring at the picture, rubbing her knuckles back and forth across her lips and teeth, she thought how her mother too had run away from home, younger than Elsa herself, no more than seventeen, and after three days let her parents know that she had married the carpenter on their place at Voss, in Norway. She risked everything for him, and got only him: he was below her, they never took her back. Within six months she was on her way to America, where for a life she had the backbreaking work of a Minnesota farm—she who had never been used to working at all. It was a short life; Elsa was fifteen when her mother died worn out at thirty-four, and it was Elsa who took up the work her mother had let go. She had father, sister, brother, to take care of; the school she had dropped out of at fourteen to nurse her mother saw her no more. And then less than three years after that lingering death they had all had to watch too closely, Nels Norgaard announced he . . .

Elsa shut her eyes down hard on the smart of tears. It isn't only that Sarah is twenty years younger than he is, she said silently to the empty, strange room. It's that she was supposed to be my best friend.

Counting up what she had left behind her forever, she saw them all as if their faces were propped on the dresser beside her mother's daguerreotype: her father's stern long-cheeked face slashed across by the guardsman's mustache, his eyes merely veiled, unreadable; Sarah in the posture she had been reduced to by Elsa's anger and scorn— stooped over, weeping, with a slack mouth and flooded gray eyes that said pity me, pity me; Erling's corkscrew red curls and red farm-boy's face emerging from the blackened towel by the kitchen cistern pump; Kristin's awed, aghast, pretty face in the bedroom when she found Elsa packing, the affected pompadour and the vain ribbons, and the whispering voice full of love, kinder than spoiled little sister had ever sounded: "Won't you take that hat I made last week? You could wear it on the train. It'd look lovely with your hair—it's green,"—and then the tempest of tears.

She knew already that she would miss them more than she had ever thought possible; she ached for them this minute, she could even have been respectful to her father and pleasant to Sarah. Maybe . . . and yet what else could she have done?

From the dresser the daguerreotype looked back at her calmly, the lips compressed. It was not a good likeness, and like all pictures of the dead it had petrified the memory of the living, so that every recollection Elsa had of her mother was now limited by this stern and pinched expression. Her mother had been ill when the picture was taken. Perhaps for that reason, perhaps because of the narrowing of memory to fit the one picture she had, Elsa had always felt the daguerreotype to be a portrait of martyrdom.

"*Mor*," she said in Norwegian, groping for some contact or reassurance. "Mom . . ."

Out the window she saw a summer whirlwind spinning across the level fields beyond the flanks of the town. The funnel of dust lifted, dropped again, whirled forward across a road, stopped and spun, moved off in jerky rushes like a top spinning on an irregular surface. It hit a mound of dumped refuse, and tin cans rolled, papers sailed flatly, slid back groundward. Beyond the whirlwind was the prairie running smoothly, the planed horizon broken by two far homesteads, ships on the calm green-bronze sea; and far beyond, the glitter from the moving blades of a windmill.

It was very big; she felt she could see a long way, even into the future, and she felt how the world rolled under her. After she had watched the summer plains for a long time, and the smarting under her lids had passed, a meadowlark sang sharp and pure from a fencepost, and she began to think that the future into which this new world of her choosing moved with her could hardly be unfriendly, could hardly be anything but good.

2

"Elsa," Karl Norgaard said, "how'd you like to go to a ballgame?"

He was sitting at the kitchen table opening a jar of *gamelost* with a screwdriver. Elsa turned from the stove.

"Are you going?"

"They couldn't play without me," Karl said. "I've closed the store for every ballgame in fifteen years."

"Sure," she said. "I'd love to."

He bore down with the screwdriver, prying at the lid. The blade slipped, and he leaped up with a startled howl. *"Fand slyta!"* he said. He shook his fingers, and the blood welling from his gouged palm spattered on the floor. *"Heste lort!"* Karl said, almost jumping up and down. For a full minute he swore savagely in Norwegian, looked at Elsa, bent his lips into a baffled, half-humorous smirk, and looked back at his hand.

She came running with the iodine bottle and soused the wound. Karl swore again. "Shame on you," she said.

"Well, hell," Karl said. He looked at the deep gouge in his palm and shook his head incredulously. "You haven't got any business knowing what I said," he said. "That's the trouble, having a Norske girl around."

Elsa giggled. "Anyway you sounded good and mad," she said. "Norwegian swearing sounds ten times worse than English, somehow. It's just like ripping canvas."

"I guess you'd swear too," he said. "Dug my whole damn hand out."

"If there was any of that smelly old cheese on the screwdriver you'll be infected sure," Elsa said. She tore a strip off a clean cloth and started bandaging.

"You mean you don't like *gamelost?*"

Elsa made a face. "Erling put some on my knife once, just stuck the knife in the jar and then laid it beside my plate, and I was sick for two hours."

"You're a traitor," Karl said. "You don't like *ludefisk* either."

"No, nor herrings."

He shook his pink head over her. "But you like ballgames?"

"Ballgames are all right."

"Vell, you batter like dem," Karl said. "You yoost batter like dem."

He went out to the store muttering, shouting back that she yoost batter be raddy at two o'clock, or a little before, and she saw him stomping through the sweet clover crosslots to the store, holding his gouged hand tenderly against his stomach.

It was a blistering day. The ground, when they walked out at two o'clock, was dry and baked, with cracks splitting through the yellow grass of the yard. What had once been a mud puddle in the road was caked into a hundred cupped plates laid together like a Chinese puzzle. Elsa picked one up; it took all the strength of her fingers to break it. Around them the sweet clover, just drying into clusters of seeds, was bone-stiff and dusty. West of the town three whirlwinds raced and dipped and lifted over the flats.

They walked past the two grain elevators, across the cindery, fire-bitten tracks. On the other side a tier of crude seats was already well filled. Buggies lined the edge of the field, crowded with women under big parasols of fringed canvas faded from the fierce sun. There was a persistent flash of paper fans. A booth wound with red, white, and blue bunting was doing a land-office business in lemonade and pop and ice cream. There were bottles and papers littered along the weedy edge of the diamond.

Standing below the plank seats, Elsa felt people's eyes on her. Men spoke to Karl, and he grinned, squinting up into the sun, saying, "Hello Gus, hello George, hello. Ought to be a hot game."

"We got it on ice," somebody said, and there was a laugh.

Feeling conspicuous, Elsa stood silently under her big hat while her uncle picked out a place in the stands. Then someone was calling from a buggy over on the first base line: "Come on over here. You'll melt down to grease in that stand."

"Ah," Karl said. "There's Helm. That'll be better."

The woman who had called beckoned. Elsa saw a broad, dark face, a wide hat, a shapeless body in a loud, intolerably hot-looking dress, a cluster of children. Then they were at the wheel of the buggy, and Karl was saying, "This is Helm, Elsa. Never call her Mrs. Helm or she'll burst a blood vessel."

Grinning with bad teeth, Helm stuck down a broad hand, her dark eyes running over every detail of the girl's hair, dress, face. At the first clutch of her hand Elsa thought her knuckles would crumble. She flushed, grew angry, and squeezed back with all her strength until she felt her knuckles slip back into line and the broad palm in hers begin to give. For an instant more they gripped each other, until Helm opened eyes and mouth in astonishment.

"My God!" she said loudly. "You're strong as a horse. Where'd you get it?"

"Milking cows," Elsa said sweetly. Give me another chance and I'll squeeze your fingernails off, she thought. She wished Karl hadn't brought her over here.

"Come on up," Helm said. She stuck down her hand again, and in one mighty heave hauled the girl up beside her, where she inspected her again, closely, with brown shining eyes.

"You ain't so light, either. How much do you weigh?"

"I don't know. A hundred and thirty or thirty-five."

"I got you by a hundred pounds, honey," Helm said. She rumbled with laughter, and her thick fingers pinched experimentally at Elsa's arm. "You don't dint easy, either. First off, I had you pegged for one of these *ladies* with fainting spells and weak chests."

Jammed uncomfortably close to Helm's radiating bulk, Elsa looked around into the box of the democrat, at the clot of children there. Helm caught her looking. "Ain't that a brood for you? They all look like their granpa. He was a Sioux Indian."

"Are you?" Elsa said.

"Half," Helm said. "The best half, if there's any choice." She picked at a tooth with her fingernail, her eyes warm behind the broad hand. "Their old man was a good-for-nothing," she said. "After he got all these he run off and left me with a shape like a bale-a hay. Good riddance to bad rubbish." She got whatever she was digging for and took her hand away. "You like baseball?"

"Very much," Elsa said stiffly. She didn't know what to make of this great vulgar woman, but Karl, sprawling on the grass beside the buggy, must have thought she was all right or he wouldn't have come to sit with her.

"This ought-a be a good game," Helm said. "We got a team, last few years. Got a catcher used to play in the Three-Eye League."

"Oh?"

"You watch him. He's a one. Bo Mason's his name."

"He runs the bowling alley next to my store," Karl said. "If he didn't have a trick knee he'd be in the big leagues."

"Oh!" Elsa said. "I think I met him the morning I came. Is he dark, sort of slim—looks slimmer than he really is?"

"That's him," Helm said. "Parts his hair in the middle and a hide like shoe leather."

A minute later she pointed. "In the blue shirt," she said. Elsa looked, and saw the young man of that first morning. As he said something to a companion his teeth were very white in his almost negroid face. She wondered how he got so dark running a bowling alley. That would keep him inside, out of the sun, she would think. And she didn't know whether she liked his looks or not. There was a kind of rolling swagger in his walk, and as the home team pegged the ball around the infield he kept making bright remarks. A little of the smart alec in him.

But he was as good as they said he was. In the very first inning he caught an Oasis man trying to steal second, caught him by three feet with a perfect ankle-high peg. After that the opposing baserunners took short leads and went down only with the crack of the bat. When he came up to bat the first time, Mason was out on a screaming grass-cutter that the first baseman tried in vain to get out of the way of, but in the fifth he drove in two runs with a thunderous triple that chased the centerfielder far back in the wild mustard. Helm, pounding Elsa on the back, announced three times that it would have been a homer sure except for that trick knee.

In the seventh inning the score was tied, eight to eight. The first two Oasis hitters were easy outs. The next one was a slugger. The stocky youngster on the mound took his time, mopping his neck with a bandanna between pitches. Squatting on his hams behind the plate, Bo Mason talked it up. Easy out, easy out! Give him the old dark one.

The pitcher wound up and threw. Strike! The hitter swung so hard he had to put the end of his bat down to keep from falling. "You need a little oil on your hinges, son," Mason told him, and the

stands hooted. Next pitch, ball. Next one, ball again. Mason's soothing voice went out over the infield. "All right, boy. Can't hit what he
can't see. Right down the old alley. Let him swing like a shutter in a
cyclone. Feed it to him, he's got a glass eye."

The next pitch was grooved, and the Oasis slugger rode it deep into
left field. The fielder lost it in the sun, and the runner went down to
second, his feet pumping quick explosions in the dust. A strained
look showed him the fielder still chasing the rolling ball, and he
legged it for third, where the players on the sidelines waved him
frantically home.

Mason, his teeth showing in his dark face, waited spraddle-legged
in front of home plate. The relay from the short stop reached him
two steps ahead of the runner, who swerved, skidded, and scrambled
back for third. He was in the box. The crowd was on its feet, yelling,
as Mason chased him carefully back, holding the throw. He faked,
then threw, and the runner reversed and tore for home again. But
the ball was there before him, and the catcher blocked the baseline.
The Oasis man put his head down and butted through under Mason's
ribs, and Mason, as he was plowed out of the path, lifted the ball and
tagged him, hard, on the top of his bare head.

The sound of ball on skull cracked in the heat, and the grandstand
let go a long, shivering "Ahhhhhhhhhh!" This might mean a fight.
They stood higher in the stands, eyes joyful and faces expectant.
"Atta boy, Bo!" they said. "Atsy old way to slow him down!"

Karl Norgaard was standing by the buggy wheel, his pinkish hair
damp. He was concentrating on the figure of the Oasis man, slowly
pushing himself up from the dust with his flat palms. Karl's voice
rose with him in the expectant hush, thin, tremulous, singsong:
"Batter we gat a doctor. Ay tank he ban sunstruck."

The stands exploded in mirth that rode the thick hot air and
echoed off the elevators. The Oasis man scowled, looking at Mason,
standing just off the baseline with the ball in his hand. Contemptuously Mason pulled off his mitt and turned his back, walking over
to the Hardanger bench. With his head down the Oasis man
started after him, pursued by the hoots of the spectators, who began
to jump down from the lower tiers to get in on the scrap. But other
Oasis players grabbed their fellow's elbows and held him while he
stood in the clover, fists balled, swearing. Then abruptly he jerked
himself loose and ran back into centerfield, and the crowd settled
back.

After that there wasn't much to the game. Hardanger batted around in the eighth; the final score was sixteen to nine. After the game Helm yelled until Bo Mason came over, and as he stood talking at the buggy wheel Elsa forgot her dislike for his smart alec streak. He was the best player there, there was no question. But his grin embarrassed her when they were introduced, and she sat back in the hot sweaty alley between Helm and the rail and let the others talk.

"What were you trying to do, kill that guy?" Karl said.

Mason laughed. "He ran me down, didn't he? He wants to play rough I can play rough too."

"I bet he can't get his hat on for a week," Helm said. "How about some beer? You look hot, Bo."

"You could fry eggs on me," Mason said. "Sure. Over at your place?"

Elsa, sitting uncertainly beside Helm, caught her uncle's grin. "You want to come along, Elsa?"

The girl flushed and laughed. "I don't drink beer," she said, and was furious at how squeaky her voice sounded. They laughed at her, and Helm patted her on the back with a hand like a leg of lamb. "You don't have to, honey," she said. "We c'n take care of that."

3

In the hot morning hush Elsa walked down the plank sidewalk toward her uncle's store. There wasn't enough housework to keep her busy more than a few hours a day, even on Mondays, when she washed, and Saturdays, when she baked. It was a problem to know what to do with her time. Unlike her father, Karl did not have many books around, and though he had given her money to subscribe to the *Ladies' Home Journal*, the first number hadn't come yet.

She could have called on Helm, but the prospect was still a little terrifying. As she thought over that afternoon with the beer drinkers she felt a little weak. They had all got a little tipsy, they had laughed uproariously, they had told jokes that she knew weren't quite clean, and she had just pretended not to hear. Before long, if she didn't watch out, she wouldn't know what was respectable and what wasn't. Fiddlesticks, she said. What was wrong about it? But she didn't quite dare call on Helm.

In the window of the hotel she caught sight of her reflection, and was pleased. The white dress, perfectly ironed, not yet wilted by the heat; the red hair puffed like a crown in front; the round, erect figure, slim in the waist, full breasted. When she walked past three young men lounging on the sidewalk she stepped self-consciously. Feeling their eyes on her, she hurried a little in spite of herself. She was ten steps past when she heard the low whistle and the voice: "Oh you kid!"

She remembered the time she had bloodied George Moe's nose for him when he got smart about her hair. Men were just the same. They'd say smart alec things and if you turned on them, even if you bloodied their noses, they'd laugh even more. But she would have liked to say something sharp to that loafer. Oh you kid! The smart alecs.

But anyway, the next window told her, she looked nice, cool as a cloud.

In front of her uncle's store she almost ran into Bo Mason, bare-headed, his pomaded hair sleek as a blackbird's breast. As he looked at her his eyes were sleepy, the full upper lids making them narrower than they really were. His voice was slow and warm. "Hel-loooo!"

"Hello."

"Going somewhere?"

"No. Just looking around."

"Seeing the city?" He lifted his head to laugh, and she saw the corded strength of his neck. He pointed down the street to the weed-grown flats dwindling off into dump ground and summer fallow. "You must take a stroll in the park," he said. "Five thousand acres of cool greenery. This is one of the show towns of Dakota. Prosperous! Did you see that magnificent hotel on the corner as you came by? Gilded luxury, every chamber in it, the fulfilled dream of one of Hardanger's most public-spirited citizens."

Elsa was a little astonished. She said demurely, "Very imposing. Bath in every room?"

"Some rooms two, so a man and his wife can both be clean same time."

"Must take a lot of water."

"Oh, they've got water to burn. Gigantic well just outside, clean pure alkali water, no more than seven dead cats in it at any time."

"You don't sound as if you liked the hotel much."

"I love it," he said. "I love it so much I live there. I love this whole town. Just the spot for an ambitious young man to make his fortune."

Curiosity uncoiled itself and stretched. She took a peek at the swinging doors behind him. Maybe he wasn't doing so well in his place. Bowling alley, was it? All she could see was a dark stretch of bar and two dim yellow lamps in wall brackets. Into the bright hot sunlight came the jaded click of pool balls.

"What're you doing, really?" Bo said.

"Nothing. I thought I might help Uncle Karl in the store."

"Let's go have a soda."

Elsa hesitated, her eyes on the darkly polished bar inside. It looked almost like a saloon, but she knew saloons were prohibited in North Dakota. Her curiosity rose on tiptoe, peering. "Why, that'd be nice," she said.

Instead of turning into his own place, he took her arm and led her down to the corner. "Why can't we have it in your place?" she said. "Then you wouldn't have to pay for it."

His look was amused. "You want to go in my place?"

"Why not?"

"Naw," he said, and moved her along. "My place is a billiard hell. It's a man's joint. You'd scare away my two customers."

"But you sell drinks, though, soft drinks?"

"Soft enough. But Joe down here makes better sodas."

She wondered if he might be running an illegal saloon. That ought, according to what the Reverend Jacobsen had always said, to make him one of the undesirable element. Looking at him again, curiously, she saw only that he looked clean, brown, athletic. She didn't ever recall seeing a man who looked so clean. Either the respectability she had been brought up in was narrow, or Bo Mason wasn't one of the bad element. But he drank beer, and told stories that weren't always quite nice. But so did her uncle, and he was respectable. And so did Helm, and Helm was a woman.

Sitting at the sticky marble slab of counter sipping sodas, they laughed a great deal and gurgled through the newfangled straws. By the time she had left him to go home she had decided that he couldn't possibly be one of the bad element, in spite of his billiard hell. The bad element were distinguishable by their evil faces, their foul mouths, their desire to trample everything decent and clean underfoot. Bo Mason wasn't anything like that. He was cleaner than anything. Even while he stood on the sidewalk just before she left he was trimming his nails with his pocket knife. She noticed too how cleanly the blade cut the thick soft nail, and she was enough a farm girl to respect a man who kept his tools sharp. Moreover, he had been all over, worked at a dozen different things, talked easily about Chicago and Milwaukee and Minneapolis, the places that had been golden towers on her horizons for eighteen years.

The thought of what her father might say if he knew she had had a soda with a man who ran a poolhall made her almost laugh aloud. Even if he ran an undercover saloon, blind pigs they called them, it didn't make any difference. She was a grown woman, and could have sodas with anyone she chose. If she found a saloon-keeper who was clean, and interesting, and pleasant, she would have a soda with him any time she pleased. The sidewalk ended and she jolted herself stepping unexpectedly down.

As she passed Helm's yard she heard the racket, the shrill, snapping snarl of a dog, Helm's voice swearing, the sudden yipe of a mongrel hurt. "Now, God damn it, will you lay still?" she heard Helm say. The dog yiped again, and as Elsa stopped at the gate its voice went up in a high wail.

She must be killing it, Elsa thought. She found herself at the side of the house, looked around the corner. In the corner of the fence Helm was kneeling. Her wide stern loomed like the gable of a barn. Then she rose, grabbed a handful of dry grass, stood back. The moment the pressure was off him the dog tucked his tail and hiked. Helm, starting back toward the kitchen, saw Elsa and scowled, red-faced. "Those sonabitching kids!" she said.

The Reverend Jacobsen, Elsa's mind said, would have told anyone to walk away from language like that. But she stayed where she was. "What was the matter?" she said.

"They're allus doing something like that," Helm said. "Tying cans to dogs' tails, or tying cats' tails together and throwing them over a clothesline, or catching frogs and blowing them so full of air they can't swim. I catch any of them I'll lay into 'em, I don't care who they are."

"What did they do?" Elsa said.

"First time I ever see this one," Helm said. "It's a dirty damn trick, even on a cur dog. They fed this mutt a ball of string, wrapped up in meat or something, I guess, and before he knows it he's trailing yards of it out behind, and ever'body stepping on it fit to pull his guts out. Ain't that a dirty trick, now?"

Elsa tried to keep her eyes up. She felt the slow red coming into her face. She ought to have gone right on by, then she wouldn't have got trapped like this. Helm, watching her with shining eyes, began to smile.

"Why honey, I believe that shocked you!"

"I . . . think it's an awful dirty trick," Elsa said.

"I forgot you was a lady," Helm said. "I didn't aim to shock you. First minute I talked to you I knew you was a lady, a natural-born lady, not one of these dames with studhorse airs. I wouldn't want to shock you any time. But I couldn't let that hound run around that way, could I?"

"No," Elsa said. "I think . . . you're very kind . . ." She escaped, feeling almost as if she were going to cry, because Helm was kind, that was a kindhearted thing to do, and all the bad language and vulgarity that went with it couldn't make it any less kind. She went about getting lunch feeling as if a bed were unmade in her mind.

Not all the people she met were as hard to assimilate as Helm and Bo Mason. Most of them she met at Helm's house, and most of them were commonplace enough. Gus Sprague, a little bandy-legged carpenter, was ordinary and pleasant; so was his wife, as little and henlike and bandy-legged as Gus. And the elevator man, Bill Conzett, was nice too. Bill's belt cut so low under his pendant stomach that small boys were always following him around waiting for his pants to fall off. There was a little group of Norwegians who sometimes came around, but they stuck together and were more pious than the rest, a little more like Indian Falls. Karl was the only Norske who seemed to have left the old country completely behind.

None of those people was disturbingly new. But Jud Chain and Eva Alsop were.

Jud Chain was a professional gambler and Bo Mason's partner. Knowing that before she met him, Elsa expected almost anything— a sinister, pale, diabolic creature with burning night-time eyes was what her anticipation finally resolved itself into. But the man she met one afternoon in Helm's cluttered parlor was a handsome blond giant, six feet three or four inches tall, abnormally wide in the shoulders. The only part of him that matched her imaginings was his pallor, and even that was not the evil midnight thing she had expected. She shook his hand in confusion, this beautifully groomed, sleek, white-handed gentleman. His smile was friendly, his eyes gentle, his manners impeccable. When he moved around bringing her a cup of coffee or pulling up a chair so that they could talk more comfortably, he moved with easy grace, and when he bent over to listen to something she was saying she smelled the bay rum on his pocket handkerchief.

He was, like Bo Mason, fascinating in a way no man in her life had ever been fascinating before. He had travelled around even more than Bo, even to Cuba and South America. He said he had been working with Bo for three years now, and when she said she hadn't seen him around town his eyes smiled. His work, he explained, kept him up all night sometimes. He was generally asleep in the daytime.

So there he was, her amazed mind said. A card sharp, another, like Bo, from the class of people all the good people of Indian Falls would consider outside the pale. Yet he was handsome, almost as imposing physically as Bo, though more willowy and fragile-looking in spite of his wide shoulders. His hands were immense, flat, slabby, with wide palms and long fingers, the nails trimmed round. She could imagine how deftly he could handle cards. A gambler, a sharper, yet more gentlemanly, deferential, polite, than anybody she had ever met. She spilled coffee on her dress at the thought of herself sitting next to this dangerous man and talking as if she had known him forever. Instantly the bay rum scented handkerchief was out, his languid ease galvanized into careful helpfulness. If she had spilled anything at home, among the men she knew, they would have stared at her with their hands on their knees and done nothing. Jud Chain could make any woman think she was both fragile and charming.

A few days later she met Eva Alsop, and that was another sort of experience. Small, doll-like, blonde, she looked the part of the Bad Woman. Her laugh was too loud, and when she was serious her mouth had a weary and petulant droop. Once in a while she placed her hand on her side, and if anyone caught her doing it she looked up with a wan, brave smile.

To her Jud Chain was as deferential as he was to Elsa, but even Elsa's inexperience detected a difference, a certain familiarity, a subtle knowingness in the way Eva looked at him, and when Jud rose to go that afternoon, saying he had business to attend to, Elsa saw the wizened petulance on Eva's mouth—a very red mouth, redder than she had ever seen a mouth before. Jud bent elegantly over her, said something the others could not hear, but Eva's eyes, as she watched him take his hat and leave, were cold.

Helm talked about her afterward. Eva Milksop, she called her. "She's a little snivelling cheap slut," Helm said. "Common as manure, making out she's the grandest lady you ever seen. Paints her face and bleaches her hair and dolls herself up like Mrs. Astor's plush horse. She makes my belly ache, her and her pains."

"Well, maybe she is sick," Elsa said.

"How would you act if you had a pain?" Helm said. "Would you go around whining and holding your belly and making ever'body feel like a sonofabitch if he didn't run right out for the hot water bottle?"

"I guess . . ."

"You damn betcha you wouldn't. You'd try to grin if you had the God-awfulest belly ache in the world. You're two different kinds of people, honey. Don't go wasting sympathy on that canary-legged little slut."

"There must be some good in her," Elsa said. "Anybody's got some good in him."

"There's about as much good in her as there is in my backside," Helm said. "And that's mainly lard. You see her shrivel up and get mean when Jud had to go?"

"Yes. I wondered."

"I wouldn't bother even to wonder, honey," Helm said. "She ain't worth it."

"Is she in love with him?"

Stacking the coffee cups, Helm made a prissy face. "If she ever decides to hook up with Jud she'll decide it when Jud makes a killing. She ain't going into no nest without a lot of feathers in it."

"Well," Elsa said. "Live and learn. I never knew there were so many kinds of people."

Helm stood with her legs planted, as if she were going to give a lecture. She was. "If you're the right kind yourself, you'll find the right kind," she said. "There's not many people'll do anything for you but kick you when you're down. I aim to save my kicks for the butter-butts and give anybody that's down a hand instead of a foot."

"Maybe Eva's down."

"She's one of the butter-butts," Helm said. "I like the kind of people that don't play they're something they ain't. I'm a sucker, honey. Don't try to learn anything from me. A fella that's down on his luck, or some simple guy that the world is kicking around, or somebody that's straight-out what he is so I don't have to keep jumping around to know what I'm dealing with, those are my kind of folks. Every hobo that ever hit this town was on my back step in half an hour." She snorted, folding freshly ironed clothes into a basket. "Jus' a softy!" she said.

She looked up under her eyebrows, still stooping. "You lonesome for home, honey?"

"Sometimes," Elsa said. "I miss the kids. They were a pest when I had to take care of them, but I miss them just the same. I miss Pa too, I guess, only he's married again, and everything."

"Married a girl a lot younger, didn't he?"

"My best friend," Elsa said. She couldn't even yet mention that without being angry and hurt.

"Yeah," Helm said. "It's funny. When you're a kid something like that can smell like a carcass, and after you get older it don't seem so bad. You liked your ma a lot, didn't you?"

"I took care of her a long time," Elsa said. "That was what made me so mad. I don't think he ever went to her grave, even. I went just before I left and it was all overgrown with weeds, right when he was going around with Sarah."

Helm sighed wheezily, stuck a thumb down inside the chafing edge of her corset and wriggled a fold of skin into place. "You're all right, honey," she said. "You stick by the things you love. Nobody can hurt you if you stick with what you know is right. They can't hurt what's inside you."

4

"That Bo Mason gets away with murder," Elsa said. "Why don't people tell him where to head in at?"

"Oh, that's just Bo," Karl said. "If it was anybody else you'd knock his head off."

"That doesn't excuse him," she said. "He was just plain mean to Eva."

"I guess Eva sort of has it coming," he said, and steered his way up the stairs to bed.

Elsa tidied up the downstairs, thinking of the way Bo had acted. The way he'd said to Eva, "For God's sake come down off your high horse and quit acting like the Duchess of Dakota. Can't you walk without looking like Dan Patch in hobbles?" The way he caught up everything anyone said all evening and turned it back, with a sting in it. The way he had sat, while Helm and Eva and Karl and Jud were playing whist, and bullied her for an hour and a half because she didn't even know how to play casino. How would she know how to play casino, when her father had never even allowed a deck of cards in the house?

She had seen him that way once before, over at Helm's, and she suspected that he was mad about the way his bowling alley was doing. Sometimes he seemed restless and dissatisfied. When he got to thinking about that too long, she supposed, it brought on one of these black and contrary moods. Or maybe it might have been only something someone had said, something he took it into his head to be mad about. He was as vain as a boastful little boy. But that didn't excuse his going through a whole evening the way he had, smiling as if he had a knife ready to stab somebody, jumping from bald insults to compliments as suave as butter that were more insulting than the insults.

He was a hard man to understand, she thought as she went upstairs with the lamp. You never knew how you'd find him. But why should she worry herself about the way he acted? Let him go on being moody and sardonic and insulting.

Yet she found herself, later, asking people about him—Karl, Helm, even Jud Chain. How could a man be so many contrary things at once? How, for instance, could anyone have grown up and never even been inside a church? He said he hadn't. Yet in a good mood he could be so very pleasant and thoughtful. There was a kind of warmth that radiated from him when he wanted to let it. And how had he come to be so good at everything he did? He was the best ball player in town. Helm assured her that he was also the best shot, the best bowler, the best pool player, and one of the two best skaters.

"But where did he come from?" Elsa asked. "What's he doing out here?"

"He's from Illinois," Helm said. "Rock River. His old man wasn't much good, I guess. Just let his family run loose. I've heard him talk about it once or twice, just odds and ends of things."

That was all Elsa got, odds and ends, scraps that could be pieced together into a skeleton biography. She did not admit to herself, did not even think about, the unusual eagerness she had to reconstruct that biography. She did not say to herself that he was the most masterful, dominating, contradictory, and unusual man she had ever met, but she picked up everything she heard, nevertheless, and she pumped Bo himself when he came over in the evening to sit on the steps and talk.

When Fred Mason came home to Illinois from the war in 1865, he had left an arm somewhere in a field hospital near Vicksburg, and most of his disposition in the Andersonville prison. In the ten years after his arrival he successively married a Pennsylvania Dutch girl of broad dimensions, begot seven children, and became the nucleus and chief yarn-spinner of the livery stable crowd.

For money he depended on his pension and a few scattered odd jobs. Working for anyone else tired him; orders were more than his irascible individualism would stand. "Nobody in my family ever took orders from anybody," he used to say. "My pap come into this state when she was nothin' but oak and Indians, and he never took no orders from any man. Neither did his pap, or his pap's pap. I'm the on'y one ever did, and I on'y did in the army. And I don't take no more."

He spent his days lounging at the stable talking bird dogs and battles. Once in a while he took over a job in a burst of ambition to augment his pension, because, though he was not especially a drinking man, he loved to eat, and his shapeless and rather sullen hausfrau couldn't make the pension stretch to cover much more than sowbelly and eggs. Often, too, he sat in the sun with the fecund stable smell about him and a coach dog dozing among the flies, and generated great schemes. He invented, on paper or in drawings sketched in the dust with a twig, all sorts of gadgets: revolvers with twelve chambers, a telescopic ramrod that could be carried in the vest pocket, a folding bootjack, an artificial arm that could be moved by a complicated system of wires and pulleys, with a minia-ture ice tongs for a hand. He even went to work and whittled out the arm, laboriously fitted it with pulleys and strung the wires, but when he had a fellow-loafer strap it on him, and tried it out before the eyes of his crowd, he got tangled up and bit himself in the ribs with the ice tongs. In a fury he threw the whole contraption in the Rock River.

His six boys and one girl grew up untended in the shambling old frame house his wife had brought him as dowry. The children learned early to avoid their father, for his one hand was quick at back-handed slaps, and his temper was hair-trigger. A crying or teasing or noisy child set him mad with irritation; he was fond of telling what a damned pest kids were—his especially, the damnedest pack of mongrels ever whelped.

But if they were mongrels, they had the mongrel's knack of making his own way. Any one of them above the age of six could have lived on what he could catch or steal. They grew like savages, black-haired, husky, broad-faced children with their mother's German features and their father's long bones. Most of their time in summer they spent roaming the wilderness of brushy woods along the Rock River, fishing, robbing garden patches, shooting rabbits and grouse with slingshots or whatever they could lay hands on.

By the time the youngest boy, Harry, was eight years old, they all had guns. One by one, mysteriously, the firearms came. Fred Mason swore they had been stolen, and stamped around the house whenever a new gun appeared, but he could never beat a confession out of any of the boys. Elmer had worked for a farmer and made the money for his. George had found his lying right out in the open on a bridge rail, and had waited all day to see if anyone would come and claim it, but nobody did. Harry had been given his by a wood-chopper up along the river. And so on.

Probably the boys felt that guns were a necessity, in order to provide food. The chances were two to one that any time they came home for a meal they would be cornered and whipped for something, if not by their father then by their mother, who sometimes flew into insane rages and drove even her hair-trigger husband from the house. So the boys stayed away, at least in summer, and lived on the fish and rabbits and corn and vegetables and watermelons of their expeditions. Sometimes they stayed out in the woods for days at a time.

In winter there was nothing much to do except go to school. It was a way of avoiding the domestic uproar, and it was a fairly painless way of satisfying parental demands. "My kids gonna have an eddication," Fred Mason was fond of saying. "They're gonna learn to read and write and figger if I have to beat it into them with a wagon tongue."

But one by one the boys dropped out, found jobs, wandered away. None of them, except Harry, remained in school beyond the fifth grade. Harry stayed till the eighth, partly because he was less indocile than his brothers, partly because he was brighter.

He was an intractable enough pupil, and the cause of much academic grief, but his intelligence and his sense of self-preservation were sharp enough to tell him when to stop, and once in a while he got a chance to outface his teacher with some monumental feat of brains.

His teacher quit picking on him, and gave him his unruly head, when Harry was in the sixth grade. From that day on she looked upon him with something like awe, tinctured with mild horror. They were reading McGuffey's Second Reader. For three or four weeks Harry slaved like a malicious little demon, reading every selection, prose and poetry, over and over until he knew almost the whole book by heart. The class, meanwhile, had spelled its way through sixty or seventy pages. Harry had ceased utterly to pay attention in reading class, loafed ostentatiously at his bench, whittled his initials, honked weirdly when the teacher's back was turned and then played he had been blowing his nose, pulled the girls' braids, pinked his fellows with a peashooter, and raised so much uproar that he was hauled up into the corner and a dunce cap set on his head. From there he grinned and made faces and commented audibly on the reading performances of the others.

The teacher was in a tooth-gnashing fury. She had tried whipping before: he was too tough to hurt. Sending him home would just be giving him a chance to go out in the woods and have some fun. So now, smelling a way of humiliating him (the only way he could be hurt), she slapped her ruler down on the desk and walked over to him with a wicked and wintry smile. "Of course, Harry," she said, "you're too brilliant to need any training in reading. But suppose —just suppose, now—you take your book and read to us for the rest of the afternoon, *pronouncing every word!* We'll let geography go, just for the pleasure of listening to you. Go on down to your desk and get your reader."

The class snickered. Harry grinned, shaking his head. "I don't need any book," he said.

"I suppose you know it all by heart!"

"I've read it over. When you're smart that's all it takes."

"All *right!*" she squealed, so outraged at his impudence that her voice cracked. "You can start right at the beginning." With her back stiff and her face tomato red, she marched back to her desk and sat down, her book open before her, ready to pounce on his slightest mistake.

At four o'clock she reluctantly turned him and the rest of the class loose. He had reached page ninety-two with only a few minor errors.

Harry Mason had good reason to hate his father, and he took advantage of his reasons. By the time the boy was fourteen he was big for his age and hard as flint from an active life of hunting and sports. Yet the beatings that had soured his childhood went on as if he were still a child. All the boys except Elmer had left, George to Chicago, Oscar and Bill to nearby farms, Dave to drive a dray in Davenport. As a result, whenever a neighbor missed a chicken, or complained of kids in his melon patch, or had his buggy wheels taken off and hung on the ridge of his barn on Hallowe'en, or found some youth toying with his daughter in the haymow, Harry had to look sharp if he wanted to avoid a tanning for it. Sometimes he was guilty, sometimes not. Sometimes he got beaten for Elmer's misdeeds because Elmer was too big at sixteen to be handled.

The procedure was monotonously reiterative. Fred Mason would lay for his one punishable son whenever he heard of a prank or theft. If he caught him (as he seldom did, and the infrequency of his success only whetted his wrath) he would take him out on the porch in full view of the offended public and administer punishment there. Because of his missing arm, he couldn't both hold and whip the boy, and so he held him by the collar and kicked his backside with brutal shoes, or hammered his head against a porch pillar. The more he kicked and hammered, the madder he got, and the more stubborn the boy's grim silence became. He never cried for pain, but sometimes after a thumping he would go off in the woods and throw himself on the ground and weep with rage and hatred. Once or twice he ran away, to be gone for two or three weeks, but he always came back, until one day in the summer of his fourteenth year.

In that July Fred Mason had had one of his occasional spells of ambition, had got together a couple of scythes, and had contracted to cut off the hay in the river meadow west of town. Elmer and Harry were impressed as free labor. They went unwillingly enough, but before they had been working half an hour they got into a race to see who could mow the greatest swath by noon. They shucked their shirts and slaved mightily in the early heat, while their father sat with his back against a tree, smoking his corncob.

Heads down, elbows bent, arms and shoulders swinging, the boys went down the field of damp grass close together, mowing almost in unison. At the fence along the road they turned and started back, still together. Then Elmer, two years older and a little bigger, began to inch ahead, and Harry strained to catch him, reaching for the exact cutting power of the scythe.

Harry never knew quite how it happened. His head was down, his eyes on the next semicircle of long wild grass that the scythe would reach. Either Elmer moved a little closer, or Harry in his hurry reached out too far, but in the warm hay-smelling quiet Elmer suddenly yelped, just as Harry, having felt the sudden solid obstruction of the blade, stood up.

Elmer sat down and rolled up his pants leg. Jets of blood pumped from the long deep gash in his inner calf. "Oh my gosh!" Harry said. He dropped on hands and knees and tried to stop the bleeding with his hands, but it burst out of the red lips of the wound and flooded his wrists. Their father came running, swearing at every step. For once Harry saw him move quickly and efficiently.

"Get me your shirt!" he said. Harry raced for it, came back on the dead run. His father had already laid Elmer on his back, found the artery above the cut, and was pressing deep with his thumb into the brown flesh. The bleeding lessened, came in feeble, choked spurts. Mason jerked his head at the twist of black eating tobacco in his shirt pocket. "Chew that up, a big hunk of it."

Harry stuffed the end in his mouth, bit off a great mouthful, and chewed desperately. Some of the juice ran down his throat; he choked, gagged, felt his bowels heave in nauseated protest, but he chewed on.

"C'mere!"

Harry knelt, helped his father fit a stone into a strip of cloth and press it against the spot where his thumb had been. A burst of blood shot from the wound, was choked down again. "Tie that around his leg," Mason said. "Tight as you can tie it."

His cheeks bulged with the evil wad, Harry tied, pulling until Elmer snapped at him. His father, kneeling on the ripped shirt, was tearing off another strip with his good hand. "All right, lessee that tobacco."

Harry spat it into the outstretched palm, watched it smeared on the wound, rubbed in with dirty fingers. Elmer winced, his eyebrows drew down, his lips pulled away from his teeth. "Gosh I'm sorry, Elmer," Harry said. "I must-a reached out too far."

"Tie that!" his father said harshly. The boy tied the strip of sweaty shirt over the daubed wound. For a moment he remained squatting beside his brother, contrite and sympathetic, and in that moment his father's anger, restrained till now by the immediacies of first aid, blew out of him like an explosion.

"*God* damn you!" he howled. The boy saw the blow coming, but couldn't duck. The back of his father's hard hand hit him across the mouth, bowled him over on his back. He arose slowly, watchfully, his sullen face sallow, his eyes burning with hatred. "I didn't go to do it," he said.

The hand hauled back again, and Harry backed away slowly. "Give me your lip!" the old man shouted. "God damn it, ain't I got enough worries without you cuttin' Elmer all to hell and bringin' on doctor bills? Who's gonna cut this hay now?"

Harry had backed away to a safe distance. "Well, I'm not, by God!" he blazed. "That's the last time you ever hit me!"

He turned and ran across the mown edge of the meadow, climbed the fence, went into town and hunted up the doctor and directed him to the place where Elmer lay, and started west out of town. He never came back.

In Davenport, three days later, he found his brother Dave. "You did just right," Dave said. "The hell with the old bastard."

"Only thing I feel mean about is running out on El," Harry said. "That was a bad cut."

Dave, while driving his dray, had learned to talk tough and smoke stogies, and he wore leather wrist protectors studded with brass nails. "Hell," he said, "what's a cut on the leg? He'll be all right. Anyway, you can write him a letter."

So Harry wrote a letter, and in a week got a scrawl back from Elmer saying that the leg was healing and itched like hell, and as soon as it was well he was going to pull out too. He was getting sick of hearing the old man moan about his hay. Maybe he'd come to Davenport himself. He'd see how things looked.

"This town ain't what it used to be when the arsenal was booming," Dave said to Harry later, "but there's a lot of building going on. Why'n't you learn a trade? That's where the wages is. Learn a trade and you're set. I haul for two-three lumber yards. Maybe I can get you on with some carpenter. Want to be a carpenter?"

"I don't care," Harry said. "That's all right."

A week later he was apprenticed to a carpenter, working for board and room and clothes. He stayed at it two years, and when he quit he was good. Even his crabbed old boss admitted it; he had never seen a kid pick up a trade any faster. He had a knack with tools; they cut straight for him, and he didn't cripple himself or them by their misuse. There was also something stubborn and persistent in him under the veneer of toughness he borrowed from Dave. He double-checked measurements, calculated angles two or three times, drew out a job till he knew what was what. Experienced carpenters seemed to go out of their way to teach him the tricks, and he was earning two dollars a day when he was sixteen.

In the evenings he hung around the fringes of Dave's crowd, learning to drink beer, sitting in now and then on a cheap poker game. From those men, teamsters and roustabouts and left-overs from the almost-vanished river traffic, he heard stories that put an itch in his feet. They knew Iowa and Illinois and Wisconsin, "Chi" and Milwaukee. One or two of them had rafted timber all the way down the Wisconsin from Wausau and down the Mississippi from Prairie du Chien to St. Louis. The life they had lived and the places they had seen and spoke of had space in them. So when the master carpenter on a big mansion job snarled at Harry for taking time off to smoke a stogie, he picked up his coat, went home to the room, shook hands with Dave, stuffed into his pocket the few dollars he had saved, and caught a ride on a shanty boat down the river.

For six months he was on the bum, sleeping in jungles and knowledge boxes, picking up scraps of useful knowledge from hoboes and transient laborers moving with the crops. He visited Chicago, and the sight of that city roaring into incredible size and impressiveness on the shore of Lake Michigan left his mind dazed with grandiose visions. Here was really the big town, here were the gangs of men creating a city out of a windswept slough, here were freight engines, passenger engines, lake boats, nosing in smoking and triumphant from every direction, here was money by the millions, a future as big as the sky. But two weeks in the big town convinced him that the days when you started with nothing and got to the top were gone as far as Chicago was concerned. All the big money was already well grabbed. And when, nosing around the freight yards, he almost got picked up by a cinder dick, he did the most direct and logical thing.

He ducked between two moving trains and swung aboard the outside one.

His wanderings took him out through the canal to the Mississippi, and down the river to Natchez on a coal barge. Then he worked north again, picking up a few weeks' work here and there on building jobs, getting offers of steady work but turning them down to hit the road again. By the end of six months he had a belly full for the time being, an ingrained and educated contempt for the law and law-abiding people, a handiness at making himself liked by hard-boiled and suspicious men, and an ambition to get somewhere where the cream hadn't been skimmed off, get in on the ground floor somewhere and make his pile. And he had the nickname of Bo.

He took the first job that offered, driving spikes in the new spur of the Illinois Central working westward through Illinois and Iowa. The heavy labor developed him into a man, sheathed his chest and shoulders with muscle, left him hard as a hound. But it brought him again into conflict with authority, with the voice of the boss. The Irish foremen on the line were drivers, loud mouthed and quick with their fists, and Bo was anything but docile. He talked back, sneered at the section boss, made no effort to keep his voice down when he beefed. That came to a climax on the graded road-bed just at the end of the steel.

The crew was bending rails for a gentle curve, locking them in the heavy vises and heaving against them with a surge of muscle. It was hot, back-breaking work in a sun over a hundred degrees. Stripped to the waist, the men launched themselves against the springy steel, relaxed, strained again. McCarthy, the foreman, stood at the end cocking his eye, estimating the curve. He had a hang-over, and apparently his cigar was nasty in his mouth, because he threw it away.

"Come on!" he roared suddenly. "Get some beef into it. You ain't bending a willow switch."

Bo wiped the sweat out of his eyes with his forearm. "I can think of a place I'd like to bend a willow switch," he said. He heaved with the rest, rocking against the rail. McCarthy stepped three paces closer, dropping his head between his shoulders.

"Where would that be, Squarehead?"

Bo heaved, grunting. "Right across your ass, Shanty-Irish," he said pleasantly.

As if at an order the men were back from the rail and dropping into a half circle. Bo and the foreman faced each other on the banked gravel, their feet shuffling lightly, their eyes sparring, their hands up.

The foreman lashed out, caught Bo beside the head, took a stiff right cross to the face in return. Like stiff-legged dogs they circled. The foreman dropped his head and rushed, swinging. For a full minute they stood and slugged it out, neither giving an inch. Then McCarthy stumbled and fell on hands and knees, his mouth hanging and his eyes amazed. The watching men howled as Bo, fighting as he had learned to fight on the road, gave him the boots. McCarthy covered up with his arms and started to roll away, and Bo, tiptoeing like a dancer, followed to crash a kick into the foreman's ribs that shocked him shudderingly still.

There was not a sound as he walked away. The men parted and let him by, and wiping his bloody nose as he went, he walked over to the bunkhouse, his head still singing with the power of McCarthy's fists, his ear swelling, but his blood pounding with a triumph so high and savage that he wanted to yell. The picture of McCarthy lying back there with his ribs caved in was raw alcohol to his soul. He was drunk on it; the toughest Irishman on the crew was back there cold as a clam.

The next day he was on his way to Wisconsin, bound for a logging camp where another section hand had worked the winter before. The food, he said, was good, the work hard but agreeable, the wages fair. They would just about be getting crews ready for the winter's cutting.

Two winters in Wisconsin gave him many skills. Either with rifle or shotgun he was the best shot in camp, so that frequently he got laid off the saw to go hunting for the cook. Those days of prowling the timber with a gun only deepened the wild streak in him as the work on the crosscut deepened his chest. He took to skis and snowshoes as if he had known them all his life, and he went out of his way to make friends.

He was genial, a good story-teller, a hearty drinker and a ribald companion in the towns where the rafts and the wanigan tied up and the men swarmed ashore for a bender. On winter evenings, when there was nothing doing in the bunkhouse steaming with the thick smell of drying socks and scorched leather and mutton tallow, he often lay on his bunk reading the one book he had found, a volume of Burns, and before the first winter was up he had added the whole volume to his fantastic collection of memorized McGuffey. He learned Paul Bunyan yarns, or invented them himself, and when half tight would sometimes take off on an extemporaneous ballad or poem that lasted half an hour. And he played poker, for higher stakes.

Those two summers, when the camps were shut down, he worked on a farm out of Portage, simply because he liked being outside better than he would have liked a carpenter's job in town. The Portage baseball team discovered him, and in the end of his second summer he leaped into local notoriety by getting a bid from the Terre Haute team in the Three-Eye League.

That winter he did not go back to the woods, for reasons which he kept to himself, and when he stood in the yard late in April ready to leave for Terre Haute, the sixteen-year-old daughter of the house burst into sudden tempestuous tears and fled to the barn.

"For gosh sakes," her father said. "What's the matter with her?"
Bo did not enlighten him.

He liked playing ball in Terre Haute. It was a wandering life, full of action, and the adulation of fans put a cocky swagger in his walk. His name in the papers pleased him, the fellowship of the gang he played with was good masculine fellowship, with many afternoons in the icehouse cooling off on beer after a game, and many evenings of quiet, intent poker. He lost money, but he learned much. If it had not been for an accident he might have stayed on as a professional ball player, might even have moved up into the big time, because his hitting was consistent and powerful, and he was a good man behind the plate in the days when catchers worked with a thin fingerless glove. But late in the season of 1896 he tried to stretch a long hit, got tangled up in a plunging fight for the bag with the opposing third baseman, and came up limping with a badly wrenched knee.

That put him on the hospital list for the rest of the season, and he had to get another job. For a while he worked in a glass factory, gave it up because it kept him inside ten hours a day, went back to his old trade as carpenter, and quit that with pleasure at the beginning of the next season. But the third day of training he wrenched his knee again; in spite of bandages it felt as if it might cave under him, and it hindered his swing at the plate. Before the middle of the first month he had been released from the club and was selling beer on the road for a Milwaukee brewery.

His territory took in all of southern Minnesota, western Iowa, and South Dakota, and sometimes was stretched to include an illicit trip into North Dakota to pick off the blind pig trade. North Dakota was then a focal point for armies of immigrants and land seekers. The trains were full of Norwegian and Russian families burdened down with masses of belongings, the station platforms were piled with bundles and boxes and trunks and farm machinery, the station walls were plastered with posters, land was for sale everywhere, new lines were pushing across the fertile Red River country and into the western part of the state.

Something in the bustle of migration stirred a pulse in Bo Mason. He was not a lazy man; his activities had been various and strenuous since he was fourteen. But the boredom of carpentry, of towns, of regular hours and wages every Saturday and orders all the rest of the week, had always made him restless. Here in Dakota there was something else. Here everybody was his own boss, here was a wide open and unskimmed country where a man could hew his own line and not suffer for his independence. Obstacles raised by nature—cold, heat, drouth, the solid resistance of great trees, he could slog through with almost fierce joy, but obstacles raised by institutions and the habits of a civilized community left him prowling and baffled.

That was partly why he loved the feel of life in Dakota. Frequently he stopped over for a day or two to go bird shooting, coming home from the wide grasslands and sloughs with a buggy full of prairie chickens, sage hens, grouse, ducks. Those days he remembered, and he remembered the sniff of something remote and clean and active in the prairie wind, the flat country leaning westward toward the Missouri Plateau, the sight everywhere of new buildings, new plowing, new grain elevators rising along the new tracks on the edges of new towns. Saloon conversations were full of tales of fantastic crops. "Sixty bushel to the acre!" men said. "Sixty bushel. I seen it, I was at the spout of that threshing machine. My God, that wheat grows tall as Iowa corn." And from train windows Bo looked out over fields of flax in flower, acres and acres of blue, and then his brewery job, full of travelling as it was, seemed trivial, picayune, confining. He wanted breath in his lungs and the sight of a flock of prairie chickens rising over his gunsights.

"Things are going on out there," he told his boss on the next home stop. "Every time I go through there the towns along the line are bigger."

His boss sat pulling a bushy eyebrow with thumb and forefinger. "You want to quit?" he said.

"How did you know?"

"You've got the itch in you," his boss said. "I've seen it before. You can stay on if you want, glad to have you. I've got no complaints about your work or sales."

Bo said nothing.

"Planning to take up a homestead?"

"I don't know. Maybe."

"Don't," his boss said, and hauled himself straighter in his chair. "You take my advice and stay away from farms. I knew a lot of people went to Dakota and Nebraska in the old days. And the ones that made money weren't the ones that sweated themselves skinny farming. The ones that made money were the storekeepers and bankers and saloon-keepers. I don't suppose you know anything about banking."

"No."

"And you wouldn't like running a grocery store."

"No."

"Then it looks like a saloon," the old man said, and grinned. "And saloons are banned in Dakota."

"Not if you believe my sales reports," Bo said. They laughed.

The old man set the ends of his fingers together and brooded. "Looky here, son," he said. "I'll make you a proposition. You go out to some new town and set yourself up a place and I'll help you out. You can draw on me for fixtures and beer, and pay me off when you get going. I think you're the kind of guy might make a go of it."

"Thanks," Bo said, and rose. "I'll let you know. I want to look around a little more first."

Two months later he wrote from Hardanger, saying that he had a good thing in a new town, no local police or anything to bother. He had bought half a building, was putting in bowling alleys himself, had three pool tables coming. He'd like a thirty-foot bar, mirrors to match it, and a shipment of beer, bottled beer. It was cleaner that way and it could be kept out of sight. "This town is only ten years old," he said, "and it's twice as busy now as it was two-three years ago. Five years from now I'll be buying out the brewery."

That was in the summer of 1899. Now it was 1905.

In September the roads were full of wagons, and on mornings when she worked around the house with doors and windows open Elsa could hear the shunt and crash of boxcars being backed under the spouts of the elevators. When the jolting and puffing stopped she could, by listening intently, hear the swishing rush as the dipped spout let go its river of wheat into the cars. Harvest excited her, as it had always excited her at home, and one afternoon, on an impulse, she left the house and went down.

There were dribbles of golden wheat below the spout, and at the bottom of the elevator wall a shining gold cone. She scooped her hand full and stood back watching, chewing and crunching the wheat kernels till they were sweet, rubbery gum in her mouth.

The last car was just being pulled away. Inside the elevator she heard the grunting of a separator engine and the occasional thud of a sack being thumped on the floor. She peeked in. A man she did not know, probably Bill Conzett's hired man, was separating seed flax, and Jud Chain, immaculate, dandified, wearing coat and vest even in the fall heat, leaned one shoulder negligently against the wall. He had his hat off, and a streak of sun through the elevator roof glinted on his blond hair.

"Hello," Elsa said. "I didn't expect to see you in an elevator."

"Come down a good deal," Jud said. "Bo and I are turning grain speculators. Buying flax this fall."

"Well," she said, and could think of nothing else to say to him.

"I'm daffy about flax anyway," Jud said. "Something about it makes me feel good. It's so slick and silky to feel." He ran his hand into the mouth of a sack and wriggled his fingers.

"We never grew it at home," Elsa said.

"Feel."

She pushed her hand into the brown, flaky seeds. They slipped smoothly up her wrist, cool and dry, millions of polished, purple-brown, miniature guitar picks. She moved her hand and the flax swirled like heavy smooth water against her skin.

"That's nice," she said.

"It's something to see in flower, too," Jud said. "Acres of blue-bells."

Her quick look acknowledged something sensitive, almost feminine, in the expression of his face as he caressed the flax with his fingers. "It's like everything else that's lovely," Jud said. "Dangerous. Boy was drowned in a flax bin here a year ago. Fell in and it sucked him down before anybody could get to him. We had to empty the whole bin to get him." He rubbed his wrist with a flat white hand. "Nice boy, too," he said. "That's the kind things always happen to. A mean, tough kid, now, he'd never know enough to appreciate the feel of flax, and he'd never get caught in it."

"I guess so," Elsa said. She let her fingers move in the satiny, treacherous seeds.

"Seen Bo lately?" Jud said.

"Not for three or four days."

"I thought he spent all his time on your front porch."

"Oh, go along!" she said.

Jud lifted an amused eyebrow; his mouth puckered into an expression almost arch. "Don't make out that you don't know the conquest you've made," he said.

She blushed. "Oh, fiddlesticks!"

"Laugh," Jud said. "You've got poor old Bo roped and hogtied. You know what he's been like for the last three weeks? When the kid that sets them up in the alleys gets his pins up, he has to jump out of there and beat it over to rack the pool balls, and then fly up to serve somebody a drink, and then hike back to the alleys to set them up again. You know why? Because Bo is standing all that time out by the door watching to see if you won't be coming down the sidewalk."

Elsa's face was hot. "Oh yes," she said sarcastically. "He's just been a regular *preste-rompe.*"

"What's a preste romper?"

"Preacher's tail. Somebody that's always tagging along. Like Bo."

"You don't mind, do you?"

"Oh no," she said. "I always feel sorry for strays. I pat him on the head once in a while."

His laugh was deep, moist, cavernous, like something alive down a cistern, a laugh that matched oddly with his polished and almost effeminate manners.

"Has Bo asked you anything lately?" he said.

She was startled. "No. What?"

"I guess he's been pretty busy," Jud said. "I know he's got it on his mind."

"Now you've got me curious."

"Oh well," Jud said. "I don't know why I shouldn't ask you. He'd get all tangled up in his tongue. How'd you like to go to Devil's Lake next Saturday?"

"Fine," she said. "What for?"

"State trap shoot. Bo's entered in the singles—would be in doubles too, but he can't stay away that long. We thought you and Eva might come along for the day. The fair's on, and there's a carnival in town. Big excitement."

"It sounds like fun," she said. "What if Bo forgets to ask me, now?"

"That," Jud said, "is the last thing he'd forget. He might forget his shotgun, maybe, but not you."

5

She saw him, from the parlor window, come up the walk with his derby already in his hand, and because they had a twenty-mile drive to make, and the shooting began at ten, she hurried to meet him at the door. He took the lunch box from her hand and held her elbow while she gathered her skirts for the step up to the axle of the buggy. "Here we go," he said, "if these old plugs can make it."

Settling herself, she said in surprise, "Why that's a beautiful team."

"Best old Handley had," Bo said. "If they ever caught up with the times in this burg they'd have horseless carriages for rent." He flicked the lines and the horses snapped into their collars; their trotting feet beat light and swift on the dust. Elsa knew they could make that twenty miles in two hours, easily. But it was like Bo to disparage anything he was proud of. Either he or Handley had worked over those horses. Their gray hides shone, their manes were roached, their forelocks tied, their tails curried smooth and glossy. She was glad they weren't docked; a docked horse was a pitiful thing when the flies were bad.

Jud was waiting in front of the hotel. Bo didn't slow down. Jud's great flat hand hooked the rail, his leg swung up, and he slid into the rear seat on the fly. The smell of bay rum came with him.

"Must be in a hurry," he said. He breathed on the ruby ring on his left hand, rubbed it on his sleeve.

"Pony Express doesn't stop for anything," Bo said.

But they stopped for Eva. In front of her house Bo whistled and Jud whistled, but nothing happened. "Still snoring," Bo said. "Go on up and break the door down, Jud."

Jud climbed out. "Not Eva's door," he said. "I prize my health." He went up and rapped, bending to listen for movement inside.

"Make some noise, for God's sake," Bo said. He lifted his voice in a bellow that shocked down the quiet, weedgrown street. "Hey, EVA!" The echo bounced off Sprague's barn.

Jud knocked again. "Must be asleep," he said.

"That's just what I think," Bo said. "Eva! Hey, Eva! Wake up!"

An upstairs window opened and Eva stuck her head out. Her left hand held a flowered kimono close to her chest. "Shut up, you big loon," she said. "You'll wake Ma."

The window slammed. They waited five minutes, ten. Jud wandered across the porch, cut off a twig from a shrub with his knife, and began peeling it. In the buggy Bo looked at Elsa, then at his watch. "Fifteen minutes," he said, and muttered indistinguishable things under his breath.

"Maybe she misunderstood the time."

"Maybe my hip pocket is a gold mine. She just likes to keep people waiting."

At six-thirty Eva came out in a white pleated shirtwaist and a dark sport skirt that just cleared the ground. Her mouth was very red, and she walked briskly, as if unaware that she had delayed anyone. Jud helped her in, waited while she got over her despairing little laughs and helpless attempts to get her skirts arranged. Bo sucked a back tooth and looked bored, but Elsa reached back and gave Eva a hand. Men ought to consider that a girl with her waist squeezed at least four inches too small couldn't move very freely. Still, she supposed Eva could have left the corset a little looser.

"Get all prettied up?" Bo said.

"I didn't even stop to eat," Eva said. "Just on account of you and your noise."

"What were you doing, then? You had time for a ten course meal."

"You needn't act so nasty," Eva said. "I didn't keep you waiting long."

Bo clucked to the team, lifted his derby and ran a hand over his hair, tipped the derby on again at a cocky angle. "No trouble at all. Do the horses good to have that hour rest."

"Oh, an hour!"

"Cut it out," Jud said genially. "We're moving, aren't we?"

He moved Bo's shotgun case from under Eva's feet and folded the buffalo robe on the floor so that her feet wouldn't dangle. Eva was always complaining that all seats were made too high for short people.

As they drove along the road the mist was rising from a slough on the left, and a half dozen ducks turned and swam away into the tules as if pulled on wires. "Getting close to bird season," Bo said, and watched them with a nostalgic eye.

The grays lengthened out in a mile-eating trot across the flats. Flickertails jerked and ran and sat up with absurd little hands hanging on their chests. The light cloud of dust behind them hung a long time in the still air, so that turning at section corners they could see it for a quarter of a mile behind. They sang, the grays went crisply, perfectly matched, heads up and tails arching a little, the mist melted from above the sloughs and the sun burned warmer. They were pulling into the carnival grounds at Devil's Lake at nine-thirty.

Jud lifted Eva down, straightened his vest. "I don't suppose there'll be anything doing till later," he said, and looked at Bo.

"I wouldn't think so," Bo said. "Not till afternoon, anyway."

"I thought you started shooting at ten?" Eva said.

Bo wagged his jaw at her. "What? Little Eva remembering the time something starts?"

"How about a stroll through the carnival?" Jud said.

Eva looked around her at the long grass. "It looks wet," she said.

Jud kicked into it, inspected his toe. There were tiny drops of water across the waxed yellow shoe. Under the trees there was still a dewy early-morning smell. "I'll carry you," he said. "Over in the grounds it's dry."

Eva giggled. "I don't trust you. You're so lackadaisical you'd probably drop me in a puddle."

"You've got us mixed up," Bo said gravely. "That's what I'd do if I was carrying you."

Eva stiffened, but his face was bland. "Come on then," she said, and stuck her hand in Jud's high elbow.

Absurdly short and imposingly tall, they stepped through the grass toward the packed carnival street and the tents set in a long semicircle around the fringe of cottonwoods. Elsa, watching them, heard the early shouts of barkers, the sodden thump of a maul on a stake. She saw the gaudy flashes of color from kewpie dolls and pennants and prizes in a concession tent open to the sun. A merry-go-round squawked for a minute into a fast two-step and then stopped, and there were six shots, sharp and steady, from an unseen shooting gallery. Along the road from town people were beginning to come on foot and in buggies.

"You shouldn't tease her like that," Elsa said.

"Why not?"

"She might think you meant it."

"I do."

"That's all the more reason for not saying things like that."

Bo grunted. "She gives me a pain. Just because Jud gives her a little whirl, she thinks she's got a lifetime lease on him."

"Jud doesn't seem to mind."

"He never minds anything. If you went up and kicked him he'd turn around and beg your pardon for having his back turned on you."

"Oh well," Elsa said. "What do you have to do now?"

"Just have to register and get a number. There's a half hour yet."

"Let's go get it done," she said. "Jud says you're going to win a prize."

"I guess not. Too many good shooters here."

"You're a good shooter too."

He grinned. "Got confidence in me, hey?"

"Of course," she said.

With the shotgun case under one arm, he steered her toward the screened street of carnival tents. Though she was tall herself, she felt his size beside her, and it pleased her to be walking with him. It wasn't just his size, either. It was the width of his chest, the smooth nut-brown of his skin, the way he walked as if everything in him moved on ball bearings. She hummed, almost skipping, and laughed when he looked at her.

At the white tent marked "Shooting Headquarters," under a limp American flag, she waited while he registered. He came back with a big paper 13 pinned on his back. "Slipped me the unlucky number," he said. One eyebrow was raised in an expression of querulous protest.

"Why, are you superstitious?"

"No, but I'd just as soon have another number."

"Friday the thirteenth is my lucky day," she said. "I'll loan you my luck."

His shoulder bumped hers as he swung to look around at the white and brown and yellow tents, the sheds housing fair exhibits, the banners of linen-paper, the pennants, the flags. The barkers were opening up all down the street, the calliope had started again, the little painted horses of the merry-go-round were rising and falling through the yellowing leaves of the cottonwoods. At the far end of the grounds a great wheel began to turn, curving up against the cloudless sky, and a girl's squeal cut through the jumble of crowd-sound.

"What in heaven's name is that?" Elsa said.

"Ferris wheel. Haven't you ever been on one?"

"I never saw one before."

"Take you for a ride when the shooting's over," he said. The corners of his eyes crinkled with a smile of pure delight. "God," he said, "I like the smell of a place like this, even. When I was a kid I was always going to run away and join a circus. Minute I get near one I start snorting and pawing the ground."

They were in the midst of a pushing crowd. For a moment their eyes met, and they stood foolishly smiling, oblivious to the push of shoulders and the jabber of voices and the danger of having an eye put out by a parasol rib. Then he grabbed her arm and pulled her along behind him. "Come on. I don't think I can miss today."

"You'd better not," Elsa said. "I'll take a sandwich out of your lunch for every one you miss."

"Give me a kiss for every one I hit?"

"Ninny on your tintype," she said, and pulled her arm away. Ahead of them, dropping toward the low shore of the lake, was a dike of earth, and behind it a little distance a crowd was lining up, sitting on newspapers, robes, bare ground. They were men mostly, but there was a sprinkling of women bright against the yellowing trees and the gray earth. Below them, on the level ground behind the five dugout traps, three men sat at a table. Men with shotguns in their hands and numbers on their backs clustered around the shooting ground. A clay pigeon hissed in an experimental arc over the water and fell.

"I mean it," Bo said, and they were stopped again. A faint, teasing smile hung on his mouth. "I won't even shoot unless you promise."

"You might as well not unpack your gun, then," she said, but his look made her feel dizzy and absurd and hot and as if she were going to fly all to pieces. She had come to the point of meeting his eyes and trying to stare him down, both of them laughing, when the man with the megaphone began to announce the opening of the singles traps, for the championship of North Dakota.

"Promise!" Bo said. "Don't be a piker. I can't shoot for any such stakes as the championship of Dakota."

Elsa got hold of the disintegrating feeling and fingered the enamelled brooch at her throat. She was delighted and a little terrified. "We'll see," she said.

They found Jud and Eva sitting among the spectators behind the second trap. Eva had a kewpie doll in her lap. "Won it on a toy horse race," she said. "That's what comes of having a beau that knows the ponies. My horse never was behind." She reached out and pinched Jud's ankle, and he moved it calmly out of reach.

One of the men at the table read off the names of the first shooters, who lined up behind the traps. Bo leaned over and began explaining to Elsa. They shot in groups of twenty-five rounds. The first was the easiest, "known traps and known angles," the shooter knowing the source and direction of each bird. There would be a clump of possibles on this one. Then came twenty-five shots at known traps but unknown angles. The bird might come straight out or to either side. That was tougher. The third and fourth rounds the shooters went out singly. In the third round they shot "reversing," standing at number one trap and getting a crossing bird from number five, then standing at number two and getting a bird out of number four, and so on. The last twenty-five rounds was "expert." You didn't know which trap the bird would come from, or in what direction.

Her eyes were on him almost in horror, but she was laughing still. "You shoot a hundred times," she said, "and you're an extra good shot, and you have the nerve . . . !"

"A hundred isn't so many." She noticed for the first time what it was that made his face so changeful and interesting. His eyebrows turned up rather than down at their outside ends. Like a devil. He was a devil. A hundred times! "I might miss as many as six," he said shyly. "That'd only be ninety-four."

"Keep the gun in the case!" she said, and waved him away.

He laughed and leaned back. A white saucer whizzed out of the first trap, the first shooter caught it with his barrels, fired. The saucer shivered to fragments, its thin splashings as the pieces hit the water clearly audible even over the echo of the shot rolling back from the shore. "Good bird," said an official clearly. The scorer at the table echoed him, "Good bird." The second shooter stood ready. "Pull!" he said.

Bo kept score with a stick on the bare ground. If anyone missed more than two he erased the whole score. "Don't need to worry about them. Guy that wins this has to shoot a possible on the first two rounds."

A man with a sheet of paper in his hand went around reading off the next names. "Simmons, number one; Carter, two; Shale, three; Gulbransen, four; Galbraith, five. Ready for the next squad. Simmons, Carter, Shale, Gulbransen, Galbraith."

"They run these off pretty smooth," Bo said. He opened the case and took out the stock and then the barrels, fitted the gun together, broke it and snapped it together again, his automatic hand going down to scratch in the tallies. He wiped off the stock, ran the ramrod through the shining barrels. His hands moved on the blue steel almost tenderly. Then he laid the gun across his feet and watched again.

"You'll be up pretty soon," Elsa said. He nodded, and she saw the tightening that had come over the muscles in his jaw and neck, the intent seriousness around his eyes. He seemed almost to have forgotten who she was, that she was even there.

Of the first two squads only two men had possibles. Carter and Olson. Bo watched Olson with a steady, almost basilisk look. "There's the guy to beat," he said. "He doesn't let down between shots at all. He's a shooter, that guy."

The squad hustler came around reading names, Bo's among them. When he stood up with the gun across his arm Elsa felt excited and nervous, weak with the desire to have him win. "Hit every one," she said, and had to hold her hands back to keep from reaching out to touch him.

He grinned at her absently. "Can't miss," he said. "See you after while."

"Five bucks you make a possible," Jud said.

Bo shook his head. "You'd jinx me."

He walked down to the table and joined the squad filling their pockets with shells. The last roar of number five's gun rolled along the shore, and number five walked back into the crowd. Then Bo was standing behind number three trap, hatless, his gun over his arm.

"Pull!" the first man said. The clay bird arced, the gun came up, the roar of the shot mushroomed in the still air. Then number two, then Bo. Each time Bo shot Elsa scratched a tally on the ground. Six, seven, eight, nine, ten, eleven, twelve. It took a long time, but every good bird was a little triumph. Glancing up from her tense concentration she saw Jud watching her. He lifted his eyebrows, and she made a face.

The thirteenth bird was coming. Thirteen! She stiffened herself, trying to loan him her luck. "Pull!" he said. The saucer shot out, but wobbly, weak, short. Bo raised the gun, hesitated, let the bird fall.

"No bird," the referee said. "No bird," said the scorer. Bo fished up a handkerchief swiftly and wiped his face. The handkerchief trailed whitely out of his side pocket as he half raised the gun again. "Pull!" he said. The bird whirred up, he caught it with the barrels quickly, too quickly, and missed it cleanly.

Elsa sat back with a noisily released breath. "Tough luck," Jud said. But Eva turned with an incredulous smile. "What do you know!" she said. "I never knew Bo was superstitious."

"He isn't."

"Don't tell me," Eva said. "He was nervous on that thirteenth one."

"He got a bad bird," Jud said. "Breaks of the game."

Bo was slow coming back. When he sat down beside them there was a clamp on his jaw and a shine of hard anger in his eyes.

"You did fine," Elsa said.

His laugh was hard and choppy, a disgusted sound. "I did fine all right. Let myself get jinxed on that thirteen ball."

"But only two hit them all," she said, "and only three others got all but one. You're tied for second."

"That isn't good enough," he said. "This Olson bird doesn't miss enough so you can afford to fool around." He sounded almost as if he were scolding her for saying he had done well. His voice was so snappish that she kept quiet.

It was after noon when he finished his second round. Going down still sore at the way things had broken in the first, he had missed the very first bird, and then in a cold fury that Elsa could see in his very shoulders and the set of his neck, had run out the remaining twenty-four as if each had been a personal enemy. Carter had dropped one, Olson none, and the rest of the field had dropped back so that Bo was third with forty-eight against Carter's forty-nine and Olson's possible.

His string of twenty-four restored his temper, and when Elsa took two sandwiches out of his lunch he groaned. "I'll be so weak I can't pull the trigger," he said.

"I guess the four you've had will keep you from starving. Besides, you lost them fair and square."

"I won forty-eight of something else, though."

"I never promised."

"What?" Eva said. "What did she promise?"

"I didn't promise anything."

"Now you're welching," Bo said.

"I'm not either welching. I never promised. Besides, you're not through yet."

"When I'm through you'll welch again."

"What I want to know," Eva said, "is what did she promise?"

"None of your business," Bo said bluntly, watching Elsa.

"You hit the next fifty and I really will promise," she said. "And when I promise anything I do it."

The full upper lids of Bo's eyes made his face look slitted like a mask, but he was smiling a fixed and concentrated smile. "Okay," he said. "I'll remember."

Jud hitched himself over until he had his back against a tree. He reached down and unlaced his yellow shoes. "What I hate about being up in the daytime," he said, "is that you have to wear shoes, and shoes hurt my feet something terrible." He pulled one off and sighed, reached for the other. Eva squealed affectedly. "Right at the table!" she said. "Put them on again, for Heaven's sake."

Bo's heavy-lidded eyes changed expression, were veiled with scorn. "I suppose you've never seen Jud's feet."

"Where would I have seen his feet?"

He shrugged. "Since he never wears anything but slippers, hardly, you might have seen them."

"Well, I don't go where Jud works," she said.

Jud sat looking down the immense length of his legs at his stock-inged toes. He wriggled them experimentally. "You talk as if my feet were an everyday attraction," he said. "Not everybody has thirteen toes. I could make a good living in a sideshow with my feet."

"Thirteen toes!" Elsa said. "Has he?"

"I never bothered to count 'em," Bo said. "They look like a couple of cartridge belts."

Elegantly relaxed, his face bland and amused, looking more than ever like an actor, Jud continued to wriggle his feet. Elsa watched him, this remote and fastidious impostor who could quite easily, without showing it in the least, change the subject, get Bo and Eva away from their outspoken dislike, make everything smooth and casual again. "Want to see?" Jud said.

"You can't scare me," Elsa said.

He took off one sock and showed seven toes. The other foot, he said, had only six, though there was a little nubbin that with applications of hair restorer or something might be made to grow. Eva covered her eyes and squealed at him to cover up his awful old feet, he looked like a centipede.

From back on the grounds, over the faint musical wheezing of the calliope, came the dull boom of a shotgun. Bo looked at his watch. "I've got to be getting back," he said.

He helped Elsa stow the scattered remains of the lunch in the buggy. Jud put his shoes back on with unhurried deliberation, rose and stretched. Eva consulted her face in a little pocket mirror.

A man, small, dark, with a red birthmark smearing one side of his face, came through the trees. He passed clusters of picnicking people, looking at them sharply as if in search of someone. Then he saw Jud, and came directly over. Eva put the mirror away and straightened her dress, but the man threw only one brief glance at the others before he led Jud out of earshot. Jud nodded, lifted his head as if musing, nodded again. They laughed together, lighting cigarettes, and stood looking back through the grounds past the colored moving specks of the merry-go-round horses. The little man bent his arm, stuck the hand out at an angle, wriggled it, his bony white hand darting like a snake's head. Jud nodded, and the little man went away.

"Who was that?" Eva said.

"Fellow I used to know in Fargo," Jud said. "Joe Theodoratus."

"What is he, an Indian or something?"

"Greek, I guess." He bent over to brush his trousers, and as he bent Elsa saw a look pass between him and Bo.

"What did he want?"

"Got a deal on," Jud said. "Wants to talk to me a little while. You wouldn't mind going to watch Bo shoot, would you, birdie?"

Eva's brows gathered. "You mean you want to run out and leave me?"

"I have to attend to this," Jud said. "Bo and Elsa will take care of you."

"So I have to stick in the mud while you go off. How long will you be?"

"We're the mud," Bo said, and winked at Elsa.

"I'll be an hour or so," Jud said. His face did not lose its bland and mannerly smile, and his voice did not lift, but Elsa thought she caught something passing between them that she interpreted as a command. Eva turned away petulantly and gave in. "You'll have more fun watching Bo shoot, anyway," Jud said. "That's what we came up here for, to watch Bo shoot." He straightened his patterned vest and settled the derby on his neat head. "Well, if you'll excuse me for a little while."

"I never knew it to fail!" Eva said, and came along unwillingly with Bo and Elsa.

Walking on the other side from Eva, Bo took Elsa's elbow and squeezed it, and glancing up she saw the glow that had been in his narrowed eyes all during lunch. When he was excited or interested, she noticed, the cool blue-gray warmed in his pupils, and his square, almost expressionless face became lively and changeful. She remembered what Jud had said in the elevator the other day, and was trying to see evidences of it in his face when she caught herself. She was just an ignorant Norske girl from the sticks. He wasn't crazy about her. He couldn't be.

All the same, when his turn came up and she watched him go down alone, to stand in the lonely focal point between spectators and traps and break twenty-five straight, holding his fire sometimes until she almost yelled for him to shoot, but always shooting in time, picking off the birds close to the water when their swift flight had slowed in the drop—when she watched him like an infallible machine scatter the clay saucers one after another, she held her breath and felt something like a prayer on every shot. When his gun missed fire on the twenty-second bird she was in an agony for fear it counted against him, for fear it would make him nervous as the bad bird had in the first round. But they gave him another, and he broke it, and then the last three.

He came back with his face as expressionless as if he had just been for a drink of water, and when she clapped her hands he pulled down the corners of his mouth. "Lucky," he said. "I'll probably miss a dozen next round."

But his eyes did not think he would. They told her privately that he was going out there and score another possible. The last three men finished shooting, and the referee called out the running scores: Olson, seventy-three; Mason, seventy-three; Carter, seventy-three; Gulbransen and Smith, seventy-one.

"Tied for first!" Elsa said. He just rubbed his shoulder, pounded sore by the kick of the gun, and kept his eye on the shooter coming up.

"I wonder where that Jud is?" Eva said. She had hardly said a word in the hour and a half they had been sitting there. She twisted and fidgeted, looking through the crowd.

"I'm going to look for him," she said. "He gets gabbing and never thinks what time it is."

Bo paid no attention to her words or her departure. He sprawled back, watching Olson shoot. His actions were faster than in previous rounds. They had to be. The birds came at sharp angles, from unexpected traps, and almost every shot was a quartering one. He ran nine, snapped a hurried side shot at a saucer spinning wide from the fifth trap. A tiny fragment zinged from the clay, its click coming back after the roar of the gun. The bird fell solidly into the water. "Lost bird," the referee droned. Olson, red in the face, protested, but the official waved him back. "Dusted target is no bird," he said.

The hustler was coming through. "Condon up, Mason on deck, Williams in the hole."

"All right, honey," Bo said softly. "Hold your right ear and pray."

He went down early, sitting at the official table while Condon shot, and when Condon was through he went out and shot another possible, shoot, relax, shoot, relax, break the breech and kick the smoking shells out on the ground, reload, shoot, relax, snap up the barrels, find the spinning disc in the split second of its rise, hands and eyes working together surely, impeccably. When he reached twenty without a miss Elsa was on her knees. When he broke the last bird hissing out at a high angle she was on her feet.

"Harder they get the easier they are for that guy," a man next to her said. She nodded, waiting for Bo to come back.

"You did it!" she said. "Bo, it was wonderful!"

His eyes were warm and intimate, his voice a purr. "I had something to shoot for," he said. He took her hand and sat down beside her while the last two unimportant shooters finished out their rounds. Then they were calling Bo Mason back to the table, and a man was standing, bellowing through the megaphone. "The winna! Harry Mason of Hardanger, singles champion of North Dakota! Harry Mason wins the fifty-dolla cash prize and the silva cup with a score of ninety-eight. That's shootin', folks! Give him a hand!"

He dropped the megaphone to clap, stopped that to pump Bo's hand. The crowd clapped and cheered. The representative of a sporting goods house was introduced and presented Bo with a shiny new repeating shotgun. Bo made a play of trying it out, winced and staggered when the butt touched his shoulder. The crowd laughed. Elsa saw that they liked him. Men went up to talk to him, and he was still speaking over his shoulder as he walked up the slope. Behind him the referee was shouting, "Runner-up, Bill Olson of Mandan. Bill Olson . . ."

"Where'll we go?" Bo said. He held a gun under each arm, a packet of new bills in one hand. "This dough'll burn my pocket out."

"Anywhere," she said. "Bo, I think it's wonderful!"

"You do?"

"Well . . . some ways." They laughed.

"Where's Eva, do you suppose?"

Elsa stopped. "My goodness, we'll never find her, in this crowd."

"Serve her right," Bo said. "Jud told her where to stay."

"But where can Jud be?"

"Jud? Jud's in a poker game."

"Is that . . ."

"He'd be a sucker to pass up a carnival like this. We probably won't see him till late."

It wasn't very nice of Jud, Elsa thought as Bo dragged her off exuberantly toward the fair. If he was going to do that, what did he bring her for at all?

They deposited the guns in the headquarters tent for safe-keeping, and three quarters of an hour later they found Eva disconsolately eating Norwegian cakes and trying to make conversation with the booth attendant, a plump, rosy Norwegian woman who spoke only a dozen words of English.

"I got hungry," Eva said. "And I lost all my money on that horse race thing, and Jud isn't anywhere around. I looked all over. If they weren't giving these cakes away free I'd be starved by now, for all he cares."

The Norwegian woman pressed *kringler* and cups of coffee on them. They ate and licked their fingers. *"Mange tak,"* Elsa said to the woman, and smiled at her. The three of them went off down the street.

"Bo won," Elsa said. "Did you know that? He's champion of North Dakota."

"That's fine," Eva said. Her eyes were roving among the passing people. She stumbled on her skirts, and flew into a vixenish rage. "That's fine," she said. "Maybe you can shoot that big fool of a Jud for me when we find him."

"Hell with him," Bo said. He winked at Elsa. "Let's go have some fun."

They bought a bag of sunflower seeds from a Russian huckster and were experimentally trying out the peanut-like taste when the ferris wheel loomed in front of them. Bo hustled them into a swinging chair. Eva squealed as the wheel began to climb, carrying them up over the trees, over the fungus-growth of colored tents. The sun, which had been just down when they got aboard, showed like a thin red plate on the horizon. They reached the zenith, and the bottom dropped out of Elsa's stomach as they rolled down into the shadow.

"How do you like it?" Bo said.

"Wonderful!" she said. "It's like flying."

"Let's go around again."

They went around three times more until the thrill was worn off it. Eva declined. From the rising, swing-like seat climbing toward twelve o'clock position Elsa saw her below in the edge of the crowd with her head turning right and left in search of Jud. She felt sorry for Eva. Such a frivolous, helpless, selfish thing. She must feel awful, being left that way.

But when they climbed out after their fourth ride Jud was there. "Oh-oh!" Bo said. "Now we'll have to referee a fight."

"I don't care!" Eva was saying violently. "You said you'd be back in a little while, and I waited hours. If there was any other way of getting home I'd go right now. I'd have gone hours ago."

"I'm sorry," Jud said. "I got detained. That was a pretty big deal Joe had up his sleeve. Turned out I made some money on it."

"What sort of deal?"

"You wouldn't understand it, birdie," Jud said. "Business." He put his arm down around Eva's shoulders and she shook it off.

"Eva got tired watching us shoot," Bo said. "We found her a while back stuffing herself with Scandihoovian cake."

"I wouldn't have had even that if it hadn't been free!" Eva said.

"Well that's too bad, birdie," Jud said. "Let's go find something to eat right now."

"I'm not hungry now."

"Quit your wrangling," Bo said. "Let's go see the show."

Lamps and Japanese lanterns were on down the carnival street, and crowds milled before booths and tents and tables. The nasal rigmarole of a barker stopped them before a long, narrow tent lighted by a half dozen lamps that threw jigging shadows on the walls. At the end, thirty feet or so from the counter that closed the entrance, a grinning Negro face bobbed and grimaced through a hole in the black curtain painted to represent a jungle river. The Negro's head came right out of the spread terrific jaws of a crocodile.

"Hit the nigger in the head, get a good ten cent seegar," the barker said. "Three balls for a dime, folks. Try your skill and accuracy. Hit the nigger baby on the head get a handsome cane and pennant." His lips moved over the drone of words like the lips of an ape kissing, and he spoke on steadily through inhalation and exhalation, never varying the penetrating nasal whine.

"Want a cane?" Bo said. He stepped over to the counter.

"Me too," Jud said.

The barker shoved over six balls from a pile stacked like cannon balls. He stood back, indifferent to his present customers, his eyes on the passing crowd, his lips moving over the nasal pour of sound. Bo motioned to Jud. "Go ahead. Knock his head off."

The black grinning face in the crocodile's throat weaved and bobbled; the curtain billowed out and in. In the inadequate light it was a deceptive target. Jud removed his coat and folded it on the counter. Then he wound up and threw, awkwardly, Elsa noticed, like a girl. The ball dented a deep shadowy hole in the canvas and dropped. The grinning face opened its mouth, cackled. Then it became fixed, its mouth stretched wide, and Elsa stared, so perfect was the illusion of a succession of red gaping mouths swallowing one another.

"Take him," Bo said. "Your bird."

Jud threw again. The face weaved easily sideward. "There's a percentage in favor of the house," Jud said. His big hand went clear around the third ball as he squinted, aiming. Beside him Bo stood ready, and just as Jud let go he snapped a quick wrist throw. The balls travelled side by side. The swivel-necked colored boy rolled away from Jud's, saw Bo's coming, rolled back. Jud's ball hit him solidly on the skull and bounced clear to the tent roof.

"Got him!" Jud said. His incongruously masculine bellow of laughter filled the entrance. The Negro face pulled back in, leaving the crocodile a dark round hole for a throat. The barker stopped his bored droning and came over angrily. "What'sa idea?" he said. "You can't both peg at once."

"You never said we couldn't," Bo said. "Come across with a cane."

"I don't pay on that. You both threw at once."

Bo's neck and shoulders stiffened as he leaned over the counter. Elsa could not see his face, but she heard his voice, soft. "This guy hit the nigger on the head," he said. "You owe him a cane."

Peaked and white with anger, the barker glared at him. "Like hell!"

"You aren't very smart, fella," Bo said. He raised one hand as the barker started to speak. "And I wouldn't hey rube, either."

"Tough guy, uh?" the barker said.

"No. I just like to see people pay off when they lose."

After a minute the barker threw a cane onto the counter. Bo took it, laid down his two remaining balls, tossed two dimes on top of them so that they rolled off the board, and handed the cane to Eva.

Walking uncomfortably beside him, Elsa said, "Do you suppose the Negro is hurt? Jud threw that awful hard."

He laughed. "You can't hurt a coon hitting him on the head."

Almost immediately came the barker's voice. "Try your luck, folks. Try your skill and accuracy. Hit the nigger baby on the head, get a good ten cent seegar . . ."

"Bo," Elsa said.

"Uh?"

"Was it fair to throw both at once like that?"

He stared at her. "Sure. Every game in this carnival is a skin game. You got to out-smart 'em."

"The percentage is always in favor of the house," Jud said.

Bo took her arm and pointed. "There's a sample. Go on over and try your luck."

Curiously she crossed the street to where a small crowd had gathered around a table. A man at the table was manipulating three half walnut shells so fast that she couldn't follow his fingers. Bo stooped to whisper. "This is one of the oldest skin games in the world. Thimblerigger." He pressed a dollar into her hand and nodded to her, go ahead.

Elsa watched the man's hands. His mouth went constantly in an unintelligible flow of sound like a barker's at the throwing tent. Finally the hands came to rest, the shells in a neat row. A tall, gangling, hayseedy man in overalls threw down a silver dollar and put his finger on one shell. "Follered her all the way," he said. He turned the shell over, and the pea was there.

"Can't win all the time," the thimblerigger said. He threw a dollar to the man, and his hands went intricately among the shells, caressing, touching, turning, mixing. Now and again he opened his hand and showed the pea, or raised a shell to reveal it. "Can't win all the time. Sometimes a quick eye beats a quick hand. Down with your bets, folks. Nothing up the sleeve, an open game of skill. Try your luck again, mister?"

The gangling man grinned and shook his head and stuck his two dollars in his pocket.

"Shill," Bo whispered.

"What?"

"Tell you later. Go ahead and bet him."

Feeling horribly conspicuous, she stepped up and laid her dollar down. The man began shifting his shells, crooning. But she knew better than to listen to his talk. She kept her eyes on his hands, distinctly saw him put the pea under a shell and then shift the shells bewilderingly, but not so rapidly that she didn't keep her eye triumphantly on the right one. She reached out and put her finger on it. There was nothing underneath.

"But where was it?" she said when they were walking again. "I saw him put it there."

"Palms it in his hand," Bo said. "A clever rigger can make you think there's a pea under every one."

"But that other man won."

"He was a shill, a booster. When business is slack he comes around and wins once in a while to keep the suckers coming."

How he could tell that the man was a shill she had no idea, but he knew all about things like this and she knew nothing about anything. And he was the trap-shooting champion of North Dakota. He was also very big and good looking. She saw women turn to look at him in the street. But there was one thing she wanted to ask him, until she forgot about it in the excitement of the games they played all up and down the street. If games like these were always fixed in favor of the house, then what about the poker game that Jud had been in that afternoon? Was that crooked too? Or were poker games like that pure games of skill where a professional gambler like Jud would naturally win? There was a great deal she didn't know, sure enough. She listened to Bo's tutoring carefully whenever he bent to tell her something in that warm, intimate voice.

It was after ten, and black dark under the cottonwoods, when they groped back to the team. Elsa went quietly, guided by Bo's hand, full to the chin with new experiences. She had ridden on a ferris wheel and a merry-go-round. She had gone for a ride around a miniature race track in a horseless carriage, the first automobile she had ever seen, a stinking, explosive, dangerous-looking affair. She had been scared to death, putting on the ulster and goggles; when the man had gone behind and spun the crank and the explosions started right underneath her, she had jumped, she thought, a mile. After the dizzy whirl around the track she had climbed out shakily and pushed up the goggles, standing laughing under the hanging lanterns, and Bo had stopped laughing suddenly and stared at her. "God, your eyes are blue," he had said.

He was just dreadfully nice, she thought. It was his day, but it was hers too. Everything he had done had been shared with her, as if he didn't care about winning the championship and the money unless she had it too. She had collected kewpies, canes, pennants with "Devil's Lake, No. Dak." across them in yellow felt. She had won a box of chocolates, eaten candy popcorn and drunk lemonade and pop until she couldn't eat or drink any more. She had seen a show where a man in rube costume came out and sang a song about two rubes who went to a circus and got in a peck of trouble. Bo had liked that. He had stamped and clapped till the man came back and did the interminable song all over again, prancing around in his chin whiskers and straw hat and red topped boots and bandanna.

Bo was singing the song himself as he helped her over the rough ground:

> *He pulled Si's whiskers so all-fired hard*
> *That his chin got as long as the neck of a gourd.*
> *All at once I see Si grin and then*
> *I knew his troubles was at an end,*
> *And sure enough, with his knife so keen*
> *He cut his whiskers close to his chin . . .*

"Where's it go from there?"

She took a firmer hold on her plunder, each article of which she had vowed she would put away and never part with. "Something about throwing them out in a hurry? I don't know. I don't see how you remember so much of it."

"They don't get thrown out yet. Something about two girls fainting. I got it." He sang three or four lines more.

"That's wonderful," she said, genuinely impressed. "I never saw such a memory."

She stubbed her toe in a root and stumbled wildly in the dark. A doll slipped from her arms and Bo fumbled for it. When he rose his arms went around her suddenly, and he kissed her. Her arms were so full of bundles that she could only twist her face away. "Wait!" she said desperately.

He kept his arms around her. "Why? They're way up ahead."

"Please. Not now."

"Don't forget you've got to be a sport. No welching."

"I won't welch," she said. Whatever happened she wouldn't welch now. That was the thing he disliked Eva so for. She wasn't a sport.

His low laugh stirred in her hair. "Ninety-seven more," he said.

The rest of the way to the buggy she was silent, wondering how she could ever do it. Ninety-seven kisses, not in fun, not the kisses of a boy in a game, but the kisses of a man seven or eight or nine years older than she was, who had been all over and maybe had a past. And a saloon-keeper, a lawbreaker, really.

Briefly, as Jud's flaring match lighted a carriage lamp and the buggy emerged in the dim glow, she was reminded of the one admirer she had ever had, middle-aged mousy old Henry Mossman, who ran the hardware store in Indian Falls and who last spring had proposed to her at a picnic. He had sandy mustaches like a haycock, and he seemed always to smell of shoe-blacking, and he was meek, apologetic, at once gentle and ridiculous. He had proposed to her in the buggy as they drove home through the firefly-streaked darkness. The situation now was close enough to that other that she had a moment of dizziness, almost as if she were dreaming, as if she had been carried in a circle and washed up in a place and time where she had been before. But there weren't, she reminded herself, any fireflies here. And there was nothing meek or apologetic about Bo Mason. Imagine Henry Mossman working it so you had to kiss him a hundred times!

"What're you laughing at?" Bo said.

"I just thought of something."

"What?"

"Nothing you'd care about."

"I care about anything you care about."

"Well, you wouldn't care about this."

Jud came around and lighted the other lamp. Bo brought in the horses and hitched up. "Want me to drive?" Jud said.

"Sure. Go ahead."

The wheels crackled through leaves and twigs as they turned into the road, leaving the calliope still wheezing and the little colored horses of the merry-go-round still rising and falling in the torchlight glare of the shore. Then hard road, the beat of trotting hoofs, the yellow blur of the carriage lamps coasting alongside, the flow of cold air around the unequal silhouettes of Jud and Eva, and the snugness as Bo tucked the buffalo robe around her feet. His arm went around her shoulders and she did not move.

She saw the shadow of Jud put an arm around the shadow of Eva, and heard the murmur of low words. Eva must be over her peeve. That was good. It would be a shame to ride all that way home mad. It would be . . .

Bo leaned close and kissed her, holding it a long time. She heard Eva's clothes rustle as she turned in the front seat to look back, but she did not even have the impulse to free herself. Instead she leaned back further in the seat and smiled into the misty sky. "Two," she said, so softly that the front seat couldn't hear.

A long time later, when her hands were cold and her feet chilled and her lips bruised with Bo's kisses, the buggy stopped and she saw the gable of Karl's house. She had given up her attempt to keep count and hold him to the letter of her bargain. He might have kissed her a hundred or five hundred times.

No one made a move. Eva, muffled against Jud, squealed once in a stage whisper. Murmured words and a giggle came back, then a breathless, hushed squeak. Bo kissed her again, and when he let her go she saw his teeth in the misty dark.

"Don't!" Eva said from the front seat, and her shadow squirmed as if trying to get away.

"Why not?" Jud said, quite loud.

"Because you tickle."

"Isn't anybody getting off here?" Jud said.

"I hate to," said Elsa, and did not move. She looked at Bo, tried to make out his eyes. She pecked him with a swift kiss, pressed him back when he started to rise and help her out. "I'll just hop out and run," she said, whispering close into his ear. "It was a beautiful day." She pressed his hands, gathered her skirts, and jumped from the tire to the ground, half falling. When she popped up again she was right beside Jud, and caught his sudden movement. Eva huddled in her coat. She said goodnight to them and ran indoors.

There was much to think about in bed, many excitements, the memory of Bo's kisses, the eagerness and frankness of his admiration when he stopped laughing beside the automobile and said, "God, your eyes are blue!" He must like her, he must like her a lot. He wasn't the sort of person to pretend anything, and everything that had happened all day had said as plainly as it could be said that he was in love with her. That was a delicious thing to sleep with, a thought that could be hugged. But there was the other thought, the troublesome one, and the complete clarity with which she had seen what she had seen gave her a minute of sacred solemnity. Where was she going, and what kind of people was she going with? Because there wasn't any doubt: when she straightened up suddenly beside Jud after jumping from the buggy he had just been pulling his hand out from under Eva's dress.

6

"It isn't any of my business," Karl said. "I just got this letter from Nels. Or maybe it is my business. I don't know. I just thought I'd come and talk to you."

"What's the matter, is he scared I'll abduct his daughter?" Bo said.

"I don't know that he's scared of anything special. He just wants to know who you are and what you intend to do. He's pretty pious. I suppose he just wants to make sure of you."

"How'd he ever hear about me in the first place?"

"Probably she wrote home," Karl said. A man going out of the poolhall slapped Karl on the back, and he turned around and grinned and nodded. "In a way I'm responsible for her," he said to Bo. "Just how serious is this, anyway?"

He watched Bo take out his knife and begin carefully paring his nails. The heavy-lidded eyes were somber and the dark face expressionless. Then he looked straight up at Karl. "Why, if you come down to that," he said, "I guess it's pretty serious."

"You mean you're going to marry her?"

"I haven't asked her," Bo said.

"But you're going to."

"I guess maybe I am," Bo said, "if I ever get up the nerve."

"I can imagine how scared you are," Karl said. "She thinks you're a little tin god on wheels."

Bo lifted his eyes again, and Karl felt the glance like something heavy, like a pressure. "You sound as if she was making a mistake to think that," Bo said. "If she does."

Karl waved his hands helplessly. He didn't want to get into this. Nels ought to have written to Elsa, or to Bo himself, if he wanted to know so much. He put a man in a bad position. "She's an awful nice kid," he said.

"I never denied that."

"But she's just a kid," Karl said. "That's the only thing that bothers me. She's never been anywhere before, she don't know much. She's just a nice good-looking kid that some careless guy could take advantage of pretty easy."

"Thanks," Bo said, eyeing him. "Thanks very much."

"I never said you were taking advantage of her," Karl said. "I just said she didn't have any experience, she's got no way of judging people because all the people she ever saw were Norske farmers with their feet in a furrow."

"Just what is it you've got against me as her husband?" Bo said.

"I didn't say I had anything against you!" Karl said. His voice rose complainingly. *"Herregud,* I've been your friend for six years, haven't I? Only she isn't nineteen yet. She shouldn't be rushed."

"I haven't been rushing her," Bo said. "I've been making myself stay away from her for a week." His eyes were still cold, uncomfortably steady on Karl's face. "Spill it," he said.

"Oh hell," Karl said. He jingled the change in his pocket and looked toward the door. A wind blew scraps of paper and gray dust past the windows. "How am I going to tell Nels what you do, for one thing?" he said. "I can't just write and say, 'Bo's a good guy that runs a blind pig here in town.' Nels won't like it." He shook his head. "He might even try to stop it," he said.

"How would he stop it?"

"He might make her come home."

"I bet you any amount of money," Bo said, "that she wouldn't go. She ran away from him once, didn't she? He's got a hell of a lot of business trying to run her now."

"Do you want to take her in to live in a room in that hotel?" Karl said. "Can you see her as the wife of a guy that runs a pig? She's just the wrong kind for you, Bo. She's cut out to have a nice house and a bunch of kids and make somebody a good wife. Your kind of life would break her heart in a year."

"Suppose I told you I'm selling the joint."

"You are?"

"I might."

"Then what would you do?"

"I've been looking over a hotel in Grand Forks," Bo said. "If that's any of your business."

Karl wrinkled his forehead. "I don't want you to get sore at me," he said. "If I was doing the marrying I'd just as soon marry you. But I don't know that Elsa should, by God if I do. You're a rambler. You might both wish you hadn't."

Bo had finished paring his nails. He shut the knife with a snick and put it in his pocket. "You're an old busybody," he said. "Why don't you go back and tend to your store?"

Karl shrugged and pushed himself away from the bar. "Give me a beer first."

While Bo got out a bottle and glass Karl watched him. He was a nice guy. He was a hell of a nice guy. But what kind of a life would it be for that innocent of an Elsa, tagging him around from one thing to another? Bo wasn't a sticker. He chased rainbows too much.

"You really gone on her?" he said. "You going to become a reformed character and settle down and be an alderman?"

Bo scraped the foam from Karl's glass with an ivory stick and dropped the bottle in a box under the bar. A man across the room was pulling the handle of the slot machine. "I told him," somebody back by the pool tables said loudly, "that I'd cut it for fodder before I'd pay any such cut to a threshing crew . . ."

"Look," Bo said. "How many times do I have to tell you? I want to marry her. I'm not pretending to be something I'm not, but I'm not saying I'm going on here sitting on my tail in this little joint, either. If she wants to marry me on those terms, whose business is it but hers and mine? Write her old man and tell him anything you please. I'll write him myself if you want. I'm not trying to pull any fast ones. Sure she's a nice girl. She's so nice I can't believe it, considering the way she was brought up. She's a peach. She deserves a lot, I know it. I want to try to give it to her."

"Yeah," Karl said. "Well, nobody could ask for more than that. I wasn't trying to break it up, you understand. It was just that I got this letter . . ."

He stopped. Bo was looking past him toward the man by the slot machine against the far wall. Moving swiftly, he raised the board and stepped out from behind the bar. He was almost at the man's shoulder before the other heard him, and turned. He was a tall, loosely-built man, a bum or an itinerant laborer with a ragged elbow in his coat. He turned and squawked almost in the same instant, and then Bo collared him.

Elsa looked up from the letter with puckered brows, looked unhappily out the window. It was a gray, unpleasant day, and the wind blew, rattling the window frame. The tight-lipped, strained face of her mother looked at her from the German silver frame of the daguerreotype. She felt miserable and discontented, and she hadn't seen Bo for days. Hardanger, her uncle's house, the people she knew here, were a foreign land and a foreign people. She had cut herself off from home, and now there was no real home here.

Her eyes went back to the letter. Sarah, Kristin wrote, was pretty hard to get along with sometimes. She was funny. One minute she'd be apologetic, and let Erling run all over her, and act as if she were a stray that had been let in, and the next she'd be snappish, trying to run the whole place. And she agreed with Pa that something should be done about Elsa, before she flew off the handle and married some good for nothing. Who was Bo Mason, anyway? Pa seemed to be worried about him. Was he nice? Where had she met him?

Elsa stood up. Let him think what he pleased. He would think the worst, because that was the way he was, but that didn't bother her. She knew Bo a lot better than he did, and if she chose to marry him —and were asked—she would. And what right had Sarah to talk! Marrying a man twice as old as she was, and then presuming to dictate the marriages of other people!

Angrily the girl threw on her coat and went outside. Until five in the afternoon she walked as fast as her legs would carry her, out through flattened weedy fields, across strips of summer fallow, over the corner of the dump-ground among wheels of old buggies, pieces of scrap iron, papers, tin cans rusted and plugged with bullet holes from the target-shooting of boys, the bones of a cow gnawed by dogs or coyotes. The slough confronted her, a saucer of stagnant water rimmed with tules, with mudhens floating close to shore and a wary flock of canvasbacks swimming out in the open water. She walked clear around it, feeling through her coat the coming of deep fall; the going away of warmth from the earth was like some loss of warmth and energy in herself.

And Kristin, wanting to get away from home too, asking if there wasn't someone in Hardanger who needed a girl—Kristin who couldn't bake, couldn't clean house without leaving the corners full of dust puppies and the wallpaper smeared where her broom had brushed down cobwebs. Indian Falls, the place she had called home and still unconsciously thought of as home, must be as bad as she had thought it when she left, if Kris wanted to leave too. But the sister she wanted to come to was lonesome in a strange and barren town.

Her feet kicked in flat brown reeds, sank in muck, squashed through wet hummocks of meadow, found dry ground again. How long would she go on living in someone else's house, eating someone else's bread, with never anything to call her own except the clothes she wore and the thoughts she thought? It would be nice, she thought irrationally, to take piano lessons. But there wasn't a piano in any house open to her. There wasn't anything she could do, no way she could use her time to improve herself, except by reading, and even finding books was difficult.

She kicked a pebble down the ruts worn by the dump wagons.

What's the matter with you? she said, and impatience put length in her strides again. Mooning around like a calf, wishing you were somewhere else, or somebody else, and wanting things you can't have.

But I know what I want, she said. I want a place of my own where I can sit down and everything there is mine and everything I do means something.

And you want Bo in it, she said.

Well what if I do? she answered.

Her feet found plank sidewalk under them. She was on the prairie end of Main Street. At the confectionery she hesitated. An ice cream soda might be nice. But the wind whipping around the corner changed her mind. A cup of coffee at home would be better. She hurried faster. The fogged sun had gone completely, and the wind had a bite.

It was too bad, she thought as she neared the bowling alley, that Bo didn't run a place women could go to. She would have liked to drop in sometimes. She would like to right now, and see why he hadn't been over. But then he would think she was chasing him. With her head down against the wind she went past his door.

She was a half dozen steps past when she heard the uproar inside, and Bo's voice, saying, "All right. I'll just fix you so you won't be tempted again."

She shrank back into her uncle's doorway just as the swinging doors of the poolhall burst open and Bo, holding a man by the front of his coat, pushed him through and backed him to the edge of the sidewalk. Though the stranger was almost as big as Bo, he looked beaten. There was a ragged hole in the elbow of his coat. The crowd that had poured out after them stood in a cluster on the sidewalk. Elsa saw Karl, still in his store apron and his black sateen cuff protectors. "Now," Bo said, "how many times did you slug that machine?"

The man's quick eyes shifted from Bo to the crowd and back. He wet his lips. "I'll make it good, mister," he said. His hand fumbled in his pocket.

"How many times?"

"Just once." The tramp's hands quit fumbling, came up to lie lightly on Bo's wrist. "That guy was right close. He c'n tell you. I only did it once. I was hongry and needed a cup-a coffee."

"Why didn't you ask for a cup of coffee?"

"I didn't think you'd hand it out, mister. Honest to God, I'll make it good."

He almost babbled, his eyes on Bo's heavy dark face. It was so changed a face from his usual one that Elsa felt her stomach draw in. Bo kept his left hand rigid in the man's coat, teetering him on the eighteen-inch drop-off into the street. "Well, turn about's fair play. That's right, isn't it? Even-Stephen," Bo said softly. "That's all I'm going to slug you, see? Only once."

The crowd snickered, then someone grunted, a startled sound, as Bo's right fist smashed up. The tramp toppled backward into the street and lay where he fell, with a smear of blood on his mouth and his hat ten feet away from him in the dust.

Bo swung to go back inside, pushing through the men whose eyes still fed on the man lying in the street. Then he saw Elsa, flattened against her uncle's door. His expression changed, the hard, tough look left his face, and he took two steps toward her, but before he could come any further she turned and ran.

She did not look back, but she heard the windy *whoosh!* of the swinging doors as someone went through then, and the voice of someone in the crowd. "Jee-suss!" the voice said. "I'll just slug you once, he says, and then he socks him. Turn about's fair play, he says . . ."

Elsa, hurrying home with her stomach sick and her mind hot with outrage, saw nothing. Her mind was too full of the image of the fear-stricken face of the tramp and the abrupt stillness of his body in the street and the smear of blood on his mouth. He had been hit when he was begging for mercy, when he was making no attempt to resist, when he was offering to make good whatever it was he had done. Any man with a bit of pity in him would have let him go.

Too furious to think, she went and sat on her bed upstairs, stooped to run icy hands through the mass of her hair. Quite suddenly, not knowing she was going to do it, she began to cry.

He appeared so suddenly that there was no way to avoid him. It was eight o'clock. She had finished the supper dishes and was sweeping the kitchen, aware of the pipe smell from the parlor where Karl was reading, aware dimly that it had started to drizzle outside, and that she ought to shut the kitchen door. But she finished sweeping first, stooping with the dustpan, and when she rose he was in the doorway, rain dripping from the curled brim of his derby and the shoulders of his coat dark with wet.

For a moment she confronted him, dustpan in hand, as if he had been a burglar. He leaned against the jamb and said nothing, but his eyes were steady and his face serious. There was no trace around his mouth of the toughness she had seen that afternoon. She looked for it in the instant she faced him, but it was his nice face she saw, the smooth skin dark and healthy looking, the jaw square, the gray eyes lighted with somber warmth. She dropped her eyes to his hand, the hand that had been a brutal fist that afternoon, hooked in his lapel: a square brown hand with long square-ended fingers, a strong, heavy wrist.

With a twist of his body he straightened away from the jamb. "Hello," he said.

"Hello," she said. She stepped to the door, brushing him as she went by, and dumped the dustpan in the can, came back and shut the door, folded the tablecloth and put it away.

"I thought I'd better come over," he said.

"Oh?"

"I thought maybe I ought to do a little explaining."

"Is there anything to explain?"

"There's plenty to explain. You saw me hit that guy."

She faced him then, furiously. "Yes, I saw you hit him! I saw you hit him when he wasn't fighting back and was begging you not to."

Annoyance brushed his face, was smoothed away again. His voice was quiet, as if he were maintaining his patience and explaining something to a child. "There's only one way you can treat those guys," he said.

"He said he'd pay you back for whatever it was he did."

"Sure. Sure he'd pay me back, long as I had him. And you know what he'd do? Next place he went into he'd slug some other machine. Guys like that will go on slugging machines till someone shows them it isn't healthy."

"I suppose you did it just to teach him a lesson!"

Bo flushed. Leaning against the door, he breathed through his nose, pressing his lips together. She couldn't keep her temper now; she had to tell him what she thought of him. "What if he did slug a machine?" she said. "It's a gambling thing, isn't it?"

"Sort of."

She took her hands from her apron pockets, shoved them back in again hard because she couldn't keep them from shaking. "Remember what you told me at the carnival?" she said. "Remember what you said about it was all right to take advantage of a gambling game because any game like that was crooked? Any gambling game is crooked. Jud said so himself. What that tramp did was just what you and Jud did when you both threw at once."

"It isn't the same," Bo said. "It isn't anything like the same."

"I don't see any difference. You bullied the man at the carnival when he objected. What if the tramp had bullied you the same way?"

"He'd have got his head knocked off."

"He did anyway." Elsa opened her hands inside her pockets. They were sweating in the palms.

"I explained to you," Bo said. "You let these guys get away with things like that and they'll cheat everybody up and down the line."

She couldn't see him any more because her eyes were blurry. "That was the most brutal thing I ever saw," she said.

He did not speak for a moment, but when he did his voice was rougher. "You shouldn't have been around there," he said. "That's a man's place. It's no place for a woman."

She looked at him, almost stammering. "Excuse me," she said. "I didn't know the sidewalks were some place I shouldn't go. But I suppose you have to have them clear so you can beat somebody up every once in a while!"

"Listen, Elsa . . ."

"Listen nothing! I thought you were big and strong and fine, and now I find out that all you use your strength for is to hit people who beg you not to. If you'd shown any mercy at all, the least bit of pity . . ."

"Just because I sock a damn tinhorn that slugs my machine, I'm that bad."

"You're worse."

He laughed, the short, choppy, contemptuous sound that meant he was disgusted. "All right," he said briefly. "That's the way you feel about it." He pulled down his derby and ducked out into the drizzle.

Very slowly the fury drained out of her. Weakness wobbled her knees. She sat down at the table and bit her knuckles and stared at the wall. After a while she picked up the lamp and made her way through the parlor past Karl, who looked up with a discreet question in his eyes that she ignored.

7

Helm stood spraddle-legged, resting her weight evenly on both feet before the kitchen table she was using for an ironing board. The room was full of the smell of steam and starch. Helm's great bare arm, solid as a sawlog, moved with weight and authority back and forth, and her tongue moved just as heavily, just as authoritatively, with the same kind of bludgeoning dislike.

"Now this," she said, "is the shirt of Mr. Gerald Witwer, the druggist. Look at it. French flannel, fine enough to wrap a baby in. Summer times he wears silk and madras. His old lady never sends his underwear, and there are only two possible reasons why. Either she don't want to give away that he wears silk panties, or he can't hang onto himself and she's ashamed to send them with the wash. I don't know which choice I'd rather take. Maybe both."

She finished the shirt and folded it onto the pile in the basket. "Sometimes," she said, "I think I'd rather sit out in front of Bo's poolhall with a patch over my eye and a tincup strapped on my leg than wash the dirt out of clothes for people like them. Even when they're clean, those clothes are dirty. There's some kinds of hypocritical dirt you can't get out."

Elsa was only half listening. She sat by the window looking out, thinking that fall wasn't the pleasant season here that it was at home. There weren't any trees to change, for one thing. The land just got brown and then gray, and one night it froze, and then it rained, and froze again so that the roads were ridged with hardened tracks, and every change from summer to winter made the place look more desolate than it had before. And the wind blew interminably, holding you back, hustling you along, sweeping at you from around corners. You weren't free of it even inside, for it whined in the eavespouts and slammed doors and eddied down the chimney and made the stove smoke. It kept you tense all the time . . .

The realization that Helm had stopped speaking made her look up. Helm was watching her, smiling with her blackened teeth, her eyes soft and shining. "Honey," Helm said, "ain't you made it up with Bo yet?"

Elsa shook her head.

"Ain't you going to?"

Elsa shook her head again.

"It isn't like you to hold a grudge," Helm said.

"It isn't a grudge!" Elsa said. "I just can't like him after what he did."

"Well, what did he do?" Helm said. "He knocked down a tramp that had slugged a slot machine. That isn't anything to break your heart over, honey. If you try to find a man that never knocked another man down you're going to be left with nothing but guys like Gerald Witwer to pick from. I'd rather have one that *could* knock somebody else down, even if he had to do it once in a while to keep in practice."

"He did it in cold blood," Elsa said stubbornly. "That was what . . ."

"Bo hasn't got a drop of cold blood in him," Helm said. "Tell me he's got too wild a temper and gets disgusted too quick and despises people if they're clumsy or puny or hypocritical, but don't tell me he's cold blooded."

"He was that day. I saw him."

Helm released the catch and dropped a sadiron onto the stove, picked up another, upended it, spat on the smooth bottom. "Well, it sure hasn't helped your disposition, either one of you," she said. "You mope around like you didn't care whether you lit butter-side up or down, and Bo goes snarling around the place like a dog that's been kicked around too much and is going to bite the next guy tries it. Why don't you call it quits and give your friends a rest?"

"I'm sorry," Elsa said, and rose. "I don't want to be grumpy and bad company. It's the darned weather. I never saw weather stay so gray and disagreeable. I never could be cheerful in bad weather."

"Honey," the big woman said, "you're talking right through the top of your hat."

But Helm didn't know everything, Elsa thought on the way home. She hadn't seen Bo hit that man. Besides, Helm, for all her big heart, was used to rough men. She thought a man ought to be rough. But he oughtn't. A man could be strong and full of courage and still be generous and kind.

But what on earth shall I do? she said, and looked with distaste at the weedy vacant lot she was passing. While she had been dreaming her idiotic dreams about Bo Mason, Hardanger had been a vivid and exciting place, but now that those were put away it was a dreary little village on the desolate flats. And the only people she knew in it were in some way tied up with Bo. The Witwers and the Schantzes and the more "respectable" part of town kept to itself; there wasn't a friend to make the place bearable except those friends who were also friends of Bo's, and she never went to Helm's any more without dreading to find him there.

She heard the train whistle forlornly as she turned in at Karl's house. She felt as lonely as the train sounded, but inside the hall she took off her coat almost angrily. What she needed was work; if she didn't do something she'd be pitying herself until she blubbered.

When she went to the kitchen and started in she found the four mallards on the table. There was no note with them, but she knew instantly who had brought them. Karl never went hunting. Neither did Jud. There was only one other person who would have left them.

Well, she thought, if he thinks he can wheedle me out of it that way! But that was the second thing that came into her mind. The first was pleasure: the very sight of the ducks lying there, and the instant recognition of their giver, was a pure warm pleasure.

Three days later, when she opened the front door to sweep the first dry snow of the year off the porch, there were four more ducks hanging on the doorknob. They had not been there more than a few minutes, for their webbed feet were barely stiff, and the bodies of the ducks when she plucked them were still faintly warm. The tracks that led to and from the porch were large tracks, the imprints corrugated like the rubber sole of a wader boot.

Karl raised his eyebrows when he saw her plucking the second batch of birds. But she gave him no explanation. There wasn't any explanation she could give him. She told herself that she was not softening one bit, that he could go on leaving ducks as long as he chose and she would not change her mind about him. Still, she looked at both front and kitchen door every morning to see if anything else was there. On the Sunday following the first mallards there was a great Canada goose.

"Don't you think we ought to have company for supper?" Karl said. "If this buck Indian or whoever he is keeps leaving game in front of the wigwam we ought at least to let him come and eat some of it, hadn't we?"

Elsa was on the point of saying yes, and letting her anger and her dislike evaporate, but when she looked up into Karl's little knowing round blue eyes she shook her head. "I'd rather not, Uncle Karl."

He shrugged and let it go, and after he had left for the store she wondered if Bo had put him up to that question. It would be just like him, and then he could come swaggering in, on her invitation. If she made the first move then his pride would be saved. But the first move had already been made, she reminded herself, and he had made it.

Oh, I don't know! she said in vexation, and stormed through the house doing her housework as if every pillow were a face to be slapped. He did hit that man in cold blood, she said, but she couldn't fix the image of the sprawling body and the bloody mouth as definitely as she would have liked. Bo's eyes kept coming in over it, gray and steady and somberly warm, and once during the morning she found herself mentally moulding the blunt angle of his jaw, almost as if she were running her fingers along it.

The postoffice was at the far end of town, a frame shanty with a wall of boxes and a stamp window. Within the past two weeks the winter stove had been set up in the center of the room and a great pile of lignite dumped against the back wall outside. There were almost always two or three men sitting around on the bench, because on these cold days the postoffice was snug.

Elsa found herself anticipating that hot, tobacco-smelling cubbyhole as she walked through the light snow. Even the few blocks' walk from Karl's house could redden her nose and whiten her breath these days. She walked fast, noticing that all the houses were banked with dirt or had tarpaper tacked along the foundations; the smokes from all the chimneys had a warm, intimate look, and the town seemed friendlier now that its ugly weedgrown lots were covered with snow. There were stubby icicles hanging from the eaves of the postoffice.

She was not thinking about Bo at all when she opened the door and stepped in. If she had been, she might have been better prepared. As it was, she stopped dead still just inside the door, with her hand still on the knob.

"Morning," he said.

A swift look showed her no one else in the room except old Mr. Blake, puttering in the room behind the window.

"Hello," she said briefly, and went to Karl's box. He was right behind her; she felt his presence with a kind of stage fright.

"Look," he said. She took the one white envelope from the box, her mind automatically registering that it was from Indian Falls, in her father's spidery, old-world hand, and with the letter held helplessly in her fingers, she looked. His eyes were so sober, so warm, so compelling, that she was confused. She ought to walk right on out, bid him good morning and open the door . . .

"Call it quits?" Bo said.

"I . . ." Her confusion deepened. He was too direct and blunt. She fought the blood back from her face.

"I'll apologize," he said. "I'll admit I was wrong, if that's what you want."

"That wouldn't make it good to the poor man you hit," she said.

"I already made that good."

"You did?"

"As much as I could. I took him in and fed him and gave him money to get out of town."

"When?"

"Right after I saw you down there, right after it happened."

"But you didn't tell me," she said.

"You never gave me a chance."

"I . . ." Elsa said again.

"I still think there's only one way to treat a tinhorn," Bo said, "but after the way you looked I got worrying about him and went out and brought him in. I guess maybe I was already mad when I spotted him. Karl had been giving me the currycomb for a half hour."

"What about?" she said curiously. She couldn't imagine Karl doing anything of the kind.

"You."

"Me!"

"You," Bo said. "He'd got a letter from your father telling him to get you out of my clutches."

"Oh!" Elsa said furiously. She turned half away from his intent stare. The letter in her fingers was like a match held too long. She looked at it, wanting to drop it as she would have dropped the match before it burned her, but she did not drop it. When she looked up Bo was looking at it too.

"That another one from him?" he said.

She nodded.

"Kind of upset, isn't he?" he said, and laughed. In spite of her rage, she had to laugh with him.

"Sometimes," she said, "I could . . ."

"He made me a little mad myself," Bo said. "I guess I took it out on that bum. Shall we call it quits?"

Elsa looked into his face, dark and square, a little curl of smile at the corners of his mouth, his eyes smoky and glowing. "All right," she said. "I . . ." She shook her head. "Everything is such a mess," she said.

Bo held up his hand, and she saw that he too had a letter. He was grinning. "Between your family and mine," he said, "we've got a nice combination."

"Your family?" she said. "I didn't know you ever heard from your family." She craned to read the return address in the corner of the envelope: Hattie Mason, Black Hawk, Illinois.

"My sister's the only one ever writes. I don't even know where any of them are now, except her and Ma."

"Are they . . . well?" Elsa said. It was a silly thing to say, but she didn't want him to stop talking about them.

"They must be, the way their appetites hold out."

"You mean you support them?"

"No. They pull the hard luck story out of the bag about half a dozen times a year, and I send them something."

"I shouldn't think they'd have the nerve, after the way they treated you."

He was amused. "They treated me all right. Where'd you get that idea?"

"But you ran away from home."

"I ran away from the old man," Bo said. "He's been dead for ten years."

"Oh." She couldn't think of anything else to ask him, and they stood in the room's heat looking at each other. Mr. Blake stuck his gray head through the window, looked around, pulled it back in with a slow munching of toothless jaws. Bo put out a hand and touched her fur collar. "Thanks," he said. "You're a sport. I haven't felt as good as this for two weeks. That feud was getting my goat."

"Me too," she said, and blushed.

"Where you headed?"

"I was going over to Helm's and give her a loaf of fresh bread,"

she said, and lifted the newspaper-wrapped parcel under her arm.
"I got something to show you." He regarded her abstractedly, his
tongue in the corner of his mouth. "You run on over, and I'll bust
past the hotel and get it and see you at Helm's. How's that?"

"Good." She smiled at him, couldn't keep the smile from breaking
into a laugh. "I'm so glad we've quit fighting!" she said, and started
back along the sidewalk. She had gone only a dozen steps when her
hat was knocked over her eye by a large soft snowball.

"One down, one cigar," Bo said as she turned. He was stooping
for another handful. "Where you want this one?"

"Quit it." She shielded herself with the bundle of bread. The
second snowball plastered itself against the newspapers, and she
started for him. Instead of running, as she had expected him to, he
grabbed a handful of snow and before she knew where she was had
washed her face with it. "Keep your complexion pretty," he said.

Sputtering, she grabbed snow and scuffled with him in the street.
Mr. Blake came to the door of the postoffice and stood watching.
"Hey," he said mildly. "What goes on, what goes on?"

Bo crunched a snowball within three inches of Mr. Blake's head
and Mr. Blake retreated. Elsa, stooping, caught Bo off guard with
a double handful of snow, wiped it around his face, grabbed her
bread by the string, and ran. The snow melted on her face, and she
wiped it off, looking back to make sure that Bo was not after her
again. He stood beside the postoffice in a burly black dogskin coat,
his teeth white in his dark face, and waved.

"Well," Helm said when she came in. "Roses in the cheeks."

"That big ape of a Bo," Elsa said. "He . . ."

She stopped, seeing Helm's smirk. "That explains everything,"
Helm said. "Don't bother to go on."

"He washed my face with snow!" Elsa said. "It isn't anything like
you think."

"Don't bother explaining," Helm said. "He washed your face, and
you're still mad. I could tell by the way you look you wouldn't speak
to him on a bet."

"Oh, go to grass," Elsa said. "I brought you some bread. In a
minute I'll wish I hadn't."

Still grinning, Helm waddled into the kitchen to put the bread
away. When she came back Elsa said, "I didn't know he was sending
money back to his family."

"Is he?"

"Every once in a while. They write and ask him for money and he sends it."

"What's wrong with that?"

"Nothing, only I wish I'd known it before. I think it's nice of him."

"Oh, he's cold blooded that way," Helm said. "Just sends money home as calmly as if he was cutting somebody's throat."

"Well, why didn't you tell me?" Elsa said. "You let me just go on . . ."

"Couldn't anybody tell you anything, last couple weeks," Helm said.

There was a stamping on the porch and Bo came in in his dogskin coat, looking as immense as a bear. He was whistling a bar of the rube ballad they had heard at the carnival. He made a pass at Helm and she lifted her great white arm.

"Feeling pretty horsy, ain't you?" she said.

"Isn't anything particularly wrong, is there?" he said.

"What's so right?" Helm said.

"Well, the *Svenske flika* has called off her dogs," Bo said. His mouth drew down as he looked at Elsa. "Then again," he said, "Jud and me just sold three thousand bushel of flax up twenty-seven cents from where we bought it."

"My goodness," Elsa said. "That's a lot of money."

"Chicken feed," Bo said. "Wait till we get going."

He was so pleased with himself and the world that he couldn't keep still. He sparred with two of Helm's boys in the kitchen, captured the pup and rolled him over to scratch his chest until the automatic hind leg was pumping, jumped up from that to go to his coat, thrown over the dining table, and bring out a package. "Forgot what I was going to show you," he said. "How do you like this?"

It was a silver shaving mug, ornately carved and moulded, with a grapevine curling around the rolled brim and three heavy clusters of metal grapes hanging down from the vine. In the unornamented metal on the side was engraved

> Champion of North Dakota
> Singles Traps
> Harry Mason, 1905

"It's lovely," Elsa said, when she had looked it over. "I didn't know they gave you a cup too." She handed it back, but he put his hands behind him.

"Keep your property."

"What?"

"It's yours. Don't you spik the English?"

"Take it, for God sakes," Helm said, "before you make him cry."

Bo scowled at her. "Seems to me there's an awful lot of low class people around here," he said. "How about going for a walk?"

Helm stood with her hands on her hips and watched them get into their coats. She shook her head. "By God, it must be love," she said.

His hand under her elbow, Bo steered her down the beaten path in the snow. "Let's go out on the flats," he said. "I've been inside so much lately I need to get some wind through me."

She lifted her skirts and plunged with him, up to her shoetops in snow. The minute they were outside he had seemed to grow somber, and he said nothing all the way out past the last straggling shacks and into the open fields. The silence began to weigh on Elsa.

"Isn't Helm a funny old thing?" she said.

His head turned, his eyes met hers briefly. Then they looked away, ahead, anywhere, across the even white plain. Their feet found ripple-marked crust over a drift that almost held their weight, but not quite, and they staggered through it awkwardly.

"Funny?" he said.

"She says such funny things," Elsa said.

"She isn't as silly as she sounds," Bo said.

They were walking across the waves of a plowed field, ribbed brown and white. A yellow cat, tender-footed, delicate, obviously disgusted at the feel of snow under its pads, obviously out of place and irritated at whatever errand took it out into the fields on such a day, crossed in front of them, stopped with a lifted forefoot, opened its mouth in a soundless mew, went delicately forward again. Bo pegged a snowball at it and it flattened against the frozen furrow. Another, and it forgot its sensitiveness and leaped across the field in great muscular wild-animal bounds.

"What on earth would a cat be doing out here?" Elsa said.

His look was sober and intent, packed with some concentrated meaning she couldn't read. "I feel about as out of place as the cat," he said.

"Why?"

He stopped and faced her. "I want to ask you something."

Over his dogskin shoulder she saw the steely sky, misted, wintry, and back of him, spreading on all sides, the flat and wintry plain, spare yellow grass poking up in places swept clean by the wind, the surface irregular with miniature mounds tailed by flat cones of drift. She couldn't lift her eyes until he took her by the elbows. His hands were as rough as his voice.

"How about it?" he said.

"How about what?" she said, refusing to let herself know what he meant.

"How about marrying me?"

Her face cold in the wind, her mind stopped by the enormity of what was happening, she looked up at him. His face was paler than she had ever seen it, and there was no foolery in it. She nodded.

He moved so suddenly to kiss her that her feet tripped in the scored field and he fell against her awkwardly. They sprawled together. Instantly the constraint was gone; their laughter shouted into the wind, and they sat kissing exuberantly with cold lips in the middle of the waste of snow.

She held him away to look at him, noticing the subtle mingling of light and dark coloring in the pupils of his eyes, and the curving firmness of his mouth. Her shoulders drew up in an uncontrollable shiver. "You've got a nice mouth," she said, tracing it with her finger. "A nice mouth and dappled eyes."

It seemed that afternoon, when lunch was over and they had told Karl and had decided to be married right after New Year, and Karl had gone back to the store and left them alone to plan things, that all the trouble with Sarah, her father, Indian Falls, all the sense of uprooting and homelessness and the multiple problems that had invaded her life, were swept backward out of her mind like straw from a thresher spout, and her world was clean and new and spotless, to be made into what she would.

Bo told her that he was going to sell the poolhall. It didn't make enough money to satisfy him. Bill Conzett had offered him a price —not high enough, but it might be better to take it and get that money for speculating in grain. And there was the hotel in Grand Forks that he and Jud had been looking over. With that, plus the annual pickings they could make on grain, they ought to make a pile. He would build her a house in Grand Forks as soon as things got rolling good, and meantime, if the hotel deal went through, there was always a place to live.

She lay with his arm around her, thinking of that house they would build, of the lawn she would plant and the trees that would make it pleasant on warm afternoons in summer, and the roses over the trellis in front and the hollyhocks high against a whitewashed back fence, and the grape arbor. . . .

"Oh goodness!" she said, and sat up suddenly. "I forgot all about that letter from Pa!"

She knew what would be in it, how much his world was set against the kind of world he thought she was getting into, and she was grateful when she opened it and saw that it was in Norwegian. Bo, looking over her shoulder, couldn't read it. All he could do was snort at the spidery hand and the unfamiliar tangle of letters. Outside the wind had risen, and pebbly snow lashed at the storm windows. Bo leaned further to see the cranky letters. "Hen tracks," he said. "What's he say?"

"He . . . doesn't think you're the right sort of man for me to be going around with," Elsa said. Her laugh was a little shrill, and she cut it off sharply. "He says anyone with a name like Bo is probably suspicious from the beginning, and Karl told him you ran a bowling alley. He doesn't want me to get mixed up with any rough crowd of people. Uncle Karl ought to take more care what people I know."

"Careful of you, isn't he?" Bo said.

"That isn't all," she said. "Listen. 'From what Karl says I do not judge this Mason the proper sort of man for you to marry. If you insist you will be going against my wishes. At the very least I hope you will bring him back here for a visit before you do anything rash.'"

Bo was fiddling with her hand, bending the thumb, releasing it. He looked up from under his upcurved eyebrows. "What's that mean? Do we take a trip to Minnesota to get looked over?"

Elsa compressed her lips. If she didn't do as she pleased now, she would never have the right of making her own decisions. "No," she said flatly. "He hasn't any right to have a say in my affairs. We'll go right ahead and let him lump it."

"That'll mean he'll disown you, or something else nice and high-minded."

"Maybe."

He snorted. He strode to the door and threw it open. The wind whipped snow in level, driving lines across his body and through the hall. "Go!" he said, pointing with a stiff finger. "Never darken my door again!"

Elsa laughed and bit her lip. "Shut the door," she said. "You'll have the hall full of snow."

"'Tis kind of blowing, at that," he said. He shut the door and came back to nuzzle in her hair. "Does it matter much?" he said.

"It's just exactly what happened to him," she said. "He was not good enough for Mother, her folks thought, and they threw her out because she insisted on marrying him. Now he acts the same way they did."

"I'm perfectly willing to go see him."

"No," she said. "He never asked any of us when he was going to marry Sarah."

"So it's all set," Bo said. "New Year's day."

She nodded, and his eyes crinkled in the full-lidded smile that hardly moved his lips. "Any idea how good that makes me feel?"

"No," she said. "Tell me."

"Makes me feel as if I could settle down," Bo said. "Seems to me I've been on the move ever since I can remember. We'll find some good proposition and dowel ourselves in and keep our nose to the grindstone and make a pile."

Later he said he ought to run down to the poolhall and make sure everything was jake. He'd be back for supper if she'd let him. She kissed him long and hard at the door, clenching her fingers in the hairy coat, begrudging even the hour or so he would be gone.

But he was not gone an hour. He had barely ducked into the wind, which now blew with heavy, gusty force, and she had barely settled down to look at her father's letter again, when he was back, stamping the snow off his feet, his nose red and leaking, his coat stiff with driven snow.

"This is going to be a buster," he said. "You can't see ten feet. The old poolhall can get along by itself. Getting cold as all billy hell, too."

"Can Uncle Karl get home, do you suppose?"

"He's a sucker if he tries it."

"Maybe we ought to get fixed," she said. "If it's going to be a bad storm."

"That's why I came back," he said. "We might be marooned three days if this keeps on."

He shouldered his way out the kitchen door with coal scuttle and bucket. It was five minutes before he came back. "By God," he said, and wiped the frozen clot from below his nose with a quick side glance of shame. "I got lost between here and the coal shed. This is an old ring-tailed roarer, let me tell you."

He dumped the buckets in the box and went out again, and a third time. When the box was full he brought in another load and filled the kitchen range and the heater, went out still once more for a last pair of buckets. Then he sat down in a kitchen chair and hung out his tongue with mock exhaustion, wiping the melting snow off his forehead with the back of his hand. His laugh filled the warm kitchen.

"How about some supper, wife?" he said.

They got into aprons and played housekeeping. It was six thirty by the time they had finished eating, and still Karl had not come. Elsa kept holding up her hand to listen for sounds. There was never anything but the pounding of the wind and the restless fluttering of the stove.

"Quit worrying," Bo said. "Karl's too wise a bird to start out in this. He'll stay snug in the store till it stops."

He was laughing, warm-eyed, the corners of his lips twitching with mirth. His big hands lay on the edge of the table before him.

"That isn't all I'm worrying about."

He leaned across the table to kiss her. "What else?"

She forced herself to meet his eyes. "If he doesn't come home, we'll be here together all night."

He laughed aloud. "Why not? We're going to be married pretty soon. And nobody can talk if people get marooned in a blizzard. It happens all the time."

He came around to her, put his hands under her chin, bent over her from behind. "It's been just like we've been married ever since this morning," he said. "Why should we worry if it keeps on?"

She shook herself loose and stood up, her chest tight and her face wrinkled as if with a pain. "Don't blame me," she said. "I . . . things come so fast, somehow. I seem to change my ideas about things from one day to the next." She put her hand on his arm. "It seems all right to me, now," she said. "Honestly it does. But can't you see what it would mean? After that letter from Pa, and the way he thinks you're not the right sort, for some reason? We'd just be giving him and people like him a chance to talk and say I told you so."

"I could slide out," Bo said. "When the storm started to let up I could vanish."

"Would you want me to be like Eva?" she said. "Do you want to be like Jud?"

For a moment he watched her face. Then he shrugged. "All right. But what if we can't help being cooped up here?"

"I don't know," she said helplessly.

His laugh chopped out, a short, mirthless recognition of the irony of what he had to do. "If I get my directions crossed and come back feet first you'll wish you'd been a little more tenderhearted," he said.

"What are you going to do?"

"Go get Karl, what'd you think?"

"Bo, you can't! You'd get lost, or frozen stiff."

"Probably will," he said amiably. "Got any rope around here?"

While she hung on his arm crying that he was insane, that he wouldn't get to the corner, that she never meant he should go out into the blizzard, she didn't know what she meant, he towed her around the kitchen poking into cupboards and drawers for rope. He was as stubborn as a mule. He was an idiot. He would die in the storm, and then how would she feel?

With a length of clothes line in his hand he looked at her quizzically. "When you convince me," he said, "you convince me for good."

"There must be some other way. Couldn't you go over to Conzett's? That's closer." Then her temper let loose. "Anyway, I should think you'd be able to control yourself even if we were marooned."

He shook his head with a hanging, mocking grin. "Wouldn't promise a thing," he said. "Us undesirable characters can't be trusted."

"All right, then," she said, and let go of his arm. "Go on out and freeze to death."

She even went into the cellar hole and found him twenty feet of rope and a length of picket chain. But when he started out the front door (he had to put his shoulder against it and heave to move the storm door through the accumulated drift) she threw herself against the dogskin coat and clung. "Oh, be careful, Bo! If you can't find your way don't try too long."

By now, she saw, his stubbornness and recklessness wouldn't have let him stay even if she had begged him to. He grinned, kissed her, throttled her with an enormous bear hug, put his head down, and ran.

He must have run, she decided afterward, all the way to the store, taking a direction and plowing ahead blind. Probably he wanted to get there and back before she had time to worry; probably he also wanted to impress her with how fast he could do it. She was surprised; she was even startled, the stamping came on the porch so soon. She ran to open the door. Karl, his face muffled in a felt cap with earlaps and a broad chin band, with a yellow icicle in each nostril and his eyebrows stiffly iced, stumbled in. The rope around his waist was a smooth, velvety white cable.

The hall was full of wind and drift. *"Herregud!"* Karl said, and grabbed the storm door to keep it from blowing off its hinges. Bo loomed through the opaque, white-swirling darkness like a huge hairy animal.

When she had untied their lifeline she led them in, inspected them under the light for signs of frostbite, rushed Bo out into the hall while she scooped up snow and held it again the leprous spots on his cheekbones. He bit at her fingers, and she slapped him on the nose.

"That's a heck of a way to welcome a guy that's just risked his neck to go get a worthless old tumblebug like Karl."

"You hold still," she said. She scrubbed his face with snow till it glowed, looked to make sure all the spots were gone, and relaxed with a noisy sigh. "Oh, I'm glad you're back!" she said, and reached up to kiss his wet, beefy, ice-cold face, right in front of Karl. "How'd you ever make it?"

"Just spread my sails and coasted down. Wind lifted me right up and set me down square in front of the alleys. Ask Karl how we got back."

Huddling close to the stove with his neck still pulled into his shoulders, Karl grumbled. "Ask me!" he said. "Pulled me along like a steer. My belly'll be sore for a week."

Tall in the doorway, full of pride, Bo grinned at her. "Once," he said, "Karl got off the path and started off toward Fargo somewheres. I thought he was stuck in the snow, when it was only the rope caught around a telegraph pole, and I yanked him half in two before he backtracked and got straight again." He put an icy hand on the back of Elsa's neck. "Satisfied now?"

She squeezed the heavy muscles of his arm. Karl went into the kitchen, and she followed to get him his supper. Bo wandered after her. "What's the use of postponing this marriage till New Year?" he said. "Why don't we get a preacher and get it over with?"

"You sound as if it was like moving the furniture, or something," Elsa said. She couldn't get married in a rush like that. There wasn't anything ready, no towels, no sheets, no clothes, no anything to keep house with. But as she looked at his cold-reddened face and his smoky, laughing eyes, and thought how nice he'd been, really, to go out in a storm like that and bring Karl back just so she wouldn't get talked about, and because she wanted him to . . .

"I guess we can at least wait till the blizzard's over," she said.

It was almost the first time she had heard real mirth in his laughter, the first time it had sounded exuberant and full instead of short and half impatient. He pulled her onto his lap on the kitchen chair, while Karl grunted and grumbled over his supper, and scuffled with her, trying to take a toothy bite out of her between the neck and shoulder, where she was most ticklish. He was so boisterous and rough and strong that she struggled, but he held her arms and reduced her to helplessness.

"Hear that, Karl?" he said. "You can give the bride away about day after tomorrow."

"I'll be giving her away, all right," Karl said. "Might as well throw a girl to the lions."

"I'm tame," Bo said. "I'm completely house-broke. You tell him, Elsa."

"About like a dancing bear," she said. He set her suddenly on her feet and stood up.

"We have to consult the oracles," he said. "See if this marriage is going to be a success. I'll play you eleven games of casino to see who's going to wear the pants in the family. And if I win I'll play you eleven more for the championship of the Chicago stockyards."

Even after Karl had been long in bed and the kerosene in the parlor lamp had given out, and the lamp had dimmed, flared, sunk, flared up again, and gone out in a stink of coal oil; even after they had quit fooling around playing cards and had settled on the sofa with the rattle of granular snow on the windows and the house shuddering under the whining strength of the wind, there was a golden light over her mind, and her senses swayed with the swaying of a ghostly hammock in an idyllic grassy backyard with hollyhocks tall against a whitewashed fence, and a redbird was nesting in the grape arbor.

II

In one way the accident was a blessing, for now, after she had swept the broom awkwardly, one-handed, across the tenthouse floor, had soused the dishes and set them to dry, and had stooped and pulled, making the beds, while the blood rushed painfully into her injured arm, there was good time to rest. For an hour or more in the mornings and for long quiet periods in the afternoons she could sit on the plank platform before the door and let the children run in the clearing and simply relax, her mind still and her senses full of the sounds and smells that the woods had always had but that she had never had time to notice before.

Cradling her right arm, spiralled with thick bandage, in her lap, she could close her eyes and hear the tapping of woodpeckers off in the forest, and sometimes the drumming of a grouse. Her lungs loved the balsam air, and her body soaked up warmth, infinitely pleasant after the weeks of rain. It was as if a blessing had fallen suddenly on the half acre of stumpy ground. For five days there had been fine weather: every morning the sun tipped the firs and poured into the open, creeping from chip to chip until it filled the clearing, leaned its friendly weight on the tenthouse door. By the time Bo went to work at seven the shadows had all pulled themselves back toward the ring of woods, and while she did her housework she could feel the warmth growing on the canvas roof. When she handed out the carrots and greens for the two boys to feed to their rabbits, and came out to stand in the full sun, it was with a sense of peace and permanence so alien that she had to smile at her own perception of it.

More than anything else, it was the rabbits that gave her that feeling of home—they and the children digging in the dirt around a big stump. Home, as she imagined it and remembered it, had always meant those things, children, permanence, the recurrence of monotonous and warmly-felt days, and animals to care for. More than once, leaning her back against the wall, she fingered the bandage caressingly. It was odd you never realized how tired you were until something made you take a rest.

Even the pain beating in her arm from wrist to elbow with a steady nagging ache was good, because it reminded her that now there was a kind of fulfillment. The pain was like something left over from the rainy winter, lying in her like the things that she could not forget. But it would pass, and the things she had thought she could never forget she would forget. Unless she stirred too fast, or got impatient at her crippling, when it would leap instantly to an immense and throbbing pressure against the tight bandage, it was even a half-pleasant kind of pain. It would pass, but the peace would not pass. While you lay against the tent wall in the sun and the children dug endlessly and happily in the dirt Bo was working, and when the arm was better you would go back to work too, and the tenthouse would not always be a tenthouse. As you got ahead a little further it would become a house, with a barn behind at the edge of the firs, and the café would bring in a little money and you could have a garden and a few animals, a cow and some chickens, and that would be a good life.

In the sun, her face tipped back and her burned arm in her lap, she let down her hair and shook it over her shoulders, as thick and wavy and richly tinted as ever, lavish and rich and good to feel when it was well brushed. That was an odd thing too. In your childhood everybody teased you about your hair and yelled, "There comes a white horse, kid!" but now everybody seemed to think it was beautiful. You got more compliments on your hair than anything. As she brushed evenly down, pulling the hair over her breast to get at it with her good hand, she thought much about how their lives would be now, how Bo seemed to be over his disappointment and his restlessness. Seven years of hard times, and the crash of 1907, had humbled his ambitions. Perhaps that was good too. It didn't do to expect too much.

It was that hotel, she thought. Five years of butting our heads against that wall! Idly she watched a half dozen chickadees fussily busy at a crust of bread one of the boys had dropped. Her brush handle lay smooth and rounded and solid in her hand. She felt it there, something she could put down if she chose, but she did not put it down. She liked its solid familiar feel. That was the way with things you remembered. You could put them down if you chose, but you didn't quite choose. Every once in a while you took them up and found them familiar and well worn and intimate, and you kept them where you could touch them when you wanted to.

But that hotel. There was little you wanted to remember about that. The musty smell of the halls, the unpleasant work of cleaning rooms after the bank went and the help had to be let go, the unfriendly masculine atmosphere of the lobby, with its faint sour smell of whiskey from the bar that had gone on in spite of her protests (How can you run a commercial hotel without a bar?). It was funny, but the things you felt most vividly about that hotel, even more vividly than you felt the birth of Chester and Bruce in the first floor front suite where you lived, even more than you felt the loss of the first one, the girl baby born dead, were the evenings when Bo played solitaire and the time Pinky Jordan came around. Those things had weight in the memory; those were what was left when you boiled down six years in your mind.

The solitaire grew on him slowly in the days when receipts and expenses chased each other in an endless circle and the big companies took their drummers off the road and the bank had been cleaned out. It became a ritual, a kind of intent solitary fortune-telling game. Every evening he sat down at the table with cards and a tablet and pencil. The game never varied. He bought the deck for fifty-two dollars and got back five for every card he put up. For hours, some nights, she heard the stiff riffle of cards, the slipping noise as he thumbed the deck, the light smack as he laid them down. Looking up, she saw his dark, intent face, dark even in winter, bent over the game. When the last card was gone he leaned over and added figures to the long string on the tablet, adding or subtracting from his total gain or loss. Then the riffle again, the expert flip of the cut, the light smack of a new layout going down. Sometimes, cleaning up, she looked with baffled wonder at the columns of figures on a discarded tablet sheet, the thousands of dollars of mythical debt, and once in a while at top or bottom a string of aimless figures elaborately penmanlike, neat sevens and nines and twos with curly tails, or signatures with strong flowing downstrokes: Harry G. Mason, Harry G. Mason. 7 7 7 7 7 7, 2 2 2 2 2 2, 9 9 9—and the debt going up in fantastic figures from page to page. She learned to know that whenever the aimless signatures and the strings of numbers appeared on the pages, he was more baffled and restless and prowling and dissatisfied than usual, that somebody had ducked on his bill or that he and Jud had lost money in a poker game in the room behind the bar.

It did no good to laugh at him or get mad at him. He wanted, he said, to see how much he would stand to make from a solitaire game if he ever had a gambling house. When she asked him if he were planning on starting a gambling house he said no, of course not. But he wanted to know. She knew that he attached cabalistic importance to his figures. If he made money off his game one night, that meant that the next day the bar would do a good business, or there would be a couple more rooms rented. If he lost, the next day would be bad. So he did his best never to lose. He would play five games more just to see if he couldn't pick it up. When he lost on those he would play five more, and then ten more, and then fifteen more, just to make it an even fifty games for the evening, and if he had a string of games in which he did not win at all he became angry and intent and touchy, and went to bed angrily leaving cards and tablet sheets scattered over the table.

When he finally threw the deck down one night and said he had lost fifty-six thousand dollars on five thousand games, she thought he might be over that streak. But the next night he was playing solitaire cribbage, with the purpose, he said, of determining exactly what the average crib hand was. But cribbage too he used like a crystal ball. If he won as often as he lost, then the hotel would pull out of it and be a decent proposition. If he lost seventy-five out of a hundred games, it was a washout, they might as well sell it tomorrow, or give it away. If he won seventy-five out of a hundred, they'd make a mint.

She shook her head and smiled, remembering that. She couldn't remember how it had ended. So many evenings were blended into one composite recollection that she didn't know for sure whether he had been playing solitaire up to the time Pinky Jordan came to town, or whether he had stopped of his own accord. All she knew was that by the time Pinky Jordan came the hotel was a hopeless weight on their backs, that even Jud was getting the look of failure and defeat that it seemed to her now lay like mildew over all of them. And Eva still living with Jud in the hotel, not married but going by the name of Mrs. Chain, having attacks of her gall bladder trouble or whatever it was that ailed her, and needing attention like an invalid half the time. They were all tired out and low when Pinky Jordan came. Perhaps that was why he seemed like a comet across their horizon.

That day Elsa remembered as clearly as if it had been last week. (And why not? she said. If it hadn't been for him we wouldn't be here in Washington now, we wouldn't have gone back to Indian Falls that winter, we wouldn't have done anything, probably, except go on trying to make the hotel pay. Why wouldn't I remember an afternoon that changed our whole lives?) At the end of an opaque, telescoped gap in her life there was a little man with a nicked ear and a whiskey voice, a kind of Pied Piper who whistled one tune and up came all the roots of the people who heard him.

She was sitting in the chair behind the desk, resting after putting the children away for their naps and trying not to hear the random talk that came through the door of the blind pig, brazenly halfway open because of the heat. Chester had been down before going to bed, and Bo had swatted him with buggy pillows and tickled him into spasms and had ended by setting him on the bar and giving him a sip of beer. When she sailed in and rescued him, Bo had been disgusted, almost nasty. "Oh for God sakes!" he said. "What's the harm in that?" Jud, tending bar, winked at her and raised his shoulders eloquently. A couple of drummers had laughed.

Then as she sat behind the desk the screen door of the lobby opened and a little hatless baldheaded man came in. His face was a fiery rose-pink, and his bald red scalp was scrawled with bluish veins above the temples. His breath, when he leaned confidentially toward her, almost knocked her down. His voice was a whiskey voice. She had learned to recognize that. "I was told," said his hoarse whisper, "that a man could get a drink in here."

She jingled the bell for Bo, not even bothering to deny that they served liquor, as she ordinarily would have. This man was obviously no officer, but only a tramp or barfly wandering in on his way through town. Bo came hurriedly to the door, looked the man over, and motioned him inside. The door he left ajar.

She heard the clump of a bottle on the bar, and a low mutter of talk. Shortly the whiskey voice rose. "I'll have another'n of those."

Altogether he ordered five drinks in the course of an hour, in his hoarse, commanding whisper. The dead summer afternoon drifted on. A boy going past opened and slammed the screen door just to hear the voice. "Gimme another'n," said the whiskey voice from the bar.

Drowsily, without much interest but with nothing else to occupy her attention, she heard Bo come over and set one up for the stranger as he always did when anyone was buying freely. After a time the whiskey voice said, "How much, barkeep?"

Jud's voice said, "One seventy-five," and change clinked on the bar.

"Ain't got the change," the whiskey voice said. "You got a gold scale?"

"Hell no," Jud said, and laughed. "What for?"

"This's all I got with me." There was a sodden thump on the wood, and for once Elsa heard excitement and haste in Jud's voice. "I'll be damned," he said. "Hey, Bo, this guy wants to pay off in gold dust."

But the rapid steps, the noise of crowding, the exclamations, were at the bar almost as soon as he started to speak. "Where in hell did you get that?" Bo said.

"Klondike," said the superior, bored whiskey voice, "if that's any-a your business."

"No offense, no offense," Bo said. "We just don't see any of that around here. Pan it yourself?"

"Right out of the gravel, boys."

He must have poured some into his palm, for there were whistles and exclamations. Elsa strained her ears, but she needn't have. The men in the pig were almost shouting. "Jumping Jesus," a drummer said. "How much is that poke worth?"

"Oh—five, six hundred."

"Quite a slug to be lugging around," Bo said.

"More where that came from," the stranger said. "Plennnty more salted away, boys. Never carry more than I need."

"I'll go try the drugstore for a scale," Bo said. "How much an ounce?"

"Eighteen bucks."

Bo laughed, a short, incredulous chop of sound. "You have to spend your money with an eyedropper at that rate."

Pinky Jordan stayed all afternoon to soak up the admiration he had aroused. After she had brought the baby down in his buggy and set Chester to playing with his blocks, Elsa heard scraps of the tales he was holding his listeners with. Three more men had come back with Bo from the drugstore, and all afternoon others kept dropping in to have a beer and listen to stories of hundreds of miles of wild timberland, hundreds of thousands of caribou, hundreds of millions of salmon in suicidal dashes up the rivers; of woods full of bear and deer and otter and fox and wolverine and mink; of fruit salads on every tree in berry time. You didn't need to work for a living. You picked it off the bushes, netted it out of the river, shot it out of the woods, panned it out of the gravel in your front yard.

"You know how much a frenna mine got for one silver fox skin?" the whiskey voice was saying as she drew near the door once with the broom as an excuse. "For one, leetle, skin?" The voice was confidential and dramatic. "Four hunnerd dollahs."

There were whistles, clickings against the teeth. "Four hunnerd dollahs," Pinky Jordan said, "an' he traded it out of a halfbreed for a flannel shirt and a sheath knife. You wanna make your fortune, gentlemen, you go on up to God's country. Flowin'th milk and honey."

It was nearly supper time when Pinky Jordan, drunk on his own eloquence and the uncounted drinks his listeners had poured for him, wobbled out of the lobby. Bo was at his elbow, telling him confidentially that sometimes they got up a little game in the evenings. Be glad to have him drop in. Just a friendly little game, no high stakes, but pleasant. They'd be glad to have him.

Pinky Jordan nodded owlishly, winked both eyes so that his naked red scalp pulled down over his brows like a loose slipping skullcap. From the desk Elsa watched him in the horizontal light of evening hesitating on the front sidewalk, a little man with a red bald head and a nick out of his right ear as if someone had taken a neat bite from it. Then he started up the walk, kicking at a crumpled piece of paper. Each time he came up behind it, measured his kick, booted it a few feet, and staggered after it to measure and kick again. On the fourth kick he stubbed his toe and fell into the street, and the men who had been looking after him from lobby and sidewalk ran to set him straight again. He jerked his kingly elbows out of their hands and staggered out of sight.

Pinky Jordan never returned for the poker game, though Bo tried all the next day to locate him around town. But he had done his work. He left behind him a few dollars' worth of gold dust in a shot glass behind Bo Mason's bar. He also left behind him a vision of clean wilderness, white rivers and noble mountains, forests full of game and fabulously valuable fur, sand full of glittering grains. And he left in Bo, fretted by hard times and the burden of an unpaid mortgage and the worry and wear of keeping his nose too long to an unprofitable grindstone, a heightened case of that same old wandering itch that had driven him from town to town and job to job since he was fourteen.

He was born with the itch in his bones, Elsa knew. He was always telling stories of men who had gone over the hills to some new place and found a land of Canaan, made their pile, got to be big men in the communities they fathered. But the Canaans toward which Bo's feet had turned had not lived up to their promise. People had been before him. The cream, he said, was gone. He should have lived a hundred years earlier.

Yet he would never quite grant that all the good places were filled up. There was somewhere, if you knew where to find it, some place where money could be made like drawing water from a well, some Big Rock Candy Mountain where life was effortless and rich and unrestricted and full of adventure and action, where something could be had for nothing. He hadn't found it in Chicago or Milwaukee or Terre Haute or the Wisconsin woods or Dakota; there was no place and no business where you took chances and the chances paid off, where you played, and the play was profitable. Ball playing might have been it, if he had hit the big time, but bad luck had spoiled that chance. But in the Klondike . . . the Klondike, Elsa knew as soon as he opened his mouth to say something when Pinky Jordan was gone, was the real thing, the thing he had been looking for for a lifetime.

"Let me show you," he said, and brought the shot glass containing Pinky Jordan's immortal dust. His mind was whitehot with visions, and he vibrated like a harp to his own versions of Pinky's yarns. There was a place without these scorching summers that fried the meat on your bones; there was a place where banks didn't close and panics didn't reach, where they had no rules and regulations a man had to live by. You stood on your own two feet and to hell with the rest of the world. In the Klondike the rivers ran gold and silver fox skins fetched four hundred dollars apiece and the woods were full of them.

She was not surprised when he proposed selling the hotel and lighting out. It took him only three or four days to arrive at that plan, but she was ready for it.

"Do you know what time of the year it is?" she said.

His look was suspicious, as if he suspected her of plotting to throw hindrances in his path. "It doesn't take any astrologer to know it isn't Christmas," he said, and ran a finger inside the sweating band of his collar.

"No," she said, "but by the time you sell this place, and get to Seattle, and take a boat to Alaska or wherever it is you go, it will be Christmas."

His look this time was as heavy as a hand pushing against her. "What of it?"

"I believe you'd take those two little kids up there right in the dead of winter," she said.

"Winter's the fur season. Jud and I could go out trapping, and you and the kids could stay in town."

"Is Jud going?"

"Sure, if we do. He's all hot to go."

"Eva too."

"I suppose."

"So you've got it all planned," she said. "It's nice of you to come and tell me about it."

"Don't you want to go? Do you want to sit around here growing roots in your tail in this damned old hotel all your life?"

"That isn't it," she said. "I'm thinking about the kids."

"Yeah," he said gloomily. "Well, I don't know. Probably we couldn't move this joint with a derrick anyway."

But circumstances pushed them faster than they would have pushed themselves. Bo had just got her promise that she would go to Alaska in the spring if they could move the hotel during the winter when the police raided them, closed the blind pig, jailed Jud, and missed Bo only because he was out of the hotel at the time and ducked out of town when he heard. Within two weeks of Pinky Jordan's meteoric passage Elsa and the two children were on their way to Indian Falls, going back ignominiously to the home she had run away from six years before, accepting whatever stiff charity her father's letter offered.

It was Bo who wrote in from where he was staying in a soddy with a homesteader and suggested that armistice with Indian Falls. Now it was a cinch they'd have to get out of the hotel, and they'd need all the money they could scrape together for passage in the spring. Couldn't they stay on her old man's farm, maybe, and earn their keep helping run the place?

Elsa made a bitter face and ruffled the bristles in her hairbrush, trying to decide how she ever humbled herself for that surrender, how Bo could have suggested it. It was the dream of what they would do in the spring, she supposed, the fire of that optimism melting everything else down until the only important thing was to get to the promised land. She supposed he would have stolen and cheated and lied to get there. When he slipped aboard the train a hundred miles out of Grand Forks and slid into the seat beside her he did not mention where they were going or remark on how mean it was to come sneaking back after defiance and repudiation to accept as charity what you had once refused as your right. All he said, breathing on the glass and rubbing a place clean to see out of, was that by God he'd never been gladder to get out of any place than he was to get out of that hotel.

The hairbrush slipped from her knees, and her quick jerk to catch it set the blood to throbbing in her arm. Carefully, with a morbid curiosity about what it looked like today, she unwrapped the bandage. The sight of the arm outraged her, and the smell made her wrinkle her nose in disgust. From above her elbow to her fingers the arm was one red piece of butcher's meat spotted with watery blisters. At the wrist the bandage stuck, and she yanked it loose; blood oozed in beady droplets from the skinned flesh.

It didn't feel better with the bandage off. It felt worse. But somewhere she had read that sunshine was good for hurts of any kind, and so every day she exposed it.

A burn was a nasty kind of injury, she thought, inflamed and disgusting. Once she had been proud of her arms, but when she stretched them out together now, the one hard, round, white, the other a peeled monstrosity, she grimaced. Maybe it never would look right again. She turned the other arm over, studying its fitness, and saw a slightly chapped spot on the elbow. She must get some cold cream to put on that. She didn't want elbows like Harriett Conzett's, or a goat's knees. Or Sarah's. The last time she saw Sarah she had been like a walking waxwork, submerged, buried, slipping into middle age before she had ever been young.

I'm only twenty-six, Elsa thought. That isn't old. And maybe now we'll be all settled down and get a house built sometime and the boys will grow up and go to school. I've got at least forty years ahead of me, she thought. It seemed a wonderful and dangerous idea. She contemplated it, shaking her head and smiling, before she got clean bandage and rewrapped her arm and got up to make the children their dinner.

2

The boys had been long in bed when she heard Bo's steps on the path, and rose to pull the curtain closer around their bed and turn up the lamp. She heard the scuff of his soles on the foot scraper. He was always careful about tracking in mud. Then the door swung inward and he came in with a lantern in his hand, a package under the other arm. As he lifted the chimney and blew out the lantern his big body blocked the door.

"You're late tonight," she said. "Any business?"

"Chicken feed. How's your arm?"

"Pretty good."

"Been picking at it any more?"

"Some more skin came off." At his frown she added defensively, "It just peels off in sheets. I can't leave it there."

"What'd you take the bandage off for?"

"It feels better."

He dumped the package on the table, keeping one hand on it. "You deserve to get blood poison," he said. "Let the doc take the skin off, if it needs taking off."

"I was just sitting out in the sun. It felt so tight I unrolled the bandage, and there was that loose skin, so I just snipped it off."

He looked at her and shook his head as if defeated.

"Have you eaten anything?" she said.

"I ate before I closed up."

"Well, what happened today?" she said, and settled back comfortably on the bed. This was the way it should be. It should be warm and pleasant and homelike like this, with your husband coming home from work and everything snug for the night and plenty of time to talk. Only it was a shame he had to work such long hours now that she was laid up. She saw his hand still protective on the package, and his eyes secret and sly. "What have you got there?" she said.

"Been bargain hunting."

"What is it?"

"Bombs," he said, and moved the package away from her reaching hand. "I joined the I.W.W.'s."

With a quick grab she hooked her fingers in the string. "Let me see!"

"Look out. It might go off."

"Oh, quit your fooling and let me see."

He surrendered the parcel and watched her, grinning, while she undid the string. "Save the store-cording," he said, and she rolled the string into a coil before unwrapping the package. Inside was a set of books in a red marbled binding, with dark red leather on spines and corners. "Complete Works of Shakespeare," the lettering on the spine said. Uncertainly she opened one and looked inside. It looked expensive.

"Well?" Bo said.

"Where on earth did you get them?"

"Fella came around. Selling bibles mainly, but I didn't think you'd want a bible."

Under her fingers the leather was smooth and cool. "How much?" she said.

"What does that matter? Do you like them or don't you?"

"Of course I like them." Her voice was low. "But I bet you paid more than we could afford for them."

Bo picked up one of the books and hefted it appreciatively, cracked back the spine in a way that would have infuriated her father, who always went through a book page by page pressing down the sheets so as not to break the binding. "Well, hell," he said. "I'm sick of not having anything decent around. We've got to have some books around the place, kids growing up and everything. I'd like to have a whole roomful."

She read him as plain as daylight. He was afraid he had been stung, he was scared she wouldn't like them, he knew he had been extravagant, but just suggest that the book peddler had skinned him and he'd blow up like a bullfrog.

"A roomful of books in a tent!" she said, before she thought. Then she saw that he was hurt, and got up and hugged him around the neck. "I love them," she said. "It was sweet of you to think of getting me something."

He pulled her down on his lap. "I don't like living in a tent any better than you do," he said.

"It's funny," she said, relaxing against him. "Since I got burned I'd loved it. Everything's been so settled and quiet it's like home all of a sudden." Through his shirt his body was like a stove. She felt warm and comfortable, cradled in affection so sure and easy that she rubbed against him. "You've been so nice lately," she said. "It's like it used to be before our luck got bad."

"It sure isn't any better now," he said, and she felt his body stir irritably. "I can't understand why that joint don't make money. It ought to, but it don't."

"It makes some."

"Some isn't enough."

"Isn't it?" she said, pulling herself back to look in his face. "Isn't it enough to make a living and get ahead gradually and make sure of things one after another and settle down in one place?"

"It'd be all right if you could make enough to live like a human being."

"It's slow," she said, "but we do make a little all the time, Bo. We'll have the fixtures paid for in a few more months, and then we'll make more. If we're careful we'll be all right in a year."

He grunted. "Being careful is what makes my tail ache. You get kind of sick of being careful after while."

"Oh, we'll make it," she said. "As soon as I'm well I'll take over and you can sleep for a week. You're all tired out."

"I'm not tired out. I'm just sick of that dinky little lumber town and seeing the same guys across the counter week in and week out."

"When we get the installments paid off we can hire somebody, maybe," she said. She kissed the side of his face. "Bo," she said, "you know you haven't got mad at either of the kids for a week?"

He grunted, but good-naturedly. "I must have forgot. I'll take care of it tomorrow."

"You watch them," she said. "They're three times better when they don't get punished a lot. They're as sweet as pie all day."

His wide chest swelled and sank under her. "Yeah, I suppose. It's been so long since I saw either of them I'll have to be introduced all over again."

"You *are* all worn out," she said. "I'll hurry up and get well so you can have a rest." Suddenly, weakly, she wanted to cry. She put her face against him and laughed instead.

"What's the matter?"

"I don't know. I'm just so happy things are as good as they are, even. After what happened in Seattle I guess I didn't ever think I could feel happy again." She smiled into his warming, half closed eyes and hugged him with her good arm. "Did you know you're a darling sometimes?"

"I've been told so," Bo said comfortably. "What am I darling about now?"

"Just being you," she said. "Just being the nice you." Her eyes went down to the book he still held in one hand. "Bo?"

"What?" As if he were methodically ringing doorbells, his fingers went down her back pushing each vertebra.

"How much did you pay for those books?"

"Eighteen dollars."

"Oh my Lord!" She lay digesting the enormity of the extravagance, but the more it grew in her mind the less she could reproach him. Because she was hurt and shut in, because he felt bothered in his conscience for letting her get burned, because he was galled by the tightness of money and needed to do something to express his contempt for penny-pinching, he spent more in one insane gesture than she had been able to spend on the boys' clothes all winter. There was nothing you could say to him when he did a thing like that. He never even said outright that they were a present for you, though you knew they were. And even if there had been a hundred presents more useful and acceptable, you had to like this one, and love him for it.

She got no news from him that night about what was happening in the settlement or the lumber camp, because she forgot to ask, but the next morning she saw him kneeling before the big black bureau he had built. He rummaged and felt in the back of a drawer. "What are you looking for?" she said.

"The gun."

"What do you need the gun for?"

"Want to load it up for you." Deliberately uncommunicative, he stooped and grunted, searching. Elsa sat up in bed. "Why should it be loaded for me?"

The boys, who had been having a pillow fight in their own bed, craned to look as Bo pulled the thirty-eight out of the bureau and slipped cartridges into the cylinder.

"I'm just going to leave it where you can get at it," Bo said. "Make you feel a little safer, maybe." Grinning at her, he laid the gun on a high shelf out of the boys' reach.

"Now tell me!" she said.

"Nothing to be scared of," Bo said. "There's been a cougar around prowling the camps, is all."

"A cougar!"

"Never bother a man. They're scared to death of a man. They just sneak around nights and steal fish and things. If you heard anything around at night you could shoo him away with this. One shot would have him high-tailing it for the next county."

Elsa looked sideways at the children, listening round-eyed. He could say all he wanted. She was scared, just the same. A cougar could get through a tent wall like nothing, and even if he was afraid of a man, he wouldn't be afraid of a child.

"Think I should keep the kids inside?"

"Akh!" Bo put the box of cartridges away. "They only prowl at night."

"Well, but . . ."

"Keep 'em around close if it makes you feel better. But there's nothing to be scared of. Bruce there could scare him clear into Oregon."

For the first hour after he left she kept glancing out into the clearing. It would be another fine day. She tried to imagine cougars lying in wait behind the sunny edge of the trees, but the thought in such fresh morning light was absurd. At mid-morning she had the children playing outside, and had settled herself with one of her new books on the step. Looking for something familiar, she found *Romeo and Juliet*.

Once or twice, lifting her head from the book to make sure that the boys hadn't strayed, she wondered about what she was reading. Shakespeare was something great and far-off, a vague magnificent name. She couldn't remember ever knowing anyone who had read any Shakespeare, though Bo had told her about one night in Indianapolis when he saw *Macbeth*, a long time ago, and about the flames flying around a dark stage and three old hags dropping the finger bones of children into their pot. Now she was reading one herself, and it was much like any other story, except that it was in poetry and there were some words she wasn't sure of. But it was a good story. She read again, and Romeo had just killed Tybalt in a street brawl when Bruce called.

He had to go to the toilet. Absorbed in her reading, Elsa told him to go by himself, he was a big boy now. Watching him with one eye, she saw him start unwillingly on the path that led back into the fringe of trees, looking back all the time, dragging his feet. He got half way, looked into the jungle of blackberry bushes, stopped, and began to cry.

Elsa put down her book. "Go on," she said. "A big boy like you shouldn't need help."

Chester, sitting on a stump swinging his legs and watching, said, "I go by *myself*, don't I, Ma?"

"Of course," she said. "All big boys do."

Bruce only wailed louder, and she stood up. He was a difficult child, cried for any little thing, grew afraid at nothing, got stubborn helpless streaks. No wonder Bo got mad at him. But it wouldn't do. You had to baby him or he got worse.

She walked out to him. "Come on, then," she said, and took his hand.

He hung back, staring fearfully into the woods.

"What are you afraid of?" she said, and pulled at him.

The child screamed and hung his whole weight on her hand. The effort of hauling at him sent a deep throbbing ache through her injured arm, and her impatience grew. "What *is* the matter with you?"

It was minutes before his screaming stopped. She had to give herself up to the job of quieting him, sit down by him, distract his attention, tell him a story. Then she took his hand again. "All right," she said. "Let's go do our business."

His round eyes swung to the woods again and his lip jutted. "Cougar'll eat me!"

"Ohhh!" Elsa opened eyes and mouth in understanding, pursed her lips and nodded. In a substratum of consciousness she felt irritation with Bo for making so much fuss about the cougar that morning. The first thing he knew, the child would be afraid to go ten feet by himself.

"The cougar's gone home," she said. "He lives way over by Lake Samamish."

"He does not," Bruce said. "He's in the woods and he's gonna eat me."

"No, he isn't in the woods." She rose, wincing at her throbbing arm. "Look, I'll go in first and show you."

She walked into the brush, slipped off the path and hid herself from him. Peeking from a thicket of blackberry she saw him sitting on the ground, his whole face set for a wail, watching where she had disappeared. After a moment she came back on the path. "See?"

"Isn't there a cougar?"

"Not a sign of one. Come on with me now."

Finally she got him to the privy and back, but her nerves were tried, and as she sat down again to read she thought in irritation that there wasn't much real peace in living in the woods a mile from town, with cougars running around robbing camps and your children afraid, almost justifiably, of being eaten by wild beasts. But that wasn't fair. Bo wasn't to blame for the way they were living now. If anyone was, she and the boys were. They had been a millstone around his neck, a jinx. If he had had only himself to think of, he would be in Alaska now with Jud, doing what he wanted to do, living the kind of life he loved, instead of working fifteen hours a day in a place he hated. Considering how much he had given up, it was no wonder he was sometimes irritable and brooding. The wonder was that he took his bad luck as well as he did. He had every excuse to be as miserable as he was that winter they went back to Indian Falls.

She couldn't remember much about the arrival home except a pattern of confusion, embarrassment, humiliation—and amazement at the change in Kristin and Erling. Kristin had grown up. Her selfishness and her lack of responsibility were gone. As for Erling, he was a great raw-boned man at eighteen, an inch over six feet and looking bigger because of his mod of red curls. He was obviously glad to see her and obviously not going to show it. She remembered the look of quick astonishment in Kristin's eyes, the sober, old-world courtesy in her father's manner, when she introduced Bo, and she remembered Henry Mossman, mild, getting a little bald, stepping up to shake Bo's hand and then stepping back as if he had just shaken hands with the President.

She felt the forced conversation as a guard against their saying what they really were thinking, and in the very quiet politeness of their manners she felt that they didn't like Bo. They had been prepared to dislike him, and now they did. He was only a big dark-faced man who had run a saloon or poolhall in North Dakota and tricked Elsa into marrying him. He was outside the pale of Christian society, son-in-law or no son-in-law. She knew also that Bo felt their careful courtesy for what it was, and that even before they reached the house he was despising them for a bunch of pious Scandihoovian hypocrites.

They were oil and water, though with the children Bo got on better. Kristin he won over to a kind of giggling liking by teasing her until she flew back at him, when he backed away waving help-less hands before him, and called her a hell-cat. She was never quite sure of him, but she thought he was lots of fun. Erling, after the first day on the farm, was his slave.

She remembered how that started. Bo, the first night, sat down after supper and lit a cigar and said well, he guessed they were set for the winter, and Erling, maliciously acute, said, "You mean stuck."

"All right," Bo said. "Stuck."

Erling was eating an apple, pounding the hard red Jonathan on the table to pulp it and then sucking the cidery juice through a hole in the skin. "You folks going to church regular?" he asked.

Bo blew out a cloud of smoke. "No."

"Swell. Then I won't have to."

"Don't go telling Pa we put you up to it," Elsa said.

"You've got the right idea," Bo said. He reached in his vest and handed Erling out a cigar. Erling took it, startled but game. Elsa started to protest, but decided to keep still. Let him play.

They sat in a haze of smoke for ten minutes. Erling took the cigar out of his mouth and looked at it, working his lips. "Good cigar."

"Just about got you whipped, hasn't it?" Bo said.

"Naw. I smoke a corncob generally."

"Not while Pa's around, I'll bet," Elsa said.

"He don't bother me. I'm running the farm myself now."

"You're the boss, uh?" Bo said.

"I'm the head man." Erling took the cigar out of his mouth again between thumb and forefinger and went to the door and spat, casu-ally.

Bo laughed. "Got any work for a good farmhand?"

"You want-a work?"

"Sure."

"You'd get so lathered out in a field you'd drownd out all the gophers."

"Sweat's good fertilizer," Bo said.

Erling looked at him doubtfully, his little bright blue eyes squinting. Elsa could see him thinking. If this big guy wanted work, he'd sure give it to him. It would be fun to get him out and run his tongue out.

On the table lay a seed catalogue half an inch thick. Casually Bo leaned over, winked at Elsa, and seemed to be reading, paying no attention to Erling. Then he rose with the catalogue in his hand. "Through with this?"

"I guess so. Why?"

"Got to make a little trip," Bo said. He took hold of the upper corner with his other hand. The blunt fingers tightened, his neck swelled and his shoulders hunched. The catalogue tore slowly, reluctantly, until with a final twist he ripped it in two and went out without a word.

Erling's eyes bulged. He looked at Elsa, who smiled.

"Holy cats!" he said. He took up the remaining half of the catalogue and tried to tear it. It was like tearing a board. "My gosh he's strong," Erling said. "Where'd he get it?"

"Don't let him fool you," Elsa said. "Running a hotel he's got a little soft, but I've seen him bend pokers with his hands."

In her brother's transparent face she saw half-contemptuous toleration giving way to awed respect. She could see him beginning to like this big guy that Elsa had married. One gesture, and the boy was his. It was hard to explain, that knack he had of making men like him (and women, she said. Wasn't I just the same after one afternoon in Helm's parlor?). It was a kind of teasing and sultry and almost dangerous charm, a feeling of power you got from him as you got heat from a stove.

She remembered the way he worked during that fall, how he set himself to go Erling one better in everything they did, how he hid his blistered hands until they were toughened and callused, how every morning he and Erling wrestled out by the mill trough. Generally those bouts wound up with Erling going head-first into the tank. Big and agile as he was, he was lost if he let Bo's hands get on him. Then he yelped like a stepped-on pup, and after the ducking he came up streaming water and blowing promises of what he would do next time he got that big goof, and ran steaming through the cold to change his overalls.

Those were good clean sparkling mornings bright with color, with popcorn drying from the rafters of the porch, and Chester was growing into such a handful that half the time they were scared to death he would kill himself and half the time proud of his adventurousness. He was always wandering off into the cornfield by himself, or crawling up into the hayloft to burrow and growl at himself playing bear, or inducing visiting children, generally girls, to go swimming with him in the mill tank. In the evenings Bo sparred with him, "toughening him up," cuffing him on the ears as he sailed in, letting himself be flailed in return.

Bruce was a different problem. Sometimes Bo would induce him to come in and fight, but one or two light flicks on the ear would set him howling. Bo got impatient then. He never could abide a child's crying. Sometimes he roared at the boy to stop his noise, and once or twice he looked as if he might haul back and knock Bruce rolling if shame, or Elsa's presence, hadn't stopped him.

"You baby him too much," he said. "I never had any of this babying. I just got thrown out in the cold and had to get along. You've got Bruce so he bawls for any little thing."

"You let him alone," she said. "You can toughen Chet up all you want. He likes being knocked around. But Bruce is sensitive. You watch his face when you yell at him sometime. Just a little difference in your voice is enough to scare him."

"Yeah," Bo said heavily. "Yeah, I guess by God it is."

It was winter, the isolation and inactivity of just sitting and waiting for word from Jud, that frayed his temper. Even when the letter from Jud came, it helped little. He had an offer of three thousand, less than half what he and Bo had paid, and he was holding off to see if something better could be stirred up. When he read it, Bo got out paper and pencil and figured for an hour, and when he got through figuring he threw the pencil across the room and went outside. Next day, in a burst of activity, he sat down and wrote nine letters, more than he had written in a year, one to a steamship line in Seattle, two to fur houses in St. Louis, one to his sister, one to Jud, one to Sears Roebuck ordering some traps, two or three others she couldn't remember. Then he sat down and played solitaire till supper time.

Inactivity was like a disease in him. He needed the excitement of starting something, getting something going. Being cooped up in the house made him grit his teeth. Haunting the mailbox for letters that didn't arrive set him swearing. And when he lost thirty-five straight games of solitaire without winning once, he threw down the cards and glared, and she knew from the look in his heavy-lidded eyes that he made an omen out of it, it was bad luck for the Klondike project. Before she could think of a way of distracting his mind from it, he was back at the table again, swearing he would sit there and play till he beat it if it took him till spring.

But even after he had whipped it a good many times the omen was not conquered. He slept uneasily, woke up sweating and whimpering like a lost pup from frightful dreams. She remembered the dream he had had three or four nights in a row, that he worried over and tried to extract meaning from. He was a boy, fishing barefooted by the creek he had grown up on, with a watermelon on the bank beside him. He was there a long time, and caught a lot of fish that came up shining from the silvery water, almost as if they flew, weightless and beautiful, each one bigger than the last. Then people started coming, his sister and his mother and all his brothers and Elsa and the children and Elsa's father and Sarah, and they all sat down and ate his watermelon, pushing him away when he protested, and asking him for nickels. They caught in their hands the gleaming fish that flew upward when he pulled in the line. In disgust he got up and moved to another hole, and the fish poured again in a silvery stream, beautiful firm glittering slippery fish that he gloated over. Then they stopped biting suddenly, and he saw the cork riding motionless on the water. It grew and grew till it filled the whole stream, and he looked up to see the people coming again, and ran. He ran across a sand beach, and by that time it wasn't people that chased him any more, but some black Thing that swooped above the trees with edges that waved up and down in the wind like the swimming motion of a flounder, and his feet stuck, and the Thing was coming, and he woke up dripping wet when Elsa shook him and cried out to see what was making him moan so.

Inactive days, haunted nights, wore out his patience and drove him against the shut doors that he wanted to burst open. He cursed Jud for not finding anyone to buy the hotel. One day he cursed the piddling nincompoop who had offered a measly three thousand,

and the next he cursed Jud for not having the sense to take it. He didn't care how much they lost, as long as they got a stake to go north on.

One day he sat in the kitchen and petted the gray housecat, rubbing behind its ears, stroking under its lifted chin, pulling its whiskers gently while it blinked and rubbed and purred. Elsa, turning at the stove to reach for the salt shaker, saw Bo's hand move down the crackling fur. The tom arched his back and tiptoed as the fingers stroked clear from ears to lifting haunches, up the raised and electric tail. Bo's face was passive, almost expressionless, and his eyes were half closed. Then the heavy thumbnail dug into the cat's tail with abrupt savagery. The cat yowled a startled, fighting yowl, turned and clawed and leaped free.

"God damn!" Bo was on his feet, his face dark with a wash of blood. "Claw me, you damn . . ."

The cat stood watchfully, yellow slit eyes on him, back humped, tail furred out and straight up. It leaped away from Bo's kick, slipped through the dining room door, dodged another kick, and vanished down the cellar stairs. Bo stood irresolute, fingering his scratched wrist. "Damn cat clawed the hide off me," he said, and sucked at the blood.

"You started it. You pinched his tail."

"Oh, the hell I did!"

"Bo, you did too. I saw you."

His heavy face, snarling, bullying, swung toward her. "And I say I didn't!"

Her blood jumping with anger, she turned away from him. She had seen his face when he pinched, the sudden, convulsive tightening of his mouth.

Through February and into a bitter March his irritability drove him from the house as if he couldn't bear to stay under a roof. He took to walking alone through the cornfield and down to the muddy little rill of water buried under the mounded snow in the creek bed, carrying a trap or two and looking for muskrat or fox or skunk sign. But all he caught was a half dozen muskrats and two skunks, and coming home from his fruitless prowling he would sit staring gloomily out the window, or try to lure Erling into a blackjack game, or get a deck and lose himself in solitaire. The sheets of tablet paper appeared again, and the strings of penmanlike signatures and figures,

*Harry G. Mason, Harry G. Mason, Mr. Harry G. Mason, Mr. Harry
G. Mason, Esq.,* with arabesques and flourishes, and pages of pictures
of animals with bodies like frame houses and heads like gables and
tails like chimneys with curls of smoke rising. The boys pounced on
those whenever they found them, but the sight of them made Elsa
feel cold and a little sick.

Brooding, the book forgotten in her lap, Elsa watched the children
riding switches among the stumps, and even in the midst of the deep
bird-twittering quiet she felt the frustration and restlessness of that
winter. All that energy bottled up without a thing to occupy it. And
then the spring, and the sale, and that wonderful week or two when
they were really on their way and the world opened out westward
into hope.

She pursed her lips and shook her head. You mustn't think about
it, she said, and looked around startled to see if she had spoken
aloud and the boys had heard. They were still playing horse among
the stumps. But she mustn't think about it, anyway. It did no good
to worry over things that were done and gone. But she wished with
all her heart that it hadn't happened, that they had caught the
boat as they intended, that Bo were doing what he would have
loved to do, playing wild man in the wilderness. She didn't like to
think of herself and the children as a hoodoo and a handicap.

3

That night after the boys were in bed she put the lamp on the
table and sat down to read. But the light, reflected off the oilcloth,
hurt her eyes, and before nine she was preparing for bed herself.
After the light was out she opened the door and stood for a minute
breathing the balsam air. It was very dark, the heavy trees a black
impenetrable wall across the lighter cleared ground, their tops trian-
gular blackness against the sky. She shivered. So lonely a place. The
Klondike couldn't have been any lonelier. Ever since her marriage
she had wanted for neighbors, in the hotel and on her father's farm
and later in Seattle when they knew no one, but now for a moment
the desire to have people nearby was like a muscular ache. If there
were only a smoke in the daytime, a light at night.

Very carefully she bolted the door, looked at the unseen flimsy canvas roof overhead, listened for a moment to the easy breathing of the children, and slipped into bed.

No noises after dark, at least none like the sounds in a town, the hoarse calling of trains, the rattle of wheels and clack of hoofs and squeak of a dry axle in the street, the unfamiliar roar of an automobile coming around a corner and diminishing, softening, disappearing again down another street you could imagine, tree-lined, pooled with shadows, perhaps a single light in the gable of some house, and the dark pitch of roofs cutting off the stars. Nothing here but the soft continuous murmur like a sigh from the trees crowding the clearing, nothing but the padded blow of an erratic, tree-broken wind on the canvas roof, the faint rustle of needles falling from the fir at the back corner of the tent and skating down the canvas incline. No noises but inanimate creakings and rustlings that you strained to hear and were never satisfied with, stealthy noises that eluded identification and kept you straining for their repetition, noises too soft to be comforting, noises without the surety and satisfaction of trains calling or freight cars jarring as they coupled in the yards beyond the dark. You lay rigidly in bed and made your breath come shallowly, noiselessly, through your mouth, and your blood slowed and pounded until you felt its pressure like monotonous light blows on your injured arm. When you had listened for a sound until you were tightened to an unbearable tension, you heard it again, and it was only the needles falling, the sigh of the moving trees, and you relaxed in the bed and breathed once more. It seemed to you then that your present was a static interval like the pause between heartbeats, and when you lay thinking you thought of the past inevitably, because you couldn't help it, because the present was without the meaning of either past or future, because the past was the thing you knew well, in image and idea, because in the past your future lay.

You remembered how the future had looked on that trip west, close and touchable and warm as it had been only once before, in the early weeks of your marriage. You remembered the oceanic plains pouring behind, the mountains, the Elbow Pass above Banff and the Three Sisters immaculate in snow behind the smoky windows; the strange smothery feeling in the tunnels, and the way the children's noses bled in the altitude, and then Seattle, with Mount Rainier floating like a great smooth cloud high above where any mountain should be.

Everything about those days was full of a kind of drunkenness; it reeled in the memory. Even the cheap boarding house where you and Eva and the children stayed while Jud and Bo went to arrange passage, even Eva forgetting to have her pains, full of laughter. The things sweet to remember—the terrier puppy you bought for the boys, and the pictures you had taken to send back to Indian Falls: Chester with a clay pipe in his mouth, looking droll and eyebrowless, holding the puppy in his arms; the two boys posed behind a cardboard screen painted to represent the cutwater of a boat, with spray V-ing out on both sides and Bruce's hands on an artificial wheel, the whole thing so convincing to the boys later that Bruce's greatest boast even yet was that he had run a big motor boat all by himself.

The day when passage was arranged and the dog assured of a trip in the hold, and the actual tickets in Bo's hands to prove that it was really going to happen. He was exalted with excitement, jumpy, full of sudden exuberances. He stood by the window looking out to where workmen with great firehoses were washing away a whole hill to make way for a street, looking out and humming, breaking into song,

> *It was at the battle of Bunker Hill*
> *There's where I lost my brother Bill.*
> *'Twas a mighty hot fight, we'll all allow,*
> *But it's a damn sight hotter where Bill is now.*

Breaking into song, standing with his hands in his pockets staring out at the activity of the city and having crazy tunes come to his lips without warning, singing,

> *Oh the Joneses boys, they built a mill,*
> *They built it up on the side of a hill*
> *And they worked all night and they worked all day*
> *To try and make that old mill pay. . . .*

When a hurdy-gurdy man came by under the window, you remembered him breaking from the window to wheel you in a clumsy waltz around the room, catching heels in the old Brussels carpet, stumbling, roaring with laughter, singing,

> *Those six Canadian boys were drowned*
> *But the oxen swam to shore . . .*

Teasing the kids, wrestling the puppy, going out in the evening for pails of beer, and you all sat around in the scrawny room, full of fun and stories and songs, growing silent once in a while as you thought of the Promised Land. You remembered evenings when Jud and Eva had gone to their room, and those nights were full of warm, low talk in bed, and lovemaking like a second honeymoon.

Ah, that dream of escape, you thought now, lying in the dark tent hearing the whisper of needles and the light breathing of the boys. That dream of taking from life exactly what you wanted—you too, not merely Bo and Jud, but all of you, drunk on that dream. Then the fall, the cracking away of the well-brink just as you were climbing out. Ding, dong, bell, pussy's in the well, you thought, and made your face smile in the dark. Whose fault? Who put her in? Who pulled her out? You knew of no one responsible, unless whoever or whatever ran the world was really what it seemed sometimes, a mean, vindictive force against which you beat yourself to rags, so that sometimes you felt like a drowning sailor trying to climb into a life boat and having your fingers hammered off the gunwale time after time, until there was nothing to do except go down or make up your mind to stay afloat somehow, any way you could.

There was Bo's face the day he came back from buying supplies for the voyage that would start now in two days, and found you tending Chester, sick and whining with a sore throat—the swift, hot, suspicious look, the look of outrage, the look as you traced it over now almost of certainty, as if he had known all along that something would happen. "God damn it," he shouted, "he *can't* get sick now!"

But he did. The next morning there was red rash in his throat. By noon it had spread all over his chest. By afternoon the man was tacking up Scarlet Fever signs on the boarding-house door, and most of the boarders had fled, and the landlady was bitter and Bo, hearing the doctor's words, had flung out of the house like a madman, the doctor shouting after him.

You expected then that he would go without you, and were bitter at him, yet even then you couldn't have blamed him much. He had set his heart so on that voyage. You sat all afternoon and evening, and late at night he came back, his footsteps creaking on the stairs, the anger gone from him and only a look of such hopeless defeat in his face that it shook you with pity. You begged him then to go, to get Jud and Eva and go, and you would join him when Chester was well, but he wouldn't. He had fought it out with himself walking, and he would stick. Maybe they could go later, all of them. But the quarantine would be six weeks, and six weeks cut half the season away. Instead of agreeing to go, he went out to find another boarding place. In the morning he would look for a job. Should he get a nurse, he asked before he left. Could you get along with both kids to mind? But you didn't want a nurse. You didn't want to add that expense to what was already bound to be a disaster. You would stay afloat till another lifeboat came by.

But no more boats. Empty ocean with a fog on it. Chester sick only a week when Bruce came down, and the quarantine lengthening through two weeks, three, four, six, seven. Bruce was barely through peeling when his ear became infected and he howled with pain so that no one slept. You remembered Bo's coming one night, slipping in after his shift of running a streetcar was done, and you sat almost wordless, beaten and tired, though you hadn't seen him for almost a month.

Even then you still talked as if you might go. You would have exposed the children to any amount of cold winter if you could have gone that fall. But Bo had turned in the steamer tickets; doctors bills and living expenses had cut down their money. And then came Jud's first letter. It was a cautious letter. It didn't say definitely that there was nothing stirring. It said merely that from all Jud could find out, the way to get in on either the gold or the fur was to go way back in the wilderness, and Eva didn't like that idea much. Living was high as a kite. Just to fill in till he had located some likely proposition for them, Jud was dealing poker in a joint. If he kept his ears open, he expected that pretty soon he'd hear of something that was worth plunging on. Until then, Jud suggested that with a family to take care of Bo might do better to stay in Seattle. It was a hell of a lot cheaper to get along there than in Seward.

You saw, with the kind of slow, inevitable movement that a high wall makes in falling, that Bo's face lost its eagerness, sagged, set hard. He crushed the letter and threw it at the wall. After a while he picked it up again, smoothed it out and read it again, and broke into a fit of foul swearing, and looking at his eyes and mouth you knew he wanted to cry.

He wore that bitterness around his mouth for months, until he heard about the little café for sale in Richmond, out in the timber, and the prospect of getting away from the carline, from the rocking platform and the swollen feet and the irritation of working for someone else, checking in and checking out, keeping still when inspectors bawled him out, was too tempting to resist. He never looked into the café at all carefully. He simply quit his job and took what little money they had and bought it, spent ten days furiously painting and cobbling and cleaning up, bought new stools and coffee urn and equipment. You flicked the shutter open on that café, and your eye saw it as you had seen it for six months, clean and painted and neat outside, where the customers saw it, its poverty plain where the poverty wouldn't show. You saw the scuffed, softened, splintery fir floor behind the counter, the floor whose slivers found the holes in your shoes and drove in, stopping you sometimes as if you had stepped in a trap; the old cupboards that no amount of soda and scrubbing would sweeten.

But even so, you said, even so. It's better. It's steady, and it does make us a living, and since I've been hurt Bo seems to be willing to stick with it. That accident, unlucky as it seemed at the time, was a point of change, a climax of the bad luck, and since it was over things were better. You remembered old lady Moe at home in Indian Falls, and her belief that whenever she broke a dish she was bound to break three, and you remembered the day you saw her drop a saucer when she was serving afternoon coffee, and how she threw down a cup and another saucer on top of it, not angrily, not in a pet, but quite carefully, as if to finish a job. That was the way the burn was.

You were getting ready for the breakfast customers, you mixing pancake batter, Bo cleaning the coffee urn. He had emptied it, wiped it out, put in the fresh coffee, and heated the water in a pail. As you stirred the batter at the other end you saw him kick a low stool into place and climb up with the steaming water in his hand. He shifted the pail, reached down awkwardly for a dishtowel, wrapped it around his right hand, and took hold of the pail again to lift. The urn was high; he had to strain to hoist the pail. The lip caught under the flange of the urn top, and he hung there, teetering on the precarious stool. "Come here, quick!" he said.

You put down the bowl of batter, wiped your hands on a towel, started. "Hurry up!" he shouted. "This is scalding my hand!"

You were over to him in three steps, looking to see what he wanted you to do. "The stool!" Bo yelled. "The stool, the stool, the stool!" He could have lowered the pail and started over, but that was not his way. Convulsed with fury and strain, he shouted at you and kept the steaming pail jammed as high as he could reach. You grabbed the stool and held its teetering legs back on the floor, and Bo staggered, stuck his hand desperately at the wall, letting go of the bottom of the pail. Hot water slopped over him, and with a yell he dropped it and leaped back to save himself. The whole bucket of scalding water came down across your shoulder and arm.

And then Bo's face again—so many times the memory projected an image of his face, the exact expression. You stood there, your teeth in your lip and your body rigid with the shock. Your bare arm, in the time you could count ten, turned fiery, clear to the fingers. His face fallen in a kind of anguish, Bo stared at the arm and then at your face, and you held yourself rigid, not quite aware yet how badly you were hurt, and looked at him. He burst out as if he couldn't bear what he saw, "Yell! God damn it to hell, yell! Cry!"

Then he was grabbing the butter can and smearing your arm, roughly, angrily. Under his fingers the skin puffed in great blisters, growing while you watched. By the time Bo closed up the place and routed out a stage driver to take you down to the doctor's little office on the mill road, your arm was twice as big as normal and so hot and painful that you staggered getting out of the stage, and Bo picked you up and carried you into the office.

His face. It was almost as if you touched it, lovingly, seeing how strongly your lives had been welded together in spite of bad luck and bad temper, how behind all the violent irritability and the restlessness and the dissatisfaction you were his wife. You had never known what that meant, really, until you saw how it shook him to see you hurt . . .

In the bed Elsa stiffened. There was something, a sound not skating needles or sigh of trees or soft blows of wind on canvas. Rigid with listening, she waited. Again, like the stealthy pad of feet at the rear of the tent, a sound as if something were prowling around the little shed where they stored food, the trunk, clothing, everything that overflowed from the tent itself. Her eyes wide upon the sightless dark, her head half lifted from the pillow, she listened, and the heavy pound of blood began in her burned arm. There again . . . She strained her ears as she had strained them a hundred times at night noises, tight with fear that was not really fear but only apprehension that wanted to smile at itself, to take a long breath and relax again and know that what had brought it upright listening was only the wind or the settling of timbers in the house or the creak of a swaying door.

A long, furtive silence, the sigh of the wind, and then the noise of a stick of firewood falling on the woodpile.

It was as if a light had flicked on and made abruptly real all the fears that she hadn't really believed in. There was something out there, prowling in the dark, and if it was friendly it wouldn't prowl at this hour. Like a shutter that clicked three times, three swift thoughts went through her mind: the automatic question of what time it was and when Bo would be home, the realization that it couldn't be more than ten o'clock, and the thought of the cougar. Propped now on her elbow, she still listened. No more wood fell, but the soft sound of steps came through the flimsy canvas, and then unmistakably the rattle of the padlock against the hasp on the shed door.

Very slowly, so as not to make a noise, Elsa laid the covers back and inched her feet over the edge of the bed. The springs squeaked, and she waited with held breath. The noise outside was still there. It sounded as if the cougar, or whatever it was, had gotten into the shed. Even while she stood up she was wondering if she had padlocked that door, but she couldn't remember. She had been out to hang the ham on its hook just after supper. . . . For a moment, standing barefooted on the cold board floor, she cocked eyes and ears at the children's bed. Sleeping. She knew what she must do. It froze her with terror, but she knew. She must drive the thing away, frighten it so it would never come back, kill it if she could, for what peace would she ever have now when she had to leave the children alone, as she often had to do when she was helping at the café?

With her hurt arm held across her body she tiptoed to the bureau, felt for the revolver on the high shelf. Her teeth were locked, and her body shivered as if with cold, but she went on, over to the door. There she stooped, laid the gun on the floor, raised up and drew the bolt very slowly with her good hand, stooped again and picked up the gun. It was awkward left-handed, but it was better that way than trying to use the burned one.

On the narrow porch she listened again. Something bumped back in the darkness by the shed. The thing was bolder. All around her the dark ring of woods pressed on the less opaque darkness of the clearing, and she saw the cloudy sky above moving with the wind as silently and almost as invisibly as a thought moves in a mind. For a moment she wondered what she would do if the thing didn't scare, if it turned and attacked her, but she shut her determination down and clenched her teeth upon it. In her bare feet, feeling the needles and tiny twigs digging into her skin, she stepped off into the yard and a dozen steps to the side, to where she could see the blob of a shadow that was the shed.

With all her will, knowing she must do it quickly or not at all, she lifted the gun and pointed it at the place where the shed door ought to be. Her hand wobbled, and she braced it with the hurt one. "Bo!" she cried out in a last forlorn hope. "Bo, is it you?"

There was a rush of movement, a half-seen moving shadow. The shed door banged back as the retreating animal bumped it, and with her teeth in her lip Elsa pulled the trigger.

The noise stunned her, the recoil threw her hands into the air and stabbed her arm with knives of pain. Slowly she let her hands come down with the gun, her mind still dazzled by the flash and the report and something else—the wild howl that still shivered against the ring of trees, an almost human howl. Before she realized that she had heard it, that the prowler had been real and that she had shot at it, perhaps hit it, she was back inside the tent leaning weakly against the slammed and bolted door.

Both boys were sitting up in bed, tousled and sleepy, shocked upright before they had had a chance to awaken. "What was it, Ma?" Chester said. His eyes, round with sleep and wonder, were on the gun hanging from her hand. Bruce whined, dug with his knuckles at the lingering sleep in his eyes. Then he too saw the gun, and his baby face slackened with the imminence of tears.

Elsa laughed, a squeaky, hysterical cackle. Forcing casualness over her panic like a tight lid over a saucepan, she went over and put the gun back on the shelf. "It was just an old skunk snooping around your rabbit pen," she said.

Chester knew about skunks. He sniffed.

"I scared him off before he had a chance to make a smell," his mother said, and laughed again, more naturally.

"D'you shoot him?"

"You bet I did. We don't want any old skunks bothering your rabbits, do we?"

Their solemn heads shook. "No."

"All right," she said, and went to tuck their covers back. "You go to sleep. If Pa comes home and finds you still awake he'll skin you alive."

They lay down again, punched one another for sleeping room, whispered together with secret giggles, and finally fell asleep. But Elsa, after playing at going back to bed, just to fool them, got up again and dressed, and she was sitting by the table with the light turned up bright when Bo's feet scraped on the steps.

She met him at the door with her finger on her lips, and when she told him what happened he whistled low. "Scare you?"

She held up her left hand, trembling again now that everything was over and Bo was back. She could even laugh a little. "Half to death," she said.

"Did you hit him?"

"I don't know. He screeched bloody murder and ran away. I didn't even see him, just a kind of rush in the dark."

"Maybe you were seeing shadows."

"He was *not* a shadow! He yelled like old Nick. He was in the shed."

"How'd he get in there?"

"I don't know. Maybe I left the door open."

"Even if you did there's a thumb latch."

"I heard the latch rattle. Maybe the door wasn't caught."

He reached down the gun from the shelf, picked up the lamp, and took her arm. "Well, let's go see if we've got a cougar rug."

While Elsa held the lantern high, Bo, with the brighter light of the lamp, went into the shed and looked. Immediately his voice came, excited. "By God, there was something in here. Stuff's all scattered around."

"Did you think I was imagining things?"

"I did, sort of," he said. He came out and searched for tracks, but the ground was so littered it wouldn't have taken a clear print. Then Elsa stooped and picked up a chip at the corner. On one edge was a dark spatter, and when Bo rubbed it with his thumb it came off red. He looked at her. "You winged him, anyway."

He searched, stooping, the light silhouetting his head and shoulders and shining yellow on the side of his intent face. He seemed to sniff like a hound; there was excitement in him. Twenty feet from the corner he found another spatter of blood on a spruce twig. After that he found nothing. "I'll get up early and try it in the morning," he said. "No use in the dark."

His arm went across her shoulders, and she giggled without knowing she was going to, a sound as involuntary as a hiccough. "Old Mamma," he said. "Pops off a lion with one shot. How'd you ever get the nerve to go right out after him?"

"I wanted to scare him good, or kill him, so he'd never come back."

He paused, stooping for a last look. "This is the best place for tracks, where there's dust," he said. The wind flawed in the light, and he cupped a hand over the chimney. There were footprints all around in the dust, but no sign of animal tracks. Then Bo bent closer. "Ha!" he said.

"What?"

"Look."

He pointed to a large footprint, set his own foot down beside it and made a track. His print was an inch longer than the other. They stared at each other. The light spread around them dimly, shone on the side of the shed, was cut off at the corner as if a knife had sliced it. The woodpile was a jumbled and criss-cross pile of shadows.

"If that was a cougar you shot," Bo said, "he was wearing number nine shoes."

There was little sleep for her that night. In spite of Bo's reassurances that no court would hold her a minute, even if she had killed the prowler, the thought of having shot a man left her weak and sick. She imagined him out in the dark, hungry maybe, rummaging among the things in the shed while he listened for noises from the tent as fearfully as she listened from her bed. Then the shout out of the dark, the terror of discovery, the desperate running, the shot, the pain, the mouth wide on a scream. She imagined him dragging himself off into the woods, perhaps to die.

There was nothing she could do, because Bo said flatly he wasn't going to lose a night's sleep hunting for him in the dark. Besides, he might be dangerous, and as for his bleeding to death, there would have been more blood than they had found if she had hit him badly. The hell with going sleepless and maybe getting shot at out of pity for any burglar. She knew that he wasn't in the least afraid to go out, that he was merely tired and needed sleep, but she could not go to sleep as he did.

Five minutes after they were in bed he had started kicking the covers off his feet—and hers. His muscles twitched as he slept. In the other bed one of the children whimpered. Dreaming. It was comforting to know that nothing worse than dreams would touch him tonight. She should try to get to sleep. Bo rolled over, the bed sagging away under his weight, and she fought him for the covers. He was like an elephant in bed. You couldn't wake him up, and whenever he moved he stripped the whole bed bare. It took savage jabs in the ribs before he would even grunt and squirm and give you enough slack to pull over you.

The child whimpered again. Which one? Bruce? You couldn't tell. Never mind. Let yourself go, feel your weight relaxing into the bed . . .

The scream brought her out onto the floor in a single leap, confused, her heart shuddering after its first great bound. Where? What? The baby. He was screaming insanely, babbling, clopping his lips. Even when she felt across Chester and found Bruce backed against the wall, and took him up to hold his face against her shoulder and comfort him, he still choked and cried. As hard to waken as a mummy, Bo stirred and grumbled a question, but she didn't answer because she was busy crooning to Bruce, running her hand up and down his shivering wet back.

"There there there," she said. "It was just a dream. Nothing's going to hurt you. Mommy's got you safe."

He pressed against her and locked his arms around her neck. "Cougar!" he said. "Great big old cougar had me."

Finally, to quiet him, she lay down between the two boys and they jackknifed their little bottoms into her body and went to sleep again, but she lay as wakeful as ever, staring upward. That fool business of loading the gun and making such a fuss. It had already caused Bruce to be afraid of going fifteen feet from the tent, had made her shoot a man, had wakened the baby from his sleep drenched with nightmare sweat. Just once, it would be pleasant to live in a place where you felt safe and secure and permanent.

The canvas roof was dingy gray, and the birds were beginning off in the woods, before she fell asleep.

4

It was broad daylight when she awoke. The children were running naked in and out of the tent, and Bo was getting breakfast on the little iron stove. The good smell, mingled with the clean scent of the woods that blew in the open door, filled the tent. There was a golden patch of sun on the floor, and the roof was dappled with gold. For a moment, not remembering, she stretched luxuriously. It was good of Bo not to wake her early, because when you woke of your own accord there was pleasure in wakening. Every detail of the tent-house was intimate and precious, the four-foot board walls, the canvas patched near the ridge with two neat, seamanlike patches, the table and bench and stools and bureau, all of which Bo had made, the light pine wood worn smooth by the rubbing of hands and clothing. The whole day ahead was full of comfortable chores, home chores.

She watched Bo at the stove. He was a good cook—better than she was at some things, and he seemed to like to sneak out of bed before anyone was up. He turned the bacon, tipped the lid of the coffee pot to look in, flipped it down again with a light clank of metal. He was whistling under his breath. Still not aware that she was awake, he turned to watch the boys scuffling in the corner over a toy boat, and she saw the skin around his eyes wrinkle. As he turned back to the frying pan his whistle turned into a hum, the hum into a song,

> My sweetheart's a mule in the mines,
> I drive her without any lines,
> Behind her I sit and tobacco I spit
> All over my sweetheart's behind.

Just that little excitement last night could make him this way, she thought. Just one unusual thing, one break in the monotony, and he chirped like a bird. His movements were quick, almost jigging, like the movements of a Negro she had seen working on

the docks at Seattle, as if at any minute he might break into a
dance. The coffee pot began to steam, and Bo opened the lid so
that a damp flaw wavered and clanged against the stovepipe like
the "witch" in the throat of a fireplace. He sang,

> *Once upon a time, boys, an Irishman named Daugherty*
> *Was elected to the Senate by a very large majawrity . . .*

The bacon fizzed, and he turned it over, the song breaking and
emerging again further on,

> *Oh they ate up everything that was upon the bill-of-fare,*
> *And then they turned it over to see if any more was there.*
> *There was blue fish, green fish, dried fish, and pa'tridges,*
> *Fish balls, snow balls, cannon balls, and ca'tridges . . .*

Then she remembered. "Bo!"

He turned around with a grin.

"Shouldn't we go out and look?"

He let his voice sink to sepulchral depths. "While you snored
like a pig I already looked," he said. "I plow deep while sluggards
sleep."

"Was there . . . ?"

"Not a sign," he said. "You couldn't have done more than
scratch his hide. I've been all around clear out to the road."

"I guess I didn't get to sleep till pretty late," she said. She
swung her legs over the side of the bed, saw Bruce watching her,
and said, "You didn't help either, you little punkin. You had a
nightmare and screamed as if you were being murdered."

Looking at Bruce, Bo said, "What'd give him nightmares?"

"You," she said, popping her head into her dress. "You and your
fool guns and stories about cougars."

"He's got teeth," Bruce said. "He *woars!*"

Bo laughed. "He woars, does he?" Standing spraddle-legged, he
winked at the child. "Tell you what. When you see that cougar
poke his nose into the open, you sail right up to him and when he
opens his mouth to eat you, stick your arm down his throat and
grab his tail and yank him inside out."

Bruce's round face wavered in a grin. "He can't eat me," he said.
"I'll kill him right down."

"That's the ticket," his father said. "Kill him right down. Pull off his leg and beat him over the head with the bloody end of it."

"You'll have them talking like toughs," Elsa said.

Bo was sitting down, cramming his mouth with bacon and fried bread. "Do 'em good. Make 'em so tough a cougar's teeth'd clinch right over if he tried to bite 'em." He made motions as if his jaws were glued together, frowned, pawed at his face, put his head down and bucked up and down in his chair, puzzled and wrathful. Both boys laughed. Bo winked at them, took a knife from the table, pried his jaws open, gulped half a cup of coffee and stood up. "Got to hustle," he said. "I'm late now."

This was her morning to go in and see the doctor. At ten o'clock she had the children washed and cleaned up, and started with them down the path toward the macadam road. They walked for a half mile under a roof of horizontal limbs, almost uniformly a dozen feet from the ground and so tightly laced over the old tote road that on rainy days it was possible to walk almost dry from the road to the tent. In that tight shaded aisle, and in the woods that thickened in brown tangles on both sides, there were no flowers brightening the mat of needles, but in the openings where the sun reached the color was spread in bright patches, flowers unfamiliar to her childhood, but looking as if they might be relatives of the windflowers and cornflowers of home. There was even one that looked like a furry-stemmed pasque flower. The boys had names for all of them, many of them the product of Bo's foolery. There was a little delicate blue blossom as low and hidden as a violet, that he had taught them to call a hocus-pocus crocus, and another, a rose blossom that grew on a sort of berry bush, which he called a blush-of-shame-for-a-life-ill-spent. If the boys ever did learn the names of things they would have to unlearn a lot of his teachings first.

Chester ran ahead, picking up cones and bending back the scales to look for seeds, but Bruce stuck close by her side, and she realized with a strange feeling of helplessness how the fear of the woods had taken hold of him. He had always been afraid of everything—horses, cows, streetcars, strange people, even the Santa Claus in the Bon Marche toy department in Seattle. Dark terrors seemed to drive him sometimes into propitiatory rituals, sending him round the tent before a meal touching with solemn babyish pats the bench, the bureau, the leg of the stove, the headboard of his bed. If he were hustled to his chair to eat, he lost his head completely, squalled, fought to get back and finish his compulsive ritual. Or he would turn against foods without warning so that one would have thought he was being offered offal, and not coaxing, not scolding, not spanking could make him eat one day what he had been ravenous for the day before.

He was a strange child. Now he clung to her skirts so closely that he hampered her walking, and she laid her hand on his head and kept it there because she knew that somewhere deep down in his prematurely old mind he lived with fear.

They came down onto the sun-dazzled white band of the macadam, and she pushed him on ahead to run with Chester, squared her own shoulders and stepped out briskly. It would be hard to know what to do with the children when she got well and went back to work, unless they could work out shifts that would let one of them be always at home. With Bruce this way, he couldn't be left alone. But she suspected that he shouldn't be left alone with Bo either. Bo wouldn't have any patience with his terrors. Maybe Bo could get permission to put an extension onto the café, and they could live there. The lumber company owned the whole town, and they hadn't been able to get any place before until Mr. Bane at the stage office let them camp on his timber tract. But if they could . . .

Oh fiddle, she said. It will all come out in the wash.

At the fork where the sawmill road turned off, she cut across the spongy meadow and entered the dirt road that ran straight as a yardstick through heavy timber. The doctor's office was visible an eighth of a mile down, a little frame shanty that he had put up midway between town and mill so as to be available to both. Just as she came into the road, a man went into the office door. That meant she would have to wait. She told the boys to play outside.

The little waiting room was empty, but the doctor poked his head around the inner door and said, "Good morning. I'll be just a minute."

She heard the noise of his moving around inside, and the mutter of voices. A high, nasal voice said, "Ow, for Christ sake!" and the doctor laughed. An instrument clinked in a pan, and after a few minutes the doctor's matter-of-fact voice again: "Leave that bandage on a couple of days, and then take it off and put on a clean one. Bake it in the oven if you can't get it sterile any other way. If it shows any signs of infecting, keep a warm wet pack on it."

The patient said nothing. The door opened and he came out, one ear and the side of his face along the temple swathed in bandage. He was a tall thin man with a peeled-looking skin and a bald head. The doctor, very young and growing a pale mustache to make himself appear older, leaned against the door and looked after him and laughed.

"How did he get hurt?" Elsa said.

"One ear hanging by a string," the doctor said. "These stiffs come in with some tall stories sometimes. An obvious bullet wound, a nice neat groove that creased his face and tore his ear half off, and he tries to tell me he snagged it on a nail in the dark, getting up to see what some disturbance was." He laughed again. "He'd have had to be going thirty miles an hour to do that on a nail."

Elsa was staring. "Do you know him?"

"No. He isn't one of the boys from the camp or the mill. Just a bum passing through. Some day he'll get shot and won't come out so lucky."

"Oh, I'm glad!" Elsa said.

"Glad?"

"You see," she said, and looked at him so radiantly that he batted his eyes. "You see, I shot him."

"Oh, come on!"

"Really. He broke into our shed last night and I thought he was a cougar."

The doctor leaned out to look up the road. "Do you want him pinched? We could still catch him, probably."

She shook her head, and he motioned her into the inner room. "Left handed?" he said as he began unwrapping her bandage. "I knew that bum was lucky. If you'd had the use of both hands he'd be worms' meat now."

Elsa shivered. "That's just what I was afraid of," she said.

Bo was alone in the café when she hurried in, and he leaned his elbows on the counter and winked at the boys. "Hi, kids," he said. "I was just hoping you'd show up."

"Why?" they said.

"Ice cream tastes funny this morning." He talked to them man-to-man, seriously. "Tastes funny as the dickens, for some reason. I need somebody to tell me what's the matter with it."

Chester's droll, eyebrowless face dropped open, and then he leered, scenting a hoax. "Which kind is it tastes funny?" he said.

"Both. Darnedest thing I ever saw. Chocolate tastes funny and vanilla tastes funny. Maybe you can tell me what's wrong with the stuff."

"I can tell quite a lot about chocolate," Chester said.

"Okay. How about you, Brucie?"

"I can tell more about vanilla," Bruce said.

Their father filled two cones and passed them over the counter. "Taste hard," he said, and waited frowning for their verdict. "Tastes to me as if they might have got a little skunk juice in them. Taste anything?"

Chester rolled his tongue in his mouth. "There's a little skunk juice in it, all right." Bruce was hesitating, not quite sure he wanted any of his.

"By golly," Bo said heartily, "that's just what I thought. Here, I'll throw them in the garbage pail for you."

He reached over the counter. Bruce, hesitating, was about to give his up, but Chester backed away, his eyes big over the suspended cone. "Don't you want me to throw the nasty thing away?" Bo said.

Chester took a lick, staying cautiously out of reach. "Aw, you're foolin'!" he said, and ran outside. Bruce followed him, the dubious cone still unlicked in his hand.

"Bo," Elsa said, "guess what I just saw?"

"What?"

"The man I shot at. He was down in the doctor's office with his ear half shot off."

"No fooling?"

"Yes. He wasn't hurt bad. He was a hobo, Miles said."

Bo's eyes across the counter were crinkling, the pupils warming. "Feel better, uh?"

"I should say so."

"Want an ice cream cone to celebrate?"

"All right."

She sat swinging her legs from the high stool, licking the cone, thinking how pleasant it was to drop into your husband's place of business and talk with him and have an ice cream cone, the way she had always wanted to in Hardanger when Bo ran the bowling alley.

"I heard something myself this morning," Bo said.

She looked at him. He had taken out his knife and was scraping absent-mindedly at the accumulated grease under the metal edge of the counter. The grease came off in a thin, curling strip. "Look at that," he said. "You'd think it would be clean, washed as much as it is." He flipped the curling strip in disgust to the floor. Elsa waited, knowing perfectly well that whatever was on his mind, it was not the grease under the counter edge. After a minute his eyes came up.

"Ever hear of the Peace River country?"

"Yes," she said slowly. "Isn't that that farming country up in Canada somewhere where people were going from Dakota?"

"Yeah. In Alberta."

Elsa had stopped licking her ice cream cone. As if someone had touched her and pointed, she saw the direction of his thoughts, and her muscles tightened with an instinctive antagonism, almost a fear. "What about it?" she said.

"Nothing about it," Bo said. "It's good country, that's all. About the best farm country anywhere, probably."

"Are you wanting to go up there?"

"Nope," Bo said deliberately. "It's all filled up." He shut his knife and slid it into his pocket. "But I know a place that's just as good or better that hasn't got a soul in it."

"But you're not a farmer!"

"I'm not a fry cook, either," he said.

"But where is it? Where is this place?"

"In Saskatchewan." They had been staring at each other over the counter almost as if they were about to quarrel. Now Elsa saw his face lose its dead expressionless stillness, the light come into his eyes, the animation appear. "There isn't a thing there but a few cattle ranches," he said. "Fella that comes in for breakfast lately was telling me. He was up through there three or four years ago drifting around working on ranches. Just wide open, big as all outdoors. But they're opening it for homesteaders, see? And the C.P.R. is going to run a branch line down through there from Swift Current. That opens it up, all that land that's as good wheat land as the Peace River country. See what that means?"

Elsa said nothing.

"It means," Bo said, watching her, "that the boys that get in there early and buy up land at the logical townsites are going to make plenty of money. In ten years there'll be dozens of towns along that line, and the ones that get in on the ground floor will be sitting pretty."

"I should think Dakota would have soured you on that kind of thing," Elsa said.

"Oh, Dakota!" he said. "You don't see the difference. The difference is that this is *new*, see? It isn't even scratched." He grew almost violent, trying to show it to her as he saw it. "Why, God knows what's up there," he said. "There might be coal, or iron, or oil, or any damn thing under that ground. Nobody but cowpunchers and the surveyors have ever been over it. And a railroad coming right through it."

When she still kept silent, he waved a pencil in the air. "Suppose you were up there and homesteaded a quarter section, somewhere along the right-of-way. And suppose you found coal on that quarter, say. Good God, all you'd have to do is snoop around a little and use your bean, and you could buy up all the likely-looking coal land and be on Easy Street in a year."

"What would you buy it with?" she said, not wanting to say it, not wanting really to throw cold water on his visions, but compelled to say it. They couldn't even afford a wooden house, and here he talked about Easy Street in a country hundreds of miles away, where they would have to start from scratch all over again and might never even get beyond their initial poverty. She saw the irritated jerk of his head when she said it, but she had to say it, and she had to keep insisting on it, because if she didn't he would drag them all off to some other get-rich-quick spot and they'd be back where they had started seven years ago, or worse.

"You've got about as much imagination as a pancake griddle," he said.

"It isn't a question of imagination," she said steadily. "It's a question of getting along. You can't just leave one place for another without knowing what's going to turn up in the new place. You wouldn't trade a sure thing for a gamble."

"I'd trade this sure thing," Bo said. "I'd trade this joint for almost any gamble you could name."

"And give up all the work we've put into it?"

"Look," he said. "I've been figuring this sure thing out for an hour, and there hasn't been a customer to interrupt me, either."

He leaned over with a sheet of paper, but she said defensively, before she would glance down at it, "It's always dead from ten to twelve. The mealtime crowds hold up."

"You'd never get rich off 'em. You know how much we still owe?" He stabbed the pencil on a column of figures. "Six hundred and twenty bucks."

"But that's pretty good," she said. "That's only half of what it was. We'll have it clear in a year or so."

"And what've we got when we've got it clear?" Bo said. "A business that brings you a hundred a month."

"It will be more than that when the payments are all finished."

"And then you'll have to spend that much more renovating."

"But we can live on it," she said. "We've been living on less."

"Out where the cougars sneak around and tramps raid the place and the kids get scared of their shadows," he said. "Do you call that living?"

He looked at the clock, turned to move a kettle onto the fire, took chalk and wrote neatly on the two-by-four blackboard, "Special Today, Irish Mulligan, bread, coffee, 20c. Ham and Eggs, 20c. Bacon and Eggs, 20c. Steaks and Chops on Short Order." He wrote a clean, neat hand, even on a blackboard.

"I worked on a railroad once," Bo said. "There's plenty of jobs for a smart guy if he keeps his eye open. Like bunkhouses. Sometimes the road puts those up, but lots of times they lease out the concession and the guy they lease it to gets it straight out of the men's pay. All clean, see. Then when the line moves on you knock down your bunkhouse and load it on a flatcar and set it up further down."

"I shouldn't think there'd be much money in that," she said stonily.

"That shows what you know about it. You know how many men a road has on a grading or steel-laying crew? Plenty. Two or three hundred. Furnishing bunks for two or three hundred stiffs isn't chicken feed, even if you flopped 'em for two bits a night. And when you're all through, in a new country like that, you can sell your beds and chairs and even your bunkhouse to somebody for almost as much as you paid in the first place." He was tapping with his finger on the counter, watching her. "There's another angle, too. What do you suppose those stiffs do for amusement at night, after work? There's no towns to go to. Suppose I wrote Jud to come on along. Don't you suppose a smart gambler like Jud could shake down a little loose change in a place like that? I just guess he could."

"You want to go awfully bad, don't you?" Elsa said. She felt sad, whipped, dependent. She was a millstone around his neck. That rough new country was where he belonged, really. But it would blow everything she wanted sky-high, uproot her again, take the children into a country where there weren't even schools.

Bo was watching her face. "And you don't," he said.

She shook her head. "No."

He shrugged and turned to getting things ready for the noon customers, and after a few minutes she went out to gather up the children and take them back for their own lunch. Bo didn't like them around eating in the café. They made it look as if they were eating up the leftovers, or something.

On Sunday Elsa was trying to wash clothes behind the tent. Laundry had piled up since she was hurt, Bo needed fresh shirts, the bed linen was soiled. She was sousing shirts in a tub of water and rubbing them one-handed on the board when she heard steps coming around the tent, and for an instant she froze with the fear of another tramp. Then Bo came in sight with his coat over his shoulder and his sleeves rolled up.

"Has something happened?" she said.

"Taking a vacation."

"Why?"

"Why?" he said. "It's about time, isn't it? I've been working sixteen hours a day seven days a week about long enough."

He seemed mad, sour, out of spirits. And he did need a rest, there wasn't any question. "Good," she said. "Did you just close up?"

"I made up about two dozen sandwiches and put 'em in a box and left a tin can with a slot in it on the doorstep," he said. "Maybe one out of three that takes a sandwich will pay for it. I don't give a damn if none of them do."

"Or if somebody steals the can," she said. "I don't either. It's nice to have you home for once. Soon as I get through maybe we can go for a walk."

He hooked his coat on the clothesline post, throwing it from six feet away, took off his shirt and threw it after the coat, and stretched in the sun in his undershirt, a lanquid, lazy, powerful stretch that moved the muscles under his milky skin. With his dark face and hands he looked like some odd cross-breed. He pushed her away from the tub. "You're an invalid," he said. "Let me swing that a while."

"I feel all right. It doesn't hurt."

"Go on," he said, and she had to back away.

"This is nice," she said. "I wish you could take a vacation more often."

He eyed her obliquely. "I'd just as soon take a good long vacation from that dump."

Instead of answering she went inside and got more laundry, and for a while they worked together, he washing and wringing shirts and children's clothes, twisting them so tight with his heavy wrists that she had trouble shaking them out to hang them up. She was standing on tiptoe at the high post-end of the line with her mouth full of clothespins when he said, "Thought any more about that Canada proposition?"

She hung the last shirt and took the clothespins out of her mouth. At this moment, when they were together, comfortable, with the sun on them and the children playing quietly in their own yard, wild enough and poor enough, God knew, but their own, he thought of nothing but getting away.

"Don't be mad, Bo," she said. "You asked me that before, and I told you what I thought. The café will keep us. We can clear it and live like other people instead of like gypsies."

"Uh," Bo said, and scrubbed a nightgown up and down the board. He said no more, but when she got the last batch of scrubbed clothes to hang up they were twisted as hard as sticks of wood, almost dry enough for ironing.

Bruce wandered into sight from the front yard and stood watching. He cocked one foot against his shin, shifted to stand on the other foot. "Ma," he said. "I got to go."

Elsa had a sheet half way on the line, and the wind pulled at it so that she had trouble keeping it in place with one hand. "You go on by yourself this time," she said over her shoulder. "You can do it."

Bruce shifted his feet, looked solemn, squinted his face, but did not move.

"Go on, bub," Bo said. "Do as your mother tells you. She's busy."

The boy moved a few feet, stopped, put his hands around the pole that supported the line, and swung on it. His eyes were on his mother. "You take me, Ma."

"Go on," his father said. "Ma's busy. You get on out there and back like a man. I bet you a penny you can't be back before I get this water dumped and the tub hung up."

Still watching his mother steadily, Bruce went a few feet, stopped to pick a flower and toss its petals into the air with a jerky little motion. He picked the leaves off the flower stem and did the same with them, very concentrated, very busy. He stood knock-kneed, holding his legs together.

"Now confound you," his father said sharply, "you move when you're spoken to! Get on out there before I have to make you."

Bruce went slowly out the path, tossing flowers and leaves and sticks into the air with his jerky, invariable motion. At the pile of slashings where the blackberry bushes grew thick he stopped. His father was hanging up the tub in the shed, out of sight. His mother was at the line. But back of him were the bushes, the shadows, and he had to walk another thirty feet into them alone to the privy. He didn't like the privy anyway. Wind blew up through the opening at the back, and flies crawled on your behind, and you didn't know what might be down there peeking at you, animals, cougars, snakes, faces with teeth . . .

Swiftly he pulled down his overalls and squatted in the weeds beside the path.

He had barely ducked when his father's yell startled him to his feet again, scuttling with hands clutching his overalls. But his father was after him. Heavy feet pounded the path. He heard his mother call out, but he couldn't get back to her now. Gasping, he scrambled into the privy and sat up on the children's hole. He cringed back when his father burst in. In one motion he was yanked upside down and spatted smartly on his bare backside.

"Now!" his father said, and slammed him back on the hole. "Now you sit there till you're through, and don't let me catch you squatting in the yard again."

Bruce bawled, and seeing his mother's face at the door bawled louder. But his father just went out and shut the door on him and he heard their steps going away.

"He's frightened," Elsa said. "That's why he doesn't like to come out here."

"Seems to me he's frightened of every damn thing in the world," Bo said. "You can't let him make a pigpen of the yard."

Elsa stopped. "I think I'll stay here and walk back with him," she said. "You've no idea how . . ."

Bo took her arm. "Let him walk back by himself."

"But he's scared, Bo."

"I was scared of water when I was a kid, too," Bo said. "That didn't keep my old man from throwing me in when I was about five, where it was ten feet deep."

"You never liked your father, either. You'll have that child hating you like poison."

"Then he'll just have to hate me," Bo said. "He's got to be trained if I have to bust his head for him on the way."

"You can't whip a child out of being afraid," she said in anger. "Bruce is sensitive, that's all. He's the most sensitive child I ever saw. But he's stubborn as a mule, too, just as stubborn as you are. You'll start something you can't finish."

"Let him keep on being stubborn," Bo said. "I'll guarantee to knock that out of him."

Still angry, she went back and finished hanging up the clothes, but after Bruce came back sniffling and Bo had started to putter in the shade of the shed, his jaw still set and a look on his face as if something smoldered in him, she didn't need to ask herself if his rage at Bruce had anything to do with the thing that had been on his mind when he closed up the café and came home for the afternoon, the proposition he had mentioned, glancing at her sideways, and then shut up about when she showed that her mind was still made up the other way.

Certainly, in the two weeks that followed, he showed less and less interest in the café. He always seemed to get there late in the morning, he closed up earlier at night, he shut up the whole place the following Sunday afternoon and made her come home when she said she would just as soon stay and take care of it. She was taking her regular turn now, relieving him at eleven o'clock and staying till the evening meal was ready. And while she was at the café, he was at home with the boys. That, she knew before two days had passed, wasn't good.

When she was at home she could take Bruce out to the privy, look after him, soothe his fears, get him interested in something else. But Bo was a martinet. The kid had been babied too much. All right, he would fix that. He made Bruce dress himself in the mornings, feed his rabbit by himself without even Chester's help, go out in back by himself, wash himself alone before meals. He insisted that Bruce eat exactly what was set before him and clean up his plate; if he didn't, it was taken away and he went hungry. When he went a whole day, stubbornly, without eating a mouthful, Elsa protested. Bo was being altogether too hard. It wasn't Bruce's fault he was finicky. The boys had been moved around from pillar to post ever since they were born. They weren't sure of anything, they had never had a home. You couldn't blame a child for feeling afraid and insecure.

But her argument got her nowhere. Look at Chester, Bo said. He hadn't had any different kind of life, and look at him. He wasn't afraid of anything. She had babied Bruce till he knew he could get anything he wanted, just by whining. Well, he would find out different.

"But he isn't even four years old yet," Elsa said, knowing with a kind of panic that she couldn't budge him. She could see him day by day getting further into that mood of restless irritability, of sullen, stubborn dissatisfaction, that had made the last months at Indian Falls a nightmare. Only this time, it seemed, it was to be Bruce and not the cat who suffered for it.

The first result of Bo's discipline was that Bruce began wetting and soiling himself rather than go out to the privy, though he had been broken of wetting for over a year. That only made things worse. If Bo were at the café, she could keep the accidents quiet, but once, when it happened during her shift, she came home to find the child sniffling against the back wall of the shed, and when she undressed him for bed she found the marks on his buttocks. Bo had used the razor strop on him.

That made her shout at him. "You can't spank a child into being dry! Haven't you any sense at all?"

He looked at her heavily. "Can't you see why he does it?"

"He does it because you've got him so scared he's half out of his mind."

"I can see pretty well," he said, "and that isn't what I see. He's doing it to dare me, by God."

"Oh, Bo," she said in despair. "You were so nice to them for a while, and they got along so well. Why don't you try being kind?"

"Sure I'll be kind, when he learns to do what he's told. Let him run over you and he'll run over you all his life. But by God he doesn't run over me." The words fell with solid, whacking emphasis, like chunks being chopped from a straight-grained block.

There was nothing she could do, unless she wanted to yield to what she knew bothered him, and take the children up into a place where Heaven knew what would turn up. So she kept quiet, but when, a few minutes later, she heard him say, "Well, I guess I'll go it one," and saw him take the deck of cards from the bureau and sit down, she wanted to scream. Solitaire was almost worse than bad temper.

On a Saturday, two weeks after Bo had first closed the café for the Sunday afternoon holiday, he came home at ten thirty in the morning. There was a barbecue over at the mill. Not a chance for a customer all day, he said. He seemed in a good enough humor, but restless. For a while he stood in the yard looking distastefully at the littered clearing. Then he called the boys and started them picking up chips and scraps of paper, piling tin cans over against the woods, straightening up the scattered woodpile. They did it lackadaisically, without thoroughness, but he didn't scold them. After a while he got hammer and nails and started repairing the porch.

"What's all the cleaning up about?" Elsa asked.

"Well, hell. Place looks like a boar's nest. If we got to live here the rest of our lives I might as well straighten it up a little."

Impulsively she put her fingers down and stirred his black hair. "Poor Bo," she said.

"Don't want to change your mind about Canada, do you?" he said. He hammered in a nail with four quick blows. "I had a letter about it the other day."

"Who from?"

"Friend of this Massey, that told me about it in the first place. I wrote him and asked for the dope."

"What did he say?"

"Said the road was coming through, all right. Already started grading."

For a moment she was almost tempted. It might be better, there might be a home there, certainly Bo would be happier if she didn't hold him back. After the way the Alaska business had fizzled, so that now Jud was still right where he had been at first, dealing in a gambling house, and after the way Bo had given up what had looked like a golden chance because of her and the boys, when Chester got sick, maybe she ought to say yes. But then her own desires would have to be sacrificed again, and the home she wanted for the children's salvation, for her own salvation, interposed itself like a fence.

She said, "If it weren't for the kids I'd say go anywhere."

He went on nailing down the loose boards of the porch, and when he had finished that he got up without a word and went to look at the well cover, which had rotted away at one side. He said nothing more about Canada, but she watched him unhappily, knowing that he was trying to do as she wished, and trying to accept the responsibility that his family laid on him, but that he still must feel chained and trapped.

Even after supper he did not mention the subject. He made an effort to be cheerful, creaking back in his chair with his pipe in his mouth and clipping Chester's ear with a back-handed cuff.

"Ow!" Chester said. He held his ear and scowled.

"Come on and fight," Bo said. "Anybody hits me, I hit him back. What's holding you?"

Chester lowered his head and sailed in, and Bo let him flail a few times before he clipped him on the other ear. As they scuffled, he got hold of Chester's wrist and bent it back, poking the tight little fist into its owner's eye. "What you hitting yourself for?" he said. "Hit me. It isn't good sense to sock yourself."

Chester squirmed and swung with the other hand. "You're doin' it," he said. "Let go and I'll . . ."

At the other end of the table Bruce sidled up to his mother, his eyes fixed steadily on the scuffling, and pulled her dress. She glanced down, saw his lips frame the words, "I got to go."

Her quick glance showed Bo still sparring with Chester, grinning, pushing the boy away with a big irremovable hand, holding him by the top of the head while Chester tried to bore in.

She nodded at Bruce, and led him quietly toward the door. Behind her Bo's voice came heavy and even. "Hey. Where you going?"

She turned around with a lie on her very lips before the absurdity of lying about such a thing made her meet his eyes. "Bruce has to go."

"Let him go by himself." Bo had quit sparring, and was holding the still-belligerent Chester at arm's length.

"It's getting dark," Elsa said.

"It isn't dark yet by a damn sight," Bo said. "He's been told often enough to go by himself. You just make him worse trying to sneak around and out-fox me."

Rebellious and angry, she hesitated. To stand around arguing about such a ridiculous thing! Why shouldn't she go out with him, if it made him feel safer? Why should he have to go out there alone when he was terrified of the woods and the dark? But Bo sat there, implacable and dominating. And that afternoon she had refused for the third time to do the thing he wanted. If this kept on, they would be at loggerheads over every little thing. . . .

"You can go out yourself like a big boy," she said. "Sure you can. Mommy's got to do up the dishes." She hated herself for that lame surrender, and saw Bruce hating her for it too. He twitched away from the door and tried putting his fingers around the lantern base.

"I don't need to," he said sullenly.

She looked helplessly at Bruce, then at Bo, and started clearing off the table without a word. But Bo half rose, and his voice was edged with a threat. "Oh yes you do. Skin on out there, right now."

Bruce's lips jutted, his eyes were dark with rebellion. "I don't need to."

The stool scraped as Bo stood up. "If you want a good hiding," he said, "just stand around there a minute more seeing how far you can go."

The child lingered at the door, his round baby face clouded with passion, but when Bo took two swift heavy steps toward him he bolted. Elsa said nothing. If Bo wanted to make that issue the most important in the world, just to assure himself that he was boss, she supposed he would do it. Bruce was trying enough. He made you want to scream sometimes. But it did no good to bully and spank. That only made the trouble loom bigger, and it was already ridiculously exaggerated. Let Bo go on and earn the hatred of his son. Secretly, she would almost have bet on the child rather than on Bo; Bruce would take scoldings, spankings, brutality, anything, and wail and howl and cry, but they wouldn't break him. All they would do would be to harden him under the surface fear and callous him to punishment.

The door opened and Bruce slipped in quickly. He shut the door as if locking something out. Bo took his pipe from his mouth and looked at him, the faint expression of petulance on his face overlaid by surface heartiness. "Get your business done?"

"Yes."

"Weren't any boogers out there, either, were there?"

"No."

"Sure not," Bo said. "Not a booger in sight. Even if there was, there's no call for a big guy like you to be scared. Chet here eats boogers for breakfast."

When he turned his chair squarely and fronted the child, his face, to his wife, was a curious mixture, as if the bluff good-natured heartiness with which he treated the children sometimes, and which he was trying to assume now, were an expression worn over at least two others, as if the underlying muscles of his face said at the same time that he was doomed and damned and leg-ironed by family responsibilities, and as if the eyes, quite independently, were appraising his youngest with an acid, prying look of contempt. But his voice was the playful voice of teasing fellowship. "Come on over and get pasted," he said. "I just toughened Chet up till you couldn't drive a nail in him."

Bruce hung close to his mother by the stove, his eyes sullen and unyielding. "I don't want to," he said.

The look of contempt for a moment obliterated the other expressions on Bo's face. He looked at Elsa, laughed a short, hard laugh, and stood up. "All right," he said. "All right, all right! You don't want to."

As he passed the stove on his way out of the tent Bruce crowded back against the box where his mother kept the dishes, and his eyes followed his father until the door shut behind him.

Elsa sighed. "You ought to play when Pa wants you to," she said, but Bruce turned his head aside and picked slivers off a stick of firewood with ritualistic care. "I don't want to," he said again.

"If you minded the first time he spoke to you you wouldn't get into trouble," she said. "Can't you try to mind better, Brucie?"

He went on picking slivers, and she turned from him to get at the dishes. After a few minutes she heard Bo's steps coming up the path, along the side of the tent. There was a surprised grunt. The footsteps paused while she might have counted five. Then Bo's voice, strident, high-pitched, insane with rage, was shouting curses. The baby jerked from behind the stove as if he were going to run, but in the middle of the tent he hesitated, his head swinging like a cornered animal's and his eyeballs distended with terror. Elsa had barely time to gather him in close to her before Bo burst in the door.

In the flash while their eyes met and held, while she crowded Bruce behind her back protectively, she knew that she had never seen Bo so furious. His face and neck were swollen and dark, his eyes glaring, his breath panting between bared and gritted teeth. His voice came in an incoherent, snarling roar.

"Of all the *God* damn, God damn! Right beside the path where

I step in it! And lie about it! Right beside the path and then lie about it . . . !"

He was crouched on the threshold as if about to spring, and she backed up a step, holding Bruce behind her. "Bo! For God's sake, keep your temper, Bo!"

The swiftness with which his big body moved paralyzed her for a split second with utter terror that he would kill the child. Before she could put up her arm he had caught her shoulder and pushed her aside, and she fell screaming, trying with both hands to hang onto Bruce, feeling his fingers torn loose from her dress even while she fell, and hearing his thin squeak of terror. She screamed, "Bo, oh my God, Bo . . . Bo . . . !"

Moving with the same silent terrible speed, he was out the door again with Bruce under his arm, and she scrambled up, silent herself now, to hurl herself after him. Around the side of the tent the child's idiot babble of fear rose to a shriek, broke, rose again, cackled in a mad parody of laughter. In the near-dark she saw Bo bending over, the baby's frantic kicking legs beating out behind him as he shoved the child's face down to the ground, rubbing it around. "Will you mind?" he kept saying, "will you mind now, you damn stubborn little . . ."

She pulled at him, clawing, but one thick arm, powerful as a hurled log, brushed backward and knocked her down again, and she fell sideways on her half-healed arm. She never even felt the pain. Her mouth worked over soundless words. Like a dog, she screamed at him without making a sound, you treat your child like a dog! Her legs kicked her to her feet again so quickly that she might never have fallen. Bo was still rubbing Bruce's nose into the ground in a savage prolongation of fury.

Hatred flamed in her like a sheet of light. She wanted to kill him. Somehow her hand found a stick of stovewood in it, and with murder in her heart she rushed him. The first blow fell solid and soft across his shoulder. The second stung her hands as it found hard bone. Then she was wrestling with him, sobbing, trying to hit him again, screaming with helplessness and fury when she felt her wrist bent backward and her fingers loosening on the club.

Now finally the long moment when the madness burned out of both of them as suddenly as it had come and they faced each other in the heavy forest twilight with Bruce sobbing on the ground between them and Chester terrified and whimpering at the corner of the tent. Bo stared at her stupidly, his hands hanging. In the dusk she saw his mouth work, and bit her own lip, her body weak as water and her burned arm one long hammering ache. She didn't speak. Gathering the threads of her strength, she stooped and picked up Bruce and carried him into the tent, motioning Chester in after her and bolting the door.

Without pause or thought she went straight to the bed and lay down with Bruce tight against her, holding his moaning into her breast and trying by the very rigidity of her embrace to stop the shudders that went through his body. While she lay there Chester crept against her, so that she rolled a little and put her burned hand clumsily on his head.

There was no sound outside the tent. She caught herself listening tensely, and the anger touched her again like a rod of bare icy metal. The shivering of the child in her arms lessened gradually, but his breath still shook him into shudders, and at every catching intake of air she held him fiercely. Like a dog. Expecting a child to learn all at once, to be told and never afterward make a mistake, never to have any feelings of his own, but to jump like a trained animal. Even a dog he treated better, lessoned with endless patience, rewarded when it did something right. She blinked her dry eyes, scratchy as if they had been blown full of sand.

Poor child, she said. Poor baby! Her hand rubbed up and down his back, and she whispered in his ear. "Don't cry. Don't cry, baby. We won't let him do it any more."

(What instant outrage that she should have to say such a thing to him! We won't let him do it any more. His father!)

"Are you all right now?" she said finally. "Will you lie here and rest while Mommy lights the lamp?"

His hands clung, and she lay back. "Chet," she said, "can you light the lamp, do you think?"

He slipped off the bed, and she heard him bump against the table in the dark. Light leaped in a feeble spurt, went out, and he struck another match. Then the steadying glow of the lamp as he brought it back to the bed in both hands, carefully.

"Good boy," she said. "Set it on the chair."

Sitting up, she smoothed Bruce's hair back from his forehead and looked at him, and the cry that was wrenched from her came from a deeper well of horror and shame and anger than even the blows she had rained on Bo outside. Bruce's face was smeared with dirt and excrement and tears. Under that filth he was white as a corpse, his face shrunken and sharpened with terror. A nerve high in his cheek twitched in tiny sharp spasms, and his whole head shook as if he had St. Vitus' dance. But his eyes, his eyes . . .

"Look at me!" she said harshly, and shook him. "Brucie, look at me!"

The mouth closed on a thin, bubbling wail, the cheek twitched, but the eyes did not change. They remained fixed in mute impossible anguish, twisted inward until the pupils were half lost in the inner corners.

"Ma," Chester said, "is he cross-eyed, Ma?" He began to cry.

She shook Bruce again, her own eyes blind. "Bruce!"

His cheek twitched and his body shuddered. "Get me a pan of water and a wash cloth," Elsa said to Chester. She said it quietly, holding her voice down as if throwing all her weight on it. He mustn't be frightened any more, she mustn't shout at him, she must be soothing, soft, safe. Holding him cradled against her bad arm, she washed his face gently with the cloth, ran it over his eyes, pressed it against his forehead under the silky light hair matted with sweat and filth. Minute by interminable minute she washed him, and heard the sobbing smooth out under the stroking, saw the cheek twitch less often, less violently.

Chester was putting wood in the stove, being helpful, his solemn teary face watching his mother and brother on the bed. Elsa took a firm hold on Bruce's shoulders. "Look, Brucie," she said. "Look at Chet over there, getting supper for us like a big man."

While she watched, not breathing, Bruce's eyes wavered, rolled outward from that fixed and inhuman paralysis; some of the glaring white eyeballs, streaked with red, slid back out of sight and the whole pupils appeared briefly. Then, as if the strain were too much, as if normal focus were an effort too great for more than a moment, the pupils rolled back again. Elsa caught her breath with a jerky sigh. Maybe tomorrow, after he had slept . . .

But oh God, she said, to treat a child that way!

She had just laid him down on the pillow and started to get something to eat for Chester when Bruce was screaming again, eyes frantically crossed and cheek twitching, his hands clawing at his face and his voice screaming, "Mama, Mama, on my face . . . on my nose . . . !"

5

There hadn't really been any decision. As she dragged the round-topped trunk up the steps and propped its lid against the table, she was thinking that you never really made up your mind to anything. You simply bent where the pressure was greatest. You didn't surrender, because surrender was annihilation, but you gave before the pressure.

A light rain fingered the canvas over her head, and she knew the move would be unpleasant, sodden, miserable. But it didn't matter greatly. To leave on a sunny day would be inappropriate; a retreat should be made in weather as miserable as the act itself.

There wasn't much to pack. Bo's clothing she stowed in his brown suitcase and put aside. That could be left at the hotel for him, in case he ever came back. Apart from that there were only her own few clothes, the children's things, the bedding and table linen. Mr. Bane would have whatever else the tent contained—stove, beds, table, bureau, dishes. Mr. Bane had been very kind. He didn't really want the things at all. It was only to help her that he bought them.

Oh, and the rabbits. She straightened, brushing back the hair that fell damply on her forehead. What to do with the rabbits? They couldn't be left, and they could hardly be taken to a boarding-house room in Seattle. She shrugged and gave up thinking about them almost before she had begun. They could be taken along part way, perhaps given to someone along the road. Any child would be glad to get them.

Chester staggered in with a quilt huddled against his chest, dragging in front so that he tripped on it. Bruce came after him, also loaded. They were excited. The move to them was adventure. They didn't know it was retreat.

"What else, Ma?" Chester said.

"You'd better go feed your bunnies," she said. "There's some carrots in the shed."

Two minutes later they were back, breathless. "Ma, the bunnies are gone!"

"Are you sure?"

"The pen's empty."

She went to look. The screen had rusted away at one side of the board floor of the hutch, and something, either the rabbits or something digging from outside, had widened the hole. The boys looked up at her, and she hid her feeling of relief. She had to appear to be sorry.

"Why don't you look around the edge of the brush?" she said. "They're tame, they'd stay around. Take the carrots and call them."

She went back into the tent and packed the remaining things. In the bureau drawer, back under a collection of odd stockings, she found the tintype of her mother, stood looking at it a moment, curiously emotionless, emptied, unable to remember, somehow, the way she had used to feel when looking at that portrait. She snapped the case shut and laid it in the trunk.

She heard the buckboard come into the clearing, and went to the door. Emil Hurla, one of the bus drivers who lived in Richmond, waved from the seat.

"I'm practically ready," she said. "The trunk's packed now, if you want to get it."

Hurla, a great, lumbering man with a gray, pock-marked face, climbed down and got the trunk, muscling it through the door on his thighs. Elsa hurriedly crammed the last rags into her telescope and crushed it shut, strapping it tight. Hurla came in and took it off the table. She looked around at the stripped beds, the empty bureau with its drawers hanging open, the trash littered on the floor, discarded socks, frayed collars, hoarded mop-rags, all the souvenirs of flight. Deliberately, under a compulsion that was more than her ingrained neatness, that was something like a defiance in the midst of panic, she took the stubby broom and swept the whole place, dumping the refuse in the stove and setting fire to it. The boys and Hurla stood in the door and watched her.

"Our bunnies got lost," Chester said.

Hurla put his hands on his knees and bent down. "Is that right, now?" he said. "That's too bad."

"They got out of the pen," Chester said. "We hunted, but we can't find them."

"Well, now," Hurla said. "Maybe we ought to look once more." He lifted his eyes to Elsa as if to ask if they had time, and when she nodded he went out, the boys after him.

She had pulled out the beds and swept up the dust puppies and had stood the broom back of the stove when she heard Bruce crying. She went to the door. Hurla stood with the well cover lifted on edge, and all three were looking down in.

"Ma!" Chester shouted. "Ma, the bunnies are down there."

Slowly she went out through the drizzle, her feet sinking soggily in the wet mound, the rain like fine mist in her face. At the well-edge she stopped and peered. Ten feet down, floating whitely, close together, their fur spread by the water like the fur of an angry cat, were the rabbits. The holes under the cover, she supposed, had tempted them in.

"Get a rope!" Chester shouted. "Get something. We got to get them out."

The sight of Bruce's immense, teary eyes as she turned away made Elsa grit her teeth with momentary fury, as if he were to blame. Then she pulled him against her and took Chester's hand. "It's no use," she said. "Your bunnies are drowned. It's a shame."

"But we can't leave them in there," Chester said. "Ma . . ."

She drew them away. Hurla let the cover fall, and Bruce burst out in a wild passionate wail. She lifted him into the buggy, letting him cry, ignoring Chester's worried "Ma, we can't . . . Ma." Hurla climbed up and took the lines. The mist had powdered the wool of his cap like a thin coating of flour.

He sawed the team around, and started out of the clearing. Elsa ducked her head to avoid the first low branches of the old tote road. She did not look back, but she could see in her mind every bush and stump in the clearing, every stain on the canvas roof, every detail of the place that had been home for a year and a half, that had still been home even after Bo ran off to Canada, that she had been fiercely determined to make home. But it was too much, she thought. She couldn't have tried any longer.

Behind her she heard Bruce's crying, furious now because she had not comforted him, and she felt in Chester's silence his grief for the death they left behind them in the well. She couldn't blame them any more than she could help them. There was too much that lay dead behind her. That well and clearing and abandoned tent-house neatly swept and locked against intrusion was a gravestone in her life. There had been other gravestones, but this was the worst, because it was more than a hope or a home that lay dead there. It was her marriage. Though she had not admitted it before, she knew that one reason she had tried so hard to keep the café going and to hold to the clearing was the hope that some day Bo would come back.

She did not look behind her, but she knew exactly how Bruce

and Chester felt when they knelt at the lip of the well and saw the white, furred-out shapes of their pets floating, lifting motionless to the motionless lifting of earthbound water in a dark, earth-smelling hole under the rain.

III

Bo came out of the Half-Diamond Bar bunkhouse with Big Horn, the foreman, and stood picking his teeth in the watery October sun. Rusty, third son of a British earl, was stapling a broken bridle at the corner of the house. Another remittance man, the boy they called Slivers, was sprawled against the horse corral playing his mouth organ. Louis Treat, a half-breed Assiniboine, lounged against a low, rock-weighted stack of prairie hay and braided at a horsehair rope. A hundred yards up through the light, leafless growth of black birch and cottonwood, the stone mansion of Jim Purcell showed. Bo spat on the ground.

"How much money has old Purcell got, anyway?" he said.

Big Horn shrugged. "He's loaded with it. He give the C.P.R. ever' other house lot to survey a townsite here, and even if he'd of give 'em nine tenths of it it'd still have been a good proposition for him."

"How many head of cattle does he run?"

"'Bout eight thousand."

"He'll have to cut that out, though, when the range gets home-steaded."

"Hell, he don't care about that," Big Horn said. "He must own forty thousand acres up the river. He was smart. He was buyin' land long before the road started down through."

"You've got to hand it to him," Bo said. "Still, he had the breaks, too."

Big Horn turned on him and laughed. "What's matter? You sore because you didn't think of it first?"

"I wasn't on the ground," Bo said. "That makes a hell of a lot of difference."

"Hell, if I had your bunkhouse business I wouldn't kick."

"I'm not kicking," Bo said. "I'm just wishing Purcell had left a little cream for the rest of us. That bunkhouse business won't last forever."

"Give you a job, thirty a month and grub," Big Horn said. "Christ A'mighty, what if you had to work? How'd you like ridin' line in a forty-below blizzard?"

"I told you I wasn't kicking," Bo said. "I'm just trying to figure some way a man could make a good thing out of this town Purcell's got started. There isn't much doubt it's going to be a town."

"Oh, it'll be a town, all right."

"Look at that Syrian peddler that's squatted here," Bo said. "Those guys are smart. They don't settle any place unless they see money in it."

"Tell me the Grain Growers' Association is going to build a elevator," Big Horn said. "Sure it'll be a town."

"There isn't anything it hasn't got," Bo said. "All that flat between the bends, that's plenty of room to grow in. Hills full of lignite, plenty of water. Hell, it'll draw trade for thirty miles around."

"Big as Chicago in ten years," Big Horn said comfortably. He yawned. "When it gets about as big as Shaunavon I'm movin' on. You and the rest of the promoters can run it then."

"Kiss my ass," Bo said. "You're scared it'll get big enough to support a cop."

"Cops don't bother me," Big Horn said. "Not Canadian cops. They're putting more Mounties at the post this winter, did you know that?"

"Sure?"

"Sure. Heard the old man talking about it the other day."

"Then that settles it," Bo said. "They aren't sticking in any new Mounties unless they're sure the place is going to grow." He looked through the trees at Purcell's stone house. There was the guy that had used his bean, gathered everything all in to himself. Stone house, forty-thousand-acre ranch, eight thousand head of cattle, real estate to hell and gone, Chink houseboy, big shots stopping in on the stage all the time to talk to him. "By God," he said, "I wish I owned about twenty lots in the middle of that flat."

Big Horn yawned. "It must be uncomfortable to be ambitious," he said. "Jaspers gnawin' at your pants all the time. Whyn't you leave all that ambition to the guys with a pack of kids to raise."

Bo looked at him. "Maybe I have got a pack of kids to raise."

"Maybe you have," Big Horn said. "How would I know?"

Two cowpunchers, Slip and Little Horn, came across the open space between the saddle shed and the corral and stopped to listen to Slivers blow on his mouth organ. He was playing something sad and shivery, flapping his fingers to get a tremolo. Out of nowhere, apparently, a small boy appeared, a dark, black-eyed boy of about eight, with a dark birthmark on the very end of his nose. Little Horn said something to him, and he looked up with an impish, white-toothed smile.

"That's Orullian's kid, one of 'em," Big Horn said. "He's the guy with a pack of 'em. Must have six or seven."

"He'll raise 'em, too," Bo said. "I never saw a Syrian yet that couldn't make money if there was any to be made."

"There you go again," said Big Horn. "Why in hell don't you open a grocery store, if you think it's such a good thing?"

"I'm after something better than grocery stores."

The Orullian boy cackled loudly at something one of the hands said. Little Horn put his hand on the boy's head, and the boy ducked away with a scornful mouth. Little Horn laughed and started away toward the corral half hidden behind the saddle shed. In three minutes he was back dragging a lassoed calf, hauling it along with upturned muzzle and braced legs. The Orullian boy stood and watched. So did Bo and Big Horn.

Little Horn went and brought an old saddle girth, threw the calf and fastened it around him like a surcingle. The calf blatted and Little Horn let it up, holding it by the ears.

"Okay, cowboy. Lessee you ride him."

The boy approached carefully, sidling; hesitated as the calf backed away; tried to get around to the side. Slip braced himself against the calf's haunches and Little Horn held its head. "Climb aboard, cowboy," Little Horn said.

The boy leaned across the calf's back and scrambled and kicked himself up. His eyes were enormous and he hung tightly to the surcingle. The two punchers jumped back and yelled, and the calf went pitching across the lot. The boy hung on for about three jumps before he sprawled headlong. For a moment he lay where he fell, while the calf bucked off toward the river. Then he pushed himself up from the ground with his mouth drawn down in a tough leer. Little Horn, before he went after the calf, shook his hand and said he'd stayed sixty seconds. Then Slip shook his hand, then Slivers. The boy was very proud.

"Pretty tough kid," Bo said. Abruptly he threw away his toothpick and pulled down his hat. "Guess I'd better go see if my Chink has burned up the joint," he said, and walked away. It was some time before he could shake out of his head the memory of the way Chet used to swagger and leer when he had done something he thought he ought to be proud of. Chet was a good kid, full of beans. He'd be just about the Orullian kid's age now, maybe a little younger.

He walked across the mouth of the east bend, cut through a straggly patch of willows, and came out on the flat where the town would be. There were already three bare frame shacks, and two derailed dining cars set up along what would eventually be a street. The raw earth where the scrapers had been working showed against the foot of the south hill, and a hundred yards on from the end of the grade was his bunkhouse, sheathed with lathed-on tarpaper. Smoke rose from the stovepipes at both ends.

Inside, he found the Chink Mah Li sitting with his hands comfortably folded in his lap. The bunks were all neatly made, there was a full scuttle of lignite by each stove. Nobody else was in the place except old Hank Flynn, sick in the lungs. The crew would begin to come around after supper, which they took at McGrannahan's boarding house a quarter of a mile back up the line.

Mah Li smiled his beaming, wrinkle-eyed smile and pointed upward. "Light all bloke," he said.

Bo looked up. The mantles on the three hanging gasoline lamps were all in shreds. "How the hell did that happen?"

"Open door," Mah Li said. "Wind blowee, all bloke."

"Well, for Christ sake keep the door shut, then," Bo said. He found a package of mantles and climbed on a chair to take the first lamp down. Hank Flynn watched from his bunk.

"I seen what was goin' to happen when they started swingin'," Flynn said, "but there wasn't nothin' I could do, sick like this. I hollered at the Chink, but he didn't savvy."

Bo said nothing. He was carefully tying new mantles around the rings, evening the tucks so that no metal touched them. He scratched a match on his foot and touched it to first one mantle, then the other. The stink of burning cloth rose. When the mantles were shrunken and ash-white, he climbed the chair again and carefully hung the lamp on its wire.

"God this is a lonesome hole," Hank Flynn said, and rubbed his gray-bristled face. "I wisht there was some place a guy could go, poolroom or something. I ain't seen a soul since the boys left this morning, 'cept the Chink."

"You couldn't go out any place even if there was a place to go," Bo said.

Hank Flynn coughed. "Ain't it a hell of a note?" he said. His voice was a thin whine that grated on Bo's nerves. "Guy gets old and sick, when he'd ought to have a place of his own and a wife and kids to look after him, and what happens but he has to lie around a damn drafty bunkhouse all day without anybody but a Chink to talk to, and he can't talk."

"If you don't like the bunkhouse why don't you move to the hotel?" Bo said.

"Oh hell, it ain't the bunkhouse," Flynn said. "This is all right, all you could expect. It's not havin' anybody give a damn whether you're sick or not. I could lay here and die and rot and nobody'd even move my bones."

"Cheer up," Bo said. "We'd move you when you started to smell."

"That's right," Flynn said. "By God, that's about the only reason anybody'd give a damn whether I lived or died."

Bo had tied the mantles on the second lamp, and scratched another match. Through the windows along the east side he could see the crew streaming across the scraped and naked earth on the way to Mrs. McGrannahan's. The light outside was bleak and cheerless, a cold, early twilight. He wished Flynn would stop his whining. It was tough to be laid up, but that was no reason to crab and grouse all day. Nobody liked to hear a guy crab all the time.

"I prob'ly *will* die here," Flynn said. He sat up and rubbed at his face again, sitting with his head hanging and his elbows on his knees.

"I sure never thought I'd wind up in the middle of nowhere without a friend or a soul that give a damn," he said. "I sure never did. I used to be strong as anybody. Ten years ago I could-a throwed anybody in that crew, straight wrastling, Marquis of Queensberry, or anything. You can sure see what sickness can do to a man. I used to have an arm on me . . ." He slipped up the sleeve of his winter underwear and pulled it high on his upper arm. "See that?" He flexed his muscle, and a hard white knob jumped under the skin. "It looks strong yet, by God," Hank said, staring at his muscle. Then he pulled the sleeve down and flinched his shoulder irritably, as if at a draft. "But it ain't," he said. "I ain't got enough stren'th left to pull my tongue out of the sugar barrel.

"If I had a sugar barrel," he added. He ran his hands over his whiskers and into his hair. "Sure is a hell of a life when you never laid nothing by," he said. "Just go hellin' around spendin' it as fast as you make it, and playin' the ladies and the horses and stickin' your feet up on bar rails. It sure makes you think when you get laid up and see what you made out-a all that stren'th you had once. You wisht you'd done a lot-a things different."

"Well, why didn't you?" Bo said.

Flynn looked surprised. "Hell, I don't know. Just hellin' around, takin' everything as it come. I don't know. When you're strong you don't ever think you can get old and sick. When you're in the jack you don't ever think you can go broke. When you don't give a damn for anybody you don't ever think you can get lonesome. But I'd sure do it different if I was doin' it over."

He stood up and scratched himself through the unbuttoned top of his underwear. "I s'pose I better get on over to the slop house," he said. "Nobody'd ever think to bring a guy anything when he's sick."

Bo looked at him, a stringy, gray-faced old man. He was pretty old to be working on a gypo gang, even if he wasn't sick. He stood there vaguely scratching his chest, mumbling under his breath and looking around for something, probably his shirt, in the mussed bunk.

"You really sick?" Bo said. "You really feel like hell, or are you just dogging it?"

Hank Flynn looked at him meanly. "I been tellin' you," he said. "I'm goin' to die right here, I know it. I'm sick as hell. I been coughin' blood for a month."

Bo looked at him steadily in pity and contempt. "Mah Li," he said.

The Chinaman was at his shoulder, smiling, bending a little forward.

"You ever have a belly ache?" Bo said. "You ever get sick, Mah Li? You're a long way from home. Ever get lonesome?"

"Lonesome long time away," Mah Li said. "Velly busy most time."

Bo grunted, eyeing the vague gray figure of Hank Flynn. "Yeah," he said. He had forgotten what he started to do. "Well, run on over to McGrannahan's and get some supper for this guy," he said. "Tell her to check it off his ticket." He turned away to prime and pump and light the lamps, turning his back on Flynn and shutting his ears to his whining and feeling a little sore, a little mad, scowling to himself with a dull pointless dissatisfaction. It was a hell of a hole, sure enough.

That night he sat at one of the two tables in the north end of the bunkhouse with a stack of papers before him and a neatly sharpened pencil in his fist. The other table was crowded with card players, seven or eight of them sitting in on one game, and he saw, when he looked up from his brooding abstraction and his figuring, that other men were hanging around as if they wished he'd clear out and leave the table empty for them. Ordinarily he would have got up and given it to them, or got up a game himself, but now he did not move. When somebody hollered for drinks he reached the key to the liquor box out of his pocket and handed it without a word to Mah Li. The Chink was good; he had savvy. He had never made as much as a ten cent mistake in the liquor sales.

He bent his head and looked at the figures before him, orderly as an accountant's books, plus and minus, expense and profit, stacked in neat columns. He was doing all right. Three months of bunking the crew, even on a sub-contract that cost him twenty percent of his profits, had paid for the lumber, the bedsprings and ticks, the stoves, lamps, tables. The liquor had brought him in two hundred dollars clear in the last month, and that was gravy. He wasn't supposed to sell it, but who was going to come around and close him up? Even the poker games that went on every night till after midnight totalled up into a surprising sum, because every game chipped in a kitty to buy cards and chips and pay for the lights. That was fair enough. He had thought a buck a game was enough; now it turned out it was three times more than enough. The accumulated kitties totalled forty-three dollars, and he had cards and chips enough to last a year. There was also the surplus that Mah Li turned up with every week. He got five dollars a week extra for dealing fan tan and monte as a house game, and he turned over his chips to the penny. In the month and a half he had been with Bo he had brought in a hundred and thirty dollars above his wages.

It was all right, he was out of the woods. He totalled up the checks he had just written and deducted them from his bank balance. He had six hundred dollars in the bank, he owned the bunkhouse and its furnishings, and he had built it so that it could be unbolted and loaded on a flat and taken on down the line on a day's notice when necessary. In three months of actual operations, with his liquor sales and gambling profits, he was that far ahead, and he had arrived in Swift Current with hardly a dime. It just went to show you that if you had any push and got into a new country you could coin money. Not the way Purcell was coining it, but Purcell hadn't started from scratch five months ago, either.

He sat hunched over his papers, hardly seeing the long smoky room with men sprawling in their bunks playing solitaire, reading magazines or newspapers, just sitting or lying, talking, arguing. He hardly smelled the thick smell of hot iron and bitter lignite smoke and tobacco smoke and socks and the heavy odor of fifty men jammed into one warm room. He hardly heard the jumble of talk, as thick and languid as the smells. Five months since he had pulled out of Washington. He hadn't written and he hadn't heard.

Well, how could she write? he said impatiently. How would she know where I was?

For a moment he had almost pulled the curtain that hung over that part of his mind, but he pulled it back. There'd be about one more month of working weather. After that there'd be only a skeleton crew on. But there'd be enough to break even, maybe enough so he could keep the Chink on to cook for him and take care of the place. He'd be close to a thousand dollars ahead of the game, and he could coast until spring, when the big gangs would be back and the steel would come on down from Ravenscrag.

Maybe another year of it, he said. Another year would leave him sitting pretty. His mind edged close to the thing he was trying to think of. If he went back to Elsa in a year or a year and a half with a good fat bankroll and a good proposition of some kind up here, would she . . . ?

Oh Jesus, he said, I don't know.

"Hey, Bo," somebody said. "You got any dice around?"

Bo looked up. Three men were standing under the lamp looking at him. "I don't know," he said. "Maybe I have."

He got up and went toward the cupboard at his back.

"We're gonna teach this heathen Chinee to shoot craps," the man said. "He's too God damn good at fan tan. That's his own game. He invented it."

Bo found a box of dice in the cupboard and picked out a pair. "You going to let yourself get trimmed, Mah Li?"

"No savvy claps," Mah Li said. "Fella can teach?"

He stood at the edge of the table in his black smock and baggy cotton pants, his yellow face bland and smiling.

Bo laughed. "Don't let 'em hook you, boy. You're playing for the house."

"Tly hard for Lady Luck," Mah Li said.

Bo sat down again. If he took part of that six hundred and bought a lot or two from Purcell he'd be paying Purcell a good profit. But the town was barely started, steel wasn't into it yet. Once the rails came in there would be a boom, and he ought to be able to sell off his lots easy. You had to keep money working or it got lazy on you.

But what about that other? he said. What about Elsa and the kids down there? Looking up at the jammed room, the bunks double-decked along both sides, the stoves squat and ugly at each end, the lamps hanging from their wires, he knew he couldn't bring them up to a place like this. He couldn't go down there and try to make things up and then bring them up to live in a bunkhouse with fifty men. He'd have to have a place to bring them to. Let it go a year and he could have a place, a good place.

And how do you know she'd come? he said. What does she feel like, left there to run that café alone with two little kids to take care of? How much does she hold that night against you? Maybe she'll never come back to you.

But good hell, she shouldn't hold a grudge like that, he said. I lost my temper, sure, but . . .

And you ran out on her, said whoever he was arguing with.

Because I was ashamed of myself, he said. Good God, how could I go back there that night? How could I go back the next morning, for that matter? How could I go back in a week, with my tail between my legs? And after I'd stayed away a week how could I go back at all?

You could have written a letter, the arguer said.

Yeah? he said. Saying what?

He looked morosely at the papers, swept them together and slipped a rubber band around them. He ought to be over seeing Purcell, or doing something useful. Or he might, as soon as the work stopped for the winter, go back to Swift Current or Regina and see what the railroad was holding its town lots at. They might sell cheaper than Purcell would.

Why didn't you write a letter? the arguer said. Why don't you write a letter right now? Are you going to let her sit there forever not knowing whether you're dead or alive? What are you afraid of?

He stared somberly at the little group between stove and bunk, down on their knees and shooting craps. Mah Li was shaking the dice against his ear. Lonesome was a long ways away, the Chink said. Velly busy most time. But how about the next six months when nothing was stirring and he had to sit in the very middle of nowhere without anything to be busy about? He'd be chewing the fat of this argument with himself every night for six months.

Well, hell, he said, and went and got a tablet from the cupboard. But when he sat down and looked at the plain white sheet it was an impossible job to put marks on it. What could he say? Go down on his knees and apologize?

Write her a letter, the arguer said. Tell her you're all right. Tell her you're thinking about her and the kids. Send her some money.

That's an idea, he said, and pulling his check book out he dated a check. How much? A hundred dollars? That would put him pretty short for any real estate deals. Make it fifty. Not expecting anything, she would be as pleased with fifty as a hundred, and it would leave him more to work with. They oughtn't to need more. They had the café, and living where they did they didn't have many expenses.

He made out the check and set the indelible pencil on the top of the tablet sheet. "Whitemud, Saskatchewan," he made the pencil write. "Oct. 17, 1913." Then he sat and looked helplessly at the white page. It was a long time, and his lip was stained with indelible violet, before he put down anything else.

2

When Elsa opened the door the statue on the stair post made her think of Helm, as it always did. The ragged boy had stood bare-legged, lifting a bunch of cherries to his lips, in Helm's hall just as he stood here. Bo had always used it for a hatrack, slinging his derby from the hall and ringing the uplifted hand. And as always, she looked at it only a moment, because she knew that if she let herself remember she would make herself miserable.

Mrs. Bohn, the landlady, looked out from the kitchen door at the end of the hall. "Letter for you, Mrs. Mason. I put it on the hall table there."

"Letter?" Elsa said. She rummaged among the half-dozen envelopes and picked hers out. The face was scrawled with pencilled addresses, from Richmond through the three or four places she had moved to in Seattle, trying to find a place where the boys would be taken care of while she worked. But the original address was in Bo's hand, written in indelible pencil smeared and running violet from some time when a postman had walked in the rain.

For a moment she stood quietly, one hand on the stair rail under the varnished pedestal of the cherry boy. Then she went on up the stairs, tiredly, lifting herself as if she carried a burden on her back and pulling with her hand to help her heavy legs.

The window of her room looked out over a plateau of roofs, over the beetle-back shapes of the carbarns caught in a spider web of tracks. Beyond the barns the land rose to a wooded hill, a better residential district with white houses and spread green handkerchiefs of lawn. Under the ceiling of high fog the air was remarkably clear, with a cool grayness in it, no shadows, no contrasts, only the pellucid transparency that left every color and every detail clean and distinct.

She had pulled the rocking chair near to the window, looping back the curtains she had carried from boarding house to boarding house in an effort to make every room seem a little bit familiar, a little bit like home. Bo's letter lay in her lap, and a check for fifty dollars on a bank in Regina, Saskatchewan.

Everything in the letter, and everything behind the letter, was perfectly clear: his shame, his unwillingness to face consequences of his own acts, his impatience at restraint and responsibility and the gnawing awareness that he was still responsible. He could neither accept those responsibilities nor run completely away from them. When he tried to shoulder them he was always chafing under the burden, and when he ran away his conscience bothered him, he worried, he finally sent a check to justify himself and persuade himself that what had happened was only an interruption, not a break. She knew too that the coming of the letter and the check would force a final decision upon her. She couldn't put it off or refuse to think what the ultimate end would be. She had to make up her mind.

The letter lay face up in her lap, and she bent her head to read it again.

Dear Elsa,

This is the first time I've had a chance to send on any money to help you out. I had to look around a while, and it took quite a while to get started up here, but I'm started now and doing pretty well. I'm running a bunkhouse for the grading crew on a sub-contract—I got in too late to pick up any contracts first hand, and probably I couldn't have got one anyway because you have to have a responsible business or post a bond, and I was pretty broke. But it's going to be a pretty good thing. Work will stop in about a month, and I'll hibernate till it opens again in the spring, and sort of keep my eye open for something permanent. This bunkhouse racket is good as long as it lasts, and will give us a stake, but I'll have to locate something to take its place when it folds up.

This is pretty fine country, flat like Dakota, with a nice river valley running through it, some timber in the valley and a nice stream. Every night when I go out and take a walk along the river I see beavers swimming around. The whole valley practically is owned by a fellow named Purcell, a big rancher. It used to be prime Indian country. A bunch of them are camped over in the bend now, with cow guts strung all over the tops of their shanties drying out. They smell like a stockyard and they'll swipe anything loose. My Chink that I've got working for me is scared to death of them, but they're harmless enough. I bought a pair of elk-hide moccasins from one the other day.

Well, Else, I hope the joint is going ok and that you've been able to clear off the payments I hope you and the kids are okay too. This winter, maybe, I can get away to come down and talk over everything with you. It's pretty lonesome up here, and I think about you and the kids a lot. I've got a lot to explain, I know, but I know we can straighten it out as soon as I get loose to come back to the States. I guess we both sort of lost our heads that night, and I'm sorry as hell for what I did. You can't ask any fairer than that.

Anyway, Else, this looks good up here, and the kids could have ponies of their own and have a fine time. I won a couple Indian ponies in a poker game over at the Half-Diamond Bar, that's Purcell's ranch, about a month ago. Won them from the son of a British earl, so they ought to be pretty hot-blooded nags. It looks as if this time we might get clear out of the woods. Let me know how you and the kids are getting along.

Love,
Bo

Through the window she watched a red streetcar crawl along a branch of the spider web and disappear under the barn. I hope the joint is going ok. If he had thought at all he might have known she couldn't take care of two children and run that place all by herself, when it was all the two of them could do when they were both there. He could make himself believe what he wanted to believe, that she was right where he had left her, secure enough, waiting to be taken back.

And what if she did go back, let him cart them off again to that wilderness he had found, a place full of cowpunchers and Indians and beavers and Chinamen and the sons of British earls? That would be giving in to what he had wanted in the first place, making herself and the children into something portable as property, like trunks left behind that could be sent for. Would it be any different up in Saskatchewan? Would there be any more permanence or satisfaction with what they had? Would he hang onto his temper any better, or forget to dream of some even better place over the hills somewhere?

"No," she said aloud, and the finality of the word in the empty room was at once proud and forlorn, so that she stood up with her breath hissing in a sigh. It was so final and awful a thing to think of doing. She knew he was sorry; there was not a doubt of that in her mind. She knew he was honestly sorry, and she knew how much it must have cost him to say so. It was hard for him to apologize. But she still couldn't risk it again. If there were only herself, maybe . . .

But if there were only myself, she said impatiently, there wouldn't
have been any trouble in the first place. I could have gone with him
anywhere. It's the boys that he's felt around his leg like a legiron, and
he shouldn't feel them that way, he ought to be glad of them, and
love them. . . .

3

Chet opened his eyes and looked straight up. His bed, the second
story of a dormitory cot, was in the east gable, and the sun lay
scrambled among the covers. Above him a great beam went from
wall to wall, and above that was a criss-cross of two-by-fours bracing the roof. There were cobwebs in the angles of the two-by-fours,
and directly above him was the dark spot on the under side of the
shingles where the rain had come in once and Mrs. Hemingway had
thought he had done it. He half closed his eyes, and the spot became
a big boat with sails. Squinting, he twisted his head, trying to find
the elephant that had been there yesterday, with his trunk in the air.
There it was; if you turned the boat on its side it became the
elephant.

"Elephant, elephant, elephant," he said, almost aloud, feeling the
shape of the word with his lips. Then he pursed his lips and imitated
Bruce. "Elphanut," he said. "Elphanut."

He snickered, peering down over the high edge of the cot, as high
as the cutbank they slid down on the way to school. If you jumped
off there you'd break your leg. That was what Mrs. Hemingway was
always saying. You boys that sleep in the upper beds better not get
frisky and jump around much. Fall off and break your leg and we'd
have to shoot you. She was funny sometimes. But sometimes she
walloped you, and then found out afterward that you hadn't wet the
bed at all, it was the rain. But she was all right. It was Mrs. Mangin
that gave him a pain. She had pretty fancy teeth, though. The gold in
her teeth was worth a thousand dollars, probably. But that didn't
make him want to kiss her any better. When Ma came on Sundays
Mrs. Mangin always called you in and patted you on the head and
stooped down so that her lavender beads clanked, and you heard
her corsets creaking as she bent while she kissed you with her mouth
that wouldn't quite close over her gold teeth. It was a funny feeling,
being kissed by all that bare gold. The heck with Mrs. Mangin. She
never kissed you when Ma wasn't around. Generally she went around

with her pencil as big as a slingshot crotch, saying, "I'll *thump* you, Chester Mason! You mind now, or I'll *thump* you!"

Stretching his legs and kicking the covers off his feet, Chet made a face, pretending his lips wouldn't meet over his teeth. He bared his teeth so they would glitter goldenly.

> *Mrs. Mangin*
> *Needs a spangin'.*

Cautiously he stood up, reaching for the big beam overhead. The springs squeaked, and he looked around. Nobody was awake yet. The beam was six inches above his upstretched fingers, but by climbing on the iron headboard he could reach it easy. Treading gingerly on the cold round iron, he crouched and jumped, got his elbows over the beam, and wriggled himself up. It was dirty up there, but it was fine, like in an airplane. He wiped a black palm across his pajamas and with his finger pushed some of the deep layer of dust over the edge. It sifted down glittering through the sunlight. Way down below him, miles below where he sat comfortably in his airplane, all the kids slept in their beds. He took his hands away from the beam and flapped his arms, flying his airplane out over the ocean.

Look at the waves! Look at the sharks! Can't get me, sharks.

He stood perilously upright, a million miles above the waves and sharks, and balanced, walking over to the wall. Then he turned around and tightroped back. He saw his tiptoe tracks in the dust on the beam. Whee, he said, and wished somebody was awake to see him.

He started to yell to wake them up, but changed his mind. He'd keep right on going, around the world. From the end of the beam two two-by-fours, one above the other, stretched out to meet another beam coming across the center of the attic. Then two more two-by-fours cut back at the reverse angle into the adjoining gable, where the girls slept.

With his tongue between his teeth Chet inched out on the lower brace, hanging with both hands to the upper one. It was easy. But when he got out over the open floor, with no beds below, it looked a lot higher. If you fell from here, probably, you'd be an hour lighting. Experimentally he spit and watched the spit curve down, heard its light *splat* on the board floor. Hanging on hard, he looked across ten feet of space to the central beam. He was pretty near halfway around the world. The big beam was China, and then he could go on around the other side on the other two-by-fours. Before starting again he pulled his tongue into his mouth and carefully shut his teeth. Pa had told him that if he stuck out his tongue to do things, sooner or later he'd get jarred and bite it off, and then he'd talk like the idiot boy, *nyahh, nyahhh*. His feet crept and his hands slid until he reached the beam.

He wanted to yell and startle somebody, but first he had to get around the world. If he didn't get clear around the world and back to Seattle before everybody woke up and saw him, he'd . . . what? He'd be put in jail. Hastily he slid out on the braces leading into the adjoining gable.

His eyes were on the two-by-four under his feet, his tongue kept getting somehow into the corner of his mouth. But he was flying. He went faster than ever now, because if he didn't get clear around and back Mrs. Hemingway would come in and . . . No, if he didn't get clear around, there would be an earthquake and the whole world would get shaken down so there wouldn't be any place to land.

The next gable had a brace just like the one across his own. He reached it, seeing vaguely, unfocussed, the line of beds below him, a million miles down. Then he sat down on the solid back of the beam and wiped his black hands on his pajamas and breathed deeply, and looking down for the first time with intent to see something, he looked straight into a pair of wide-awake blue eyes.

The shock almost knocked him off the beam, and he grabbed the bracing rafters, ready to run. But the blue eyes—it was Helen Murphy, he saw, the new girl who had come only last week, and about his own age—winked rapidly at him, both eyes (he could wink with either eye, one at a time) and Helen's finger came up to her lips. On the brink of falling or flight, he hung on the beam and stared.

Helen slept in a top bed, like his. The top decks on both sides of her were empty, but the ones nearer the window were mounded with covers. Not a soul seemed to be awake but Helen. He must have waked up awful early.

He grinned at her, whispering, forming the words wide and round with his lips. "I'm a aviator. I'm flying around the world." He let go with one hand, then with both, and flapped his wings.

Helen lay quiet on her back, her eyes as steady as the eyes of a bird on the nest. Then she folded her arms over her chest and hugged herself, smothering a giggle. "You're dirty," she whispered. "You're dirty as a old pig."

Chet wiped his hands again, looking down at the broad smears he had made. "I don't care." He looked at his palms, evenly black, at the soles of his feet, the same way. Dust had sifted up between his toes.

"Mrs. Hemingway'll fix you. You ruined your pajamas. You'll have to sleep nekkid."

"I don't care," Chet said. He spoke too loud, and darted his eyes around. Nobody stirred. It must be awful early. With Helen giggling and watching him he had to do something. He stood on tiptoe and flapped his wings hard, making soundless crowing noises. The sharp eyes in the bed watched him, and when he sat down again she clapped her hand over her mouth and turned her face into the pillow. She was a nutty girl, he thought. Always acting silly.

One hand came out and a finger pointed at him. One eye, peeping up from the pillow, gleamed like a rabbit's, and there were muffled shakings of the bed. Now what? He stared at her, baffled.

The whole face came out again. The finger still pointed, and the face was twisted up with her silly laugh. "I see you," she said.

"Huh?"

"I see you. Your pajamas are unbuttoned."

He jerked around, saw that what she said was true, and buttoned himself up. When he looked back at the bed, doubtfully, she was still stifling giggles. A vague excitement stirred him. He swaggered from the waist up, straddling the beam, and wiped his hands again on his shirt.

Helen sat up. "You sure are dirty," she whispered. "You'll have to sleep in a nightgown, like a girl."

"Aw!" he said hoarsely.

"You'll have to sleep in a nightgown like me," she said. "Or nekkid." She shook with noiseless laughter.

Chet stared at her, his fingers prickling like growing pains. He ought to be getting back, before the earthquake shook everything down. He tried to imagine himself getting back too late and having no place to land on, but he couldn't quite imagine it any more. Helen was looking at him. She twisted around and looked at the other beds, turned back and winked both eyes at him. He winked back with one eye, to show her.

"Look," she whispered. Her eyes were like quarters, and her smile had got tangled up so that her teeth were over her lower lip.

Squirming, she pulled her nightgown up around her neck and lay back on the bed.

Chet hung onto the beam with both hands. His heart went way up in the air without beating at all and then came down again, *kerchonk*. Then he grabbed for the rafter and fled, shuffling sideways out along the two-by-four, stretching and clawing to get across the angle where it joined the central beam, then on again, back to the beam above his own bed.

Win Gabriel, in a lower bed by the window, reared up in bed. "Look!" he screeched. "Look at Chet!"

In a minute all the kids were awake and staring, but Chet didn't stay on the beam to show them how he could fly. He let his feet down over the edge and dangled, feeling for the headboard, just as the six o'clock bell rang. His toes groped frantically, he twisted his head to try to see the thing. Mrs. Hemingway's steps sounded on the stairs, the bell in her hand ringing, ka-*dang*, ka-*dang*, ka-*dang*. Chet found the iron, let go with his hands, and threw himself sideward to alight on the bed. The springs bounced him right out again, and he was hanging by his elbows, scrambling to get back up, when Mrs. Hemingway came in and caught him.

There was no chance to think up a story or try to pretend he had just been getting out of bed. The evidence was all over him, and he didn't say a word when Mrs. Hemingway, after one indignant look, upended him and pulled down his pajamas and swatted his bare bottom a dozen times. She upended him again before he knew which end he was on and had him by the ear, leading him toward the washroom.

But at least, he thought, dragging along with automatic yelps when she yanked on his ear, she hadn't caught him on the beam up over Helen Murphy's bed. If she had caught him there, good night! Oh my!

The washroom was full of steam and the smell of soap and the noise of two dozen boys all washing at once. Chet crawled out of the bathtub where Mrs. Hemingway had dumped him and looked around for Bruce. He was supposed to make sure Bruce washed good every morning, because Bruce was afraid of soap in his eyes and didn't do it right. The kids were pushing him and yah-yah-ing him about getting paddled, but he didn't care. He was still groggy from what Helen had done. Mrs. Hemingway had swatted him pretty hard, though. He twisted to see if his bottom was red. It was, and he felt proud.

He found Brucie at the end washbowl dabbling his hands in the water. His face was dry, and he hadn't taken off his pajama top. "Come on," Chet said. "You're just a darn baby."

He grabbed the washrag and swabbed Bruce's face, splashing him, dripping on the floor. "You cut it out!" Bruce said. "I can wash."

"Hurry up then. It's pretty near breakfast time."

Boys flooded out through the door, racing upstairs again to get dressed and make their beds. Mrs. Hemingway stood at the door inspecting them as they went through. As Chet squeezed by with Bruce she caught him, looked behind his ears, cuffed him lightly. He looked up and saw her smiling. "Our big acrobat!" she said, and let him go.

His bed was tracked with dirt, and he brushed it off as well as he could. Then he went down to the end where Bruce slept in a lower bunk. Bruce had messed up the blankets worse trying to make the bed. He always did. Chet pushed him aside and yanked at the blankets. Little kids were a nuisance. They couldn't do anything.

The long tables in the dining room were already full when they got down. Chet caught a glimpse of Helen Murphy in the middle of the girls' table, but he ducked his head and ate. Mrs. Mangin moved ponderously behind the chairs, and he kept his head down, spooning his oatmeal. It was like a storm coming up to feel Mrs. Mangin creaking up behind you. He spooned desperately, sucking his lower lip to get the drip of milk. The storm moved close behind him and stopped. Chet ducked lower, his automatic elbow going. Any minute now that big pencil might come down on his head like a club, and he'd hear her say, "Ruining your pajamas, Chester Mason! There's only one thing to do with a disobedient dirty boy like you. *Thump* you!"

But it was Bruce she was after. "Eat your oatmeal, Bruce Mason," she said. Chet felt her there, one foot going, her lips as close over her golden teeth as she could get them. He smelled the faint flowery smell of her lavender beads, and heard her breath coming and going in her nose. Brucie would catch it if he didn't start eating his oatmeal.

"I don't like it," Bruce said.

Mrs. Mangin's hand came down across Chet's shoulder and took hold of Bruce's. "Eat it!" she said. "You know what I told you."

"I don't like it," Bruce said.

"Nonsense. It tastes good."

"It don't either."

"Bruce Mason!" Chet ducked until his chin was almost on the table, as Bruce was whisked out of the chair beside him.

"We learn to eat what's put before us," Mrs. Mangin said, "or we do without."

"I want some bread!" Bruce said. His voice started low and ended high and loud.

"Eat your oatmeal."

"No," Bruce said flatly. He started to bawl as Mrs. Mangin hustled him out of the room.

"Get out," she said. "Leave the room! Finicky, stubborn, insolent child . . ."

The storm cloud moved off and Chet straightened a little. He stole a grin at Win Gabriel, on the other side of Bruce's empty chair. Win was a year older than Chet, and could swear, and knew how to braid shoe laces into watchfobs.

"Damn old crab!" Win said, out of the corner of his mouth.

"Damn old stink!" Chet said.

They snickered, their eyes wary to spot Mrs. Mangin moving like a thunderhead along the back of the girls' table. Chet saw her stop behind Helen Murphy's chair.

"Comb your hair before you come to the table after this!" she said, and moved on.

Across the two tables Helen caught Chet's eye, and hunched over to clap her hand across her mouth the way she had done in bed. Chet looked away. When he looked back she was still watching him. She winked rapidly several times. Both eyes.

With his mouth full of bread and butter, Chet leaned over to Win and whispered, "I saw Helen Murphy without any clothes on."

"You're a liar," Win said.

"I ain't a liar. I did so."

"When?"

"This morning."

"I don't believe it."

"All right," Chet said. "Don't believe it then."

The bell rang to end breakfast, and they grabbed their plates to carry them to the kitchen. Just before the bread and butter plate was taken away Chet hooked a piece for Bruce. Ignoring Win, who trailed along behind him, he went to the door and out into the back yard, where he leaned against the wall and watched for Helen Murphy. Bruce was nowhere around, and before he thought Chet ate the bread and butter. He discovered his loss just before the last two bites, but there was no use saving two bites, so he finished them and licked his fingers.

"I don't believe you seen her at all," Win said at his elbow.

"Did so."

"Well, how?"

"Up on the rafters this morning. She just pulled up her night-gown and showed me."

At that minute Helen came out and went by as if she didn't see them, swinging her hands against the sides of her skirt.

"Shame shame double shame everybody knows your name," Win said. Helen jerked her head and went around the corner toward the teeter-totters.

"You're just a big liar," Win said. He stared at the corner where Helen had disappeared. "What's she *look* like?" he said.

At ten o'clock Mrs. Hemingway came to the door with the brass bell in her hand and waved it up and down, ka-*dang*, ka-*dang*, ka-*dang*. In the half minute during which she turned back inside to put down the bell and pick up the big granite dishpan, children materialized from everywhere. Up from the basement, pouring out of the sloping half-doors, stumbling and sprawling on the upper step; out of the orchard where they had been searching for left-over apples; up from the gully behind, where the bigger boys were digging a cave; around the corner from teeter-totters and sandpiles, they came like Indians from an ambush, forty of them in pell-mell haste, three- and four-year-olds galloping, six-year-olds with chests out and fists doubled, girls of all ages shrieking, their pigtails whipping behind.

Chet had been digging in the cave. He was the first one up the bank, and as he ran he saw figures streaming from orchard and yard. Breakfast was pretty early at St. Anne's, and the oatmeal and bread-and-butter didn't hold you long. You were always hungry before Mrs. Hemingway came out on the step to ka-*dang* her bell.

Only the kids who had been playing in the basement beat Chet to the step. He rushed up, tiptoeing, crowding, to get his hands into the dishpan full of buttered crusts, pieces of dry bread left over, sometimes with single bites taken out of them, sometimes whole and untouched and precious. He jammed in close, tramped on a girl's heel, and edged ahead of her when she turned to yell at him. His right hand found the edge of the pan, and he felt Mrs. Hemingway brace herself backward to keep the whole thing from being torn out of her grasp. His first grab netted only a nibbled crust that someone had left under the edge of a plate. Dropping it, unable to see over the packed heads and reaching arms, he felt around frantically, feeling other hands, edges, the soft oily smear of butter. His fingers closed on a large piece of something and he caught a glimpse of it through the tangle. A whole half piece, unbitten. Before anyone could grab it from him he jerked his arm down and ducked out of the press, nibbling, smelling the breadbox smell of bread and faint mold and rancid butter.

There were still children hopping up and down, crowding to get close, when Mrs. Hemingway lifted the pan upside down to show that everything was gone, and disappeared inside. Chet stood against the wall with his slice, and as he nibbled around the edge delicately, like a rabbit, he saw Bruce. Bruce hadn't got anything. Chet watched him somberly. In a minute Bruce would start to blubber, prob'ly, and want a bite. Chet bit into the slice, deeply, just as Bruce saw him.

"Gimme a bite," Bruce said.

"Go on," Chet said. "You should of got here sooner."

"George Rising pushed me," Bruce said. "I was here early as anything, but he pushed me." He came close, his eyes steady on the bread in Chet's hand. "Just one bite, Chet," he said, and reached out. Chet pushed him away.

"You big pig," Bruce said. "Gimme a bite!"

"Go on, or I'll bust you one in the nose," Chet said. He turned to avoid Bruce's lunge, and made a threatening motion with his fist.

Helen Murphy, brushing crumbs from her hands, came swinging across the back of the house, humming to herself. She looked right through Chet, smiled as if at something she had thought of, and paused at the cellar doors. Chet watched her, pushing Bruce off with one hand. Win Gabriel was hanging around at the corner.

"Let's see now," Helen said, her finger against her cheek. "I'll play house, I guess." She smiled the vague smile that included Chet without recognizing him, and skipped down the stairs.

"I'll tell Ma," Bruce was saying. "I'll tell Ma you wouldn't give me any."

"Oh, for the love of Mike," Chet said. He shoved the remains of the slice at Bruce, wiped his hand across his mouth and went down-stairs after Helen. He was on the bottom step when he heard Win Gabriel behind him.

They stood in the doorway a while watching Helen play house with two other girls. Helen was bossy, and she paid no attention to Chet and Win. "I'm the mama," she said. "You've got to be my two kids, and when I come home and find you messing up the kitchen, I spank you and then we get supper and then I'm the papa, and I come home . . ."

"You can't be mama and papa both," one of the girls said. "I want to be papa."

"You will not," Helen said. "First I'm mama, and then I'm papa."

Win looked at Chet. "My God," he said, like a grown man, and spit on the floor.

They climbed on boxes and jumped for the pipes running along under the floor. Win caught a pipe that was hot, and let go with a yelp. He hit a box and sprawled halfway across the floor.

"You're terrible," Chet said. "Watch a great acrobat." He jumped and caught a pipe and hung warbling, his eyes on Helen and the girls. But they still squabbled. Helen had a rag-plugged basin they were playing was a kettle, and another girl was tugging at it.

"I'll tell Mrs. Mangin," the girl said.

"Go ahead and be a tattle-tale."

"I *will!*"

"Go head. Go on and tattle."

The other girl started to cry and fight, and Helen pushed her so she fell down. Then both the other girls went out, the one crying and saying she was going to tell Mrs. Mangin and Mrs. Hemingway and everybody.

"Bawl-baby titty-mouse
    Laid an egg in our house!" Helen said after her.

Win jumped and swung beside Chet, swinging with his knees bent, making faces. Helen put down her basin and put her hands behind her back. "You two are silly," she said.

Win dropped down, and Chet followed him. "I know what you did this morning," Win said.

"What?" Helen said, daring him. "You don't know anything."

"*I* know."

Win jerked her pigtail and they wrestled. In a minute he had her backed against the cement wall, penning her in with his arms. She giggled. "Chet ran away," she said.

"Aw, I did not," said Chet. "I heard Mrs. Hemingway coming."

"I bet you we wouldn't run away if you did it again," Win said. She stuck out her tongue at him, but she was smiling, watching Chet.

"I bet you would. I just bet you would!"

"Like fun," Win said. "I double-dare you."

Helen watched them both. She sucked her thumb briefly, looking up from under her eyelashes. She winked both eyes. "Not for nothing," she said. "You have to too."

Win looked at Chet, fished uncertainly in his pockets. "You're scared," he said.

"I'm not either scared," she said. "You do it and I will."

Win promptly slipped his overall straps down and let the overalls fall around his ankles. He was not wearing any underwear. Helen looked at him slyly, two little white teeth hooked over her lower lip. "Chet too," she said.

A glaze was over Chet's eyes. He moved jerkily, afraid and ashamed and shaken with excitement. "You first," he said.

"No. I won't till you do."

Through eyes strangely misted, Chet looked at her shining eyes, her red cheeks, her teeth hooked over her lip. Her breath whistled a little out of the corner of her mouth. "You're afraid," she said.

"Oh, I ain't either afraid!"

"Well, do it then."

"Come on," Win said, standing in the puddle of his overalls. "You're both a-scared. I'm the only one ain't a-scared."

Excitement grew in Chet until he could hardly breathe. Just as Helen was tossing her head and turning away in scorn he whipped down the overall straps and fumbled at the buttons of his underwear. He saw Helen reach up under her dress and pull her black drawers down, saw her hands gather the skirt and lift. Then he saw her face change, her eyes fix in a frightened stare. Her hands still helplessly held up the skirt, but her mouth dropped as if she were going to yell. Win jerked around with a squawk, grabbed for his overalls and started to run, and Chet did the same. But there was nowhere to run to. There was only one entrance to the basement room, and Mrs. Mangin was standing in that.

He was glad they had sent him out into the hall. He didn't want to stay in the company parlor and have Mrs. Mangin look at him as if she could just barely keep from vomiting, and he didn't like to see Ma sitting there. He hated Mrs. Mangin. That morning after she caught them she had taken them all up into the kitchen, just dragged them up with their clothes still hanging off them, and turned them up one by one and beaten them on the bare bottom with a yardstick. Chet wished he'd had as much nerve as Win, to fight her, even if he had got beaten over the head with the stick the way Win had. He wondered where Win was now, and Helen too. Prob'ly still locked up, the way he had been all day without anything to eat.

The hall still held the smell of supper, and he swallowed. He wished he had a belt to cinch tight, the way Indians did. Or he wished he had, right in his overalls pocket, a great big chocolate bar with peanuts in it. The vision and the taste came together, so delicious and overpowering that he felt in the pocket almost hopefully. There were only four slingshot rocks, a rubber band, a couple of carpet tacks he had been saving to put on seats in school, and an empty brass cartridge case.

Sitting on the hall seat in the dark he took the cartridge and blew in it experimentally. It made a thin, breathy whistle. He wished he had a gun. He'd put in this bullet and aim it right through the wall at where Mrs. Mangin was sitting inside talking to Ma, and he'd shoot it off and shoot a hole right through Mrs. Mangin. He aimed the cartridge, squinting. Bang, he said. Bang, bang, bang! There . . . I guess you won't ever lick me again, you old stink of a Mrs. Mangin.

His bottom was still sore from the whipping, and he shifted to get comfortable. He would be an Indian, and some morning he would come to the door with his gun under his blanket and say to Mrs. Mangin, "Last week you spanked Chet and Win and Helen right in the kitchen in front of everybody, and you're always going around thumping kids with your pencil. Well, I'll fix you." Then he would shoot her with his cartridge and whip out his scalping knife and snip off her scalp, zing, and pull out her gold teeth and sell them and give the money to the kids to buy marbles and candy with.

The voices in the parlor had grown louder, and he listened. It sounded as if Mrs. Mangin was mad. Carefully he slid off the hall seat and sneaked up to the door. By the time he got there and held his breath to listen, it was his mother's voice.

". . . that you're not being fair to him. You can't lay all the blame on him. He's not a bad boy."

Now Mrs. Mangin's, heavy and triumphant. "What do you call climbing on the rafters and peeking at the girls in bed? If that isn't bad . . ."

"You don't know he did that. Mrs. Hemingway doesn't think he did."

"What else would he be doing up there? I'm sorry to say it, Mrs. Mason, but I think we are dealing with a corrupt and filthy-minded child."

"Oh, nonsense!" Ma said, almost as loudly as Mrs. Mangin. "He's not quite seven years old yet."

Mrs. Mangin said, "My experience lets me know many more children than you can have known, Mrs. Mason . . ."

There was the scrape of a chair, as if someone had stood up, and Chet started to scuttle for the hall seat, but stopped when he heard his mother's voice again. "I know that when I brought Chester here he was as clean and nice a boy as anyone could ask for."

Mrs. Mangin's voice cut in, rising, "Mrs. Mason, if you mean to insinuate . . ."

"So if there's any evil in his mind now, he learned it at this home. I won't stand for your putting him in jail for two weeks, making him feel as if he's done something horrible. There's no evil in a child that age. The evil is read in by other people."

"There is only one way to treat a rotten-minded child," Mrs. Mangin said. "If our methods don't suit you . . ."

"There is only one kind of rotten-minded child," Ma said, almost shouting, "and that's the kind that exists in a rotten mind. You can just bet your methods don't suit me."

His ear against the wood, Chet shook his shoulders and crowed silently. Ma was just giving it to the old stink. "I looked at Bruce tonight, too," Ma was saying, and her words sounded jumbled and fast as if she were trying to say two or three things at once. "He's thin as a rail, all shoulder blades and eyes."

"If he won't eat his meals," Mrs. Mangin said, "he gets nothing else here. We don't coddle children, Mrs. Mason."

Ma didn't say anything for a minute, and Chet stretched his neck, trying to see through the crack in the door. But all he could see was the tiled fireplace, and the stone dog set above the opening. He jerked back when Ma's voice came, much closer to the door.

"There's not much point in discussing it, is there?" she said. "I'm taking the children out, right now."

Chet ducked back against the hall seat and the door opened, letting out a wide stripe of light across the hall. Ma stepped out and came over to him quickly. Her shirtwaist smelled like ironing as she stooped to hug him. "Wait here," she said. "I'm going up and get Bruce and we're going to get out of this place."

Ten minutes later she was down carrying Bruce; he was dressed, but sleep had not entirely left him, and his knuckles dug into his eyes. Mrs. Mangin stood in the parlor door, drawn up high, with her teeth not quite covered by her inadequate lips. Chet sidled past her, watchful for a thumping, till he got his hand in his mother's.

"I'll be back tomorrow for their clothes," Ma said.

Mrs. Mangin, with her wintry and goldenly-gleaming smile, watched them out the door. Chet stuck out his tongue from the porch, and then Ma set Brucie down and they walked together down the aisle of black spruces. It was the latest Chet had ever been out, and the yard looked funny in the dark. He wouldn't have known it was the same place.

"Where we going, Ma?" he said.

Her hand closed on his. "To my room."

"Are we gonna live there?"

"No."

"Is Pa coming back and get us?"

"No."

"What are we gonna do then?"

Ma sounded tired. "There's only one thing we can do," she said. "We'll have to go back and visit Grandpa."

4

That house—the dark, quiet little parlor, the library table stacked with Norwegian newspapers, the glass-fronted bookcases full of sets, Ibsen, Bjørnson, Lie, Kjelland, the folksongs of Asbjørnson and Moe, the brass-and-leather Snorre, the patriotic *landsmaal* songs of Ivar Aasen—she knew the feel and look of everything there, the wallpaper, the curtains, the stained dark woodwork. Nothing had changed a particle. She knew on what page of the great Snorre she would find the engraving of the death of Baldur that had made her cry as a child because Good was being destroyed by Evil, and she even felt some of her old hatred of the unstable and mischievous Loki. The most wonderful thing about the place was that sense of everything just where it had always been.

Kristin's arm was around her all the way upstairs, as if she were an invalid. The affection and sympathy in her sister's face was almost too much. She hadn't found it in her father or in Sarah; they were polite, dutiful, a little cold, and she knew they didn't want her, she knew their disapproval cut so deep that even now, in her desperation, when she had no other place to turn to, they suffered her merely, without real welcome. She smiled a little wearily, going upstairs, at what her pride had come to. Not once only, but twice, she had come back on them like a charity case.

Her room was just as it had always been. The roses still clustered in the wallpaper, the curtains hung crisply against the window whose bars were outlined by early snow, the carpet still took its streak of sun, and she saw the mark where it had faded through the years. On the wash stand was the big red and white bowl, the pitcher inside it, just as they had stood through her childhood, and through the misted window was the same quiet street and the same three white houses and the same gentle swell of open country dotted with bare trees.

Like smoke that rose and filled a room the feeling swelled in her that she had never breathed properly since she had run away from home. Dakota had been too open, a place of wind and empty sky. Seattle had been tenements in crowded streets and the interminable drifting rain. The tent-house where she had almost got the feeling of home had been huddled closely within a circle of woods. But here there was both shelter and space, here was home even if she was unwelcome in it. The changelessness of the house and the strip of quiet street and the swell of farmland was like an open and reassuring door.

She heard Kristin talking without being fully aware of what she said. There was a sad-sweet relaxation in all her bones, as if she had just taken off a rigid corset after hours of formality. Then Kristin's talk paused, and Elsa looked up to see her holding a dress she had just taken from the telescope. The dress was cheap, too-much-laundered, and the instant defensive words jumped to Elsa's lips. "I've had that dress ever since we lived in Hardanger. I ought to have thrown it away, years ago, but you know how you hang onto things."

"Yes," Kristin said quietly, and hung the dress in the wardrobe, but there was a vague hostility between them. Elsa had no idea what they all thought about her leaving Bo. Maybe they thought she had left because he wasn't a good provider, as if she were as disloyal and selfish as that! She shut the empty telescope and shoved it under the bed.

"Is there any hot water?" she said. "The boys ought to have baths."

"So should you," Kristin said. "They're out playing around the barn. You look after yourself first."

"Maybe I will," Elsa said. "A bath will feel good."

"I'll bring the tub up here."

"I can get it."

"Let me," Kristin said. "Please." She was out the door, and Elsa let her go. Slowly she unbuttoned her blouse and took it off, unhooked her corset, unlaced her shoes. Kristin labored in with two pails of steaming water, went out again after the tub. As she set the tub down she looked at Elsa, and Elsa saw her eyes widen and her mouth twist. She was looking at the burned arm. Elsa raised it and laughed a little.

"Oh, Else, how did you do it?" Kristin said.

"The coffee urn tipped over."

Kristin came up and touched the smooth whitish scar that prevented the arm's being completely straightened. "It must have been awful," she said. "Were you alone?"

"Do you want to blame that on him, too?" Elsa said.

Kristin stammered, flushing.

"He was there," Elsa said. "He carried me down to the doctor."

"Oh." Kristin stood twisting her engagement ring around on her finger.

"He isn't as bad as all of you always thought he was," Elsa said bitterly.

"I'm sorry, Elsa. Honestly, I didn't mean to . . ."

"Oh, let's not," Elsa said. "Please, Kristin. I didn't mean to snap at you, either. I just get tangled up. I can feel it all through the house, the way they blame him for everything. I'm as much to blame as he is."

"Do you know what Dad said to me after we got your wire?" Kristin sat down on the bed and took both of Elsa's hands. "He'd talked it all over with Sarah, and you know what he said? He said he wanted me to keep you occupied, and stay around and do things with you, because this whole thing was going to be pretty hard on Sarah. On *Sarah!* Oh, Else, she's still ashamed of marrying Dad, and she dislikes you for it, somehow, I know she does."

"Does she?" Elsa said. "I gave up disliking her a long time ago. She married Dad because she was alone and didn't have any place to turn. I couldn't dislike her for that very long. And besides, he's doing me a favor if he asks you to look after me. Isn't he?"

"I think Dad would be all right if it weren't for her," Kristin said. "She's just got so *good*. He missed you after you went away, but she keeps reminding him of all the sins she says Bo does. When you came back before she didn't want Dad to let you. That's the only time I ever heard him get mad at her and bawl her out."

"Oh well," Elsa said. "I'll try to find work somewhere, and then we won't have all this. I'm just so tired now I guess I don't care what they think."

"When George and I get married in April you come and live with us," Kristin said.

Elsa smiled. "I guess I don't want to wish that on you," she said. "I thought maybe I could keep house for Erling on the farm."

"You don't want to go out on that farm and get snowed in all winter. You stay right here. You've got more right here than Sarah has. I wouldn't let her drive me out."

"We'll see," Elsa said. She didn't, actually, want much to go out to the farm. The farm was the one part of home that was spoiled for her. The winter when Bo had nearly gone crazy out there would keep coming up and reminding her of things she didn't want to remember.

"You're thin," Kristin said, on the second morning. "You need to rest and eat a lot."

After that things were set beside her at the table casually, slyly. Her plate was heaped before she could refuse. She got second helpings she didn't want. She tried, she ate till she was stuffed, she let herself be supinely carried off for naps after lunch, but all the time she was aware that her father and Sarah were not a part of this plan. They were like strangers on a bench, making room for her to squeeze in, but asking no questions, inviting no confidences, interesting themselves in what had absorbed them before her arrival. They would not welcome her, but they would make room out of Christian charity.

Still she could forget, often, that they didn't want her. She could forget Bo and the café and Seattle and the orphanage, could look at the children and see them blooming, and be thankful at least for their sakes. Chester was in school, Bruce was teasing to go too, devoting himself for hours to crayons and slates, curled on the floor in the dining room. In the mild, brooding, early-winter days Elsa often sat in the dining room sewing and watched his absorbed play-learning and was grateful.

On Sunday afternoons her father took his nap in the dining room, on a couch crowded into the corner, his fingers trailing on the floor among the trailing fringes of the cover. The boys, unable to subdue themselves to Sunday, were in and out, pestering. They sneaked up to tickle Grandpa with feathers, and he played with them as Elsa had never seen him play with his own children. Even the unrelaxing sternness of his face, after the first few uncertain days, could not fool them. On the pretense of having protection against the flies, he took a fly-swatter with him to his nap, waving it up out of his doze occasionally. He seemed to sleep, his mustaches faintly blowing as he breathed, and the boys crept forward smothering giggles, stretching their feathers far out. They would be right at his nose, only an inch away, when one blue eye would open like a shutter, the stern eyebrows would scowl, and the fly-swatter would swish around their legs.

"Preacher's tails!" he would roar at them. "Mosquito-shadows!"

Watching that, or watching the boys playing with the neighborhood children, Elsa hadn't the heart to look for work yet. She couldn't take them away just when they were tasting normal childhood, making friends, feeling themselves secure. So she kept her own feelings quiet and made herself useful in the house. She helped preserve meat at butchering time, made head cheese and sausage and tried lard. And when there was nothing else to do she could help Kristin with her trousseau.

Most of her clothes had to be made, for her father would stand for no nonsense like shopping tours in Minneapolis. So Elsa made nightgowns and dresses and petticoats and blouses, hemmed sheets and pillow cases, crocheted lace, working as if it were her own hope chest that was being filled, and not her sister's.

"You're wonderful at sewing, Else," Kristin said once. "Why don't you make things for yourself, instead of helping me all the time? You could stand some new clothes."

Elsa bit off a thread, threaded the needle, and pulled the end down. "I don't need any new clothes."

"You do too."

"What for?"

There was no answer to that.

But even the unfailing recourse of sewing for Kristin could not occupy more than her hands, and to keep from thinking she often sang. Sometimes in the midst of a song she would break off abruptly, wondering why she sang at all. She wasn't happy enough to sing, certainly, only dormant, as if half of her slept. She remembered times when she had been happy enough to sing, the old days when she had sung alto in the church choir, evenings in Hardanger, even in Grand Forks, so miserably burdened with the weight of that hotel. She remembered evenings coming home from somewhere in the buggy, when she and Bo had sat together with their voices going up in old tunes. Bo had a nice voice, she thought wanly, full and rich. She remembered the nodding tip of the buggy whip against the sky, the windy freshness of the air of those lost evenings, and Bo's laughter, his rich, warm, possessive laughter, and the fool songs he knew, dozens of them, as if his mind were flypaper to catch all sorts of buzzing tunes. When she got that far in her remembering she always broke off, sang some other song, one that had no echoes except those that sounded down the green avenue of her childhood.

Sometimes Henry Mossman came to call, and everybody always assumed that he came to see Nels Norgaard, and the two men sat in the parlor while the women worked or darned or chatted in the dining room. But Elsa knew why he came, and she sat sometimes studying his stooped, apologetic figure with a kind of regret, remembering that once he had wanted to marry her, that if she had she might have got what she now so desperately wanted. With a little shake of the head she would let amazement run through her mind at the way people changed. Nine years ago, silly and young and full of confidence that she knew just what she wanted to do with her life, she had run away from Indian Falls and Henry Mossman and the stodgy uneventful life of the town, and now she almost wished she had chosen the other way.

Henry was so mild and inoffensive and docile, so unwilling even to say straight out that he came to see her, not her father, and he sat in the parlor half a dozen evenings talking to Nels Norgaard and saying hardly more than ten words to Elsa. He was steady, incapable of a harsh word to anybody, kind, unattractive, dependable. She wished once, with a sigh, that Bo, with all his arrogant ease, his sharpness, his powerful and well-tuned body, might have had just a touch of Henry's dependable quietness. But before she had half thought it she was thinking almost proudly that Bo could never be like Henry. He wasn't a domestic animal, he wasn't tame, he couldn't like halters, no matter how hard he tried—and he did try, had tried, often. It just wasn't in him; she had probably helped along his unhappiness and her own by trying to turn him into something he was never cut out to be. Just by marrying him she had done that. Karl had known it, right from the beginning. Bo was a rambler, and the responsibilities of marriage would never sit easily on his back.

George Nelson, blond, laughing, very much in love with Kristin, came down from his Minneapolis law office and stayed for two days at Thanksgiving, and when he was gone Kristin folded up and put away the dress she had stolen out of her trousseau and threw herself into crocheting pillow-slip lace.

"You must be planning to spend all your life in bed," Elsa said. "You've already got six or eight pairs done."

Kristin blushed, let her hands stop, and looked up with her face strained as if she were about to cry. "I should think you'd hate me, Elsa."

"For goodness' sake, why?"

"Because I'm so happy."

Sympathy again, Elsa thought. Poor Elsa. But she wasn't angry. Kristin was so full of her happiness and she had to be spendthrift, share it with everybody. "I'm as glad as I can be," Elsa said.

They were on the edge of the old forbidden ground. A silence like a drawn curtain came between them.

"You like George, don't you?" Kristin said from the other side of the curtain.

"Very much. I always did."

"You think he'll make a good husband, don't you?"

Kristin picked at a knot in the lace, her eyes hiding. "I think he's wonderful," she said.

"So do I," Elsa said, crocheting steadily. "Not as wonderful as you do, but wonderful enough."

"I suppose every bridegroom seems wonderful to the bride," Kristin said. "Oh Elsa, I wish . . ."

"What?"

"I wish you were as happy as I am. You deserve such a lot, and you never got a thing."

"Maybe I don't deserve very much," Elsa said, "and how do you know I never got anything?" She straightened a square of lace and laid it aside. "That's fourteen," she said. "Eighty-two more and you'll have your bedspread."

Kristin stood up. "I've got to run down to the postoffice. George said he'd write the minute he got back."

She stood in the doorway, struggling into her coat. "Don't you think it's cute the way his hair curls up above his ears?" she said. She went out, letting the storm door bang.

In a few minutes the door slammed again, and Kristin blew in in a cloud of snow. She was some time taking off her coat and hanging it in the hall. Out in the kitchen Sarah was rattling pans. Then Kristen came in.

"Get your letter?" Elsa asked.

"Uh-huh."

"You don't seem very excited. Didn't he put any kisses at the bottom?"

"Oh, it's a nice letter," Kristin said. She went to the table and ruffled through the papers there.

"Is anything wrong?"

"No." Kristin turned around. "There's a letter for you, that's all." She took it out of her pocket.

"For me?" Elsa's hand came out halfway. Her eyes jumped to meet Kristin's.

"From him," Kristin said. She seemed unwilling to give it up. "Oh, I wish he'd let you alone!" she said. "When it's all over with, he ought to have decency enough . . ."

She threw the letter at Elsa and went out into the kitchen, leaving Elsa alone with the envelope a warm, speaking, dangerous thing under her fingers. The letter was postmarked Seattle. He had come back to Washington, then, and found her gone. She tore open the end and very slowly drew out the letter, a fat one. There was a money order folded into it. Two hundred dollars. Straightening the sheets, she read:

Dear Elsa,

If this letter doesn't reach you I don't know what I'll do. I've been about crazy since I came down here a week ago and found out you'd left the place in Richmond a long time back. I've been hunting all over Seattle, had a detective on the job and everything, and finally I found out you'd worked in that store, and got your address from a guy there, but the landlady said she didn't know where you'd gone. So I just have to shoot in the dark and hope you went home. You should have written me and told me about the cafe. I thought you'd make out there all right, and after you shut me out that night I was so mad and sick I didn't know what I was doing. I wrote a letter a month ago, with a check in it. Did you get it? Oh, damn it, Elsa, I don't know what to say. I'm getting along fine up in Canada, bought some real estate and ought to make some dough in the spring, but I'm lonesome for you and the kids all the time. If you've gone home to stay with your folks I wish you'd think it over, and in the spring come up here with me. I'm really in on the ground floor here, even if Purcell does own the whole valley. This road is opening up a country as big as Dakota, and there's plenty of homestead land open yet. I'm looking out for a half section in a good place, with water. Sometimes you can pre-empt another quarter along with the homesteaded quarter if the guy who homesteaded it first hasn't made his improvements. This land will grow wheat six feet high, and if we could get into some business in town and have a half section for farming in the summer we'd be set. This town, or this place where they will be a town, is going to have a lot of opportunities in it. As we get rolling we could buy up more land in the townsite and clean up a bbl. of money from the people who'll be flocking in here in six months. There is white clay along the river that a fellow from Medicine Hat says is just right for pottery. Coal too, lignite, the hills are full of it, and some fellows were around there when I left, snooping for oil. If we owned some land and oil was struck on it we'd be on Easy St. for life. We can't make any mistake on this place. It's what I've been looking for all my life. It isn't all skimmed off and gobbled up.

Elsa, I miss you and the kids, and this proposition looks so good I hate to think that now we stand a chance to make some money you aren't with me any more. Its no satisfaction to make money just for yourself. I can't seem to get steamed up about it alone. I guess if you're really set on leaving me I can't kick, because I had it coming the way I acted, but I wish you'd think it over. In a new country like that we could start all over. This town will be a nice place to live. It's on the Whitemud River, and there'd be swimming and hunting and riding for the kids, and plenty of brush for them to run in. The country reminds me some of my old home town in Illinois, only there aren't any trees except in the river valley. I caught four beaver and a half dozen muskrats in traps in the week before I came down to the States. That shows you how wild it still is. Beavers swim right out in the river under the railroad bridge.

You think it over, Elsa. We don't want to go breaking up the family and not give the kids a chance. I have to go back to Whitemud right away, but if you get this, write me and let me know you're all right. I'm sending on some money, if you need more let me know and I can rake it up. I was going to invest this two hundred in another lot, but then I thought you'd probably need it, especially when I found out you hadn't been able to make the cafe go. And you'd better decide to come up here in the spring. I promise you nothing like that other will happen any more. I guess I learned something from that night.

All my love,

Bo

P.S. I want to send on something for a Christmas package. Can't tell much what you need, but I'll try to find something useful. I know you never did like jewjaws.

So he had finally struck something that promised to pay off. She had always believed that some day he would. If you tried enough things, sooner or later something was bound to turn out. But she mustn't, she thought almost desperately, she mustn't let herself be softened. It was a nice letter, and it made her want to do just what she knew she shouldn't do. But she would hang onto what she knew: she knew he couldn't promise to change what he was. The thing she feared in him, the thing that had made her shut him out that night, was still there, deep in his violent and irritable and restless blood.

Or was it? Was there a chance that only poverty, bad luck, dissatisfaction, brought that out in him? Was there a chance that in a new place, living the way he wanted to, making enough money to satisfy him, that side of him would never come out any more?

She looked up to see Kristin standing in the sliding doors between dining room and parlor. Her eyes were accusing. Pugnaciously she came in and sat down, her whole expression saying that she was not going to get up again until this thing was talked over and settled. Elsa sat still.

"What did he say?" Kristin said.

Elsa shrugged. "Sent some money. Wants me to come up to Canada in the spring."

"He would," Kristin said. "That's the kind he is. He'd abuse you for eight or nine years and then expect you to come crawling back for more. I wouldn't even have opened his letter."

"He's still my husband," Elsa said. "I wrote Dad once about helping me get a divorce, but he wouldn't do anything unless I had the one reason the church accepts. And Bo's never looked at another woman. You dislike him too much, Kris. He sent me two hundred dollars in this letter."

"It's a bribe!" Kristin said. "He'll send you money to get you back and then you'll have rags and beatings again."

"Beatings!"

Sitting forward on the edge of her chair, Kristin let her eyes bore into Elsa's. "He did beat you, didn't he?"

"My goodness, no."

Kristin sat back reluctantly, only half believing. "But you aren't going back to him, are you?"

"I was just wondering," Elsa said. She stared at the cherry-red mica squares in the door of the parlor heater and shook her head tiredly. "No, I don't think so."

"Because you don't know what he's done to you," Kristin said. "When you went away you were young, and pretty, and healthy, and everything, and you come back with your arm hurt so it'll always show, and without decent clothes, and . . ."

"And looking like an old woman," Elsa said.

"That isn't what I meant. You're pretty yet, only you look so tired, and thin. Sometimes when you don't know anybody's looking at you you look so worn out you scare me. Elsa, you look . . . just the way I remember Ma!"

She gave the spring handle of the poker a hard kick, and it rattled against the stove legs.

"I guess I can still manage to get around," Elsa said. "People needn't wear themselves out worrying about me."

"He's taken the heart out of you," Kristin said helplessly. "Even if he didn't beat you or burn your arm, he led you such a life that he's taken the heart right out of you. You used to be so spunky and independent, and make Erling and me toe the mark, and now you're so quiet and kind you make me want to cry!"

She was crying as she said it. Elsa put out a hand and touched her. "Then he's been good for me," she said. "At least I may have learned to keep my temper."

"It isn't a matter of keeping it. It's having it to keep. You don't seem to ever want anything for yourself any more, and that's not natural, Elsa."

"Let's not talk any more about it," Elsa said.

"Why don't you get a divorce in spite of Dad?"

Elsa laughed a little. "I don't know how. I don't even know how to begin, and I haven't any money for a lawyer."

"George would help you."

"And get him and you in dutch with Dad."

"George wouldn't care. Then you'd be free of him. You wouldn't always be getting letters . . ."

"One since I came," Elsa said drily.

". . . and worrying yourself about him. You're thinking about him all the time, and worrying."

"And then what would I do?" Elsa said, rising. "A divorce wouldn't change things any."

"You could get married again."

After a short, incredulous stare, Elsa laughed. "Don't be silly."

"Henry would still marry you."

"You make him sound very charitable," Elsa said. "I remember what you used to say about Henry."

She held the indignant eyes for a minute. "Don't you like Henry any more?" Kristin said.

"Certainly. I always did like him."

They stared at each other, and by a sudden emotional shift in the wind they were both close to anger. As they stared, Kristin's face changed, her eyebrows lifted, her lips came together.

"Elsa," she said, "you're still in love with Bo!"

Elsa turned away. "Well, what of it?" she said harshly.

5

Elsa stood above the kitchen range, the glow of its slow heat on arms and face, making Christmas pastry. It was the day before

Christmas. Kristin, Sarah, and the boys were doing some last-minute shopping; her father had gone out to the farm after Erling.

On the table behind her a mound of sugar-dusted *fattigmands bakkelse* almost poured off on the floor, the back of the stove was sheeted with gray *lefse*, a wide crock in the cupboard was heaped with *goro brød*. She turned over a *lefse* sheet, browning in spots like broad freckles, and dropped a new batch of *fattigmand* into the kettle of fat. The kitchen was full of rich smells. She smiled a little, remembering how excited the boys were. This would be a Christmas they would remember, the kind of Christmas kids ought to have.

She thought too of what Bo's Christmas would be like in that raw little settlement in Saskatchewan: a few drinks with some other men, probably; perhaps a bowl of tom and jerry batter in his bunkhouse the way they used to have it in Dakota. Just that, and her own futile, wept-over parcel with the knitted muffler and the gloves and the heavy home-made socks. One parcel to be ripped open in the postoffice or wherever he got his mail, and instead of the warmth and ritual and color, the tree and the decorations and the bountiful eating that brought the old country close that one day of the year, and the reunion of people tied by blood and traditions, there would be only his drinks with a few other men as lonely as himself in a little unformed unhistoried town of a half dozen frame shacks.

But that was what he wanted, that was the natural result of the itch in his bones and the restlessness in his mind. She thought it odd that he should be lonely, as his letter said he was, as she herself knew he was. For all his strength and violence he was oddly dependent in some ways, like a child. Like Bruce, she thought in surprise. He was really more like Bruce than like Chester, though they had both always thought Chet the image of him.

The doublings of her own mind wearied her. As she lifted the *fattigmand* brown and cake-smelling from the fat, she saw her bare right arm, the ridge of white scar in the bend of the elbow. She would always, apparently, wear Bo in her as she wore that scar, yet she had to make up her mind. She had to answer his letter, let him know what she would do. And she had to decide what to do about this house that echoed constantly of home but was home no longer.

The front door slammed, she heard the stamping of feet in the hall, Sarah's admonitions to the boys to clean the snow off their shoes. They all came in together, the boys rosy with the cold, Sarah pulling a wisp of hair up under her net, Kristin carrying packages. She dumped them on the floor by the cistern pump.

"Else," she said, "could you . . ." She stopped, looked at the piles of pastry, pulled off her gloves. "You're awful busy, though."

"I'm just about done. What is it?"

"George is going to be here at six o'clock, and that green dress doesn't fit right around the neck."

"Sure, just a minute."

Elsa moved the kettle of fat off the stove, gave a sugared *fattigmand* to each of the boys, standing with their tongues between their lips at the table, and shooed them out. Kristin picked up three or four big packages and followed her upstairs. While Elsa worked on the dress she said nothing, but when the collar was going back on, she jerked her head at one large parcel. "That came for you in the mail," she said.

They looked at each other, then at the square package. "Yes," Elsa said. "He said something about a Christmas parcel."

Though she wouldn't have shown it to Kristin, she was excited. Bo would have some part in this Christmas. He hadn't forgotten, and he wouldn't be forgotten.

She was so busy getting Kristin ready for George that she had no time to open it then, and later there was supper, and then the dishes, and then a quick change into a dress-up dress for the Christmas tree. But that was all right. Let it be a surprise, to her and to all of them. They thought he was so low and vicious, let them see right out in the open that he could be thoughtful too.

The house was full. Sarah's two sisters had come over, George was down from Minneapolis, Erling in from the farm. Groaning full with *ludefisk, kjodkager, risengrot, anschovy salat,* a half dozen kinds of pastry, pleasantly warmed by the grape wine traditional with Christmas feasts, they crowded into the parlor, sitting on chairs and floor wherever there was room. George and Kristen sat on the floor under the Christmas tree, Sarah on a straight chair, Nels Norgaard on the couch between Sarah's sisters. He quizzed them in Norwegian and smiled a little grimly at their halting and giggling answers. Erling had slipped out immediately after supper.

Chester stuck his head in between Grandpa and Hilda Veld. "There ain't any Santa Claus, is there?"

"Hoo!"

"There ain't any Santa Claus that comes down the chimney, is there?"

"I knew a boy once that didn't believe in Santa Claus," Grandpa said. "You know what he got for Christmas? An orange, and the orange was spoiled."

"Aw!" Chet said. He retreated to whisper with Bruce.

When Elsa came in Bruce ran up to her. "Mom."

"What is it?"

"Chet says he ain't going to come."

"Isn't. We don't say ain't. But he'll come. Chet's just trying to be smart."

"Aw, I know," Chet said. "*I* know!"

There was a knock on the door, and Elsa went to open it. It was Henry Mossman, stooping and smiling and apologetic. "Merry Christmas," he said. "Can I butt in on the celebration?"

"Sure thing. Come on in."

Henry bowed and spoke all around, the parcel he carried looking uncomfortably prominent in his hands. Elsa told him to put it under the tree.

"When do the festivities start?" he said.

"Any time now. Erling's out getting ready."

Henry looked at the boys, secretive in their corner. "They don't look half excited, do they?" he said, and laughed.

Elsa half turned away and smoothed the papers on the library table. For an instant a thought had sneaked into her mind. Just the sight of Henry's unaffected kindness, the way he looked at the boys as if he loved them both, made her see him for an instant as their father. They'd have walked all over him from the time they were born, but they would have loved him, they wouldn't ever have known what it was to hate or fear him . . .

Outside there was the faint jangle of sleigh bells. Nels Norgaard rose and shooed them all toward the kitchen, reached over and picked up the lamp. "All out," he said, "all out, all out. He won't come in if he sees us." The boys, frantic with excitement, hung back, escaped, had to be rounded up and herded. George and Kristin were hurriedly lighting the tree candles in their pink clamp-sockets. The tree glowed, the strings of popcorn gleamed white, there was a rich red glitter from the long festoons of cranberries, a shimmer from the glass bubbles and ornaments.

Motioning Henry to go in with the others, Elsa ran upstairs and collected her packages, piled her arms, stooped and caught her fingers in the cord of Bo's parcel, felt her way down the dark stairway again. Kristin was pushing packages under the tree. In the three minutes since the lamp had been removed the floor under the tree had been mounded with gifts. Elsa pushed her packages in with the others, turned and saw Erling's face grinning in through the window over a bushy white beard. "Hurry up," Erling said, his voice faint through the storm windows. "It's cold out here in this monkey suit."

The boys burst loose when she slipped into the kitchen. "Is he *here?*" Bruce said.

"I heard him up on the roof," she said. "He got stuck in the chimney for a minute or I'd never have got out in time."

She peered out the door. The partition between dining room and parlor cut off the tree, but she saw the flutter of its lights on the wall. There was the soft sound of the front door opening. She turned to her father. "Blow out the light," she said. "Then we can let the boys creep out and peek at him."

The kitchen went dark in a puffed breath. Sarah's sisters, somewhere in the dark, whispered and giggled. "Shhhhhhh!" Chester said fiercely, three times as loud as the whisper had been.

Taking the boys' hands, Elsa tiptoed them carefully into the dining room, where she stood with finger on lips and leaned to look through the double doors. Erling in a Santa Claus suit was standing in front of the fireplace cramming long scrolls of candy into the stockings. From a bag he poured streams of peanuts and butternuts and almonds, and crowned each stocking with a tangerine. The tree was barricaded with new packages, brightly wrapped. Candy canes hung from the tree, and there was a shimmer, a glitter, the whole fairy wonder of childhood, in the room. She pulled the boys close so they could peek.

They bent, stared; she felt their bodies rigid with awe. Even Chet, the unbeliever, did not breathe for minutes. Against their will they were tugged back into the kitchen. Sarah lighted the lamp again, and the roomful of people stood looking at the two boys, every pair of eyes watching the dazed entrancement in their faces. Bruce looked up at his mother, crowded against her legs, smiled wanly, and began unaccountably to cry.

Sleigh bells jangled again loudly, diminished as if moving away. "There he goes!" Chet said. They piled out of the kitchen, and the boys stopped short for a moment when they saw, well-lighted now and in plain view, the piles of gifts. Then they fell upon the loaded tree.

For a half hour there was pandemonium as they ripped open parcels, exposing Indian suits, revolvers, pencil boxes and crayons, tricycles (her father's gift, lavish, unheard of). The room was full of birdlike chirps of joy. Henry and George went around salvaging packages from the boys' rapacious hands and distributing them to their rightful owners. With surprise, Elsa found herself pressed with gifts. It had not occurred to her, in her desire to make this Christmas one that the children would always remember, that she would herself be remembered. Christmas before had always been a kind of hurried pushing-back of the world's leanness, a hasty and dutiful gift-giving always soured just a little by Bo's contempt for the whole business. (Spend a lot of money and get people things they'd never buy themselves and would never use.) She wished he could see this, the fine wholeheartedness of this feast. Her lap was full of things, gloves and a new dress from Kristin, a lavalière from Erling, a sternly practical sewing basket from Sarah and her father, even a brush and comb and mirror, backed with ivory, from Henry Mossman.

She stammered on her thanks, and her eyes betrayed her, so that she got up and began picking up scattered wrappings and feeding them into the heater. If Bo could only see it, just once, could only know just once that feeling of family loyalty and love and thanksgiving that was like a song sometimes, when Christmas went right, he would know what she missed, and why she missed it. Then she thought of Bo's package.

Chet collided with her, riding his tricycle around the room, and she caught his shoulder. "There's a package from Pa," she said, and steered him toward the tree. Bruce wheeled up, avid for more plunder, while she groped under the low branches and found the parcel.

The babble of voices went on behind her while she cut the string. The lips of the cardboard box spread apart. Wadded newspaper came first, then a package wrapped in brown paper. She wished she had had time to open the things first and re-wrap them prettily. Bo wouldn't have had any chance, where he was, to get nice wrappings, and now his presents looked shoddy by comparison with the others. She supposed Sarah and her father, even Kristin, would notice that and hold it against him.

The boys were clamoring at her shoulder. George Nelson, his eyes crinkled with a smile at the corners, bent to help her. For a moment, with the brown and dowdy package in her hand, she felt a twinge of fear, a tiny cold premonition. The voices behind her had dropped, and she knew they were all watching.

"It looks . . ." she said. "It looks as if it had been opened."

"Customs," George said. "They'd have to open anything coming in from Canada."

"Oh," she said, relieved. Her fingers unrolled the paper. A pair of overshoes came in sight, and her eyes went blurry, her whole body stiff with disappointment, as she looked at them. On her knees, the children over her shoulder, she hung as if clinging for her life. The overshoes were smeared with yellow mud from top to sole.

Frantically, telling herself it was a joke, a bad joke, but meant to be funny, she unrolled the second package. Another smaller pair of overshoes, smeared like the first ones. Bruce's voice, shrill, angry at being cheated, cut through the room. "Why they're *old!*" he said.

Elsa's face was hot as fire, her blood so wild with rage that she felt smothered. Violently she tore the paper off the third parcel and shook out the contents. It was a coat with a fur collar. There was mud spattered on it, and the collar, ripped half off, hung askew.

Not a person in the room said a word as she stood up. She fought to smile, fought to make her voice bright. "All right," she said. "That's all. They must have got dirtied by the customs inspectors. We'll wash them off tomorrow. Time for bed, now."

Henry Mossman picked up one of the overshoes and rubbed with his fingers at the dried mud. "That's about the worst I ever saw," he said. "Open packages and ruin everything in them." He looked at Elsa, and his eyes dropped. "I'll wash them off at the pump," he said. "They must have thrown them down in a puddle and stamped on them."

"Thank you, Henry," Elsa said. The stiff smile still on her face, she motioned to Chet and Bruce. Chet looked at her solemnly, hanging to the handlebars of his tricycle. "Is that all Pa sent?" he said. "Is that all, Ma?"

Sick and humiliated, furious at the people in the room who sat silently and watched her shame, she herded them off to bed. She did not come down again, but went to bed to lie wakeful, bitter and raging, cringing at the thought of facing all of them tomorrow, beating against the brutal, unanswerable question of why he had sent things like that for Christmas gifts. Because she didn't believe, any more than the people downstairs did, that the customs inspectors were responsible.

Even the explanation, when it came, only made her bite her lips in vexation. That was the way Bo was, and there was no changing him. Everything he did was characteristic, blind, yet from one point of view reasonable, practical, full of insensitive logic.

The letter came two days after Christmas. The envelope had been stamped "Return to Sender," and stamps had been stuck on over the post office lettering. It was meant to reach her before the package, but he had forgotten the stamps, again characteristically.

She read it coming home from town, where she had fled to escape the house, get clear of Sarah's closed and vindicated face and the children's sullen reluctance to wear their scrubbled overshoes. The day before, she had sat a long time mending the ripped collar of the coat, and her whole mind had been one impossible question, Why? It was a nice coat, with a fox collar. It had cost a good deal. But the smears of mud, the rips. To buy new things and then spoil them before putting them in the mail.

Dear Elsa, the letter said.

There hasn't been any answer to my letter except that post card saying you were staying at home. What's the matter, honey? I've been up here working my head off to get a stake, and you won't even write more than a post card. I know you had a tough time in Richmond, but I honestly thought the joint would give you a living. Anyway I'm sorry, but I told you that before. You don't know how lonesome a place like this can be, just sitting around the stove and spitting in the door with a lot of section hands that don't know their behinds from thirty cents a week. The place is dead as a doornail, with winter here, and so cold you can't stick your nose out without freezing it off. The foreman of the Half-Diamond Bar and I got the Chink cook to stick his tongue on a cold doorknob the other day and he like to tore all the hide off it trying to get away. You never heard such a jabber. But there isn't much doing. I've been drawing plans for a house I might build if you don't spoil everything by staying mad. Four gables, a bedroom in each one, and a big verandah. I've got three lots along the river on the high side where it won't ever flood out, and I'm sort of reserving one for us. You and the kids would like it up here. It's a swell climate in summer, sunshine sixteen hours a day.

I sent a box for Christmas today. When you open it you'll find the overshoes dirty and the coat torn a little, because I found out that new clothes sent across the line had a big duty slapped on them, but you can send second-hand ones without any duty. Money don't grow on trees so thick that I could afford to miss foxing the customs guys. The collar ought to sew right back on, and you can wash the mud off the boots easy. I got the coat when I came through Moose Jaw after I left Seattle. The collar is gray fox. I hope you think of me once in a while when you wear it, and that you'll write me a decent letter and say you'll come up here in the spring.

Love
Bo

P.S. Merry Christmas. Tell the kids Merry Christmas too. If Chet is in school now maybe he has learned to write and can write his old man a letter.

Elsa leaned against a tree and sighed, and laughed aloud, and crushed the letter in her hand. Every word from him was full of the tangle of emotional pulls that had wearied her mind for months. He missed her, he missed the boys, he would love a letter from Chet—she could imagine his pride as he showed such a letter around—he honestly wanted her back, he would promise anything. And he sent her gifts that were not gifts, but slaps in the face that shamed her for him in front of everybody, yet the gifts had been well meant. It was only the saving of a few miserable dollars of duty that had made him spoil them. And his optimism, his incurable conviction that this time he was going to make his pile, the old, endless, repetitive story of his whole life . . .

A letter from him always weakened her resolution, made her wonder if she were doing right to stay away from him. Before she could soften herself too much with thinking she went home and wrote him a letter, a letter she could not help making kind. But she couldn't come back. The boys were coming out of their kinks, they had something like a home for the first time, they had friends and playmates and were healthy and happy. She was dreadfully sorry and unhappy, but she couldn't risk their futures any more. If he wanted a divorce she would agree, because she couldn't expect him not to want to be free under the circumstances. She had used the two checks he sent for the boys, and was keeping what was left to be spent on them when they needed things. He needn't feel any responsibility for her. The kids talked about him a lot, they hadn't forgotten him.

Across the bottom she wrote her thanks for the Christmas gifts, and she could not bring herself to mention how they had been received. It was a lovely coat, the overshoes were very useful in the deep snow they were having. The thought of how much he might be hurt if she told him the truth, how he had spent a lot of money on the coat and was staying up in a lonesome village hoping she might come back to him, kept her pen in the easy platitudes of thanks. She would lie before she would hurt him that way.

6

It was almost as if the necessity of protecting him, of keeping from him the knowledge of what a catastrophe his gifts had been, made the problem of living under the shadow of her family's unspoken condemnation harder to bear. She found herself on the brink of flaring out and defending him a half dozen times when their talk or their gestures or their very silence steered close to the disapproval they felt. They had known it all the time, their silence said, and now they were half pleased to have their judgment vindicated. Sometimes she felt like shouting at them, and as Kristin's marriage came closer she felt more and more how impossible it would be to stay on after her one friend was gone from the house. If it hadn't been for the children, she would not have stayed a week.

Then in mid-April Kristin was married, and after she and George had fled in a shower of rice and old shoes for a honeymoon in Florida that made Sarah lift her eyes in deprecation of such ungodly extravagance, the house was the dull burying ground she had known it would be. Her life went on from day to day by sufferance, not by any will or direction of its own. The weeks crept through their routine of housework and Sunday quiet. Sarah went beside her through the house like a mute, walked the four blocks to and from church like an automaton, spoke hardly ten words a day. Even the lavish flowering of the wild plum tree by the side of the house, and the misty green spread below her bedroom window, were tinged with the melancholy of something long-lost and past reclaiming. Her heart was no longer in this house, there was nothing for her here.

On the last day of April, when she was sweeping the porch, Henry Mossman came by and stood with his hat in his hand and asked her if she would like to bring the boys and come on a picnic the next Saturday afternoon. He asked her lamely, not knowing how she, a married woman, would feel about going out with him, humbly ready to assume that probably she wouldn't want to.

"I just remembered that other picnic we went on once," he said. "Pretty near ten years ago. When we had the buggy race and your dad walked on his hands."

"That was a lovely day," she said. "I've never forgotten it."

"Like to come this time? We might be lucky and get another perfect day."

"I shouldn't," she said. "I might get you talked about, Henry."

"That's what I was wondering," Henry said. "Not about me, about you."

"It wouldn't bother me."

"Then let's go," Henry said. "Nobody who ever knew you would talk about you a minute, and the rest of them don't matter." He lifted his face and smiled. She noticed how fine his eyes were, what a sweet and quizzical and gentle expression he always wore.

"The boys ought to have fun," Henry said. "I'll come around about one, then."

Standing with her back to the unfriendly house she felt the sudden trembling as if tears were fighting to emerge. She said, "I guess I've never known anyone as kind as you, Henry."

Henry quirked his lips in his half-humorous, self-derogatory smile. "I'd rather hear you say that than anyone I can think of," he said.

That was on Wednesday. On Friday the boy from the station came up with a telegram for Elsa Mason. It was from Bo, and he was in Minneapolis. He wanted her to meet him there Saturday afternoon.

"I'm dreadfully sorry, Henry," she said. "It's just that . . . he's come a long way . . ."

"Sure," he said. "Of course. You want to go."

He stood behind the counter of his hardware store in a black alpaca jacket, stroking the ends of his mustache, and her own uncertain state made her clairvoyantly sensitive to the stages by which he put away his disappointment.

"You were banking on it," she said. "I'm awfully sorry."

Henry reached out and swung the handles of three rakes hanging from the rafter. "Well, I won't say I'm glad he came just when he did."

She felt driven to explain, to justify Bo and herself. "I guess he won't come down here," she said. "He knows they don't like him. But when he comes all that way I can't just . . ."

"Why sure," Henry said. "You want to go right up. Don't worry about me."

Full of obscure and stubborn shame, Elsa started for the door. "Thank you, Henry," she said. She always seemed to hurt him, no matter how hard she tried not to. It always came down to a choice, and she always chose against him.

Henry came around the counter and followed her to the entrance. The street outside lay sleepily dead, a tired horse drooped on three feet a few doors down. "Elsa," Henry said.

She stopped.

"I want to tell you something," Henry said. "I had a half idea I might tell you at the picnic, sort of reproduce that one ten years ago." He was perfectly serious, perfectly self-assured. The awkwardness had fallen away, even his stoop wasn't noticeable. "I don't want to butt into anything that isn't my business," he said, "but I can't help knowing a few things. Maybe what I've heard is right and maybe it isn't. I don't care. I just want you to know what I think."

She watched him. "One thing I want to tell you," he said, "is that no matter what other folks think of your husband, I always liked him. I never saw Mr. Mason except that one winter a little, but I liked him."

Elsa wet her lips. "It's kind of you to say that."

"I don't know what's the trouble between you and Mr. Mason. That's none of my business either. Sarah said something once, but I didn't listen much." He looked out into the street. "I don't know what the trouble is and there's no reason I should know. Sarah said you wanted to get a divorce and couldn't. I don't know. But if you did do anything like that, and you didn't want to stay on with your folks . . ."

His face turned to meet hers. "I am no better than I was ten years ago," he said, "and I'm not any younger. But I'd be proud to ask you the same thing I did then, if you should find yourself free."

Elsa bent her head. Every little thing lately seemed to make her cry.

"I like Mr. Mason," Henry was saying, "and you know I'm not prying at you to get you to divorce him. I just wanted you to know, just in case, so you would have it in mind as a possibility."

She was crying quietly with her head down.

"Don't," Henry said. "Please, Elsa. You don't have to say anything, or make up your mind, or anything. You go on up on Saturday and see him and I'll take the kids to the picnic."

It was that last kindness that put her to flight. She nodded and walked away before everything flew out of control.

It was difficult, telling Sarah. She simply announced that she was going up to see Bo in Minneapolis. Sarah stared at her, her placid, smooth face the color of dough, her slightly-bulging gray eyes hard and disapproving. She looked, Elsa thought, twenty years older than her real age, she looked unhealthy, like a fungus.

"Your father won't like it," Sarah said.

"I'm sorry," Elsa said. "Why should he object?"

"You know he doesn't want you to have any more to do with that man."

"Then why wouldn't he help me get a divorce?"

"You know why. You didn't, or said you didn't, have the Reason."

Elsa laughed, and she heard her laugh unpleasantly harsh in her own ears. "I had reason. I just didn't have the little narrow reason the church recognizes."

"Elsa!"

"Don't shout at me," Elsa said. "I don't know what you want me to be. I'm nothing the way I am. You won't help me divorce him, and you don't want me to go back to him, but still you act as if I were unclean when I come home to stay."

"I'm sorry," Sarah said stiffly. "We've been as kind as we know how to be."

"With a poker up your back," Elsa said. "You hush-hush around me as if he had given me some awful disease."

"He's not a good man," Sarah said.

Elsa sighed and shrugged. "Maybe not. I don't know what a good man is any more. But he wasn't all to blame. He . . ."

She stopped, looking at Sarah's faded hair, the plump colorless face, the quenched and somehow petulant look in the eyes. She said before she thought, "I loved him once, we were awfully happy at first."

Sarah turned away and went into the kitchen, and Elsa looked after her, thinking. As she went upstairs to dress for the train trip she knew that unhappy as she was she was not as unhappy as Sarah, and that seemed a strange thing.

She saw him before the train had fully stopped, and as people began crowding to the ends of the car she sat in the seat gripping the handle of her suitcase. Slowly, with a vise on her mind, she stood up. A porter took her bag and she let it go, though she would have liked it to hang to. The steps, the black hand helping her down, the momentary confusion of turning and searching among the crowd, and then Bo's eyes, gray and sober and intent. He stepped a half step forward, as if unsure of himself, started to speak and stopped, and then lifted her and held her close. His voice was whispering in her ear, "Oh, Elsa, Elsa!"

She shook her head, pulling away from him. Through the weak tears that came to her eyes she saw that he was well dressed, really handsome again in a good gray suit, and when she bent her head to blink the tears away she saw his hand, brown, scarred with signs of labor, still holding her elbow. The hand was more definitely Bo than the handsome man in the gray suit. She knew his hands, lovely big square long hands.

He drew her aside, she mindless and voiceless and almost without power to move her feet, rescued her bag from the porter, and stood her against a post to look at her. His eyes were warming, he was beginning to smile. "Ah, Elsa," he said, "you had me scared to death!"

She wet her lips, trying to grope back among the fragments of what she had been going to say to him. "Bo."

"Don't tell me you meant it," he said, and laughed. "Maybe you meant it when you wrote it, but you don't now. Where are the kids?"

"I left them at home. But Bo . . ."

"Come on," he said. "We've got a lot of talking to do. We're going to talk so much your tongue'll be tired for a month. You know what I've been doing the last three weeks?"

She wanted to tell him that he was taking too much for granted, that she was still determined, that she couldn't come back, but all she said, feebly, was "What?"

"Ever since the frost started working out of the ground," Bo said, "I've been building a house."

"A house!" She still had the feeling of idiocy, as if all she could say was senseless sounds, monosyllables, parrotings of his words.

"A two-story, eight-room house. When I left the foundation was

in and the frame up. Full cement basement. Four bedrooms upstairs, living room, dining room, kitchen, big front hall. I sold the
two lots and kept the best one for us."

"But Bo, I wrote you . . ."

They were outside the station. Bo raised his arm at a taxi and it
pulled up to the curb. The street was of cement, and when they got
in and started riding Elsa sat marvelling idiotically at how smoothly
they went, not a bump or a sway. She brushed her hand across her
mouth, trying to get hold of herself, forget how things had started
falling in her mind the instant she saw him. But his voice was in her
ears, warm, reassuring, and his arm lay across the seat above her
shoulders.

"Look, honey," he said. "I started building the house in spite of
your letter. We might have had a lot of hard luck, and what we did
and said, me especially, might not be very pretty. But we're going
to start all over, see? That's why I got the house going, just for a
kind of guarantee."

"I don't know," she said. "I don't think . . ."

"I'll tell you something," Bo said, and pulled her around to face
him. The taxi stopped in front of a hotel, but Bo paid no attention.
"I'll tell you something. When I left Richmond I thought I was leaving you for good. I thought I really was, after that night. You know
how long it lasted? About three weeks. I've been so lonesome and sick
for you I can't sleep. Then when I thought I had a good start I came
back for you and you weren't there."

He tightened his hold on her shoulders, and his eyes were so urgent
that she wavered. "I just can't live without you," he said. "That
sounds dippy, but it's true. And you can't live without me, either.
Can you?"

She did not answer.

"Can you?"

"I . . ."

"How do the kids feel about it?"

"I don't know. Kids forget so quick."

"Meaning you can't forget," he said. His hands loosened, and he
sat back. The little thing like a clock went on ticking in the taxi.
The driver was looking straight ahead, whistling through his teeth.

"I'll tell you something else," Bo said. "I'll never let myself go like
that again, as long as I live. I got on top of all that when I found
out how much I missed you."

"But how can you promise a thing like that?" she said. "You'll forget, and lose your temper again, and there you'll be."

"All I can do is promise and mean it."

Because she needed time to think, and because she didn't like talking in front of the driver, she opened the door. Bo paid the driver and led her into the hotel lobby. It was one thirty by the clock over the desk.

"How about dinner?"

"I ought to be getting back," she said, and for an instant, looking at his face with her own absurd words slowly making their meaning plain, she laughed.

"What did you bring the suitcase for, then?"

She looked at the bag. In it she had packed nightclothes, a change of clothes, stockings, clean underwear. Her mouth was open and dry, and she swallowed. "I don't know," she said.

In the middle of the lobby he burst into loud, triumphant laughter, the kind of full, deep-chested laughter he so seldom voiced. "See?" he said. "I told you you didn't mean it. You're coming back with me tomorrow."

"Oh no," she said. "No, I couldn't."

"Why not?"

There were a dozen reasons why not. She had been over them a hundred times. But when she opened her mouth her treacherous tongue betrayed her again. "Chester couldn't just leave school," she said.

Bo motioned her toward the dining room and she went as if sleepwalking. The waiter pulled out a chair for her and she sat down in it as if afraid it would collapse the way everything else had collapsed. Bo's eyes across the table were full of mirth, but warm, excited, loving, a look like those she remembered from years back, like the day they had become engaged, when they went walking in the snow and fell down in the middle of a field and sat laughing and kissing. "You've got a nice mouth," she had told him then, "a nice mouth and dappled eyes."

"Ah, Bo," she said, smiling at him, unable to think of a single one of the things she had been so resolutely going to say.

"If you come in June," he said, "I can have the house all finished for you." He reached for her hand across the table, and his face was twisted with a smile that looked as if it hurt him. "Lordy," he said, "you don't know how much you had me scared."

"Is it really good up there?" she said curiously. "Do you really think we can make some kind of a home there?"

"Listen," he said. "Canada's in a war, and they're howling for more wheat, more wheat, all the time. Homesteaders are already coming into that place by the hundreds. Know what I did? I homesteaded a quarter and pre-empted a quarter right next to it. That's a half section of wheat land, and wheat is going to be worth its weight in gold."

"But what about the railroad? I thought . . ."

"Oh, the railroad," Bo said. "That's died. Saving steel for war factories. The steel came into Whitemud and stopped. But it's all right. We've got a start, and a house and lot, and a farm. Wait till wheat gets to be three bucks a bushel and we have two hundred acres in and get sixty bushel to the acre."

In early June, 1914, Elsa loaded the children into the train under the brown eaves of the station, said goodbye to Sarah and George and Kristin and Erling and her father, all attending her dutifully as they would have attended her funeral, shook hands with Henry Mossman, holding his fingers in one last relinquishment of what he stood for and had offered her, and set her feet on the iron steps. The boys were already climbing on the seat inside and sticking their tongues out against the glass. For the third time (and each time forever, each time certain she would never return) she left home to hazard herself and her hopes in a new and unknown country.

And oh God, she said, looking through the windows at her family, Kristin with her handkerchief out, her father straight and grim with his hat formally off, Sarah placid with pursed mouth and hands folded across her stomach—oh God, let it be final this time! Let the house Bo is building be the place we'll stay in the rest of our lives, let it be the real home that the boys can look back to without a single regret.

Because she knew she was surrendering completely this time. She knew that she would stick to Bo now no matter what came. She had made her bed, and this time she would lie in it.

The train jerked. She waved, and as they moved up the platform she seized the window catches and shoved up the glass, and with her arm outside the window waved once more, the last time, at the place that had been home.

IV

In the summer it was the homestead, the little round-roofed shack that looked like a broad freight car with one side extended into a sleeping porch where the two beds were, the single room with the kerosene stove against one wall and the cupboards built up beside it, the table and the benches and the couch where the cat slept all day long, curled up dozing, but sleeping so lightly that a finger placed on one hair of him, anywhere, would bring him instantly awake with a *pr-r-r-rt!*

The homestead was the open, flat plain, unbroken clear to the horizon on every side except the south, where the Bearpaw Mountains, way down across the line in Montana, showed in a thin white line that later in summer turned to brown. In August, when the heat was intense, the mountains faded out of sight in the haze and heat waves, but almost any day in June and early July they could be seen, and they were an important part of the farm.

There were other important things about the farm, the intimate parts like the pasture, a half mile long and two hundred yards wide, fenced with three tight strands of barbed wire on peeled cedar posts, the whole thing a pride to Bruce because there was no fence anywhere near as tight and neat on the other farms nearby. His father was a thorough man on a job; when he put in a fence he put in a fence that he need not be ashamed of, he set the posts deep in the ground and tamped them in tight, he bought a wire-stretcher and strung the strands like guitar strings.

The pasture was cut diagonally by the coulee, and just below the house was the reservoir, and across the reservoir and through the fence was the long sixty-acre wheat field and the smaller field of flax, and the end of those fields was both the south line of their property and the international boundary. The farm was that feeling, too, the sense of straddling two nations, so that even though you were American, living in Canada, you lost nothing by it, but really gained, because the Fourth of July was celebrated in Canada and Canadian holidays like Victoria Day and the King's birthday were celebrated in Montana, and you got in on both. And you lived in Saskatchewan, in one nation, but got your mail in Montana, in another.

The farm was every summer between June and September. It was the long trip, in the first year by wagon but later by car, from Whitemud out; it was the landmarks on that trail, the Frenchman's house with a dozen barefooted children streaking for the barn, the gates that had to be opened, the great horse ranch where they travelled hours without seeing a living thing except herds of horses as wild as coyotes. It was Robsart, a little clot of dwellings with a boarding house that they generally tried to make for the noon meal, and then scattered farms again along the grass-grown wagon-track, and a couple of little streams to ford, and Gadke's where they always stopped while Pa talked things over with Mr. Gadke because Mr. Gadke was a smart dry-farmer, until finally the last gate and the last ford just past the twin tarpapered shacks that all the homesteaders called Pete and Emil, and then their own house, and the familiar-unfamiliar look of the fence and fireguard and pasture the first time in the spring.

Farm was the shut-up, mousy smell of the house, the musty smell of packed quilts, the mattresses out in the sun on the first morning. It was the oil that had to be wiped off his gopher traps, and the first walk out along the pasture fence to the edge of the field with the traps over his shoulder. It was trouble with water, sometimes, when the well-hole beside the reservoir had caved in and they had to haul drinking water in barrels for two miles, and stories like the one his father told about the Picketts, down in Montana. The Picketts had no well, only a little creekbed that often dried up on them, and then they hoarded water, according to Pa, like nothing you ever saw. A pan of water would be used to boil eggs in the morning. Then the dishes would be washed in it. Then all the family would wash, one after the other. Then the water would be strained to get the grease and dirt out, and saved to put in the radiator of the Picketts' old car. Pa swore you could tell whether the Picketts had had cabbage or beans or sweetcorn for dinner just by smelling the boiling radiator of that old McLaughlin.

Farm ordinarily was the things he and Chet did together, the guns they whittled out of sticks, the long campaigns in the coulee and the patch of sweetcorn when it got high enough to make good cover. It was the Russian thistle they hoed out of garden and fireguard, and the swearing his father did when the thistle got a good start in the wheat field. It was long days of blazing sun, and violent rains, and once it was a cyclone that passed a mile south of them. That was when they were still living in the tent, before Pa got the house built, and Pa roped them all down in the section hole until he was sure the twister wasn't going to hit them.

In this summer of 1918, because Chet was staying in town to be delivery boy for Mr. Babcock in the confectionery store, the homestead was isolation and loneliness, though he never felt it or knew it for what it was. Only when his mother looked at his father and said they should never have let Chet take that job, it left Brucie too much alone. Then he felt vaguely disturbed and faintly abused, but he never did really believe he was lonely, because he loved the homestead, and the Sunday school hymns he sang to himself down in the flowered coulee meant to him very definite and secret and precious things, meant primroses and space and the wet slap of a rare east wind, and those tunes would mean those things to him all his life.

Still he was almost always alone, and that summer he somehow lost his identity as a name. There was no other boy to confuse him with; he wasn't Bruce, but "the boy," and because he was the only thing of his kind in all that summer world he needed no name, but only his own sense of triumphant identity. He knew the homestead in intimate and secret detail because there was so little variety in it that the small things took the senses. He knew the way the grass grew curling over the lip of a burnout, and how the prairie owls nested under those grassy lips. He knew how the robins tucked their nests back under the fringes of the prairie wool, and their skyblue eggs were always a wonder. He could tell, by the way the horses clustered in a corner of the pasture, when something was wrong, as when Dick got wound up in the lower strand of the fence and almost cut his leg off trying to break loose. He could tell instantly when a weasel was after the hens by the kind of clamor they made. Nothing else, for some reason, ever caused that fighting squawk from the mother hens. He could tell a badger's permanent burrow from the one he made in digging out a gopher. The yapping of coyotes on a moonlit night was lonely and beautiful to him, and the yard and chicken house and fireguard and coulee were as much a part of him as his own skin.

He lived in his own world in summer, and only when hail or wind or gophers or Russian thistle threatened the wheat on which he knew his father yearly gambled everything, was there much communication with the adult world whose interests were tied down to the bonanza farming and the crop. Wheat, he knew, was very high. The war did that. And he knew too that they were not well off, that every spring his father scraped together everything he had for seed and supplies and hoped for a good year so that he could clean up. He knew that they had less than most of the homesteaders around: they didn't have a barn, a cow (they had two in town, but it was a hard trip to bring them out), a seeder, a binder, a disc, a harrow. They didn't have much of anything, actually, except a team, a plow, and a stoneboat. Anything he didn't have tools for his father either borrowed tools to do, or hired done. But that frantic period of plowing and seeding came early, before his senses had adjusted themselves completely to the homestead, and later, in the period when they did practically nothing but sit and wait and hope that the weather would give them a crop, he moved in a tranced air of summer and loneliness and delight.

At the end of the first week in this summer he caught a weasel in one of his gopher traps, and brought it, still twisting and fighting in the trap, to the house. His father and mother came to the door; his mother made a face and shivered.

"Ugh!" she said. "Ugly, snaky thing!"

But his father showed more interest. "Got something special, uh?" he said. He came down and took the ringed chain from the boy's hand, held the weasel up. The weasel hissed in his face, trying to jump at him, and he straightened his arm to hold the swinging trap away.

"You've got to hand it to them," he said. "There isn't anything alive with more fight in it."

"Take it and kill it," Elsa said. "Don't just keep it in the trap torturing it."

Bruce was looking at his father. He ignored his mother's words because this was men's business. She didn't understand about weasels. "Maybe I could keep him till he turns into an ermine," he said.

"Why not?" his father said. "You could get three bucks for his pelt, these days. We ought to be able to make a cage that'd hold him."

"Oh, Bo," Elsa said. "Keep a weasel?"

"Give Boopus here something to do," Bo said. "You've been telling me we ought to get him a pet."

Bruce looked from one to the other, wondering when they had talked over getting him a pet. "We've got old Tom now," he said.

"Old Tom," his father said, "is so full of mice his mind is all furry."

"We ought to get a dog," Elsa said. "Not a vicious thing like a weasel."

"Well, we've got the weasel, and we don't know any place to get a dog." Bo looked down at the boy and grinned. He swung the weasel gently back and forth, and it arched its long yellow body against the trap and lunged. "Let's go make a cage for this tough guy," Bo said.

"Can I have a dog too?"

"Maybe. If I can find one."

"Holy catartin," Bruce said. "A cat, a dog, and a weasel. Maybe I can catch some more and start a weasel farm."

"I'd move out," his mother said. She waved them away. "Hurry up, if you're going to keep that bloodthirsty thing. Don't leave it in the trap with its broken leg."

They made a cage out of a beer-case, screened under the hinged top and with a board removed at the bottom, leaving an opening over which they tacked a strip of screen. They had trouble getting the weasel out of the trap, and finally Bo had to smother him in a piece of horse blanket and spring the jaws loose and throw blanket and all in the cage. For three days the weasel sulked in the corner and would eat nothing, but when the boy said he didn't think it was going to live his father laughed at him. "You can't kill a weasel just by breaking his leg. Put a mouse in there and see what happens."

Next day the boy rescued a half-dead mouse that Tom was satedly toying with under the bed, and dropped it in the cage. Nothing happened, but when he came back later the mouse was dead, with a hole back of his ear and his body limp and apparently boneless. The boy fished the carcass out with a bent wire, and from then on there was no question of the weasel's dying. The problem was to find enough mice, but after a few days he tried a gopher, and then it was all right.

There had been a wind during the night, and all the loneliness of the world had swept up out of the southwest. The boy had heard it wailing through the screens of the sleeping porch where he lay, and he had heard the wash tub bang loose from the outside wall and roll on down the coulee, and the slam of the screen door, and his mother's padding feet as she rose to fasten things down. Through one half-open eye he had peered up from his pillow to see the moon skimming windily in a luminous sky. In his mind's eye he had seen the prairie outside with its woolly grass and cactus white under the moon, and the wind, whining across that endless oceanic land, sang in the screens, and sang him back to sleep.

Now, after breakfast, when he set out through the pasture on the round of his traps, there was no more wind, but the air smelled somehow recently swept and dusted, as the house in town smelled after his mother's cleaning. The sun was gently warm on the bony shoulder blades of the boy, and he whistled, and whistling turned to see if the Bearpaws were in sight to the south. There they were, a tenuous outline of white just breaking over the bulge of the world; the Mountains of the Moon, the place of running streams and timber and cool heights that he had never seen—only dreamed of on days when the baked gumbo of the yard cracked in the heat and the sun brought cedar smells from fenceposts long since split and dry and odorless, when he lay dreaming on the bed with a Sears Roebuck or a T. Eaton catalogue before him, picking out the presents he would buy for his mother and his father and Chet and his friends next Christmas, or the Christmas after that. On those days he looked often and long at the snowy mountains to the south, while dreams rose in him like heat waves, blurring the reality of the unfinished shack and the bald prairie of his home.

The Bearpaws were there now, and he watched them a moment, walking, his feet automatically dodging cactus clumps, before he turned his attention to the scattered stakes that marked his traps. He ran the line at a half-tort, whistling.

At the first stake the chain was stretched tightly down the hole.

The pull on its lower end had dug a little channel in the soft earth of the mound. Gently, so as not to break the gopher's leg off, the boy eased the trap out of the burrow, held the chain in his left hand, and loosened the stake with his right. The gopher tugged against the trap, but it made no noise. There were only two places where they made a noise: at a distance, when they whistled a warning, and in the weasel's cage. Otherwise they kept still.

For a moment he debated whether to keep this one alive for the weasel or to wait so he wouldn't have to carry a live one all the way around. Deciding to wait, he held the chain out, measured the rodent, and swung. The knobbed end of the stake crushed the skull, and the eyes popped out of the head, round and blue. A trickle of blood started from nose and ears. The feet kicked.

Releasing the gopher, the boy lifted it by the tail and snapped its tail fur off with a smart flip. Then he stowed the trophy carefully in the breast pocket of his overalls. For the last two years he had won the grand prize offered by the province to the school child who destroyed the most gophers. On the mantel in town were two silver loving cups, and in the cigar box under his bed in the farmhouse were already seven hundred forty tails, the catch of three weeks. In one way, he resented his father's distributing poison along the wheat field, because poisoned gophers generally got down their holes to die, and he didn't get the tails. So he spent most of his time trapping and snaring in the pasture, where poison could not be spread because of the horses.

Picking up trap and stake, Bruce kicked the dead gopher down its burrow and scooped dirt over it with his toe. They stunk up the pasture if they weren't buried, and the bugs got into them. Frequently he had stood to windward of a dead and swollen gopher, watching the body shift and move with the movements of the beetles and crawling things in it. If such an infested corpse were turned over, the carrion beetles would roar out, great, hard-shelled, orange-colored, scavenging things that made his blood curdle at the thought of their touching him, and after they were gone and he looked again he would see the little black ones, undisturbed, seething through the rotten flesh. So he always buried his dead, now.

Through the gardens of red and yellow cactus blooms he went whistling, half-trotting, setting his traps afresh whenever a gopher shot upright, whistled, and ducked down its hole. All but two of the first seventeen traps held gophers, and he came to the eighteenth confidently, expecting to take this one alive. But this gopher had gone in head first, and the boy put back in his pocket the salt sack he had brought along for a game bag. He would have to trap or snare one down by the dam.

On the way back he stopped with bent head while he counted the morning's catch of tails, mentally adding this lot to the seven hundred forty he already had, trying to remember how many he and Chet had had this time last year. As he finished his mathematics his whistle broke out again, and he galloped down through the pasture, running for very abundance of life, until he came to the chicken house just within the fireguard.

Under the eaves of the chicken house, so close that the hens were constantly pecking up to its door and then almost losing their wits with fright, was the weasel's cage. The boy lifted the hinged top and looked down through the screen.

"Hello," he said. "Hungry?"

The weasel crouched, its snaky body humped, its head thrust forward and its malevolent eyes steady and glittering.

"Tough, ain't you?" the boy said. "Just you wait, you blood-sucking old stinker, you. Won't I skin you quick, hah?"

There was no dislike or emotion in his tone. He took the weasel's malignant ferocity with the same indifference he displayed in his gopher killing. Weasels, if you kept them long enough, were valuable. He would catch some more and have an ermine farm. He was the best gopher trapper in Saskatchewan. Why not weasels? Once he and Chet had even caught a badger, though they hadn't been able to take him alive because he was caught by only three hind toes, and lunged so savagely that they had to stand off and stone him to death in the trap. But weasels you could catch alive, and Pa said you couldn't hurt a weasel short of killing him outright. This one, though virtually three-legged, was as lively and vicious as ever.

Every morning now he had a live gopher for breakfast, in spite of Elsa's protests that it was cruel. She had argued and protested, but he had talked her down. When she said that the gopher didn't have a chance in the weasel's cage, he retorted that it didn't have a chance when the weasel came down the hole after it, either. When she said that the real job he should devote himself to was destroying all the weasels, he replied that then the gophers would get so thick they would eat the wheat down to stubble. Finally she had given up, and the weasel continued to have his warm meals.

For some time the boy stood watching his captive. Then he turned and went into the house, where he opened the oatbox in the kitchen and took out a chunk of dried beef. From this he cut a thick slice with the butcher knife, and went munching into the sleeping porch where his mother was making the beds.

"Where's that little double-naught?" he said.

"That what?"

"That little wee trap I use for catching live ones for Lucifer?"

"Hanging out by the laundry bench, I think. Are you going trapping again now?"

"Lucifer hasn't been fed yet."

"How about your reading?"

"I'ne take the book along and read while I wait. I'm just going down by the dam."

"I *can*, not I'ne, son."

"I can," the boy said. "I am most delighted to comply with your request of the twenty-third inst." He grinned at his mother. He could always floor her with a quotation out of a letter or the Sears Roebuck catalogue.

With the trap swinging in his hand, and under his arm the book —*Narrative and Lyric Poems,* edited by Somebody-or-Other—which his mother kept him reading all summer so that "next year he could be at the head of his class again," the boy walked out into the growing heat.

From the northwest the coulee angled down through the pasture, a shallow swale dammed just above the house to catch the spring run-off of snow water. Below the dam, watered by the slow seepage from above, the coulee bottom was a parterre of flowers, buttercups in broad sheets, wild sweet pea, and stinkweed. On the slopes were evening primroses pale pink and white and delicately fragrant, and on the flats above the yellow and red burgeoning of the cactus.

Just under the slope of the coulee a female gopher and three half-grown pups basked on their warm mound. The boy chased them squeaking down the hole and set the trap carefully, embedding it partially in the earth. Then he retired back up on the level, where he lay full length on his stomach, opened the book, shifted so that the glare of the sun across the pages was blocked by the shadow of his head and shoulders, and began to read.

From time to time he looked up from the book to roll on his side and stare out across the coulee, across the barren plains pimpled with gopher mounds and bitten with fire and haired with dusty, woolly grass. Apparently as flat as a table, the land sloped imperceptibly to the south, so that nothing interfered with his view of the ghostly mountains, looking higher now as the heat increased. Between his eyes and that smoky outline sixty miles away the heat waves rose writhing like fine wavy hair. He knew that in an hour Pankhurst's farm would lift above the swelling knoll to the west. Many times he had seen that phenomenon, had seen Jason Pankhurst watering the horses or working in the yard when he knew that the whole farm was out of sight. It was heat waves that did it, his father said.

The gophers below had been thoroughly scared, and for a long time nothing happened. Idly the boy read through his poetry lesson, dreamfully conscious of the hard ground under him, feeling the gouge of a rock under his stomach without making any effort to remove it. The sun was a hot caress between his shoulder blades, and on the bare flesh where his overalls pulled above his sneakers it bit like a burning glass. Still he was comfortable, supremely relaxed and peaceful, lulled into a half trance by the heat and the steamy flower smells and the mist of yellow from the buttercup coulee below him.

And beyond the coulee was the dim profile of the Bearpaws, the Mountains of the Moon.

The boy's eyes, pulled out of focus by his tranced state, fixed on the page before him. Here was a poem he knew . . . but it wasn't a poem, it was a song. His mother sang it often, working at the sewing machine in winter.

It struck him as odd that a poem should also be a song, and because he found it hard to read without bringing in the tune, he lay quietly in the full glare of the sun, singing the page softly to himself. As he sang the trance grew on him again, he lost himself entirely. The bright hard dividing lines between senses blurred, and buttercups, smell of primrose, feel of hard gravel under body and elbows, sight of the ghosts of mountains haunting the southern horizon, were one intensely-felt experience focussed by the song the book had evoked.

And the song was the loveliest thing he had ever heard. He felt the words, tasted them, breathed upon them with all the ardor of his captivated senses.

The splendor falls on castle walls
And snowy summits old in story . . .

The current of his imagination flowed southward over the shoulder of the world to the ghostly outline of the Mountains of the Moon, haunting the heat-distorted horizon.

> *Oh hark, oh hear, how thin and clear,*
> *And thinner, clearer, farther going,*
> *Oh sweet and far, from cliff and scar . . .*

In the enchanted forests of his mind the horns of elfland blew, and his breath was held in the cadence of their dying. The weight of the sun had been lifted from his back. The empty prairie of his home was castled and pillared with the magnificence of his imagining, and the sound of horns died thinly in the direction of the Mountains of the Moon.

From the coulee below came the sudden metallic clash of the trap, and an explosion of frantic squeals smothered almost instantly in the burrow. The boy leaped up, thrusting the book into the wide pocket of his overalls, and ran to the mound. The chain, stretched down the hole, jerked convulsively, and when he took hold of it he felt the life on the other end trying to escape. Tugging gently, he forced loose the digging claws and hauled the squirming gopher from the hole.

On the way up to the chicken house the dangling gopher with a tremendous muscular effort convulsed itself upward from the broken and imprisoned leg, and bit with a rasp of teeth on the iron. Its eyes, the boy noticed impersonally, were shiny black, like the head of a hatpin. He thought it odd that when they popped out of the head after a blow they were blue.

At the cage he lifted the cover and peered down through the screen. The weasel, scenting blood, backed against the far wall of the box, yellow body tense as a spring, teeth showing in a tiny soundless snarl.

Undoing the wire door with his left hand, the boy held the trap over the hole. Then he bore down with all his strength on the spring, releasing the gopher, which dropped on the straw and scurried into the corner opposite its enemy.

The weasel's three good feet gathered under it and it circled, very slowly, along the wall, its lips still lifted to expose the soundless snarl. The abject gopher crowded against the boards, turned once and tried to scramble up the side, fell back on its broken leg, and whirled like lightning to face its executioner again. The weasel moved carefully, circling, its cold eyes hypnotically steady.

Then the gopher screamed, a wild, agonized, despairing squeal that made the boy swallow and wet his lips. Another scream, wilder than the first, and before the sound had ended the weasel struck. There was a fierce flurry in the straw before the killer got its hold just back of the gopher's right ear, and then there was only the weasel looking at him over the dead and quivering body. In a few minutes, the boy knew, the gopher's carcass would be as limp as an empty skin, with all its blood sucked out and a hole as big as the ends of his two thumbs where the weasel had dined.

Still he remained staring through the screen top of the cage, face rapt and body completely lost. After a few minutes he went into the sleeping porch, stretched out on the bed, opened the Sears Roebuck catalogue, and dived so deeply into its fascinating pictures and legends that his mother had to shake him to make him hear her call to lunch.

2

Things greened beautifully that June. Rains came up out of the southeast, piling up solidly, moving toward them as slowly and surely as the sun moved, and it was fun to watch them come, the three of them standing in the doorway. When they saw the land east of them darken under the rain Bo would say, "Well, doesn't look as if it's going to miss us," and they would jump to shut windows and bring things in from yard or clothesline. Then they could stand quietly in the door and watch the good rain come, the front of it like a wall and the wind ahead of it stirring up dust, until it reached them and drenched the bare packed earth of the yard, and the ground smoked under its feet, and darkened, and ran with little streams, and they heard the swish of the rain on roof and ground and in the air.

They always watched it a good while, because rain was life in that country. When it didn't stop after twenty minutes or a half hour Bo would say with satisfaction, "She's a good soaker. That'll get down to the roots. Not so heavy it'll all run off, either." Then they would drift away from the door, because it was sure to be a good rain and there was another kind of satisfaction to be gained from little putter jobs while the rain outside made a crop for you. Elsa would carry her plants outside, the wandering Jew and the foliage plants and the geraniums stalky like miniature trees, and set them in the rain.

During that whole month there was much rain, and the boy's father whistled and hummed and sang. The boy lay in bed many mornings and heard him singing while he fried the bacon for breakfast. He always fried the bacon; he swore no woman knew how to do anything but burn it. And these days he always sang, fool songs he had learned somewhere back in the remote and unvisualizable past when he had worked on the railroad or played ball or cut timber in Wisconsin.

> *Oh I was a bouncing baby boy,*
> *The neighbors did allow;*
> *The girls they hugged and kissed me then,*
> *Why don't they do it now?*

He had a deep, big-chested voice, and he sang softly at first, rattling the pans, or whistled between his teeth with concentrated pauses between sounds, so that from the bed you knew he was slicing bacon off the slab. Then a match would scrape on the tin front of the stove, and he would be singing again,

> *Monkey married the baboon's sister,*
> *Smacked his lips and then he kissed her.*
> *Kissed so hard he raised a blister . . .*

You lay in bed and waited, feeling fine because it had rained yesterday but today was fair, a good growing day, and you could almost feel how the wheat would be pushing up through the warm and steaming earth. And in the other room your father sang in great good humor,

> *She's thin as a broomstick, she carried no meat.*
> *She never was known to put soap on her cheek.*
> *Her hair is like rope and the color of brass—*
> *But Oh, how I love her, this dear little lass!*
> *Dear Evelina, Sweet Evelina . . .*

After a minute or two he would poke his head into the porch and frown blackly, turn his head and frown even more blackly at the other bed where your mother lay stretching and smiling. "I plow deep while sluggards sleep!" he would say sepulchrally, and vanish. Then the final act, the great beating on the dishpan with a pewter spoon, and his singsong, hog-calling voice, "Come and get it, you potlickers, or I'll throw it away!"

It was fun to be alive and awake, and wait for your father to go through his whole elaborate ritual. It was fun to get up and souse in the washbasin outside the door, and throw the soapy water on the packed earth, and come in and eat, while Pa joked at you, saying he thought sure you were dead, he had been in there five times, pinching and slapping like a Pullman porter, but no sign of life. "You sure do sleep heavy," he would say. "It's a wonder you don't break down the bed. I better put some extra slats in there."

You joked back at him, and after breakfast you had a sparring match that left your ears all red and tingling, and then Pa went out to harrow to keep the earth broken up and the moisture in, and you went around your traps.

All through June there were good mornings, but the best of them all was the day Bo went down to Cree for the mail, and when he came back there was a dog sitting in the car seat beside him, a big-footed, lappy-tongued, frolicsome pup with one brown and one white eye and a heavy golden coat. The boy played with him for an hour, rolling him over and pulling his clumsy feet out from under him. Finally he lay down on the ground and the pup attacked his ears, sticking a red tongue into them, diving for openings, snuffing and snorting and romping. When the boy sat up, his mother and father were standing with their arms around one another, watching him. He went up very seriously and hugged them both in thanks for the pup.

"You'll have to teach him tricks," his father said. "A dog's no good unless you educate him. He gets the habit of minding you that way."

"How'll I do it?"

"Show you tonight." His father reached out and cuffed him on the ear and grinned. "Anything you can think of you'd like to do next week?"

The boy stared, wondering. "What?"

"What? What?" his father said, mimicking him. "Can't you think of anything you'd like to do?"

"I'd like to drive the stoneboat next time you use it."

"I don't think you know what fun is," his father said. "Don't you know what date it is?"

"Sure. It's June 27. No, June 28."

"Sure. And what comes after the week of June 28?"

The boy wondered, looking at first one, then another. They were both laughing at him. Then it hit him. "Fourth of July!" he said.

"Okay," his father said. He cuffed at him again, but missed. "Maybe we'll go into Chinook for the Fourth. Fireworks, ballgame, parade, pink lemonade sold in the shade by an old maid."

"Whee!" the boy said. He stooped and wrestled the pup, and afterward, when he lay panting on the ground, resting, and the pup gave up lapping his ears and lay down too, he thought that he had the swellest Ma and Pa there was.

That night his father showed him how to get the pup in a corner and make him sit up, bracing his back against the wall. For long, patient hours in the next few days he braced the pup there and repeated, "Sit up! Sit up! Sit up!" while he shoved back the slipping hind feet, straightened the limp spine, lifted the dropping front paws. You had to say the command a lot, his father said, and you had to reward him when he did it right. And you had to do only one trick at a time. After he learned to sit up you could teach him to jump over a stick, roll over, speak, shake hands, and play dead. The word for playing dead was "charge!" He would teach him, Bruce thought, to do that next, so they could play war. It would be better than having Chet there, because Chet never would play dead. He always argued and said he shot you first.

When he wasn't training the pup he was dreaming of Chinook and the ballgame and parade and fireworks, sky rockets, Roman candles, pinwheels. He was curious about pinwheels, because he remembered a passage in *Peck's Bad Boy and His Pa* where a pinwheel took after Pa and cornered him up on the sofa. But he was curious about all fireworks; he had never seen any except firecrackers. And the finest thing of all to imagine was the mountains, because Pa and Ma decided that since they were that close, they might as well drive up to the mountains too, and take the whole day.

His father teased him. Probably, he said, it would rain pitchforks on the Fourth. But his mother said Oh Pa, don't talk like that.

Then on the afternoon of the third day they all stood in the yard and watched the southeast. Thunderheads were piling up there, livid white in front and black and ominous behind. Thunder rumbled like a wagon over a bridge.

"It'll pass over," Elsa said, and patted Bruce on the back. "It just wouldn't be fair if it rained now and spoiled our holiday."

The boy looked up and saw his father's dubious expression. "Do you think it'll blow over, Pa? Hardly any have blown over yet."

"Bound to blow over," his father said. "Law of averages. They can't all make a rain."

But the boy remembered three rains from that same quarter that same month that had gone on for twenty-four hours. He stayed in the yard watching, hoping against hope until the wall of dark was almost to the fireguard and the advance wind was stirring dust in the yard, stayed until the first large drops fell and puffed heavily in the dust, stayed until his mother pulled him inside with dark speckles all over his shirt. "Don't you worry," she said. "It'll be clear tomorrow. It has to be."

That night he stayed up until nine, waiting to see if the steady downpour would stop, hating the whisper of the rain outside and the gravelly patter on the roof. The tomcat awoke and stretched on the couch, jumped off with a sudden soft thud and went prowling into the sleeping porch, but the boy sat up. His parents were reading, not saying much. Once or twice he caught them looking at him, and always the house whispered with the steady, windy sound of the rain. This was no thunder shower. This was a drencher, and it could go on for two days, this time of year. His father had said so, with satisfaction, of other rains just like it.

When his mother finally sent him off to bed he went unwillingly, undressed slowly to see if the rain wouldn't stop before he got his shoes off, his stockings off, his overalls off. But when he was in his nightshirt it still rained steadily and insistently, and he turned into his pillow wanting to cry. A big tear came out and he felt it hanging on the side of his nose. He lay very still for fear it would fall off. He strangled the sob that jumped in his throat because that would make the drop fall, and while he was balancing the drop he fell asleep.

After the night's rain the yard was spongy and soft under the boy's bare feet. He stood at the edge of the packed dooryard in the flat thrust of sunrise looking at the ground washed clean and smooth and trackless, feeling the cool mud under his toes. Experimentally he lifted his right foot and put it down in a new place, pressed, picked it up again to look at the neat imprint of straight edge and curving instep and the five round dots of toes. The air was so fresh that he sniffed as he would have sniffed the smell of cinnamon.

Lifting his head, he saw how the prairie beyond the fireguard looked darker than in dry times, healthier with green-brown tints, smaller and more intimate somehow than it did when the heat waves crawled over scorched grass and carried the horizons backward into dim and unseeable distances. And standing in the yard above his one clean footprint, feeling his own verticality in all that spread of horizontal land, he sensed that as the prairie shrank he grew. He was immense. A little jump would crack his head on the sky; a stride would take him to any horizon.

His eyes turned into the low south sky, cloudless, almost colorless in the strong light. Just above the brown line of the horizon, faint as a watermark on pale blue paper, was the tracery of the mountains, tenuous and far-off, but today accessible for the first time. His mind had played among those ghostly summits for uncountable lost hours: today, in a few strides, they were his. And more. Under the shadow of those peaks, those Bearpaws that he and his mother always called the Mountains of the Moon, was Chinook, the band, the lemonade stands, the parade, the ballgame, the fireworks.

The pup lay watching, belly down on the damp ground. In a gleeful spasm the boy stooped to flap the dog's ears, then bent and spun in a wild wardance while the dog barked. And when his father came to the door in his undershirt, yawning, running a hand up the back of his head and through his hair, peering out from gummed eyes to see how the weather looked, the boy's voice was one deep breathing relief from yesterday's rainy fear.

"It's clear as a bell," he said.

His father yawned again, clopped his jaws, rubbed his eyes, mumbled something from a mouth furry with sleep. He stood on the step scratching himself comfortably, looking down at boy and dog.

"Going to be hot," he said slyly. "Might be too hot to drive."

"Aw, Pa!"

"Going to be a scorcher. Melt you right down to axle grease riding in that car."

The boy regarded him doubtfully, saw the lurking sly droop of his mouth. "Aw, we are too going!"

At his father's laugh he burst from his immobility like a sprinter starting, raced one complete circle around the house with the dog after him. When he flew around past his father again his voice trailed out behind him at the corner. "Gonna feed the hens," he said. His father looked after him, scratched his knee, laughed suddenly, and went back indoors.

Through chores and breakfast the boy moved with the dream of a day's rapture in his eyes, but that did not keep him from swift and agile helpfulness. He didn't even wait for commands. He scrubbed himself twice, slicked down his hair, hunted up clean clothes, wiped the mud from his shoes and put them on. While his mother packed the shoebox of lunch he stood at her elbow proffering aid. He flew to stow things in the topless old Ford. He got a rag and polished the brass radiator. Once or twice, jumping around to help, he looked up to see his parents looking at each other with the knowing, smiling expression in the eyes that said they were calling each other's attention to him.

"Just like a racehorse," his father said, and the boy felt foolish, swaggered, twisted his mouth down, said, "Aw!" But in a moment he was hustling them again. They ought to get going, with fifty miles to drive. Long before they were ready he was standing beside the Ford, licked and immaculate and so excited that his feet jumped him up and down without his own volition or knowledge.

It was eight o'clock before his father came out, lifted off the front seat, poked the flat stick down into the gas tank, and pulled it out dripping. "Pretty near full," he said. "If we're going to the mountains too we better take a can along, though. Fill that two-gallon one with the spout."

The boy ran, dug the can out of the shed, filled it at the spigot of the drum that stood on a plank support to the north of the house. When he came back, his left arm stuck straight out and the can knocking against his leg, his mother was settling herself into the back seat among parcels and waterbags.

"Goodness," she said. "This is the first time I've been the first ready since I don't know when. I should think you'd have done all this last night."

"Plenty time." The father stood looking down at the boy. "All right, racehorse. You want to go to this shindig you better hop in."

The boy was up in the front seat like a squirrel. His father walked around to the front of the car. "Okay," he said. "Look sharp, now.

When she kicks over, switch her to magneto and pull the spark down."

The boy said nothing. He looked upon the car with respect and a little awe. They didn't use it much, and starting it was a ritual like a firedrill. The father unscrewed the four-eared brass plug, looked down into the radiator, screwed the cap back on, and bent to take hold of the crank. "Watch it, now," he said.

The boy felt the gentle heave of the springs, up and down, as his father wound the crank. He heard the gentle hiss in the bowels of the engine as the choke wire was pulled out, and his nose filled with the strong, volatile odor of gasoline. Over the slope of the radiator his father's brown strained face looked up. "Is she turned on all right?"

"Yup. She's on battery."

"Must have flooded her. Have to let her rest a minute."

They waited, and then after a few minutes the wavelike heaving of the springs again, the rise and fall of the blue shirt and bent head over the radiator, the sighing swish of the choke, a stronger smell of gasoline. The motor had not even coughed.

The two voices came simultaneously from the car. "What's the matter with it?"

His brow puckered in an intent scowl, Bo stood back blowing mighty breaths. "Son of a gun," he said. Coming round, he pulled at the switch, adjusted the spark and gas levers. A fine mist of sweat made his face shine like dark oiled leather.

"There isn't anything really wrong, is there?" Elsa said, and her voice wavered uncertainly on the edge of fear.

"I don't see how there could be," Bo said. "She's always started right off, and she was running all right when I drove her in here."

The boy looked at his mother sitting erect and stiff among the things on the seat. She was all dressed up, a flowered dress, a hat with hard green varnished grapes on it pinned to her red hair. For a moment she sat, stiff and nervous. "What will you have to do?" she said.

"I don't know. Look at the motor."

"Well, I guess I'll get out of the sun while you do it," she said, and fumbled her way out of the clutter.

The boy felt her exodus like a surrender, a betrayal. If they didn't hurry up they'd miss the parade. In one motion he bounced out of the car. "Gee whiz!" he said. "Let's do something. We got to get started."

"Keep your shirt on," his father grunted. Lifting the hood, he bent his head inside. His hand went out to test wires, wiggle spark-plug connections, make tentative pulls at the choke. The weakly-hinged hood slipped and came down across his wrist, and he swore. "Get me the pliers," he said.

For ten minutes he probed and monkeyed. "Might be the plugs," he said at last. "She doesn't seem to be getting any fire through her."

Elsa, sitting on a box in the shade, smoothed her flowered dress nervously. "Will it take long?"

"Half hour."

"Any day but this!" she said. "I don't see why you didn't make sure last night."

Bo breathed through his nose and bent into the engine again. "It was raining last night," he said.

One by one the plugs came out, were squinted at, scraped, the gap tested with a thin dime. The boy stood on one foot, then the other, time pouring like a flood of uncatchable silver dollars through his hands. He kept looking at the sun, estimating how much time there was left. If they got started right away they might still make it for the parade, but it would be close. Maybe they'd drive right up the street while the parade was on, and be part of it . . .

"Is she ready?" he said.

"Pretty quick."

He wandered over by his mother, and she reached out to put an arm around him. "Well, anyway we can get there for the band and the ballgame and the fireworks," he said. "If she doesn't start till noon we can make it for those."

She said, "Pa'll get it going in a minute. We won't miss anything hardly."

"You ever seen skyrockets, Ma?"

"Once."

"Are they fun?"

"Wonderful," she said. "Just like a million stars all colors all exploding at once."

His feet took him back to his father, who straightened up with a belligerent grunt. "Now!" he said. "If the sucker doesn't start now . . ."

And once more the heaving of the springs, the groaning of the turning engine, the hiss of the choke. He tried short, sharp half-turns, as if to catch the motor off guard. Then he went back to the stubborn, laboring spin. The back of his shirt was stained darkly, the curving dikes of muscles along the spine's hollow showing cleanly where the cloth stuck. Over and over, heaving, stubborn at first, then furious, till he staggered back panting.

"God damn!" he said. "What you suppose is the matter with the thing?"

"She didn't even cough once," the boy said, and staring up at his father's face full of angry bafflement he felt the cold fear touch him. What if it wouldn't start at all? What if, all ready to go, they had to unload the Ford and not even get out of the yard? His mother came over and they stood close together looking at the car and avoiding each other's eyes.

"Maybe something got wet last night," she said.

"Well, it's had plenty of time to dry out," Bo said.

"Isn't there something else you can try?"

"We can jack up the hind wheel, I guess. But there's no damn reason we should have to."

"Well, if you have to, you'll have to," she said briskly. "After planning it for a week we can't just get stuck like this. Can we, son?"

Bruce's answer was mechanical, his eyes steady on his father. "Sure not," he said.

His father opened his mouth to say something, looked hard at the boy, and shut his lips again. Without a word he pulled out the seat and got the jack.

The sun climbed steadily while they jacked up one hind wheel and blocked the car carefully so it wouldn't run over anybody if it started. The boy let off the brake and put it in high, and when they were ready he sat in the seat so full of hope and fear that his whole body was one tight concentration. His father stooped, his cheek pressed against the radiator as a milker's cheek touches the flank of a cow. His shoulder dropped, jerked up. Nothing. Another jerk. Nothing. Then he was rolling in a furious spasm of energy, the wet dark back of his shirt rising and falling. Inside the motor there was only the futile swish of the choke and the half-sound, half-feel of cavernous motion as the crankshaft turned over. The Ford bounced on its spring as if its front wheels were coming off the ground on every upstroke. Then it stopped, and the father was hanging on the radiator, breathless, dripping wet, swearing: "Son of a dirty, lousy, stinking, corrupted . . . !"

The boy stared from his father's angry wet face to his mother's, pinched with worry. The pup lay down in the shade and put its head on its paws. "Gee whiz!" the boy said. "Gee whiz!" He looked at the sun, and the morning was half gone.

Jerking with anger, his father threw the crank halfway across the yard and took a step or two toward the house. "The hell with the damn thing!" he said.

"Bo! you can't!"

He stopped, glared at her, took an oblique look at Bruce, bared his teeth in an irresolute, silent swearword. "But God, if it won't go!"

"Maybe if you hitched the horses to it," she said.

His laugh was short and choppy. "That'd be fine!" he said. "Why don't we just hitch the team to this damned old boat and pull it into Chinook?"

"But we've got to get it started. Why wouldn't it be all right to let the team pull it around? You push it on a hill sometimes and it starts."

He looked at the boy again, jerked his eyes away exasperatedly, as though he held his son somehow accountable. The boy stared, mournful, defeated, ready to cry, and his father's head swung back unwillingly. Then abruptly he winked, mopped his head and neck, and grinned. "Think you want to go, uh?"

The boy nodded. "All right," his father said crisply. "Fly up in the pasture and get the team. Hustle!"

On the high lope the boy was off up the coulee bank. Under the lip of the swale, a quarter of a mile west, the bay backs of the horses and the black dot of the colt showed. Usually he ran circumspectly across that pasture, because of the cactus, but now he flew. With shoes it was all right, and even without shoes he would have run. Across burnouts, over stretches so undetermined with gopher holes that sometimes he broke through to the ankle, skimming over patches of cactus, soaring over a badger hole, plunging into the coulee and up the other side, he ran as if bears were after him. The black colt, spotting him, lifted his tail and took off in a spectacular stiff-legged sprint, but the bays merely lifted their heads and watched. He slowed, came up walking, laid a hand on the mare's neck and untied the looped halter rope. She stood for him while he scrambled and kicked himself up, and then they were off, the mare in an easy lope, the gelding trotting after, the colt stopping his wild showoff career and wobbling hastily and ignominiously after his departing mother.

They pulled up before the Ford, and the boy slid off to throw the halter rope to his father. "Shall I get the harness?" he said, and before anyone could answer he was off running, to come back dragging one heavy harness with the tugs trailing. He dropped it, turned to run again, his breath laboring in his lungs. "I'll get the other'n," he said.

With a short, almost incredulous laugh Bo looked once at Elsa and threw the harness over the mare. When the second one came he laid it on the gelding, pushed against the heavy shoulder to get the horse into place. The gelding resisted, pranced a little, got a curse and a crack across the nose, jerked back and trembled and lifted his feet nervously, and set one shod hoof on his owner's instep. Bo, unstrung by the heat and the hurry and the labor and the exasperation of a morning when nothing went right, kicked the gelding in the belly. "Get in there, you damned big blundering ox! Back, back up. Whoa now, whoa!"

With a heavy rope for a towline and the disengaged trees of the wagon for a rig he hitched the now-skittish team to the car. Without a word he stooped and lifted the boy to the mare's back. "All right," he said, and his face relaxed in a quick grin. "This is where we start her. Ride them around in a circle, not too fast."

Then he climbed into the Ford, turned the switch to magneto, fussed with the levers. "Let 'er go!" he said.

The boy kicked the mare ahead, twisting as he rode to watch the Ford heave forward off the jack as a tired, heavy man heaves to his feet, and begin rolling after him over the uneven ground, jerking and kicking and growling when his father put it in gear. The horses settled as the added weight came on the line, flattened into their collars, swung in a circle, bumped each other, skittered. The mare reared, and the boy shut his eyes and clung. When he came down, her leg was entangled in the tug and his father was climbing cursing out of the car to straighten her out. His father was mad again and yelled at him. "Keep 'em apart! There isn't any tongue. You got to keep Dick over on his own side."

Now again the start, the flattening into the collars, the snapping tight of the tugs. This time it went smoothly, the Ford galloped after the team in lumbering, plunging jerks. The mare's eyes rolled white, and she broke into a trot, pulling the gelding after her. Desperately the boy clung to the knotted and shortened reins, his ears alert for the grumble of the Ford starting behind him. The pup ran beside the team yapping, crazy with excitement.

They made three complete circles of the back yard between house and chicken coop before the boy looked back again. "Won't she start?" he yelled. He saw his father rigid behind the wheel, heard his ripping burst of swearwords, saw him bend and glare down into the mysterious inwards of the engine through the pulled-up floor-boards. Guiding the car with one hand, he fumbled down below, one glaring eye just visible over the cowl.

"Shall I stop?" the boy shouted. Excitement and near-despair made his voice a tearful scream. But his father's wild arm waved him on. "Go on, go on! Gallop 'em! Pull the guts out of this thing!"

And the galloping—the furious, mud-flinging, rolling-eyed gallop-ing around the circle already rutted like a road, the Ford, now in savagely-held low, growling and surging and plowing behind; the mad yapping of the dog, the erratic scared bursts of runaway from the colt, the boy's mother in sight briefly for a quarter of each circle, her hands to her mouth and her eyes sick, and behind them in the Ford his father in a strangling rage, yelling him on, his lips back over his teeth and his face purple.

Until finally they stopped, the horses blowing, the boy white and tearful and still, the father dangerous with unexpended wrath. The boy slipped off, his lip bitten between his teeth, not crying now but ready to at any moment, the corners of his eyes prickling with it, and his teeth locked on his misery. His father climbed over the side of the Ford and stood looking as if he wanted to tear it apart with his bare hands.

Shoulders sagging, tears trembling to fall, jaw aching with the need to cry, the boy started toward his mother. As he came near his father he looked up, their eyes met, and he saw his father's blank with impotent rage. Dull hopelessness swallowed him. Not any of it, his mind said. Not even any of it. No parade, no ballgame, no band, no fireworks. No lemonade or ice cream or paper horns or firecrackers. No close sight of the mountains that throughout four summers had called like a legend from his horizons. No trip, no adventure, none of it, nothing.

Everything he felt was in that one still look. In spite of him his lip trembled, and he choked on a sob, his eyes on his father's face, on the brows pulling down and the eyes narrowing.

"Well, don't blubber!" his father shouted at him. "Don't stand there looking at me as if I was to blame for your missed picnic!"

"I can't—help it," the boy said, and with terror he felt the grief swelling up, overwhelming him, driving his voice out of him in a wail. Through the blur of his crying he saw the convulsive tightening of his father's face, and then all the fury of a maddening morning concentrated itself in a swift backhand blow that knocked the boy staggering.

He bawled aloud, from pain, from surprise, from outrage, from pure desolation, and ran to bury his face in his mother's lap. From that muffled sanctuary he heard her angry voice. "No," she said. "Go on away somewhere till he gets over it."

She rocked him against her, but the voice she had for his father was bitter. "As if he wasn't hurt enough already!" she said.

He heard the heavy quick footsteps going away, and for a long time he lay crying into the voile flowers. When he had cried himself out, and had listened apathetically to his mother's soothing promises that they would go in the first chance they got, go to the mountains, have a picnic under some waterfall, maybe be able to find a ballgame going on in town, some Saturday—when he had listened and become quiet, wanting to believe it but not believing it at all, he went inside to take his good clothes and his shoes off and put on his old overalls again.

It was almost noon when he came out to stand in the front yard looking southward toward the impossible land where the Mountains of the Moon lifted above the plains, and where, in the town below the peaks, crowds would now be eating picnic lunches, drinking pop, getting ready to go out to the ball ground and watch heroes in real uniforms play ball. The band would be braying now from a bunting-wrapped stand, kids would be playing in a cool grove, tossing firecrackers . . .

In the still heat his eyes searched the horizon for the telltale watermark. There was nothing but waves of heat crawling and lifting like invisible flames; the horizon was a blurred and writhing flatness where earth and sky met in an indistinct band of haze. This morning a stride would have taken him there; now it was gone.

Looking down, he saw at his feet the clean footprint he had made in the early morning. Aimlessly he put his right foot down and pressed. The mud was drying, but in a low place he found a spot that would still take an imprint. Very carefully, as if he performed some ritual for his life, he went around, stepping and leaning, stepping and leaning, until he had a circle six feet in diameter of delicately exact footprints, straight edge and curving instep and the five round dots of toes.

3

His father's voice awakened him next morning. Stretching his back, arching against the mattress, he looked over at his parents' end of the porch. His mother was up too, though he could tell from the flatness of the light outside that it was still early. He lay on his back, letting complete wakefulness come on, watching a spider that dangled on a golden, shining thread from the rolled canvas of the blinds. The spider came down in tiny jerks, his legs wriggling, and then went up again in the beam of sun. From the other room his father's voice rose loud and cheerful:

> Oh I'd give every man in the army a quarter
> If they'd all take a shot at my mother-in-law.

The boy slid his legs out of bed and yanked the nightshirt over his ears. He didn't want his father's face poking around the door, saying, "I plow deep while sluggards sleep!" He didn't want to be joked with. Yesterday was too sore a spot in his mind. He had been avoiding his father ever since the morning before, and he was not yet ready to accept any joking or attempts to make up. Nobody had a right hitting a person for nothing, and you bet they weren't going to be friends. Let him whistle and sing out there, pretending that nothing was the matter. The whole awful morning yesterday was the matter, the missed Fourth of July was the matter, that crack on the ear was the matter.

In the other room, as he pulled on his overalls, the bacon was snapping in the pan, and he smelled its good morning smell. His father whistled, sang:

> In the town of O'Geary lived Paddy O'Flanagan
> Battered away till he hadn't a pound,
> His father he died and he made him a man again,
> Left him a farm of tin acres o' ground.

Bruce pulled the overall straps up and went into the main room. His father stopped singing and looked at him. "Hello, Cheerful," he said. "You look like you'd bit into a wormy apple."

The boy mumbled something and went out to wash at the bench. It wasn't any fun waking up today. You kept thinking about yesterday, and how much fun it had been waking up then, when you were going to do something special and fancy. Now there wasn't anything to do except the same old things: run the traps, put out some poison, read the Sears Roebuck catalogue.

At breakfast he was glum, and his father joked him. Even his mother smiled, as if she had forgotten already how much wrong had been done the day before. "You look as if you'd been sent for and couldn't come," she said. "Cheer up."

"I don't want to cheer up."

They just smiled at each other, and he hated them both.

After breakfast his father said, "You help your Ma with the dishes, now. See how useful you can make yourself around here."

Unwillingly, wanting to get out of the house and away from them, he got the towel and swabbed away. He was rubbing a glass when he heard the Ford sputter and race and roar and then calm down into a steady mutter. His mouth opened, and he looked up at his mother. Her eyes were crinkled up with smiling.

"It goes!" he said.

"Sure it goes." She pulled both his ears, rocking his head. "Know what we're going to do?"

"What?"

"We're going to the mountains. Not to Chinook—there wouldn't be anything doing there today. But to the mountains, for a picnic. Pa got the car going yesterday afternoon, when you were down in the field, so we decided then. If you want to, of course."

"Yay!" he said. "Shall I dress up?"

"Put on your shoes, you'd better. We might climb a mountain."

The boy was out into the porch in three steps. With one shoe on and the other in his hand he hopped to the door. "When?" he said.

"Soon as you can get ready."

He was trying to run and tie his shoelaces at the same time as he went out of the house. There in the Ford, smoking his pipe, with one leg over the door and his weight on the back of his neck, his father sat. "What detained you?" he said. "I've been waiting a half hour. You must not want to go very bad."

"Aw!" the boy said. He looked inside the car. There was the lunch all packed, the fat wet canvas waterbag, even Spot with his tongue out and his ears up. Looking at his father, all his sullenness gone now, the boy said, "When did you get all this ready?"

His father grinned. "While you slept like a sluggard we worked like a buggard," he said. Then Bruce knew that everything was perfect, nothing could go wrong. When his father started rhyming things he was in his very best mood, and not even flat tires and breakdowns could make him do more than puff and playact.

He clambered into the front seat and felt the motor shaking under the floorboards. "Hey, Ma!" he yelled. "Hurry up! We're all ready to go!"

Their own road was a barely-marked trail that wiggled out across the burnouts along the east side of the wheat field. At the line it ran into another coming down from the homesteads to the east, and at Cree, a mile inside the Montana boundary, they hit the straight section-line road to Chinook. On that road they passed a trotting team pulling an empty wagon, and the boy waved and yelled, feeling superior, feeling as if he were charioted upon pure speed and all the rest of the world were earth-footed.

"Let's see how fast this old boat will go," his father said. He nursed it down through a coulee and onto the flat. His finger pulled the gas lever down, and the motor roared. Looking back with the wind-stung tears in his eyes, the boy saw his mother hanging to her hat, and the artificial grapes bouncing. The Ford leaped and bucked, the picnic box tipped over, the dog leaned out and the wind blew his eyes shut and his ears straight back. Turning around, the boy saw the blue sparks jumping from the magneto box and heard his father wahoo. He hung onto the side and leaned out to let the wind tear at him, tried to count the fenceposts going by, but they were ahead of him before he got to ten.

The road roughened, and they slowed down. "Good land," his mother said from the back seat. "We want to get to the Bearpaws, not wind up in a ditch."

"How fast were we going, Pa?"

"Forty or so. If we'd been going any faster you'd have hollered 'nough, I guess. You were looking pretty peaked."

"I was not."

"Looked pretty scared to me. I bet Ma was hopping around back there like corn in a popper. How'd you like it, Ma?"

"I liked it all right," she said comfortably. "But don't do it again."

They passed a farm, and the boy waved at three open-mouthed kids in the yard. It was pretty good to be going somewhere. The mountains were plainer now in the south. He could see dark canyons cutting into the slopes, and there was snow on the upper peaks.

"How soon'll we get there, Pa?"

His father tapped his pipe out and put it away and laughed. Without bothering to answer, he began to sing:

> *Oh, I dug Snoqualmie River*
> *And Lake Samamish too,*
> *And paddled down to Kirkland*
> *In a little birch canoe.*
>
> *I built the Rocky Mountains,*
> *And placed them where they are,*
> *Sold whiskey to the Indians*
> *From behind a little bar.*

It was then, with the empty flat country wheeling by like a great turntable, the wheat fields and fences and the weathered peak of a barn rotating slowly as if in a dignified dance, wheeling and slipping behind and gone, and his father singing, that the strangeness first came over the boy. Somewhere, sometime . . . and there were mountains in it, and a stream, and a swing that he had fallen out of and cried, and he had mashed ripe blackberries in his hands and his mother had wiped him off, straightening his stiff fingers and wiping hard. . . . His mind caught on that memory from a time before there was any memory, he rubbed his finger tips against his palms and slid a little down in the seat.

His father tramped on both pedals hard and leaned out of the car, looking. He swung to stare at the boy as a startled idiot might have stared, and in a voice heavy with German gutturals, he said, "Vot it iss in de crass?"

"What?"

"Iss in de crass somedings. Besser you bleiben right here."

He climbed out, and the boy climbed out after him. The dog jumped overboard and rushed, and in the grass by the side of the road the boy saw the biggest snake he had ever seen, long and fat and sleepy. When it pulled itself in and faced the stiff-legged dog he saw that the hind legs and tail of a gopher stuck out of the stretched mouth.

"Jiminy!" he said. "He eats gophers whole."

His father stooped with hands on knees to stare at the snake, looked at the boy, and wagged his head. "Himmel!" he said. "Dot iss a schlange vot iss a schlange."

"What is it?" the mother said from the car, and the boy yelled back, "A snake, a great big snake, and he's got a whole gopher in his mouth."

His father chased the pup away, found a rock, and with one careful throw crushed the flat head. The body, as big around as the boy's ankle, tightened into a ridged convulsion of muscles, and the tail whipped back and forth. Stooping, Bo pulled on the gopher's tail. There was a wet, slupping noise, and the gopher slid out, coated with slime and twice as long as he ought to have been.

"Head first," Bo said. "That's a hell of a way to die."

He lifted the snake by the tail. "Look," he said, "he's longer than I am." But Elsa made a face and turned her head while he fastened it in the forked top of a fencepost. It trailed almost two feet on the ground. The tail still twitched.

"He'll twitch till the sun goes down," Bo said. "First guy that comes along here drunk is going to think he's got d.t.'s." He climbed into the car, and the boy followed.

"What was it, Pa?"

"Milk snake. They come into barns and milk cows dry, sometimes. You saw what he did to that gopher. Just like a suction pump."

"Gee," the boy said. He sat back and thought about how long and slick the gopher had been, and how the snake's mouth was all stretched, and it was a good feeling to have been along and to have shared something like that with his father. It was a trophy, a thing you would remember and tell about. And while he was thinking that already, before they got to the mountains at all, he had something to remember about the trip, he remembered that just before they saw the snake he had been remembering something else, and he puckered his eyes in the sun, thinking. He had been right on the edge of it, it was right on the tip of his tongue, and then his father had tramped on the pedals. But it was something a long time ago, and there was a strangeness about it, something bothersome and a little scary, and it hurt his head the way it hurt his head to do arithmetical sums without pencil and paper. When you did them in your head something went round like a wheel, and you had to keep looking inside to make sure that you didn't lose sight of the figures that were pasted up there somewhere, and if you did it very long at a time you got a sick headache out of it. That was the way it felt when he almost remembered, only he hadn't been able to see what he knew was there . . .

By ten o'clock they had left the graded road and were chugging up a winding trail with toothed rocks embedded in the ruts. Ahead of them the mountains looked low and disappointing, treeless, brown. The trail ducked into a narrow gulch and the sides rose up around them, reddish gravel covered with bunch grass and sage.

"Gee whiz," the boy said. "These don't look like mountains."

"What'd you expect?" his father said. "Expect to step out onto a glacier?"

"But there aren't any trees," the boy said. "Gee whiz, there isn't even any water."

He stood up to look ahead. His father's foot went down on the low pedal, and the Ford growled at the grade. "Come on, Lena," his father said. He hitched himself back and forth in the seat, helping the car over the hill, and then, as they barely pulled over the hump and the sides of the gully fell away, there were the real mountains, high as heaven, the high slopes spiked and tufted with trees, and directly ahead of them a magnificent V-shaped door with the sun touching gray cliffs far back in, and a straight-edged violet shadow streaming from the eastern peak clear to the canyon floor.

"Well?" his father's voice said. "I guess if you don't like it we can drop you here and pick you up on the way back."

The boy turned back to his mother. She was sitting far forward on the edge of the seat. "I guess we want to come along, all right," she said, and laughed as if she might cry. "Anything as beautiful as that. Don't we, sonny?"

"You bet," he said. He remained standing all the way up over the gentle slope of the alluvial fan that aproned out from the canyon's mouth, and when they passed under the violet shadow, not violet any more but cool gray, he tipped his head back and looked up miles and miles to the broken rock above.

The road got rougher. "Sit down," his father said. "First thing you know you'll fall out on your head and sprain both your ankles."

He was in his very best mood. He said funny things to the car, coaxing it over steep pitches. He talked to it like a horse, scratched it under the dashboard, promised it an apple when they got there.

Above them the canyon walls opened out and back, went up steeply high and high and high, beyond the first walls that the boy had thought so terrific, away beyond those, piling peak on peak, and the sun touched and missed and touched again.

The trail steepened. A jet of steam burst from the brass radiator cap, the car throbbed and labored, they all sat forward and urged it on. But it slowed, shook, stopped and stood there steaming and shaking, and the motor died with a last lunging gasp.

"Is this as far as we can get?" the boy said. The thought that they might be broken down, right here on the threshold of wonder, put him in a panic. He looked around. They were in a bare rocky gorge. Not even any trees yet, though a stream tumbled down a bouldered channel on the left. But to get to trees and the real mountains they had to go further, much further. "Are we stuck?" he said.

His father grunted. "Skin down to the creek and get a bucket of water." The boy ran, came stumbling and staggering back with the pail. His mother had climbed out and put a rock under the hind wheel, and they stood close together while Bo with a rag made quick, stabbing turns at the radiator cap. The cap blew off and steam went up for six feet and they all jumped back. There was a sullen subterranean boiling deep under the hood.

"Now!" Bo said. He poured a little water in, stepped back. In a minute the water came bubbling out. He poured again, and again the motor spit it out. "Can't seem to keep anything on her stomach," he said, and winked at the boy. He didn't seem worried.

The fourth dose stayed down. He filled the radiator till it ran over, screwed the plug in, and threw the pail in the back end. "You two stay out," he said. "I'll see if she'll go over unloaded."

She wouldn't. She moved two feet, strangled and died. The boy watched with his jaw hanging, remembering yesterday. But his father wasn't the same today. He just sat in the car and didn't swear at all, but winked at the boy and made a closing motion with his hand under his chin. "Better shut that mouth," he said. "Some bird'll fly in there and build a nest."

To Elsa he said, "Can you kick that rock out from under the wheel?"

"Sure," she said. "But do you think . . . Maybe we could walk from here."

"Hell with it," he said cheerfully. "I'll get her up if I have to lug her on my back."

She kicked the stone away and he rolled backward down the hill, craning, steering with one hand. At the bottom he cramped the wheels, got out and cranked, got in again, and turned around in the narrow road, making three or four angled tries before he made it. Then his hand waved, and there was the Ford coming up the hill backwards, kicking gravel down from under its straining hind wheels, angling across the road and back and up, and the motor roaring like a threshing engine, until it went by them and on up to the crest and turned around with one quick expert ducking motion, and they got in and were off again.

"Well!" said Elsa in relief. "Who would have thought of coming up backwards."

"Got more power in reverse," Bo said. "Can't make it one way, try another."

"Yay!" the boy said. He was standing up, watching the deep insides of the earth appear behind the angled rock, and his mind was soaring again, up into the heights where a hawk or eagle circled like a toy bird on a string.

"How do you like it?" his mother shouted at him. He turned around and nodded his head, and she smiled at him. She looked excited herself. Her face had color in it and the varnished grapes on her hat gave her a reckless, girlish look.

"Hi, Ma," he said.

"Hi yourself." He lifted his face and yelled with the pressure of happiness inside him.

They lay on a ledge high up on the sunny east slope and looked out to the north through a notch cut as sharply as a wedge out of a pie. Far below them the golden plain spread level, golden-tawny grass and golden-green wheat checkerboarded in a pattern as wide as the world. Back of them the spring they had followed up the slope welled out of the ledge, spread out in a narrow swampy spot, and ran off down the hill. There were trees, a thick cluster of spruce against the bulge of the wall above, a clump of twinkling, sunny aspen down the slope, and in the canyon bottom below, a dense forest of soft maple. His mother had a bouquet of leaves in her hand, a bunch of spruce cones on the ground beside her. The three lay quietly, looking down over the steeply-dropping wall to the V-shaped door, and beyond that to the plain.

The boy wriggled his back against the rock, put his hand down to shift himself, brought it up prickled with spruce needles. He picked them off, still staring down over the canyon gateway. They were far above the world he knew. The air was clearer, thinner. There was cold water running from the rock, and all around there were trees. And over the whole canyon, like a haze in the clear air, was that other thing, that memory or ghost of a memory, a swing he had fallen out of, the feel of his hands sticky with blackberries, his skin drinking cool shade, and his father's anger—the reflection of ecstasy and the shadow of tears.

"I never knew till this minute," his mother said, "how I've missed the trees."

Nobody answered. They were all stuffed with lunch, pleasantly tired after the climb. Bo lay looking off down the canyon, and the sour smell of his pipe, in that air, was pleasant and clean. The boy saw his mother put the stem of a maple leaf in her mouth and make a half-pleased face at the bitter taste.

Bo rose and dug a tin cup from the picnic box, walked to the spring and dipped himself a drink. He made a breathy sound of satisfaction. "So cold it hurts your teeth," he said. He brought Elsa a cup, and she drank.

"Brucie?" she said, motioning with the cup.

He started to get up, but his father filled the cup and brought it to him, making believe he was going to pour it on him. The boy ducked and reached for the cup. With his eyes on his father over the brim he drank, testing the water to see if it really did hurt his teeth. The water was cold and silvery in his mouth, and when he swallowed he felt it cold clear down to his stomach.

"It doesn't either hurt your teeth," he said. He poured a little on his arm, and something jumped in his skin. It was his skin that remembered. Something numbingly cold, and then warm. He felt it now, the way you waded in it.

"Mom," he said.

"What?"

"Was it in Washington we went on a picnic like this and picked blackberries and I fell out of a swing and there were big trees, and we found a river that was half cold and half warm?"

His father was relighting his pipe. "What do you know about Washington? You were only knee-high to a grasshopper when we lived there." He looked at Elsa, and she made a curious puzzled, almost-warning face. They were both watching him.

"Well, I remember," the boy said. "I've been remembering it all day, ever since you sang that song about building the Rocky Mountains. You sang it that day, too. Don't you remember, Mom?"

"I don't know," she said doubtfully. "We went on picnics in Washington."

"What's this about a river with hot and cold running water?" his father said. "You must be remembering some time you had a bath in a bathtub."

"I do not!" the boy said. "I got blackberries mashed all over my hands and Mom scrubbed me off, and then we found that river and waded in it and half was hot and half was cold."

"Ohhhh," his mother said. "I believe I do. . . . Bo, you remember once up in the Cascades, when we went out from Richmond with the Curtises? And little Bill Curtis fell in the lake." She turned to the boy. "Was there a summer cottage there, a brown shingled house?"

"I don't know," the boy said. "I don't remember any Curtises. But I remember blackberries and that river and a swing."

"Your head is full of blackberries," his father said. "If it was the time we went out with the Curtises there weren't any blackberries. That was in the spring."

"No," Elsa said. "It was in the fall, just after we moved to Richmond. And I think there was a place where one river from the mountains ran into another from the valley and they ran alongside each other in the same channel. The mountain one was a lot colder. Don't you remember that trip with the Curtises, Bo?"

"Sure I remember it," he said. "We hired a buckboard and saw a black bear and I won six bits from Joe Curtis pitching horseshoes."

"That's right," the mother said. "You remember the bear, Brucie."

The boy shook his head. There wasn't any bear in what he remembered. Just feelings, things that made his skin prickle.

His mother was looking at him, a little puzzled wrinkle between her eyes. "It's funny you should remember such different things than we remember," she said. "Everything means something different to everybody, I guess." She laughed, and the boy thought her eyes looked very odd and bright. "It makes me feel as if I didn't know you at all," she said.

She brushed her face with the handful of leaves and watched Bo gathering up odds and ends and putting them in the basket. "I wonder what each of us will remember about today?"

"I wouldn't worry about it," he said. "You can depend on Bub here to remember a lot of things that didn't happen."

"I don't think he does," she said. "He's got a good memory."

He picked up the box. "It takes a good memory to remember things that never happened. I remember once a garter snake crawled into my crib and I used it for a belt to keep my breechclout on. They took it away from me and I bawled the crib so full of tears I had to swim for shore. I drifted in three days later on a checkerboard raft with a didie for a sail."

The boy stood up and brushed off his pants. "You do too remember that river," he said.

His father grinned at him. "Sure. Only it wasn't quite as hot and cold as you make it out."

It was evening in the canyon, but when they reached the mouth again they emerged into full afternoon, with two hours of sun left them. Bo stopped the car before they dipped into the gravelly wash between the foothills, and they all looked back at the steep thrust of the mountains, purpling in the shadows, the rock glowing golden-red far back on the faces of the inner peaks. Elsa still held the bouquet of maple leaves in her hand.

"Well, there go the Mountains of the Moon," she said. The moment was almost solemn. In the front seat the boy stood up to look back. He felt the sun strong against the side of his face; the mountains sheering up before him were very real and solid. In a little while, as they went north, they would begin to melt together, and the patches of snow would appear far up on the northern slopes. His eyes went out of focus so that he saw the mountains as they would appear from the homestead on a clear day, a ghostly line on the horizon.

He felt his father twist toward him, but the trance was so strong that he did not look down. When he finally did, he caught his mother and father looking at each other, the look they had for moments when he had pleased them or made them proud of him.

"Okay," his father said, and stabbed him in the ribs with a hard thumb. "Wipe the black bears out of your eyes."

He started the car, and as they bounced down the rocky trail toward the road he sang at the top of his voice, bellowing into the still, hot afternoon:

> *I had a kid and his name was Brucie*
> *Squeezed black bears and found them juicy.*
> *Washed them off in a hot-cold river,*
> *Now you boil and now you shiver.*
> *Caught his pants so full of trout*
> *He couldn't sit down till he got them out.*
> *Trout were boiled from the hot-side river,*
> *Trout from the cold side raw as liver.*
> *Ate the boiled ones, ate the raw,*
> *And then went howling home to Maw.*

The boy looked up at his father, his laughter bubbling up, everything wonderful, the day a swell day, his mother clapping hands in time to his father's fool singing.

"Aw, for gosh sakes," he said, and ducked when his father pretended he was going to swat him one.

4

There were days in July when they went out together along the wheat field, the long narrow strip stretching almost a mile from the pasture fence to the Montana line. They all carried pails of wheat wet and swollen and sweet-smelling from strychnine, and dropped a tablespoonful at every gopher hole they found. This was the crucial time, as far as the gophers were concerned. The wheat was a foot high, and the gophers liked it best at that stage, when they could break down the spears and get at the tender joints. Already, in spite of the boy's trapping and snaring and poisoning, there were patches as big as a table along the edges of the field where the wheat was broken and eaten down close to the ground.

"You ought to get out here with your traps more," Bo said. "You spend too much time in the pasture, where it doesn't matter."

"They come down for water, though," the boy said. "There's one hole by the dam where I've caught nineteen already."

"Well, you aren't catching them all," said his father. "If this poison doesn't thin them down you'll have to trap all up and down this field."

"I'll get 'em. I sort of hate to poison them because then I don't get the tails."

"Forget about the tails. You've got to keep this field from looking as if it had the mange."

They went clear to the line, to the heavy iron post that marked the international boundary, along the foot of the field, and back up the other side between the wheat and the flax. Bo was sweating heavily under his wide straw hat. "I was a sucker to make that field so long and narrow," he said. "It'd be a lot handier if it was wider and not so long."

Elsa looked at him and smiled. "You wanted to plow a furrow a mile long and straight as a string," she said.

"Well, I plowed her. Maybe I'm no farmer, but I plowed her a mile long and six inches deep and straight as the team could walk."

"I know," she said, and lifted her straw hat from her red hair to let the wind cool her. "You've done fine with it."

Reaching down for a clod, he crumbled it between his fingers. "Dry pretty far down," he said. "We could stand a rain."

"It'll rain," she said. "It has to. Even so, I think the wheat looks awfully good." She wiped her forehead on her sleeve and smiled.

"It better," he said. He looked down the green shimmer of the field and set the edges of his teeth precisely together. "By God," he said, "if it doesn't make for us this year I'll . . ." He could think of nothing bad enough to do. "It sure better rain," he said. "With wheat two and a half a bushel it better rain."

"If we get a crop will you fix up the house a little?" she said.

"Fix it up how?"

"Paint it, maybe. And rig some kind of water system so I could plant flowers and things."

"Old Mama," he said. "Wants a cottage with roses round the door."

"Well, I do. It's so barren the way it is. It's like camping in the place. Ever since we went to the mountains I've had the itch to fix it up."

"I tell you one thing," he said, "if we don't make it this year we won't even be camping in it. We'll be going some place where we can make a living."

"We've made a living. Even with the drouth last year and the rust the year before we made a living."

He stooped to lay a spoonful of poison at a gopher hole. "When we came up here," he said, "we didn't come up just to make a living. We came up to make a pile."

They watched the sky those days, watched the southeast where the June rains had come from. Nothing but the fitful glare of heat lightning rewarded their watching, but even without rain the wheat grew strongly. From day to day the boy thought he could see the difference, for the days were warm and endless, and when he dug into the ground it was warm for five or six inches down.

The gophers were under control, though there were still hundreds of them. He had almost fifteen hundred tails in the cigar box, tied into bundles of a hundred so that he didn't have to spend all afternoon counting them. And he had taken to drowning out gophers along the coulee by the dam. There were always some there, now that the dry spell was on, and it was fun to sic Spot on the hole while he ran with buckets. Spot learned fast. He would stand quivering with excitement, with his nose down the hole, while the boy was gone, and when the water came he backed up one step and waited, whining and watching the hole. When the gopher popped out, wet and slick and dark with the water, Spot would snap once, and that was the end of Mister Gopher.

There were days, during that hot July, when they got into the Ford and went down to the little stream by Pete and Emil and had a swim in the lukewarm, barely-running water. Those were good days. But as July passed and the rain held off a tension came into the house. His father sang less at breakfast-making, and he was likely to stand in the door facing another cloudless morning and swear under his breath. His mother went around often with her lips pressed together and her eyes worried, and he saw how she avoided talk whenever she could.

When thunderheads did build up, the tension pulled harder, and there was a difference in the way they stood and watched. In June they had waited confidently, because if this one blew over the ground was still good and moist, and there would be another one soon anyway. But now there was a half expectation that the clouds would come to nothing, because there had been false alarms a half dozen times. Once or twice they watched storms get near enough to drop a few heavy pellets of rain in the baked dooryard, and whistle their winds through the screens of the porch so that they ran to roll down the canvas blinds. But by the time they got the porch snug the pelting would have stopped, and they would stand in the doorway again and see blue sky coming like a falsely-smiling enemy behind the hopeful dark of the cloud.

That tension invaded the private life of the boy, too. The farm was no longer a world invented simply for his exploration and delight. Seeing his father glum, his mother silent, he felt a compulsion to do something. The only thing he could do was to destroy gophers, and though they were not the real danger now, their decimation at least gave him the sense of helping. He was in the pasture and along the field three or four times a day, and from his lookout in the sleeping porch he kept the coulee bank always under his eye when he was in the house. The minute a gopher showed on the tawny slope he was out with a bucket as if he belonged to a volunteer fire company.

"By God," his father would say irritably, looking up at the brassy summer sky, "there isn't a drop of rain in a thousand miles."

The boy's mother told him privately that there wasn't enough for Pa to do. If he had had stock to care for, or odd jobs to do, or anything, he wouldn't be so nervous. On an ordinary farm, if one crop failed, others would come through all right, and you would have your hogs or your cattle or your cowpeas or whatever even if your big crop didn't make. But here it was just sit and watch, and it was pretty hard on Pa, and if the wheat didn't make there was nothing.

He took to going out into the field alone, and they would see him walking along the edge of the wheat, green-bronze now, stooping and straightening and taking little excursions into the grain that reached around his waist like green water. The first year they had come out, his mother said—1915, that was—the wheat had been higher than Pa's head. He had just walked into Gadke's field and disappeared. Ever since then Pa had had a great respect for Gadke as a farmer. But he hadn't had much of a field in that year himself, just twenty acres, because he was building the house and getting the fence in and getting the sod broken and everything. Even so, they had made over a thousand bushel of wheat that year, more than they had made since with two or three times the acreage in.

The boy dreamed about the wheat at night now. Once he dreamed that he went out across the coulee and there was the grain grown enormously, a wilderness, a woods of wheat, taller than tall, with great fat heads nodding far above him, and he ran back to the house with his mouth shouting words, calling his father to come and see, but when they got back the wheat had shrivelled and blackened and died, and the field looked like a dark and smoky place that fire had passed over. His father flew into a rage and cuffed him for lying, and he awoke.

As August moved on day by cloudless day, they began to watch the southwest rather than the southeast. The days were hot, with light hot fingering winds that bent the wheat and died again, and in the evenings there was always a flicker of heat lightning. The southwest was dangerous in August. From that direction came the hot winds blowing for two or three days at a time, that had withered and scorched the wheat last year. They were like Chinooks, his father said, except that in summer they were hot as hell. You couldn't predict them and you couldn't depend on their coming, but if they came you were sunk.

What a God damned country, his father said.

The boy heard them talking in bed at night, when they thought he was asleep, but even without that he couldn't have missed how his father grew darker and more sullen and silent. The good humor was less frequent and never lasted. Even when he proposed a swim down by Pete and Emil he did it as if it were a last resort to keep from flying all part with worry and impotence. "Let's get out of here and do something," he would say. "Sit around here much longer and the roof'll fall in on us."

"It's just this not being able to do anything," the boy's mother said. "It's this sitting, without being able to do anything but sit . . ."

That was why, the boy knew, she proposed the visit to the Garfields, who had come two years before to take up a homestead four miles east of them. "We ought to know our neighbors better," she said. "They've lived there two years and we've never even met them."

"I've met him," Bo said.

"Where?"

"Down at Cree. He's a prissy-faced long-nosed Englishman."

"Well, but he's our nearest neighbor. And she might be nice."

"Have they got any kids, Ma?" the boy asked.

"I don't think so. I wish they had." She looked at Bo and wheedled him. "You'll drive us over on Sunday, won't you?" she said. "Just to be neighborly. It'll do you good."

He shrugged and picked up a magazine, four months old and dogeared from long use.

The boy was excited by the visit to Garfields'. The hot afternoon was still and breathless, the air harder to breathe than usual. He knew there was a change in weather coming, because the ginger-snaps in their tall cardboard box were soft and bendable when he snitched a couple to stick in his pocket. He could tell too by his father's grumpiness that something was coming. If it was rain every-thing would be dandy, there would be humming and singing again before breakfast. Maybe his father would let him ride the mare down to Cree for the mail. But if it was hail or hot wind they'd have to walk soft and speak softer, and the crop might be ruined, and that would be calamity.

He found more than he looked for at Garfields'. Mr. Garfield was tall and bald with a big nose, and talked very softly and politely. The boy's father was determined not to like him right from the start.

When Mr. Garfield said, "Dear, I think we might have a glass of lemonade, don't you?" the boy saw his parents look at each other, saw the beginning of a smile on his father's face, saw his mother purse her lips and shake her head ever so little. And when Mrs. Garfield, prim and spectacled, with a habit of tucking her head back and to one side while she listened to anyone talk, brought in the lemonade, the boy saw his father taste his and make a little face behind the glass. He hated any summer drink without ice in it, and kept his own beer at home deep in the cellar hole where it would keep cool.

But Mr. and Mrs. Garfield were nice people. They sat down in their new parlor and showed the boy's mother the rug and the gramophone. When the boy came up curiously to inspect the little box with a petunia-shaped horn with a picture of a terrier and "His Master's Voice" painted on it, and when the Garfields found that he had never seen or heard a gramophone, they put on a cylinder like a big spool of tightly-wrapped black thread, and pushed a lever and lowered a needle, and out came a man's voice singing in Scotch brogue, and his mother smiled and nodded and said, "My land, Harry Lauder! I heard him once a long time ago. Isn't it won-derful, sonny?"

It was wonderful all right. He inspected it, reached out his fingers to touch things, wiggled the big horn to see if it was loose or screwed in. His father warned him sharply to keep his hands off, but Mr. Garfield smiled and said, "Oh, he can't hurt it. Let's play some-thing else," and found a record about the saucy little bird on Nellie's hat that had them all laughing. They let him wind the machine and play the record over again, all by himself, and he was very careful. It was a fine machine. He wished he had one.

About the time he had finished playing his sixth or seventh record, and George M. Cohan was singing, "She's a grand old rag, she's a high-flying flag, and forever in peace may she wave," he glanced at his father and saw that he was grouchy about something. He wasn't taking part in the conversation, but was sitting with his chin in his hand staring out the window. Mr. Garfield was looking at him a little helplessly. His eyes met the boy's and he motioned him over.

"What do you find to do all summer, young man? Only child, are you?"

"No sir. My brother's in Whitemud. He's twelve. He's got a job."

"So you came out on the farm to help," Mr. Garfield said. He had his hand on the boy's shoulder and his voice was so kind that the boy lost his shyness and felt no embarrassment at all in being out there in the middle of the parlor with all of them looking at him.

"I don't help much," he said. "I'm too little to do anything but drive the stoneboat, Pa says. When I'm twelve he's going to get me a gun and then I can go hunting."

"Hunting?" said Mr. Garfield. "What would you hunt?"

"Oh, gophers and weasels. I got a pet weasel now. His name's Lucifer."

"Well," Mr. Garfield said. "You seem a manly little chap. What do you feed your weasel?"

"Gophers." He thought it best not to say that the gophers were alive when he threw them in. He thought that probably Mr. Garfield would be a little shocked at that.

Mr. Garfield straightened up and looked around at the grownups. "Isn't it a shame," he said, "that there are so many predatory animals and pests in this country that we have to spend our time destroying them? I hate killing things."

"I hate weasels," the boy said. "I'm saving this one till he turns white and then I'm going to skin him. Once I speared a weasel with a pitchfork in the chicken house and he dropped right off the tine and ran up my leg and bit me after he was speared clean through."

He finished breathlessly, and his mother smiled at him, motioning him not to talk so much. But Mr. Garfield was still looking at him kindly. "So you want to make war on the cruel things, the weasels and hawks," he said.

"Yes sir." The boy looked at his mother and it was all right. He hadn't spoiled anything by talking about the weasels.

"Now that reminds me," Mr. Garfield said, rising. "Maybe I've got something you would find useful."

He went into another room and came back with a .22 in his hand. "Could you use this?"

"I . . . yes *sir!*" the boy said. He had almost, in his excitement, said, "I hope to whisk in your piskers."

"If your parents will let you have it," Mr. Garfield said, and raised his eyebrows at the boy's mother. He didn't look at the father, but the boy did.

"Can I, Pa?"

"I guess so," his father said. "Sure."

"Thank Mr. Garfield nicely," his mother said.

"Gee," the boy said. "Thanks, Mr. Garfield, ever so much."

"There's a promise goes with it," Mr. Garfield said. "I'd like you to promise never to shoot anything with it but the bloodthirsty animals, the cruel ones like weasels and hawks. Never anything like birds or prairie dogs."

"How about butcher birds?"

"Butcher birds?"

"Shrikes," said the boy's mother. "We've got some over by our place. They kill all sorts of other things, snakes and gophers and other birds. They're worse than the hawks, because they kill just for the fun of it."

"By all means," said Mr. Garfield. "Shoot the shrikes. A thing that kills for the fun of it . . ." He shook his head and his voice got solemn, like the voice of Mr. McGregor, the Sunday school superintendent in town, when he was asking the benediction. "There's something about the way the war drags on, or maybe it's just being in this new, clean country," Mr. Garfield said, "that makes me hate killing. I simply can't bear to shoot anything any more, even a weasel."

The boy's father turned cold eyes away from Mr. Garfield and looked out the window. One big brown hand, a little dirty from the wheel of the car, rubbed against the day-old bristles of his jaws. Then he stood and stretched. "We got to be going," he said.

"Oh, stay a while," Mr. Garfield said. "You just came. I wanted to show you my trees."

The boy's mother stared. "Trees?"

He smiled. "Sounds a bit odd out here, doesn't it? But I think trees will grow. I've made some plantings down below."

"I'd love to see them," she said. "Sometimes I'd give almost anything to get into a deep shady woods. Just to smell it, and feel how cool . . ."

"There's a little story connected with these," Mr. Garfield said. He spoke warmly, to the mother alone. "When we first decided to come out here I said to Martha that if trees wouldn't grow we shouldn't stick it. That's just what I said, 'If trees won't grow there we shan't stick it.' Trees are like the breath of life to me."

The boy's father was shaken by a sudden spell of coughing, and his wife shot a look at him and then looked back at Mr. Garfield with a light flush on her cheekbones. "I'd love to see them," she said again. "I was raised in Minnesota, and I never will get used to a place as barren as this."

"When I think of the beeches back home in England," Mr. Garfield said, and shook his head.

Bo lifted himself heavily out of his chair and followed the rest of them out to the coulee edge. Below them willows grew in a thin belt along the almost-dry creek, and farther back from the water there were perhaps twenty cottonwoods a half-dozen feet high.

"I'm trying cottonwoods first because they can stand drouth," Mr. Garfield said.

Elsa was looking down with all her longing plain and naked in her face. "It's wonderful," she said. "I'd give almost anything to have some on our place."

"I found the willows near here," Mr. Garfield said. "Just at the south end of the hills they call the Old-Man-on-His-Back, where a stream comes down."

"Stream?" the boy's father said. "You mean that spring-mouth trickle?"

"It's not much of a stream," Mr. Garfield said apologetically. "But . . ."

"Are there any more there?" Elsa said.

"Oh yes. You could get some. Cut them slanting and push them into any damp ground. They'll grow."

"They'll grow about six feet high," Bo Mason said.

"Yes," said Mr. Garfield. "They're not, properly speaking, trees. Still . . ."

Bo Mason looked at the southwest. "It's getting pretty smothery," he said, rather loudly. "We better be getting on."

This time Mr. Garfield didn't object, and they went back to the car with Mrs. Garfield and the boy's mother exchanging promises of visits. Bo turned the crank and climbed into the Ford, where the boy was sighting along his gun. "Put that down!" his father said. "Don't you know any better than to point a gun around people?"

"It isn't loaded."

"They never are. Put it down now."

The Garfields were standing with their arms around each other's waists, waiting to wave goodbye. Mr. Garfield reached over and picked something from his wife's dress.

"What was it, Alfred?" she said, peering.

"Nothing. Only a bit of fluff."

The boy's father coughed violently and the car started with a jerk. With his head down almost on the wheel, still coughing, he waved, and the mother and the boy waved as they went down along the badly-set cedar posts of the pasture fence. They were almost a quarter of a mile away before the boy, with a last flourish of the gun, turned around to see that his father was not coughing, but laughing. He rocked the car with his joy, and when Elsa said, "Oh, Bo, you big fool," he pointed helplessly to his shoulder. "Would you mind," he said. "Would you mind brushing that bit o' fluff off me showldah?" He rocked again, pounding the wheel. "I cawn't stick it," he said. "I bloody well cawn't stick it, you knaow."

"It isn't fair to laugh at him," she said. "He can't help being English."

"He can't help being a sanctimonious old mudhen, either," he said. "Braying about his luv-ly, luv-ly trees. They'll freeze out the first cold winter."

"How do you know? Maybe it's like he says—if they get a start they'll grow here as well as anywhere."

"Maybe there's a gold mine in our back yard, too, but I'm not going to dig to see. I couldn't stick it."

"You're just being stubborn," she said. "Just because you didn't like him . . ."

He turned on her in a heavy amazement. "Well my God, did you?"

"I thought he was very nice," she said, and sat straighter in the back seat, speaking loudly above the jolting of the springs and the cough of the motor. "They're trying to make a home, not just a wheat crop. I liked them."

"Uh huh." He was not laughing any more now. Sitting beside him, the boy could see that his face had hardened and that the cold look had come into his eyes again. "So I should start talking like I had a mouthful of bran, and planting trees around the house that'll look like clothesline poles in two months."

"I didn't say that."

"You thought it, though." He looked irritably at the sky, misted with the same delusive film of haze or cloud that had fooled him for three days. "You thought it all the time we were there. 'Why aren't you more like Mr. Garfield, he's such a nice man.'" With mincing savagery he swung around and mocked her. "Shall I make it a walnut grove? Or a sugar orchard? Or maybe you'd prefer orange trees."

The boy was squinting down his gun, trying not to hear them quarrel, but he knew what his mother's face would be like—hurt and a little flushed, and her chin trembling into stubbornness. "I don't suppose you could bear to have a rug on the floor, or a gramophone?" she said.

He smacked the wheel hard. "Of course I could bear it if we could afford it. I'd love it. But I don't know what you think is going to give us the dough for things like that if a wind comes up out of that heat-hole over there. And I'd a damn sight rather do without than be like that old sandhill crane."

"I don't suppose you'd like to take me over to the Old-Man-on-His-Back some day to get some willow slips, either."

"What for?"

"To plant down in the coulee, by the dam."

"That dam dries up every August. Your willows wouldn't live till snow flies."

"Well, would it do any harm to try?"

"Oh, shut up!" he said. "Just thinking about that guy and his fluff and his trees gives me the pleefer."

The topless Ford lurched, one wheel at a time, through the deep burnout by their pasture corner, and the boy clambered out with his gun in his hand to slip the loop of the three-strand gate. It was then that he saw the snake, a striped limp ribbon, dangling on the fence, and a moment later the sparrow, neatly butchered and hung by the throat on a barb. He pointed the gun at them. "Lookit!" he said. "Lookit what the butcher bird's been doing."

His father's violent hand waved at him from the car. "Come on! Get the wire out of the way."

The boy dragged the gate through the dust, and the Ford went through and up behind the house framed by the fireguard overgrown with Russian thistle. Walking across that yard a few minutes later, the boy felt its hard heat through his sneakers. There was hardly a spear of grass within the fireguard. It was one of his father's prides that the dooryard should be like cement. "Pour your washwater out long enough," he said, "and you'll have a surface so hard it won't even make mud." Religiously he threw his water out three times a day, carrying it sometimes a dozen steps to dump it on a dusty or grassy spot.

Elsa had objected at first, asking why they had to live in the middle of an alkali flat, and why they couldn't let grass grow up to the door. But he snorted her down. Everything around the house ought to be bare as a bone. Get a good grass fire going and it would jump that guard like nothing, and if they had grass to the door where would they be? She said why not plow a wider guard then, one a fire couldn't jump, but he said he had other things to do than plowing fifty-foot fireguards.

They were arguing inside when the boy came up the step to sit down and aim his empty .22 at a fencepost. Apparently his mother had been persistent, and persistence when he was not in a mood for it angered his father worse than anything. Their talk came vaguely through the boy's concentration, but he shut his ears on it. If that spot on the post was a coyote, now, and he held the sight steady, right on it, and pulled the trigger, that old coyote would jump about eighty feet in the air and come down dead as a mackerel, and he could tack his hide on the barn the way Mr. Larson had one, only the dogs had jumped and torn the tail and hind legs off Mr. Larson's, and he wouldn't get more than a three-dollar bounty for its ears. But Mr. Larson had shot his with a shotgun, anyway, and the hide wasn't worth much even before the dogs tore it.

"I can't for the life of me see why not," his mother said inside. "We could do it now. We're not doing anything else."

"I tell you they wouldn't grow!" his father said, with emphasis on every word. "Why should we run our tongues out doing everything that mealy-mouthed fool does?"

"I don't want anything but the willows. They're easy."

He made his special sound of contempt, half-snort and half-grunt. After a silence she tried again. "They might even have pussies on them in the spring. Mr. Garfield thinks they'd grow, and his wife told me he used to work in a greenhouse."

"This isn't a greenhouse, for Chrissake. Go outside and feel that breeze if you think so."

"Oh, let it go," she said. "I've stood it this long without any green things around. I guess I can stand it some more."

The boy, aiming now toward the gate where the butcher bird, coming back to his prey, would in just a second fly right into Dead-eye's unerring bullet, heard his father stand up suddenly.

"Abused, aren't you?" he said.

His mother's voice rose. "No, I'm not abused! Only I don't see why it would be so awful to get some willows. Just because Mr. Garfield gave me the idea, and you don't like him . . ."

"You're right I don't like him. He gives me a pain right under the crupper."

"Because," his mother's voice said bitterly, "he calls his wife 'dear' and puts his arm around her and likes trees. It wouldn't occur to you to put your arm around your wife, would it?"

The boy aimed and held his breath. His mother ought to keep still, because if she didn't she'd get him real mad and then they'd both have to tiptoe around the rest of the day. He heard his father's breath whistle through his teeth, and his mincing, nasty voice: "Would you like me to put my arm around you now, *dear?*"

"I wouldn't let you touch me with a ten-foot pole," his mother said. She sounded just as mad as he did, and it wasn't often she let herself get that way. The boy squirmed over when he heard the quick hard steps come up behind him and pause. Then his father's hand, brown and meaty and felted with fine black hair, reached down over his shoulder and took the .22.

"Let's see this cannon old Scissor-Bill gave you," he said.

It was a single-shot, bolt-action Savage, a little rusty on the barrel, the bolt sticky with hardened grease when he removed it. Sighting up through the barrel, he grunted. "Takes care of a gun like he sets a fence. Probably used it to cultivate his luv-ly trees."

He went out into the porch, and after a minute came back with a rag and a can of machine oil. Hunching the boy over on the step, he sat down and began rubbing the bolt with the oil-soaked rag.

"I just cawn't bear to shoot anything any more," he said, and laughed suddenly. "I just cawn't stick it, little man." He leered at the boy, who grinned back uncertainly. Squinting through the barrel again, his father breathed through his nose and clamped his lips together, shaking his head.

The sun lay heavy on the baked yard. Out over the corner of the pasture, a soaring hawk caught wind and sun at the same time, so that his light breast feathers flashed as he banked and rose. Just wait, the boy said. Wait till I get my gun working and I'll fix you, you hen-robber. He thought of the three chicks a hawk had struck earlier in the summer, the three balls of yellow with the barred mature plumage just showing through. Two of them dead before he got there and chased the hawk away, the other with its crop slashed open and wheat spilling from it to the ground. His mother had sewed up the crop, and the chicken had lived, but it always looked droopy, like a plant in drouth time, and sometimes it stood working its bill as if choking.

By golly, he thought, I'll shoot every hawk and butcher bird in twenty miles. I'll . . .

"Rustle around and find me a piece of baling wire," his father said. "This barrel looks like a henroost."

Behind the house he found a piece of rusty wire, brought it back and watched his father straighten it, wind a piece of rag around the end, ram it up and down through the barrel, and peer through again. "He's leaded her so you can hardly see the grooves," he said. "But maybe she'll shoot. We'll fill her with vinegar and cork her up tonight."

Elsa was behind them, leaning against the jamb and watching. She reached down and rumpled Bo's black hair. "The minute you get a gun in your hands you start feeling better," she said. "It's just a shame you weren't born a hundred years sooner."

"A gun's a good tool," he said. "It hadn't ought to be misused. Gun like this is enough to make a guy cry."

"Well, you've at least got to admit it was nice of him to give it to Bruce," she said. It was the wrong thing to say. The boy had a feeling that she knew it was the wrong thing to say, that she said it anyway just to have one tiny triumph over him. Even before he heard his father's answer he knew Pa would be mad again.

"Oh sure," he said. "Mr. Garfield's a fine man. He can preach a better sermon than anybody in Saskatchewan. God Almighty, I get sick of hearing his praises sung. If you liked it so well why don't you move over there?"

"If you weren't so blind stubborn . . ."

He rose with the .22 in his hand and brushed past her into the house. "I'm not so blind," he said heavily in passing. "You've been throwing that bastard up to me for two hours. It doesn't take very good eyes to see what that means. It means I'm no good, I can't do anything right."

She started to say, "All because I want a few little . . ." but the boy cut in on her, anxious to help the situation somehow. "Will it shoot now?" he said.

His father said nothing. His mother looked down at him, sighed, shrugged, smiled bleakly with a tight mouth. She moved aside when his father came back with a box of cartridges in his hand. He ignored her, speaking to the boy alone in the particular half-jocular tone he always used with him or with the dog when he wasn't mad.

"Thought I had these around," he said. "Let's see what this smoke-pole will do."

He slipped in a cartridge and locked the bolt, looking around for something to shoot at. Behind him Elsa's feet moved on the floor, and her voice came purposefully. "I can't see why you want to act this way," she said. "I'm going over and get some of those slips myself."

There was a long silence. The angled shade lay sharp as a knife across the baked front yard, and a breeze stirred in the Russian thistle of the fireguard. Bo's cheek was pressed against the stock of the gun, his arms and hands as steady as stone.

"How'll you get there?" he said, whispering down the barrel.

"I'll walk."

"Five miles and back."

"Yes, or fifty miles and back. If there was any earthly reason why you should mind . . ."

"I don't mind," he said, his voice soft as silk. "Go ahead."

Close to his mother's long skirts in the doorway, the boy felt her stiffen as if she had been slapped. He squirmed anxiously, but his desperation could find only the question he had asked before. His voice squeaked on it: "Will it shoot now?"

"See that sparrow out there?" his father said. "Right out by that cactus?"

"Bo!" Elsa said. "If you shoot that harmless little bird!"

Fascinated, the boy watched his father's dark face against the rifle stock, the locked, immovable left arm, the thick finger crooked inside the trigger-guard almost too small to hold it. He saw the sparrow, gray, white-breasted, hopping obliviously in search of bugs, fifty feet out on the gray earth.

"I just . . . cawn't . . . bear . . . to . . . shoot . . . anything," his father said, his face like dark stone, his lips hardly moving. "I just . . . cawn't . . . stick it!"

"Bo!" his wife screamed.

The boy's mouth opened, a dark wash of terror shadowed his vision of the bare yard and the sharp angle of shade. "Don't, Pa!"

The rocklike figure of his father never moved. The thick finger squeezed down slowly, there was a thin, sharp report, and the sparrow jerked and collapsed into a shapeless wad on the ground. In the instant of the shot all its clean outlines vanished. Head, feet, the white breast, the perceptible outlines of the folded wings, disappeared all at once, crumpled together and were lost, and the boy sat beside his father on the step with the echo of the shot thin in his ears.

He did not look at either of his parents. He looked only at the crumpled sparrow. Step by step, unable to keep away, he went to it, stooped, and picked it up. Blood stained his fingers, and he held the bird by the tail while he wiped the smeared hand on his overalls. He heard the click as the bolt was shot and the empty cartridge ejected, and he saw his mother come swiftly out of the house past his father, who sat still on the step. Her hands were clenched, and she walked with her head down.

"Ma!" the boy said dully. "Ma, what'll I do with it?"

She stopped and turned, and for a moment they faced each other. He saw the dead pallor of her face, the burning eyes, the not-quite-controlled quiver of her lips. But her words, when they came, were flat and level, almost casual.

"Leave it right there," she said. "After while your father will want to hang it on the barbed wire."

The boy dropped it and went straight away, as if by inspiration, to run his trap line. He hated his father and he would not even stay in the same yard with him, and he hated him all up through the pasture and back along the north end of the wheat field where the grain drooped in the withering sun. The wind, by the time he got back to the house toward evening, was blowing quite strongly from the southwest.

5

So the year that began in hope ended in bitterness. The rains that came after the blistering winds were ironic and unwanted, the crop was ruined, the prospect of a hard winter was there again, like an old unwelcome acquaintance come upon around a corner.

For the boy, the farm was spoiled. The reservoir had dried up almost completely, and now was a smelly, hoof-pocked, muddy hole. The creek by Pete and Emil was almost as bad. The trapping had palled, and the smell of his almost-two thousand tails when he opened the cigar box filled the sleeping porch and sickened him. There was no water for drowning gophers out, he had no more cartridges for shooting at hawks. And one night, in a blustering wind, the weasel's cage got tipped over and the weasel got away.

Everything was stale. Because his father went down to Cree three or four times a week now and spent all afternoon talking with other lost and prowling homesteaders, there were practically no trips to the store any more. The only thing that saved him from empty moping was the advent of the Fall Sears Roebuck catalogue and the coming of the thresher crew to rescue the remnants of the wheat.

But then nothing again, the lackluster hours of hanging on the pasture gate and looking south toward the Bearpaws, without pleasure particularly, without longing, without anything but a dull wish that they'd go into town pretty soon.

"What's the matter, son?" his mother said to him. "You go around looking like a lost soul."

"I don't know," he said. He ran a finger up the rough face of a stud behind the sofa where he lay, got a sliver under the nail, and listlessly pulled it out again. "When we going into town, Ma?"

"Right away, soon as Pa can get the rest of the wheat hauled. You anxious to get back?"

"Uh huh. I guess so."

"Oh Lord," she said. "Me too. The change would do us all good."

Then his father came back from his trip with the wagon crews, so bitter that he wouldn't even say how much he had got for the little wheat the winds had left him, and the morning after that he said they were going to get out of this God-forsaken buffalo-chip flat as quick as they could pack.

They worked all that day stowing in the bed of the wagon quilts, clothes, odds and ends of furniture needed in town, spare cans of gasoline and kerosene, some sacks of wheat saved for chicken and cow feed. The wagon box was more than level full when they went in to supper, and when the boy went to bed that night and lay thinking about the loaded wagon outside, the trip coming up tomorrow, the excitement of town again, school again, Chet again, the house in town and the river and the brush and Hallowe'en again, it seemed to him that the lonesome whining of the wind through the sleeping-porch screen, the lonesome slatting of a half-unrolled canvas curtain, had in them all that frightened and depressed him about the home-stead. It was so big outside, the stars so high and cold, the land so flat and mysterious lying still as a shadow-earth under the remote sky. You could go out in the yard and stare in every direction and never see a light unless one of the few neighbors within five miles was out in the yard with a lantern, or an infrequent car was mov-ing on the Cree road, and then it was almost worse than seeing no light at all, because it was such a faint lost glimmer that it spread the horizons further than ever and deepened instead of lightening the loneliness of wind and dark and stars and empty prairie.

And tomorrow would be the fifty-mile trip in, Gadke's and the horse pasture and the Frenchman's, La Pointe's, and all the kids peeking around the stone foundations of the barn, and then there would be the south bench, the dipping of the road that angled down into the flat river valley, and below them the green belt of willows crooked as a snake-trail in sand, the dull glitter of the river and the folded brown draws down the north bench opposite, and then the town, almost a hundred houses, dozens of kids, greetings and late shivery swims and playing run sheepy run again, and hare and hounds through the river brush.

Before daylight he was awakened by his father's swearing and stamping around in the other room. He lay listening. The stove had run out of kerosene, and all the spare coal oil was packed far down under the mass of household goods in the wagon. The boy got out of bed and dressed swiftly, not wanting to be yelled at for oversleep-ing on a busy morning. But the morning was pretty well spoiled. Pa had got up on the wrong side of bed.

The sun was not yet up, and the prairie outside lay gray and desolate. He turned from the screen and went into the other room, hardly responding to his mother's good morning. There was a dull and dispirited weight on his mind. He couldn't wake up properly, and his mouth kept opening in jaw-cracking yawns.

His father came inside with the kerosene can, saw him standing there stupidly, and told him sharply to do something, for God sake. Did he think the world moved on wheels to get his breakfast and carry him into town? Go up and get the horses.

He went sullenly in the gray light, searching the corners of the pasture for the outlines of the team. In the east light grew, and turning his head he saw the pearly band along the horizon touched with rose. He stumbled in a badger hole and cursed like his father, kicking the mounded earth.

When he returned with the team, breakfast was on the table and his mother was already eating. His father was frying slices of bread in bacon fat. The boy slid into his chair, and his father turned to glower at him. "Have you washed?"

"No," the boy said sullenly. At the bench outside, in the full rosy light, he dabbed his face and hands and threw out the water. The sun's glaring saucer slipped over the flat horizon and touched him. That, and the dash of cold water on his face, made him feel better. The headachy feeling he had waked up to, the sort of feeling he had when a bilious spell was coming on, was almost gone. In a little while, his mind said, they would be heading for Whitemud, and that would be fine.

"Are we going to leave right after breakfast, Mom?"

"I am. I'm going to start with the wagon, and you and Pa are going to finish up here and then you're coming in the car."

The boy looked toward the stove. His father's dark face, even in profile, looked grouchy, dissatisfied, mad. "Ma, I want to go with you."

"I'm afraid you can't," she said. "Pa needs you to help him." She smiled at him, squinting her eyes and warning him, reminding him —not to make a fuss, not to whine, not to get Pa's temper started. He understood her look but he fussed anyway. The prospect of riding all the way with his father was suddenly dreadful to him.

"Well, I want to!" he said. "I want to go in the wagon with you."

"You do as you're told," his father said, and slapped another slice of bread into the pan. The boy sat pouting, accusing his mother silently. She had betrayed him. Her face was weary as she reached out to pat his hand.

"Don't worry," she said. "I won't get very far before you catch me. You can change off then."

He was carrying old boards up to the house for shuttering when his mother climbed into the wagon seat atop the monstrous load and gathered up the lines. He dropped the boards and ran to open the gate, and as the wagon went through with his father walking at the wheel his mother smiled down at the boy and blew him a kiss off the ends of her heavy gloves. She looked so funny up there with a straw hat on that he laughed.

"Don't try to hurry it," his father said. "You've got a heavy load and a colt along. Let the team make its own speed. We'll probably catch you the other side of the horse pasture somewhere."

"All right." Sitting on her high seat, she smiled down on them. "'Bye, son." Her eyes went back to the little round-topped shack on the other side of the coulee, and she stood up to raise an arm. "So long, homestead," she said. "We'll be back!" She met Bo's eyes briefly, held them, and flapped the lines over the horses. The laden wagon creaked heavily, rocking through the burnouts. A hundred feet away she turned and waved, and the boy waved back, mechanically, watching the wagon crawl into the blazing east.

"All right," his father said. "Let's get a move on."

Back at the house he started nailing boards over the two windows, rolling down the porch blinds and cleating them fast. He sent the boy for the three chicken crates saved from the spring, and they ran down all the hens and put them squawking into the boxes. The boy loaded them in the Ford while his father lugged the rain barrel and all the loose tools inside. The plow went into the chicken house, the stoneboat was leaned up against the wall.

Then there was the last-minute gleaning of the house, the loose bundles of odds and ends, the left-over food in a cardboard box, the cat, the dog, the almost-forgotten cigar box of gopher tails, and finally the moment when they stood in the door looking back into the darkened, unfamiliar cave of the house, and the last shutting of the door.

"Want anything to eat before we start?" his father said. He had the box of left-over food, ready to load it into the Ford.

"No," the boy said. "I don't feel very good."

His father looked at him sharply, and his brows drew down. "What do you mean, you don't feel very good?"

"I feel kind of sick to my stomach," the boy said, and stood lugubrious and resentful under his father's harsh glare.

"Oh Jesus," his father said finally. "You would. Well, get in."

The boy walked out to the gate, closed it when the Ford passed through, and climbed in. His father needn't act as if a person got sick just for fun. He belched, testing himself, and thought with forlorn satisfaction that he would probably have to throw up pretty soon. He could feel his insides rolling as the Ford lurched, and he tasted deep inside himself for that old familiar awful bitter taste of a sour stomach. He thought that the belch had had it, just a little.

"How're you feeling?" his father said as they passed Pete and Emil.

"Kind of sick," the boy said. He tasted again, thinking how bad it was that his mother had gone off and left him, and now here he was going to have a bilious spell, and nobody with him but Pa, who didn't ever have any patience with sickness even though he had plenty of sick headaches himself. He belched again, and the gall burned his throat. Misery went through him. He was sick, and all Pa would do about it was to get mad and think he did it on purpose to make things unpleasant. Brine flooded his mouth, he swallowed, belched again, felt the blood drain from his face, and hung onto the side of the car.

"Pa," he said. "Pa, I got to throw up!"

Through his fear and misery he saw his father's sideward face, the exasperation, the irritation just short of swearing, but no sympathy, no pity. He began to bawl, and as the Ford rolled to a stop in the narrow wagon-track he leaned out and vomited over the side.

When Elsa turned to look for the last time she saw the broad body of her husband, the slight one of her son, standing together at the gate, and behind them the shanty and the vanishing line of fence dipping down the coulee. Bruce's figure looked thin, spidery, somehow pathetic, and she waved, watching his arm come up. His face remained steadily fixed in her direction. Poor lamb, he'd had a lonesome summer. It would be a treat for him to get back to town.

The sun's glare was bright in her eyes, and she bent her head away from it. Almost fifty miles to go, and no roads to speak of for the first fifteen, just wagon tracks that split and branched and wandered through the buffalo grass. It would have been much nicer if Brucie could have come with her. Someone to talk to. And he didn't want to ride with Bo. He'd been a little sullen with Bo ever since the shooting of the sparrow. She sighed, wondering if all boys held things against their fathers as a kind of natural reaction against authority, or if Bruce were going to be a grudge-holder, or if maybe —she thought of the hot-cold river and the picnic in the Bearpaws —if he might remember something about that time back in Washington.

She put her foot on the trailing lines and wriggled out of her coat. Letting the team plod on, she pushed up her sleeves and opened the throat of her blouse. It was already hot. The scar on her right arm caught her eye. In six years the shiny red had faded, but it always reacted to sunburn violently, and was redder than the tan of the unharmed skin. There was a ridge of tight scar in the elbow that wouldn't quite let her straighten the arm out. That was one relic of the days she wanted to forget. Could there be, she wondered, another relic in the mind of that child? Would he, at four years, have hatred and fear so burned into him that the scar would never leave?

She laughed at herself and picked up the lines. Put me by myself, she said, just let me sit alone for a few hours, and I'll sure worry something up.

She sat looking at the base of the wagon tongue, watching the singletrees jerk, staring half-seeing at the black hairs snagged in the bolt of the doubletree. Her mind doubled on itself, avoiding things as a horse shies. She didn't want to think of those things. But there was the look on Bruce's face as he watched his father, the old familiar feel in the air of hard times and restlessness, as definite and recognizable as a weather change to a rheumatic old man.

The prairie lay around her, withered and pitted and brown like a very old face, but she didn't see it. Her eyes were fixed on the space between the horses, and her mind went back, beyond Washington, beyond Dakota, back to Minnesota where it started, back to Indian Falls when she was eighteen and had run away from what she couldn't bear, or thought she couldn't bear. Her mother might have stayed and borne it and made some kind of triumph out of it, but when you were eighteen you didn't know what you knew when you were thirty-two, and because you were eighteen and proud and blind and full of high notions you ran away like a coward and called it the only decent thing to do.

She couldn't run away from this, and wasn't going to. Only she wished that the still, breezeless air didn't carry that threat of storm, and that the rheumatic joints of her old worrying mind didn't ache with the fear of something.

She looked up. She was approaching Gadke's, and Mrs. Gadke was in the yard, her apron full of chicken feed. She came to the road to meet the wagon, her greeting so warm and hearty that Elsa heard the loneliness and isolation in it. Farm women were always lonely. There were never enough visitors to satisfy their itch to talk, and up here there were probably not a half dozen a year. She leaned down to shake Mrs. Gadke's hand.

"Well, well!" Mrs. Gadke said. "Moving in again."

Elsa took off her hat and fanned herself and laughed. "Seems like we're always loaded up going somewhere."

"I wish I was," Mrs. Gadke said. She looked at the loaded wagon with envy. "Come in and have a cup of coffee and a bite."

"I shouldn't," Elsa said. "Bo and Bruce are coming in the car, and I ought to be covering ground."

"Oh, come on in," Mrs. Gadke said. "You can spare twenty minutes. We don't see you folks more'n twice a year."

Elsa let herself be tempted down. She sat in the kitchen and had a cup of coffee and looked at Mrs. Gadke's brilliant row of geraniums, more than a dozen, in a wooden box under the window. "Your plants are pretty," she said. "Moving as much as we do, I can't seem to keep flowers going. I just get some nice plants started in town and we have to leave them with somebody or bring them out here, and if we leave them they get forgotten and die, and if we bring them they get broken."

"They're a comfort," Mrs. Gadke said. "But if I could talk Gadke into going in for the winter I'd sure be glad to do without."

"I notice you've got a rose bush outside."

"Gadke put that in for me last spring. It seems to be doing all right. I dump my dishwater on it every day. It's a climbing kind, white blossoms."

"It'll be lovely when it blooms," Elsa said. "There are some people over by us, some English people named Garfield, that have planted trees in their coulee. He used to work in a greenhouse and he thinks they'll grow."

She knew while she said it that she was envying Mrs. Gadke her geraniums and that rose bush, and that she envied the Garfields their trees. But what she really envied in both of them was the permanence they had. They had both made up their minds to settle down and stick, they weren't bonanza farmers gambling against the rains. Or if they gambled, they risked their whole lives, and it was only on that assumption that you could be comfortable in a place.

She rose. "I really have to get on," she said. "It's a long drive in the wagon."

"I s'pose you'll be out again come spring," Mrs. Gadke said. "Plan to stop off and stay the night. Then you could get a good start and have the morning to shake down in your own place."

"Thank you," Elsa said. "That's nice of you." She put her foot on the hub and took hold of the dusty iron tire, hoisting herself up. "I don't know," she said, looking down. "Bo's so discouraged about the crop this year that I don't know whether we'll ever be out again. I had a kind of feeling this morning when I drove off that I was saying goodbye for good."

"Of course you'll be back," Mrs. Gadke said. She stood back as the wagon started, and Elsa turned three times to wave to the stout aproned figure before she dipped down into the first rolling country and climbed off to open the horse-pasture gate. Ahead of her was fifteen miles without house or field, just one immense pasture with herds of horses thundering away from the wagon, standing on high ground to stare with ears up, whickering loudly, curiously, and putting the team into a state of nervousness and scaring the colt so that he hugged his mother's side.

The wagon rocked, the road over the rolling ground was rougher and rockier, and the seat was hard. She folded her coat and sat on it, and the team went steadily. The trees seesawed, the tugs slacked and tightened, the doubletree bolt squeaked, and she felt the weight of the wagon like a falling thing whenever the wheels rolled solidly over a hump and jounced down.

You never like what you've got, she was thinking. Mrs. Gadke, with something permanent and good started there, wanted to leave it and come to town for the winter. You had to stay in a place to make it a home. A home had to be lived in every day, every month, every year for a long time, till it was worn like an old shoe and fitted the comfortable curvatures of your life.

It was almost eleven before she heard the tooting of the Ford's horn, and looked back to see it behind her. She turned off the road and stopped, and Bruce got out of the car and into the seat beside her. Elsa took one look at his greenish-white face and wrapped her arms around him.

"Oh, what's the matter?" she said.

"Sick to his stomach," Bo said from the car. His lips went down in a wry, deprecatory grimace.

Stroking the boy's thin back, Elsa said, "Maybe he should go on with you. I'll be hours behind."

"He doesn't want to go with me," Bo said, and pressed his lips together.

She saw that he was irritable, sore, exasperated, ready to bite. "All right," she said. "You go on then."

She watched him pull ahead in the trail. Bruce lay down with his feet in her lap and his straw hat over his face. Within a mile they came to the other edge of the pasture. Bo had left the gate open, and she knew from that how cranky he was. He was usually as fussy as an old woman about gates.

When she got up again after closing it, Bruce was sitting up, looking forlorn and pinched around the mouth.

"Feel better?"

"No," he said sullenly.

"You'd better lie down again."

"I don't want to lie down."

She let him have his contrary way while they rocked over the last mile of ruts to the junction with the Robsart road. He wanted, she knew, to be sympathized with, and if he wanted that, he wasn't as sick as he pretended to be. When he got a real sick headache he was in bed for two days.

Bruce squirmed sullenly. He said, "Pa got mad at me for being sick."

"You couldn't help being sick," she said. "He wouldn't get mad at you for that."

"Well, he did."

"Pa's just disappointed about the crop," she said. "He's got a lot of worries on his mind. He wasn't mad at you."

The boy pulled his straw hat down over his eyes and glowered under the brim. "I hate Pa!" he said.

Elsa reached out and shook him hard. "I don't want you talking like that. Understand?"

His shoulders contracted under her hands, and bending to look at his face she saw his old expression of stony, stubborn implacability. It was useless to try to talk to him when he wore that look, but she shook him again anyway, and said, "Pa's doing the best he can. That's all any of us can do. We've all got to do the best we can and help all we can."

She said no more to him for a long time, and there was nothing on the road to interest him. He sat for a while slumped, lurching with the wagon, thinking how he hated his father and how when he got big enough he would run away and after a while he would come back rich and well dressed and grown up, and take Chet and Ma away to live with him, and if Pa wanted to come too he'd just turn his big McLaughlin around and drive off and leave him standing there.

After a time he lay down, and his mother said, "Feeling sick again?"

"No."

"You might as well keep lying down anyway," she said. "It'll be three hours at least before we're there. You can go right to bed when we get back."

"I feel all right."

He lay quietly, his straw hat over his face and his legs sprawled over the boxes piled in front of the seat. His mind slipped away from how he hated his father, caught for a spiteful minute, wandered off again to consider what he would do when they got to town. The thought of town made him squirm his back and keep his eyes shut the way he did when he was having a nice dream and didn't want to wake up. He nursed the pictures that came to him, went painstakingly around and through everything that town meant, and everything that made summer and winter different.

In summer it was the farm, and freedom and loneliness and the clean sharpening of the senses, the feeling of strong personal identity in the midst of a wide, cleanly-bounded world; but the rest of the year it was the town, sunk in its ancient river valley hemmed in by the bench hills, and that was another life.

That life centered around the three houses on the cutbank side of the west bend, and the bath houses behind, on the bank, that the boy got to use only for a short time in the spring. In winter they were used as storehouses by the three families in that end of the town. His feet knew the path, rutted hard with frost or deep in snow, that went out past the barn to the bath houses; his fingers knew the cut of the bail and the icy slop of water as he lugged buckets from the chopped hole in the river ice, staggering lopsidedly up the dugway from the footbridge head. His fingers knew too the sticky bite of a frosty doorknob, they knew the clumsy fumbling with the bath house key when he was sent out to bring a chunk of frozen beef or pork in from the still, cold, faintly urine-and-wet-bathing-suit-smelling shanty. His nose knew bath house smell and barn smell and kitchen smell and the smell of baking paint behind the redhot parlor heater, and those were town.

Town was Preacher Morrison and the Sunday school parties where they played beanbag and crocinole. It was birthday parties the girls gave, and the bolt of hair-ribbon that Mr. Orullian cut from when you went in to spend your two bits for a present. It was McGregor's hardware store with the smell of stove blacking and turpentine and the tallowy smell of the baled muskrat skins on the back counter. It was the Pastime Movie Theater where every Friday night there was a new installment of *The Black Box* or *Tarzan of the Apes* or *The Red Ace*. It was the boys, Weddie Orullian or Preacher-Kid Morrison that the cave caved in on last spring, or Bill Brewer or the Heathcliff kids from across the river, the bunch he went skating with around the river's bitter bends, spreading his mackinaw to the wind on the way back and skimming like a bird up to the fires and slush and noise by the cutbank.

Town was many things, was the irrigation dam of old man Purcell where they trapped muskrats and weasels and once a mink, the willow breaks where in late fall the gang of little kids built huts of branches, playing they were holing up for the winter—huts which the Big-Kid gang, Chet among them, always discovered and tore down. It was the smell of dry willow leaves crushed and rolled in tissue paper and smoked, the taste of wild rose hips nibbled on an October afternoon, the numb blue-white of snow moons when the crowd of them rode on a bob behind Pete Purcell's pony up the long Swift Current hill, their handsleds stretched out in a black line behind. It was the game they played after a heavy blizzard, when they tun-

neled down through the overhanging drifts piled against the cutbanks, making a smooth packed burrow through which they could
dive in a breathless belly-ride and skid snowy and yelling onto the
river ice.

The town was Whitemud, Saskatchewan, what Bo Mason, when he
was disgusted, was likely to call a dirty little dung-heeled sagebrush
town. But to the boy it was society, civilization, a warm place of home
where his mother sat sewing long hours under the weak light of the
north windows, singing sometimes to herself, making dresses for girls
who were going to be married or for women who lived up on Millionaire Row. The town was school, the excitement of books, the Ridpath
History of the World that he had read entirely through by his eighth
birthday. His mother, telling that to neighbors, always spoke with
awe in her voice, and her pride in his brains sent him scrabbling for
anything else in the old bookcase upstairs that he had not already
read. Mostly it was novels like *The Rock in the Baltic* and *Graustark*
and *The Three Musketeers*.

Town, home, was that and more. It was the steel engravings in
Ridpath, the "Rape of the Sabine Women" that he puzzled over
and finally asked his mother about, to be told that he shouldn't be
so everlastingly curious. It was the sixth grade room where they
sang "God Save the King" and "In Days of Yore from Britain's
Shore" and "The March of the Men of Harlech," and the boy sang
with tears in his eyes because the songs were heroic and Miss Crow's
brother was in the army and Canada was at war with the Huns.

Bruce was a better scholar than Chet, but Chet was a better singer,
and in all the cantatas the school gave. Chet was strong, too, and had
licked Weddie Orullian and Pete Purcell and had almost licked Tad
McGovern.

Town was things that had happened, like the time he had shot
himself through the toe with Chet's .22, the numb moment before he
knew he was hurt, when he thought somebody had hit him in
the foot with a rock, and stood there with the .22 in his hand wondering what had made the noise, until he saw the sole ripped clear
off his shoe, and the leather bloody.

Town was winter, the river ice full of air bubbles like silver coins,
and the wonder of a Chinook in the midst of bitter cold, when he
woke to the wail of a blizzard and looked out to see no blizzard at
all, but a thaw, the eaves of Chance's house dripping, the roof melted
black, the ground a lake of slush and water, and the wind coming

through the three little portholes of the storm windows warm as milk. Town was the four-gabled white house his father had built when the town was first settled in 1914, the room where he and Chet lay in bed making pictures of dragons and trains and animals and angels among the blotches left by the firemen's chemicals when the attic had caught fire. It was the parlor downstairs, the piano his mother was so fond of, the big-bellied Round Oak stove with the asbestos pad underneath and the scuttle of lignite behind it.

It was his mother darning, and sometimes his father reading or reciting Robert W. Service:

This is the law of the Yukon, and ever she makes it plain.
Send not your foolish and feeble, send but your strong and your
  sane . . .

Sometimes too it was stories, when his father was feeling good, exciting stories about the Wisconsin woods and the Terrible Swede and little Pete the Wanigan boy and Paul Bunyan and Hot Biscuit Slim. When the boys were finally shooed off to bed, going reluctantly up the cold stairs and looking back wanting more, Bruce always had a strong feeling of home and warmth and security on nights like that, when his father was jovial and full of yarns. He knew his mother liked those too. She never had the tired look in her shoulders, the puckery squint around her eyes, the habit of looking as if she saw something through the wall.

His mother's hand touched him, and she said, "Well, son, there's the big city."

He sat up and looked. They were starting down the dugway. Below them lay the river valley and the looping bends, and at the top of the big U-bend the houses of Whitemud. He pushed his hat back and watched as they went down carefully, the wooden brake shoes sizzling on the tires like sandpaper, the horses' rumps hunched back, braced into the breeching against the push of the load. The colt limped along beside Daisy, fell behind, trotted tiredly to catch up.

"Poor little thing," Elsa said. "That's an awful trip for a poor little colt."

Bruce snapped his fingers and whistled at the lagging colt. "Come on, Peggie," he said. "We're pretty near there."

"Glad?" his mother said.

"Uh huh."

"So am I," she said, and laughed. "Or I would be if I knew what we were going to live on this winter."

V

What, said Bo to himself, sitting and thinking, trying to figure away the winter that stretched ahead, would an Indian do to make sure of eating for those seven months? How would some pioneer off in the wilderness provide for his family?

There were the cows and the chickens. He had already figured them, one cow fresh and one due to freshen in two months. There might be a little milk to sell, and there might be a few extra eggs from their dozen hens. But that was almost all. The jobs he could do he had done. He had spent three frantic weeks cutting fall hay on the north bench, had borrowed a baler so that he'd be able to get more into the small loft he had. There might be some of that to sell, if he turned the horses loose on the range and kept only the cows and the colt inside. And he had hauled five wagon-loads of lignite from the hillside west of the railroad bridge, enough to keep them warm for the winter. It was lousy fuel, half ash and half rock, but it was better than nothing, and it was free.

So, he said, figuring, they could keep warm and they could depend on milk and eggs. They might make a dime a day from their extra milk, maybe thirty cents a day when the muley freshened. There might be thirty or forty dollars' worth of extra hay. The town owed him ten dollars for his annual job of taking out the footbridge before the river froze over.

And that was all. That was absolutely, by God, he thought angrily, that was absolutely all. The little money he had got from the wheat would pay their bills and buy a few necessities, but there wouldn't be anything left in the spring for seed, for summer supplies, for anything.

Grind your own wheat? he said. Slaughter your own hogs? If you had a hog. Might be a good idea to try picking one up, even this late. It was cheaper on the hoof than it was in Heimie's shop. A beef was out, but he might find some farmer who was slaughtering and had a quarter to spare. But what else? There had to be something else. What would an Indian do?

Game? He considered it, weighing the cost of shells against the possible addition to the food supply. In Dakota they had sometimes frozen ducks and geese down. And fur. There were all those traps of the kids', and the north bench was full of muskrat sloughs. And fur was high. It would be small pickings, maybe, but better than sitting on your pratt.

He rose from the table, went to the window and looked into the square of front yard that two years ago had been hopefully seeded to lawn. The two spruces that he had gone clear up to the Cypress Hills for stood withered and dead at the corners of the house. That was the way with everything in the whole damn town. It started out big and just dwindled away.

He compressed his lips, breathed in a great lungful of air, went to the cellarway and took out his shotgun. The hell with just sitting around wondering and figuring. He would fill that bath house so full of meat, by God, that they'd eat duck three times a day and have some left over for the Fourth of July.

So through the waning days of mid-October, in the chill, leaden, snow-spitting weather, he spent days on the north bench after ducks. He built a blind and sat patiently for whole mornings at a time with his feet slowly going dead through the heavy socks and waders, watching the sky and the bobbing decoys riding the shallow, riffled water. He sat in the wind with the mangy dogskin coat around his ears, and when a flock circled and came back he crouched lower, shaking the coat off onto the packed damp tules, and as they came in he let them have it, taking no chances, trying no fancy shots, letting them come clear down even, shooting sitting birds, because there was no limit in this kind of hunting. He was after a winter's meat.

The first day, red-nosed and windburned, he brought in fourteen ducks. The next day he got only eight. The day after that he had a carful of teal and mallard and spoonbill, and one goose. In a week he brought in over a hundred birds. They had eaten duck until the very sight of one turned their stomachs, Elsa and the boys had plucked ducks until their fingers were sore (because duck down, Bo said, made good pillows, and pillows were things people always wanted. Elsa could get some ticking and make a lot of pillows and you ought to get a buck apiece for them).

He was driven by such a furious compulsion to fill the house with game that Elsa laughed at him, asking him when he was going to start saving tea-lead and string, and he was irritated and hurt that she couldn't see how necessary it was to save every penny. For himself, he was a miser. The thought of all the money he had squandered in the past ten years tortured him. The necessity of saving everything, making use of everything, living off the land, was an obsession that hardly let him sleep. Elsa tried to make him stop. People were talking about the flu that was spreading around the country. John Chapman said that if it came anywhere close he was hitting for California. It would be a hard and cold and long winter even if the flu didn't get to them, and Bo's going out and catching pneumonia in a slough wouldn't make it any easier.

She might as well have saved her breath. He kept up his hunting, she picked a dozen or two dozen ducks every day, there were gunny sacks full of duck feathers waiting to be made into pillows when she got time. The ducks themselves they hung out to freeze, and then strung up in long lines in the bath house, but it was early in the season for freezing down meat, and Elsa eyed them dubiously, afraid they might all spoil.

They did. The weather turned warm, the frozen ground softened and turned to mud. Bo was in a frenzy. A hundred ducks out there, enough for fifty meals, two months' meat, and the damned thermometer jumped up to forty-five degrees. He rushed down to Heimie Gross to see if they could be packed in Heime's ice-house, but Heimie's ice-house was nothing but damp sawdust. There wouldn't be any ice until the river froze.

"God damn!" Bo said. He stood for a minute, thinking, and then started toward home, took the key from the kitchen door, and went out to the bath house. It felt cold inside when he stepped in, but not cold enough. He felt one of the ducks hanging from the wire. Beginning to soften. He swore again, his eyes darting around the bare room with the benches, the dirty inscriptions, the nails where clothes and bathing suits were hung in the summer.

There was a step outside, and Elsa looked in. "How are they?" she said. She held her hand up, feeling the air. "It feels pretty cold yet. Maybe they'll last till night, and it'll get colder then."

He shook his head, looking at the strings of ducks, fat, meaty, their necks stretched from hanging and their webbed feet dangling. "Have you got any empty fruit sealers?"

"A dozen or so, maybe." She looked doubtfully at the ducks. "Would that work?"

"Well, something's got to work!" he shouted at her. "Have you got any better ideas?"

"It seems a shame," she said. "The jars I've got wouldn't save more than a few."

"I know that." He clicked his teeth, wanting to cut loose and kick the bench away from the wall. Violent impulses jumped in his hands and feet, and he went abruptly outside. Elsa came after him.

"I'll go get the jars boiling," she said hurriedly, and with a side glance at him went back to the house.

Bo stood where he was, looking out over the cutbank, across the river to the low thick scrub of willow and alder and black birch. It never failed. You worked your head off and then something went sour. His mind groped for an object to curse, something to vent his anger on. A tin can lay at his feet, and with one swing he booted it thirty feet into the river.

Well, there were only four ways of preserving meat that he knew of. Freezing was out because of the thaw, canning would take care of only a few ducks, and jars were too expensive to buy. Drying was out of the question in this weather. So there was only smoking left. He had never heard of smoked duck, but by God there was going to be plenty of smoked duck this winter. He locked the bath house door, and lurching in his haste, started for the barn to get tools and boards to knock together a smokehouse.

At the end of five days he gave up. The ducks which had hung in the smoke, wizened, dried, blackened things, were rubbery and evil-tasting. The combination of gamy flavor and smoke was enough, he said, to turn the stomach of a vulture. He tasted them raw, and they sickened him. He boiled one, and the smell drove him from the house. Finally he threw the whole lot of them in the river, and all they had from his furious hunting was a dozen jars of canned duck and a few of duck soup.

By October 28 the river was filmed with brittle ice under the wagons coming down from the bench and fording below Purcell's. There were many wagons. Bo, driven to prowl the town and sit in Anderson's poolhall, saw two dozen men he did not recognize, and the street was full of strange women and children. The town wore a look of unaccustomed activity, as if for Thanksgiving or Christmas, but there was little holiday feeling. Faces were long and talk somber, and they talked of three things: the war, the price of food, and the flu.

Bo had been too busy to pay any attention to the flu, but listening to the farmers who hung around the poolhall he heard the fear in their talk. Out on the prairie, miles from town or a doctor, a man got thinking. There was never a winter that some homesteader didn't get snowed in, or break his leg or cut himself with an ax and then sit there in his shanty unable to help himself, sitting with his sheepskin on and all his blankets over that, hoarding his fuel, while his wound festered and swelled and the shack got colder, and almost every spring some such homesteader was found frozen stiff. Suppose, then, a whole family got sick with this flu, and no help around, and winter setting in solid and cold three weeks early?

It was supposing things like this that drove in the homesteaders in wagons piled with goods, to settle down on some relative or friend or in vacant rooms. Three families had gone together and cobbled up a shack, half house and half tent, in the curve of the willows east of the elevators. Even a tent in town was better, in these times, than a house out on the bitter flats.

The papers they read didn't reassure them. On both coasts the hospitals were jammed, the army camps were crowded with sick soldiers, whole inland parts of the country were virtually isolated. Because there was no safe place to run to, people stayed, but they took it easy about going outdoors, they doctored colds as if they were pneumonia, they kept their children home from school if a sniffle was heard in the primary room, they soused their handkerchiefs with the eucalyptus oil that Henderson the druggist said was a preventative. And they sat in Anderson's poolhall and talked.

Once Bo sat for a solid hour hearing how the disease turned you black as ink just before it killed you, and how people in the last stages rose from their beds and ran screaming and gibbering through the streets, foaming at the mouth and biting anyone who got in their way. Bo hawked in disgust and got up to take a drink from the waterpail in back. As he lifted the dipper he saw the yellow-green moss coating the tin bottom, and dumped the water angrily on the floor. With his fingernail he traced a skull and crossbones in the bottom of the dipper, digging the scum off clear to the stained metal, and hung the thing up again. No wonder these guys were scared of the flu. They had a right to be, with things like that left around to drink out of.

Back at the bar, sticky and smelling sweetly of strawberry pop, he drummed his fingers on the counter and looked at Ed Anderson. Ed had had an eye knocked out by an exploding pop bottle the year before, and wore a black patch. "I don't suppose you've got a bottle of beer in the joint," Bo said.

Mopping off the counter, Ed turned to spit at a hidden spittoon. "I would if I could, boy," he said. "You just can't get it, even if the cops would let you sell it."

Bo drummed again, looking out the dirty windows into the street. He turned his head and inspected the half dozen men hanging around the front end, and cleaned his teeth with his tongue. Bunch of dung-footed dirt farmers. He contemplated them with contempt, wondering if it would do any good to try getting up a little stud game. But he gave it up immediately. If they were too leaded to play pool, they wouldn't play poker. They didn't even have spirit enough to crab about the prohibition law that kept them from having a schooner of beer.

"What's the matter with this town?" he said irritably. "Isn't there anybody in it with gumption enough to start a blind pig, even? What's the matter with you, Ed? You don't look like a Christer."

"I ain't any Christer," Ed said. "But I'm telling you, you can't get it. Where'd I buy it?"

"There must be somebody got it for sale. When I was selling beer on the road in Dakota I did my whole business with blind pigs."

The half dozen loungers were all looking at him. "What I wish," one said, "is that you could get a bottle of good strong liquor-sauce in this place. If that old flu lights around here I want to crawl in bed with a bottle."

"Ain't it the truth," Ed said. "If I had ten cases behind this bar I could sell out in three days."

"You could get five bucks a bottle for it, too," Bo said.

Ed's one eye, pale, with strained red streaks in it, opened in agreement, and he jerked his head sideways to shoot at the spittoon again. "You tell 'em," he said. "If a guy wants something bad enough, he'll pay anything."

Bo stood up. "Well," he said, "if bullshitting around would get a man a drink, I'd be stiff as a plank now. Anybody want to shoot a game of pool?"

Nobody did. Dissatisfied and aimless, he got into the dogskin and wandered outside. Weddie Orullian's great wife, thick and pillowy and wide as a sidewalk, the mother of nine children and enormous now with her tenth, went up the street on the other side and waved a bulky arm, grinning and yelling at him. Bo waved back. That old squaw, common as manure, but she had fun. About the only cheerful thing in the whole damn town.

He was disgusted, vaguely grouchy, irrationally sore at the farmers who sat around Anderson's all day and couldn't think of anything to do but tell bear stories about the flu. Every one of them wanted a drink or a bottle, but would they do anything to get it? They'd sit on their behinds and cry, that was all they'd do. It was only a hundred miles to Chinook, less than that to some of the smaller Montana towns. If they wanted a drink as bad as they said, they could drive over any time, get a carload, bring it back into Canada over any of a hundred little unwatched wagon-track trails . . .

In the middle of the plank sidewalk he stopped short. An incredulous laugh burst out of him. "Holy jumping Jesus!" he said softly. "I've been sitting right on top of a gold mine!"

Briefly, automatically, he wished for Jud. Jud was the only partner he had ever had, a guy you could depend on to come in on anything worth a gamble. But Jud was dead in Alaska, and there was nobody in town he could go to for money, nobody he wanted to cut into this proposition. The only possibility was Chapman, at the bank, and Chapman would have to be talked to like a Dutch uncle.

As he passed McKenna's store on the way to the bank another thought struck him, and he turned up the stairs to Dr. O'Malley's office. The doctor was in, sitting on his desk. He had a young, fresh face and an easy grin, and his sleeves, even in the chilly office, were rolled up above the elbows. Bo noticed that his arms were brown and corded with muscle. The kid was more man than he looked.

"Want to ask you a question," Bo said.

"Shoot."

"About this flu."

O'Malley's eyebrows lifted. "I've been answering that one for three weeks. Stay out of drafts, avoid catching cold, don't go outside when you're overheated, don't hang around in crowds or go to the picture palace." He grinned. "And pray," he said.

Bo grunted. "That isn't the question. I want to know if whiskey is good for the flu."

"Whiskey's good for almost anything," O'Malley said. "Except d.t.'s. Why?"

"It's a medicine, isn't it? You'd say it was good medicine for this influenza."

O'Malley laughed. "I guess it must be medicine. The druggist's the only person in town allowed to sell it. I've worn out a prescription pad helping him."

"That's all I want to know. Thanks."

The doctor's puzzled frown followed him to the door. With one hand on the knob Bo turned. "How's your own stock?"

"I haven't got any," O'Malley said. "I'm not in the liquor business. Sell you some nice ipecac."

"I don't want to buy any. I'm asking you if you want to buy any." He shoved his hands deep into the pockets of the dogskin. "They've been saying that if the flu hits here the town'll be quarantined. Is that right?"

"Yes."

"And if it's quarantined there won't be any trains in or out."

"No."

"And if there aren't any trains there won't be any more supplies for Henderson."

"I asked him already to lay in a lot of salts and quinine and eucalyptus oil. We'll be cut off for a while, sure."

"But you didn't have him lay in any whiskey. Want me to bring you some?"

O'Malley sat down on the desk and slowly rolled down his sleeves, buttoning them neatly around his wrists. "It's against the law, you know."

"This is an emergency," Bo said.

"If it weren't," O'Malley said, "I wouldn't be talking to you. How much do you want for Irish?"

Bo guessed, guessing plenty high. "Six dollars a bottle."

"I'm used to paying around three and a half," the doctor said.

"But you haven't been able to get any."

The doctor stood up and reached for his coat on the hanger. "How much for a case?"

"Make it to you for sixty-five."

O'Malley rummaged in a drawer, came out again empty-handed, and faced Bo. "All right," he said. "Only there's this. Are you going to Montana after it?"

"I didn't say."

The doctor's voice sharpened. "I have to know, just the same. A lot of towns in Montana are quarantined already. I can connive to break the liquor law in an emergency, but if you're breaking quarantines to bring this whiskey in, I'm out."

"You needn't worry," Bo said. "The place I'm getting this isn't quarantined."

O'Malley held his eyes a minute. "All right," he said shortly. "A case of Irish, Bushmill's or Jameson's."

Bo nodded and went downstairs again, his mind jumping with figures. It was a dead immortal cinch. If he couldn't buy a case of Irish for thirty-five at the most, he'd kiss a pig. Maybe less, if he bought a lot, ten cases or so. His mind jumped again. Ten! The old Lizzie ought to carry twelve or fifteen. Maybe get a pony cask and decant it, sell plain old corn for three bucks a bottle . . .

John Chapman was sitting alone in the bank, peeling an apple carefully, the unbroken spiral peel hanging like a shaving as he turned the fruit. Bo watched him till the peel fell into the waste-basket, watched him halve and then quarter the white meat, and then asked for his loan: two hundred dollars for two weeks.

Chapman deliberated. There was already a mortgage on Bo's house, and no payment on the principal for a year and a half. "What security?" he said.

"How about my team?"

Very tall and bulky, Chapman sat and spread his hands. "If you didn't meet your obligation I couldn't get two hundred for a team. I couldn't get a hundred, this time of year."

"Listen," Bo said. "This is no bread-and-butter loan, see? I'll have that money back to you in a week, maybe less. You can have the team, the colt, two cows, and anything else you think you want if you'll let me have two hundred right now, American money."

"You sound pretty sure of yourself," Chapman said.

"It's foolproof," said Bo. "I don't even give a damn what interest you charge me, because I'll be paying this back before you know it's out of your safe."

A half hour later he went home carrying a bag of American silver dollars and some bills, all the American money Chapman had.

He kept the bag hidden under the hall seat until after supper, when the boys were sent up to bed. Even then he did not bring it out, but sat figuring. He ought to be able to get fifty dollars a case for good liquor, and if he couldn't buy it for around twenty-five there was something wrong. He could double his money. And suppose he got a twenty-gallon keg of corn. It shouldn't cost more than five dollars a gallon that way, and he could get three dollars a quart just like spitting in a stove door. Gold mine! he said. I hope to whisk in your piskers it's a gold mine.

He lifted his eyes and looked at Elsa, her head bent over her darning. "How much money have we got?"

She smiled. "Figuring again?"

"There's nothing wrong with knowing where you stand. Have we got any left?"

"I paid McKenna and the hardware store," she said, "and I laid out what we owe Hoffman for seed. There's not much left."

"Well, let's count it up and see. The less there is the easier it is to count."

While she was upstairs getting her purse he slipped into the hall, got the bag, and concealed it under his chair. Elsa came down and laid the purse on the table. "There's our worldly wealth," she said, and laughed.

Bo opened the purse and counted out a hundred and twenty-two dollars. The hundred he smoothed out, folded, smoothed again, and laid aside. The twenty-two he put back in the purse. Elsa watched him. He could see the curiosity and the anxiety in her face.

"What would you say," he said, "if I told you I could turn that hundred into two hundred and forty in three days?" He lifted the bills between his fingers, passed the other hand over them, waved his fingers. "Nothing up the sleeve," he said. He opened his right hand. "Nothing in the hand. Presto, chango, pffft!" He palmed the bills and showed her his empty hands and grinned. "Three days from now I'll make it return with a hundred and forty more."

The anxiety had not left her face. "You've got some deal on. What is it?"

"Starting with three hundred dollars," he said, "I can be worth over six hundred by the end of the week."

"But you haven't got three hundred to start."

He reached under the chair and got the bag, set it with a metallic clump on the table, untied the neck and poured a flood of silver dollars on the cloth.

"Well, where on earth . . . !" she said.

Expertly he stacked two piles of dollars, shuffled them, melted them into one pile with a smooth drawing motion. "We're out of the woods," he said.

She was facing him with her hands on the table, as if ready to rise. "Where did you get this?"

"Borrowed it."

"Who from?"

"Chapman."

"But . . ."

He got up and went around to her. "This is how it is," he said with his hands on her shoulders. "The flu'll hit us sure. It's already in Regina. And when it comes there won't be any way of getting in and out, or of bringing medicine in. So I'm going after some, to Chinook. I talked with the sawbones this afternoon."

"But why should you have to borrow all this money?"

"Because I'm making the profit. You know what the best medicine for flu is?"

"Eucalyptus oil?" she said. "I don't know."

"Good old-fashioned corn whiskey. So I'm going out like an old St. Bernard with a keg around my neck."

He felt her stiffen under his hands, and she leaned forward. "Whiskey business!" she said.

"It isn't whiskey business," he said in irritation. "Their damn fool prohibition law might kill off the whole town. Ask Doc O'Malley. He wants a case of Irish himself."

She stared across the table at the stacks of dollars. "What if you get caught?"

"Oh, caught! Who's going to be running around that prairie trying to catch anybody? Anyway it's a medical emergency."

When she said nothing for a long time he pulled her chair sideways and looked at her face. "You still don't like it," he said.

"I hate to see you get into that illegal business again," she said. "And it's dangerous. What if a blizzard came up, or you got sick on the road?"

"I might dislocate my jaw yawning, too," he said. "Hell, I can drive over there and back in less than two days."

"I wonder," she said. "I bet you it's snowing right now."

He went to the window and looked. The yellow panes of Chance's house, next door, were streaked with wavering white. "It isn't even the end of October yet," he said. "This'll be gone by morning. Even if it isn't I can wait a day."

Elsa came up and took his arm, and he looked down at her worried face. "Bo," she said, "I wish you wouldn't."

For a moment he stood, almost hating her, hating the way she and the kids hung on him and held him back, loaded him with responsibilities and then hamstrung him when he tried to do anything. His teeth clicked, but he waited till the anger passed. "Look," he said wearily. "This town's played out. It played out two or three years ago. Do you think I'd be sticking around here if it wasn't for you and the kids? I'd be off somewhere where there was money to be made, wouldn't I? Well, I'm sticking here, but you can't expect me not to make a living any way I can."

"You brought us up here," she said. "You said you didn't want to live anywhere without us. I believed you then, Bo."

In spite of himself he heard his voice rising, and he faced her, shaking-handed. "I'm sticking," he shouted. "I haven't run away, have I? I built you a house and made you a home, didn't I? But how in hell are we going to live in it without any money?"

Elsa looked at him, silent for a moment. "All right," she said. "I said when I came back that I'd never try to interfere with you again. I made up my mind that I was your wife and I'd stay your wife, no matter what. But I just want you to remember, Bo, that I never asked for more than we had. I'd have been satisfied with just a bare living, if we could only keep what we've had up here. So don't ever say you did this for me or them. Don't ever forget that I was against it."

Their eyes held for a moment, and he turned half away to look out the window. After a minute Elsa's hand touched his arm lightly. "Poor Bo," she said. When he turned back her eyes were shining with tears.

"Poor Elsa, you mean," he said. "Oh damn it, honey, you think I like to see us down to a hundred bucks with a whole winter ahead?"

"I know you don't," she said. She moved against him and he put his arms around her. "What you don't see," she said, "what you'll never see, is that there are things ten times worse than being poor."

"I guess I never will," he said. "Maybe you think it would be fun to go hungry, but I don't."

"So you still think you'll go."

He held her tightly against him, looking over her head at the open sack of money on the table, and his mind shut hard and tight. "I've got to," he said. "Whether you see it or not."

It still snowed in the morning, not heavily, but persistently, with a driving wind. For a few minutes Bo contemplated going away, but it was too thick, and with all the homesteaders crowded into the towns there would be no place to stop along the road if anything went wrong. So he spent the day canvassing the town discreetly, getting orders for five cases more without even propositioning the crowd at Anderson's. They were bulk-rye prospects anyway.

That afternoon he worked on the Ford in the shed. Under the seat he put a half dozen cans of canned heat, two spare sparkplugs, a couple pair of chains, and a little bottle of ether, trying to prepare for any sort of emergency. When a car wouldn't start, he had heard, a little ether in the sparkplug wells was like turpentine on a balky mule. With all that whiskey aboard he wasn't going to run any chance of getting stuck. He even cut up an old horse blanket, doubled it, and sewed it into a crude cover for the radiator. If the weather turned cold the radiator could freeze even with the motor running, and you wouldn't know it till you cracked the head or did some real damage.

There was gasoline left from the drum to fill the tank and a five gallon can. At the last minute, looking around for final preparations, Bo took out the back seat and set it against the wall. The car would hold more with the seat out.

After supper he sat in the kitchen while Elsa fried a chicken for his box lunch. It was Hallowe'en, and the boys were both out. Bo kept going to the door and looking out. The snow had stopped, but the ground was humped with drifts, and it was still blowing. From the direction of town he heard the distant yelling of kids.

"If those shysters come horsing around the shed and bung up that car I'll fill their behinds with birdshot," he said.

"It's locked, isn't it?"

"Locks don't stop kids when they get going on a tear."

"I'll stay up and watch," she said. "You should get to sleep early."

He looked at her curiously, wondering how much she still objected, how much she was swallowing. She had a habit of swallowing things, and then years later you discovered that she hadn't forgotten them.

The kitchen door swung open, and Chet and Bruce rushed in. Their noses were red and leaking with the cold, their eyes starting out.

"The flu's hit town!" they said in a breathless burst. "Old Mrs. Rieger's got it."

Bo shut the door. "How do you know?"

"Mr. McGregor said. We were out behind the Chinks', and he called us and said not to play any tricks because the flu was in town, and now all the kids are distributing flu masks and eucalyptus oil and we're going back right now."

"No you're not," Bo said. He looked at Elsa. "You chase these snickelfritzes up to bed. I'm going uptown to see what's going on."

"You won't be able to go now," she said, and the relief in her voice made him mad. "The town will be quarantined."

"That quarantine's nothing but a word," he said. "The town really needs the stuff now."

"Go where?" Chet said.

His father pushed him into the dining room. "None of your beeswax. Go on up to bed, both of you."

An hour uptown told him nothing he didn't know. Nobody would be allowed in or out of town, but that just made him grin. He could imagine people sitting out along the roads in the cold to warn people. Like hell. They'd be sealed up tight in their houses. At ten o'clock he went home from the darkened and deserted main street, stoked the parlor heater for the night, and went up to bed. All the actual coming of the flu did was to make it surer that he could sell all the whiskey the Ford would carry.

2

In the clear, gray-and-white morning he carried blankets and lunch box out to the shed. The snow had blown during the night, and a foot-deep drift with a deep bluish hollow at its inner edge curved around the corner of the barn. The thermometer read twenty-two above zero. The Ford smelled cold; it was hard to imagine that anything so cold would ever start.

Dumping the blankets and lunch, he went back to the house, dipped two steaming pails of water from the waterjacket of the range, and lugged them back out. They took careful pouring in the tiny hole, and he squinted in the gray indoor light, concentrating. When he had the radiator full he bent to feel the crank, engaged it, tried a half turn. It was like trying to lift the car with one hand. The cold oil gave heavily, reluctantly, to the crankshaft's turning. Whistling through his teeth, he went around to adjust spark and gas levers and switch the key to battery. Then with one finger hooked in the choke wire he bent and heaved, fighting the stiff inwards of the motor around. On his cheek he could feel the dim warmth of the water he had poured in.

Three minutes of laborious heaving loosened the crankshaft a little. He pulled the choke full out and threw his whole weight into the spin. After two ponderous twirls the motor coughed.

"Ha!" he said. He spun again, and again it coughed. It was a good feeling to have that stubborn frozen block of complicated metal giving before his pressure. He felt strong, heavy, able to twist the Ford any way he wanted to. The muscles hardened in his shoulder, and he heaved.

The motor coughed, caught, roared, died again in spite of his frantic coaxing of the choke wire. Another spin and it roared again, banging his knuckles against the mudguard. He choked it in quick bursts, laid his shoulder against the radiator to hold back the Ford's trembling, nuzzling eagerness, and watching his chance, ran around to pull down the spark and push up the gas lever. Only a frantic grab at the choke kept it from dying, and he nursed it carefully, leaning far inside the side-curtained darkness of the front seat. The switch to magneto was crucial: she survived it. He slipped the gas lever up and down, and she roared.

Okay, you old bugger, he said, and leaving it running, went back to the house sucking his skinned knuckles.

The boys were up, crowding their bottoms into the oven door and regarding the preparations with blurred and wondering eyes. Bo warmed his hands briefly before pulling on the big double mitts. When he picked up the bag of money he met Elsa's sober look.

"Now don't you worry, Sis."

"How can I help worrying? A thousand things could happen."

"You never saw me get into anything I couldn't get out of, did you?"

"There's always a first time," she said.

"Where's Pa going?" Chet said.

"Just on a little trip," Elsa said. She reached up to touch Bo's cheek. "Be awfully careful," she said.

He bent and kissed her, sparred a moment with the boys in farewell, and eyed them all seriously from the doorway. It wouldn't do to get into any trouble on this trip, with the flu in town. "You stay close," he said to Elsa. "I ought to be back tomorrow night, but if I'm not, don't worry. Something might hold me up till the day after."

He ducked out, swinging the heavy bag of dollars, and ran down the path, feeling light, agile, like a boy again. As he drove out of the shed and bucked through a drift into the road up past Van Dam's toward the oil derrick he booped once on the rubber horn to Elsa, standing in the doorway with her arms folded across her breast and watching him.

The wind had blown from the north all night, and the dugway up to the south bench was almost bare. But on the bench the snow lay in long, ripple-marked drifts, not deep, but deep enough to hide the road in spots. There had been no guard or hindrance, not even a sign, along the road as he left town. Bo folded a blanket on the floorboards to set his feet on. It was cold, but not too cold, and he was glad for the absence of wind. The sun, flat along the bench, burned on the crests of the drifts and the air in front of the car glittered with sunstruck motes of frost.

Close in, the fences and the Russian thistle jammed against them had kept the road fairly clear, and even where the fences gave out the drifts were nowhere more than a foot deep. The snow was so granular, almost like coarse sand, that he rode over it as he might have over a hard-packed beach.

There was no sign of life, no smoke, in the homesteads he passed; the pastures were empty of stock. As the farms thinned out and the fences broke off at right angles to leave the road unmarked, the drifts were more frequent, and he had to look far ahead to the spots blown bare to make sure of staying on the trail. Once, bucking across a long drift, he dipped down in a swale and bogged down. Three minutes after he had shovelled out he ran smack into a fence, and there was no gate.

He got out to look around, but there was nothing to tell him where he was, only the dazzle of sun on snow and the patches of beaten and frozen grass. Climbing in again, he cramped the wheels sharp left and bumped along the fence. Within a half mile he came to a gate, and recognized it. He was at the edge of the horse pasture. That wasn't so bad. He'd be at his own homestead by noon, could stop off and have lunch inside, warm up a little before going on. Experimentally he moved his toes inside the heavy socks and elkhide moccasins. Not cold yet, just a little stiff from sitting still.

He was lost twice in the horse pasture, finding his way back into the road each time by following the water ditch. Once he had to shovel out. When he pulled up toward Gadke's at eleven-thirty he decided to stop there rather than go on to the homestead. Any story would do to tell them. He was being sent for flu medicine, that was all.

But there was no one at Gadke's. The barn doors were nailed shut with cleats, the blinds in the house were drawn. Bo swore, kicking his numb feet together, and pulled out again. It was the homestead for lunch after all.

For a while he pounded his feet on the blanket and sang to keep warm, but it was too hard to follow the trail and sing at the same time. The biggest branch of the trail turned off just past Gadke's, and left only a pair of shallow ruts. In undrifted snow he could have followed them, but the drifts changed everything. In ten more minutes he was off the road again.

He swung left in a wide circle, but there were only drifts and bare grass. Under one wheel the bottom fell out of a drifted burnout, and the shock rattled his teeth. The motor died and he had to get out and crank. It infuriated him to be lost in a country he had driven through two dozen times. It was the damned snow; everything looked different.

All right, he said, and climbed in again. Lose the road, drive by ear. The sun was straight ahead of him. He couldn't go far wrong if he headed straight south, unless he hit a coulee he couldn't cross. The burnouts were enough to kink his neck, but if the Ford could stand them he could.

Within a mile he came to the edge of a coulee ten or fifteen feet deep and a hundred wide. "Damn!" he said, and sat peering through the windshield. The snow was deep in the coulee bottom, too deep. So it was go around. He cramped the wheels to the right and bucked drifts along the top till he got to the rounded, windswept edge where the grass was bare. All the coulees in this country ran east and south. If he went far enough west he ought to head this one.

He came to the head and saw the shack at the same time. It was a one-room, slant-roofed lean-to, covered with tarpaper outside and striped vertically with lath. He had pulled into the yard, his eye on the thin smoke from the stovepipe, before he recognized the place as Ole Pederson's. He swore unbelievingly. He was within six miles of his own farm, and hadn't recognized a thing till he bumped into Ole's yard. But at least he was somewhere. Ole Pederson was a dumb Swede, but his fire was as warm as anybody's.

Feeling good again now that he had passed the bad part, now that Montana lay ahead of him, with marked roads, he hammered on the door. Inside he heard movement: he hammered again. "Hey, Ole!" he said.

The door opened and Ole Pederson, taller than the door by a good two inches, stood there stooping. He wore a black sweater with a wide orange stripe around the middle like the stripe of a Poland hog. His pale hair was wispily on end, as if he had been lying down, and his eyes were suspicious.

"Hi," Bo said. He started in, but Ole half closed the door, keeping his long melancholy face in the crack.

"Ay don't tank you batter coom in har," he said.

"Why, what's the matter?"

"Anyt'ing," Ole said wearily. "Ain't anyt'ing matter. But Ay don't tank you better coom in."

"What the hell?" Bo said. He peered at Ole's pale, long-cheeked face. "You sick?"

"No," Ole said. "Ay ban't sick. Ay yust don't vant to gat sick. Ay don't vant to run you out, but you batter go on."

"Hell," Bo said. "I couldn't give you the flu. I haven't got it."

"Var you coom from? V'itemud?"

"Yeah. And there's no flu there. Come on, let me in, I'm cold."

"Val, Ay don't know . . ."

With one quick step Bo crowded into the shack. "Hell's afire," he said. "You don't need to be scared of me. I'm healthy."

Ole backed up till he sat down on the bunk in the corner. He ran a great splay hand through his hair. "Ay vish you didn't coom in har," he said.

Bo had his mitts off, warming his hands over the stove. "Take it easy. How long have you been holed up?"

"Two veeks."

"Haven't you seen anybody all that time?"

"Two farmers," Ole said. "Ay rather be alone than catch flu."

Bo eyed him half in contempt. His fingers tingled with the heat, and he felt his toes, stiff and deeply aching when he set his weight on one foot or the other. Opening the box of lunch, he spread bread and butter and chicken on the table. A half sandwich went down in two bites, and he sank his teeth in a drumstick, cold and meaty and succulent. "Help yourself," he said with his mouth full.

Ole looked, but made no move, so Bo picked up the other drumstick and tossed it to him. He caught it clumsily in his lap and sat holding it, lugubrious and stubborn. Bo dropped the leg bone in the pail behind the stove and started on a second joint.

"Why don't you go into town where the doctors are, if you're scared of the flu?" he said.

Ole shook his head. "Ay don't vant to go to town." His face, which had been pale as cheese when Bo came in, was flushed now, clear to the roots of the yellow hair. Maybe the big dumb guy was sick and didn't know it.

"I'm going into Chinook, if you want to come along," Bo said.

When Ole shook his head again, Bo shrugged and pulled on his mitts, rolling the remains of the chicken in its napkin. "Well, that's your lookout," he said. "Thanks for the hospitality."

Ole sat on his bunk and with obvious relief watched him get ready to go.

"How do I get to the Chinook road?" Bo said. "Up along your fence?"

"It's a half mile," Ole said. "Turn right at the corner."

"Sure you don't want to come in?"

"Ay tank Ay stay har."

Bo shrugged and left him. He bumped down across the flats, turned right at the fence corner, and found the road. Fifteen minutes later he was on the narrow graded road coming up past Cree, in Montana, and with a contented sigh he settled back to let the Ford plow ahead. It was easy from here. Three hours and he'd be in Chinook. Eight hours for the whole hundred miles. That was good time, considering. And coming back he'd have his own tracks to follow.

At four o'clock, the sun already a dry yellow ball in the haze, he pulled into the empty street and stopped before the Palace Hotel.

With the bag of money under his coat he climbed out, stiff and clumsy with cold, and stepped up on the plank sidewalk. It was funny there wasn't anyone around. Not a man, not a horse, not a sleigh or a car, was in the street. The hotel front was blank; he saw his own fur reflection coming to meet him in the front window. And the door, when he thumbed the latch and put his shoulder against the panel, was locked.

"Well I'll be . . ." he said. He cupped a hand over his eyes and put his nose against the glass. The desk was there, deserted. The chairs were there, the big-bellied stove, but there was no sign of life. Bo stepped back, his chest beginning to churn with slow rage. Now what if the flu had closed up the whole place? What if the saloons were closed? With narrowed eyes and lips compressed he started walking.

He saw the white flutter of paper on the saloon door before he reached the corner. "Closed while the flu is on," it said. "City Ordernance."

Savagely, his feet beginning to ache as walking brought the blood back, he cut across the deserted street to the other saloon where he had bought beer last summer. There was no sign up, but the doors were locked.

Involuntary swearing broke out of him. No place to sleep. Not a joint in the whole stinking, cowardly town open. No place to buy the whiskey he had driven a hundred cold miles for. But by God, somebody would have to open up, or he'd beat their door down.

He had knocked without success on three doors, up the street past the business section, when he saw a man hurrying along the opposite sidewalk. The man wore a white mask over his face, and his head was covered by a heavy fur cap with deep earlaps. Bo crossed over.

"What's the matter around here?" he said.

The man's eyes, sharp black holes between brown fur and white mask, darted at him, looked him up and down. "Where'd you come from?"

Bo let his face go dead and stupid. "I just come in off the farm. What's the matter, there ain't a place in town open."

"We got the flu," the man said. "The place is quarantined."

"Good gosh," Bo said. "Is that right?" He kept the man standing impatiently while he fingered his chin. "Hell, I wanted to buy me some whiskey," he said. "I heard there was this flu around, but I didn't know it was in town here."

"Everything's closed," the man said. "You can't even leave town, now you're in." He seemed rather pleased to see Bo stuck. "You got to get a mask, too. That's orders."

"How'd I get a mask if nothing's open?"

"Hospital," the man said. "Block up the first cross street on the right."

He started off, but Bo laid a hand on his arm. "Look," he said. "If I can't get out of here I still want a bottle or two. Where's a barkeep or somebody live?"

The man laughed. "The whole bunch from the Last Chance is in the hospital."

"Isn't there another one?"

"There's the Silver Dollar. Frank Selby lives right back of the joint. But you won't get him to open up."

"Well, I guess I'll try anyway," Bo said. He watched the man's slight hurrying figure go up the street, and wrinkled his lip and spat in the snow.

The Silver Dollar saloon ran back from a two-story false front for seventy or eighty feet, a bare blank wall for half its length. At the back end, where it became living quarters, there were two windows and a door approached by three wooden steps. The green shades were drawn on the windows.

Bo went up the steps, the bag of money under his coat, and knocked. For two minutes he waited without an answer. He banged on the storm door with the whole weight of his fist. One of the blinds, he thought, twitched slightly, but no one came to the door. He lifted his fist and thundered on the wood.

"Who's there?" a woman's voice whined suddenly. She must have tiptoed to the door, for the voice came directly through the boards in front of him.

"I have to see Frank Selby," Bo said. "It's important."

"He isn't seeing anybody," the woman said.

"He's got to see me," Bo said. "The doctor sent me."

There was a moment's silence, then the inner door was opened and the woman's face looked at him through the little window in the storm door. She had a red, wet-looking harelip. "What's the doctor want?" she said.

"I'm from Harlem. The doctor there sent me over for whiskey for medicine."

The woman shook her head. "You'll have to get it somewheres else. We're closed."

Quietly, out of her sight, Bo put his thumb on the storm-door latch, depressed it gently. As she started to shut the inner door he opened the outer one swiftly and stuck his foot in the crack. The woman confronted him furiously, shoving at the blocked door. "Go away!" she said. "You can't come butting in here!"

Bo took the bag from under his coat. "Look," he said. "I was sent over here in an emergency. I want three hundred bucks' worth of liquor for that whole town. And I'm not going back without it. You think I drove over here for fun?"

The woman stared at the bag, then at him. She licked the red split in her lip. Still exerting pressure on the door, she called, "Frank!"

In a minute her husband's face appeared over hers in the crack, a fat face, bartender-pale, with drooping sandy mustaches. "What is this?" he said. "What you trying to do?"

Lifting the bag before the man's hard eyes, Bo said, "I was sent over from Harlem for a carload of whiskey. They need it for flu medicine."

Both faces remained stuck behind the door's edge. "Jesus, man," Frank said, "I can't sell you nothing. The law's closed me up on account of this-here epidemic."

Bo rattled the bag. "I guess three hundred bucks ought to be worth opening up for."

"What's the matter with Joe's place in Harlem?"

"He's burned down. That's why I had to come over here."

Frank eyed the bag again. "All right," he said finally. "You wait right there." Bo took his foot out of the door and it closed smartly. He laughed. In five minutes Frank came out, a sheepskin around his ears, the strings of a flu mask dangling inside it and a muffler wrapped around mouth and nose.

"Afraid of freezing your handlebars?" Bo said.

"Go ahead and laugh," said Selby, through the muffler and mask. "You stay six feet away from me if you want me to sell you anything. Where's your car?"

"In front of the Palace."

"Drive it around behind the joint, clear around the house part and halfway up the inside. I don't want anybody snooping around."

When Bo brought the Ford around Frank opened a side door and backed away to a safe distance. "All right," he said. "What you want, now?"

"Got any kegs of rye?"

"Couple."

"How much?"

"I'd have to figure," Frank said. He figured. "Ninety-six."

"Okay. One of those. How about Irish?"

"How much you want?"

"Case."

"I'll see." He rummaged among a stack of case goods against the wall. The air in the storeroom was still and cold, full of the smell of whiskey and straw and burlap. "Here she is," Frank said. He swung the case out by its burlap ear. "What else?"

"Seven cases middle-price bourbon," Bo said. "What you got?"

He took a bottle of beer out of an opened barrel and yanked the cap off on a nailhead. The beer was icy cold and faintly skunky. "You ought to keep the light off beer in white bottles," he said. Frank, lifting cases around, only grunted through his muffler.

"I'll have to split up on you." he said finally. "I ain't got seven cases all one kind."

"Okay, long as it isn't rotgut." Sitting on a box, Bo tipped the beer and watched Frank pull cases together, watched him roll a keg from behind some barrels of beer.

"How much does that come to?" he said.

Frank figured on a barrel head. "Two hundred and ninety-four even."

"Sharpen your pencil a little," Bo said. "This is a wholesale deal."

"I already figured it wholesale. I don't make more'n a buck or two a case at that price."

"Tell you what," Bo said. "If it was for me, I'd never buy a bottle of it till I got a jobber's price. When a town buys whiskey for medicine it ought to get the lowdown. But you throw in another case of bourbon and I'll give you three hundred even."

Frank shook his head. "I couldn't do it. That's a whole case for six bucks. I wouldn't make a dime."

"That's the only kind of a deal I'm interested in," Bo said. "I went over to the hospital and talked to the guy from the Last Chance, because I couldn't raise anybody out in front here. He wanted to sell me the stuff, but I'd have to hunt up a relative of his to get it. I thought it'd be easier here. But if you don't want to talk business . . ."

Frank backed away further. "You been over to the hospital?" he said. His voice was a squawk. "What the hell do you come around me for?"

"You don't want to do business, uh?"

"All right, take it," Frank said. "Take your nine cases and get out of here."

"Now you're talking sense," Bo said. He held out the bag, but Frank put his hands behind him. "Put it on the table," he said. He stood back while Bo carried the sacks outside. "I'm not sticking my nose in the car you're driving, even," he said.

Bo worked swiftly in the late gray light. The seat took three flat cases neatly, and three more on top of those brought the load level with the sides. The keg, heavy and clumsy, he wrestled into the footspace in front of the back seat, and one of the three remaining cases he wedged beside the keg, padding it with a blanket. The last two he put in front, one in the seat and one on the floor. Then he covered the whole load with blankets and threw the gasoline can on top.

Frank was still standing back. "You count out the money," he said. "I'm not touching it till the wife bakes it in the oven."

"Okay," Bo said. "Strike a light."

Selby lighted a candle, and very carefully and contemptuously Bo counted out the stacks of dollars and the roll of bills. "Okay?"

"Okay," Selby said. "Dump 'em back in the bag."

The last thing Bo saw, as he backed out of the alley, Frank was carrying the sack before him as if it might explode. He would probably bake the glove he had touched the bag with, too. Bo laughed. As he bumped across the intersection of alley and street he whistled. The springs hit bottom on the slightest jar. No batting over burnouts on the way back. That was another reason for not starting back now. He'd need daylight to find the road and keep on it.

He slept that night at the livery stable, where he found two men taking care of a whole barnful of stock belonging to people in the hospital. They didn't want him at first. He loosened them up by going back to the car and breaking out a bottle of bourbon. After that they let him drive into the grain shed and make himself a bed of hay beside the car. When he lay down in his clothes, the fur coat wrapped around him under the blankets, he heard their voices loud through the partition, heard the stamp and blow of horses and the knocking of a cow's horns against the stanchions. The hay he had piled on the floor rustled under his weight, and sometime during the night he heard a dog sniffing under the shed door. The thought of food for tomorrow crossed his mind, but he let it drift. There was some bread left, and a wing of chicken, and if he got an early start he'd be back in Whitemud by early afternoon. Everything was jake. The bottle to the stablemen was a good investment. Keep them from getting too curious.

It was barely daylight when he woke. There was a yellow-spoked wheel directly in front of his eyes, and he lay wondering for a minute. His shoulders and hips were stiff and his feet cold. The wheel revolved a little, stopped, went around a little the other way, and he blinked his eyes clear and saw the car, the crack of light under the shed door.

He stood up, stamped his feet, swung his arms. A look into the Ford showed him the load untouched. In the other room he heard the stablemen snoring. Driven by ravenous hunger, he went through the partition door and into the stable. There were a half dozen milk pails on a bench. Four cows, in improvised stanchions, swung their heads to look at him. He hunted up a stool, tipped straw out of a pail, and sat down to the nearest one. The quart of milk he drew down was foamy and warm and slightly sickening, and it spilled on his coat as he tipped the pail to drink, but it laid the devil in his stomach. He drank it all, resting between gulps.

The stablemen were still asleep when he went through to the shed. There was the question of warm water for the Ford. He turned the radiator petcock and went out in back with a pail. The pump was there, a wide smooth icicle hanging like a white tongue from its mouth. The pump complained stiffly, but finally brought up water, and with the bucket in his hand he went in and started a fire in the sheetiron stove. When he came in with a second pail one of the stablemen was sitting up. His face was contracted and his eyes bloodshot. He looked incuriously at Bo for a few minutes and lay down again with his face to the wall. The other one snored on. They were still in their bunks when Bo poured the hot water into the rust-smelling gullet of the Ford and bent to crank.

At eight o'clock he was headed out of town, following his own solitary tracks of yesterday. There was not a soul anywhere about except for a woman who pulled back her front curtains to look as he went by.

It was not as clear as it had been the day before. The sun, straight ahead of him for the first two miles, before the north road switched off, was pale behind a thin screen of mist. Occasional snake-trails of snow moved in the road, wriggled a few yards, and died. Inside the sidecurtains it did not seem cold.

As he drove, Bo was juggling figures. Sometimes, having difficulty keeping them straight in his head, he took his hands off the wheel and drew them in the palm of his mitt. The case to Doc O'Malley would bring him sixty-five; the keg, at three dollars a quart, would be another two hundred and forty. That was his original investment, right there. The whole eight cases of bourbon were gravy. At four dollars a bottle—and there were ninety-six bottles, or ninety-five since he'd given one to the stablemen—and four times ninety-five was. . . . He figured on his mitt, one eye on the road. Three hundred and eighty, all clear profit. Not so bad, he said to the Ford, not so bad. He remembered the time only a couple of weeks ago when he had nearly lost his mind because his ducks had spoiled. That all seemed very childish and primitive, something out of the backwoods. One good break, and he was past all that scrabbling for a living.

He ate the fragments left in the lunch box and threw the box out the window. There were no tracks on the straight road except his own. The sun, on his right now, was barely visible through the mist. He took a firmer grip on the wheel and pulled the gas lever down a notch. It might snow, and he needed those tracks. Ahead of him the erratic wind lifted a trail of dry snow across the road.

His feet, unprotected now by a folded blanket, felt the cold first. When he stamped them he realized that they had been getting colder all the time. In one way cold was good. There wouldn't be much snow if the temperature dropped. But the road ahead was now crawling with lifting ropes of drift. He swore. Wind was just as bad, worse. It would cover his tracks in an hour if it blew. The sky was grayer now, too, the whole world darkening over the white waste. He dropped the gas lever another notch.

Where the road turned off to Cree he stopped, hesitating between choices. He ought to stop somewhere and get warm, have a cup of coffee, before tackling the last fifty miles. But there might be no one left at Cree. His own place would be like an icehouse, and the kerosene stove wouldn't do more than warm his hands. The only place he was sure of was Ole's, and Ole wouldn't be tickled to death to see him. He jammed his foot hard on the low pedal. Ole would see him anyway.

Rather than risk losing his way he followed his own tracks, going carefully across the roadless flat and stopping in Ole's yard. The wind blew smoke down to the ground, making him turn his head. The barometer must be clear to the bottom, if smoke wouldn't rise.

Ole didn't answer his first knock, and he put his shoulder against the door. Locked. He pounded again, listened. "Coom in," the Swede's voice said.

"The door's locked!" Bo yelled.

He waited, leaning his weight impatiently against the homemade door. In a minute the latch clicked and Ole, still in his orange-banded sweater, backed away to let him come in. The minute he looked at the Swede's face a slow, climbing rage tightened in Bo's stomach and chest. Ole's face was drawn and sick, his eyes glittering like blue ice, his mouth chapped and stained in the corners.

"What's the matter?" Bo said sharply. "You sick?"

"Ay don't feel gude," Ole said. "Ay ant felt gude for couple days."

"Well for Christ sake why didn't you come into Chinook with me yesterday?"

Ole didn't answer, and Bo stood with his hands spread over the stove, watching the drawn face. He was sick all right. He was sick as a horse. His hands shook, and when he stooped to sit down in the bunk he had to reach back and ease himself down. So now, Bo said, I suppose I've got this big ox on my hands with the Ford already so loaded she hits bottom on every bump!

"You were a damn fool to stay out here alone in the first place," he said.

Ole shook with a heavy chill, grabbed his hands together and held them to still their trembling, but said nothing.

"Got any coffee?"

Ole's eyes lifted to the stove. Bo took the top off the pot, saw that there was a good pint of black liquid inside, and shoved it onto the hot part of the stove. While he waited for it to boil he went out and got a bottle of bourbon. "Where's your corkscrew?" he said.

"Ay an't got vun."

"Oh for . . . !" Angrily Bo pawed through the half dozen knives and forks and spoons on the cupboard shelf. Nothing, not even a paring knife. He tipped the bottle neck down and gave the bottom a stiff, flat-palmed smack, hitting it so hard that pain jolted up his wrist. You had to hit it just right to jar the cork loose, and it was a damn fool stunt anyway. He had seen a man cut his hand half off trying it. But if this big dumb Ole didn't have a corkscrew there was nothing else to do. He jolted the bottle again, savagely. On the fifth try he caught it right. The cork started a quarter of an inch, and he got the blade of his knife under it and lifted carefully till it came out.

He poured a tin cup a third full and handed it to Ole. "This is supposed to be medicine," he said. "See what it does for you."

He had a swig himself out of the bottle, corked it and stuck it in the pocket of his coat. The coffee pot was steaming, rocking a little on the stove.

"Got a cup or anything you haven't used lately?" Bo said. Ole's mouth opened helplessly, he wrinkled his forehead, looking at the cupboard.

"Well, what the hell," Bo said. He found a saucepan and poured coffee into it for himself, filled the Swede's cup. "Drink that damn quick," he said. "We got to get out of here."

His own coffee was black and bitter, with grounds floating in it, but he drank it in gulps, scalding hot. In ten minutes he had the bundled Swede outside with a quilt around him. The two cases of whiskey in the front seat had to be shifted to the back. That was bad, because they were loose and might bounce and break, but there was nothing else he could do. He boosted Ole inside and tucked the quilt in, went inside to snatch two blankets off the bunk, dumped the coffee pot into the fire and kicked the draft shut, and closed the door.

There was a definite wind now, a creeping, close-to-the-ground wind that he could feel as a steady pressure from the northwest. The drifting didn't seem to be much worse. The snow was packed, and only the top dust blew. But it was cold. It was cold as all billy hell. And if it hadn't been for this jinx Swede he'd be almost to Gadke's by now. As he climbed in he looked with distaste at Ole's muffled face. A guy that big ought to be all man.

Ole was definitely a jinx. At the first coulee head, still within sight of his shack, they had to run through a shallow swale drifted a foot deep on one side. Bo took it charging, but something under the snow, burnout or badger hole, rocked them with a solid, bouncing shock, and the Ford hit bottom and died in the drift. The inside filled with the smell of whiskey.

"*God* damn!" Bo said. He yanked the sidecurtain loose, ripping one of the eyelets, and swarmed over the side. God knew how many bottles were busted. There wasn't even time to look now. That wind was too dangerous. Hard pebbles stung his face, and he looked up to see that they were not drift, but snow.

Shovelling like a dynamo, he cleared the wheels and threw the shovel inside. "Can you drive?" he said to Ole.

Ole shook his head. "You're going to anyway," Bo said. "Shove over here." He showed Ole how to let the brake off and push down on the low pedal, feeding gas at the same time. "When I say go, let her have it," he said.

He braced himself against the body, said "Go!" and heaved forward. The Swede jammed on the pedal, forgot to feed gas, and killed the engine.

"Gas!" Bo yelled. "Give it the gas!"

Ole dropped his hands from the wheel and leaned away. His face was pitiful, as if he were going to cry. Bo took a deep breath and swallowed his rage, cranked, braced himself again. "Now take it easy," he said. "When I say go, let her in slow and give her plenty of gas."

This time the Swede gave her too much, and went roaring and spinning up the coulee side, out of control, scared to death and with his foot frozen to the gear pedal, so that Bo, encumbered with his heavy coat, had to sprint alongside and jump on the running board to yank on the hand brake. He was breathing hard when he climbed in, and his mind was red hot. The air inside the curtains was so thick with spilled whiskey it was almost intoxicating.

By the time they reached Gadke's the tracks were drifted half full, only the top edges clear, and the gray sky was spitting snow as hard as hail against the windshield. The wind increased steadily, pushing against the bellied sidecurtains, pouring in the V-shaped hole where Bo had torn the eyelet. And it was getting colder. He could feel it getting colder by the quarter-hour, feel it in his bones and in his mind. This was going to be a regular old he-blizzard, and he was still forty miles from home. At the horse pasture gate he stopped long enough to fit the radiator blanket on, thanking his stars he had had sense enough to make it.

There was no worrying about the trail now. The best he could do was to follow his yesterday's tracks, hoping to God they held out. His jaw clenched on him automatically as he drove, and at intervals he sat back and loosened it. Then the tense concentration of trying to see ahead through the drift and the murky white darkness crept into his muscles again, until he came to and forcibly relaxed once more. Ole sat beside him, humped in the quilt.

They passed through the horse pasture faster than Bo had been able to go coming out. The not-quite-covered tracks did that for them, at least. But at the far gate of the pasture Bo stood outside the Ford, his eyes slitted against the drift, and wondered whether to stay with the tracks, off the road, or try to pick up the trail. He hadn't been far off that time. If he started straight out from the gate he ought to hit his tracks again within a half mile. It was taking chances, but there wasn't much time. The wind by now was a positive force, a thing you fought against. Drift and falling snow were indistinguishable, the air was thick with stinging pebbles, the visibility hardly fifty feet. It was so cold that his eyes stung and watered, his nose leaked. When he wiped it with the back of his mitt he felt the slick ice on the leather.

He piled in beside the Swede. "How do you feel?" he said. "Okay?"

Ole nodded, and they started again. Bo was driving partly by sight, partly by feel now. The wind was from the northwest. He wanted to go almost exactly northeast. If he kept the wind square against the left sidecurtains, kept them stiff and strained as a sail, he couldn't go far wrong. The minute they flapped or slackened he was circling. Either that or the wind was shifting. But you didn't think about that.

Ahead of him was a whirling blur of light, the whole world driving, moving, blowing under his wheels. It was like driving on fast water, except when bumps or holes or burnouts bounced them clear down to the axle. Bo squinted, peering, his stiff hands clenched on the wheel. There were almost-effaced tracks ahead. He'd hit it, right on the nose. But the tracks turned off left, and the slack in the sidecurtains when he started to follow them stopped him. He had almost followed his own tracks the wrong way. That would have been a nice one. He backed and started in the other direction.

He knew he was off the road. The feel of the tires told him that. But as long as he kept the wind there, he'd eventually run into the graded road paralleling the south bench. He'd get her in, by the gods, if he had to drive the last twenty miles by ear.

The tires hit the road again. He could feel it, smooth and hard and sunken, though his eyes showed him no difference. Within five minutes the ruts were gone. He swung into the wind, feeling for them like a blind man, his body tense, one with the body of the car. And in the moment when he turned, feeling, the wind burst furiously against the sidecurtain and tore it loose, and he was blinded and muffled in cloth and icy isinglass.

Cursing, he stepped on the pedals and fought the frantic flapping thing out of his face. The eyelets were all ripped now, and there was no fastening it down. Wind and snow drove into the hole, hammering his eyes shut, peppering his face. His fury ripped out of him in shouted swearing as he twisted, trying to fasten the curtain somehow. The Swede was a hindrance to his movements, and he shoved him over in the seat with one fierce hunch of the shoulder. Eventually he had to grope in the back seat and find one of Ole's blankets, poke it up over the metal bar along the top, pull it down through, and sit on both ends. It wasn't as good as the curtain, and it made the car almost as dark as night, but it kept that paralyzing wind out of his face while he drove.

The thing became a nightmare. He sat within the dark cabin of the car, his numb feet ready to jump on the pedals, his mitt slipping up and down the smooth wheel to feed or retard gas, his eyes glued on the flowing, dirty-gray-white world ahead. In an hour he was on and off the road a dozen times.

The strain and cold stiffened his legs and arms, but the excitement got into him, too. He turned to look at Ole, only his long nose and white eyebrows showing above the quilt, and in the steady motor-sounding and wind-sounding and snow-pebble-sounding silence of the car he opened his mouth and yelled.

"Yippee!" he yelled. "Powder River, let 'er buck!"

The Swede jumped six inches, and his lugubrious, startled face turned. "You tank ve make it?" he said.

Bo laughed, jamming the Ford recklessly through a drift. "You're God damned right Ay tank ve make it," he said. He leaned back, stretching, relaxing his tightened muscles for the twentieth time. The whirl of snow visible through the windshield lifted briefly, showing him a drift deeper than most, long and crested and fringed with blowing tatters of snow. He stepped on the low pedal and dragged down the gas, and then when they were halfway through the drift, slugging through it like a boat through a wave, he saw the fence dead ahead.

His hands yanked the wheel around and his feet stabbed at brake and reverse at the same time. The Ford shuddered, swung, skidded, caught, hit something big and solid under the drift, and very slowly, as if careful not to hurt or break anything, turned over on its side.

The Swede's two hundred pounds came down on Bo, smashing him against the blanket curtain. He felt the snow under the blanket crush and give, heard bottles smash, and then he was fighting back against Ole's dead weight, reaching out through the clumsy coat and mitts and blanket to turn the switch and cut the motor, still running on its side.

"Get off!" he roared. "Get your damned dead carcass out of here!"

3

Elsa saw the storm coming by mid-morning. At noon, when she was certain it was going to be bad, she sent the boys out after buckets of lignite, and herself went out to the barn, broke open two bales of hay with the pliers, and tumbled the packed dusty slabs down into the mangers. If the wind blew hard for very long she might not be able to get out for a while.

The wind was up strong when she closed the barn doors; she had to wrestle them with all her weight. Worry about Bo drove her to sit by the kitchen window afterward, staring across the vacant lot toward the south road. The air was striated and thick with driving snow. Sometimes such a gust drove in from the river bend that Van Dam's house and shed and the low windmill tower were blotted out, and only the madly-whirling blades remained in sight. Jim Van Dam ought to do something about that mill. It would blow to pieces if he didn't.

She was about to call Chet and send him over to tell them their mill was up, but another look at the wind and snow outside made her hesitate. And the boys should be kept in because of the flu. She reached for her coat, stooping to see if the blades were still there.

"I'm going over to Van Dam's," she called into the other room. "You stay in the house, both of you."

Her eyes screwed shut, body doubled against the gusts, she made her way across the lot and up to the Van Dam's kitchen door. Her knock went rattling down the wind. No one could possibly have heard it. She pushed on the knob, and the wind blew her into the kitchen.

Jim Van Dam, a lumpy quilt around him, was sitting on the oven door with a dishpan between his feet. He did not look up, but his wife, holding his forehead, turned a white face and made a sick grimace with her mouth. Then he gagged and retched, and she clung to him, holding him upright.

"He just took sick this morning," Mrs. Van Dam said. "He was all right till after breakfast, and then he said he felt queer and I gave him some calomel, and he's been throwing up for a half hour."

She didn't say, "Now he's got it!" but she might as well have. Elsa took off her coat. "Where's little Jimmy?" she said.

"Upstairs. I wouldn't let him come down too close."

"Haven't you got a couch in the parlor?"

"Yes."

"We ought to get him to bed," Elsa said. She looked at Jim Van Dam, contracted in a heavy chill. But when she stooped to help Mrs. Van Dam get him to his feet and lead him in to the couch, the other woman's eyes met hers. "Oh Lord," Mrs. Van Dam said. "Now you've got close to him."

"I'd have got close, one way or another," Elsa said. "None of us can hide away, I guess."

She stayed until the sick man was in bed. Then she brought in a good supply of coal and kindling and two buckets of water from the well. The windmill, she saw, was already ruined, its whole broad tail gone. But it was no time to be worrying about windmills. When she sat inside again having a cup of coffee with Mrs. Van Dam she tried not to see the tears that dropped on the oilcloth, or the scrawny thinness of Mrs. Van Dam's arms. But even more than that she tried not to see the picture that her mind kept trying to uncover, a picture of Bo fighting his way back through this blizzard, maybe sick himself. If Jim Van Dam was all right at breakfast and was this sick by noon, Bo could have had the same thing happen . . .

"I'll go call up Doctor O'Malley," she said. "He'll probably want to send a rig to take Jim to the schoolhouse. They've got the school-teachers nursing, and he'd get better care there."

"Thank you," Mrs. Van Dam said. "I guess that'd be better. I'm no good. When I knew he had it I just went all to pieces. I . . ."

"Don't worry," Elsa said. "Give him a hot lemonade and some salts when he can hold them down, and I'll see if I can't get somebody. They may not be able to get around till tomorrow, if this keeps up, but I'll run over and see if you need anything."

It was not until the odd jobs, the telephoning, the grim preparatory look through the medicine cupboard, were all done that worry crept up on her and stayed. It came obliquely, discreetly, while the wind leaned its weight against the house, howled around the eaves, strained the frame until the walls creaked. No car could get a mile in such weather. She had confidence in Bo, he could get through if anyone could, but that was just the trouble. He might very well have started from Chinook while there was only that pre-storm haze, that ominous coppery blurring over the sun, thinking that he could run through before it broke. And once it broke he wouldn't stop. He'd butt right ahead, stubborn as a mule, no matter how cold it got or how the wind blew.

She went to the front window and looked at the thermometer hung on the outside frame. Two below. An hour ago it had been five above, at noon ten above. The longer he drove—if he was driving—the worse it got.

Her nervousness wouldn't let her sit still. She went to the sewing machine and got out the dress she was making for Freda Appleton, who was getting married next month. One way to keep from worrying was to stitch buttonholes. But every few minutes during the two hours she sat sewing she kept getting up to stoke the stove, shake down ashes, walk to the window and see the temperature down to four below, to five, to eight. The boys squabbled over the Erector set on the dining room table, and she separated them and punished Chet with only half her mind on what she was doing. If Bo had started after breakfast he ought to be in now. The clock said a quarter to five. Still, he hadn't promised to be home tonight. He would certainly have stopped along the road, at Cree or Gadke's, or maybe at Robsart if he had chosen that road. He was probably sitting by some fire not two hours away from home, waiting for the storm to blow out.

But suppose the snow blocked the roads and stayed. There would be no moving the car till spring.

Oh fiddle, she said. He can take care of himself. He could get a bobsleigh or something.

With all that liquor aboard? her mind said. What would he do with that? Suppose he stopped somewhere and they called in the police . . .

She spun it back and forth, stitching steadily at the monotonous buttonholes that went from neck to waist down the back of the dress. The stove glowed dull red in the corner, but over where she sat under the lamp, needing light now to see, it was cold. Occasionally attention stiffened her body as she thought she heard noises that were not the wind. Once she was sure she heard a car, but the window showed nothing, and when she tried to look out the back door it was nailed fast by the wind. For a minute she stood listening: the sound did not come again. Before she quite gave it up she went out on the front porch, half blocked by an angled drift laid in on the side-swipe of wind, and stood for a minute with the snow buzzing in the air around her, settling on hair and dress.

He wouldn't try to come through today. There was no use worrying. Besides, it was time to get the boys' supper. Shut in, they did nothing but eat. They had been piecing all day, and still they said periodically, every ten minutes, "Ma, when do we eat?"

Still she went back to the buttonholes for a few more minutes, unwilling just yet to break her listening. But what if, her mind said slyly, Bo stopped somewhere along the road and they had the flu there? Or what if he got so sick on the road he couldn't make it to shelter?

For one catastrophic instant she saw the image of cattle frozen by the roadsides in the spring, still frozen but bloated, horrible, obscene as the spring thaws softened them for the final decay, and she gritted her teeth and stood up. It was then that she heard the unmistakable thumping on the porch.

When she opened the door a short, involuntary cry was wrenched out of her. A man was stretched out on the steps, feet trailing in the broken snow, and another man was pulling at his shoulders, trying to drag him. He turned his head at her cry, and his grim face, only nose and eyes showing from the fur cap, brought her flying out to help him. Together they dragged the heavy figure of the other man into the hallway. The boys were in the door. "Get out of the way!" Bo said harshly, and shouldered through them.

They laid the man down, and in the light from the front room Elsa recognized Ole Pederson. His cheeks and rose were leprous white, and he had evidently been crying, because his eyelids were stuck fast with ice. Her eyes darted to Bo. "Oh, I was afraid . . . !" she said. "Where . . . ?" She was noticing twenty things at once—the rattling icicles beaten into the hair of the dogskin coat, the monstrous hulk of Bo's shoulders, the harsh jut of brows and nose from the fur cap, the way he stood with feet wide apart, swaying, the telltale white patches on cheeks and nose. In one quick glance, while she moved to shut the door on the curving lee-side wind, she saw all those things, and her hands and feet and voice leaped into action all at once.

"Lie down on the couch," she said to Bo. "Chet, get a dishpan full of snow. Bruce, run upstairs and get some blankets and quilts, anything." Reaching outside, she scooped a handful of snow and slammed the door. The boys were still stupidly staring at Ole's corpse-like body; Bo stood in the hall door, swaying a little and grinning at her. She hustled the boys off, slapped the handful of snow into his face and held it there. He stood for it quietly, and when the last white patch had disappeared, wiped his face clumsily on a towel, his hands still cased in the icy mitts. He was stooping to look at Ole when Elsa got the pan of snow from Chet and came up. He motioned her away.

"Stay away from him, all of you," he said.

Deliberately, as if contemptuous of his own samaritanism, he smeared snow in Ole's face with a mittened hand, found it clumsy, and held out his hands to Elsa. "Pull these off," he said.

The leather was frozen stiff, curved from the wheel, and the mitts came off hard. When they came, Elsa cried out again. Bo's fingers were white clear to the second joint. She tried to push them down in the pan of snow, but he snarled at her and brushed her away. She watched helplessly while his frozen fingers rubbed snow on the frozen cheeks and nose and chin of the Swede. In a minute she had started forward to pull at him. "Let me," she said, "if he has to be fixed first."

"Get back!" he said. He waved at the boys, crowding on the stairway to look down. "You too. Get away on back."

"What's the matter with him?" she said. "Is he hurt?"

Bo didn't answer. He tried to take off Ole's mittens, could not grip them with his own wooden hands, and ended by pulling them off with his teeth. Ole's hands were all right.

On his heels beside the Swede, Bo squatted and washed his hands in the pan. "I don't know what to do about this big sucker," he said finally. "I don't want you tending him. He's got the flu, I guess."

"Chester," Elsa said without turning her head. "Call up Doctor O'Malley and tell him if he's going to pick up Jim Van Dam as soon as the storm stops, he'd better pick up Ole here, too."

"Van Dam got it?" Bo said.

"I was over there helping this afternoon."

Their eyes met, and Bo shrugged. "Then I guess there's no use taking care. I didn't want to bring him home, but there wasn't anything else I could do with the guy."

"Brucie," Elsa said, "you start taking off Pa's moccasins. Chet, soon as you telephone, get a new pan of snow and a bucket of water."

Leaving Ole on the floor under a quilt, she led Bo in to the couch. He walked awkwardly, his face fiery red now, and his hair on end. Coming out of the bearish bulkiness of the coat, his head and neck had a curiously frail human look that made Elsa shake her head. You got used to thinking of Bo as capable of anything, but this drive must have been close. She steered her mind away from how close it must have been. His hands and face frozen, maybe his feet . . .

"Hurry!" she said to Bruce. "Hustle!"

Her own hands were busy kneading his fingers in the pan of snow, working them, stripping them like the teats of a cow, rubbing down the wrists. "Feel anything?" He shook his head.

"Let's get a little closer to the fire," he said. He started to rise, but she pushed him back.

"You stay away from the fire!" She rubbed at the cold, curved, inhuman fingers, and relief brought tears to her eyes. "Oh Bo!" she said. "You shouldn't have tried to come through!"

Bruce was pulling with both hands at the heavy socks, their tops stiff frozen. One came off, and Elsa, looking down, winced. The feet too, waxen and ribbed by the ribs of the socks like something hardened in a mold. She looked at Bo's red, unshaven face, and he winked at her, drawing down the corners of his mouth. "Too many patients for you, Mama," he said.

Elsa dumped snow in Chet's pail of water, rolled up Bo's trouser legs, and set both feet in the pail. The water slopped over, but she went on working, shifting from fingers to toes. "Feel anything yet?"

"Hands a little. I haven't felt my feet since we tipped over."

That brought her head up. "Tipped over? How did you get in then?"

"I drove in," Bo said. His mood seemed to have changed suddenly; he looked and sounded savage, as if the very memory made him mad.

"But," she said, still rubbing. "If you tipped over . . ."

"I tipped it back up," he said harshly. "Don't ask me how. I don't know how. I don't know how I got in, either, so you needn't ask me that. I didn't know I was here till I ran into the fence."

"Oh my Lord," Elsa said softly. "You're lucky!"

He grunted irritably. "Yeah. I'm lucky I ran into that big dumb Ole and had to bring him in. I'm lucky I froze my face and hands and feet. I'm lucky I broke God knows how many bottles of hooch. I'm lucky as hell, all right."

She kept still, and later, when the pain came like fire into his hands and feet and he roared at her to let him alone, she did as he asked. There was nothing she knew about the care of frost-bite except to keep it from thawing out too fast, to prevent gangrene. Maybe he'd get gangrene anyway. It had taken a long time to get the blood back into his feet. And all, she said in one spiteful instant, for a load of whiskey and a few dollars!

Because Bo was in too much pain now to put his weight on his feet, she got the boys to help knock one of the upstairs beds apart and set it up again in the dining room. Ole Pederson came out of his stupor and moaned, and she tugged and dragged and rolled him onto the couch in the parlor. Then she fed the boys and sent them off to bed.

Curiously, that night was one of almost blissful peace. Her worry was gone, Bo was home and safe. The blizzard whined and howled and pounded around the house, and the thermometer on the porch dropped steadily until at ten o'clock it hovered around twenty below. But the parlor stove was brick red, there was a comfortable, lazy smell of baking paint from the asbestos mat in the corner. She sat on the edge of the bed in the dining room and talked to Bo quietly, remembering the other time she had had to rub his frosted face with snow, the day she and Bo had decided to be married. Ole Pederson, in the other room, drank the duck soup she fixed for him and sank into a light, mumbling sleep, and with the lamp blown out she and Bo talked.

He told her about Chinook, and the fear that was chasing everybody inside to hibernate.

"A lot of people wouldn't have brought Ole in," she said, and smoothed the hair back from his forehead.

Bo grunted. "All this running away. If it's going to get you it's going to get you."

"Funny," Elsa said. "Once it comes right into your own house you're not scared any more. It's just like any sickness, and it doesn't paralyze you the way it did at first."

"If you're not scared you're the only person in Saskatchewan that isn't." He reached out to pull her down for a kiss, and flinched back. She felt the jerk of his body, and a slow, warm, tender amusement filled her. He could overcome almost anything, do almost anything, but give him a little pain and put him in bed and he was the biggest baby on earth. A woman could stand twice as much. It was like the way the flu seemed to take the biggest and strongest men, as if their very strength was their weakness.

She moved, and Bo hissed at her through gritted teeth to go easy. When she dragged the covers over his feet that way she liked to killed him.

"What will you do about the things in the car?" she said. "You can't walk, and you can't hold anything in your hands."

"I don't know. Unless maybe you and the kids can get it in. None of it's very heavy but the keg, and that'll roll."

"We'll get it," she said. "Are you sure it's all right out there to-night? Won't it freeze, or something?"

He roared with laughter that clicked off against his teeth when the pain hit him. "Old Mama!" he said. "It'll freeze about as quick as the thermometer will."

"How about the car radiator?"

"Have to get a new one," he said. "That'll be froze solid before now. I wasn't in very good shape to drain her when I pulled in."

"No," she said, and stooped carefully to kiss his raw, hot face. "You couldn't have gone on much longer, could you?"

"It was pretty touchy for a while."

"Mmmm," she said, quiet now, at rest, warm and peaceful and in possession of her husband and her home, and not afraid of anything because somehow they'd pull through it. They always did. She lay down beside him, and he turned to nuzzle in her throat. His lips nipped softly at the skin under her jaw.

"Take off your clothes," he whispered.

"How about Ole?"

"He's dead to the world."

"Don't talk that way. He might really be."

"He's all right. Take them off."

"But your hands," she said. "Your feet . . ."

"I don't need any hands or feet."

"Well," she said, softly laughing. "If you want to hurt yourself . . ."

"I want to hurt you too," he said, and bit her suddenly in the side of the neck. "I want us both to lie here and love and hurt together and then I want to sleep for twenty-four hours."

But in the morning the peace was gone, along with the violence of the wind. When she slid out of bed, Bo still slept, one swollen hand up to his cheek. His breath was quick and noisy. She started to feel his forehead, but didn't for fear of waking him. In the other room Ole Pederson was blazing with fever, his voice so weak that she could hardly make out what he said. Blood had oozed in tiny droplets through the pores of his cheeks and nose, and the inert helplessness of his body alarmed her. In slippers and robe she padded into the kitchen to make up the fire and get some breakfast going.

The rattling of the stove when she shook down the ashes woke Bo. He felt hot, he said, and his eternally God damned hands and feet were killing him. His back felt as if a log had dropped across it, and his bones ached. For a while she went on trying to believe that his fever was from the frost-bite and the terrible trip, but after breakfast he gurgled frantically, waved his arm, grew purple. She ran with a pan and he leaned out of bed to vomit, every joint tortured with retching, his eyes shut and the sweat standing out on his forehead in great drops. She remembered Jim Van Dam yesterday, the big man helpless as a stunned calf, and she couldn't pretend any more.

The sleigh from the livery stable came just after she and Chet had finished getting the liquor in from the Ford. The house stank with the smell from the seven broken bottles when Lars Poulsen knocked on the door and said to get the patients ready, he'd go get Van Dam and be back. He stood on the porch and chewed tobacco rhythmically, watching her from under his felt cap.

"See your car got left out."

"Yes."

"Bo out driving when the wind come on?"

She hesitated a moment. "Yes."

"Where's he now?" Poulsen said. "Like to see him a minute."

"Come in," she said. "He's sick. I was just going to ask you to take him in to the schoolhouse."

Poulsen came in, stood at Bo's bedside. "Fella told me you had some hooch for sale," he said.

"Who told you that?"

"I dunno. One of the guys." He lifted his head and sniffed. "Smells like he had it about right."

"What do you want?" Bo said. "I'm sort of laid out. Sis'll get it for you."

"How much is it?" Elsa said. "I don't know anything about it."

"I can tell you, can't I?" he said. "Get a pencil and I'll make you a price list. You'll have to run this thing if I'm getting lugged off to the hospital."

She got paper and pencil and made a list at his dictation, and sold Lars Poulsen a half gallon of rye and watched him tuck it carefully under the seat of the bobsleigh and turn his horses toward Van Dam's. It was almost funny, the way her dislike for the whiskey business boomeranged. She was the operator of a blind pig now, all by herself. She could be arrested if anyone wanted to turn her in. But there was no time now to worry about that.

Poulsen was a long time at Van Dam's. When everything was ready for him she sat on the bed. "I hate to see you go up there," she said. "I'd rather take care of you here, but I think for the kids' sake . . ."

"You'd be up all night," Bo said. "You stay home and take it easy and I'll be back in a few days. This isn't anything but grippe."

"It's worse than grippe. You be careful, and do what they tell you to up there. I can imagine you ranting around and refusing to take your medicine."

He grunted. "Some of that hooch ought to be delivered," he said. "The sawbones gets the case of Irish, and there's a list of guys who get bourbon. In my pocket, somewhere."

She found the list. "I'll see that they get it."

"Chet could take it on his sled," he said. "But tell him not to leave it without the money. Not for anybody."

"I won't be sending Chet," she said. "I won't have the kids mixed up in this."

For a minute he looked at her, red-faced and puffy-lipped. Then he grunted.

But he was tender with her when Poulsen's knock sounded. "Take it easy," he whispered. "I got a hunch that as soon as we get past this flu we're out of the woods."

Her lip was trembling, and she bit it down. "Bo, get well right away. Do what they tell you, and don't get mad at anything."

"What would I get mad at?"

"You always get mad when you're sick. You get mad at people for trying to help."

"Oh bull!" he said, grinning. To Poulsen he said, "How you going to get me out there? Got another man?"

"Nope. Can't you walk a few steps? I'll hold you up."

"My feet are froze," Bo said, instantly irritable. "Walking out there would be like walking on broken glass. Why the hell can't they send two men on a job like this?"

"Ain't got 'em to send," Poulsen said. "How about riding on my back? How much you weigh?"

"Two ten," Bo said. He snorted, a short, violent sound. "Feel like lugging two ten out there?"

"Now come on," Elsa said. "I can take your feet if Lars will take your shoulders."

They got him out finally, and he lay in the hay of the wagonbox with his forehead white and dewed, his jaw tight and his eyes furious. Then Ole, almost as heavy, but easier to carry because they didn't have to be careful of hands and feet. Poulsen climbed to the seat and Elsa leaned against the tailgate, looking at the bundled sick men, all of them big, strapping men, and she thought again of the thing people said, that the flu took the strongest first, the ones with the deep chests and wide backs. The tears in her eyes were like pebbles of ice.

"Goodbye," she said. "Get well quick, all of you." She said it to all, but she looked only at Bo. She saw his jaw relax a little. "Take it easy, Mama," he said. "I got enough meanness in me to poison any germ."

"John Chapman died this mornin'," Poulsen said from the seat.

Bo sat up, and the stab he made to catch his balance with his hand made him grit his teeth. "What did you say?"

"John Chapman's dead. Funny thing, Doc O'Malley says his heart was all out of place, clear over on the right side. Been that way all his life. Never think it, a big tall guy like that."

Bo's eyes sought Elsa's. "By Godfrey," he said, "I almost forgot about something."

"Shall I do anything about it?" She too had forgotten that they owed Chapman two hundred dollars. Now Chapman was dead. But they could pay it back as soon as she delivered those cases . . .

"No," Bo said. "Let it go. Everything's closed up anyway. Let it go." He lay back on the hay and stared upward. "John Chapman," he said, as if he didn't believe it. "I talked to him three days ago and he was as well as I was."

"Bo . . ." Elsa said.

Poulsen flipped the lines and the sled started, the runners creaking in the dry snow, breaking down through the drift as he swung around toward the school. "Goodbye!" Elsa shouted. "I'll be up to see you every chance I get. And please be careful, do what they say . . . !"

For just an instant, as the sled slid away and she saw the schoolhouse two blocks beyond in the middle of the white field, the symbol now of plague and death because it housed in its four square rooms dozens of sick men and women, Elsa was shaken by utter panic. Then the moment passed and she turned back to the house. Bo would be better there. The doctor was living there now, and there were nurses on duty day and night. She would have plenty to do trying to keep the boys safe, and taking care of Bo's whiskey.

For an hour she went about the house cleaning up all the leavings of the two men, throwing Bo's clothes in a tub of water and starting them to boil, hanging out all the blankets and quilts that had been over him and Ole, scalding the used dishes with triple doses of boiling water. Then she stood and looked at the stack of sacked whiskey in the corner, the keg on the kitchen chair with its bung up. That next, the sooner the better.

Altogether she made three trips, taking two cases at a time on Chet's sled, going boldly through the main street because she believed literally Bo's story of the emergency. She knocked on doors and was greeted suspiciously from inside, until she told her errand, when the doors came wide and eager hands reached for the ears of the sacks. "I'll have to have the money right now," she told them stolidly. "Bo's sick, but he told me not to leave anything without the money, because he borrowed the money to get it and has to pay it back right away."

Two of her customers paid at once. A third grumbled about the price. Elsa said, quite honestly, that she knew nothing about that except what Bo had told her. If the price wasn't all right, she would take it back. But Bill Patterson, who was doing the grumbling, didn't want it taken back. He went and found forty-eight dollars in every denomination down to pennies.

At the fourth house Jewel King wanted the whiskey but didn't have the money. The bank was closed, Chapman was dead, he couldn't pay till he could get into the bank again.

"I'm sorry," Elsa said. "Bo said not to leave it without the money. I can't."

"But good Lord, Elsa," King said. "We need that stuff. If Bo was here he wouldn't hold out. I'd give you the money in a minute if I could lay hands on it."

If it had been her own doing she would have let him have it. But she didn't want to do anything that Bo could find fault with. She hated this job, so she would do it impeccably. "I wish I could, Jewel," she said, "but Bo said not to."

"Well, let me have some of it," Jewel said. "I got enough money for a bottle or two. I got to have something around, with all these germs in the air."

"You come down," Elsa said. "Bo tipped over on the way in and broke quite a few, and that left some loose bottles. I'll sell you all you want of those, or there's some bulk in a keg."

"Okay," he said. "I'll come down. Bo tipped over, you say? How'd he get back up?"

"I don't know. He wouldn't tell me."

King, scratching himself thoughtfully under the arm, laughed. "Old Bo," he said. "He's quite a boy."

"He brought a homesteader named Ole Pederson in with him," Elsa said. "He had the flu, and now Bo's got it."

King eased his weight onto the other foot. He obviously did not care to continue the conversation. Gregariousness had suddenly ceased to be pleasurable to Whitemud. "Yeah," he said. "Tough. Well . . ."

So Elsa pulled the case of bourbon back to the house, unloaded it, put the Irish on the sled, and went to the schoolhouse to see Bo. They wouldn't let her in. Visitors were not allowed. The best she could do was wait in the vestibule while Regina Orullian went to find O'Malley. When he came, he didn't have the money either. "If you want to leave it anyway," he said, "I can have a check for you tonight."

For just an instant, looking at his young, tired, sleepless-eyed face, she hesitated.

"Don't leave it if you don't want to," he said. "I can see why you might not. I might die, and you'd never be able to distill it out of me."

"I guess I'll take a chance," she said, and smiled at him.

The doctor ducked out of the storm door and carried in the sack. "I suppose you want to know how your husband is."

"I'd like to, yes."

"I wouldn't worry," O'Malley said. "He's too ornery to be hurt much. I tried putting packs on his hands and feet and he about tore the ward down. He'll be all right."

Elsa saw that he didn't like Bo. He didn't like him and yet he had a sneaking admiration for him. A lot of people reacted to him that way, they saw only his hard side . . .

"Well, thanks," she said. "Can I come back here every day and find out how he is?"

"Or call up," he said. "That's better." He looked at her speculatively. "How many of you at home now?"

"The two boys and I."

"If any of you get it," he said, "call up here right away. I can't do a thing unless I have everybody in one place. And if you hear of anyone else, call me, will you?"

"I will," she said. "And you're sure Bo isn't really very sick?"

"He's sick enough," O'Malley said, "but I think he'll be all right."

On the way back home again through the crusted drifts, she saw the sun break through the mist and shine for a few minutes thin and watery on the snow. She was glad O'Malley was there instead of old Doctor Barber. She remembered Barber, sag-cheeked, shaking-handed, riddled with dope or whatever it was he took. He must have been pretty far gone to drink denatured alcohol on a bet, the way he did. It occurred to her that everywhere she and Bo had lived there was somebody like Doctor Barber, lost and derelict and painful to see. Were they all over, she wondered, or was it just that Bo took them always to the fringes of civilization where the misfits and the drifters all congregated?

After lunch there was the problem of keeping the boys in the parlor while she served the continuous stream of people who came, some with milk pails, some with fruit jars, some furtive, some loud. The kitchen was headachy with the barroom smell of rye slopped from the keg. By suppertime she had taken in, from case goods and bulk, two hundred and sixty-five dollars. At eight o'clock that night she bundled up and walked to the schoolhouse, found that Bo was sleeping and doing as well as could be expected, collected the sixty-five dollars from the doctor, and came home again. She put her afternoon's total of three hundred and thirty along with the six she had got from Poulsen in the morning, tucking it down in a box at the bottom of her bureau drawer. Tomorrow, if things went right, she would be shut of the whiskey job.

She knew the moment she woke that she was sick. Her bones ached, her head throbbed, her throat was inflamed and sore, and her tongue, when she stuck it out in front of the mirror, was coated with gray-green moss. For a minute, desperately, she tried to pretend it wasn't true. She was just tired; she hadn't slept well; she was coming on toward her time, and that always made her feel low and draggy. But she hadn't been up ten minutes before the staggering weakness in her legs made her sit down. She called for Chet and Bruce, raising her voice painfully over her sore throat, and in a few minutes Chet came racing downstairs. "Ma!" he said. "Brucie's got it! He threw up all over the bed!"

"Oh my Lord!" she said. Driving herself, she stood up and started for the stairs. "Call Doctor O'Malley," she said. "Tell him Brucie and Mommie have both got it. You'll have to hold the fort alone, son."

"Jeez!" Chet said. For a moment she thought he was going to run and cling to her legs as Brucie sometimes did. But he stood still, running his tongue around his upper lip. "I can do it," he said. "I can milk old Red and sell the whiskey and do everything."

"Sell the whiskey!" she said. "You don't know what you're talking about."

Within an hour she lay in the hay-filled box of Poulsen's sleigh, with Bruce, pinched and delirious, against her side. Poulsen was not driving the sled today, but a young man she did not know. He said his name was Vickers, and he had just got in from the south the night before. Why, he must be a sort of neighbor of ours, out on the farm, she thought. But she was too weak and tired, and Chet was standing beside the sleigh too consciously brave in his mackinaw. The devil could have been driving the team and she wouldn't have paid very much attention.

She made Chet promise to call up twice a day and report to the hospital how he was getting along. She asked Vickers to look in once in a while on his trips around. When they pulled away she couldn't even kiss Chet, or hug him, for fear of the death her lips might carry. She could only wave, sitting up weakly with her muttering younger son under the blankets beside her, and say, "Goodbye, Chet, goodbye. You're the man of the family now, you've got to hold the fort."

Too weak and hurried to do anything else, she had left the whiskey in plain sight in the kitchen. The bundle of money she carried in a knotted sock in her purse.

4

Until afternoon Chet stayed indoors. The silence of the house bothered him, and the thought of what if Mom and Pop and Brucie never came back at all lay big as a sob in his throat. On his back was the burden of being the man of the house, responsible for the fires, the stock, for getting his own meals and keeping the house clean. He accepted those duties solemnly. For a while he was attentive to the fires as though they were in danger of flickering out every ten minutes. He made the beds. He got the broom and stirred a dust in parlor and dining room.

As he was eating his second bowl of bread and milk for lunch, the young man named Vickers came back and said he needed some beds and bedding, so Chet helped him knock down both double beds and load them on the sleigh. He would sleep on the couch in the parlor. It was warmer there anyway, and it would be pretty nice to undress right by the fire and pop into bed without any cold old floors and stairs.

In the kitchen, making a list of things he had taken, Vickers saw the keg, the sacked bottles. "Your dad doesn't want to sell any of that, does he?" he said.

"Sure," Chet said. "That's what he got it for, to sell for flu medicine."

"What have you got?"

"Rye and bourbon," Chet said promptly. "There isn't much bourbon left, I guess." He rummaged. "Five bottles is all."

"How much?" Vickers said, and reached for his wallet.

"Four dollars a bottle," Chet said. He caught himself, shot a look at Vickers' face. If he got more than the regular price, they'd have to admit he had held the fort to a fare-thee-well. "Or is it four and a half?" he said. "I forget."

Vickers' face was expressionless. "Sure it isn't five? I wouldn't want to cheat you." Under his eyes Chet broke and fled into the other room. "I'll go look," he said. "I think there's a list."

He stood in the front hall a minute before he came back with his face business-like and his mind crafty. "Four-fifty," he said casually. "I thought prob'ly it was."

Vickers counted twenty-two dollars out of the wallet, dug in his pocket for fifty cents, and picked up the ripped sack. He stood by the door and looked at Chet and laughed. "What are you going to do with the extra two-fifty?" he said.

Chet's heart stopped. His face began to burn. "What two-fifty?"

"Never mind," Vickers said. "Have you got all you need to eat here?"

"I got crocks of milk," Chet said in relief. He grinned at Vickers and Vickers grinned back. "Ma baked bread the other day, and there's spuds. I can go out and shoot a rabbit if I need some meat."

"Oh," Vickers said. His eyebrows went up. "You're a hunter, are you?"

"I shot rabbits all last fall for Mrs. Rieger," Chet said. He tried to make it sound matter-of-fact. "She lent me the shotgun and shells. She had to have rabbits and prairie chicken and stuff because she's 'nemic."

"Mmm," Vickers said. "I guess you can take care of yourself. How old are you?"

"Twelve."

"That's old enough," said Vickers. "Well, Mervin, if you need anything you call the school and I'll see that you get it."

"My name isn't Mervin. It's Chet."

"Okay," Vickers said. "Don't get careless with the fires."

"What do you think I am?" Chet said in scorn. He raised his hand stiffly to Vickers and went back to his bread and milk, excited and triumphant. That two and a half would look pretty good. He wondered how Vickers knew he had been euchred. Because he changed the price, probably. Next time he'd know better than that. He took the money out of his pocket and counted it. Twenty-two fifty was a lot of dough. He'd show Mom and Pa whether he could hold the fort or not.

But holding the fort got tiresome. The house was too empty. Sitting in the parlor with a book he heard the walls tick and the floors creak as if under stealthy feet. He looked up every thirty seconds.

Then he stood up, stretched his arms elaborately, yawned, and walked through the whole house, basement to attic, as if he were just strolling around. But his eyes were sharp, and he stepped back a little as he threw open the doors of closets and bedrooms. He whistled a little between his teeth.

Downstairs again, his suspicions laid but his boredom even greater, he remembered suddenly that he was the boss of the place. He could go where he liked and do what he pleased, as long as the cows got fed and milked and the house was warm. He thought of the two traps he had set at muskrat holes under the river bank. The flu had kept him from visiting them. It might be a good idea to take the gun and go out on a little hunt.

"Well," he said in the middle of the parlor rug. "I guess I will."

For an hour and a half he prowled the brush with his father's shotgun. Over on the path toward Heathcliff's he shot a snowshoe rabbit, white and furry and big-footed, and lugged it triumphantly toward home. One of his traps yielded a stiffly-frozen muskrat, and the weight of his game made him proud as he came up the dugway swinging the rabbit by a foot, the muskrat by its plated tail.

Coming past the barn, he looked toward Van Dam's, then the other way, toward Chance's, hoping somebody would be out and see him. He whistled loudly, sang a little into the cold afternoon air, but the desertion of the whole street, the unbroken fields of snow where ordinarily there would be sled tracks and fox-and-geese paths, let a chill in on his pride. He came up the back steps soberly and opened the unlocked door.

The muskrat's slippery tail slid through his mittened hand and the frozen body thumped on the floor. Two men were in the kitchen. His chest tight with surprise and shock, Chet looked from one, standing by the whiskey keg, to the other, at the table with a cup before him. One he didn't know. The one at the table was Louis Treat, a halfbreed who hung out at the stable and sometimes worked a little for old man Purcell. All Chet knew of him was that he could braid horsehair ropes and used to sing a lot of dirty songs.

"Aha!" Louis Treat said. He smiled at Chet and made rubbing motions with his hands. "We 'ave stop to get warm. You 'ave been hunting?"

"Yuh," Chet said. He stood where he was, his eyes swinging to the other man by the keg. The man was looking at Louis.

"Ees nice rabbit there," Louis said. His bright black eyes went over the boy. Chet lifted the rabbit and looked at the drops of frozen blood like red beads on the fur. "Yuh," he said. He was thinking about what his father said. You could trust an Indian if he was your friend, and you could trust a white man if his pocketbook wasn't involved, and you could trust a Chink more than either, but you couldn't trust a halfbreed. He looked at the man by the keg and decided that he looked tough.

Louis' voice went on. "You 'ave mushrat, too, eh? You lake me to 'elp you peel thees mushrat?" His hand dipped under his sheepskin and produced a long-bladed knife that snapped open with the pressure of his thumb on a button.

Chet stayed where he was. "No thanks," he said. "I can peel him."

Louis shrugged and put the knife away. Then he shook his shoulders inside the sheepskin, drained the cup he had been drinking from, and turned to thump the bung hard into the keg. "Ees tam we go," he said. "We 'ave been told to breeng thees w'iskey to the school."

"Who told you?" Chet said. He felt his insides growing tighter and his mind setting like plaster of Paris. If Pa was here he would throw these robbers out in a minute and scatter them from here to Chance's. But Pa wasn't here. He dropped the rabbit on the floor beside the muskrat, watching Louis Treat. You couldn't trust a halfbreed as far as you could throw a bull by the tail.

"The doctor, O'Malley," Louis said. He nodded to his companion. "You tak that end."

The other man stooped to lay hold of the keg. Chet's breath had left him. He bit his lip, and then in one jump he was around the kitchen table, out of reach of them in the dining room door, and he had the shotgun pointed straight at their chests. Without taking his eyes from them he cocked both hammers, *click, click.*

Louis Treat swore. "Put down that gun, you fool!"

"No sir!" Chet said. "I won't put it down. You drop that keg and get out of here."

The two men looked at each other. Louis set his end gently back on the chair and the other man did the same. "We 'ave been sent," Louis said. "You do not see w'at I mean. The doctor . . ."

"Like hell!" Chet said. "If Doctor O'Malley had wanted that he'd have had Mr. Vickers get it this afternoon."

The second man ran his tongue over his teeth and spat on the floor. He looked at Louis. "Think he knows how to shoot that thing?"

Chet's chest expanded. The gun barrels trembled so that he braced them against the door frame. "I shot that rabbit, didn't I?" he said.

Louis Treat's teeth were bared in a thin smile. He shrugged. "You are a fool."

"And you're a thief!" Chet said. He covered the two carefully as they backed out, and when they were down the steps he slammed the door and bolted it. Still carrying the cocked gun, he raced for the front hall, made sure the night lock was on, and peeked out. Louis and his friend were walking side by side up the bank of the irrigation ditch, the stranger pulling an empty box sled, Louis talking, throwing his hands around.

Very slowly and carefully Chet unlocked the hammers. Ordinarily he would have unloaded the gun, but not now, not with thieves like those around. He hung the gun above the mantel over the .30-30, looked in the door of the stove, threw on some lignite, went to the window again to see if he could still see the two men. Then he looked down at his hands. They were shaking. So were his knees. He sat down suddenly on the couch, unable to stand.

The days of holding the fort were long days. There was no one to talk to, no one to go hunting with, and he wouldn't have dared go hunting anyway, after what had happened that first day. The only people he saw were those who came to buy whiskey. Once his school teacher, Miss Landis, came apologetically and furtively with a two-quart fruit jar. He charged her four dollars a quart for rye and watched her hurry away toward the school with the jar under her coat. The men who came generally sat a while in the kitchen and told him about people who had died or got sick. They brought occasional news about the war. People were betting it would be over by Christmas.

But after three days people stopped coming for whiskey, and then there was only the twice-a-day telephone call to the school. His father was pretty sick. Then a day or two later his father was better but Mom had had a relapse because they got so short of beds they had to put Brucie in with her.

He moped around the house, milked the cow night and morning and couldn't possibly drink all the milk, so that the crocks piled up in the cellarway, all of them staying miraculously sweet, until he told the schoolhouse nurse about all the milk he had and Doctor O'Malley sent down old Gundar Moe to get it for the sick people.

Sometimes he stood on the porch on sunny, cold mornings and

watched Lars Poulsen's sled go out along the river toward the grave-yard, and the thought that maybe Mom or Pa or Bruce might die and be buried out there on the knoll by the sandhills made him swallow and go back inside where he couldn't see how deserted the street looked, and where he couldn't see the sled and the steaming gray horses move out along the river. He prayed earnestly at night, with tears, that none of them would die. He resolved to be a son his parents could be proud of, and sat down at the piano determined to learn a piece letter-perfect before Mom came home. But the dry silence of the house weighed on him; he lay sometimes with his forehead on the keyboard, and listened to the sound of the monotonous note. It sounded different with his head down, and he could concentrate on how different it sounded so that he didn't get afraid.

Nights were worst. He lay awake on the couch and stared into the sleepy red eyes of the heater and heard noises that walked the house. The death watch ticked in the walls, and there were crosses in the lamp chimney when he lighted it to drive away the dark and the fear.

For a week he lived alone, eating rabbit and duck soup and milk and bread, counting the tedious hours, playing with the Erector set until he lost interest in it entirely. On the fifth day he decided to write a book. In an old atlas he found a tributary of the Amazon called the Tapájos, and wrote his title firmly across the top line of a school tablet: "The Curse of the Tapájos." All that afternoon he wrote enthusiastically. He created a handsome young explorer and a sinister halfbreed guide very like Louis Treat. He lived for hours in the steaming Amazonian jungles, and when he got tired of those and the snakes got a little too thick even for his taste, he let his explorer emerge into a wide grassy pampa and see in the distance, crowning a golden hill, the lost city for which he had been searching. Then suddenly the explorer clutched his breast, reeled and fell, mysteriously stricken, and the halfbreed guide, smiling a sinister smile, disappeared quietly into the jungle. The curse of the Tapájos, which struck everyone who had ever set out in search of that lost city, had struck again. But the young hero was not dead . . .

Chet chewed his pencil and looked up. It was going to be hard to figure out just how his hero escaped the curse, and was only stunned by it, not killed. He rose, thinking, and wandered over to the window. A sled came across the irrigation ditch bridge and pulled on up to the Chances'. Out of it got Mr. Chance and Mrs.

Chance and Harvey and Ed Chance. They were well, then. People were starting to come home cured. He rushed to the telephone and called the hospital. No, Regina Orullian said. His family weren't well yet, but they were getting better. How was he doing? Did he need anything? No, Chet said. He didn't need anything.

He was disappointed, but not too much so. The sight of the Chances coming home gave him new spirit. He wasn't the only soul on the street any more. That night after milking he took a syrup pail full over to the Chances. They were all weak, all smiling, and Mrs. Chance cried every time she tried to speak. They were awfully grateful for the milk. He promised them that he would bring milk every day, and chop wood for them until they got strong. When he went home wearing a halo of big words that Mr. Chance, whom everybody called Dictionary, had laid upon him, he felt virtuous, kindly, charitable, like a knight helping people in distress. He wondered if it might not be a good idea to have his explorer run onto a group of people, or maybe just a girl, in distress, and rescue them or her from some awful fate, cannibals or head hunters or spider men or something.

On the afternoon of the tenth day he was over at Chance's. He had spent a good deal of time there the last day or two. His own house had got heavier and heavier to bear, lonesomer and lonesomer in its dead stillness. Besides, there wasn't much there to eat any more. So he took milk to the Chances, chopped their wood, sat for hours in their warm kitchen listening to talk about the schoolhouse and the Death Ward where they put people who were going to die. The Death Ward was the seventh grade room, his own room, and he and Ed Chance speculated on how it would feel to go back to school there where so many people had died—Mrs. Rieger, John Chapman, old Gypsy Davy from Poverty Flat, lots of others. Mrs. Chance, still so weak she could barely totter around, sat by the range and wiped the tears from her eyes, and when anyone spoke to her she smiled and shook her head and the tears ran down. She didn't seem unhappy about anything; she just couldn't help crying.

Mr. Chance said, solemnly, that there would be many familiar faces missing when this was over. The old town would never be the same. He wouldn't be surprised if an orphan or two had to be adopted by every family in town. He pulled his sagging cheeks and said to Chet, "I'll tell you what, son, you're fortunate yourself. Many times in that hospital I said to myself that those poor Mason boys were going to lose a loving father, certain as grass is green. I'd lie there, and the first thing I'd hear, some old and valued friend had passed in the Death Ward. I gave your father up when they moved him in . . ."

Chet's throat was suddenly dry as dust. "Pa isn't in there!" he said.

"Ira," Mrs. Chance said, and shook her head and smiled and wiped the tears away. "Now you've got the child all worked up."

"He isn't there now," Mr. Chance said. "I never hope to see again a spectacle as heartening as Bo Mason coming out of that Death Ward alive. Hands and feet frozen, double pneumonia—what a picture of fortitude that was! You should be proud, son."

"Is he all right now?" Chet said.

"Right as the rain," said Mr. Chance. "You needn't worry about your family, my boy. Take your father, I'd bet on him to live through anything. But then on the other hand you take a man like that George Valet. I dislike speaking of such things, but he couldn't even hang onto himself in bed. Those girls cleaned up his bed four times a day while he lay there red as a beet for shame, but did he improve? No." Mr. Chance closed his fist and made a decisive motion into the air. "A man like that, there's no *push* in him," he said. "Everything about him is as loose as his bowels."

"Ira!" Mrs. Chance said.

"I'll make you a bet," Mr. Chance said. "I'll bet you he doesn't live through this epidemic."

"I wouldn't bet on a person's life that way," she said. "And I wish you'd keep your language clean in front of the children."

"Ma," Harvey called from the next room, where he was lying down. "What's all the noise about?"

They stopped talking and listened. The church bell, far uptown, was ringing madly. Then the bell in the firehouse joined it. The heavy bellow of a shotgun, both barrels, rolled over the snowflats. A six-shooter went off, *bang bang bang bang bang bang,* and there was a sound of distant yelling.

"Well, what in Heaven's name," Mrs. Chance said. They were all at the window by then, trying to see.

"Here comes somebody!" Ed said. The figure of a boy was streaking across the flat. He hesitated as if undecided whether to go up by Van Dam's or down at this end of the street. Mr. Chance opened the door and shouted at him. The boy ran closer, shouting something unintelligible.

"What?" Mr. Chance yelled.

Chet recognized the boy now. Spot Orullian. He cupped his hands and yelled from the road as if unwilling to waste a moment's time.

"War's over!" he shouted, and wheeled and was gone up the street.

Mr. Chance closed the door slowly. Mrs. Chance looked at him, her lip jutted and trembled, her weak eyes ran over with tears, and she fell into his arms. The three boys, not quite sure how one acted when a war ended but knowing that it called for celebration, stood around uneasily shooting furtive grins at each other, staring at Mrs. Chance's shaking back.

"Now Uncle Joe can come home," Ed said. "That's what she's bawling about."

"I'll be back in a sec," Chet said. He bolted out the kitchen door, raced over to his own houee, pulled the loaded shotgun from above the mantel, and burst into the yard. He blew the lid off the silence in their end of town and split his throat with a wild long yell. Ed and Harvey answered from the open windows of their house, and another shotgun *boom-boomed* from downtown.

Still carrying the gun, Chet went back to Chance's. He felt grown up, a householder, able to hold up his end of any community obligations. Mrs. Chance was still incoherent. Broken ejaculations of joy came out of her, and she put a big red circle with a crayon around the date on the calendar. "I don't ever want to forget what day it happened on," she said.

"Neither you nor anyone else is likely to," said Mr. Chance. "This day history has come to one of its great turning points." Chet looked at him, his mind clicking with an idea that brought his tongue out between his teeth.

"Mrs. Chance," he said, "would you like a drink to celebrate?"

Mr. Chance looked startled, interrupted in a high thought. "I beg pardon?"

"Pa's got some whiskey left. He'd throw a party if he was home. Come on over."

"I don't think we should," Mrs. Chance said. She looked at her husband dubiously. "Your father might . . ."

"Oh, Mother," Mr. Chance said, and laid his arm across her back. "One bumper to honor the day. One toast to that thin red line of heroes. Chester here is carrying on his father's tradition like a man of honor." He bowed and shook Chet's hand. "We'd be delighted, Sir," he said, and they all laughed.

Nobody knew exactly how the party achieved the proportions it did. Mr. Chance suggested, after one drink, that it would be pleasant to have a neighbor or two, rescued from the terrors of the plague, come around and join in the thanksgiving, and Chet said sure, that was a keen idea. So Mr. Chance called Jewel King on the telephone, and when Jewel came he brought Chubby Klein with him, and a few minutes later three more men came to the door, looked in to see people gathered with glasses in their hands, and came in with alacrity. Within an hour there were eight men, three women, and the two Chance boys, besides Chet. Mr. Chance wouldn't let any of the boys have any whiskey, but Chet, acting as bartender, sneaked a cup of it into the dining room and all three took a sip and smacked their lips. Later, Harvey called Chet into the parlor and whispered, "Hey, I'm drunk. Look." He staggered, hiccoughed, caught himself, bowed low and apologized, staggered again. "Hic," he said. "Had a drop too much." Ed and Chet watched him, laughing secretly while loud voices rose in the kitchen.

Mr. Chance was proposing toasts every three minutes. "Gentlemen," he would say, "I give you those heroic laddies in khaki who looked undaunted into the eyes of death and saved this ga-lorious empiah from the clutches of the Hun."

"Yay!" the others said, banging cups on the table. "Give her the other barrel, Dictionary."

"I crave your indulgence for one moment," Mr. Chance said. "For one leetle moment, while I imbibe a few swallows of this delectable amber fluid."

The noise went up and up. Chet went among them stiff with pride at having done all this, at having men pat him on the back or shake his hand and tell him, "You're all right, kid, you're a chip off the old block. What's the word from the folks?" He guggled liquor out of the sloshing cask into a milk crock, and men dipped largely and frequently. About four o'clock two more families arrived and were greeted with roars. People bulged the big kitchen; their laughter rattled the window frames. Dictionary Chance suggested periodically that it might be an idea worth consideration that some liquid refreshments be decanted from the aperture in the receptacle.

The more liquid refreshments were decanted from the aperture in the receptacle, the louder and more eloquent Mr. Chance became. He dominated the kitchen like an evangelist. He swung and swayed and chanted, led a rendition of "God Save the King," thundered denunciations of the Beast of Berlin, thrust a large fist into the lapels of new arrivals and demanded news of the war, which they did not have. Within five minutes Mr. Chance and Jewel King were off in a corner holding a two-man chorus of "Johnny McGree McGraw," keeping their voices down, in the interest of decency, to a level that couldn't have been heard past Van Dam's.

He did not forget to be grateful, either. Twice during the afternoon he caught Chet up in a long arm and publicly blessed him, and about five o'clock, while Mrs. Chance pulled his sleeve and tried to catch his eye, he rose and cleared his throat and waited for silence. Chubby Klein and Jewel King booed and hissed, but he bore their insults with a reproving eye. "Siddown!" they said. "Speech!" said others. Mr. Chance spread his hands abroad and begged for silence, and finally they gave in to him, snickering.

"Ladees and gen'lemen," Mr. Chance said. "We have come together on this auspicious occasion. . . ."

"What's suspicious about it?" Chubby Klein said.

"On this auspicious occasion, to do honor to the gallant boys in Flanders' fields, to celebrate the passing of the twin blights of pestilence and war . . ."

"Siddown," said Jewel King.

". . . and last, but not least," said Mr. Chance, "we are gathered here to cement our friendship with the owners of this good and hospitable house, our old friend Bo Mason and his wife, a universally loved woman." He cleared his throat and looked around. "And finally, my friends, our immediate host, the boy who in the absence of father, mother, and brother, kept the home fires burning and finally, out of the greatness of his heart and the knowledge of what his father would do under similar circumstances, opened his house and his keg to our pleasure. Ladees and gen'lemen, the Right Honorable Chester Mason, may he live to bung many a barrel!"

Embarrassed and grinning and not knowing quite what to do with so many faces laughing at him, so many hands hiking cups up in salute, Chet stood in the dining room door and tried to be casual, tried to hide the fact that he was proud and excited and had never had such a grown-up feeling in his life.

And while he stood there with their loud and raucous approbation beating against him, the back door opened and the utterly flabbergasted face of his father looked in.

There was a moment of complete silence. Voices dropped away to nothing, cups hung at lips. Then in a concerted rush they were helping Bo in, limping heavily on slippered feet, his hands bandaged, his face drawn and hollow-eyed and bony with sickness. After him came Elsa, half-carrying Bruce and staggering under his weight. Hands took Bruce away from her, set him on the oven door, led her to a chair. All three of them, hospital-pale, sat and looked around. Chet saw that his father did not look pleased. His jaw was set harshly.

"What the devil is this?" he said.

From the dining room door Chet squeaked, "The war's over!"

"I know the war's over," his father said. "But what's this?" He jerked a bandaged hand at the silent ring of people. Chet swallowed and looked at Dictionary Chance.

Dictionary was not unequal to the occasion, after his temporary shock. He came up to clap Bo on the back; he swung and shook Elsa's hand; he twinkled at the white-faced, big-eyed Bruce on the oven door.

"This, Sir," he boomed, "is a welcoming committee of your friends and neighbors, met here to rejoice over your escape from the terrible sickness which has swept away to untimely graves so many of our good friends, God rest their souls! On the invitation of your manly son we are here not only to celebrate that escape from the plague, but the emancipation of the whole world from the greater plague of war." With the cup in his hand he bent from the waist and twinkled at Bo. "How's it feel to get back, old hoss?"

Bo grunted. He looked across at Elsa and laughed a short, choppy laugh. The way his eyes came around and rested on Chet made Chet stop breathing, but his father's voice was hearty enough. "You got a snootful," he said. "Looks like you've all got a snootful."

"Sir," said Dictionary Chance, "I have not had such a delightful snootful since the misguided government of this province suspended the God-given right of its free people to purchase and ingest intoxicating beverages." He drained his cup and set it on the table. "Now neighbors," he said, "it is clear that the Masons are not yet completely recovered in their strength. I suggest that we do whatever small jobs our ingenuity and gratitude can suggest, and silently steal away."

"Yeah," they said. "Sure." They went in a body out to the sleigh and brought in the one bed that had been sent back, lugged it through the kitchen and set it up in the dining room, piled the mattress on it, swooped together bedding and sheets and left them for the women. Before the bed was made people began to shake hands and leave. Dictionary Chance, voluble to the last, stopped long enough to pour into Bo's ear the virtues of his first-born. "We have enjoyed your hospitality, extended through young Chester," he said. "If we may be of any service during your convalescence, please do not hesitate to call upon us. I am happy to say that, thanks in good part to the excellent medicinal waters I have imbibed at your house, our family is almost completely recovered and at your service."

Mrs. Chance said goodbye with a quick, pleading smile and led Dictionary away, and there was nothing for Chet to do but face the eyes that had been waiting for him all the time.

"All right," his father said. "Now will you tell me why in the name of Christ you invited that damned windbag and all the rest of the sponges over here to drink up my whiskey?"

Chet stood sullenly in the door. He had already given up any hope of explaining. Under his father's hot eyes he boiled sulkily. Here he had held the fort all alone, milked the cows and kept the house. Everybody else praised him and said he was doing a keen job. But you could depend on Pa to fly off the handle and spoil everything.

"The war was over," he said. "I asked them over to have a drink and celebrate."

His father's face and neck began to swell. "You asked them over! You asked them over. You said come right on over and drink all the whiskey in the house! Why God damn you . . . !"

"Bo," Elsa said quietly. Chet slid his eyes toward her long enough to see the pain and sympathy in her face, but he didn't move. He set his mouth and faced his father, who was flapping his hands and looking upward in impotent rage. "Leave the house for ten days," he said. "Go away for as much as a week and by Jesus everything goes wrong. How long were they over here?"

"Since about two," Chet said. He met his father's hard look with one just as bitter, and his father started from his chair as if to thrash him, but his sore hands and feet put him back, wincing. Two hot angry tears started from Chet's eyes. He wished the old man wasn't all crippled. It would be just fine if he tried to whip him and couldn't make him say a word. He'd bite his tongue out before he'd make a sound, or say he was sorry, or anything.

"How much did they drink?"

"I don't know," Chet said. "Three crocks, I think."

His father's head shook back and forth. "Three crocks. At least a gallon. Twelve dollars' worth. Oh Christ, if you had the sense of a pissant . . ."

Laboriously, swearing with pain, he got up and hobbled to the keg. When he put down his bandaged hand and shook it his whole body stiffened. "I thought you only sold six gallons out of this," he said to Elsa.

Her glance fluttered toward Chet. "I don't know," she said. "I thought that was all . . . Now Bo, don't fly off the handle. We're lucky to be alive . . ."

"I sold some out of there," Chet said. "I've got the money in here." His body stiff, his mind full of self-righteous, gloating hatred, he went in and got the money from the jar. With it was the list itemizing each sale. He laid it all on the table.

"So you've been selling liquor," his father said. "I thought your mother told you to let that alone."

"People came wanting it. It was medicine, so I thought I ought to sell it to them."

His father laughed unpleasantly. "Probably sold it for a dollar a bottle," he said, and picked up the list.

Now! Chet said. He waited, his blood beginning to pound with triumph. His father's eyes went down the list, stopped. "What's this twenty-two fifty?"

"That's five bottles of bourbon to Mr. Vickers."

"That should only be twenty."

"I know it," Chet said. "But I got twenty-two fifty." He met his father's eye and almost beat it down.

"I ought to whale you within an inch of your life," his father said. "You had no business selling anything. Now you spread my affairs all over town, you charge people too much and ruin good customers, you ask the whole damned town over here to drink up twelve dollars' worth of stuff. . . ."

"All right!" Chet shouted. "All right, I'll tell you something!" He batted at his eyes with his forearm, seeing his father's sick-thin face and seeing nothing else. "The day Ma and Brucie left, Louis Treat and another guy came in here and were going to steal the whole keg and I run 'em out with the shotgun." He stood with his fists balled, the tears blurry in his eyes, shouting at his father's stiff, gray, expressionless face. "I wish I'd let 'em take it!" he said, his face twisting. "I wish I'd never done a thing to stop 'em!"

His father's face was dissolving, running, melting, and the bandaged hands were coming up in the air, and then his father was laughing, flung back against the kitchen table and shouting with uncontrollable mirth. Chet looked startled, and then sneered. His father's hands pointed at him, his father's breath came wheezy with laughter from spent lungs. "Okay, kid," he said. "Okay, you're a man. Nobody's going to take it away from you. If you looked at Treat the way you just looked at me he's running yet, I'd bet on it."

Everything had dissolved so suddenly, the defiant stand he had made had produced such unlooked-for results, that Chet went grouchily into the parlor and sat by himself. After a minute his mother came in, her lips twitching with the beginning of a smile, and put her arms around him.

"Don't be mad at Pa," she said. "He didn't understand at first. He's proud of you, proud as he can be. So am I. You did just fine, Chet. It was more than a boy should have had to shoulder . . ."

"If he's so proud," Chet said. "why does he have to *laugh?*"

"Because you looked so fierce you struck him funny, I guess."

Chet scowled at the .30-30 and the shotgun hanging one on top of the other above the mantel. He shook his shoulders irritably inside his mother's quick tight squeeze. "Well, there's no call to laugh!" he said.

5

A week after their return from the hospital, Bo sat counting his money in the dining room. Elsa was already in bed; he could feel her watching him. Deliberately he counted out fifty dollars and pocketed the rest, almost six hundred dollars, a fine fat roll with a rubber band around it. He sat down on the edge of the bed and shook off his slippers.

"Coming to bed already?" Elsa said.

"Lot to do tomorrow."

"What?"

He slid his pants off one leg, pulling at the cuff. "Change the wheels to bobs, for one thing."

He knew she was lying there stiffly, accusing him with her eyes, but he pulled his shirt over his head and pretended not to know. Finally she said, "To go to Montana?"

"Yep."

She lay stiff and straight on her side of the bed as he got into his nightgown and stretched out. Her voice went flatly up toward the ceiling. "So it wasn't the epidemic. You're in the whiskey business."

"Look," Bo said. He put his arm around her but she didn't yield or turn her face. "I've still got six hundred, and it'll be over a week before they get the bank open again and I have to pay that note. I can take the wagon and bring back twice as much as I did before. Double my money again."

They lay in silence, with bitterness between them. Then Elsa said, "Fourteen years ago you were in the liquor business and you got out. Now you're back in it worse."

"What's wrong with the liquor business?" he said. "Almost anywhere it's perfectly legal. Just because this crackpot province passes a war measure . . ."

"Even where it's legal it isn't respectable," she said.

In exasperation he turned his back on her, turned over again just as abruptly to say, "You sold some a while ago. Did it burn your fingers? Did the money you got for it poison you? I suppose you think you and Chet are a cinch for hellfire because you both sold whiskey."

"It isn't hellfire that bothers me," she said. "I just want us to have a good solid place in the world where nobody can shame us with anything."

"That's sure ambitious," he said. "That shows a lot of imagination, that does. Any dirt farmer in the province can claim that, practically."

"But we can't," she said.

"Okay," he said. "Okay, I'll go down tomorrow and get the job of driving the honey-wagon. That's a nice solid place in the world. That's a steady job. And Heathcliff's dead, they'll need somebody."

"Bo," she said, "I'd rather see you doing that than what you're going to do."

"By God," he said, almost in wonder, "I believe you would." He turned away from her and settled himself to sleep. As long as he remained awake he did not feel her stir. When he woke in the morning he felt the antagonism still between them, but he went ahead anyway. And when he had returned with the load, and had peddled it in town and in all the little towns along the line, and had turned the whiskey into cash and paid back the note to the bank, he took

off again with team and bobsled in January, and brought back enough
to last through the rest of the winter.

Now the long closed winter, blizzard and cold snap and Chinook,
delusive thaws in February and iron cold in March and heavy snow
in April. Two line-riding cowpunchers from the Half-Diamond Bar
froze to death on St. Patrick's day in a forty-below blizzard. Mrs.
John Chapman, widowed by the flu, created a sensation by taking
strychnine for the lost affections of Hank Freeze, the most prosperous farmer on the north bench. As soon as it was clear that Mrs.
Chapman had taken an overdose and would recover, people had a
good deal of fun with that. What could you expect of a guy named
Freeze?

In formal meeting, the town council voted to collect money for
a bronze plaque to be erected in the firehouse in honor of the four
local boys who had died in the war and the eleven others who had
served. The Reverend Charles Evans, successor to the Reverend John
Morrison who had died of the flu, bought a half column of space in
the Whitemud *Ledger* to deplore, more publicly than he could from
his pulpit, the falling away of Sunday school and church attendance.

Early in April Howard Palmer, who had hung up a shingle reading "Barrister" two years before, stood up in church to denounce the
wickedness of the town. He thundered, his head shook, his eyes went
bloodshot with passion, foam gathered at the corners of his mouth.
He called down hellfire on three sinful women, and named their
names. He blasted the person who had brought liquor in in defiance
of provincial law, and named his name. He took a passing swipe at
Ed Anderson's billiard hell and the Pastime Movie Theater. When he
had cracked his damnation blacksnake over most of the town's backs,
he fell down between the pews in a fit, and that night, while Bo
Mason was winning a pearl-handled jackknife for figure skating at
the annual ice carnival, they carted the barrister off to Saskatoon
to the bughouse, and that was a nine-days' wonder.

Until finally there came a time when the sun was up before most
of the townspeople, and by the time breakfasts were over the eaves
began to drip. They dripped all day, and after a day or so women
emerged on front porches and swept out the accumulated rubbish
of the winter. The nights froze hard, but before eight in the morning water was running again, and anyone walking below the bench
hills was likely to break through the sodden crust and fill his shoes

with icewater, and if he stood quietly and listened he could hear the streams under the snow. Thermometers stood at forty-five, ninety degrees above where they had stood a time or two during the winter. Dogs ran dirty-footed through the town, boys felt the misty, warming air on their faces and hated school. Because this was it: this was the real spring thaw. It might freeze every night, it might even snow again, but the weather had broken. The awakening was like a sunny morning after long rain, or light after long darkness, and the blood leaped to the sound of the spring freshets coming down the gullies from the hills.

After a week of thaw Bo went downtown and brought back the Ford from Bert Withers' garage, where he had left it to get a new radiator put on. Three days later, as soon as the sun had dried the roads a little, he was ready to go.

"Keep an eye on Daisy," he said to Elsa. "She'll throw her colt any time now. I asked Jim Enich to come around every other day or so."

"Are you going to be gone long?"

"I might be gone ten days."

"But why? With the car . . ."

"I'm going to peddle this in the other towns," he said. "The quicker I get rid of this the fatter the stake gets. I want to build up a good one before two or three other guys get the idea the roads are passable."

"Is there anything you want me to do?" she said.

He looked at her quickly. "Like what?"

"Like selling any stuff you've got left over."

"I thought you didn't want anything to do with it?"

"I didn't," she said. "But I'd rather be in it with you than have you going off on these trips without telling me anything. We always did things together, till now."

"Old Mama," he said, and put his arm around her. "Now you're playing ball."

An hour later he climbed into the Ford and drove out toward the bench, his tracks like parallel wriggling ditches in the thick gumbo mud.

For eleven months of the year the Whitemud River was a sleepy, slow, clear stream, looping in wide meanders between the bench hills, shallowing to brief rapids, deepening along the cutbanks in the bends. But for a week or two around the end of April it was a flood thirty feet deep, jammed with ice cakes and driftwood and the splintered timbers of bridges. It completely covered the willows across the channel from the Mason house, and what had been a wilderness of brush and scrub was a chocolate expanse of water, moving in places with terrible quiet speed, stalling at others into eddies and backwashes.

It began with the first sudden thaw, when every little drainage gully from the hills began pouring water down onto the river ice, and it kept on until the channel was gorged and overflowed by this new river on top of the old. In the sun, in the wet, exciting wind, groups of people lined the banks waiting for the breakup. Somebody reported that she was going below the dam; in ten minutes there was word that ice was backed twenty feet high behind the upper railroad bridge. By the time the townspeople arrived, a section gang working cautiously from a handcar was dropping dynamite into the moving, sliding, ponderous pressure of the pack. They might as well have dropped firecrackers.

After one look, some of the men went home for pikepoles. In a timberless country, those forty- and fifty-foot piles and those heavy hemlock timbers were worth fishing for.

Bruce, coming home from school at four, was told to take Daisy out and picket her for a couple of hours, give her a breath of air and some exercise. He led her out, rubbing down along her shoulder, working off some heavy winter hair. He wished she would hurry up and have her colt, so he could feed it and try to teach it tricks.

He led Daisy down into the northward loop of the river, drove in the picket pin, and snapped the chain into her halter ring. "Okay," he said. "You take a little stroll around and get a bite of grass and I'll come for you about dark." He slapped her haunch and rubbed her poll when she poked her head at him. She was so round with her colt that her legs spraddled.

Coming back, he heard the blasting out by the bridge, and saw the people moving that way. Harvey Chance was just starting to sprint down the muddy road. "Come on," he said, and jumped up and down waiting. "The bridge is going!"

Together they raced past Van Dam's, through the south pasture fence, out toward the abandoned oil derrick on the town side of the bridge. There were boys on the derrick's top, the bank was black with people, men with pikepoles were posted along the lower side.

"There she goes!" The crowd's voice rose, an enormous, exciting, soaring yell. Bruce and Harvey ducked in to the cutbank edge just in time to see the handcar scuttle off the bridge. The spindly structure was already buckling and kneeling above the white ice and brown water. Timber groaned. A cake of ice was hurled against the yielding piles of the upper side, snapped two of them off, and split in two, falling with a heavy double crash. The bridge buckled more, the right rail split loose from a half dozen ties and snapped straight, the left one was bent inexorably downward. From then on the measure of the bridge's yielding was that widening rift between the rails. The ice growled heavily upstream. A few cakes, released by the snapping of the two piles, slid through edgewise and splashed in the open water below.

There was another heaving, straining, wood-splitting, nail-and-spike-bending, ice-burdened groan from the bridge. The left hand rail broke loose and snapped almost upright, humming like a mighty tuning fork, and the crowd sighed, a noise like a sudden wind, as the ice mounted the upper piles and the whole toothpick structure bent over very slowly toward the river, held together momentarily against the seethe of edgewise, endwise, flatwise, twisting and righting and grinding and overflowing icepans and dirty floodwater. Then the whole middle section fell apart, went out in a spider-legged tangle of timbers. The townward side held except for three cabled-together piles that were gnawed off by the ice. But the excitement by then was gone from the bridge. The excitement was in the log fishing downriver. The whole crowd fled, even the impotent section gang, to help the men with pikepoles.

One man, hanging to a willow bush, his feet on the slippery edge of the rising water, leaned far out and hooked a pile with his pikepole, hauled it closer, lost it to a driving ice cake and yelled to the next man downstream, who hooked it and snaked it halfway in, where a dozen hands laid hold and dragged it up the bank.

"God bless the C.P.R.!" somebody yelled. There was laughter and noise, more yells as someone else snaked in a pole. A detachment left for the next bend, racing the pounding icepans and the match-like logs, to fish in less troubled water farther down.

They stayed for hours, virtually the whole town, men, women, children, and dogs. The bigger boys went along the cutbanks kicking great undermined blocks of earth into the river. Women went home at supper time and came back with coffee and sandwiches.

Men split firewood and built up a bonfire. Every ten minutes the bridge would obligingly drop off another timber or group of timbers, and they were dragged out of the water and ice with a "Heave! Heave! Heave!" and yells of laughter. It was a picnic, a spontaneous spring overflowing. It was ten o'clock before Bruce and Chet and their mother walked home all together, arm in arm, singing.

Bruce went to bed late, drunk and exhausted with excitement. Through his sleep, a faint and disturbing titillation of his eardrums, he heard the noise, and when he stirred and woke in the morning he realized that he had not been dreaming it. The window, open clear to the top of the sash for the first time in months, let in a shivery draft of fresh damp air, and with it the faint yelping, far off.

Chet was already up and gone. When Bruce got dressed and went down into the kitchen the dogs were still yapping down in the bend. "What's the matter with all the pooches?" he said. "Where's Spot?"

"He's out running with them," his mother said. "Probably they've got a porcupine treed or something. Dogs go crazy in the spring."

"It's dog days they go crazy."

"They go crazy in the spring, too," she said, and hummed a little as she set his breakfast out. "You'd better run out quick and feed the horses. I told Chet to, but he went right on by the barn as if he'd never seen it."

Bruce stood still in the middle of the kitchen. "Oh my gosh!" he said. "I left Daisy out all night!"

He saw from his mother's face that it might be serious. "Where?" she said.

"Down in the bend."

"Where those dogs are?"

"I think it was higher up," he said, but he was sick and afraid. In a minute they were both running. Bruce broke ahead, around Chance's shed, and searched the brown wet meadow at the head of the U. No sign of the mare where he had left her. He opened his mouth, half-turned, running, to shout at his mother coming behind him, and sprinted for the bottom of the bend.

As soon as he rounded the bay of brush fringing the cutbank behind Chance's he saw the mare, a brown spot against the gray brush, and on the ground beside her another smaller spot. There were six or eight dogs leaping around, barking, sitting in a circle. He saw his own dog and the Chapman's airedale.

Shouting, he pumped on. At a gravelly patch he stooped and clawed and straightened, still running, with a handful of small pebbles. In one pausing, spraddling, aiming motion, he let fly at the distant pack. The rocks fell far short, but the dogs drifted out in a widening circle, sat on their haunches and let out defiant short barks, each bark a sharp muscular contraction of their whole bodies. Bruce yelled and threw again, watching the colt at Daisy's feet. The colt jerked its head up and down; the mare's ears were back and her eyes rolled. She pricked her ears once at Bruce and laid them back again.

As Bruce came up slowly the colt struggled, raised its head with white eyeballs showing, spraddled its white-footed legs, and tried to stand. It was sitting like a dog on the ground when Elsa came up, getting her breath, her hair half down. Bruce reached out and succeeded in touching the blazed face. "Gee!" he said. "Isn't he a pretty colt, Ma?"

He patted Daisy, slapped her wet neck, scratched under her mane and felt her tremble. She must have got chased hard. But there was the colt, sitting comically on the ground, and his happiness that nothing had gone really wrong bubbled out of him. "Lookit his feet," he said. "He's got four white feet, Ma. Let's call him Socks. Can I? Isn't he a nice colt, though?" He reached down to pull the colt's forelock, and the colt bobbed his head away.

Then Bruce saw his mother's face. It was quiet, too quiet. She hadn't said a word to all his jabber. Instead she was kneeling about ten feet in front of the squatting colt and staring at it. Bruce's eyes followed hers. There was something funny about the way . . .

"Ma!" he said. "What's the matter with its feet?"

He left Daisy's head and came around. The colt's pasterns looked bent—*were* bent, so that when its weight came on the front hoofs the whole pastern touched the ground. His shifting frightened the colt, and with a flopping effort it floundered to its feet and pressed against its mother. And it walked, Bruce saw, flat on its fetlocks, its hoofs sticking out in front like a comedian's too-large shoes.

Elsa pressed her lips tight, shook her head, stood up, moving so gently that she got her hand on the colt's poll. He bobbed against the pleasant scratching. You poor little broken-legged thing, she said. You poor little friendly ruined thing! Still quietly, she turned on the circle of dogs, sitting with hanging tongues out of range, even Spot staying away as if he knew he had outlawed himself. God damn you, she said, God damn your wild hearts, chasing a poor mother and a newborn colt.

To Bruce, standing with trembling lip, she said just as quietly, "Run and find Jim Enich. Tell him to bring a wagon or a democrat. And don't cry. It isn't your fault."

Bruce bit his lip and drew his face down tight, trying to keep his eyes from spilling. "It is too my fault!" he said, and turned and ran.

Jim Enich was a bandy-legged little man who had been a horse wrangler for Purcell for many years. He was slow, gentle, mild; there were deep creases down each side of his mouth, with a brown mole hiding in one of them. He had Bruce wait while he hitched up, and they drove together past the picnic ground and the ballfield and the swings. Bruce's mother had the colt on the ground again, and the mare was nosing her impatiently.

Enich climbed out, walked around the mare. He squatted by the colt's head and scratched around its ears. His fingers went down to press and probe and bend the broken arch of the pasterns. He whistled tunelessly between his teeth while Bruce stood around with his feet on fire, aching to do something, ask something, but not daring to interrupt Enich's deliberate professional concentration.

Without saying anything, Enich examined the mare, still whistling.

"What do you think?" Elsa said.

"Mare's all right."

"What about the colt?"

"Lessee him try to stand up."

With one hand in the colt's topknot, he helped it to its feet. It spraddled wide, fetlocks sunk to the ground. The dropping of the weight there threw its fine, long-legged body out of proportion. Enich plucked a blade of short grass and chewed it and shook his head.

"Ruined?" Elsa said.

"'Fraid so."

She grimaced, and her hand tightened on Bruce's. He hadn't realized till then that he had been holding her hand. "Well, let's get them back to the barn, at least," she said.

Enich tied the colt's feet, heaved and pulled and pushed it into the wagon. It lay there with terrified white eyes rolling, and the mare toe-danced behind the endgate, butting Enich around with her nose.

"All right, gal," the wrangler said. "You can put your face right in, if you're that worried."

When they started, Daisy was left momentarily standing. She chuckled with instant apprehension, trotted quickly after the wagon, stuck her neck over the endgate and touched the colt, the breath vibrating in long wheezy solicitous nickerings in her throat.

Bruce sat between his mother and Enich, his head twisted back to watch. Every time they hit a bump and the colt's raised head thumped on the boards, he was stricken with pity and contrition. "Gee whiz," he said. "Poor old Socks." He tried to reach back and touch the chestnut haunch. His mother put her arm around him to keep him from leaning too far. Absorbed in his pity for the colt, he didn't watch where they were going or notice anything ahead of them until he heard his mother say in surprise and relief, "Why, there's Bo!"

Terror tightened him rigid. He had forgotten and left Daisy out all night. It was his fault that the colt was ruined. From the narrow space between Enich and his mother he watched like a gopher from its burrow. He saw the Ford pulled up beside the barn and his father's big body leaning into it pulling out blankets and straw. There was mud from top to bottom of the car, mud all over his father's pants. The boy slid deeper into his crevice.

Then his father was at the wheel, Jim Enich was climbing down, Elsa with puckered lines in her forehead was saying that Daisy had had her colt while she was staked out, and the dogs had smelled her out and chased her and broken down the colt's feet. Pa said little. He went around and helped Enich lift the colt out onto the ground, stooped to feel its fetlocks with square muddy hands, looked once at Bruce.

"Would've been a nice colt," he said. "Damn a pack of mangy mongrels anyway." He brushed at the mud on his pants and said to Elsa, "How come Daisy was staked out?"

"I told Bruce to," she said. "The barn's so cramped for her, I thought it would do her good to stretch her legs. Then the ice went out, and the bridge, and we all forgot what we were doing . . ."

Bruce heard her trying to smooth it out and take the blame off him, but in his own mind it was perfectly clear, as it had been from the beginning. He was to blame.

"I didn't mean to leave her out, Pa," he said squeakily.

His father's somber eyes rested on him briefly, turned to the colt and then to Enich. "Total loss?" he said.

Enich shrugged.

Bruce thrust himself into it again, not wanting to, but unable to stay out. "Pa, it won't have to be shot, will it? Give it to me, I'll take care of it. I'll keep it lying down and heal its feet up."

"Yeah," his father said, and laughed, but his mother said quickly, "Jim, isn't there some kind of brace you could put on it, to hold its legs straight? I remember once at home my dad had a horse that broke a leg below the knee, and he saved it that way."

"Might try a hobble-brace," Enich agreed. He plucked a weed and stripped off the branches. "I wouldn't expect much from it, though."

"But it would be worth trying," she said. "Children's bones knit so quick, I should think a colt's would too."

"Would, if you could make a colt savvy he had to lay down."

"Bo," she said, "can't we try it? It seems such a shame, a lovely colt like that." She nodded at him slightly, and then both of them were looking at Bruce. He felt the tears coming up, and turned away.

"How much this hobble-brace cost?" his father said.

"Two-three dollars. Blacksmith can make it."

"All right," Bo said. "Let's go get MacDonald." He laid his hand on Bruce's shoulder. "It's your responsibility," he said. "You left Daisy out, and now you've got to take complete care of the colt."

"I will," Bruce said. "I'll take care of it every day."

Big with contrition and shame and gratitude and the sense of sudden, immense responsibility, he watched his father and Enich start for the house to get a tapemeasure. When they were almost to the kitchen door he said loudly, "Thanks, Pa! Thanks ever so much!"

His father half turned, laughed, said something to Enich. Stooping to pet the trussed colt, Bruce caught his mother's eye, started to laugh like his father and felt it turn into a sob. As he swung away he saw Spot, one of the pack that had done all this to Daisy and the colt, looking around the corner of the barn. Spot took three or four steps forward and stopped, wagging his tail inquiringly.

Very slowly (never move fast or talk loud around animals) Bruce stooped and found a stone as big as a pigeon egg. He straightened casually, brought his arm up, and threw with all his might. The stone caught Spot in the ribs. He yiped, tucked his tail, and ran. Bruce chased him, throwing clods and stones and gravel, yelling, "Get out of here! Go on, get out of here! Beat it! Go on!"

6

Chet sat in the sun on the back step, cleaning his .22. In the yard Bruce was plucking handfuls of fresh grass from the fence corners to feed into the nibbling lips of the hobble-legged colt. It was Saturday in mid-May. Flies hummed in the yard, and a swallow, skimming like an arrow, hit the tiny hole in the barn eaves and disappeared at full speed.

"Hey Brucie," Chet said. "Get your gun and let's go shoot gophers."

"I'm going to take care of Socks," Bruce said.

"Aw, come on. He can take care of himself."

"He gets excited," Bruce said. "He tries to run if I don't watch him."

Chet grunted, threw away the oiled rag, and replaced the bolt in the gun. Bruce was nutty. He'd rather stick around and watch his old colt than go out and do anything. Chet spit off the porch and went in to hang the ramrod on its nail. His mother was looking at the calendar.

"He doesn't stop to think how a person might worry," she said.

"Uh?"

"Your dad should have been home day before yesterday."

"Where's he gone? After more whiskey?"

She looked at him long and steadily, and her mouth moved as if she had something bad-tasting in it. "Chet," she said, "you don't ever talk about what Pa's doing, do you?"

"Naw. I know better'n that."

"I hope you do. Don't say anything to anybody." She laughed and shook her head. "I guess that's one trouble. A person can't talk to anybody. Where were you going?"

"Oh, out."

"Run up to the postoffice and get the mail before you go."

"Gimme two bits?"

"What for?"

"I need some cartridges. These old b-b's are no good for anything. If I saw a rabbit I'd need longs."

"All right." Chet followed her into the dining room.

"Can I have a dime for some chocolate bars too?"

"Why a dime? Won't nickels buy anything any more?"

"Well, a nickel then."

She gave him a quarter and a nickel, and as he went out he was thinking that it was kind of good to have Pa gone. He crabbed when you asked for money. Ma was better about things like that.

He was carrying the gun as he went uptown, and by the time he reached the postoffice he had picked up Bill Stenhouse and Pete Armstrong. Pete had his Daisy pump gun, and Bill had no gun at all. Chet felt both superior and magnanimous, letting them tag along.

There was no mail except a letter from Aunt Kristin, from Minnesota. In McGregor's hardware Chet bought a box of longs, and at Henderson's drug, while he took a long time deciding what kind of chocolate bar he wanted, Pete swiped a package of spearmint gum and Bill got a vial of perfume.

They clotted briefly outside, around the corner, to count their wealth and decide where they were going. "I got to take this letter home," Chet said. "Come on, I'll make Bruce lend us his old .22. He's going to stay home anyway."

He left Bill and Pete leaning on the fence looking critically at the crippled colt while he took the letter inside. "Oh, good," his mother said automatically, seeing the return address. "Nothing from Pa?"

"That was all," Chet said. "Ma, can Pete and Bill and me have a little lunch to take along hunting?"

"I suppose so. You want me to fix it?"

"I'll fix it." Chet sliced off some thick slabs of bread, buttered them, found three doughnuts gummed with powdered sugar, and dropped them all in a bag. From the cellarway he got Bruce's .22.

"Brucie," he said out the door. "Can we borrow your gun?"

"No," Bruce said. He had been quarreling with Bill and Pete, who said the colt would always be an old wreck that couldn't walk. Bruce was almost crying. "No, sir!" he said. "You leave my gun alone."

"Give you a stick of gum for the loan of it," Pete said.

"No."

"Two sticks."

"No."

"Aw, come on, Brucie," Chet said. "You aren't going to be using it."

"I'm not going to lend it anyway."

Chet came clear out on the step. "What you want to be so stingy for? We won't hurt your old blunderbuss."

"If it's an old blunderbuss," Bruce said, "what do you want to borrow it for?"

"I'll punch your nose in a minute," Chet said. He started out, but his mother's voice stopped him.

"Let him alone," she said. "If he doesn't want to lend it, that's his right."

The three started away. "I know where you little squirts got your shanty," Chet said. "Wait and see what happens to that."

"You leave it alone!" Bruce yelled after them. "If you touch that shanty I'll drop rocks through your old boat."

"You do and you'll get your nose busted," Chet said. He walked with long, Leatherstocking strides, and the others fell into single file behind him, walking in his footprints. Bill, having no gun to occupy his hands, took out his snitched vial of perfume and began dosing his shirtfront.

A half hour later, in the exciting, growth-heavy spring wind, the three sat on pinnacles of the sandhills halfway up the bench and looked down over the river valley, the looping brown river, the willows fresh green, the valley grass a deeper, brighter green, the houses sharp-edged in the strong light. On both sides of the washed-out railroad bridge Chet saw the black dots of men moving; and the railroad itself, the double line of rails and the criss-cross of ties and the spiderweb lines of fences along the right-of-way, was drawn straight east and west along the valley.

Hooking his legs around the sandpapery stone of his pinnacle, he twisted to look back of him at the slope. The aspen came down in three bright tongues, one behind the summer cottage of Howard Palmer, one directly behind the sand hills, and one behind the shanty of Tex Davis. Tex was a cowpuncher who came and went, appearing sometimes in the spring and staying a few weeks, then disappearing again, nobody knew where. Some said he followed the rodeos and stampedes, others said he was a road agent. Chet had peeked into the one window of the shack plenty of times, but his peeks had told him nothing except that Tex was a dirty old buzzard and never swept his floor.

He turned again, looking out across the railroad to Heathcliff's place in the bottom, across Heathcliff's to Purcell's dam. The air blew across him warm and soft, and all around the bottom of the pinnacles the ground was misty purple with crocuses. He could smell sweet pea perfume floating across from the peak where Bill perched.

"There goes somebody on a bike," Bill said.

Chet looked and saw the smooth, floating motion of the wheel, the blaze of a white shirt as it caught the sun. "It must be Frankie Buck," he said. "Old Man Lipscomb must have given him Saturday off."

He took a firm grip with his legs, shot off his .22 into the air, yelled, "Hey, Frankie!" Pete and Bill yelled too, and the figure below, almost a mile away, stopped moving. The white-shirted arm waved, and they yelled to him to come up. Frankie rolled along to the gate where Angus MacLeod's road came across the tracks, and came walking his wheel through. He left both gates wide open as he started up. Chet and Bill and Pete slid down off the pinnacles and went over to Tex's shack to meet him.

He was puffing when he came up the hill, and his stockings had slid down, leaving his bowlegs bare. Frankie was adopted by Mr. Lipscomb, who ran the *Ledger,* and he had to work a lot, setting type and delivering. "Hi," he said. "What you kids doin'?"

"Horsing around," Chet said. "How come you don't have to work?"

"I have to this aft," Frankie said. "Have you shot anything?"

"Chet couldn't hit anything if he saw it," Pete said.

"Oh, couldn't I?" Chet said. He looked around for something to shoot at, found an old demijohn behind the shack, and set it up on a fence post. From fifty feet away he aimed and fired. There was a *spann-n-n-g!* but the demijohn didn't break. Pete haw-hawed.

"Well, I only had a b-b in," Chet said. "I hit it, didn't I?"

"I can do as good as that with my air gun," Pete said. He pumped his gun and shot, and again there was a noise, a higher, lighter noise, *spinn-n-n-g!* The demijohn was still intact.

"You guys are terrible," Frankie said. "Leave me have a shot, Chet."

He shot and missed. Then Bill shot and missed. Chet slipped a long into the .22 and waved them back. "Lemme show you how it's done," he said. He shot high and broke the neck off the jug. Bill and Frankie started pegging rocks at it, and in a minute it was in a dozen pieces. Inside was the dried body of a mouse.

"Lookit that," Frankie said, picking it up by the tail. "I bet he died happy."

He threw the mouse at Pete, who fell on him. They wrestled till they were both winded and lay sprawling on the warm ground.

Then they were all lying on the ground looking up into the empty, pale, sunny sky. Pete lifted his head as if that was all the strength he had left. "Gosh I'm hungry!" he said. So they ate the sandwiches and split the doughnuts and the chocolate bar and all had a drink at the spring behind the shack. On the way back, Frankie chinned himself up to the high little window and peeked in. He banged his hand against the sash, and the sash gave a little.

"Hey!" he said. "I bet we could get in here."

He pried and hammered at the sash, but it wouldn't give far enough to give him any leverage. "Stand back a minute," Chet said. "I bet I move her." He jammed the gun butt against the side, but the butt slipped, and there was a shattering tinkle of glass.

Chet pulled back and looked at the others. Bill looked scared. Frankie and Pete looked as if they didn't know how to look. "Now you've did it!" Bill said.

"Oh hell!" Chet said. He reached up the barrel and knocked another of the four lights out. In an instant the other kids were clattering and banging and pounding, and the window was a total loss.

Excitement was in them now. "Gimme a boost," Frankie said. He jumped for the sill, but Chet pulled him down. "I busted the winda first. I get to go in first."

There was an argument, but Pete gave him a hand and he popped his head into the musty twilight of the shanty. He picked the glass out of the road, got his leg over, and slid inside to the littered floor. He was hunting plunder before Pete's face was in the window, and he had found the horse pistol before Pete was halfway inside.

With the treasure in his hand he snapped the door lock and let in a flood of sun. The pistol was an enormous single-action Colt .44 with a great arching wooden butt. It was so heavy that he needed two hands to aim it. The other kids crowded around and wanted to handle it, but he kept them off. It was his prize. And it was even loaded, five shells in it and the hammer carefully down on the empty chamber. Chet broke it and looked through the barrel. Clean.

Pete and Frankie were turning the shanty upside down looking for more, but Bill was a little scared. He said, "You ain't gonna keep it, are you, Chet?"

The word touched Chet's mind briefly: Stealing. But the gun was in his hands, ponderous, heavy, a real honest-to-goodness man-sized six-shooter. "You bet your life!" he said.

The other two, having found nothing but a rusty butcher knife and some tin dishes, were looking under the bunk. Pete lifted the mattress, and field mice dropped and scattered.

"Whee!" Frankie yelled. He leaped sideways out of a half dozen twittering, frantic mice that skittered and scurried and hid and popped out again and jumped up and down. Frankie grabbed an old alarm clock almost as he jumped, and as he alighted he turned and threw it. The thing smashed like a bomb, scattering glass and hands and wheels and springs halfway across the room.

"Oh Lordy!" Bill moaned. He stood back, but the other three kept on. Pete threw the butcher knife and it stuck quivering in the wall. Frankie skimmed a plate and cup after the clock. The mice were all out of sight by now.

"I know what," Chet said. "Here, Frankie, you take my .22. I'll use the horse pistol and Pete's got his air gun. Bill can yank the mattress up and jump back and we can all blaze at once."

Bill said, "What if old Angus MacLeod came around here and caught you? He looks after this place for Tex."

"Oh, Angus!" Chet said. "He's so tight every time he farts he whistles."

They all laughed. He looked around and saw them laughing, and with a Dead-Eye Dick draw he yanked up the horse pistol and aimed it at the bed. "Come on, Bill," he said.

"You'd shoot me," Bill said. "I don't want to bust up Tex's shack anyway."

"You helped bust the winda," Chet said. "What are you such a sissy for?"

"I ain't a sissy."

"You sure act like one," Pete said.

"It ain't fair," Bill said. "You'd all get to shoot and I wouldn't."

"You can have second shot with my .22," Chet said. "Frankie'll shoot, and then you can."

Bill hesitated. "Well, all right," he said. "But don't any of you shoot till I get out of the way."

He walked over to the bunk, eyeing them. "Wait till I get clear out of the way, now." He stooped, still watching them, yanked the mattress over the edge, and jumped clear. Two mice dropped out of a wide hole and darted for the corner. Another one dashed from under the bed. The air rifle went off, then the .22. The mice switched back toward the bed. Chet held the pistol with both hands and pulled the trigger.

There was a tremendous roar, the gun kicked clear up over his head and almost out of his hands. The four stared. The mice had vanished, but there was a great splintered gash in the floor.

"Holy cow!" Chet said.

For a moment the damage that that one slug had done to the boards shocked them silent. How would you like to get shot with a thing like that? It would make a hole through you you could put your hand into. Bill was staring with his eyes wide and scared. "Jiminy!" he said. He looked at Chet. "I'm gonna get out of here!" he said, and bolted.

Frankie reached out a toe and scuffed at the splinters the .44 bullet had ripped from the floor. They looked at each other, almost holding their breath. Then the impulse struck them almost simultaneously. They yelled. They fired their guns into the sodden mattress. They tipped over the table and spilled magazines and candle-ends onto the floor.

"Let's burn the damn place down," Chet said. He shot the .44 into the bed again, and a mouse ran out. They cornered and killed it, ripped the mattress into the middle of the room, kicked at the mice that scattered frantically. Frankie wrenched till he got a leg off the table, and with that for a club he beat down the shelves. From the doorway the scared face of Bill watched them.

"Burn 'er down!" Chet said. "Break 'er all to pieces!" He smashed a chair against the wall and splintered one leg, threw the whole thing on the pile. Pete was bending down trying to light the mattress, soggy with winter damp. "I need some paper," he said.

The air was immediately full of crumpled sheets of paper. Pete twisted a handful, lighted the feathered end, and stuck it under the pile of broken furniture and rubbish. The flame caught, grew. Chet looked at Frankie and wet his lips. He shifted the .44 to his other hand and moved over by the door.

"You guys are gonna catch it," Bill said from outside.

"Aw bull," Chet said. He wet his lips again and watched Frankie doing a wardance around the fire. The shack was beginning to get smoky, and the smoke was exciting. Chet leaped after Frankie, waving the gun. He struck a pose by the window and stood crouching, the gun in his belt, his hand like a claw. "I'm Buck Duane," he said. "I'm the old Lone Star Ranger. Any-a you outlaws lookin' for me?"

He looked around the shack slowly, contemptuously, eyes narrowed and mouth a slit. The others were all watching. "I guess I'll just shoot your lights out anyway," Chet said, "seeing you're all too yellow to come on." He snatched for the gun in a lightning draw, but the front sight caught in a belt loop and he had to tug it loose. He fired twice into the ceiling, and Pete, by the door, pretended he was shot, clutching at his breast and staggering loosely around the floor. Frankie stuck out his foot and Pete almost fell into the fire. He arose full of wrath.

"Watch out who you go tripping."

"Oh bushwah," Frankie said.

Pete shouldered him sideways. "Bushwah nothing. You watch out who you go tripping around into fires."

"Who'll make me?"

"I'll make you."

"You and whose army?" Frankie said.

"I don't need any army."

Their hands were up, they were sparring lightly, shuffling around in the corner where the table had been. Chet coughed in the smoke. "Come on outside and settle it," he said. "We're gonna get our pants burned off in here."

The quarrelers started out just as Bill, his eyes bugging out and his jaw so loose that he could hardly speak, stuck his head inside and shouted something. "What?" Chet said. He pushed past Bill, Frankie and Pete on his heels, shouldering each other angrily in the doorway. Bill yelled again and pointed. A wagon was coming up the hill, hardly more than two blocks away, and in the wagon was Angus MacLeod and his whole family. Even as they stared Angus was tossing the reins to his wife and jumping to the ground.

Bill and Frankie broke together around the smoking shack, Chet and Pete a step behind, hitting for the aspen coulee that came down close. After ten steps Frankie stopped, digging, and legged it back, to come after the other three in a moment pushing his bicycle on the dead run.

By the time Frankie reached the edge of the protecting brush Angus, tall, red-headed, and surprisingly fast, was around the house. He didn't even stop to look inside or put out the fire. Fists doubled, red hair blowing, he covered ground like a galloping horse, so that there never was a chance of getting the bike away. A block inside the brush Frankie wheeled it into a clump of bushes and came pounding after Chet, burdened down with his two guns. Bill and Pete were out of sight, maybe still running, maybe hiding.

The grade got steeper. Chet's mouth was dry, his eyes bulging, his chest on fire for air. Once, when the trees thinned, they heard Angus yell, and looked back to see him coming with that terrible unsuspected speed. They ducked up a side trail, raced across a stretch of level ground, slid off to the left through straggling brush, and huddled up under the bank of the watercourse, completely spent, trying to swallow the heaving of their breath. They waited, hoping that they had fooled Angus, and in a minute they heard him go thundering by. Even then they stuck where they were. Chet started to whisper to Frankie, but a sound above made him huddle close up against the bank, so close that little clods of dirt broke loose and rolled down past his cheeks.

Angus was coming back. They heard his steps, heavy, not running now, and his hoarse breath. The steps went straight on down the path, and after three minutes Chet peeked through the roots on the lip of the bank and saw the farmer just disappearing into the trees. Keeping out of sight under the bank, they went back up the coulee, crossed through it onto the east side near the top, and came down through the other coulee to the sandhills. At the edge of the hills they found Bill and Pete, scared to go on any further till Angus left. They had run clear up onto the bench and then come down under the cover of the trees.

"Well, by Jeez," Chet said, "he never caught any of us."

In the low sumac between the aspen and the sandstone pillars they lay sprawling on their backs. Chet began to feel pretty good. They had got away slick as a whistle, and he still had the six-shooter, too. "Never laid a hand on a one of us," he said.

"No," Bill said, "but he's got Frankie's wheel."

Frankie sat up, was pulled down instantly. He opened his mouth and squawked. "What?"

"I seen him," Bill said. "I seen him come out of the brush pushing the bike. It's stood against the shanty now."

They all stared at Frankie. His lip trembled, and a tear popped into each eye. "What'll Mr. Lipscomb do?" Chet said.

"He'll kill me," Frankie said. He dashed his forearm across his eyes and bit his lower lip. "You don't know. When he gets mad he's just as likely to hit me with a stick of type."

On hands and knees he crawled to the very edge of the sumac. The others wriggled up and they lay in a row looking across the green slope to the shack. The smoke wasn't going up any more, but there was a smoldering pile of stuff outside, where Mrs. MacLeod and the kids had thrown it. Mrs. MacLeod and the children were sitting by the wagon, Angus was hitching his horses to the plow he had brought along, and Frankie's wheel was leaning against the corner of the shack.

"Oh damn!" Frankie said. He lay down in the brush with his face on his arms.

Chet, looking over the six-shooter, rolling the empty cylinder, peering down the fouled barrel, thought darkly that they ought to go right down there and throw a gun on old MacLeod and take the bike and tell him to hit the grit. He would do just that, if he had any more bullets. He would throw his gun from low on his thigh, and it would come so fast Angus wouldn't even see it. "All right, MacLeod," he'd say. "Give the kid back his bike, and don't take your time, either!"

He stole a look at Frankie. Once, on a hike, he had seen old man Lipscomb, who was the scoutmaster, get mad at Frankie and slap him so hard on the jaw that the red mark stayed there for an hour. Frankie would get hail columbia now.

Frankie raised up a little. "We got to get it back," he said doggedly. "I wouldn't dast go home without it, and I ought to be there now."

"Well, how?" Chet said.

"I ain't gonna help," Bill said. "I didn't want to bust up Tex's shack in the first place."

"You're a coward," Frankie said.

"I ain't either. I just don't want anything to do with it."

"Me neither," Pete said. "Any guy that'd shove you in the fire."

"Oh, quit arguing," Chet said. He was remembering an Indian story he had been reading in the *American Boy* where one hunter had drawn the Indians' fire while the other got away and went for help.

"Lookit," he said. "Come on over here." They all crawled to the edge again. "See? If you could get into the brush on this side, then the rest of us could go around on the other side and make a racket and get Angus chasing us and then you could dash out and get on your bike and beat it."

"I'm game," Frankie said. His face was smeared and his mouth tight. "Who's coming?"

"Not me," Bill said.

"Me neither," said Pete. "I'm not helping any guy that tries to push a guy in the fire."

Frankie half raised up. "Oh for gosh sakes," he said. "I'll smack you in the nose."

"Try it," Pete said. "I dare you. Go on and smack me."

They lay on their elbows glowering, and Chet got mad at both of them. "You can fight any old time," he said. "We got to get that wheel."

So he and Frankie went alone, Chet feeling loyal and heroic and contemptuous of the two left behind. He left his two guns with Pete, so he could run faster if Angus took after him, and he and Frankie worked back down through the coulee until they could hear the cries of Angus' two little girls playing.

"Now I'll sneak on across," Chet whispered. "You watch, and when you see the bushes jerk, get ready. Then I'll jump up and see if I can get him after me, and you grab the bike."

Stealthily he snaked through the golden bright shadows of the aspen and into the fringe of sumac. Lifting his head carefully, he could see Angus plowing the potato patch he grew on Tex's land every year, and Mrs. Angus spreading out some lunch in the shade of the wagon. None of them was within a hundred feet of the bike. He jerked the bushes, and a bush across the opening, hardly fifty feet from the shack, twitched back.

Chet drew a long breath, trying to un-knot his stomach. He waited until Angus was plowing in his direction, as far from Frankie and the bicycle as he would get. Then he jumped to his feet, yelled, waved his arms, thumbed his nose.

Angus did not hesitate a second. He dropped the reins from around his neck, turned the plow on its side, and started like a foot-racer for Chet. Out of the corner of his eye, before his legs could answer his command to bolt, Chet saw Frankie run crouching to the corner of the shack, and then he himself turned tail and dug for the woods.

He had gone only a few steps when Mrs. Angus yelled. He threw a scared running look over his shoulder. Angus had turned, and was trying to cut Frankie off as he pushed the wheel desperately across the bumpy ground toward the road. Chet stopped and watched, hardly breathing.

Frankie had fifty yards to go before he hit the trail and ground smooth enough to ride on, and Angus, coming down at an angle, had a good chance to cut him off. Frankie sprinted, bouncing the wheel, his bare legs and fallen stockings twinkling, but Angus was coming like a thunderbolt. Chet's heart stopped for a full two seconds as Frankie hit the road and made a running leap onto the seat. It looked as if Angus could reach out in one more stride and grab him. He had looked terribly fast before, coming uphill. Now, going down, he was all legs. He opened up clear to the neck like a clothespin, he ate up twenty feet at a stride. Frankie's head was down, his feet on the pedals were a blur, his shirt was ballooning out behind, but he did not open up any daylight between himself and Angus. One bump, one spill, and Frankie was a goner.

But he didn't spill, and he didn't let up, and even at the tracks, where he had with providential carelessness left both gates open, he pedalled right on, bumped perilously over the planks of the crossing, and legged it out the other side and up the road to town. Angus stopped at the fence.

Chet yelled, cheered, waved to Frankie far down below. When he took his eyes off the flying white figure and woke up to where he was, Mrs. Angus was only a few rods away, bearing down on him with her face puckered in anger. Like a scared antelope Chet cut for the woods. At first he didn't really fear her much. Then, a little way inside the aspen, he glanced back to see her almost upon him. She was almost as fast as Angus. Fear put a spurt of speed in Chet's legs, but he couldn't shake her. He heard her feet pounding on the path behind, close upon him. In a minute her hand might reach out . . .

Like a flash he dropped to hands and knees. Mrs. Angus' heavy knee hit him solidly, knocking his wind half out, and she went over him ponderously, grabbing for him as she fell. But Chet scrambled loose and escaped like a limping, winded fox into the brush.

When Chet got home from that expedition he hid the six-shooter in the cellar and kept his mouth discreetly shut, waiting to see what would happen. A time or two he slipped home from school at noon, when he knew his mother would be down at the postoffice seeing if there was a letter from Pa, and took out the gun to snap and fondle it. But it came Monday, Tuesday, Wednesday, and nothing happened. Angus wasn't going to raise a fuss, or maybe he didn't know who to raise it at.

He and Frankie had started building an elaborate shanty in the brush by the east ford. Pete came in, over Frankie's protest, when he produced a full bag of Bull Durham stolen from his father. Bill came in too on the strength of half a raisin pie he had got from home. They camouflaged the shanty with brush, disguised the path in. And on Thursday afternoon Chet proposed that they take the six-shooter down and have some target practice. Shells for a .44 probably cost plenty, so everybody'd have to divvy in.

A quick foray under the plank sidewalk in front of the hotel turned up a dime and a good deal of tea lead. Crawling out, they scattered to their homes to see what could be raised.

In half an hour all were back. Bill had a dime. Pete had hooked seventeen cents from his father's second-best pants. Frankie had only four pennies. Mr. Lipscomb wouldn't give him any money, and he was scared to hook any. Chet had bummed a dime from his mother. Altogether they had fifty-one cents.

"I should think that'd be enough," Chet said. He shifted his pants, because the .44 was inside them and kept slipping down. On their way to the hardware store they ran into Bruce, going to mail a letter for Ma. That was the second one she had sent in two days.

"Don't you go following us," he warned Bruce.

"Why? What you gonna do?"

"None of your business. You just stay away, is all."

"I guess I can walk where I want to," Bruce said.

"You're too little to hang around with us," Chet said, and hitched his pants. The string that hung the gun around his neck was cutting into him; he walked a little spraddling to keep the pistol from banging against his stomach.

They ditched Bruce and went into the hardware. Mr. McGregor's pale egg-like bald head came forward along the dark counter. On a nail keg sat Jewel King, hugging his knees.

"Hi, Mr. King," Chet said.

"Hi, boy," King said. "Been throwing any parties lately?"

"No sir," Chet said. He wished he could forget that Mr. King was town marshal, and he wished he hadn't brought the gun along in here. It was so dark that probably the little bulge it made wasn't noticeable, but it bothered him anyway, and he crowded against the counter. "Have you got any .44 cartridges?" he said to Mr. McGregor.

Mr. McGregor bent over the counter. "You mean .45, don't you?"

"No. .44."

"That's an old-fashioned size," Mr. McGregor said. "If you really want anything that big you must want .45's. What do you want them for?"

"It's for a gun of Pa's," Chet said. "It's .44, I know."

Mr. McGregor looked across at Jewel King. His toothless mouth wrinkled up like the mouth of a paper bag. "You ever see a .44, Jewel?"

"Sure," Jewel said. "They make 'em, all right." He let his knee down and said to Chet, "You haven't got the gun handy, have you? Maybe we could tell."

Chet swallowed. Jewel King was looking at him from one side, Mr. McGregor from the other. Bruce had come in and was standing by the door. "No," Chet said. "I haven't got the gun. I just wanted some to . . . to . . ."

Jewel's hand came out suddenly and patted him around the waist, felt the gun, dragged it out, broke the string. He looked the pistol over and showed it to Mr. McGregor. Mr. McGregor nodded his head up and down. "Give themselves away every time," he said.

Jewel spoke sadly to Chet, who was standing frozen, not trying to run. "I'm sorry to do this, boy," Jewel said, "but I've got to arrest you. You stole that gun from Tex Davis' place. Didn't you?"

Chet swallowed. The door slammed and he turned his head quickly. Frankie and Pete and Bill had all skipped, and only Bruce stood inside the door.

"Yes sir," Chet said.

Mr. McGregor munched his gums together and cackled. "'Y God it's funny," he said. "Both in jail the same time. That's a funny one."

"What?" Chet said.

Jewel King looked at him soberly. "Don't you know?"

"Know what?"

"Never mind," Jewel said. "I'll have to take you over to the jail, and then I'll have to go see your mother. I don't like to see you in a mess like this, Chet. I had a pretty high opinion of you, up till now."

As they started for the door Bruce, pale and weeping, turned and fled. When they got out on the street Chet saw him streaking along the irrigation ditch toward home.

7

"He said that?"

Elsa rose slowly from the chair in the kitchen and stared at Bruce. He nodded, sniffling.

"But how could he know," she said, half to herself, "when I just got the letter today?"

"He just took hold of Chet and said, 'I'm sorry, boy, but I've got to arrest you,' and then Mr. McGregor said that about both of them at the same time. Is Pa in jail, Ma?"

Elsa put her hand in her apron pocket and felt the letter. "No," she said.

"What are they going to do to Chet?"

"Never mind," she said. "You run out and play. I'll go get Chet straightened out."

"I want to come, Ma."

She said, "You stay as far out of this as you can get. I'll be back pretty soon."

Along the ditch bank, as she went uptown, there were purple crocuses, and the primroses were just beginning to fold their petals together. A chilly little wind blew in from the river. So now everything's falling apart, she said. Now Bo's in jail in Havre and Chet's in jail at home, and we're right back where we started in Dakota, only worse now, with the kids in it.

Walking, she pulled out the letter and read it again. Two policemen had been waiting at the line, picked him up before he could get across. He was full of shame, he couldn't blame himself enough for bringing this on her. They had confiscated the car and the load and had him charged with smuggling. "I should have listened to you, Sis," he wrote, "but I wanted so damned much to get out of the hole. If I could have made a good stake at this we could have gone anywhere you wanted, and settled down to some steady business. I was just sick of living on sowbelly and beans in a dirty little jerkwater town, I guess. They've got me in jail with a nigger, but I'm not complaining. I'm no better than a nigger, the way I've made you live. I hope you won't think you have to tell the kids. If this turns out all right I'll make it up to you, that's a promise . . ."

She put the letter away again. Don't tell the kids.

At the jail she found Jewel King. "I was just going to call you," he said, "but I thought I better let Chet stew a while in the jail- house." He chuckled, and his belly shook. "He's got guts, that kid," he said. "Most kids would of bawled, but he just sits there and grits his teeth. I like to see a kid like that."

"Do you like to see a boy steal?"

"Oh, steal," Jewel said. "This wasn't really stealing. Any kid would snitch a gun if he found it in a deserted shanty. He's just full of beans. I wouldn't of put him in the cooler only Angus MacLeod was pretty hot, said a bunch of them swiped the gun and some other stuff and then tried to burn the house down."

"Oh Lord!" Elsa said. "Did they?"

"Naw. Angus come along and put it out." Jewel fished up a bent cigar. "I wouldn't worry, Elsa. Chet wasn't the only one. We got the gun back, and if you give Angus four-five dollars damages every- thing's all right."

"Who are the others?"

"I don't know. Chet wouldn't tell."

"But he stole the gun himself."

"I guess so. He had it on him."

"All right," she said. "I'll give you five dollars for Angus. Chet was the ringleader. He always is. I want him to spend the night in jail."

"Oh now, that ain't necessary," Jewel said.

"I want him to stay in jail anyway," Elsa said. "I want him to learn what it means to break laws and get in trouble."

She met Jewel's queer, sidelong look steadily. "Now can I see him a minute?" she said.

He led her into the little cell back of the firehouse, where Chet slumped on a bench. He rose when the door opened, and Elsa felt a pang at the sight of his face, white and set and too old for him. Like father like son, she thought. Shame and sullenness and eager- ness for sympathy and determination to act like a man whatever happened—his face said exactly the same things as Bo's letter.

"Well, Chet," she said.

"Hello, Ma."

"I never expected to see you in a jail," she said.

He stood sullenly silent. He would not, she saw, attempt to deny his guilt or plead with her. There again he was like Bo. He was what he was, and he wouldn't pretend to be anything else. Bruce would have lied, in the same situation. Chet might much more likely go clear wrong, but he'd go in his own way, with a kind of pride.

"I hope you realize what you've done," she said. "I wouldn't like to see a boy of mine grow up a thief."

She stopped then, because she didn't want to add the humiliation of tears to his punishment. "Mr. King will let you out in the morning in time for breakfast," she said. "You come home and eat and get ready for school."

Chet turned and sat down on the bench, and to keep from crying herself she brushed past Jewel and went outside. "I'd rather spend the night in there myself than make him do it," she said.

"Yeah," Jewel said. "Well, I'll see that Diamond Dick gets back home all right. Don't worry about the jail. That's a good clean jail. No bugs or anything."

"Will he have to sleep on that bench? I didn't see any bed."

"Bed in the firehouse part," he said. "He'll be okay."

"All right." She looked hard at Jewel. "But don't you be too easy on him. Don't give him the idea that what he's done is smart, or manly, or anything. I want him to know that being in jail is a disgrace."

So now there would be waiting again, as it seemed to her she had waited all the time she had known Bo. Now there would be sitting day after day busying herself with little unimportant things, but jumping at the slightest noise, running to the window at the slightest flash of movement along the south road. There would be getting through the day somehow, anyhow, getting the boys to bed, sitting in the evenings to do fancy work or to read, and her ears twice as alert as in daylight, her mind twice as receptive to frettings and worry. There would be dragging off to bed with the worries waiting for her to lie down, hanging over her like mosquitoes on a warm night.

There would be the escapes she had used before, the daydreams and the memories of childhood that sometimes were so similar that they confused her: pictures of quiet streets, apple trees heavy with fruit or white with blossoms in a green back yard, her children scuffling leaves under the maples and running to greet Bo when he came down the sidewalk on a summer evening, coming from work with his coat on his arm and the six-o'clock sun on his face. That dream expanded indefinitely: neighbors dropped in for root-beer and whist, Bo told stories, did card tricks, sang songs, kept them all laughing. There were good nights of tenderness and love, and in the mornings Bo's voice singing a fool song.

She didn't want much. Yet it seemed to her sometimes as if life had conspired to keep from her exactly that one thing that she desired, and as if her husband and her children, who were the single indispensable part of her daydreams, should be the ones to destroy what she had been working for.

One night she sat reading a novel that someone had loaned her. It was all about castaways on a cannibal island, and war with wooden swords between the tribes, and it was romantic and exciting and a little silly, but she kept at it because if she didn't she would have to think. Once her head lifted: it sounded like someone out behind. But there had been too many of those false alarms lately. Her ears were like the ears of a dog pricking in sleep at phantasmal noises.

Then she heard it again, distinctly. She stood up just as the door between dining room and kitchen opened and Bo's grinning face looked in.

She dropped the book and ran to him, was swept into his bear-hug. When he set her down and she could look at his face his eyes were sly and warm.

"Hi, Mama," he said. "How've you been?"

"Oh, all right," she said. She had him by the arms, looking him over. There was something different about him, something gayer and younger. His clothes . . .

"Why, you've got a new suit," she said.

"Like it?"

"It's lovely. But what . . . I thought . . . How did everything come out?"

"Did you think they'd hang me?" His laugh was so open and amused that she stared. There was no such shame as she had expected, no hangdog look of creeping home in disgrace, and she realized instantly, though the idea had never entered her head before, that she had been counting on that, expecting to steer him with it as she had steered Chet.

"What happened over there?" she said.

He laughed again. "They had to turn me loose. Didn't have any business pinching me in the first place. The American prohibition law isn't in effect yet, see? They pinched me on the wrong side of the line. The cops just got all snarled up about what their job was. So after they'd kept me in jail a week or so they had to give me back the car and the load."

"But how could they be so stupid? If there wasn't any law . . ."

"They don't know what the law is yet, that's their trouble. Neither did I. I was piping pretty small till my lawyer put me wise. He was a smart little shyster." He shook her fondly by the shoulders and narrowed his eyes, grinning. "Want to see something?"

"Sure. What?"

"Where's the lantern?"

"I'll get it. What've you got?"

"Wait and see." With an air of great secrecy he lighted the lantern.

"And you didn't have to pay a fine or anything?" she said, going out.

"Nary a nickel. Go on, keep moving, right on out to the shed."

The shed doors were open, but Bo muffled the lantern so that she could see nothing. "Open your mouth and shut your eyes," he said.

"You're just like a child," she said. "Unexpected returns, and surprises, and mysteries. What is this?"

"Now you can open."

She opened. There was a car in the shed that was not the old Ford. It was new, expensive looking. Bo had turned on the headlights, which burned with a white brilliance against the shed wall and reflected back on the gleaming dark green of the body.

"My goodness!" Elsa said. "Where did you get this?"

"Bought it."

"Bought it! With what?"

"With seventeen hundred dollars."

"*What?*"

"Take it easy," he said. "There's plenty more where that came from."

"Well, I just don't understand," she said. She inspected the mysterious dials on the dashboard, wiggled the gear-shift knob, read the name on the plate: Essex. It was by all odds the finest car she had ever seen. The seats were grained leather, the top was black and rakish as a taut sail. "A new suit and a car that cost seventeen hundred dollars," she said. She lifted the blankets in the back of the car and looked under. "And another load!"

"And that isn't all," Bo said. "Come on back inside."

He shut off the headlights and locked the shed doors. On the way to the house he laid his arm across her shoulders and shook her again. "Got your eyes bugging out, haven't I?"

"You've mystified me enough," she said. "I give up. Now tell me, quick."

Inside the kitchen he blew out the lantern with a sharp puff of breath and let the chimney down. In the light of the lamp on the table his eyes were bright as a cat's.

"I had almost two thousand when I left here," he said.

"And you've spent it all."

"Don't get ahead of yourself. I put fifteen hundred in a Havre bank and got a load and started back. That's when they pinched me and took me back to Havre. And in jail I met a guy that put me wise."

"The nigger?"

He looked at her in disgust. "No, not the nigger! All he did was teach me to play coon-can. This was a guy that got pinched in a gambling raid. After I got through talking to him, and they let me out, I went out and traded old Lena in on this boat, and moved the load from one to the other, and bought some more to fill this one up, and there she is."

"But if it cost seventeen hundred . . ."

"I got four hundred and fifty for Lena," Bo said, "and I gave them two-fifty cash. We owe a thousand on her."

"But what are we going to use it for? I'd feel silly, riding around this town in a car like that."

"Maybe you won't be riding around this town," Bo said. "This boat will go twice as fast as old Lena, and she holds half again as much. She'll pay for herself before you can spit twice."

"You're going on running whiskey," Elsa said.

He nodded, watching her. "Till I get so far ahead I can afford to get out," he said. "You know what we're going to do?"

"I can imagine."

"We're going to move."

"Where to?"

"One of the Montana towns. Havre or Great Falls."

"And leave the homestead, and this house, and the stock . . ."

"Hell with all of it," Bo said. "The hell with this little burg, too. Soon as that prohibition law goes into effect in the States there'll be millions to be made. There is now. Some of the states are already dry, and there's always a market in a dry state. We're going to run whiskey where there's money to pay for it in wholesale lots."

Elsa stood quietly, everything in her sagging, as if she had worked all day and saw more work ahead that had to be done before she could rest. "I wish . . ."

"Uh?"

"What if they *had* convicted you in Havre?"

"They didn't," Bo said. "And they won't ever get the chance again, not as long as I've got a fast car."

His eyes were steady on hers, as if he dared her to raise an objection, as if he had arguments and statistics and proofs to counteract anything she could say. She sighed and gave it up. Bo seemed to feel the moment when her resistance disintegrated. He swung around the kitchen as if shaking the whole thing from his back, and yelled for food. While she got him something he sat at the table, natty and citified in his new clothes (he told her that he had stopped out on the bench and changed, so as to come in with all flags flying) and watched her slyly. His hand was in his coat pocket. Absently, when she set the food before him, he picked up her left hand and looked at it, bent the knuckles tentatively forward and back, smoothed out the skin. "Nice little hand you've got there."

"Nice and red and rough."

"No," he said. "You've got nice hands."

"Now what do you want?" she said.

"Just want to prettify it a little," Bo said. He brought a small package out of his pocket. Inside the paper was a jeweler's plush box, and inside the box was a tiny gold watch. She looked at it, at him, back at it, and suddenly she was crying. Bo came around the table and put his arm around her, whispering into her hair. "Take it easy," he whispered. "I just wanted you to know how much . . . I appreciate . . . you've been swell."

She said no more that night about the whiskey business she had been determined to steer him out of. She couldn't. Instead, she sat and listened to him talk about what they were going to do and see, the money they were going to make. He opened up the future like a Christmas package for her delight, and he was so delighted himself that she couldn't be otherwise.

"We've been stuck in this backwater too long," he said. "You're going back where there are lawns and trees and cement sidewalks and automobiles that make that one out there look like a donkey cart. You're going to have a fur coat and nice clothes—and you aren't going to make them yourself, either. The kids are going to a high school and I'm smoking nothing but two-for-a-quarter cigars, starting now. We've been chasing pipedreams too long. This is the time we make it go."

8

For a week they were a wonder. When Bo drove the Essex downtown and parked it a crowd gathered. Boys ran their hands over the finish, men lifted the hood and bent in over the motor, stood back respectfully when Bo climbed in and stepped on the self-starter. They examined it from front to rear, their faces closed, their eyes veiled. They kicked the tires. They listened to the idling motor. They unscrewed the radiator cap and looked in. They asked, casually, how fast she'd go and how good she was on hills. They commented on her lines, her color, her mechanical perfections. Some said oh hell, she wasn't anything but a cheap Hudson, but they watched like the others when she went by.

In that week Elsa had a thousand things to do. There was the house to clean out, clothes to pack, books to box. Bo sold the two cows to Hank Freeze, on the north bench. The horses he couldn't sell, so he left them with the oldest Heathcliff boy to keep for half the increase. For the house there was no market at all; George McKenna at the store finally agreed to try to sell it for them.

The wholesale sell-out brought up the question of Bruce's colt. It was getting no better. As it grew it threw more weight on the broken legs, and its walk was the same floundering lunge it had had when they found it in the bend. Jim Enich came over to see Bo about it, and with Bruce hanging anxiously on the fringes of their talk they looked the colt over.

Bo's eyes went to Bruce, rubbing the colt's neck under the long sorrel mane. He drew Enich aside, but Bruce left his pet and followed.

Patting his pockets, Bo pretended to hunt for something. "Run inside and get me a couple cigars."

Bruce looked suspiciously from one to the other, hesitated, then turned and darted away.

"Worth anything at all?" Bo said.

Enich spat. "Hide."

Bo breathed angrily through his nose. "I never should have let the kid get attached to it," he said. "He's all wrapped up in it now."

"It ain't a very pleasant thing to do," Enich said. "I'll take it off your hands, if you want. The hide's worth about three bucks."

Bruce came running back with the cigars, his eyes swinging from one face to the other. Bo cleared his throat. "Well," he said, "Jim's willing to make a deal for your colt."

"Couldn't we . . . ?" Bruce said. "Couldn't we take him along? Ship him, or something?"

"No," Bo said. "We couldn't do that. He'll be better off here. Jim'll take care of him for you. He'll give you three dollars for him."

"Oh gee!" Bruce said. "I don't want to sell Socks!"

"Well, it's either sell him or give him away," Bo said. He squatted down and put his hand on the boy's shoulder. "Look," he said. "Maybe we'll be coming back here sometime. Your colt couldn't get along running with the herd over at Heathcliff's. So you'd better sell him to Jim, and if we come back you can buy him back."

"Sure thing," Enich said.

Bruce broke loose from his father and went over to the colt. He reached up and hugged it around the neck, and it nuzzled his shirt, leaving flecks of moisture on the cloth. The boy reached up to whisper something private in the colt's ear. Then he turned and said, "All right, I'll sell him to you, Mr. Enich. He'd rather stay with you than anybody else. He knows you."

He took Enich's three silver dollars and held them uncertainly in his hand. "Can I come and see him before we go?" he said.

"I'm taking him out to the ranch," Enich said. "That's pretty far."

Over his head Bo made a motion at Enich, and Enich went out to drive his wagon around in back. In ten minutes he pulled out again, the half-raised head of the trussed colt showing above the endgate. Bruce ran after the wagon, rubbing the sorrel's nose, the tears shaking big down his face, until almost the east ford. There he stood waving, seeing through a blur of crying the high-wheeled wagon and the sorrel hide and the blazed white nose and one rolling scared eye over the endgate as the wagon went on down the trail and around the curve behind the willows.

They gave Spot to the Chance boys. Old Tom was wheeled away one morning in a doll buggy by three excited little girls who had dressed his languid, sleepy gray body in petticoats and tucked him under the covers, where he lay in a most uncatlike position, flat on his back, and purred like a teakettle.

"I hate to see old Tom go," Elsa said. "He was such a comfortable, sleepy old cat."

"Except when a dog got after him," Chet said. "Remember when Chapman's airedale treed him in the barn? He went right up in the air and came down on that old airedale's back with his claws digging like sixty. He rode him clear up past Van Dam's."

"He wasn't so sleepy out hunting, either," Bruce said. "Remember when we saw him dive into the river on top of the mudhen?"

That was the way of their uprooting. "Remember the time . . . ?" Five years in that town had made it home. Elsa wondered if her boys would have the same homesick memories of that barren little river-bottom village as she had of the maple-lined streets and the creamery and the white-steepled church in Indian Falls. Home was a curious thing, like happiness. You never knew you had had it until it was gone.

You never knew either how many people you thought of with kindness, the people who now met you on the street as you went about pulling up all the little roots that had gone down in five years, and shook your hand, and said don't forget us, don't get so prosperous over there in the States that you never remember your old friends . . .

There was no time for regrets. Maybe this whiskey business, for all its illegality, was as good as anything they could have chosen. There were no places on earth any more where opportunity lay new and shining and untouched. The old days when people used to rush to Dakota or California or Alaska in search of easy wealth were gone forever; she and Bo together had tried one or two of those worn-out dreams, to their sorrow. But if he could do as well as he said he could at this business, and then get out, he at least would have been preserved from his own irritability and restlessness and bad temper.

So she went carefully pulling up the little roots that gave with a slight unwilling tug, and left the future to Bo. He was so sure of it.

In the sun-slanting, dew-fresh morning they stood for the last time on the porch, the loaded car nosing the front fence. Not even the rush of packing had ruffled Bo's temper this time. He locked the door, tossed the key in his hand, looked at Elsa, puckered his lips in a jigging whistle, and winked. He rubbed his finger down the doorframe.

"Goodbye, Old Paint," he said. Elsa was looking through the front window at the bare room, its raw floor showing inside the frame of painted border. The mantel Bo had put in with the intention of some day building a fireplace under it was empty of knickknacks, the picture of three white horses floating-maned against a background of storm was gone, and only its clean oval shape remained on the wall.

She touched Bo's arm. "Let's try," she said. "Let's try awful hard this time."

They went out to the car, the boys half hysterical with excitement, singing loudly, "Goodbye, Old Paint, I'm leavin' Cheyenne, I'm leavin' Cheyenne, I'm goin' to Montana, Goodbye, Old Paint . . ."

"You want to wake up the whole town?" Bo said. He shoved them into the back seat, where they squirmed their way neck-deep into the luggage. Their heads stuck out like the heads of young owls in a nest.

"Open your mouth and I'll drop in a mouse," Bo said.

They had to leave the key with George McKenna, out on the east edge of town. At the low swampy spot that had been made into the dumpground the road split, leaving the dump like an island in the middle, and as they bumped over the right-hand fork they smelled the foul stench from the garbage and bones and offal thrown out there.

"Pee-you!" Elsa said, and held her nose. The boys echoed her. "Pee-you! Pee-you-willy!" They clamped their noses shut and pretended to fall dead.

"I better get to windward of that coming back," Bo said.

They left the key with McKenna, shook hands with him twice (he was very affable now that Bo had paid up the long-standing grocery bill) and started back, really leaving now. The things they saw as they passed had the sharpness of things seen for the last time.

They noticed things they had never consciously noticed before, the way the hills came down into the river on the north like three folds in a blanket, the extreme height of the stovepipe on the Chinaman's shack below Poverty Flat. The boys chanted at everything they saw, "Goodbye, Old Chinaman, Goodbye, Old Whitemud River, Goodbye, Old Dumpground, Goodbye."

"Hold your noses," Bo said. He eased the car into the windward fork around the dump. "Somebody sure dumped something rotten."

He stared ahead, bending forward a little, and Elsa heard him swear under his breath. The car jumped ahead over the bumpy trail.

"What?" Elsa said. She looked at his set face, the dark look of anger in it. Then she saw too, with a hard, flinching pain, and closed her lips tight over her teeth. Hurry, she said. Oh, hurry, get by before he sees it!

But the boys were not missing anything. They were half standing, excited by the burst of speed and the reckless bouncing. She knew he saw it before she heard him cry out; she could feel his seeing it like a bright electric shock, the way she had once felt the pain of a woman in the travelling dentist's chair when the dentist dug a living nerve out of the woman's tooth and there was a livid tableau, the woman sitting with face lifted, half rising from the chair, the dentist scrambling stupidly on hands and knees looking for the wire of pain he had dropped. Then she heard Bruce's cry.

"Oh!" he said. "It's Socks! Ma, it's Socks! Stop, Pa, there's Socks!"

His father drove grimly ahead, not turning or speaking, and Elsa shook her head. Bruce screamed, and neither of them turned or spoke. And when he dug down into the luggage, burrowing in and hiding his head, shaking with long smothered sobs, there was no word in the car except Chet's "Gee whiz, he still had his hobbles on!"

So they left town, and as they wound up the dugway to the bench none of them had the heart to look back on the town they were leaving, on the flat river bottom green with spring, its village snuggled in the loops of river. Their minds were all on the bloated, skinned body of the colt, the sorrel hair left below the knees, the iron braces still on the broken front legs.

Wherever you go, Elsa was thinking, whenever you move and go away, you leave a death behind.

VI

It was two o'clock in the morning when Bo hit the outskirts of Great Falls. Through the uncurtained front of the car the air was cold, with a faint remembrance of leaf-fires in its smell. Across the river on his left, the high stack of the copper smelter went up like a great dark lamp chimney above the huddled houses of Little Chi. Downriver he could see a glow of light from the power station on Rainbow Falls.

Bumping across the cartracks, easing the car over a rutted intersection, feeling the built-up springs sink heavily, clear down, on a slow bump, he swung left to avoid the main streets. His headlights, knocked out of line somewhere on the trip, glared along front porches, fences, up into the thinning color of the maples. Then the street, the alley, the turn, the branches of the crabapple tree over the garage, and he swung in, dimming the lights and climbing out stiffly to fumble among his keys. From Govenlock to Great Falls, on that kind of road, was all you wanted to drive.

For a moment, standing inside in the glow of the dimmed lights, he wondered if he ought to unload, but the weariness of driving ached in his shoulders, and he snapped the padlock on the garage doors, opened the wire gate in the fence, and went up to the back door.

He heard the bell ring far inside the house, and as he waited under the frosty, star-spiked sky a little wind stirred the creeper over the back porch trellis. Probably Elsa would be scared to death. She always jumped a yard when the doorbell rang.

The window above him opened, and her voice called down, "Who is it?"

"Me," Bo said.

"Oh good!" she said. "Just a minute."

The key turned in the kitchen door and he stepped inside, still in the dark. His hands reached out and felt her, pulled her close. She was in her nightgown. "Mmmmm!" he said, and kissed her. She snapped on the light.

"I bet you're tired," she said. "Do you want something to eat?"

"I might use a sandwich at that. How've you been?"

"All right. Chet got his nose broke."

"Fighting?"

"He's out for football, gone clean crazy about it. I never see him from morning till night except when he drags home after dark with half the skin off him."

"That won't hurt him," Bo said. He sat with his overcoat on, his legs sprawled wide, watching her pad around the kitchen. The way the silk lay close to hips and breasts made him stir with a comfortable, warm unease. Silk nightgowns, big house, gas stove, electric lights, icebox, lawn and trees. You couldn't kick.

"Heimie come over after his stuff?" he said.

"Yes. Day before yesterday."

"Pay you?"

"No. He said he'd see you when you came back."

Bo grunted.

"I wish you didn't have to work with that crowd," she said.

"They've got contacts. It would have taken me a long time to work in here alone."

"You'd have made more."

"Once I got in. But we weren't doing anything very wonderful till the last few months. Besides that, if you work with those guys a little you're safer. They'd as soon stool you off as look at you."

She went to the icebox, and he saw the corrugated metal interior, a package of sliced bacon, bottles of milk, oranges, a roast of some kind, a glass-covered dish of butter.

"Quite a bit different from the old cellar hole," he said. The fat richness of the food, the clean crinkled metal, the kitchen with white woodwork and linoleum floor, filled him with a sense of luxurious prosperity. Elsa ought to like it. She'd been hollering for a nice home for fifteen years.

"Yes," she said. "Only I never had to be afraid that anyone would come and take the cellar hole away from me."

"For God's sake," he said disgustedly, and filled his mouth with bread. "You wouldn't be satisfied if you were a calf and your ma was giving liquid gold."

"Oh, I'm satisfied," she said. "I've got everything I could want here, sure enough." She started out into the hall.

"Where you going?"

"To get a kimono. It's chilly."

"Heck with it," Bo said. He reached out and pulled her onto his lap, eating with one hand while with the other he caressed the creased softness of her stomach. "You feel pretty nice through silk," he said.

Elsa laughed. "I should think you'd be too tired to feel anything."

"Never too tired," Bo said. "Is there any hot water?"

"I think so."

"Hot dog," he said. "Hot running water, bath tub six feet long, and a chicken in a silk nightgown. I'd have been home hours ago if I'd thought of that."

She smiled, arching away from his arm, and he saw that she was very glad to have him home, that she liked his hand on her, that the beauty parlor he had made her go to had done things for her hair and skin. He bit her. "You hit the grit," he said. "I'll be along before you can say Ishmael Rabinowitz."

When he woke in the morning he lay watching the sun that lay like a wide yellow board under the blind. There were noises downstairs—Elsa getting the kids off to school. He stretched luxuriously in the wide bed, kicked the covers off and inspected his white feet, his heavy, white-skinned calves with the black hair worn nearly off where the garters went around.

"Old piano legs," he said, but he liked his legs, the way the muscles hardened into flat plates when he wiggled his feet.

Chet, with the whole middle of his face bandaged, came in and stood looking at him, eyes solemn over the gauze. "Hi, Pa."

"Hi," Bo said. "Who you been mixing it with, Jess Willard?"

"Football," Chet said. "I got my nose broke."

"Somebody must've kicked pretty high."

"Oh, you don't kick in football. Just once in a while."

"What do they call it football for?"

"Because . . . I don't know." Chet's eyes wandered around the bedroom. He seemed at once indifferent and ill at ease.

"Pa."

"What?"

"Could I have four dollars?"

Bo stared. "You don't want much. What are you planning to do, go into business?"

"I want a football. If I had one of my own I could practice around after school."

"Yuh," Bo said. He swung his legs over the edge of the bed and sat in his nightshirt, looking at Chet. It didn't take long to give a kid millionaire ideas. A year ago a dime would have looked like a fortune to this one.

"I might make the first team next year," Chet said. "I'd be a sophomore, and if I gained ten pounds or so and got so I could throw passes good I could . . ."

"You could get your behind in a sling," Bo said. "Do all the other kids get busted up the way you do?"

"This isn't anything," Chet said. He passed his fingers tenderly over the taped gauze. "Sloppy Johnson bust his collarbone last week. He's on the team."

"So if you could have a football and practice a lot maybe you could get on the team and break a leg," Bo said. He laughed, tickled at the solemn earnestness of this little squirt with the patched face. "Hand me my pants," he said. He fumbled in the pants, found the wallet, leafed off a five-dollar bill. "I'll want change."

"You bet," Chet said. "Thanks, Pa, a lot. I'll bring the change after school."

He scooted out, went downstairs like a falling safe. Bo laughed. It was a good feeling to give a kid something when he wanted it that much. Sitting on the bed leisurely pulling on his socks, he thought, I'll give it to him, too. I'll have it to give all of them. Give me another few months, let the roads stay open a few weeks longer . . . He began dressing more purposefully. He had to see Heimie, get a half dozen things, get things organized so he could pull out tomorrow. And if Heimie wanted part of this load he'd have to be satisfied with two or three cases. There was more in it the other way.

"Got anything to eat for a starving Armenian?" he said in the kitchen.

"Oh, a few odds and ends." She took bacon and toast from the oven and set them before him. "How many eggs?"

"Make it three. I've got a lot to do."

"Going to unload?"

"No. I'm leaving it right there. I'll be pulling out again in the morning."

"Where?"

"Right on down to Nebraska."

She turned to watch the frying eggs, but he could see by the set of her shoulders and the angle of her head that she was going to protest.

"I'm scared of that trip," she said. "It's so long."

"That's why there's money in it."

"And more risk," she said.

"That's the chance you take," Bo said. "I want to get this sold and get back to Govenlock for another load before the roads get too bad. Then we can live off the fat of the land the rest of the winter."

He wolfed his breakfast, wiped his mouth, kissed her, and went out, walking fast. At the drugstore on the corner he bought four two-for-a-quarter cigars and turned into Central Avenue, letting the fragrant smoke fill his mouth. At the door of Chapell's Garage he slowed, looking in. Frank Chapell was burning waste in the office stove.

"Mornin'," he said. "Thought you was out of town."

"Was," Bo said.

"Anything stirring up north?"

"Quiet as a church."

"Same here," Frank said. "Anything I can do for you?"

Bo gave Chapell a cigar. "I'm looking for a Wyoming license plate. Got any?"

"Might have."

Chapell looked under the bench at the rear of the shop. "Pair of Utahs, pair of Oregons, couple sets of Montanas."

"It's better when there's only one plate. Couldn't pick me up one, could you?"

"When you want it?"

"This afternoon."

"Come around sometime after three," Frank said. "I think I can smouge you one."

From Chapell's Bo went to Strain's Department Store and found a floor walker. "I want to buy a clothes dummy," he said.

The floor walker looked baffled. "You mean a regular dummy? Window dummy?"

"Yes."

"I'll get the manager."

"I'd rather have a dead one," Bo said, and laughed at the floor walker's startled face.

He waited for the manager, waited again while that polite gentleman looked back among the invoices to see what dummies cost, and finally bought one for sixteen dollars, twice what he thought it was worth. Across the street at Gill's Hardware he bought two boxes of large-headed roofing nails, and with those in his overcoat pockets walked the last block and a half to the Smoke House, guarded by its wooden Indian and flanked on either side of the door by peephole slot machines saying "Adults Only."

Heimie Hellman was eating breakfast at the counter with his overcoat and hat on, and while he ate the shine from the barbershop next door sat jackknifed on a portable stool and shined his yellow shoes. Bo, coming in the door, let his lip curl slightly. Ladies' man, probably pimp. He was too God damned elegant in his yellow shoes and tan silk shirt and velvet-collared coat.

Heimie looked over, lifted his head and half shut his eyes and opened his mouth, the whole gesture like an act. He lifted a hand, and as Bo slid onto a stool beside him, he tossed a quarter to the shine, who grinned and went.

"Well," Heimie said. "How they hanging?"

"Okay."

Heimie shook his head in an admiration that might have been ironic. "How do you do it?" he said. "Every other guy I know has been knocked over at the line one time or another. You just go up and come back like you was driving in the park." He smiled at Bo, thumping a cigarette on the counter gently. "You must have a rabbit's foot," he said.

"I just happen to know roads the law never heard of," Bo said. "Things moving here?"

"Little slow yet. We'll start turning it over when people begin buying for Christmas."

Bo looked down the counter and watched the waiter draw a cup of coffee. "You won't want anything for a while then."

"What did you bring?"

"White Horse and Haig and Haig."

"You can't get what good Scotch is worth around here," Heimie said. "Most of our customers are pikers, 'sa fact. Rather rot their guts out than pay for good stuff."

"Yeah," Bo said. "Well, I guess I can get rid of it."

Through hands cupped to light the cigarette Heimie watched him. "Running it on down?"

"I didn't say," Bo said. "I could spare you two or three cases if you wanted them. Probably I'll be making another trip before Christmas. Let me know what you want and I'll bring it then."

"How soon'll that be? The rush might start quicker than we expect."

Leaning over, Bo dropped the cigar butt in a spittoon. "I could get it to you within two weeks."

Heimie frowned, tapping his fingers on the counter. He looked at himself in the mirror and took off his hat to smooth his beetleshell hair. "Two weeks is pretty late," he said.

"That's as quick as I can make it."

"Well," Heimie said, "we might have to draw on somebody else. I thought you'd have some plain stuff this trip."

"Send somebody up," Bo said contemptuously. "Somebody that always gets knocked over at the line, with a lot of your hooch aboard."

Heimie shrugged. "Maybe two weeks will do. But I'll give you a tip about running that Scotch south."

"I didn't say I was running it anywhere."

"Just the same," Heimie said, "I know damn well you didn't think you could sell a whole load of White Horse and Haig and Haig in this burg." He smiled and tapped a finger on Bo's chest. "If you do go south, stay away from Sheridan," he said. "They're getting tough as hell around there. Prohis at all the bridges and ferries, stopping every suspicious car. Friend of mine was knocked over down there last week with a new Marmon and a thousand dollar load."

"Well," Bo said, "I guess we'll let the guys around Sheridan worry about that." He slid off the stool. "Do you think you can move two or three Scotch, or shall I unload them myself?"

Motioning to the waiter, Heimie slid a half dollar down the counter and stood up, tightening the overcoat across his chest. He walked to the door with Bo, his head bent. "What's it going to come at?"

"It's up. Cost me eight dollars a case more at Govenlock this time. I'll have to pass that on."

"That would make it sixty-two," Heimie said. He stood picking his teeth, looking down across the shoulder of the wooden Indian. A boy of twelve or so, standing on tiptoe before the eyepiece of one of the "Adults Only" slot machines, jerked his head away and pretended to be interested in the window full of pipes and razor blades and tins of tobacco.

"I've been thinking," Heimie said. "You take a lot of chances running it on down. You get a better price, sure, but with Wyoming hot you take chances. What about making a deal for the whole load?"

"I've got other customers I have to take care of," Bo said. "I thought you couldn't sell Scotch in this town anyway."

"Little water'll do wonders to the price of Scotch," Heimie said. "Brings it down where pikers can buy it."

"That'll lose you customers, too, in the long run." Bo reached out another cigar and bit off the end. "No, I guess I better stick with the arrangements I already made."

"I'll take the whole load," Heimie said. "That saves you a lot of trouble. I'll take the whole load at the old price, fifty-four a case."

"I'd be a sucker," Bo said. "I can sell it for seventy-five in wholesale lots."

"Not here in town."

"What does that matter? I can sell it for that—got it sold."

"Well, I can't pay any price like that," Heimie said. "I can't get that selling it by the bottle."

That, Bo knew, was a lie. Heimie had been getting seven and eight a bottle for watered Scotch for six months, ever since people's stored-up liquor had begun to run out. And at Christmas time he'd hike the price.

"I might make it sixty," Heimie said. "But I wouldn't stand to make anything much. Customers kick like steers even at the old price."

"We'd better let it slide," Bo said. "You can have the three cases if you want."

"Fifty-four?"

"Sixty-two. I can't absorb that eight-buck raise."

Heimie considered. "All right. Can you bring them over to the house tonight?"

"Can't you come after them?"

"I'm tied up. Got to see a guy from Kalispell out at the tourist park. Matter of fact, you might be interested in what's in the wind."

Bo waited, but Heimie apparently was not going to say what was in the wind, so Bo shrugged. "All right," he said. "I'll be over around nine."

As he went down the street he cursed Heimie's deviousness. He might just as well have said in the beginning that he wanted the whole load—at a cut price, on credit!—instead of beating around the bush with bear stories about Wyoming being hot, and maybe they'd have to draw on somebody else for stuff. At the same time, there was just enough possibility that Wyoming was hot so that it would pay to be careful. There was only one decent road south unless you went clear over into Dakota and then down. And ever since the Federals got organized they had been making trouble. It might be a good idea to go clear around Sheridan, at that.

Then he thought of having to unload the whole car, just to take three cases over to that damned lazy Heimie. If it wasn't for the certainty that Heimie would stool on anybody who told him off, he would have liked to back out even on the three cases.

He unloaded, put the rear cushion in, threw three sacks of sand in the back end along with Heimie's three cases, to bring the built-up springs down, and went in to lunch. While they were eating the dummy arrived over the shoulder of a grinning delivery boy. "Just put her on the couch," Bo said. He went into the hall and called Elsa. "Here's your dummy," he said.

"My what?"

"Your dummy. Come on in here."

"What on earth are you talking about?" she said. "I haven't ordered anything." She came into the room and stopped. "Now what?"

"Look," Bo said, boxing his ankles and scuffing his toe. "I didn't know how you'd feel about it, so I didn't say anything about it before, but this girl wants to ride down to Nebraska with me."

"Take that silly look off your face and tell me," Elsa said.

"No fooling. She wants a ride. Only she hasn't got any clothes to wear."

Elsa laughed. "Where did you get this thing?"

"This is camouflage," Bo said. "It's too easy to spot a car with one man in it, travelling fast. Henriette here is coming along to look after me."

"But anyone could tell in a minute . . ."

"Put a veil on her. Just seeing us go by, nobody is going to spot her."

"You're like a little kid playing detective," Elsa said. "I'll bet anything you're doing this because it tickles your funny bone. You'll be talking to her all the way down."

"Why not?" he said. "Put some classy duds on her and she'll be worth talking to."

"Well, I'll see."

She went upstairs, and in a few minutes came down with an armful of clothes. "She'll have to wear hand-me-downs," she said. "I'm not giving away any of my good clothes to a girl no better than she should be."

"She'll need an overcoat."

"I can fix that all right."

She dressed the dummy quickly, while he stood watching. "No underwear?" he said. He whistled, wagging his head. "How about the veil?"

"I'll have to cobble one."

She found a small black hat and dug out of the sewing machine some black net. When she had the dummy veiled and pushed back on the couch Bo cackled. "That's the goods," he said. "Put her behind sidecurtains and guys'll be flirting with her."

Elsa looked at him and shook her head. "For a man in a dangerous business, you try more fool kid tricks than anyone I ever saw," she said.

At nine that night he pulled up in front of the house Heimie and his outfit had rented the month before. It was an old house that had formerly had some connection with a silver smelter. The two-hundred-foot stack, all that still stood of the smelter, soared out of the bottom of the lot close to the river.

Bo sat in the car, in the shadow of the overgrown lilac bushes, looking the place over. It was a good house, way off the main track. The only thing Heimie would have to watch would be kids prowling around in the summertime. But it was extra good as far as the smell was concerned. Heimie had never said he was running a still, but it was plain enough.

His feet crunched in broken glass and rubbish in the path. The house was completely dark. When he tapped with the heavy brass knocker the noise echoed inside. He waited.

"Who is it?" a voice said through the door.

"Mason."

The bolt was shot, and the door opened. "You got the stuff here?" the man inside said.

"In the car."

"Just a minute, I'll help you." The man stepped back and shut the basement door, from which a little light and a strong smell of mash came up. "Heimie said you'd be along," he said, coming out on the porch. "He wants you to wait till he gets back."

"When'll he be here?"

"He ought to be along pretty quick."

They took a case apiece inside, and Bo went back for the third. The man locked the door and took Bo's arm. "Come on down here."

He led Bo down the basement steps, the light brightening as they went, the mash smell thickening. The furnace, like a great octopus, hid the source of the light. When they got around it Bo saw a row of oak kegs, two oak barrels with boards across them to form a table, two men sitting against the wall with glasses in their hands. The light came over a low partition, where the still must be.

One of the men, the small dark one, made a motion with his glass. "Hi," he said. The other slouched back against the wall and barely nodded. He had a heavy-jawed face with a smudge of black beard, and he looked tough. The one who had brought him downstairs, now that he saw him in the light, he recognized. Beans McGovern, a small-time thug.

"Got it snug down here," Bo said, and shook off his overcoat.

"Furnace makes it nice," McGovern said. "Have a drink?"

"Thanks."

"This is Joe Underwood," McGovern said, waving at the heavy-jawed man. "Used to work out of Butte. This is Blackie Holmes. Bo Mason." He poured a glass from a jug and handed it across the boards.

Underwood was watching Bo steadily. He had a slight cast in one eye. Bo was instantaneously reminded of the cop who had been killed in Little Chi a week before. This was the kind of cookie that might have done that sort of job. At best he was a bouncer. At worst he might be a hatchet man.

"Heimie tells me you just been north," McGovern said. He squatted on a keg and tipped it back carefully against the wall.

Bo nodded.

"Still doing the old land office business in Govenlock?"

"They got a warehouse big as a freight yard," Bo said. "And their ideas are getting as big as the warehouse. Hiked the price of Scotch eight bucks a case this time."

"There wasn't any raise last time I was up there," Underwood said. He spoke flatly, without lifting his voice or changing his position against the wall, but there was a challenge there, a hard deliberate will to pick a fight. The thought that he might be in a trap, that Heimie might have fixed all this up, made Bo slow to answer. He sipped his drink, getting a look all around through half-closed eyes over the rim of the glass. He moved a little so that his back was to the furnace. "When were you up there last?" he said.

"Ten days ago."

"They raised it on the first, they said."

"I hadn't heard about it from anybody else," Underwood said.

Bo deliberately drained his glass and put it down. "Then you haven't been talking to the people that know."

McGovern cut in. "Heimie says you're slick at getting back and forth."

"I manage to make a few trips," Bo said.

"Sixteen loads without a knock-over," McGovern said. "You must have all the cops fixed."

"I was talking with a prohi that works the Chinook territory," Underwood's flat voice said. "He was telling me he chased a guy a month or so ago, so close he could hear the guy banging over the bumps up ahead, running without lights, and then all of a sudden the guy vanished. The prohi tried every crossroad for ten miles up and down, no go. Just evaporated."

Bo looked at him steadily. This bird knew something. His tone, however, had got less nasty since McGovern had cut in a minute ago. Still it wasn't good. Something was behind that first tone, and behind this little probing, apparently aimless, conversation. "That was me," Bo said. "That sonofabitch cost me three cases in breakage."

Blackie Holmes squirmed his back against the wall. "What did you do, take a disappearing powder?"

"I missed a bridge," Bo said. "I was loaded so heavy behind I just sailed out flat as an airplane and lit in the bottom on all four wheels. Blew out every tire. So I sat there while the prohi ran up and down a while, and then I came in on the rims."

McGovern wagged his head and spat at the base of the furnace. "Lucky!" he said.

"That was the one time," Bo said, his eyes steady on Underwood, "when I took advice about a road. From a guy at the warehouse in Govenlock. He wouldn't be a friend of your prohi friend from Chinook, would he?"

He held Underwood's eye, or tried to, but Underwood had the advantage of the slight cast. It was hard to tell whether he was looking at you or past you. "I don't keep track of any prohi's friends," Underwood said.

After a minute Bo took his eyes off him. He had lost the feeling of being in a trap, but he was surer than ever that this Underwood was not only dangerous, but was deliberately making himself look dangerous. It was perfectly possible that Underwood was the stool who was responsible for all the knock-overs at the line. He was in the business, he would have hot tips on who was coming through, and when.

McGovern raised a hand. "Somebody on the door?" he said.

He went upstairs fast, his sneakers thudding softly on the treads. Bo heard the door open. Steps came down the stairs, and Heimie appeared around the furnace, ducking his head and shuddering his shoulders together.

"Jesus, it's getting cold," he said. "Hi, Bo. Hi, boys. How's every little thing?"

"Can't kick," Bo said. Underwood nodded. Holmes raised his glass. Heimie rubbed his hands together, reached up and felt the furnace pipe over his head, stood reaching with both hands against the warm tin. "I just been talking to Bill Burman from Kalispell," he said. "You remember, I told you this morning I was going to see him."

Bo nodded.

"He's a bright boy," Heimie said. "Made me a proposition sounds pretty good."

"Better take it then," Bo said. Heimie took his hands from the pipe, flapping and slapping them from loose wrists. He moved around jerkily, smiling.

"He's got a lot of know-how," he said. "There's only one way this racket can be made to pay big and keep on paying big. This'll interest you, Bo."

Bo waited. He looked at Underwood, slumped down, almost lying, against the wall, his face in shadow.

"This is how Bill lays it out," Heimie said, "and it ain't bushwah. The Federals are getting tough, and the state and city are beginning to work with 'em. You can pay off the city and maybe some of the state, but the Federals are hard to get at, and every once in a while they're going to knock you over. Lose your car, lose your load, pay a big fine. There's no percentage in it."

"Not unless you stay out of their way," Bo said.

"Yeah," said Heimie, "but you can't. So Bill lays out a proposition for some big-time distribution that's a honey. We've got the connections here, see? Here and in Havre. Bill's got 'em in Kalispell and Helena. That's four good towns. We can work into Butte later, after we get organized. We have a bunch of guys to bring it in from the line, we have another bunch to truck it around where it's needed. When one town gets loaded up we drain it off to the others. Take about ten guys, we could supply the whole state with stuff. Anybody gets in a jam, we spring him, hire a lawyer that can play all the cards. How's that sound?"

"Sounds all right for the guys that don't take the chances," Bo said.

"It's all right for everybody," Heimie said. "Look what you get: You get protection in town, and that'll be foolproof. And if the state or Federals gets hot and you get knocked over, the organization pays your lawyer, pays your fine, sets you up to a new car and puts you back to work. You can't lose."

"How much would a man make?" Bo said. "That's the angle I'm interested in."

"That'd have to be figured out."

"It looks like a guy could make about twice as much alone."

Heimie put his hands up to the pipe again, took them down to remove his overcoat. He had changed clothes since morning, and the shirt he wore now was whitest silk. When he opened his coat to smooth out his shirttails Bo saw the blue embroidered butterfly on the shirt pocket. "A guy alone could make more," Heimie said, "until he got knocked over. Then he could lose about five times as much. And it's a cinch that any man working alone is going to get knocked over oftener than if he works with us." His eyes strayed over to Underwood, sprawling against the partition, and Underwood met his look.

Bo sat still, as if considering. They made it clear enough. The threat was doubly underlined. Rising and stretching, Bo smiled into Heimie's pale, widow's-peaked face. "Yeah," he said. "It sounds like a good layout. You want me to come in, is that it?"

"You'd be doing yourself and us both a favor," Heimie said.

"When you planning to get going?"

"Right away. We've already got this place for a depot. Bill's got another in Kalispell. We've got everything we need except the organization, and that shouldn't take long."

"Well, you let me know," Bo said. "When you get things moving, call me up."

"I'm asking you in right now," Heimie said. "There's a beautiful chance to get rid of this Scotch of yours in Helena. Bill could move it like water down a drain."

Bo let his eye drift over the others as he reached out a cigar. Underwood was sitting up. Holmes had his glass to his lips, watching Heimie over the rim. McGovern was slouched against a barrel, watching.

"I couldn't come in with this load," Bo said. "I've got this promised. Suppose I think it over and let you know next week."

The point of Heimie's widow's peak moved down, then back, and he shrugged. "There's such a thing as waiting too long."

"I guess I'll have to take that chance," Bo said. "I can't go back on the promises I've already made."

For a moment they looked at each other, then Heimie shrugged again. With his overcoat thrown around his shoulders like a cape he followed Bo up the stairs and into the dark hall. The cold pushed in in a solid, moving mass as Heimie shot the bolt and opened the front door.

"There's one thing I want to know before I do anything," Bo said. "That's about this Underwood cookie."

"What about him?"

"He's a stool."

He could not see Heimie's face, but Heimie's low laugh filled the hall. "He knows which side his bread is buttered on," he said. "You don't need to worry about him."

"Far as I'm concerned," Bo said, "a stool pigeon is like a clay pigeon. He can fly any way he's pushed."

"I said don't worry," Heimie said. "I've got enough on that bruiser to make him be a good dog."

"Yeah," Bo said. "Well, long as you're sure."

"If that was what bothered you, why don't you come in now and get on the gravy boat?"

In the dark Bo stood for a minute silent. "I'll have to see you about that next week," he said. "And I'll have to have the dough for these three now. I need it."

Without a word Heimie shut the door, snapped on a little blue light, and counted out the money. He laughed. "Anything you ask for you get," he said. "That's the way this new outfit works."

"That's a good start," Bo said. "Well, see you next week."

"You going to be in town all week?"

"Yeah," Bo said. "I'll be around."

"I'll call you if anything hot comes up."

"Okay."

He went out down the rubbishy path, the night very dark, with a chilly, searching wind. His eyes were narrowed and his blood hot with rage. Come in with us little shyster crooks or get run out of business. Come in and be our errand boy, driving a truck in our transfer business. Take all the chances for little piddling wages and we'll bail you out of the hoosegow when you get caught! Wasn't it a dandy! Why, the dirty little pimping son of a bitch . . .

But it would pay to be careful. It would pay to be careful as hell. Underwood had been planted there to scare him, but if he didn't scare then Underwood might be used for other things. It was complicated and dangerous, and by the time he pulled into the garage he had decided not to leave the next morning as he had planned. It wasn't too far-fetched to believe that Heimie might try to stool him off. That might happen either at home or on the road, but he had to take that chance. He'd better lie low for a day and slip out when the coast looked clear.

2

From the back door Bo looked out across the yard, across the alley to the back hedge of a house on the next street, up to the corner where the street light had just come on, dim and popping in the

November dusk. There was no one in sight; the fresh and slightly smoky air made him anxious to start. He had already been lying around the house too long, just because of Heimie and his gang of two-by-four toughs. The car was loaded, the Wyoming plate installed, the dummy in the front seat.

He went back into the kitchen and picked up his overcoat. "Guess I'll be going," he said. Elsa dried her hands and left the sink to call the boys in from the front room.

They came out, Chet tossing his new football. "Goodbye, Pa," they said, like parrots. Bo looked at them, Chet husky, stringy with muscle, the younger one thin, puny actually, with staring hungry eyes and spindly legs.

"So long, kids," he said. "You mind your mother now, while I'm gone."

As they stood looking at him he had a feeling that they were a thousand miles away, unreachable; they were strangers who studied him critically and without affection. He reached back into his hip pocket and got the wallet. "Brucie, you didn't get anything to match Chet's football. What do you want?"

"I don't know," Bruce said. A wavering grin split his face and he threw a quick, triumphant look at Chet. "A Boy Scout hat, maybe."

"You aren't old enough to be a scout," Chet said.

"Well, I can wear a scout hat, can't I?"

"How much this hat cost?" Bo said.

"I don't know."

"Here," Bo said, and laid a five-dollar bill in Elsa's hand. "Get him his hat. That'll make everything even."

He stooped and kissed both boys, and under his hands their slight bodies were stiff and unemotional. Obscurely baffled, he roughed their hair once, put his arm around Elsa, and led her to the door. He kissed her long and hard, the boys watching. "I'll be about a week," he said. "Don't worry, now. All I have to do is unload and turn right around and come back. I'll be hightailing it all the way."

"Goodbye," she said. "Please be careful."

He squeezed her arm and ducked out under the trellis, and she followed to close the garage doors after him. As he drove out the alley he saw her standing with her hand on the door, watching after him, and the picture struck him as somehow pathetic. These trips were pretty hard on her.

And that was the last he thought about his family. He let them slide out of his mind, concentrated on getting out of town, covering ground. If Heimie had posted any prohis on the road they'd be tired of it and gone by now, after a day and a half. Just the same, he wouldn't go down the good road to Helena and Three Forks. He'd cut over the Little Belt Mountains and hit Livingston that way. It was a bad road to run with a load on, but it was shorter.

"How about it?" he said to the dark dummy at his side. "Want to take a little trip through the mountains?" He nudged her, and she tilted stiffly against the side. "Okay," he said. "You don't have to be scared of me, chicken."

Out of town, past street lamps and houses, the road clear now and deserted, planing into whiteness under the lights, the weeds brittle in the passing glare along the roadside, the country ahead and aside and behind all dark and lost and only the ribbon of glare-lighted road slipping visible into invisible, real into unreal. The driver of an automobile on a lonely road is a set of perceptions mounted in the forehead of a mechanical monster. The air that comes through the sidecurtains is the air of another planet, the only real world is the narrow cabin from which he sees unreal shapes writhe by, fences and trees and bridge rails, the mouths of culverts jammed with tumbleweed, the snaky road with its parallel-and-then-unparrallel lines, the ruts of rainy drivers still unerased and serpentining between the even boundaries of the grade. Those flashes of the unreal world become before long completely absorbing; the eye clings to them, is filled and satisfied by them; the brain asks no other business than to see. A car approaches with glaring lights, and the world broadens momentarily into an alley of pasture and creek bottom and three sleeping horses behind a three-strand fence, and then dark again, the headlights fingering the unknown sides of the world as it slips by. I see, said he, the elephant is very like a wall, like a board fence, like a man with a flashlight in an immense dark barn, like a moving picture reel unwinding too fast, catching fire, going black again. I see, said he, the elephant. I see . . .

The Essex rides heavily, rolling with the dips like a laden barge. The speedometer shows, on this stretch of fairly smooth grade, forty miles an hour. The ammeter, with the lights on, reads minus five. In the cold night the motor sounds sweet, sounds contented and purring. And the eyes sit above the wheeling car, immensely lofty and percipient watching the irregular unravelling of the road. The hands are loose on the wheel, the body relaxed. The lights of a car a good distance behind glint in the cop-spotting rearview mirror, and the hand reaches up to turn the mirror sideways.

A hundred and seventy-five miles to Livingston by this road, fifty less than by Helena, but a steep pull over Kings Hill Pass and a bad road down the other side. Seven o'clock when he started: budget eight hours to Livingston. With luck he might better it.

The streets of Belt, a few men on the sidewalk before a poolhall, their breath white under the arc light; a block of stores, square false fronts, then shacks, weeds, sweet clover fields, the town dump, the highway again. Little towns were all alike. You could be dropped into any one of them anywhere and swear you'd lived there one time or another.

As he swung into the little village of Armington, the lights from the car behind glinted again in the mirror, and a tiny, watchful alertness awakened in his mind. The outskirts, the dump, the foot pressing down harder on the round button of the accelerator, and the eyes watchful in the readjusted mirror. Then the brakes, the hard shuddering stop, the craning from the dark cabin to see which of the two forks, and the swing to the right, leaving the hard high-crowned road. Now the perceptive apparatus mounted in the fore-head of the beast tightened and quickened, because those lights behind might mean a chase, and a chase on this unmarked trail was dangerous. There was every chance that when you came to a bridge there would be a plank out, or the bridge itself gone, or that the approach on either side might have a chuckhole hell-deep that would drop your heavy breakable load like a jug into a quarry, snap your brittle and overloaded springs, break an axle. The speedometer now, even with the lights behind to drive him on, read only twenty-five.

He watched the mirror, saw the lights break into the open around a hill, saw them move on past the forks and on down the main highway. His breath came easier, and he eased up on the throttle. False alarm.

No more towns now till Neihart, up in the mountains forty miles or so, and beyond Neihart nothing till White Sulphur. He crossed a creek, and after ten minutes crossed it again. A hundred yards further on he recrossed it on a wobbly log bridge. The road tilted under the lights. He was starting to climb. On his left he saw a hill blacker than the sky. He shifted his weight in the seat and took a new grip on the wheel.

"Wouldn't be so bad," he said to the silent dummy, "if there was any way of knowing what's up ahead of where your lights hit. Keeps you on a strain all the time. Or are you interested?"

"Sure," the dummy said. "Get it off your chest."

"It's the worst part of this business," Bo said. "You have to make time, and you're always having to do it on roads that'll break your neck if you go over twenty. Still you got to do thirty or thirty-five on them. You can't stop anywhere and take a snooze because somebody might come snooping around. Sometimes you have to drive thirty hours at a stretch, and every damn mile of it full of bends and chuckholes and narrow bridges and mud. It's the roads that make this business tough. Give me good roads and I'd make two thousand a month without turning a hair."

"You don't say," said the dummy.

Bo's foot smacked on the brake pedal, the loaded tonneau surged up behind him, the dummy lurched sideways. He shifted, crawled through a wash, flattened out again, reached out to straighten the tipped dummy.

"I've learned a hell of a lot about automobiles since I got into this, though," he said conversationally. "One time I broke an axle in Wolf Creek Canyon above Helena, and I had to cache the load in the sagebrush and tear down the rear end and walk back to where I could telephone for a new ax, and then I had to put her in and reload. And I only lost seven hours altogether."

"You're good," the dummy said. "Why don't you post these things up on a billboard?"

"The hell with you. Another time I broke a spring leaf and didn't know it till it slipped in against the brake drum and locked me tighter than a clam. And over by Havre I blew a gasket and had to pull the head in the middle of the night by the light of a candle and a box of safety matches."

"My word!" the dummy said.

Bo, leaning over the wheel, peering into the unreal darkness ahead, trying to jump his vision ahead of the lights, anticipate the curves, guess the bumps, his foot tender yet insistent on the throttle-head, saw his own face dimly reflected in the windshield, and thumbed his nose at it.

"You're a pretty smart girl," he said to the dummy. "But you don't know how much I've made in the last six months, just by being able to get over roads better than most, and patch up a car better than most, and stay awake longer than most."

"I couldn't begin to guess," the dummy said. "A million?"

"Just give me time," Bo said. "Give me a little more time."

"Well, how much have you made?"

His eyes and his mechanical hands and feet still busy, Bo let his mind turn into an adding machine. Sixteen loads, and he must have averaged five or six hundred dollars profit a load. That was around eight thousand, and expenses and breakage and a little fixing of a deputy or two would knock off about fifteen hundred. Say sixty-five hundred, and he owned this car and this load, and here was thirty cases of Scotch all arranged for at seventy-five a case. He'd come back from Omaha with a cold two thousand in his jeans, and his bank balance of cash was already over four thousand.

"It's better than picking gooseberries at a dime a quart," he said. "If they leave me alone for a year I'll be in the money good and plenty."

"I wish I'd ever meet them after they got into the money instead of when they're just going to get in," the dummy said. "Every guy I meet is right on the edge of making a killing. I'm jinxed, I guess."

"Stick around," Bo said. "Stick around a year."

"Uh-huh," the dummy said. "And what about Heimie Hellman and his little band of Boy Scouts? Are you going to play ball with that outfit?"

With a wrench of the elbows Bo pulled the Essex around a hook in the road. His headlights, bursting into space, touched a steep wall with small black spruces toe-nailed into it, and his nose, joining his perceptive faculties for the first time, sniffed at the balsamy smell. He was in the pass. The motor labored. He shifted into second and gave it a good goose before shifting back.

"I don't know," he said. "I don't know what about that bunch. They can make trouble if they try."

"But you don't think they'll try," said the dummy. "You'll say 'Boys, you're going to make me uncomfortable if you try any squeeze plays,' and then they'll back away and say, 'Beg pardon, we wouldn't want to put you out.' "

"Yeah, like hell," Bo said.

"Well, what are you going to do?"

"I don't know," Bo said. "If I buck 'em, they stool me off, and if I try stooling them off to protect myself I run into a lot of cops and prosecutors Heimie and his gang own."

"And if you play ball with them," the dummy said, "you don't get anything but wages out of it, and you're all tied in with a bunch of pimps and strongarm men."

"Yeah," he said. "Suppose you take a nap. I can think of people I'd rather talk to."

"And if you try to buck them," the dummy said, "you haven't got enough customers without using Heimie's outlets, even if you could keep out of the law's way."

"I guess I could get customers," Bo said. "I guess good straight stuff at a fair price would take Heimie's customers away from his watered-down Scotch and rotgut moon."

"And some guy like Underwood might take you away from the bosom of your family, too," the dummy said. "Those guys wouldn't stop at murder. How long would you last? You make me laugh. You and your big money. You know what I think?"

"I don't know that I care," he said.

"I think they've got you," the dummy said. "I think this is your last trip on your own."

"Oh, shut up!" he said. "I'll be running whiskey when you're back in some department store window showing off your legs."

"You'll be running it for Heimie," she said. "You and your big ideas of being your own boss. Bushwah. You'll be taking orders from that pimp in the embroidered shirts."

"Shut up!" he said again, and for a half hour he drove in silence, sullenly, his mind edging up to the problem, finding a wall, blowing up in anger, edging up again at a different point. But it was all wall. His eyes strained out through the windshield, splashed and pebbled now with muddy water from a wash he had forded. The world unrolled in steep blackness beyond the fleeting glow of the lights, and the beam picked up an occasional timbered or rocky slope, a bank rose perpendicularly on his right and the road narrowed to two rocky ruts that apparently ended dead against the mountain. I see, said he, the elephant is very like a wall. I see, I see . . .

If you could only know what was on the other side of the light's beam, if you could see far enough ahead to take the strain off, you could make two thousand a month without turning a hair. His mind crept out toward the wall again, and he jerked it away. Through the slits in the sidecurtains came the strong smell of pines, and the Essex labored on the grade.

Entering Neihart, up in the pine woods, he eased up on the throttle, looking for a garage where he might get gas, a café where he could wash away the fuzzy feeling in his head with a cup of coffee. There was only one garage, with two gas drums on wooden supports and another drum marked "Oil." As he pulled in he caught the reflection from the headlights of a car parked against the side, facing out. He swung a little to bring his lights on it. Empty.

A man came to the door holding a lantern shoulder high. "Gas," Bo said, and climbed out, shutting the door on the shrouded dummy.

"You bet," the man said. He took a five-gallon can and began to fill it at one of the drums. "How many?"

"She'll hold five all right."

"You bet." He concentrated on the pour from the drum's spout. "Just closin' up. Don't many people come through this late."

Bo grunted, standing by the door to block off the man's view of the dummy.

"You're the third in the last hour," the man said. "Funny how some nights they come all in a covey and some nights I sit from supper time till eleven and not a one shows up."

"The others go on through?"

"One did. The other's right here against the wall. Couple fellas in it. Went on over for a cup of coffee."

His mind instantly alert and suspicious, Bo dug a couple of silver dollars from his pocket and laid them in the garage man's hand. Two men, driving a back road at night, parking nose out by a garage wall, didn't look good. It looked like law, either law or another bootlegger. And a bootlegger wouldn't leave his car like that. He watched the café across the street, but there was only the shadow of the counter man moving up and down behind the dirty window.

He took his change, gathered his overcoat around his hips, and slid in. "Come again," the garage man said. Bo pulled away. The trail climbed steadily, second gear much of it, and many curves, the roadbed deeply washed, exposing the solid rock in places. It was no road to make time on, but he rode the throttle anyway. Whoever was waiting back there was asleep at the switch, there was that to be thankful for.

But at the top of a long swinging hairpin he looked back and saw the moving lights of a car.

He swore, clicked off the dash light in order to see better. The road climbed up and up and up, a rocky shelf in the mountain's side. Sometime soon he should hit the top of the pass and start down, and on the other side it was better, not so steep or crooked. But he had to make the pass first: on this side, with a load on, he was at a disadvantage.

When he next looked back the lights were out of sight, but at the next bend he saw them burst around a corner, already closer, coming up on him like a house afire. He swore and slid the Essex into low, got a start over a steep pitch, slipped into second and stayed there, gunning it, the speedometer needle trembling around thirty. His arms and shoulders were set like cement. "By God," he said to the dummy, "if that's the law they're going to have a ride."

Skidding on a curve, he felt the weight of the car haul him sideways, settle, come back to center. The tires shot gravel like bullets up under the fenders. Then there was a flattening, a dropping, the road ahead tilted flat, tilted down. He shifted and settled himself. It was a horserace now. With one eye on the mirror he counted, waiting for the lights. He was up to thirty-eight when they blazed over the rim, diffused among the pines. That settled it. They hadn't lost much, if any. And nobody would drive as fast as he was driving without good reason, on that road.

He felt in his overcoat pocket for a box of roofing nails. "Looks like we've got to give these prohis a headache," he said to the dummy.

Driving with one hand, he ripped the end out of the box and shook into his palm a heavy weight of nails, big-headed, an inch and a half long. He unbuttoned the sidecurtain all down one side, losing time in doing so, and when he was ready he saw that the lights had gained more.

"Well, let's see if you can be slowed down a little!" he said. With a twisting, upward heave he threw the handful of nails back over the car's top, so that they would land in the center of the road. Another handful, then another, then another, until he had emptied the box and gathered up all the loose nails in his lap. Then he threw the box out the window and started crowding it again.

"It'll take a little while," he told the dummy. "The nails'll plug their own holes for a while. But pretty soon they start ripping the tube, and then those guys are going to have a nice long walk."

"You're pretty cagey," the dummy said. "You got out of that better than I thought you would."

"Let's hold the celebrating for a while," Bo said. "We may have to sow a few more seeds of kindness."

The light was still behind them, growing, snuffing out again, seeming not to move very fast, but keeping up, not more than a half mile behind. The road levelled out, and he took the stretch at a run, hitting it up to fifty, pouring his weight recklessly on the throttle. At the slightest beginning of a bend he eased up. The quickest way to get nabbed was to wreck yourself.

He could see no lights now. The road swung left, then right, and his own lights showed him rounded grassy hills instead of the rocks and pines of the pass. He was getting down. He watched the mirror, waiting for the flash. None came.

"You must have got 'em," the dummy said.

"Maybe."

He kept looking back, but all the way down out of the hills the road behind was black, part of that unknown and unreal world the single lighted reality of the Essex hurtled through. It was all right. Those cookies were sitting on their running board right now cussing. And he hadn't even hit a bump hard enough to shift the load or break a bottle.

Still, he had been chased, and the pit of his stomach was even yet a small, pulsating, sensitive hole. He breathed his lungs full and yelled aloud, letting off pressure. After a while he began to sing.

When he had sung himself normal again he slid down in the seat, pulled the gas lever down, and rested his throttle foot, wiggling it to limber the ankle. "I wonder," he said to the dummy, "if those prohis were tipped off by our friend Heimie."

"He'd have had to work fast."

"It doesn't take long to put in a telephone call," Bo said. "Only thing is, how would he know what road I was taking, and when I was leaving?"

"He could have had your house watched," the dummy said. "And for that matter, remember the lights that followed you down to the fork past Armington? Suppose one of Heimie's boys was in that, just tailing you to see which road you took? Once you were on this road you couldn't get off."

"By God," Bo said, "there might be something in that."

"But if that's the way it was," the dummy said, "those guys in Neihart would have known within a few minutes when you'd be there. Wouldn't you expect them to be parked across a bridge waiting to stop you?"

"Yes," Bo said. "I would. I don't savvy this business at all. You'd say those guys were chasing us, wouldn't you?"

"They weren't out driving for their health."

"No. So they must just have got careless and let me get through and then tried to catch me."

He began snapping up the sidecurtain, hearing through the opening the noise of the tires, the flip and pop of pebbles, the swish of running rubber. It would have been the easiest thing in the world for him to blow a tire himself hitting that road the way he had. A last look behind showed him only the empty face of the dark, and he buttoned himself in.

He came to a fork and stopped. There were no signs, but the main travelled road led on. The other must cut off to Harlowtown. There was only one thing to do, when he didn't know the country. He took the main road.

His watch said a quarter of one. He must be more than half way to Livingston. He might make Billings for breakfast. Or he might, if he found the road good that way, cut down through Yellowstone and angle across Wyoming until he hit the Lincoln Highway. That would put him a long way around Sheridan, just on the chance Heimie's tip had been worth anything.

"How about it?" he said. "Want to see Yellowstone Park, baby?"

"It wouldn't be open," the dummy reminded him.

"We could circle around it. There's a road down the west side. Or there's one cuts over into Wyoming near the east entrance, around Cody. That'd be better."

"Save your plans till we get past Livingston," the dummy said. "Once we're that far we're past anything Heimie might have had up his sleeve, and then we can really make it a honeymoon."

Bo settled back, relaxed into the torpor of driving, the unthinking suspension of mind; became once more the set of faculties in the forehead of the beast, eyes and ears for the road and the motor, hands for the steering. He noticed that they were in a flat of some kind, probably a river valley. Thin willows slid by, the road became wallowed sand. He shifted as a precaution, and a moment later came to a peering stop as the road disappeared and became merely two planks with two-by-four flanges, a skimpy skeleton of a bridge walking a foot above the deep sand of the riverbed. It was hardly wider than a railroad track, but perfectly safe and solid if taken easy. He eased out onto the planks. It was like driving on an extended grease rack.

The new sensation jogged him, and he sat up. "This is one way to make a road," he said to the dummy. "Damn if it isn't a pretty good idea, long as nobody's coming the other way."

He peered out, trying to see if there was water underneath, but all he could see was dimly luminous white sand and the occasional dark blob of willows. But he stared so persistently, trying to make out what it was he was crossing, that he almost ran into the obstruction in the road.

His foot slapped on the brake, the Essex halted with its nose almost against the barrier, and in the light he saw the stack of railroad ties three feet high laid across the planks. A trap. He knew it instantly, coldly, furiously, even before he saw the shadows start up from beside the road. Before he heard their shout he had slammed the Essex into reverse and was backing up, tightrope-walking the narrow planks, driving blind, by ear, by feel, his breath stilled in his chest and one arm rigid across the wheel, the other ripping the sidecurtain out so that he might lean out and crane, steering by the gleam, the glimmer of his tail light. He felt the tires start up on the low flange of two-by-four and then pinch down again, but his foot on the throttle didn't relax. The car roared full speed backward into the dark along the car-track road.

The figures which had leaped from the roadside were running after him. Out of the very periphery of his vision he saw one stumble and go headlong off the runway, and he heard them yelling. The first shot throbbed in his ears, but it didn't mean anything. All that meant anything was the tight wire of plank unreeling under his left hind wheel. If he could hold her on it, get back to the road, he had a chance yet. They would lose time getting to their car, wherever it was. He could run back to the Harlowtown fork, cut down on that . . .

Lights blazing, he was beautiful target, but he didn't dare switch them off. He needed their glow. Pink flashes stabbed the dark, but the running figures were dropping behind, and his blood leaped. Another hundred feet, and he would have outrun them, even in reverse. Then a quick turn, a dash back to the forks . . .

The wheel kicked out of his hand, numbing his locked wrist, and the front wheels were wrenched up and sideways, swerving the car, bucking it up over the flange, dropping it down awkwardly angled across the tracks. There was a heavy crunch from the shifting load, and for a moment the car hung uncertainly, about to go over, before it settled back.

Before it had quite settled Bo was on the ground, crouching. The Essex sat with its front wheels high, the tires still revolving slowly. The headlights burned like furious eyes up into the black. He heard the pound of feet sodden in the sand, and with no more than a second's hesitation he turned and ran.

3

He came so quietly that she didn't hear him at all. She simply looked up and he was there, his face blackened with new beard, his overcoat ripped from one pocket halfway to the hem. In the instant when their eyes met it crossed her mind that if he had not been her husband she would have been frightened to death at his face.

"Bo . . . ?"

He sat down and stared at her. His trousers, she saw, were also ripped, and there were scabbled scratches on hands and wrists. He made a disgusted sound and spread his hands. "Kapoot," he said. "Gone. Load, car, everything."

She said the thing that was instantaneous in her mind. "But they didn't catch *you!*"

His stare was almost contemptuous. "They weren't after me. They could have had me if they'd half tried."

"I don't understand," she said.

"It wasn't the law."

"Then who?"

"Hijackers."

He had straightened it out in his mind on the way back. The pieces fitted. First that car tailing him out of Great Falls, seeing which road he went. Then the two waiting in Neihart, letting him go by, closing in behind him. Then the barricade. It was neatly planned, and far enough away from everything so that there was no chance of anyone blundering by and spoiling it.

"I should have caught on in Neihart," he said. "That's where I saw the car parked against the garage." He rubbed his emory-paper jaw, the story coming out past the tips of his teeth. "I still thought they were law, then. By Christ, I don't know what was the matter with me. I ought to have my head examined."

"But . . ." she began, and even that one word of expostulation or lack of understanding made him furious.

"Does it stand to reason that two cops would sit in a town waiting for me, knowing I was coming in a few minutes, and then go over for a cup of coffee and let me slide right on by? Does that sound like sense?"

"No," she said. "I just . . ."

"It isn't sense," he said. "Those guys didn't want me there, either. They just wanted to let me pass so I could run down into their little trap. They weren't taking any chances of me getting away, I'll say that for them."

"But how could they know so well?" Elsa said. "It sounds as if they knew every minute what you were going to do."

"They did."

"But who could have?"

"There's only one son of a bitch in Montana that could have known or guessed that much."

"Heimie?"

"Heimie."

"Now what?" she said, watching him steadily. "Are they after you?"

"I don't know. I doubt it."

"What will we do if they are?"

"I don't think they are. I think this is Heimie's little way of inducing me to come in with his crowd."

"You won't," she said.

"I don't know. If we want to stay in this town we may have to."

"Then let's not stay in this town!" Elsa said. There were tears in her eyes. "I don't want to see you mixed up with those people. They're criminals, they'd rob and murder and do anything. You don't want to go in with them, Bo. You know you don't."

"You're exactly right," Bo said. "But what are we going to do?" He stood up impatiently, fingering the gash in his overcoat, his eyes vague and troubled. "I don't know," he said. "I've got to figure it out. All I know is that if there's a good chance to get even with that little silk-shirted bastard I'm going to."

"You'll get yourself killed."

"Not if I'm careful."

She shivered and half turned. "You didn't tell me how you got away."

"No," Bo said, his words heavy as iron. "I didn't tell you and I'm not going to." The fury in him broke out, and he swung around shouting. "How would I get away? I ran like a God damned jack-rabbit. I plowed through sand and tore through brush and walked a thousand miles and hooked a ride on a homesteader's wagon. How the hell would I get away? Fly?"

"I'm sorry," she said quietly. It didn't do to question him when he was sore. Whenever anything went wrong he butted against it like a ram, and the worse it went the more violent and stubborn he got, and though he generally got through, the effort outraged something deep and furious in him. He would never learn to climb over or go around. He had to butt right through, and when he got his head hurt he was untouchable.

But the car gone, and the whole load, two or three thousand dollars gone as surely as if they had taken the sum in hundred dollar bills and touched a match to them. It served her right. She had been thinking of that bank balance almost in the same terms Bo had. She had been seeing ultimate security and emancipation in it. It was just as well for her to learn that security was not there, that the whole thing could disappear like mist touched by the sun.

"I'm going to bed," Bo said. "If anybody calls or comes around, I'm out of town and you don't know when I'll be back."

Three days later he hunted up Heimie in the Smoke Shop. Heimie, elegant in a lavender silk shirt, pinstripe suit, yellow shoes, had a greeting as mellow as syrup. He led Bo into the back room and sent the counter man for a bottle.

"You made a quick trip," he said.

"What makes you think I've been anywhere?" Bo said, and stared at Heimie hard. Heimie shrugged and let it go.

The bottle came and Heimie poured two shots. "Here's how," he said. Bo drank, watching him. It would have been a pleasure to reach across the table and slap that light secretive smile off Heimie's mouth, but it wouldn't do. You had to know when somebody had you, or you'd wash out fast.

Heimie's smile deepened. He twirled the whiskey glass slowly. "Thought any more about that proposition?" he said.

"I'm willing to listen."

"Ah," Heimie said. "That's what I've been wanting to hear. You're too valuable a man to waste your talents working alone." Steadily smiling, inviting Bo to make a double meaning out of that if he chose, he leaned his impeccable elbows on the table and dropped his voice. "What is it you want to know, now?"

"I want to know what the proposition is," Bo said impatiently. "How do I know whether it's any good or not?"

"You want to go on hauling down from the line?"

"That's my racket," Bo said. "I don't want anything to do with any still, if that's what you mean."

"Beans can handle that all right." Heimie pursed his lips, thinking. "What would you say to a proposition like this: You haul down to us here, whole loads. You don't have to fuss around with deliveries or collections or anything. Just whole loads, dump them off and you're clean. *And* protected."

"What would I get out of it?"

"What's it worth?"

"I can make six hundred a load at least, hauling for myself."

"But you take chances," Heimie said. "You take a lot more chances. Law all over the place, and getting thicker. And they have to pinch somebody, see? They're fixed not to pinch our boys, so they have to make their reputations on the stragglers and lone wolves. It's a good setup to be in on."

"How much?" Bo said.

"What about two hundred a load?"

"Don't make me laugh."

"That's high pay, boy, for a job that's safe as a church."

"But it isn't high enough," Bo said, "and it isn't as safe as you make out. What if I got hijacked?"

He watched Heimie's face closely, but Heimie didn't tumble. His face was still smiling, faintly amused.

"The organization will take that chance, not you," Heimie said.

"But I don't think it's much of a risk." He grew more confidential, huddling across the table and squinting as he figured in his head. "Now look," he said, "you're the best man I know at getting in and out with stuff. We can use you, and you can use us. We'd be suckers to work against each other, but that's what we'd be doing if you didn't come in. But two hundred a load—well, make it two fifty—is damn good for what you'd be doing."

"We aren't getting anywhere," Bo said heavily. "Now I'll make *you* a proposition. I'm willing to come in, on any kind of terms that gives me a decent cut. I'll haul down from Govenlock for you for fifteen bucks a case, no less, you putting up the money for the stuff and paying me cash on the nose when I bring it in. You guarantee protection, and let me be the judge of when it's safe to make a trip. And if I don't haul for anybody but you, you'd have to furnish me a car."

"Say, now, wait a minute!" Heimie had his hands up, warding off imaginary blows. "Fifteen a case? And protection? *And* a car? You want a gold mine."

"That's what you've got," Bo said. "Why shouldn't I want one?"

"You've got an exaggerated idea of how much there is in this business," Heimie said, still playfully. He took out a pencil and figured on an envelope. "Make it twelve a case, and you furnish the car, and it's a go."

"Couldn't do it," Bo said.

"Fifteen a case would be four hundred and fifty a load."

"That's a whole lot less than I'm making now."

Heimie shook his head, at first slowly, then emphatically. "We couldn't afford that kind of money."

"Listen," Bo said. "That is a business deal, isn't it?"

"What else?"

"And I'm going to be a kind of hired man in it."

"Not exactly."

"Exactly," Bo said. "And I'll be doing the hard and the dangerous part, and you know it damn well. So I'm worth wages enough to keep me interested in working hard for you, and it's up to you to put up the car. You don't ask a truck driver to furnish his own hack."

"Suppose we did put up a car," Heimie said after a pause. "Would you haul for twelve?"

"Fifteen."

"Then I guess we can't get together." Heimie's voice grew crisp. "Twelve a case, and we'll put up a car. That's as deep as we can go. Take it or leave it?"

For a moment Bo hesitated. He didn't like it at any price, but there wasn't much else he could do. "Okay," he said finally. "I'll take it."

4

Toward the end of May Bo came home from town with his special look of excited secrecy, his air of being possessed by great schemes, which could only be divulged little by little, with suspense and the aggravation of Elsa's curiosity. He began asking, quite casually, if she wanted to go on a little trip.

"Up to Govenlock?" she said.

"No. A real trip."

"Sure. Where?"

"Yellowstone, maybe. Salt Lake City. All around."

"You mean—just for the trip?"

"Sure."

"Kids too?"

"Kids too."

"That would be wonderful!" she said. "Can we afford it?"

Bo's wink was almost grim. "I'm going to see that we can afford it. This is where I catch up a little on Heimie and his outfit."

"Oh," she said, and her animation faded. "You mean we'll be hauling a load."

"For the love of Mike," he said, "did you think we could go off touring just for the fun of it?"

"Some people do."

"Some people are richer than we are, too. Come on out in the garage, I want to show you something."

He took her out and showed her: an auto tent, folding beds that hooked to the running boards, a food box bolted to the right front fender, with shelves and boxes and a lid that folded down for a table. "Everything the very latest," he said. "This is due to be a trip in style."

"But the kids," she said. "What if we should get caught?"

"That's just it. With the kids along we wouldn't even get stopped. No prohi is stopping families on a tour. He'd lose his job the first time he searched some big shot's car."

She was silent, and her eyes came up to meet his. "It's so much like *using* them," she said.

He snorted. "They'd have the time of their lives. We'd camp out, see some scenery, take it easy. There isn't a chance for a hitch."

"Where would we be hauling to?"

Bo smiled, his lips tight across his teeth. "Heimie wants to open up some new territory. Salt Lake City, especially. And I've been such a good dog he's sending me. It's only incidental that if I get knocked over down there he'd wash his hands of me and not know anything about any agreement. But that's all right."

"Why?" she said. "Why would you go?"

"Because I can get even with the son of a bitch," Bo said. "I'm taking his load in the car, all right, but I'm hooking on a trailer of my own."

"That's double-crossing him."

"You're damned right," Bo said. "The old double-x, just what he pulled on me."

He pulled her back to the house, talking all the time. "I'm going up to Govenlock day after tomorrow. You'll have to pack up and store what stuff we've collected. We've lived in this house long enough. Can you be ready soon as the kids are out of school?"

"I guess so," she said, "but . . ."

"But nothing. This is going to be the nicest trip you ever had."

"I know it would be fun for me. I was thinking about the kids."

"I'll bet you a hundred dollars they'd stow away if we tried to leave them behind."

She laughed uncertainly. "I guess they would, at that." Her laugh died, and she threw him a pained and anxious look. "I keep thinking of that dummy you took along once," she said. "Now you're taking all of us for the same reason. We'll all be camouflage."

He looked at her with such utter lack of comprehension that she gave up.

They pulled out in broad daylight, with the neighbors out to see them off, going publicly like any tourists, their lunch box high on the right fender, the rest of that whole side wedged with suitcases in the luggage carrier, the tent and camp beds strapped on the iron grill back of the spare tire. In the tonneau the boys' heads stuck up through a mountainous load. Bo laughed as he packed them in. "Whiskey to right of them, whiskey to left of them, whiskey on top of them gurgled and thundered," he said. Sixteen cases of whiskey, camping equipment, food, and four people were in the car. They sat on dynamite and waved goodbye to the neighbors and pulled out boldly through the town on the road to Fort Benton, and at Fort Benton, back in a dusty alley behind a warehouse, they picked up the loaded trailer carrying fourteen more cases of whiskey, and crossed the Missouri and started south. The detour to Fort Benton took them almost a half day out of their way, but it made the trailer safe. Eventually, that night, they wound up in the pass above where Bo had been hijacked in November.

The next night, after slogging all day through heavy gumbo mud, they camped in the clear evening with the sun pink on the Crazy Mountains east of them, and the next day they were in Yellowstone, one loaded car among dozens of dusty loaded cars, one family of tourists among the hundreds who peeked into the smoking caverns of geysers and tossed chocolate bars to bears and strung out behind the road construction gangs on dusty unsurfaced grades through the timber. All of that was fun. Elsa never failed to wave at cars they met or passed; they rarely failed to wave at her, and the feeling of being free and open and in society again, part of a good-natured fraternity of gypsies, pleased her almost more than the scenery.

Yellowstone took them exactly one day. In spite of his belief that he was taking it easy, seeing the sights, Bo pushed the Hudson along. A half hour was enough for the canyon, fifteen minutes apiece sufficed for two or three of the more notable geysers, ten minutes was enough to stop and feed some old robber bear. Elsa and the boys looked enviously at parties starting out on horseback, at enticing trails leading off to Mount Washburn or Cody or the Tetons. For all that, they were outside the boundaries of the park by seven the next morning, and that night they were creeping through heavy construction again on the edge of Blackfoot, Idaho.

The roadbed was almost impassable, the detours worse. When they were within sight of the trees of the town they hit a chuckhole that rocked them clear to the axle. Bo winced and gritted his teeth, and the boys whooped from the back seat, pushing the shifted load back off them.

"Smell anything?" Bo said.

Elsa sniffed. "No."

"I do," Chet said.

"God damn!" Bo said. He stopped the car and got out, sniffing over the load. "Busted one, that's sure," he said finally. "But it would be like hunting for a needle in a haystack."

"What can you do?"

"Nothing now. If we get to a good out-of-the-way camp I can unload."

Ahead of them the late sun burned through the tops of a long line of Lombardy poplars, and the roadside was deep green and cool-smelling with alfalfa. "This is a pretty town," Elsa said. "I don't know when I've seen a town so green."

"Irrigation," Bo said.

There were ditches along the road, a wide canal running off across the meadow toward the north. When they pulled past the big U.S. ROYAL CORD scroll bearing the history of Blackfoot, Elsa said, "It would be nice if we could camp here somewhere, it's so cool and green," and five minutes later, when they came to the town tourist park, green-lawned under a canopy of trees, Bo looked at her once and pulled in. Broken bottle or no broken bottle, this was too pleasant a camp ground to miss.

They found a spot under the trees near the irrigation ditch, and after supper Bo rummaged a little in search of the broken bottle. But the load was too solid, and he didn't dare unload completely now, with tourists pulling in every few minutes and settling down for the night. A car was parked and a tent went up hardly fifty feet away. All he could do was settle everything back in and tuck quilts and blankets in tightly all around, to keep the smell as muffled as possible. By nine o'clock they were in bed.

It was barely daylight when Bo sat up abruptly, creaking the iron framework of the bed. "Hey!" a voice was saying outside the tent. "Hey, wake up!"

He poked his head through the tent flap. A man on a horse was outside, and as the horse moved, its feet splashed in the sodden grass. "What's the matter?" Bo said, wide awake now, his mind stiff with the prospect of the law.

"Ditch has busted loose," the man said. "There's already two inches of water running through here. You better pack up and get out or your car'll bog down." In the gray light he kicked his horse closer. "With that trailer, you might have trouble," he said. "I can get you a team after while if . . ."

His nostrils pinched in, dilated once. Bo sitting up to get shoes on, saw his attention wander. That God damned smell . . .

"Thanks," he said. "We'll get out of here right now." He shouted to the boys and shook Elsa. As the rider turned away, looking back over his shoulder, Bo said, "How's the road to Ashton?"

"'Sall right. Might be some snow up high, but the road's open."

"Thanks," Bo said again. He swung on Elsa the minute he let the tent flap fall. "Hustle!" he said. "We've got to get out of here damn fast."

"Ashton?" Elsa said, still only half awake. "Isn't that back up in Idaho?"

"Yeah."

"But . . ."

"Let it go!" Bo hissed. "That damn snooper smelled us, see? We've got to move."

He set his feet down and felt cold water as high as his ankles. The thought of the slippery lawn, the soaked topsoil, under the heavy wheels of the overloaded Hudson made him want to knock somebody down. The Hudson was no good in mud anyway. Too much power, too much weight. A lighter car would walk right through the mud that would mire this elephant . . .

In ten minutes they were packed, the tent and beds and blankets thrown in hastily, any which way, on the load. Bo slid in and stepped on the starter.

"You get out and be ready to push," he said to Chet and Bruce. Elsa climbed out too, and the three braced themselves in water that flowed in a silvery sheet over the whole lawn. It had been almost fifteen minutes since the rider had left. He would have had time to get a cop and come back, if he was the kind that would turn you in. Five minutes more might be too many to delay. They had to make it out the first time or they were sunk.

A gravelled driveway circled the park, fifty or sixty feet to their left. If they could make that . . . Bo leaned out the window. "Push like the devil," he said. "Now!" He let out the clutch and felt the Hudson strain, roll. At the first sign of spinning he eased up, feeding only enough gas to keep the car moving. He heard one of the boys yell and fall down, but he kept easing it, inching it, heavy and lumbering, toward the drive. Ten feet, fifteen, three car lengths. It was like driving a loaded wagon over thin ice. The minute the wheels started to spin in mud instead of on grass, they would be in to the hubs.

The lawn sloped slightly downward, a barely perceptible dip, and then upward again to the drive. He would have to run for it. He stepped down on the throttle, felt the clumsy car spin and swerve, but gain momentum. As long as it was downhill it was all right.

But he had to gun it up that slope. In fury he stamped down on the accelerator and went roaring, throwing mud and water, skidding and whipping back into line, his hind wheels digging in and his speed slowing, slowing, until he barely crept for all the noise of the motor and threshing of the wheels. His front wheels made the gravel, he swung left to ease the hill, and his hind wheels spun, dug, found something solid and pushed him two feet, spun again. Elsa and the boys came panting, threw themselves against the fenders, and gradually, painfully, inch by inch, the car crept up on hard surface until one wheel caught. Elsa jumped aside to avoid the trailer. Bruce was flat on his face in the mud, his upraised forehead spattered. Chet trotted triumphantly alongside.

Bo started again before they were half into the car. "Keep your eye peeled," he said over his shoulder. "If you see any cars behind us, you tell me."

"If he believed that Ashton business we may be all right," he said to Elsa, "but if he didn't we may have to run for it."

She looked at him with her mouth set, turned her head and looked at the boys, muddy and wet, crowding their faces against the spattered back window. They didn't look scared, they weren't bothered by what might happen. They were only excited. She sighed.

"There's a car!" Bruce said. Chet crowded him aside to see better, and they fought for the window.

"Nope," Chet said. "It's turned off again."

They clung precariously balancing on their knees while Bo drove fast down the straight road to Pocatello. On smooth stretches he took it up to sixty, and gravel spanged under the fenders, the tires whined on little curves, the trailer behind wove from side to side, the car rocked with a monumental, dangerous weight on the punished springs.

"Whoopee!" Chet yelled. He grabbed for the top brace to steady himself. Bruce, a little white around the eyes, yelled in echo, and they both screeched hysterically, drunk with excitement and speed, until Bo turned and yelled at them to shut up.

"Sit down," Elsa said quietly. "I don't think there's anybody coming now." She looked back a long time. The road was clear as far as she could see, and a white curtain of dust blew eastward to meet the sun. "You can slow down," she said to Bo. "I'm sure it's all right."

Bo let the Hudson back down to forty, looked once at her, and pressed his lips together. "That could have been bad," he said. "Scare you?"

"Yes."

So that, her mind was saying, is the end of a pretense that this is a picnic trip. Now at least we aren't trying to fool ourselves any more.

It was a day when, having started wrong, they could not do anything right. After the first hundred miles, which they made before breakfast because Bo would not stop until he was clear of possible pursuit, they made bad time. At breakfast Bruce cut himself deeply with the butcher knife, and in his surprise and pain swore furiously out loud, and Bo slapped him end over end. An hour after they had started again it clouded over and began to rain, a slow, insistent, misty drizzle. At three o'clock, after a cold lunch huddled in the car, they were descending a dugway into a river valley. A yellow delivery truck was coming up the grade toward them, hogging the road. Bo rode the horn, pulled the Hudson as far over toward the edge as he dared, and bent, swearing, to peer through the streaming windshield. At the last minute the truck saw them, swerved, skidded, slewed around, and shot by in second gear, and at the instant the soft clay shoulder of the bank began to give under the Hudson's rear wheels. Bo swung in and stepped on the throttle, but the weight of the car bore them down, the trailer slipped half over the edge and the Hudson balanced precariously on its universal housing like a balancing rock.

Very carefully they climbed out the upper side into the rain. Bo's jaw was set, his whole face smouldering. He went to the edge and looked down, walked rapidly up to the next curve and looked back. When he came back to Elsa he was already shooting out orders. "Chet, you run on over to that farm, see, over there on the river. See if they've got a team to pull us out of here. Bruce, you go up to the curve and watch for cars. The minute you see one, wave and yell." To Elsa he said, "There's a sheepshed or something right below us. We can maybe camp there tonight, but first we got to get this damn load off and ditch it."

He was lifting a sack out of the upper side, and Elsa moved to help him. He went plowing down the slope with the sack, and even before she could get another out of the wedged load he was back. His energy was enormous. Put him in a tight spot, she thought, let him get into a place where something serious might happen, and he didn't even waste time swearing. An intense and terrible concentration came upon him. He was driven, furious, violent, but his violence got things done. In twenty minutes he cleaned out the car and cached the sacks in the sagebrush, and in another twenty he had the trailer emptied, had unhooked the coupling, and pulled the trailer by hand up onto the road. No cars or wagons had showed up. Bruce still stood huddled under a blanket at the upper curve.

"You and Bruce go down and start a fire if you can," Bo said. "I'll wait and see if Chet had any luck."

So she took blankets and quilts and went through the rain to the shed. It was open on one side, and the floor was paved with dry and trampled sheep dung, but the roof was decently sound. With damp paper and a loose board she got a fire going and hung the blankets around to dry out. Bruce stood chattering and shivering beside the little blaze, and the sight of his misery epitomized so completely her own disillusion and discomfort that she laughed.

"Well," she said. "How do you like touring?"

They looked at each other. Bruce's solemn face cracked, grinned, and they stood giggling at each other. When Chet and Bo came in to report that the farmer was gone for the day and no one had come by on the road, they were sitting half dressed drying out their clothes and eating a chocolate bar and laughing as if at some uproarious joke.

Late in the afternoon a passing wagon pulled the car off the edge, and that night, in the persistent rain, Bo lugged the sacks one by one over to the sheepshed and reloaded. Early the next afternoon they rolled around the base of Ensign Peak and looked upon the city of the Saints.

"Gee," Bruce said, standing up to see better. "This is a big town."

"Isn't it nice?" Elsa said. "It's like all the towns through here, so green and nice."

Bo stirred and sat up behind the wheel, filling his eyes with wide streets, gutters running with clean mountain water, trees in long rows down the parkways. "This is something like," he said. "There ought to be plenty doing in a town this size."

They coasted slowly through the traffic, swung eastward up a broad avenue leading to the mountains that went up sheer from the edge of the city. A gas station attendant told them there was camping in any of the canyons, and following his directions they climbed a long hill to a ledge under the steep bare peaks, from which they could look back on the city like a green forest below them, and beyond that the white salt flats and the cobalt water of Great Salt Lake far to the west.

"Quite a town," Bo said. "There'd be some point living in a town like this. This makes Great Falls look pretty dumpy."

"Onward and upward," Elsa said. "Excelsior!" As long as they had lived together they had lived in little towns, with only that one bad year in Seattle to break the pattern, and as long as they had lived together he had hated the little burgs. He wanted to get into the big time. The few months he had spent in Chicago, a cocky youngster from the sticks in the incredible metropolis, had been a scented memory all these years. The very name of a big city lighted a fire in him. "Why don't we move on down?" she said.

She said it as a joke, to twit him about the way he itched for somewhere else, but the serious stare he turned on her said that he did not think it was so funny, or even so impossible.

In the next three days she could see the idea working in him, see the progress from speculation to conviction to enthusiasm. Everything he saw and did in the city fed that fire. The three names which Heimie had given him, a shine-parlor operator, a head bellhop, and a brakeman on the D. and R.G.W., were all names that meant solid business. There was a whiskey famine. A reform administration, an active city prohibition force called the Purity Squad, and a consistent record of prosecutions and convictions for bootlegging had steered the whiskey supply to other points. The shine parlor man thought he could use four cases. The bellhop could definitely use two cases immediately, and probably more tomorrow. The brakeman could dispose of three cases as soon as they could be delivered. And all three had their fingers on the places which were good outlets for whiskey. That night Bo loaded the car with the five cases he had definitely sold, and after dark buried the rest of the load deep under the oak brush. Then he took the whiskey and his family to town, treated the four of them to a show and a sticky ice cream orgy in a confectionery store, and drove them home all singing under an incredible round moon that tipped the valley with light like an underwater forest. In his pocket was a roll of three hundred and seventy-five dollars.

In the next two days his brakemen outlet got busy, and before he was through moved twelve cases. The bellhop and the shine parlor man moved another four between them. None of them had even blinked at his asking price of eighty dollars a case. On the fourth day, by dropping the price five dollars a case, Bo unloaded all he had left on the brakeman and the bellhop and was clean.

"My God!" he said to Elsa. "Look at the bead on that." He sat in the tent on a folding stool and spread the money on the bed, smoothed every bill out, separated them into piles of fives and tens and twenties. He got out an envelope and began to figure—his old game. She had seen him, when other figuring palled, sit for three hours computing the ultimate fate of a hundred dollars left in the bank to bear interest at four percent computed semiannually for a hundred years. He had once even bought a copy of Coffin's *Interest Tables* just for the fun of looking up things like that.

Now he stopped figuring to count out five hundred and sixty dollars, the cost of Heimie's sixteen cases, and laid it aside. Heimie's profit on that was twenty-two fifty a case. He multiplied it neatly, laid out another three hundred and fifty. That left him fourteen hundred and forty-five as his own share. He counted it to make sure, bundled up Heimie's roll and put a rubber band around it, figured again. His own net profit was nine hundred and fifty-five dollars.

"Holy cats," he said. "I could sell whiskey in this town as fast as I could haul it in. I guess you're not going to have as long a vacation as you figured on."

"Well," she said, a little tartly, "we might take two or three days to see the place. You said Heimie didn't expect you back for two weeks."

"Yeah," he said. "Sure, we can stay a while and look around." He looked at the brown canvas wall, his fingers tapping lightly on the bed. "Say!" he said, "did it ever occur to you . . . ?"

"What?"

Excitement lifted him to his feet. His head lifted, eyes narrowed, he stood hefting the roll of bills in his palm. "Could you get along here for a week or so, you and the kids?"

"For a week? Why?"

"Because," Bo said, "I'm going back up to Canada after another load."

"But why can't we all go?"

"I want to crowd it. Heimie expects me to take two weeks. All right, I'll take two weeks. But in the meantime I'll haul in a load on my own hook."

"It's his car," she said, "and you're supposed to be working for him."

"Yeah," Bo said, "and he owes me a car and a load of Scotch."

In the glare of the gasoline lantern his eyes were glowing slits. Elsa noticed again how the upward curve at the outer edge of his eyebrows gave him a curiously devilish look. "Besides," he said, "I've got a feeling our dealings with Heimie are almost over."

"I don't know," she said. "If you make this trip you'll be as bad as Heimie."

"Oh for hell's sake!" he said, and turned away. In a moment he was back, not to argue, because his mind was made up, but to pursue another strand of the idea. "I might take Chet along. You and Bruce could stay here and be comfortable."

"How comfortable do you think I could be with him along on a trip?"

"He came down this last trip, didn't he?"

"I was along," she said. "I'll tell you right now, Bo, you can't take him. I wish you wouldn't go yourself."

He tossed the roll impatiently in his hand and stared at her. "We'd sure get rich if we followed your line," he said. "I can make us fifteen hundred bucks cold."

"I'm not thinking about that," she said stiffly. "I'm thinking of what you'll get yourself into. What'll you do afterward? Go back, or stay down here, or what? And if you stay down here what'll you do with Heimie's car? Steal it?"

"I'd just as soon."

"Oh you fool!" she said. "You'll get shot dead in some alley some day." Tears gathered on her lashes and she shook them off. "Go ahead," she said. "Put yourself on Heimie's level, take all the chances you want. But you can't take Chet."

"All right," he said. "I won't take Chet."

Just at evening, seven days later, Bo bumped off the road into the campsite under the maples. He was red-eyed, sleepless, unshaven, weary, but he had thirty-five cases on the car and trailer, and the car was a brand new Hudson Super-Six, a mighty seven-passenger behemoth that even under the mud and dust gleamed with an expensive luster. He had not broken a bottle, had a spot of trouble, or been so much as looked at suspiciously, and he was loose from Heimie for good. Heimie's Hudson he had left at Fort Benton. At first he had been tempted, he said, to keep all of Heimie's roll, drive the car over a bridge somewhere, and make out to have killed himself. He could have changed his name and they could have started out as Mr. and Mrs. Johnson, or Mr. and Mrs. Davis, with a nice fat bankroll. But he had got thinking of what Elsa would say to that, and in the end he had sent Heimie a cashier's check for his share of the first load, and had left his car in a Fort Benton garage with a message that he was through, quitting the business and going back to Dakota.

Now, he said, they could really roll. Now their hands were untied and the world ahead of them.

During the ten days in which he was disposing of the second load he bought clothes, two new suits and three pairs of shoes and two Panama hats. He sent Elsa into town to outfit the boys and herself, and in the evening, a two-bit cigar in his mouth and the top of the new, washed, polished car down to air their prosperity to the world, he drove them all out to Saltair and blew the lid in a Coney Island spree. He tossed silver dollars to the boys whenever they ran out of money, he took them over the roller coaster, through the Fun House, into the restaurant where they had lobster which none of them either liked very well or knew how to eat. Once or twice he looked critically at Elsa's dress, and on the way in, driving with the cool night wind stirring their hair above the plate-glass wind wings, he told her she'd better go in tomorrow and get something dressy. The stuff she'd bought was all right for every day, but she ought to have something snappy to step out in.

"Isn't this all right?" she said. "Just camping the way we are, I should think this would do. It's a nice little dress."

"Sure it's a nice little dress," he said. He fished for a cigar. "It would do all right in Great Falls, but you can't step out in it around here. You're in the big leagues, Mama. You're out of the bush leagues now."

"Can I have a house to live in?" she said. "Now that we're rich and can have new clothes and a new car and can throw money around at resorts, can I have a house? I'd like to be dry when it rains, and have a bath out of something besides a pail for a change."

"Tomorrow," he said, "we'll go house hunting. And we won't be hunting any little dump, either."

"When we're poor," she said, "you're as miserly as old Scrooge, and when we make a few dollars you throw it around with both hands. You need a manager."

"Only thing I need a manager for," he said, "is to add up my money for me. I get so I can't add that high after while." He blew a whiff of expensive smoke into the air and put his arm around her, driving one-handed like a young buck stepping out on a flapper date, and when she stabbed him in the ribs to make him quit playing the fool he quelled her with a smoke screen.

VII

Long afterward, Bruce looked back on the life of his family with half-amused wonder at its rootlessness. The people who lived a lifetime in one place, cutting down the overgrown lilac hedge and substituting barberry, changing the shape of the lily-pool from square to round, digging out old bulbs and putting in new, watching their trees grow from saplings to giants that shaded the house, by contrast seemed to walk a dubious line between contentment and boredom. What they had must be comfortable, pleasant, worn smooth by long use; they did not feel the edge of change.

It was not permanence alone that made what the Anglo-Saxons called home, he thought. It was continuity, the flux of fashion and decoration moving in and out again as minds and purses altered, but always within the framework of the established and recognizable outline. Even if the thing itself was paltry and dull, the history of the thing was not.

If one subscribed to the idea of home at all, one would insist on an attic for the family history to hide in. His mother had felt so all her life. She wanted to be part of something, an essential atom in a street, a town, a state; she would have loved to get herself expressed in all the pleasant, secure details of a deeply-lived-in house. She was cut out to be a wife and mother as few women were. Given half a chance, she would have done well at it.

But look, he said, at what she had to work with. Twelve houses at least in the first four years in Salt Lake, each house with its taint from preceding tenants, each with its own invulnerable atmosphere and that spiritual scent that the Chinese call the *fêng shui*. Twelve houses in four years, in every part of the city. They moved in, circled around like a dog preparing to drop its haunches, and moved out again, without any chance of ever infusing any house with the quality of their own lives.

He remembered some of those houses: the first one, the pretentious place with the two cement urns like enormous pustules flanking the front walk. To that place his father brought ball players for beer-busts after the games, not for any commercial purpose but because he liked ball players and because now, feeling prosperous and meeting players who had been famous once in the big leagues, he liked to expand and play glad-hand host. That was about all there was left of that house in Bruce's memory: the brown men laughing with glasses in their hands, and his father circulating around with a pitcher. That house held them five months.

Then an abrupt declension in style. Perhaps Bo Mason had been knocked over or had lost a load or got in trouble somehow. Bruce never knew. But the second house was a ratty old place on the edge of a weedy field. The front door, decorated down its sides with lozenges of colored glass, had a bullet hole through it at the level of Bruce's eyes. In the back yard was a barren pear tree, and the lawn was mangy and run down. In this house, during the spell of hard times, his father started selling liquor by the drink. Bruce remembered coming home from high school and going into the kitchen to avoid the people crowding the parlor. Once in a while, when there was a rush, he had to serve drinks. He hated it. So did his mother. There was almost always a quarrel after one of those afternoons. Then the Purity Squad raided the house next door and poured barrels of stinking mash out the second-story windows, and Bo Mason moved out quick. He never went back to the speakeasy business, perhaps because Elsa objected so much. Before long he was running liquor in from the coast.

A house by the municipal playground, a good one, with big trees and a wide back lawn, a house his mother liked and wanted to stay in. That was the year when a woman named Sarah Fallon boarded with them while she studied beauty culture, and Bruce remembered the dimes he used to earn every afternoon massaging her incipient double chin. The feel of that soft, moist skin clung to his fingers yet, a sharper memory than any other he had of the house. They moved from there because his father got suspicious of the pious Mormons next door. A man who drove a big car and came in and out with suitcases a good deal, but never seemed to have any regular working hours, was too likely to get the neighbors talking. You couldn't stay too long in one place.

So they moved, and moved again. A brick bungalow up on the avenues overlooking the long wooded sweep of the city; a two-story frame house where they boarded a ball player's wife and family one summer; another undistinguished bungalow; an old adobe house almost as old as the city, but cool and pleasant under its locust trees. They melted and flowed together in the mind, a montage of houses, crowding the recollections of four years. An apartment in a big brick block, a little doll house near a gully where the mocking birds sang madly on moonlit nights, a vague and telescoped memory of some time spent living with an automobile salesman on a chicken ranch south of town . . .

What other houses? What else? They blurred and ran together. Things like the places you had lived got lost. They had importance in one context, but in the daily process of living they dwindled. There was school to take Bruce's time, there was the constant impatient agonized wish that he would ever start growing, get some muscle, get to be an athlete like Chet. There was the habit of walking on tiptoe all the way to school to develop his calves, the secret exercises in the basement to harden his neck and arms. There were his envy and pride, oddly mixed, when Chet did something spectacular and got his name in the papers, and his moral horror when he found that Chet and all his gang of big-chested boys smoked cigarettes and played penny ante poker.

There was his pride in his grades at school, his caddying at the golf club and his growing interest in the game of golf. There were his fear of girls, his tormenting dreams, his adolescent agonies, his constant furious expenditure of energy in the effort to be a top scholar, an officer in the ROTC. His whole private life took up his time, and the life in his home he noticed only when it irritated or balked him. Moves from one house to another meant to him only the necessity of finding new cross-lot ways to school.

It was only in retrospect that the moves had any significance, only when he thought of what his mother's life must have been all that time; and even there, he realized, his memories were probably colored by a sentimental pity that had little relation to his mother's real feelings. She never complained, except humorously, about the life she led. Probably much of the time she was almost contented except for her constant nagging worry that Bo would get into trouble that he couldn't get out of. But there was nothing really unhappy about her life, in spite of its rootlessness, until the spring when Chet was seventeen.

2

It was cool in the locker room after the sun outside, and it felt good just to sit and feel the tiredness run down his arms and legs. His spikes scratched a little on the cement floor as he hunched his shoulders to lean forward with elbows on knees. His mind was full of visions.

They would have that one in the papers all right. Through the open windows he could hear the last ragged yell for West High, and the babble of voices and clack of spikes coming down the hall. The cheers he had got as he trotted off at Muddy's wave, not even stopping to lean into the huddle and give three for his beaten opponents, were still sweet in his ears, but he did not look up as the doors slammed open and the team swarmed in. Hands hit his back, knocking him further down in his slump on the bench, but he paid no attention. His eyes were fixed on the floor in a steady, completely-faked look of despondency or exhaustion.

Hands seized his bowed head and roughed it, and he looked up as if mad. Muddy Poole, the coach, stood there grinning. "Great stuff, Chet," he said. "You really got in there and pitched that one."

Chet glowered, then winked. "Guess I smacked a couple too, didn't I?" he said. He could see the newspapers now. "Mason Holds West to Three Hits." "Chet Mason, star portsider of East High, held the strong West team to three meager bingles yesterday while his mates were collecting eight off the combined offerings of Rudd and Jenkins to win, 5–0. Two of East's hits were rousing doubles by Mason which drove in three runs . . ."

Muddy shook his two hands at him and went in behind the lockers. Shoes were dropping all over the room, bodies were squirming out of sweat shirts and pants, somebody yelled as a flipped sock garter spatted against his skin, and in an instant there was a towel fight in the aisle, Pinky DeSerres and Jerry Knowlton cracking them off like bullwhips. Pinky took refuge behind Chet, using him as a shield, and Chet watched his chance to smack him a beauty across the rump. He saw the red mark start and swell almost before the yelping Pinky was out in the aisle again and being chased toward the shower room.

Van Horsley, the catcher, came out from the lockers in jock strap and socks. His face was waggling in astonishment. "Looky," he said. "Look what that potlicker Rudd almost did to me when he beaned me in the fifth."

He pulled his supporter down and showed the aluminum crotch guard, dented as if someone had hit it with a mallet.

"Oh well," Chet said. "Nothing there to get hurt."

"Yeah," Van said. "I guess I can take care of myself. What've you got you're so proud of?" He ripped Chet's buttons and ducked the return kick.

"Come on," he said, reappearing with a towel. "You can't sit around here all afternoon and gloat. There's a couple hot numbers waiting outside."

"I got a date."

"I know it," Van said. "She's waiting with my date by the gym door."

"She is, ha?" Chet said. He dug a sweaty towel from his locker and started for the showers. "Well, let her wait."

But he took only a short shower, and he was dressed before Van. The girls were sitting on the steps in the afternoon sun, amusing themselves by tossing scraps from scattered lunch boxes to the seagulls that coasted with cocked heads over the lawn. Laura Betterton, slim and quick, brown-haired, brown-eyed, waved her hand at Chet and started over. She was older than the high school girls, wasn't a high school girl at all, but a student at a business college downtown. "Oh Chet," she said, "I think it was just simply *swell!*"

Chet looked at her, looked away vaguely. "Oh, I don't know," he said. "West's not so hot. L.D.S. is the tough one in this league."

"But only three hits!" Laura said. Her enthusiasm embarrassed him.

"Been feeding the gulls?" he said.

"Yes. Aren't they tame?"

"Show you something."

He scouted around till he found a scrap from a lunch box, tied a length of string on it, and walked onto the lawn. Three gulls hung over his head, crying, and he made elaborate gestures of protecting his head from droppings. The three watching him laughed. "Watch him now," Chet said. He tossed out the scrap, keeping hold of the string, and a gull swooped and grabbed and flapped up again. Chet let him get about fifteen feet up before he pulled the string. The gull turned almost a complete somersault, a startled squawk was yanked out of him along with the scrap, and in a confusion of feathers and indignant cries he lit out straight for Great Salt Lake.

They were all laughing. "I think you're mean," Laura said.

"My hero!" Van said.

"Aw, shut up."

"I thought you were the hero," the other girl said. She was taller than Laura, rather thin, with a bright spot of rouge on each cheekbone.

"Sure," Chet said. "Van got heroically injured in the front line trenches."

"What do you mean, trenches?" Van said. He was burbling with secret laughter, and his girl's face wore a sly, sidelong smile that she couldn't quite conceal. Laura was looking at Chet and didn't seem to be listening.

Van, Chet was thinking, was a real slicker. His hair was always Sta-combed ·back, he could toss the old bull around, his suit was pretty snazzy, pinch-waisted coat with four pearl buttons set close together under the breastbone, bell-bottom pants with straight-across pockets and a broad belt band. The next suit Chet got was going to be one like that, even if his old man did call them "four-button pimp suits." There was no percentage in going around looking like an old sack of laundry. You had to have style, like Van. Van had a stripped-down Ford bug, too.

"Where we going?" Van's girl said.

Chet looked at Laura, and she took his hand and tucked it under her elbow. "I don't care," she said.

"I'm hungry," Van said. "Let's go have a dog."

"I know what," Chet said. "You got your car, Van?"

"Yeah."

"Let's go out to Saltair."

"Is it open?"

"Sure. Opened the fifteenth. I'm going to work out there soon as school's over. We can get in anywhere for nothing. I know all the guys."

"I ought to call home," Laura said.

"Okay," Chet said. He looked at Van's girl. "How about you?"

"I ain't got no home," she said, and puckered her face into a gamin's grin.

"Me neither," Van said. "Come on, let's go over to Mad Maisie's and get a dog and call."

Ten minutes later they piled into Van's red bug, a home-made racing car with a souped-up carburetor and a Rajah head and a Ruxtell axle. It had no muffler, no top, no fenders, no windshield, no seats except folded blankets.

Chet and Laura were in the back cockpit. They went down South Temple as if propelled by rockets, slowed a little crossing the business section, and swung out past the fair grounds and the airport on the Saltair Speedway. The speedway was a dirt road, but smooth and straight across the salt flats. Chet and Laura ducked further down out of the tearing wind, their eyes close to the sign scrawled in white paint across the red metal: "No mugging aloud." They looked at each other and smiled, and he slid his arm around her. Her hair blew across his face, tickling, as she relaxed against him.

Van was horsing the bug all over the road, unable to see much for the glare of the dropping sun, and pretending not to be able to see anything at all. He drove on the left side, held his course in the face of approaching cars until his girl shrieked, and then swung wildly toward the right-hand ditch. Other cars almost went off the road avoiding him, drivers turned and yelled, and one car even stopped to turn around in the road.

"Hey!" Chet said. "He's after you."

Van looked back, raised his eyebrows, and yanked down the gas lever. The bug tore up the straightaway, the wide-open exhaust roaring so loud that no one could hear what anyone else yelled. They hung onto the bucking seats and laughed. By the time they reached the salt works the other car had dropped back out of sight.

"Safe at last!" Van yelled. He pulled his girl over to him and hugged her, let go the wheel to use both arms, grabbed it again just as the bug was careening toward the ditch. Laura was frowning. "He's crazy!" she shouted, close to Chet's ear, and he nodded. He had been a little scared himself when the other car started to chase them. The old man would raise some hell if he wound up in jail.

There were not many people at the Moorish pavilion built on piles out into the lake. It was too early in the season, and the Coney Island of the West was having a moderately dull Saturday afternoon. Chet took them around to the bathing houses, winked at the attendant, and got them all in for a swim free. At the hot dog stand he ordered four hot dogs and got eight.

Laura hung onto his arm above the elbow, and he liked the way her hand didn't go more than halfway round his muscle. On the roller coaster a little later she hung onto him in panic, and he scared her pants off, he told Van afterward, by standing up on the first steep pitch.

They toured the Fun House, rolling drunkenly in front of distorting mirrors, yelling encouragement when Van's girl got caught in a whole battery of air blasts and had her skirts blown up around her ears. Her efforts to keep them down were not very successful, and Van dug Chet with an elbow. "Did you see that?" he hissed. "No pants!"

"Not bad!" Chet said. He hadn't seen anything, because he had been watching Laura edge along the walk with her dress clutched down in both hands so that only the hem blew. Van's girl was standing at the other end laughing. "That's a dirty trick," she said, but she was still laughing when they went outside.

The sun was flat along the lake, and the heavy brine sloshed against the piles. From the left came the shriek of a girl on the roller coaster, and the roar of a car avalanching down the first incline. Ahead of them the barker was just helping two couples out of the square-ended barge at the mouth of the Tunnel of Wonders. He saw Chet and waved.

"Hi," Chet said. "Packin' 'em in?"

"Not so fast. Hasn't really got going yet."

"How about a ride?"

The boy looked right and left across the pavilion. "Get in," he said. "I'll shoot you through."

Van's girl pretended to hesitate. "Are there any blow-holes in there?" She looked at the watery tunnel, the water dotted with wrappers from candy bars, gum, Eskimo Pies, popcorn.

"What's the diff?" Van said. "It's dark in there."

"That might be worse," she said, and stepped into the barge. The look she flashed back over her shoulder at Van made Chet shift his feet. Van was getting there, all right. He was a little uncomfortable with Laura at his elbow. She wasn't any little cheap chippy like Van's squaw, but just for a minute he almost wished she was. You could get away with plenty in that tunnel with a swamp angel like Gladys.

They slid smoothly, silently, into the mouth of the *papier maché* tunnel. The opening was a blurred glow behind them, and then as the flame curved the glow was gone and they moved in velvet blackness.

"Eeee!" Gladys said. "This is spooky!"

Sitting in the rear seat, Chet couldn't see either Van or Gladys, couldn't even see Laura a foot away. He felt for her hand, got it, felt her crowd against him. His lips felt stiff. Up ahead he heard rustling, a giggle, soft exciting noises. Van's voice, an insinuating whisper with a burble of laughter in it, said, "How'd you like to walk home from here, baby?" and Gladys' voice said, "I could swim, I guess."

"That's what the mermaid thought," Van said. "You know what happened to her." The voices stopped, and there were only the soft noises that Chet listened to with held breath, trying to interpret them. He swallowed and leaned sideways until his lips felt Laura's hair. She turned up her face and they kissed. In the hot velvet black the kiss lengthened and tightened, and their bodies crowded together. An alcove with a dim red light and a phosphorescent death's head broke them apart momentarily. The barge crawled on, around another bend. In just a minute the surprise lights would flash on. Chet kept his arm around Laura's waist but raised his head, focussing on the dark ahead. Van's activities up there fascinated him. Would the lights catch them dead to rights? He squinted so that he wouldn't be blinded when it happened.

The gray tunnel walls leaped instantly out of the dark, the square ends of the barge were there, the water with floating papers and bits of popcorn, and the two: Their heads jerked apart as if pulled by ropes, and Gladys' hands grabbed downward. Chet saw the white gleam of skin, heard Van's startled grunt, and then the lights went off and dropped them into blackness blacker than before.

"What the hell!" Van said. "That's kind of hard on the heart."

Chet laughed out loud, and startled them all with the thunderous reverberation in the tunnel. "I thought that'd catch you," he said.

"You might have said something, if you knew it was coming," Gladys snapped.

"Oh bushwah," Chet said. He was a little disappointed. They had only been necking, then. But her skirt was up over her knees. Van must have been giving her a working over.

Laura's body moved against his, and he bent to kiss her again. There was a light throbbing all through her, as if she were shivering. He slipped his hand up over the swelling of her breast, and when her hand came up again to push it down he whispered, "It's all right. There's nothing but little red lights from now on. There's three or four minutes more."

She let his hand stay, and he forced her up against him in a fierce embrace, forgetting the soft noises from the front seat. When they coasted around the last bend into the growing glow of light he was taken by surprise. He straightened and looked at Laura. In the half dark her eyes had a curious shine, and her lips were parted. Before she shifted over on the seat and with a pat or two made herself demure she squeezed his hand once, hard. On the front seat Van and Gladys untangled.

"Holy cow!" Van said. "Let's go around again."

"Want to go again?" Chet said. Laura shook her head at him quickly.

"Oh, come on," Van said. "I never got much of a look at the wonders last time."

Laura rose teetering and stepped out on the platform, clinging to Chet's hand. He looked back at Gladys and Van in the barge. "You go ahead," he said. "We'll meet you."

"Where?"

"At the car?"

"All right. When?"

"I don't care. Say an hour?"

"Okay," Van said. He dug thirty cents out and held it up to the barker, and Gladys settled herself on the seat, tilting her head away from him to look at him with her sidelong smile.

Alone, Chet stood a little uneasily watching Laura. The shine was gone from her eyes. She looked quiet, almost severe. "What do you want to do?" he said.

"Couldn't we go somewhere and just talk?"

"How about going swimming again? We could float around and have a regular old gab fest."

"All right," she said. "It was hot in that tunnel."

Lights were on all over the resort, an umbrella of white dazzle. The potted palms moved a little in the first night wind; the cement floor of the pavilion was still radiating warmth from the sun. At the bathing concession the attendant was just closing his shutters.

"Sorry, Chet," he said. "I got to be checked in and have everything closed up by nine."

"Hell, you could let us go out," Chet said. "I don't need any lifeguard."

The boy hesitated. "Come on," Chet said. "It's no skin off you. I'll be quiet."

"Oh, all right," the boy said. He looked curiously at Laura as he passed out two keys with rings of elastic on them, two towels, and two gray cotton bathing suits. "You'll have to undress in the dark," he said. "I can't leave any lights on."

"That's okay," Chet said. He held the gate open for Laura and raised his hand to the attendant. "I'll do as much for you some day," he said.

Going back through the rows of dressing rooms Laura clung to Chet's arm. "Are you sure it's all right? We could have gone and sat in the car."

"Sure it's all right. Everybody hangs together out here. It's okay."

He found her dressing room for her with the help of a match, and by the door he pulled her to him and kissed her again. "You're pretty nice," he said.

"Am I?" Her head was back, cocked, and her eyes glinted a little in a flake of light wavering across from the pavilion. "You're pretty nice yourself."

"Like me better than anybody?"

"Oh," she said, shivering. "Much!" She stood on tiptoe, pecked him with a kiss, and whipped laughing inside the dressing room before he could grab her. He was remembering the soft resilience of her body all the way over to his own room. She had a nice shape, more roundness to her, a better armful than any of these high school kids. She was a woman, not any little half-baked kid. There was no percentage in playing around with kids.

They went barefoot together out the long pier. To their right the pavilion was a blaze of light, the Moorish minarets lifting like green mushrooms from the glare, people moving around, the sound of barkers and the roar of the roller coaster and the yells of girls in the shake-up concessions coming loud and yet unimportant across the oily water. The air was cool, but when they slipped down the stairs and into the brine it felt warm, almost lukewarm, with a slippery, half-sticky feel to it from the salt.

For a while they floated quietly, the buoyant water holding them cradled, their feet lifting helplessly high in the water. Paddling himself like a canoe, Chet came close to Laura's vague pale shape. Heavy-sounding as cement, the water slopped against the salt-crusted piles under the pier.

"This is nice," Laura said. "This is ever so much nicer than sitting in the car."

"This is a pretty good place," Chet said. "It's fun working out here."

They drifted and paddled. "Wonder what Van and Gladys are doing now?" Chet said.

Laura said nothing for quite a while. "Do you like Gladys?" she said finally.

"I guess so. I don't know. Why?"

"I think she's cheap."

"Yuh, I guess she is, a little." He rowed himself around in a circle and came back to position with his feet pointing toward Laura. "She's probably giving Van quite a workout in that tunnel."

"That's just it," Laura said. Her voice was sharp. "I don't think a place like that is decent. They just fix it so all sorts of things can go on, and people like Van and Gladys like it."

"Oh well," Chet said. "Van can take care of himself. He's a pretty handy boy with the women."

They were silent again, floating under the blurred noises of the pavilion. "Chet," Laura said.

"Uh?"

"You're not like that, are you?"

"Like what?"

"Like Van. Chasing girls all the time just to see what he can get. Picking the cheapest ones because they're easy."

"I picked you," Chet said. "Not for that reason, though."

"I know you're not like that," she said. She waded toward him, the brine shining around her white shoulders. "You're clean," she said, standing close to him and speaking with a shiver in her voice. "Just to look at you I could tell you were clean. Just to look at your hands."

"My hands?" he said stupidly.

"You've got beautiful hands," she said. "So big and long and square. I noticed them before I ever knew you, when I just saw you at a ballgame."

Chet laughed self-consciously. "Big hands are a help playing ball."

She reached out and took one, stroking it. "The skin is just like satin on them," she said. "Like a girl's skin. I think you can judge people by their hands, don't you? Better than by their faces. I watch the hands of people down at school. Most of them are skinny, like claws, or else big fat wads of things."

Her voice in the dark praising him, flattering him; the feel of her fingers moving on the skin of his hands, their skins touching with the slightly-sticky, slightly-slippery feeling of the salt water on them, excited him. He pulled her close, hard against him. "You're . . . beautiful," he said. The word was hard to get out.

Playfully she leaned back against his encircling arms and swayed as if she were in a hammock, and every movement brushed her body against his. He licked his lips, tasting salt, and cringed away a little from the intimate kiss of their skins under water.

"How old are you anyway, Chet?" she said.

"Nineteen," Chet said. He had lied about his age so consistently at school, because he hated being the youngest member of the football team, that he almost believed it himself.

"Only nineteen," she said, almost as if disappointed. "I'm twenty-one, did you know that?"

"I could tell you weren't any punk kid," he said. "These little high school flappers give me a pain."

"They're no worse than the boys," she said. "They all go around pretending to be so grown up, necking and fooling around. They've got no more intention of getting married than the man in the moon."

"Married!" Chet said. The word was like the word "beautiful," a solemn and importunate and scary sound. "There's plenty of time to get married," he said.

She had stopped swinging, and seemed to be searching his face, but in the dim light that flaked off the water he couldn't see her well. Then her head turned. "I never thought very much . . ." he was saying, before he realized that she was crying.

"Good hell," he said. "What's the matter, Laura?"

She continued to cry silently, standing with her face twisted away from him, and he gathered her unprotestingly close. "You shouldn't cry," he said. "What's wrong?"

"I just . . . keep thinking . . . how impossible it is," Laura said.

She wiped her eyes on her upper arms to keep from getting salt in her eyes.

"How impossible what is?"

"You're only nineteen."

"What difference does that make?"

"You won't want to get married for a long time," she said, the words strangling out sideways, ending in a wail. "If I can't marry you I don't ever want to get married!"

Chet swallowed, standing very still, his arms like wood around her. "Well, good hell," he said. "I love you, you know that, don't you?"

She was hard against him again, her fingers clenched on his arms. "Oh, I do!" she said. "I do, and I love you too, Chet. Terribly. I love you more than anything in the whole world."

Chet lifted his head and looked over her white cap at the thick, glimmering water and the lights curving up along the roller coaster scaffolding in an intricate tracery that wavered in reflection toward him across the moving surface. "Aw honey," he said, and patted her back.

"Chet," she said, and put her face in the hollow of his shoulder. "I'm such a baby. I've been thinking and thinking, and I didn't know how you felt, whether you thought of me the way I did of you. A girl can't go on forever not knowing. I hate my home, and school, and everything but you. The only fun I have is watching you play ball and being proud of you, and seeing you afterwards."

Chet swelled his chest, got self-conscious, and pushed her backward with it until she half laughed. He swung her around in the water like a pinwheel, and his strength seemed like something superhuman, something that could break down anything, tear things up by the roots, give him whatever he wanted. "I tell you what," he said. "Soon as I'm out of school I'll get a job and we'll save, and pretty soon we'll get married. We don't have to wait till I'm twenty-one. I could pass for twenty-one most places."

"Oh, Chet," she said, her breath against his skin. "Oh, Chet!"

They stood in the deep shadow of the pier, their bodies locked together. Laura made tiny whimpering noises as he kissed her, breaking her mouth away and bringing it back eagerly. A chill not from the water shook Chet till his teeth chattered. With one hand he unbuttoned the shoulder strap of her suit.

Above them, as they stood in the water to their shoulders, the noise of merrymakers in the concessions drifted unmeaningly, and the light splintered and shook over the moving water.

"Where can we go?" he whispered. "Up on the pier?"

Her hands pushed against his chest and she waded backward, stooping for the fallen suit around her ankles. "No," she said. "No, Chet, not now, I don't want to, please!

"*Please,* Chet," she said, as he reached for her again. He stopped, watching her pull the dark suit on again. She came up to him, ran her hands up and down his sides, pulled them away with a little laugh and put them behind her. "Oh Chet," she said, "you'll think I'm one of those like Gladys."

"Bushwah," Chet said sullenly. "You couldn't be like Gladys if you tried. But I don't see why you won't. We love each other, don't we?"

"If we didn't I'd be so ashamed I could die," Laura said. "If I didn't know we'd be married, sometime soon . . ."

"It can't be too soon for me," Chet said.

She laid her hand against his shoulder, and instantly the blood leaped up in his veins, hot and throbbing. "That'll be lovely," she said with a little sigh.

"Then why not? There's nobody around. It's dark up there. Come on."

"No, no please."

"Why not?"

"Chet," she said.

"What?"

"You don't carry anything around with you, do you?"

"What do you mean?"

"Those . . . protection."

"Oh," he said. "No. But . . ."

"See?" she said. "I knew you didn't. I knew you were clean. So you see, it wouldn't be safe, Chet." She laid her hand on his arm. "Please wait."

"Oh, all right," he said. "But you're driving me crazy."

They climbed the ladder to the pier. Walking back to the dressing rooms he had his arm around her under the suit, and by the time they reached her door they were stammering, stopping every five feet to kiss passionately. "Why not in here?" he said.

She beat her fists against his chest, but there was laughter in her voice, and she punctuated every four words with a kiss. "You great big impatient bullying thing!" she said. "Can't you even wait till I get used to the idea of being engaged?"

"No."

"Well, you'll have to," she said, and whisked in the door. He jumped after her, but the latch had clicked. A dim foot and ankle poked out below the swinging door. "Here," she said. "You can kiss my big toe."

Chet stooped and took her ankle, caressed it a moment, bent and bit her big toe savagely. She squealed, smothered the sound quickly.

"That'll teach you," he said, and stalked off. But while he was dressing he was thinking how he had almost had her. Jeez, it was hard to imagine that it had been him out there in the water with her, and her suit off . . . But it was all right anyway. She thought he was the clear goods, and now that they were engaged it was going to be hunky-dory, no fooling. And she was a real woman, none of your fifteen-year-old hallway flappers, and Jesus, Jesus, it was wonderful.

It was already too late, he knew, to meet Van and Gladys at the car. They'd probably be off somewhere in the dark getting in their licks. He and Laura would have to ride home on the train, but that would be all right too, sitting on the steps of the open car with the wind off the salt flats, and the smell of the flats that was like no other smell on earth, a stink almost, so that the first time you smelled it you held your nose, but it grew on you, and before long you found yourself sniffing it, liking it, a salt, exciting, sea-smell that was wonderful to take in great gulps when you were driving or riding the train at night. And now there'd be Laura right next, snuggling against him with her head on his shoulder.

Engaged, he said. Holy cats.

Back in his mind was a door that he could open any time he wanted to but he didn't want to now. Behind the door was a sign, and it said in big letters—but he didn't look at the letters because what was the point?—"Chet Mason isn't nineteen, he's only seventeen." He didn't open the door and he didn't look at the sign, but he knew it was there and he knew what it said.

3

The papers had it. Chet sat at breakfast eating by feel, his eyes pasted to the sport page of the *Tribune*. That had all that about the stingy East southpaw and about only two West runners reaching second, and about his two doubles. But what held his attention longest was the Sports Chatter column. Bill Talbot, the manager of the Salt Lake Bees, had seen the game from the stands, and had remarked to the reporter that he had seldom seen a high school pitcher with more promise. A good curve ball, the reporter said. But it wasn't the curve that interested Talbot. Anybody could learn to throw a hook. "The kids you want to watch," he said, "are the ones that can throw a baseball a mile a minute and keep it up all afternoon. When their fast one hops, you want to watch them extra close. This kid's fast one hops."

Spooning his breakfast food automatically, Chet looked through the wall, which opened suddenly to show him trying out on a green diamond with the Bees, striking out the head of the lineup one— two—three while Bill Talbot stood on the third base line watching. He saw the headlines at the end of a season, when Mason was announced as the standout pitcher in the Coast League with a record of twenty-five won and six lost. He saw the Big League scouts coming, heard the prices they quoted to Talbot, saw his picture on a sport page snapped at the top of his windup with his spikes in the air, and underneath the legend, "Seventy-five Thousand Dollar Beauty goes to Cardinals." He saw himself playing ball with Collins and Sisler and Ruth and Schulte. He saw himself starting a game in the World Series, and the headlines and the chatter about that: "Miller Huggins, masterminder for the New York Yanks, has his work cut out for him to think up some magic to counteract the stuff his Yanks will have thrown at them today via the good left arm of Chet Mason, brilliant young freshman hurler who this season set a record for strikeouts in the National League . . ."

He pushed the cereal bowl away and reached for a roll. His mother, clearing up the rest of the dishes, looked at him and smiled. "Got it memorized?"

"Oh, bushwah," Chet said. He grinned and waved the paper in her face. "See what Bill Talbot said? Did you get an eyeful of that 'promise' stuff? You'll grin out of the other side of your face when I'm pitching in the big leagues and drawing down twenty-five thousand a year and splitting a World Series melon every fall."

He didn't know his father had come into the room until he heard him grunt. "Maybe you'd better get out of short pants before you start swallowing all of Bill Talbot's guff," he said. "What was the matter with those guys yesterday? All sick?"

"I was just throwin' it past 'em," Chet said.

His father laughed and looked across at his mother. "Modest, isn't he?"

"Terrible," she said. "But I guess he must have been just a little bit good."

"Just a little bit my eye," Chet said. "I was terrific. My fast one was hopping four inches."

"You know me, Al!" his father said.

"Well, it was."

"How about those six bases on balls?"

"I didn't walk six guys."

His father's big blunt hand came down and took the paper and held it in front of his nose. "Bases on balls, off Mason, six," he read from the box score. Chet took the paper and read it for himself. "They must have got it wrong," he said. "Even if this is right, how about those eleven strikeouts?"

"I don't care how many you strike out. If you walk six guys you put six possible runs on base."

"None of 'em got past second."

"But they might have," his father said. "Six walks are as good as six singles."

"Well, the umpire was blind in both eyes," Chet said. "You had to groove it or it was a ball."

"Now we've got an Alibi Ike around the place," Bo Mason said. He chopped out a laugh from down below his belt. "Come on out in the yard," he said. "Let's see this hot one of yours."

"You couldn't hang onto it," Chet said. "It takes a good catcher to catch me."

"I was catching guys faster than you when you were nothing but a vague idea," his father said, "and doing it with my bare hands."

"You won't need the mitt then," Chet said.

His father looked at him. "Come on, Smarty," he said. "Get that pillow and a baseball and get out and let's see what you've got."

Chet dug the mitt, his own glove, and a ball from the hall closet. "Bo," Elsa said as they went past her, "I don't think you've played catch with the kids for ten years."

Chet winked. "This'll be the last time. I'm going to blow him over backwards."

He would show the old man whether or not he had a fast one. They laid down a folded dishtowel from the clothesline for a plate, and Chet stepped off the distance. He put his toe on an imaginary rubber, took an easy windup, and lobbed one over. It plunked into his father's mitt and came back smartly. For a few minutes they tossed the ball back and forth, warming up. "All right," his father said. "Let one go."

Chet wound up and threw. The ball smacked into the mitt with a flat, wet-leather sound. The return throw stung. "High and outside to a right hander," his father said. "Ball one. Come on now, quit babying them."

Chet pitched again, a perfect waist-high strike. "Okay," his father said. "Pitch to me."

He held his mitt for a target, low and inside. Chet threw him a hook that broke a little late, and he had to move the mitt six inches. "Hit where I call for 'em," his father said. "Never mind the round-house stuff."

He moved the mitt thereafter only when he had to to stop a pitch, and Chet threw at the target, really trying to put it squarely in the pocket, bearing down as if the bases were loaded and nobody out. He walked the first imaginary batter, struck out the next two, walked another, and everything he threw his father took handily, peppering the ball back with a sharp wrist throw.

"You must have had a pretty fair peg to second when you were playing ball," Chet said.

"Fair," his father said drily. "I used to stand on home plate and throw balls into a barrel in center field on the first bounce."

He pulled off the mitt, examined his pink palm, and tossed the mitt to Chet. "That's enough," he said, and took a cigar from his leather case. He squinted at Chet speculatively, and Chet, wondering what the old man thought of his pitching, looked off down the street as if expecting someone.

"Your fast one is pretty fast," his father said. "You're no Walter Johnson, but you can burn one in. But it doesn't hop as much as you think."

"I can't get a good toehold without spikes. It was hopping yesterday."

"Forget the alibis," his father said, watching him steadily. "What I'm telling you I'm telling you for your own good. You might make a ball player. You've got the build and you've got the arm. But it's awful easy to think you're Christy Mathewson when you're only some little busher. You'll never make a class-A league till you buckle down to throwing baseballs at a knothole in a barn. You're wild as a steer."

"Well, I'll practice up and pitch me a no-hitter with no walks next time," Chet said. He grinned, but his father did not grin back.

"And forget to be so proud of what the papers say," his father said. "You'd have got knocked out of the box yesterday if those kids didn't all step in the bucket. They're scared of a fast ball. Throw 'em up that way to a hitter and he'll lose your ball for you."

"You just think they step in the bucket. That's a heavy-hitting outfit."

"I know they step in the bucket," his father said, "because I was there. I was sitting right beside Bill Talbot. One or two heavy hitters who weren't scared of a fast one, and you'd have had half a dozen runs scored against you, with all those walks. You got to remember one thing about a fast ball. If a guy even meets it it's likely to go for two or three bases."

"Yeah," Chet said, a little sullenly. The old man could never say anything without sounding as if he was daring you to contradict him. Well, maybe he knew a lot of baseball and maybe he didn't.

He tossed the ball up and caught it, wishing the old man would go on inside or somewhere and get this catechism over, when the other thought cut into his mind like a car cutting into a stream of traffic. Chet Mason, it said, is not nineteen. He's only seventeen. But just the same in two or three years he may be playing in the big leagues, and this morning, now, he is engaged to a woman twenty-one years old. This is not, he said, any punk kid you're dishing up free advice to. It's about time you got next to that notion.

But it was funny about the old man being at the game yesterday.

"Pa," he said, "can I have the car for a couple hours this afternoon?"

"What for?"

"Van and I have got a line on summer jobs at the Magna smelter. They put you on the bull gang or something, but what you really do is play ball for them. We have to get out and see a guy about it."

That about the smelter job was true enough, but it was not true that he and Van had to see anyone. The smelter man was coming up to school to interview four or five team members on Monday.

Chet's lips had gone over the lie smoothly, but he felt sullen and defensive under his father's eyes. He hated to be made to explain.

"What's the matter with the streetcar?"

"You can't take a streetcar to Magna."

"You can't take the car either," his father said. "I need it myself."

"But Jeez, I want that job, Pa!"

He felt aggrieved, as if his father were keeping him from a real appointment. His mother, out on the back porch and listening, looked at his father.

"Why not?" she said. "If it's a chance to play ball . . ."

"Maybe we can all drive out," Bo said.

Chet opened his mouth, shut it, fished up another excuse. "But I have to pick up Van, and we may have to hunt all over Magna for this fella. We haven't got a regular appointment, he just said come out any time and see him." He shot a look at his father's suspicious face. "I know you," he said. "If you had to wait around for me ten minutes you'd be sore as a boil."

His mother laughed. "That touched you, Papa," she said.

His father was staring at him somberly. "If I let you have it," he said, "I want it understood that you don't go over forty and that you're back here by four o'clock. I've got a delivery to make."

"Okay," Chet said.

"Remember now," his father said, and went inside.

"Good gosh," Chet said to his mother. "You'd think that car was made of solid gold. Other guys can get their dads' cars when they need them."

"You're getting it," she reminded him. "It's Van more than anything that makes Pa careful. He thinks Van is wild. Is he?"

"No," Chet said. "He's all right."

"He looks like a kind of girl-chaser. You don't want to get mixed up that way."

"Well, I'm not."

His mother smiled. "You don't have to bite my head off. You didn't get enough sleep last night. Can't you try to get in earlier?"

"I couldn't," he said. "We were with Van and his girl and we had to wait for them for an hour."

"What'd you do after the game?"

"Just went out to Saltair and fooled around."

"That's one thing that made Pa grumpy," Elsa said. "He went to the game and thought you were real good, and he was expecting to talk it all over with you last night. And then you didn't come home. He was proud of you yesterday, Chet."

"He sure doesn't act like it."

"That's just his way," she said. "He's been around a lot more than you have, and he knows what it takes to be a good ball player, and how a boy can be ruined by getting off to the wrong kind of start. He thinks if you'd quit smoking and train more you'd make something big out of baseball."

"Well," Chet said. "If this smelter job pans out I can get some experience this summer, anyway."

He went down to the drug store and bought the *Telegram* and the *Deseret News,* read their accounts of the game, clipped them both carefully, along with the one from the *Tribune,* and brought his scrap book up to date. At one o'clock, before the family were more than half through dinner, he got the keys and drove out of the garage. But he didn't head either for Van's house or for Magna. He headed for South State Street and Laura.

She met him at the door, and her smile so clearly asked him to remember last night that he slipped into the hall and took her in his arms. She leaned back and put her finger on her lips. "Come in and meet the folks," she said aloud.

He had never been in her house, only in the hall at night. It was not, he saw now, a very good house. Neither it nor her family looked prosperous. Her father looked him over pretty sharply, put out a big rough workman's hand, and sat back. Her mother was excessively fat, almost as broad as she was tall, and fully as thick as she was broad. Her mouth disappeared in great buttery cheeks. The two kids in the kitchen were her brother Jim, about twelve, and her sister Connie, eight. It seemed funny that Laura should be so grown up and still have brothers and sisters as little as that.

"Chet's the fellow that pitched the three-hitter yesterday," Laura said. Her father raised his eyebrows, but he didn't say anything.

"I saw what Bill Talbot said about you," Laura said.

"Oh well," Chet said. "You can't believe all that stuff. I just had a lucky day. I walked so many guys that a few solid hits would've sunk me."

He waited for a denial of this from any of the Bettertons, but none came. "Going to play ball this summer?" Laura's father asked.

"I'm talking to a fellow on Monday about a job at Magna, playing in the Copper League."

"I thought you'd be working at Saltair," Laura said.

"Not if this other job turns up."

"Would it pay more?"

"Quite a bit more, I think," Chet said. "I'll know Monday."

He was getting uncomfortable. He kept stealing looks at Mrs. Betterton, the fattest woman he had ever seen. The parlor seemed warm. His eye flicked around looking for ashtrays as he thought of lighting a cigarette. There weren't any ashtrays. Mormons, he supposed. He had never thought to ask Laura.

"I've got the car," he said to Laura. "Want to take a little ride?"

"Fine," she said. "When's dinner, Mom?"

"About three. I got a chicken, so you'd better get back."

Laura threw Chet a peculiar pleading look and went into the hall. "Well, goodbye," Chet said in the parlor. "It's been nice to meet you."

They stood up and watched him out, and he had a feeling of relief when he and Laura got into the air. "Do they know?" he said.

"No."

"They seemed to be looking me over pretty sharp."

"They always do that," Laura said. "They're so darned afraid I'll start going with somebody they don't like. They just sit and stare at people I bring home."

The edge in her voice warned him to shut up about her family. Maybe she was ashamed of them. It would make you squirm, all right, to walk along the street with that fat woman and have everybody turn and stare.

"When we get married," Laura said, "I want to move clean away from Salt Lake."

"I don't know why not," Chet said. "It's a dump, far as I'm concerned." He opened the door of the car for her, and she stopped dead still.

"My goodness!" she said. "What is it, a Lincoln?"

"Cad."

"Gee!" She admired it as she got in, sat down almost uncomfortably on the leather and looked at the dashboard. "I didn't know you were rich," she said.

"We're not."

"But a Cadillac!"

"My old man just likes good cars," Chet said.

"Well, he must be able to afford them," Laura said. "What does he do, Chet? You never told me anything about your family."

Chet sat pumping up the gas tank, his eyes fixed on the radiator cap across the gleaming hood. "He fusses around with mines," he said. He couldn't have told why he gave that answer. It made the old man sound richer than the Cadillac did.

"Oh," Laura said. Chet locked the pump and stepped on the starter. The motor purred.

"Where do you want to go?"

"I don't care."

"Up the canyon?"

"All right."

She moved over closer to him, and he dropped one hand to squeeze her knee. "Still love me?"

"Um," she said, and smiled her intimate, inviting, remember-last-night smile.

"You were pretty stingy last night."

"Was I?"

"You bet your cockeyed hooley you were."

"Maybe that's the way I am."

"Maybe that's a pretty lowdown way to be."

She looked up at him sideways. "Did you suffer?"

"I didn't sleep all night."

Her laugh rang out, and two girls walking along the sidewalk looked up with envy in their faces. Laura patted his arm. "Poor itty-bitty baby," she said. "It suffered."

"But I'm not going to suffer any more," Chet said. He watched her with excitement mounting in his blood to see if she'd say anything to that. But she only smiled and dug her fingers into his muscle.

They drove up on the east bench and started out toward Big Cottonwood. At Thirty-Third South Chet hesitated, pulled the Cadillac over to the curb. He looked Laura steadily in the eyes. "I want to stop in the drug a minute," he said.

If she understood she made no sign. But after what had happened last night she ought to understand. She did understand, by the Lord. She was just pretending to be dumb and bashful. Exultation carried him out of the car and up to the door of the drug store. It was only after he got inside that the fear of the bald-headed clerk almost stopped him. He looked at the candy counter for a minute, and then, covering up the unease with a swagger, he went back to the furthest, most intimate corner.

It was already three-thirty by the dashboard clock when they came down out of the canyon. Laura, although she sat close, seemed miles away, her face still and her eyes remote. Chet kept stealing looks at her, a little ashamed because he had shown up his own inexperience, a little afraid she was distant because she was disappointed in him. He gnawed his lip.

"Still love me, honey?" he whispered.

Her smile this time was slow and deep, and it thrilled him so that he could hardly sit still. "Ummm," she said. That was better. He was still shaky from her tears up on the mountainside, from her passionate clinging and her stumbling words. He wouldn't think badly of her, he musn't! He knew it was only because she loved him so much, because she loved him till it choked her to look at him . . .

"Me too," he said, sitting rigidly behind the wheel. His eye lighted on the clock. A quarter to four. Laura had missed her dinner, and he would be late with the car. God damn. Something was always getting in the way. He didn't want to take her home now. It would have been perfect to go somewhere to eat and then go up the canyon again in the evening, with plenty of time and everything dark all around, and the lights winking down the valley.

"I guess you're late to that chicken dinner," he said.

"I guess so."

"What'll we do tonight?"

"I don't care. Can you come down?"

"Sure."

"The folks will be going to meeting at six thirty."

They were Mormons all right, then. "Don't you go?" he said.

"I haven't gone for a year," she said. "They think I'm a lost soul." Her eyes flicked up to his, and she turned her face to lay her cheek against the seat. "I guess I am."

"I guess you're not."

"Sometimes I think I could almost die, living at home," Laura said. "They're both suspicious all the time, and Pa's grouchy, and the kids are always getting into trouble and stealing things. I almost hated to have you meet them. You're so strong and clean and you don't know what all that nagging can mean."

"It won't be for long," Chet said. He drove like a lord, weaving the Cadillac through the Sunday afternoon traffic, conscious of his hands and wrists on the wheel. He was glad she liked his hands. Great big old paws, he said. Mentally he flexed one, feeling how it could go almost around a baseball. "You won't have to live in that much longer," he said.

He turned into State Street and up toward her house. As she got out of the car she hesitated, her brown eyes searching his face. "You *do* love me, don't you?" she said. "We *are* engaged?"

"We're married," Chet said. "All but paying the preacher."

Secretly she grabbed his hand and bent over to kiss it. She was biting her lips when she looked up. "You're wonderful!" she said breathlessly. "Oh darling, I think you're perfect!"

He watched her run up the sidewalk. Then he swelled his chest and cramped the car around. She was his woman, and she thought he was perfect, and she was wonderful herself. The way she'd hardly made any fuss up there on the mountain, never pretended or made him coax . . . Oh sweet patootie, he said, and wished it was six thirty.

That made him think of his father and look at the clock. Twenty minutes past four. He'd be a half hour late. The rest of the way home his mind struggled between the need of inventing excuses for the old man and the need of remembering with wonder how fiercely Laura had met his lovemaking in that pocketed hollow under the maples and the sumac just leafing with high spring. Almost as if she were afraid he'd get up and run, as if she were scared she had to hold him to keep him . . .

His father was waiting on the back porch, his watch in his hand, his face like a thundercloud. "Is this your idea of four o'clock?" he said.

"We ran into some construction," Chet said. "I'm sorry, Pa. I got home as quick as I could."

"It isn't quick enough," his father said. "When I say four I mean four, not twenty minutes to five."

"It's only four thirty," Chet said.

"Let's not waste any more time," Elsa said quietly. "We can still make it down by five."

She motioned for Chet to go inside, but he remained standing by the porch. He wasn't going to run from the old man's blustering. The hell with him. He watched his father carry the suitcase down the steps and put it in the car, watched his mother settle herself.

His father's head bent to look at the dashboard, then jerked up. His hard eyes looked across the lawn at Chet. "I thought you said you were going to Magna."

"I did."

"You did like hell," his father said. "I'm getting sick of your lies. You haven't driven but thirty-three miles, and it's more than that to Magna and back."

"I don't care how far it is," Chet said. "That's where we went."

"And I say that's a lie!"

"Don't call me a liar," Chet said.

"Why God damn you . . . !" His father opened the door and started to get out, but Elsa's hand was on his arm.

"Bo."

His lips together, his breath snorting through his nose, Bo looked at Chet, standing defiantly by the porch rail. "The next time you want a car to chariot some cheap floozie around," he said, "don't come to me. This is the last time."

"That's all right with me," Chet said. He locked eyes with his father, who swore and jerked the car into reverse. On the way out he backed off the twin strips of red concrete that served as a drive, and gouged up a stretch of lawn. Chet didn't even bother to laugh. He just looked contemptuously until they were out of sight.

4

On Monday he got his job at Magna, twenty dollars a week and a five dollar bonus to every player when they won a game. "You don't have to do much but play ball," the man from the smelter said. "Mornings you'll putter around, do whatever the foreman of the bull gang finds for you. Lots of the guys spend half the morning in the can. But we want you to play ball for keeps. You'll go to practice at three every afternoon, and twice a week you'll play. We're making it plenty easy for you so we can walk away with that league this summer."

It was pretty nifty, Van and Chet agreed. If they won most of their games they would make close to a hundred a month. They were on the gravy boat. Plenty of dough to spend.

Chet was already back-tracking on the marriage business, postponing it in his mind. You couldn't really bank on it, he told Laura. It wouldn't pay to go getting themselves in a hole.

But it was not really money that was making him cautious. It was the sign behind the door in his mind, the sign that said, "Chet Mason isn't nineteen, he's only seventeen." It was easy to forget that when he was with Laura, but it kept coming back when he lay in bed and thought about things before sleeping.

There was one more week of school, one more game in the high school league. Two days before he was to pitch against L.D.S., Laura came up to school after practice, and she and Chet and Van went over to Mad Maisie's for a root beer. They were sitting there smoking cigarettes just off the edge of the school grounds when Muddy Poole came by. The next day both Chet and Van were dropped from the squad.

That was a blow, no matter how the two tried to swagger it off. It made them celebrities of a kind, got them kidded in the halls, even made them the center of a righteous and indignant group. Muddy ought to have more loyalty to the school than to throw off his first-string battery right before a crucial game. If East lost this one, and West took Granite, then L.D.S. would win the championship. Muddy ought to be able to overlook smoking. What was a cigarette anyway?

All that was pleasant enough, but still Chet was sullen when he went up to the field and sat in the bleachers to watch the game. He didn't even bother to hunt up Van. Obscurely he hoped that something would go wrong, that the team would get in a hole and Muddy would have to come up in the stands and ask him to get in there and save the day. At the end of the second inning he saw his father come down the cement steps and find a seat, and before the end of an inning rise and go out again. Probably he had found out from somebody why Chet wasn't pitching. Now there'd be a big blowup at home.

God damn, Chet said, and sat glumly watching his team pound the L.D.S. pitcher for three runs in the third and two in the fourth. Hench, a little squirt with not half the stuff Chet had, settled down after giving up one run in the first, and had yielded only four hits by the time Chet got disgusted and left.

"It serves you right," his father said at supper that night. "It serves you damn well right. You had a chance, and you blew it. Maybe it'll teach you something."

"Rub it in," Chet said.

"Maybe I need to rub it in. Maybe if it isn't rubbed in it'll run right off your thick hide."

"Oh, let it drop," Chet said. "It isn't worth making all this fuss about."

"It doesn't matter to you, uh?"

Chet raised his eyes. "Not very much."

"No," his father said. His voice was acid with contempt. "I guess it wouldn't, at that. The only thing that'd matter to you is running around with this flapper of yours every night till one-two o'clock."

"Don't you call her a flapper!" Chet said.

His father looked at him a moment. "All right, she isn't a flapper. She just doesn't know when to go home to bed. Hasn't she got anybody to tell her she can't stay out all night every night?"

"Oh, all night!"

"Two last night," his father said. "One-thirty the night before. Three the night before that. You haven't been in before midnight for a week."

"Oh bushwah."

"Yes, bushwah. You haven't."

"Bo," Elsa said. To Chet she said, "You have been staying out awful late. It's not good for you while you're growing, and you don't get your studying done."

"I do my studying at school," Chet said. "And for gosh sake, I'm through growing."

"Well," she said smiling. "We'd like to see you once in a while. You might stay home one night a week."

"Okay, okay," he said. "I'll stay home tonight. I'll sit here and twiddle my thumbs till ten o'clock and go to bed."

He had a date with Laura, but he was so mad at his family for grinding him down, and so sore about the game, that he just called her instead, sitting in the hall from eight fifteen till nine o'clock with his lips confidentially close to the mouthpiece and his voice secret and soft. When he finally hung up he stretched elaborately and yawned. "Well, it's almost nine," he said. "Time for big athletes to go beddy bye."

His father did not rise to his sarcasm, and his mother only said, smiling, "I guess it wouldn't do you any great harm."

So he went, and for an hour lay imagining how it would have been if L.D.S. had cracked down on Hench right at the beginning, and the sub catcher had let a pitch through him and allowed a run to come in, and the whole battery had fallen apart, and runs had kept coming across, so that Muddy had to come leaping up in the stands and get Chet and Van right down in their street clothes to save the day. He could hear the crowd yelling, nine for Mason, nine for Horsley, and he saw himself toeing the rubber in street shoes, rolling up his sleeves and going to it, and the succession of strikeouts, his fast one burning in there so fast that Van shook his mitt hand and grinned when he tossed the old apple back. Not a hit, not a walk, after his appearance in the fifth. Not an L.D.S. runner to reach first, while East whittled away at the big lead and got two here, one there, till they tied it up. It would have been something to come up in the eighth or ninth with the score tied and slam one down the right field line for two or three bases, driving Van in from second with the winning run, and have Van wait at home to shake his hand and pound him on the back. Then the two of them would walk off with the crowd yelling. Muddy would have to come up and stick out his hand and admit that when he threw them off the squad he threw away his ball club, and then they would have shaken hands and lighted up a cigarette right in his face.

But instead of that East had won seven to two, the sub catcher hadn't made a single error, and Hench had held L.D.S. to six hits. The little pipsqueak.

Then graduation, he and Bruce graduating together, the assembly hall full of parents and all the little high school girls running around halls and lawns in their first formals, the long meeting when you sat and waited your turn to go up on the stage and get your football sweater, walking across and taking it from Muddy's hand and going back and sitting down while the applause died for you and started for the next one. Muddy couldn't cheat him out of that sweater, anyway. He'd earned that one, catching that fourth quarter pass and beating Provo six to nothing, and taking a kickoff eighty yards against Brigham City, and completing seven passes for three touchdowns against Granite. He'd earned that one, and plenty. And he sat in the row of athletes holding the sweater box in his lap, wondering if just maybe they'd give him a baseball letter too. He'd earned that too, the potlickers. East wouldn't have taken the championship if he hadn't won three games for them. But probably Muddy would hold a grudge and not even read his name off.

The football candidates were finished, the basketball team had gone up one after another, the midget basketball team had climbed the stage to the accompaniment of polite clapping and snickers from the audience. Bruce was one of the little guys. He looked puny and skinny, even though he had suddenly started to grow in the last year and had shot up a couple of inches. Chet felt a little ashamed that his brother was such a runt. Probably he could have done all right in high school if he'd been bigger. He wasn't bad at anything for his size.

The Superintendent of Public Instruction was introduced, and stood up to present the silver loving cup representing the baseball championship to Muddy Poole. Muddy made a little speech, it was all due to the fellows, they had got in there and worked like mad and played the game clean and hard, and sat down. The names of the baseball team started, and the line where Chet sat began to shift as boys worked their way out to the aisles. Chet crossed his hands on his football sweater box and sat still. He almost caught himself breaking into a whistle. Van, down the row, turned and winked.

Then Muddy read off Van's name. Van shot a look at Chet, stood up, marched down the aisle, and was given a sweater. Muddy read off others: Longabaugh, Mackay, Mason. Chet stood up and marched. Muddy, his face perfectly straight, held out the box and said without moving his lips, "I ought to charge you ten bucks for this, you stinker." Chet grinned, conscious of the audience at his back, the row of teachers and dignitaries along the stage. "Horse collar," he said, in the same stiff-lipped deadpan whisper. Muddy shoved the box hard in his belly, as a quarterback tucks the ball into the arms of a halfback coming around on a reverse, and Chet put his head down and made a play of running it off-stage for a touchdown. There were some smiles, some looks of formal surprise on the faces along the stage, some laughter from the audience. Chet skinned back into his seat over the crowded legs. Muddy was all right, a good guy.

That was the cream of the assembly, as far as Chet was concerned, but there were a lot of other awards, pins for publications and opera and glee club and student offices. Chet was up twice more, for opera and glee club, and then once again with the glee club when it sang. Then the speakers, the valedictorian and the salutatorian and the Superintendent of Schools and the Commencement speaker, and the long queues forming for the passing out of the diplomas, and that was the end of that.

That was the end of school, of stinking chem labs, of physics classes where you experimented with the laws of the pendulum, swinging plumb-bobs on strings down the stairwell from the third floor to the basement, so that girls going into the door of the girls' gym could be bopped with them. Now was the end of practices after school, of showers in the steamy old shower room and towel fights between the lockers, of snake dances through the streets to celebrate victories, of operas in the old Salt Lake Theater where you sang tenor leads in *Mademoiselle Modiste* or *The Red Mill*. This was the end of lunches on the lawns while the gulls flew over crying, of butts snitched behind the corner of Mad Maisie's, of hot dogs and mustard and rootbeer over her messy counter, of toting a gun in ROTC drills and marching on hot spring days up through the lucerne toward the mountains, a whole battalion breaking ranks sometimes and tearing through the alfalfa when a racer snake slid from under the file-closer's feet, all of them chasing the swift snake while the student officers yelled their heads off and howled commands that nobody minded and tossed around demerits that nobody listened to, and the commandant started back from Company A to see what was the matter.

Now was the end of a lot of things. He held the rewards of the year in his hands and lap, sat among his fellows as he could now no longer, in quite the same way, sit among them. He was through school, grown up. It had been all right, but he didn't want any more of it. Bruce said he was going on to college. Let him be the grind of the family. There was more fun in the world than that. There was his ball-playing job this summer, the possibility in the future of a tryout with the Bees, and the big leagues ahead.

And in back of the hall somewhere, back where the first sharp spats of clapping started whenever his name was called to go up for an award, was Laura, and Laura was somehow the symbol of the end of all this. He turned his head and looked at the boys along the row, whispering together, snickering, telling jokes. Kids. Nothing but kids.

His mother and father and Bruce were standing together near the arc light under the row of little planted maples when he came out with Laura. For a moment he would have slipped away if he could have. But the crowd was shoving behind him. He took Laura's arm. "Come on," he said, "you want to meet my folks?"

"Oh gee!" Laura said. She made quick dabs at her hair and peeked into her compact mirror. "Do I look all right?"

"You look swell."

"I'm scared," she said. "What if they don't like me?"

"If they don't, that's their tough luck."

He was a little nervous himself, for fear his old man would make some break, be grouchy about something. But it was all right. His father was dressed up fit to kill, black and white shoes, Panama hat, diamond in his tie, and his mother wore her best dress, the one that had cost eighty dollars and had been bought over her protests when the old man had a fit of generosity. Chet was glad she had it, anyhow. It looked nice. And you could always depend on Ma to be kind. She smiled at him and took Laura's hand, and it was all right. His father kidded them. Didn't Laura feel a little funny, going around with a Big Shot? She'd be lucky to kiss the hem of his garments now. He took off his Panama and clapped it on Chet's head. "How's the head size?" he said.

"All right."

"Good," his old man said. He kept looking out over the crowd, standing big and broad as a bridge pier while the crowd swirled around him. He seemed abstracted, almost embarrassed. His eyes met Chet's, wandered away, came back again. "Well, you've got more education now than either your mother or I had," he said to Chet and Bruce. "Let's see what you can do with it."

They looked at him and moved their lips, murmuring something.

"It's a big night for both of you," Elsa said. "I'm proud of you both." She turned to Laura. "They're pretty good boys, both of them, even if they are so homely," she said, and her smile asked Laura into the family, made her part of the circle.

"Homely!" Laura said. "I think they're two of the best looking boys in school."

"Now my head size is going up," Chet said.

Bruce kept looking at Laura. "I hate to be classed with him," he said. "He looks like something you'd find in a rat trap. Like old second-hand cheese."

"I could think of something you look like," Chet said, "but I'm too polite to mention it here."

"You look a good deal alike to me," Elsa said. "How does that suit you?"

"Rotten," Bruce said.

"Lousy," said Chet. He reached over and took a poke at Bruce. "So you graduated from high school!" he said. "When you gonna get your first long pants?"

"Horse collar," Bruce said.

They were all grinning, and it was a good feeling to be standing there all dressed up, something accomplished, everybody friendly and horsing around. "Mama," Bo Mason said, "maybe we ought to take these young fry out to celebrate. Where shall we go?"

"Where do they want to go?" Elsa said.

"Where do you want to go?" Chet said to Laura.

"Gee," she said, "I ought to go home, really."

"Oh bushwah. How about a show?"

"It's pretty late, isn't it?"

"Not late at all," Bo Mason said. "I often stay out after ten."

"Well, all right," she said, laughing.

"Haven't you got a girl, Bruce?" Elsa said. "Wouldn't you like to take somebody?"

"No, I guess not."

"Bruce's scared of girls," Chet said. He tucked Laura's arm boldly under his. "There's a half dozen chase him around all the time, but he dowanna."

"Go lay a nice rough firebrick," Bruce said.

They went to the movies, and after the movies they stopped for ice cream, and on the way back to the car they passed a shooting gallery and Bruce and Chet and their father shot for kewpie dolls. Bruce won, and his father looked at him in something like amazement. "He's been practicing up all spring on the rifle team," Chet said.

"Yeah," his brother said. "And even when I'm out of practice I'll take you on any old time."

"This seems funny," Elsa said. "Remember back in Dakota when you won me a lot of kewpies and pennants and things at the carnival in Devil's Lake?"

"I was shooting a little better that day," Bo said.

"I guess. That was the day you won the state traps championship."

"Really?" Laura said.

"He just looks that way," Chet said, and poked his father's shoulder, solid as a wall. "He used to be a shooter and a ball player and all sorts of things. Never think it to look at him now."

His father let loose a stinging cuff that just grazed Chet's ear, and they sparred on the sidewalk, horsing around like kids, until Chet got self-conscious and quit. His father's iron arm stuck out to jolt him one. "Get on any time," his father said, holding the arm out straight. "Do some trick bar stuff. Chin yourself. Let me know when you do, though, so I don't forget you're there and drop you."

"Gee," Laura said later, when he took her in. "I think your family's swell. Your dad is a good egg."

"He's all right," Chet said.

"And your mother's so sweet. I just love her."

"So do I," Chet said. "See you tomorrow?"

"After class?"

"Okay, I'll meet you there."

He went back to the car and got in, and on the way home they all sang. It was funny, Chet thought as he got into bed. It was darned funny how the old man changed. One minute he was the damnedest old crab on earth, ordering you around and bawling you out, and the next he was a hell of a good guy. You could depend on Ma to be right in there, any time, even if she felt lousy, but you could never tell about the old man.

He guessed that the old man was pretty proud of his kids to-night, maybe that explained it. He stewed around and raised hell, but he wanted you to be something all the time, and because he had never got past the eighth grade himself he thought education was the clear stuff. That was a laugh. He ought to go into a study hall sometimes. Still, it was sort of nice to know that the old man was proud of you. It made you feel as if everything was all right. As he dropped off to sleep he had a curious feeling that his old man's pride was somehow the best thing in the whole day.

Now summer, the best part of the year. Rising at six thirty you could hear the birds making a great clatter in the back yard, and see robins running, their heads cocking sideways to listen, their beaks digging down hard and their legs bracing, and the night-crawlers coming out of the grass stretching and hanging on. You could smell the morning smell of sprinkled lawns, and hear from across the street the whir of a lawnmower, and as you ate breakfast alone in the kitchen the *Tribune* thudded on the front porch and you went to get it, propping it against the milk bottle as you ate.

You went out tiptoeing, so as not to wake the family, and your chest couldn't hold all the air it wanted, and at the corner, in the first light of the sun just breasting the Wasatch, you leaned against a tree and had your first cigarette of the day. In the early morning the sounds that at mid-day were an indistinct and blurred overtone were distinct and clear. The rumble of a truck coming down the unpaved hill past the old brewery, the even clop of a milk-horse, the whistling of the little sheeny opening his doors and running down his awning half way up the block, the thud of a flat wheel on the streetcar as it came around the upper curve and started down toward your corner. As you swung aboard your nose gave up the whiff of honey locust it had been smelling and smelled instead the familiar dust-and-ozone-and-oil smell of the streetcar, and you went to find a seat between the men with lunchpails like your own on their laps.

At Third South and State you got off to join the other guys waiting for the smelter truck. If merchandise was being unloaded into the sidewalk doors of Auerbach's store, you ran hurdle races over bales and cartons. If you got there early, and there was nothing else to do, you could horse the deaf-and-dumb newspaper vendor who came up to wave his papers in your face and make his ungodly noises. "Umwaooo! Umiayah!" When you just stood looking across the street and pretended you didn't hear, he would get furious, thrust a paper right under your nose, almost jump up and down. Then you could act surprised, eye him coldly, say "What?" put one hand up around your ear. You could always get a laugh from people going by, and it sure made the old guy mad.

Work at the mill was a joke. Half the time you couldn't have found anything to do if you'd wanted to. You just sat and threw the old bull around, or chucked rocks at tin cans, or went up to the roofless backhouse and read a magazine until somebody hammered on the door and threatened to tip you over if you didn't get the hell out.

About three you went out and peppered the ball around, held battery practice, batting practice, infield practice, fungoed out flies. Generally you got up a game of rounders for the last half hour before the five-thirty truck pulled out. On the way in to town you could generally talk the driver into stopping at Otto's, on Thirty-Ninth South, for a pitcher of home brew, the whole gang of you storming into Otto's parlor to guzzle his cold black beer, pouring some into a saucer for the cat and watching him get tight, hanging around till the truck driver got scared he'd be called for staying on the road too long.

You got home about six thirty in time for a shower before supper, while Bruce crabbed at you for not getting home in time to do your share of lawn mowing, and your old man sat on the porch reading the *Telegram* and going out once in a while to move the sprinkler around the lawn. If you didn't have a date with Laura, you telephoned her until someone wanted the phone. It made the old man sore sometimes to have you hang onto the phone for an hour, but what the hell.

It was a swell life, and he was pitching good ball, never got into trouble once except when Tooele rooters started shooting a mirror into his eyes from the stands. That made him so mad he blew up entirely, walked two men, allowed three hits, and wild-pitched another run home before the manager jerked him. All the Dagoes and Greasers and Wops and Bohunks in the Tooele stands razzed the hell out of him, giving him the old hip-hip as he walked off. But that was the only time anything had gone wrong. He had won two games, saved another for Pearson, and lost only that one, and his team was tied for the lead at six won and two lost. It was a swell life.

The best part of it was the secret part, the nights with Laura at Lagoon, at Saltair, at movies—times when they borrowed Van's bug, or went out with Van and some girl and drank beer, coming home loud and late, parking under the poplars of some dark street and growing quiet, necking. It was hard to find anywhere to go to make love really. The cockpit of a bug was no place, especially if you were really in love and your girl didn't like the idea of being jammed up in a seat and maybe some snooper or cop come by and flash a light on you. Laura was always cautious when Van was around anyway. She thought he talked too much.

Then they moved. It made little difference to Chet except that now he had to walk two blocks to the carline. But it made a difference when his mother broke down and had to go up in the mountains to Brighton for a rest. That meant he was camping in the house with Bruce and his father, and when Bruce went up to Brighton too to live in a tent below the inn, then Chet and his father were the only ones left. They got their own meals or ate out: because of his father's business they had never had a maid or a cook. After a while, when Chet had got home too late, and the supper his father had fixed was all cold and the old man mad about it, they quit making believe they were keeping house. Chet left before his father was up, came home often to find the house empty, went out again to see Laura and came home late, and often for two days at a time they didn't even see each other. The old man couldn't stay around the house much. It gave him the jim-jams, so that often he stayed out till midnight just to avoid being in the place alone.

"The damn place is like a morgue," he said. "I wish to hell your mother would get well."

"So do I," Chet said. "You going up Sunday to see her?"

"Yes."

"Maybe I'll come along," Chet said. He really ought to. She'd been up there two weeks and he hadn't even written her a letter. He'd been going to, but then Bruce went up, and there didn't seem any point in a letter as long as he was there. "Maybe Laura could come along," he said. "Is that all right?"

"Can't you go anywhere without her in your hip pocket?"

"I don't see that it'd be so awful to take her along."

"All right, take her along. Only don't forget you're going up there to see your mother, not squire your Laura around."

"Don't worry," Chet said. "I guess I appreciate Ma as much as you do."

5

The sun was slow coming over the mountains. The bedroom in the log lodge was cold, and she dressed shivering. But there was always a fire in the huge rock fireplace on the mezzanine where she had breakfast, and when she went out on the second-floor balcony and around the corner into the early sun she stepped from cool to warm instantly, as if the bar of shadow the corner threw was an insulating wall. There was a dewy smell of balsam fir, and the air was so high and pure that it made her lightheaded.

Sitting on the balcony in the mornings, waiting for Bruce to come up from his camp, she could see out over the whole little settlement, the old collapsing frame hotel, the glint of Silver Lake beyond it, the Twin Lakes foot trail a brown line against the green mountainside. It was fun to sit and look up a half mile, past timberline, to the snow that still lay in northern crevices, and to let her eyes swing around the whole circular rim of the divide, over the fir and

aspen that floored the cirque, over the peaks sharp and clean between her and the farther sky. A smoke always went up from the
girls' camp on Lake Katherine, a straight feather among the trees,
and sometimes there was a distant rumble of blasting from Park
City, nine miles over the divide. Chipmunks ran along the top rail
of the balcony looking for peanuts or crumbs: the first time she got
one to come into her lap for a nut she laughed aloud for the pure joy
of having made friends with something.

She felt guilty for having so much fun. Poor Bo and Chet were
batching down in town in the heat, the house probably a mess, nobody to get their meals. She ought to go back down and take care
of them. But she didn't really want to. The way she lived up here—
everything done for her, the balsam smell good in her nostrils even
while she slept, reading a little and walking a little and napping a
little in the afternoons—was a condition so unusual and pleasant that
the thought of breaking it off was like Sunday-morning awakening
to a lazy sleeper. Let it go on a little while longer.

Bruce came whistling along the road and stopped under the balcony to look up at her, his face a thin brown wedge. He had a camera
on a strap over his shoulder, and a loose, almost-empty knapsack in
his hand. "Howdo, Modom," he said. "Feeling pretty spry?"

"Spry as a cricket," she said. "I think every morning is more
wonderful than the last one."

"How'd you sleep?"

"Like a log."

"Eat a good breakfast?"

"Enormous," she said, and patted her stomach.

"Lessee your tongue."

She stuck her tongue out, leaning over the balcony rail, and he
squinted up at it. "I guess you're all right," he said. "Want to go
for a walk?"

"I was just hoping you would. It's such a lovely morning."

"I know a good trail up around the edge of Mount Majestic.
Once you get up the slope you walk along under the aspens for a
mile or so. It's pretty nice, only it's a little far."

"Let's go," she said. "I feel as if I could walk all day."

Up the long trail through the firs they walked slowly. In openings
along the trail the columbines were pure and tall and white, sometimes a space of half an acre solidly white with them. Farther up, as
they climbed a brown rooty path around the flank of the mountain,

the columbines were not so large, not so tall, but their petals were touched with the palest blue and pink, like the blush of blood through a transparent skin.

"It's the altitude," Bruce said. "When you get up high they get that tinge."

"I know I shouldn't pick any," Elsa said. "But do you suppose one each would matter?"

"I guess not," he said seriously. "They only reproduce from seed, and a lot of old dames come up here and pick an armful and then there aren't any more."

"I don't want to be an old dame, then, I guess," she said.

"Here." He picked her one of each color, and she folded them into her book, amused at his solemn air of being the personal caretaker of the whole mountain, and very fond of him.

They came over a steep hump that had her warm and breathless, her legs tired, and before them lay a level trail cut through the aspen. Through the thin trees on the lower edge of the trail she could look over a long oceanic roll of ridges and peaks, a forested valley stretching southward, the blue glimmer of water. Clouds like cottonwool coasted over the peaks on the Alta side, snagged on spines of rock, blew eastward in frayed strings.

"Those are the Ontario Lakes," Bruce said, pointing. "The valley is Bonanza Flat."

Elsa sat down on a stone, filling her eyes with green and blue distance. The sun through the thin aspen leaves was warm, the earth was fragrant with bark and mould and bitter leaf smell.

"Oh dear!" she said. "I don't ever want to go back."

"How'd a cabin be right here?" Bruce said. "With that view in your eye? You could ski on over to Park City when you needed supplies in winter, and stay the year around."

"You build it sometime and I'll come be your housekeeper."

"I'd like to," Bruce said. "Don't ever think I wouldn't." His eyes, she thought, were strangely dark and brooding. You could never tell what he was thinking. He steered you off when you got close.

"What made you say that?"

"What?"

"What you just said."

"I don't know," he said. "I'd like it. Wouldn't you?"

"It might be a pretty hard life."

"That kind of a hard life is easier than a lot of other kinds," he said. He stared down over the twinkling trees, flowing like bright water down the slope into Bonanza Flat. "Last time I came across here it was raining cats and dogs," he said, and Elsa understood that he had changed the subject. That was all he was going to say about the other, whatever it was.

"When was that?" she said.

"Last year. That was the day after we spent the night in the Park City jail."

"What?"

"Sure. We went over to a ballgame, walked over along the old tramway, and in the afternoon it rained so we couldn't walk back. We didn't have any money, so we asked a cop what to do and he let us sleep in the jail."

"For goodness sake," she said. "You never told me about that."

"Sure I did."

"You never did." She shivered her shoulders. "That's the last place I'd ever want to sleep," she said. "I'd rather walk in the rain."

"It was all right. The cockroaches were a little bad."

Arms hooked around his hunched-up knees, he looked down across the valley, and Elsa watched him with pity, knowing that what had been in his mind a minute before was sullenness about his father's business, bitterness that the days weren't always like this. She couldn't have told how she knew what was in his mind. Perhaps that reference to jail. There had been a shadow on her own thoughts, instantly, at that word.

"Well," she said, "shall we walk some more?"

"I don't care. How do you feel?"

"Maybe we'd better start back," she said. "Pa may come up to have Sunday dinner with us, and it's getting on toward eleven now."

It was a curious feeling for Elsa to come down the trail and see Bo and Chet pitching horseshoes beside the inn, with Laura watching. She saw them objectively, as she would see strangers. Bo big and dark, getting a little heavier, his Panama on the back of his head and the diamond glittering in his tie when he turned sideways in the sun; Chet not as tall, but broad, very deep in the chest, his arms heavy and muscular under his rolled-up sleeves. Almost in surprise she thought, "Why, he's really a very handsome boy!" Everything about him looked clean and strong. And there was Laura along.

That was getting to be quite a romance—almost too much time spent on one girl.

Laura turned and saw her, waved. The horseshoe pitchers stopped.

"Hi, Ma," Chet said. "How you feeling?"

She kissed him, then Bo, put out her hand to Laura. "Oof, we've walked a long way," she said, and sat down on the step to fan herself.

"You're up here for a rest," Bo said, frowning. "You don't want to overdo it."

"I'm having a lovely rest," she said. "How do you two get along at home?"

"I never see this guy from one week's end to the next," Bo said.

"Oh horse," Chet said. "I'm home more than you are."

"Neither one of us wears the place out living in it," Bo said. "When you going to get well and come home, Mama?"

"I don't know. The doctor said two months, but I feel fine now, rested as can be."

"You look better, I think," Laura said. "I noticed it right away. Lots better."

"Really?" Elsa said. "I'm glad I don't look worse. That would be pretty hard on my family."

"When do they eat around this place?" Chet said.

"It ought to be pretty quick now. Did you make a reservation?"

"I'd better go do that," Bo said, but Elsa rose. "I'll do it. I have to go tidy up anyway. You want to come with me, Laura?"

"Sure," Laura said.

A very quiet girl, Elsa thought. Yet there was something there she vaguely disliked. As if her quiet were put on, as if it wasn't quite her own face she wore. Or maybe the hungry way she looked at Chet, or the very slight dissatisfied wrinkle between her eyes.

While she took off her walking dress Elsa could see her in the mirror. "How's Chet been pitching?" she said. "I don't see the paper very often up here."

"He's done swell," Laura said. "He's only lost one game."

"Fine," Elsa said with her mouth full of hairpins. She shook her hair down and brushed it hard.

Laura sat with her hands in her lap, nervously swinging her foot. "You've got beautiful hair," she said.

"It's the one thing I ever had that doesn't seem to fade or wear out," Elsa said. She looked at Laura in the mirror, saw her hungry eyes, the look almost of weeping around the mouth. "Don't you feel well?" she said, turning.

Laura wet her lips. "Oh yes, I feel all right."

"I thought for a minute you might be ill," Elsa said. To her dismay the girl jumped up from the bed and threw her arms around her, her face twisted.

"Oh Mrs. Mason!" she said.

"Why, what is it?"

"I wish I had a mother like you!" Laura said. She buried her face in Elsa's shoulder and clung when Elsa tried gently to break her loose.

"Let's be sensible," she said. "You have your own mother."

"But she isn't like you!" Laura wailed. "She's always after me for something, and suspicious of me, and she isn't pretty at all. She's *fat!*"

"Well," Elsa said. "I'm sure she's . . ."

"You don't know," Laura said. She turned and sat on the bed again, dabbing at her averted eyes. She said without looking up, "You just don't know how it is to have a family that's vulgar and bullying. I see how pleasant everything is in your family, and how kind you are, and how they all love you and you love them, and how nice Mr. Mason is, and I can't help it. I wish I had a family like yours."

"Why you poor child," Elsa said. The thought of anyone's envying their family life was so wild that she wanted to laugh. "We have to be satisfied with what we have," she said. "Maybe your mother is tired, or overworked." She watched Laura's bent head. "Maybe you're poor," she said. "I know all about that. It's hard to keep pleasant when things go wrong all the time."

"We aren't poor," Laura said sullenly. "We have enough. But we're just not kind like you, we don't get along. I don't know why it is."

"Love is a thing that works both ways," Elsa said quietly. "We have to give other people a chance to love us before we find them lovable, sometimes."

Laura stood up and tried to laugh. "I'm silly. I don't know what got the matter with me all of a sudden."

Elsa went back to putting up her hair, watching the girl in the mirror. She was a rather helpless, pretty thing, and obviously unhappy. But her unhappiness was obscurely annoying too. There was the edge of spite in it, the eagerness to blame someone else for her misery, that would have made one want to shake her if she had been one's own. She turned and faced the girl squarely. "Is it because you're in love with Chet?" she said. "Don't your family like him?"

"Oh, they like him all right."

"But you *are* in love with him," Elsa said.

Laura nodded, keeping her head down.

"How does Chet feel about it?"

Laura nodded again, unwilling to meet Elsa's eyes.

Elsa sighed. "There's no reason you shouldn't go together, as long as you aren't foolish about it. When you're both old enough to get married you probably won't even like each other any more, but if you do nobody will try to stop you from marrying in a few years."

Laura lifted tragic eyes, but said nothing, and Elsa frowned. "You children aren't serious, now?"

Her eyes full of utterly disproportionate terror, Laura pushed herself back on the bed. "I . . . that is . . . I don't know . . ."

Elsa took her hand and pulled her to her feet. "Good heavens, don't be afraid of me! I didn't mean to scare you. I just wanted to be sure you and Chet weren't going to be foolish about waiting. Waiting isn't too hard, when you can see each other all the time. Nobody's trying to keep you apart, child."

"Oh Mrs. Mason!" Laura said, and began to cry. "I'm so unhappy!"

Elsa stood waiting, but the girl said no more, so Elsa said it herself, the words heavy and sodden and hard to lift. "You and Chet haven't got in trouble, have you?"

"No," Laura said. "Oh no, nothing like that."

"Well then, everything will turn out all right. You've got your whole lives ahead of you. You shouldn't be unhappy, at your age."

But she was thinking as they went downstairs that Laura had been playing some kind of double game, had been trying to say something she was afraid to say, and at the same time had been angling for sympathy, trying to ingratiate herself by appearing miserable and picked on, as if to justify that other thing that she hadn't dared to say.

Poor child, she thought automatically. Kids in love gave themselves endless troubles for nothing. But she didn't like the idea of

Chet's being involved with this girl as deeply as he apparently was. He was too young, he didn't know enough. She had hardly phrased her automatic pity for Laura before the phrase had twisted itself in her mind into something else: Poor Chet.

She watched Chet at dinner, kept glancing up to intercept looks between him and Laura. They did not act like kids out for a good time. They were sober, their eyes and their occasionally-touching hands eloquent of secrets. The thing was obviously serious, but how serious it was hard to tell. But two children like that! she thought. Chet was only seventeen. Still, he was in deep. He wasn't full of horseplay the way he ordinarily was, he hardly laughed at all except with his sly, sidelong look at Laura. There was something brooding and almost deadly in the way the two looked at each other.

Oh Lord! she said, why are they so intent on ruining their own lives?

After dinner Bo was playing the slot machines while Laura and Bruce watched, and she crooked her finger at Chet. As they walked away she felt Laura's eyes on her back. Everything that happened, the slightest incident, was significant to those two, pertinent to some guarded secret of their own.

"Let's sit down," she said. The mezzanine was empty. The other guests were all out on the porch, their voices a dim buzzing through the doors. Finding it hard to begin, not knowing exactly what she had brought him up here to say to him, Elsa took his hand.

"You've got paws just like your father's," she said. "It doesn't seem any time at all since they were making mud pies."

Chet said nothing. He waited.

"Chet," she said. "What about Laura?"

She could feel the stiffness of his body through his hand. His eyes were veiled as if she were an enemy. "What about her?"

"She talked to me a little before dinner, up in my room."

Instantly there was life in the veiled eyes. "What did she say?"

"What could she have said?"

The eyes went dull again. "I don't know," he said, and shrugged slightly.

"She said she was in love with you," Elsa said.

Chet tried to laugh. "Good," he said. "She never told me that."

"Oh Chet!" his mother said, and stood up impatiently. "You

needn't try to duck and hide from me. I just want to talk to you openly and see if I can't give you some good advice."

"People are always awful free with advice," Chet said.

"Have I been?"

"You're always worrying about what time I come in, and stuff like that. You can't get over thinking of me as a kid."

"I was thinking more about your health than anything else."

"Oh, my health! I'm healthy as a horse. No guy wants to be mothered and babied around. I've got to grow up sometime."

"Not too soon," she said softly. "Not so soon you spoil your whole life by it. I'm not trying to hold you back, Chet. You're old for your age, in some ways. But you're still only seventeen, and you can ruin your life by getting too serious with a girl too soon. I'm just asking you to remember that you aren't really a man till you're twenty-one. Lots of boys aren't till later than that."

His ears were pink, his brows pulled down in a black frown. At least she had got the mask off him, she thought wearily. But it didn't do any good.

"I can look after myself," he said. "I know enough to come in out of the rain." He said it angrily, but he did not quite meet her eyes, and she read him as if he were an eight-year-old trying to bluster his way out of trouble. Underneath that anger he was uncertain and scared. He knew he was in deep.

"We're getting altogether too serious," she said lightly. "I didn't bring you up here to croak at you. I just wanted to remind you to keep yourself free and clean. If you want to be a ball player you'll have to be free for a few years, Chet."

"Yeah," he said. "I don't know what got you thinking I wasn't going to be."

"Laura."

"Oh," he said. He looked past her, the dull and sullen look on his mouth. "Shall we go on down again?" he said.

For a moment Elsa looked at him feeling that she wanted to cry. He was just like Bo, as stubborn and immovable as a wall, as unwilling to admit a mistake. What he did was right. It had to be. Out of her anger and irritation came a curious desire to reach out and hug him, but that would have been as embarrassing and bothersome to him as her attempt to give advice. She turned and went downstairs. She did not want to be an interfering mother, but she was determined that if there was anything she could do to prevent his making a fool of himself she would do it, short of actual compulsion.

"What about speaking to Bill Talbot about Chet?" she asked Bo out on the porch later. "Couldn't you get him a chance to try out with the Bees? He's been doing so well out in the Copper League."

"He isn't ready for any Double-A league," Bo said. "When he's ready, they'll be after him themselves. Besides, you don't try out in the middle of the summer. They look over the young guys in the spring, in training camp."

"But . . ."

"What do you want him pushed so fast for?" Bo said, irritated. "Let him grow up a little. He'd just blow his chance."

"Bo," she said, "I wish you'd talk to Bill, just the same."

His brows drew down, and he turned to stare. "What's on your mind?"

With her eyes she indicated Chet and Laura leaning over the balcony rail. Chet was pointing at something, and Laura was bent close to him, trying to see. "I think it would do Chet a lot of good to get away from Salt Lake for a while," Elsa said. "Bill's a good friend of yours. He'd do it for you as a favor. Even if we had to pay Chet's expenses . . ."

Bo jerked his head at the oblivious two. "You think . . . ?"

"I don't know. I'm afraid they're both pretty far gone."

"At seventeen!" he said, and snorted through his nose.

"It doesn't do any good to talk to him," Elsa said. "I've tried. If you tried you'd just make him bull-headed. But if you could get Bill to let him go along with the team, maybe pitch for batting practice or something . . ."

"Yeah," Bo said. "Well, I'll see. But I wouldn't expect too much. Bill's the best judge of when he wants to look anybody over."

They looked at each other, and both laughed. It was funny, in a way, how they schemed on one end of a balcony while Chet and Laura plotted heaven only knew what on the other. "I guess they never get too old to need taking care of," Elsa said. "How's business going?"

"Yesterday," Bo said, "I bought another thousand bucks worth of U. S. Steel."

"How much does that make?"

He winked. "Mama," he said, "we may not be as rich as we'd be if we played the market right, but we've got eighteen thousand dollars' worth of stock in that safety deposit box, and we own every nickel's worth of it."

"Eighteen thousand," Elsa said. It seemed an enormous sum.

"I figured up our assets the other day," Bo said. "We're worth pretty close to thirty thousand, counting everything. Give me time to multiply that by ten and we'll retire."

Elsa smiled. "Remember when you first started you said you'd make a few trips and get a stake and get into some business. Then you got knocked over and had to make it up. Then Heimie spoiled things for you in Great Falls and we had to make *that* up. But you always said when you got ten thousand dollars ahead you'd get out of this business, Bo."

"You know what the interest on ten thousand would amount to?" Bo said. "Even if you had it in seven percent preferred stock you'd only get seven hundred a year off it. How long could you live on seven hundred?"

"But you've got more than ten thousand. You've got two or three times that much."

"You never figure right when you're down," Bo said. "Ten thousand looks like a million from where we used to be. But you can't get into any kind of business with only that kind of capital. You got to put up dough."

"But you'll have to get out sometime," she said. "It isn't fair to the kids. Bruce'll be going to college this fall. What if you got into trouble and all his friends knew what you did? What if all Chet's friends knew it?"

"What do you want?" he said, eyeing her somberly. "Want me to sit on my tail and let what we've got dribble away?"

"You know what I want. I want you to find some business that we don't have to be ashamed of. The kids feel it, Bo. They don't like to bring their friends around the house. They have to lie about what you do. It isn't fair to them."

"Well, I'm keeping my eyes open," he said. "You can't just rush into a thing blind."

He moved impatiently and stood up at the rail to watch two boys ride hell-for-leather around the trail and out of sight into the woods. "Ho hum," he said. "Here I thought you'd be excited at the idea of another thousand socked away."

"Did it ever occur to you," she said, her eyes on his, "that there are things that would make me feel better than any amount of money?"

6

The game had started when Bo got there. He slipped the usher a half dollar and moved down to a box on the first base line. At the end of the fourth Bill Talbot came out of the dugout to take a turn coaching at first, and Bo waved to him. After the third out Bill came over.

"How's tricks?" he said.

"Can't complain. Looks like you got a ball club this year."

"They look pretty good, don't they?" Bill said. "You never saw a bunch of guys hit like these kids. If we had the pitching we'd be in first place by ten games."

"You're only three games off the pace. You can make that up."

"I got my fingers crossed," Bill said. "Anything stirring in your league?"

"Nothing except a favor I want to ask. Maybe you can't do it, I don't know."

"What is it?"

"You know that kid of mine."

"The pitcher? I been seeing his name in the Copper League. Doing all right."

"Doing pretty good," Bo said. "I went out and caught him in the back yard one day. He's got a fast one that whistles, and a pretty good hook."

Bill bowed himself to spit carefully in the dust and then erase the spit with his spikes. "What's the favor?"

"I was wondering if you could take the kid along on a road trip."

Bill shook his head. "Got my quota. We can't have any extras on the payroll after the middle of May."

"Trouble is," Bo said, and bit the end off a cigar, "trouble is, the damn kid's got a crush on a girl and I'd like to shake him loose till he cools off, and there's nothing he'd leave her for but maybe baseball."

Bill opened his mouth to laugh, raised his cap to cool his bald head, slipped it back on again. "You don't want me to put him on the team then."

"He isn't ready for that, hell no."

"Tell you what," Talbot said. "Would he come as batboy, do you think?"

"I don't know. I should think so."

"He wouldn't get any money, only expenses. But you could tell him I'll be looking him over. He could work out with the boys, nobody'd fuss about that."

"I should think that would do it," Bo said. He lighted the cigar and chuckled out a cloud of blue smoke. "It would do him good to be a batboy. He thinks he's ready to pitch to Ruth right now."

"Tell him to come down and see me," Bill said. "I'd like to get a longer look at him, for a fact. We need pitchers so bad that even a green one with stuff looks pretty interesting. He might set himself up for a tryout next spring."

"Good," Bo said. "You leave next Monday?"

"Gone for two weeks, then back for two, then gone for three. He could go this trip or wait till the August one. What about his smelter job?"

"If I know him," Bo said, "he'll throw that overboard in a minute. And the sooner he's got out of here the better."

He watched Bill go back to the coach's box at first, and after another inning he rose and went home. He felt so good about the way he had used his influence to give Chet a chance and at the same time to get him away from Laura that he got out a bottle of Scotch and wrapped it up and put it aside for Chet to take down to Bill when he went.

His slight fear that Chet would stick up his nose at a batboy's job lasted only the first minute of their conversation. Chet saw the possibilities all right.

"Jeez, let me at him!" he said. "Did he say I could work out with them?"

"Yeah. He wants a look at your stuff. But he has to put you on as batboy because his quota's full. You keep your eyes open and your mouth shut and try training a little and you might get a break out of this, boy. Bill's short of pitchers."

Chet looked up at the ceiling and cracked his knuckles together. "Maybe somebody'll get hurt and they'll have to put me in a game," he said.

"You won't get in any games," Bo said shortly. "You're not on the team, for one thing. For another, you wouldn't last a third of an inning. But you might learn something."

"If I don't I'll kiss a pig," Chet said. "Can I take the car now?"

Bo laughed. "Don't let any grass grow under you. Yeah, if you get it back here by seven."

"Okay."

"What'll you do about the smelter?"

"That can fry," Chet said. "I can't pass this up just to pitch in that league."

"Then what'll you do all winter? Sit around on your tail?"

"That shows how much you know about it," Chet said. "I already lined up a job at the International Harvester. I'm going to play basketball for 'em this winter."

"Okay, okay," Bo said. The kid had enough ambition. Wean him away from his Laura and he'd do all right. "You better get along," he said. "Give this bottle to Bill."

Chet took it, stood in the doorway jingling loose change in his pocket, looked up once, then out the door. "Well, thanks, Pa," he said uncomfortably, and went out.

He was back promptly in an hour. "All fixed," he said, and took a basketball shot at the top of a lamp with a sofa cushion. The lamp teetered and started to fall, and he leaped to grab it. "Caught him and half the team at dinner," he said. "Bill said I could stick around till the end of the season if I wanted."

"I never saw anybody quite so overjoyed at getting a job as batboy," Bo said.

"Stick around, boy," Chet said. "I'll be on that team when it starts training next spring."

A few minutes later Bo heard him talking on the telephone in the hall. He held his paper still, listening. "Yeah," Chet was saying. "Bill wants to look me over this summer. No fooling. Yeah, Monday night. No, just to look me over, sort of a preliminary tryout. That's what I was thinking, you bet your life. I'll do what I can. Old John can't go on catching forever. His legs are all shot. I don't know why not. I'll sure talk you up, anyway. Tell 'em I can't pitch to anybody but you . . ."

Bo waggled the paper and grinned to himself. Big Shot, he said softly. The batboy getting jobs for his friends. He looked at his watch and got up. That half case was due down on South Temple at seven thirty.

After his father had gone out Chet wandered restlessly around the house. Jeezie Kly, it was all right. Two months with the Bees, sitting in the dugout with them, eating with them in diners and hotels, meeting players from all the other clubs, guys like Lefty O'Doul and Chief Bender and Walter Mails. There was the guy with the fast one. Old Bill Talbot was no bush leaguer, for that matter. He'd been one of the best outfielders in the business in his day, and he was still good enough at forty to hit over three hundred and play a good left field more than half the games. He'd been up in the big time a long while, and he knew them all. Ruth and Hornsby and Walter Johnson and Grover Alexander and Casey Stengel and Sisler and Collins and all of them. You ought to be able to learn plenty just sitting and listening to Bill.

It was darn nice of Bill to take him along—though probably he thought he'd get his money back in a year or so when Chet made the team and strengthened the pitching staff. It was nice of the old man to speak to Bill, for that matter. Every once in a while he cropped up with something like this that made you think he was all right for sure. Like the night he took them all out on the night of graduation. Laura was still talking about what a good egg he was.

Well, he said, you made up for plenty this time. This'll make you a good egg for a long time.

He had a date with Laura at nine, but he'd stick around now till the old man came home, just on the chance that he could get the car. Laura was going to feel bad about his going, but after all he'd only be away two weeks, and then back for two, and then away three. He went into the hall to call her up. Her eyes would stick out on stems.

The doorbell rang, a faint muffled tinkling in the kitchen. Chet looked through the window in the front door, but whoever was ringing was off to the side and he couldn't see anything. He turned the knob, and the door swung in hard against his chest, pushing him against the wall.

"Say, what in . . ." he said.

He was looking into the muzzle of a gun.

The man holding the gun came around the door and let two others in behind him. Pushing Chet into the front room he took a quick look in bedrooms and kitchen to make sure no one else was at home. He came back and patted Chet's pockets perfunctorily and motioned him over into a chair. "You sit down and take it easy," he said. "This is a raid. Want to tell us where it is and save yourself trouble?"

"I don't know what you're talking about," Chet said.

The other two men were already in the kitchen. Chet heard the feet of one go thumping down the cellar stairs. Because he could do nothing else, he sat in the chair while they went methodically through the house and cellar. All the time they were below Chet sat still under the eyes of the officious detective with the gun, his ears strained to hear any sound of moving. The preserve cupboard that his father had built so that it looked like a solid wall out from the furnace room, with a little six by six room back of it packed with liquor, bottles, labels, seals, alcohol, would be a find if they had sense enough to try to move the shelves. But the two came upstairs with nothing in their hands but a sack and some straw bottle sheaths. The three of them stood looking at Chet. "Where's your old man?" one said.

"He's out of town."

"Went kind of suddenly, didn't he?" the man with the gun said sarcastically. "I saw him this afternoon."

Chet shrugged.

"Hell with the old man," the second man said. "Where do you keep the whiskey? You'll get off easier if you spill it."

"What whiskey?" Chet said.

"Oh for Christ sake," the first man said. "Don't be as stupid as you look. You aren't pulling anything off."

The blood had drained from Chet's face. He could feel his skin dead and stiff on his bones. "Go to hell," he said flatly.

The tableau of the three glaring at him was interrupted by a jerk from the little hook-nosed man in the middle. He held up a hand. "Shhh!" he said. In the garage beside the house a motor was cut. A car door slammed.

"Round in front, you, Ted," the man with the gun whispered. "Joe and I'll wait for him at the back door."

Chet wet his lips. He ought to jump and shout a warning. But the deputy had his gun out again. The old man wouldn't have a chance to run for it, and he might get shot. He closed his mouth, but he couldn't stay sitting down. As the back door opened he saw the deputy spring forward, his gun out. "I got you!" he said. He was so excited that his mouth frothed. "Don't you make a move, I got you, by God!"

Caught entirely unaware, Bo stood in the doorway, the sack of whiskey he had been unable to deliver in his arms. His eyes shot from the deputy with the gun to Chet, standing white and still in the other doorway. His lips came together and he breathed once, audibly, through his nose.

"All right," he said. "You're Tom Mix. You got me. What do you want?"

The deputy grabbed the sack and Bo let it go in contempt. It crashed on the floor with a thudding clink of smashed glass. The deputy, showing his teeth, let it lie there. "You're under arrest," he said. "Possession and transportation."

Bo's voice was perfectly controlled, the voice of a good citizen annoyingly bothered by officious officers. "Since when have you started arresting people for having a little liquor around for their own private use?"

"Own use my ass," the deputy said. "Come on, you too." He motioned to Chet, took a pair of handcuffs from his pocket and shook them.

Bo's eyes went narrow and black. "He's got nothing to do with whatever you're charging me with," he said. "He's just a kid."

"Would you like to handle this?" the deputy said. He handcuffed the two of them together, and for just an instant their eyes met, Chet's smoky, sullen, a little scared, Bo's bleak and gray. "Don't worry, kid," Bo said. "This smart bastard is just showing off. You'll be out of this in an hour."

"That's all right," Chet said. He went along out to the deputies' car, feeling his chained hand brush against his father's as he walked, and his whole mind was emptied as if water had washed through it.

7

For an hour after lunch she had been sitting on the balcony with two women from Salt Lake, one a dancing instructor at the university, the other the wife of a professor. They were very pleasant women, easy to know, their voices quiet. The things they talked about let her for a little while look into a world that had been completely closed to her. The professor's wife had been reading a book by a man named Sinclair Lewis.

"You must read it," she told Elsa. "It's priceless. I should think every Rotarian in the country would be squirming."

"I think it's rather pathetic," the dancing instructor said. "After his boy has run off and married the girl, you remember, Babbitt has to accept it and give the two his blessing. When he said that about never having been able once in his life to do what he really wanted to do, I could have wept."

"The Civil War didn't abolish slavery," Mrs. Webb said. "We're all slaves to something, just like Babbitt. I hate to think of what somebody might write about college professors, plugging along with their minds half on their work and half on a promotion. There are a thousand things George would like to do, but there he goes on reading themes and getting up lectures and going through the same old grind year after year, just getting acquainted with his students' minds and then having them pass the course and vanish. I should think that must be the worst feeling on earth, teaching freshmen in college. You'd never meet any minds but seventeen-year-old ones. Eventually your own mind must freeze at that level."

"Have you noticed George deteriorating?" the instructor said.

"I notice he never gets his book done. That's where my slavery comes in. He's a slave to his classes and I'm a slave to the duty of driving him in to work on his book." She smiled at Elsa. "What's your husband a slave to?"

"I don't know," Elsa said. "Cigars, maybe."

She could have come much closer than that, but it wouldn't do. Any consideration of his slavery or her own had to be kept for the nights when sleep wouldn't come and the thoughts went around in their circular paths, pacing the mind like animals caged. Neither she nor her thoughts had any place in the society of these women who could talk shop freely and openly, criticize their husbands because nobody would dare to think for a moment that their husbands were not respectable and estimable men. You criticized in public only when you hadn't really much to object to.

For an instant, sitting in the sweet afternoon sun with these women who read books, went to plays, knew music, moved in an atmosphere of ideas, she felt a pang of bitter black envy. It had never occurred to her why the world of criminals and lawbreakers was called the underworld, but it was clear now. You were shut out, you moved in the dark underneath, and if you came up for a brief time, as she was doing now, you knew, better than these women who accepted you in friendship as something you were not, that you were an uneasy visitor in a place where you didn't belong. Under other circumstances these women might really have been her friends. They could have played bridge or Mah Jong in the evenings, visited at each other's houses, loaned each other books, gone to plays or movies or musicals together.

"That's dreadfully true," she said. "That about the slavery."

The mail truck from Salt Lake came up across the bridge and stopped under the balcony. A boy carried the mail sack inside.

"There's what I'm a slave to," the instructor said. She put away her petit point and stood up. "I just exist from one mail to the next. If the truck broke down some day and didn't get here at least with my newspaper I think I'd die."

She went down after her mail, and the professor's wife held out the Lewis book. "Would you like to read this? I think you'd like it."

"Why thank you," Elsa said. "My son and I have been reading things aloud in the evenings. He'll be going to the university this fall."

She riffled the pages, wondering when Bruce was coming up. He generally came around three, after he had gone through all his rituals of being a good camper. She stood up to look down the road, and it was then that she saw the Cadillac coming. It pulled into the parking lot and Bo got out, and she could tell from the very way he walked that something was wrong.

"Excuse me," she said to Mrs. Webb, and laid the book down in her chair. "Here comes my husband . . ."

In her room she heard him through in silence. "Well," she said when he was done, "I guess I'd better start packing my things."

"Do you think you ought to?" Bo said. "The doc said a couple months, at least."

"Did you come up just to tell me to stay on here?" she said. Then she saw that he was hurt. He had run to her the minute he got into trouble, and he had come to take her back, but he didn't like to be told why he had come. "I wouldn't think of staying," she said. "I feel worlds better. A month has been more than enough."

"I want you to stay right here if you think you need to," Bo said. "There's no point in coming down if you're going to get all run down again."

Out of the weariness that had come back on her, Elsa smiled. "We'll be moving again, I suppose."

"I guess we'll have to."

He sat on the bed and watched her put her clothes in the bags. He was nervous and fidgety, stood up to look out the window, lit a cigar, let it go out, lit it again. "That damned show-off prohi," he said. "Waving a gun around as if he was catching horse thieves. I wish to hell Chet hadn't been there."

Elsa turned sharply. "Was Chet there?"

"Didn't I tell you?" Bo said. "They took him down to the station with me, but they let him loose right away. It was just that prohi trying to get himself a reputation. I don't think he'd ever made a raid before."

Elsa only half heard him. She wanted to say "Oh my God!" and sit down on the bed and cry. Instead she said, quietly, "How did Chet take it?"

"All right. He was pretty white. He just kept his mouth shut till they turned him loose."

"Have you seen him since?"

"No. I didn't get out till eleven-thirty. They didn't take the car, because they didn't have any evidence I'd been transporting in it, so I gave Chet the keys. When I got back this morning the car was in the garage and Chet was gone. I suppose he went to work, or else out to make some arrangements."

"Arrangements for what?"

"I guess I didn't tell you that, either. I saw Bill Talbot and he's taking Chet along this trip."

So it was better, she thought. That would keep him from thinking too much about it. But it was bad enough to have had him dragged off to jail. "That's the part I hate worst about this business," she said. "To have the boys mixed up in it . . ."

"Do you think I like it?"

"You could have prevented it if you'd quit a long time ago."

His face flushed darkly. "Kick me," he said. "I'm down."

"That isn't fair," she said, almost crying.

"Is it fair to gouge me when I'm down? I'd have done anything to prevent that, if I could have."

"Bo," she said, "let's not fight. I'm sorry. I'm just sick about Chet, that's all."

So you've given up again, her mind said. You've backed away when you knew you were right. You used to have more spirit than that.

Will you go on, she said, will you keep on backing away until your children are both blackened by this dirty business, or driven to something worse? She looked at Bo, his face haggard, almost old, the faint lines of bitterness and violence deepened around his mouth. He was miserable too, as miserable as she was.

But then why! she said. He could have got out of this business years ago.

What is your husband a slave to, Mrs. Mason? To himself, Mrs. Webb, to himself. To his notion that he has to make a pile, be a big shot, have a hundred thousand dollars in negotiable securities in his safety deposit box, drive a Cadillac car, have seven pairs of shoes with three-dollar trees for each pair, buy three expensive Panamas during a summer and wear a diamond worth fifteen hundred dollars in his tie. He doesn't know, he wouldn't know, what to do with money when he has it. Would he ever think of going to the theater, or reading a good book, or taking a trip somewhere just for the trip? He gave up reading books ten years ago, and even when he goes to a movie he goes only to kill three hours . . .

"Chet'll be all right," he said. "I wouldn't worry about him, Else."

"I hope so," she said. "He's more sensitive than you think, though. He has to show off a lot, and pretend he's older than he is. He lives on the admiration of his pals. And if this gets in the paper it'll hurt his pride so bad. . . . Is it in the paper?"

"Not very big," Bo said. "It's there, though."

"Poor Chet," she said.

"We'll have to stop at Bruce's camp," she said. "Maybe we could let him stay up here."

"Moving, we could use him," Bo said.

"Well, we'll see." She took one bag and Bo the other. At the top of the stairs Elsa remembered Mrs. Webb and the book. "I have to run up again," she said. "I'll meet you in the car."

Up on the balcony she spoke to Mrs. Webb. "I'm sorry," she said. "I guess I won't be able to read your book after all. My husband just came up and I have to go down with him."

"I hope it isn't anything serious," Mrs. Webb said.

"No. Nothing serious. I may come back in the next few days. I . . . hope so. It's been a wonderful place."

"If you don't," Mrs. Webb said, "don't forget to come and call. I'd love to see you. Did I give you my address?"

"Yes," Elsa said. "I hope you'll come and see me too."

Mrs. Webb put out her hand. "It's been ever so nice to know you," she said. "Be easy on yourself. You don't want to get sick again."

"I feel almost as if I were leaving home," Elsa said. "Will you say goodbye to Miss Sorenson for me?"

She broke away and went, and on the stairs she met Miss Sorenson and had to go through it again. Miss Sorenson had the paper under her arm, and as she got into the car Elsa thought miserably that now, probably, up there in the sun on the balcony, the two would read that news item, not very big but there all right, and know her for what she was. Next to her worry about how Chet was taking everything, that was the most miserable of many miserable thoughts. The only consolation was that the address she had given Mrs. Webb would be useless after a day or two. So even if Mrs. Webb missed that item in the paper, and came to call, she would find only blank windows and a closed door. At the very least, the underworld could hide.

She found more to worry about than even her worse anxieties could have anticipated. When, at the end of a week that left her sick and spent, she sat down in the afternoon with all of it settled, Chet gone, Bruce off with a friend's family on a tour of the southern parks, Bo downtown making the last of his undercover arrangements that would get him off lightly with a fine, she felt as if she had gone through an earthquake, and the world was still tipsily rocking. Moving hadn't helped any, either. Her curtains weren't up yet, there were boxes still unpacked in the kitchen, the linen was piled on top of the bed in the spare bedroom. The house, like her own life, was upside-down, but she couldn't do any more now. She just wanted to sit and cry. Even the realization of how burnt-out she felt sent a twinge through her, and she rested her forehead on her hand. Ah Chet, Chet, she said, blinking the tears. She had cried enough already, she thought in wonder, so that she shouldn't be able to cry any more.

She looked up at the uncurtained room. It was a pleasant enough room, far pleasanter than many she had lived in, but the windows were streaked, the shades hung a little crookedly in their brackets, the rug wasn't down yet and the furniture was arranged anyhow. It struck her as a cold room, an unlived-in room, as unfriendly to its new occupants as a barn. Whenever she moved anything the sound echoed. Outside, in the stretch of vacant lots that went for a half block down the street, children were yelling, and cars went up and down on the new pavement, but the sounds too were remote and indifferent. She was shut up here in this half-lived-in house, hidden behind its dirty windows, in isolation as complete as if she lived in Labrador.

The mantel clock said four o'clock. It would be pleasant, she thought, to have somebody drop in (her eyes took in the amount of cleaning and straightening still necessary, and she retreated from her wish, then came back to it again. What difference did the condition of the house make? They had moved in only yesterday. Whoever would be coming would be a close friend). They would have a glass of iced tea and a cookie or cake, and sit and talk a while. It would be a relief to talk. For five days she hadn't talked to anyone but furious people, sullen people, stubborn people, tearful people. She had had to play peace-maker to the whole bunch of them when she would rather have gone to her room and cried.

Somebody to talk to. What if Mrs. Webb came around?

Don't be stupid, she said. You couldn't talk to her, or to anyone except Bo or Bruce, and Bruce is gone for a week and Bo is still mad enough to fly off the handle at a word. You can sit and let it simmer inside you, that's all you can do.

Now, she said, you really know what it is to be uprooted. You're as homeless as a tramp on a park bench. You've pulled away from all your family and you're alone in a room that isn't really yours. You have a father, a step-mother who used to be your best friend, a sister, a brother, uncles and aunts and cousins, but you don't know any of them any more except maybe Kristin.

Psycho-social isolation, her mind said. That was what Bruce had said about the way they lived, one day when they were talking in the parlor by the fire. She had laughed then at the big words, and at the half-playful venom with which he spat them out. Something he had got in school—another mysterious world that she saw only in reflections and heard only in echoes, through her children. Psycho-social isolation.

"Well, whatever you call it," she said to the empty room, "I hate it!"

And oh, Chet, Chet, she said why did you let it hit you so hard? You were strong enough to bear burdens and strains and fatigue. Why weren't you strong enough to bear shame?

She rose and wandered around the room, picked up the metal elephant on the mantel, brushed the dust on it experimentally, set it down again. There was a box of stationery, two or three bottles of ink, some pens and pencils in a carton on the other end of the mantel, waiting for time when she could put them away. The clock said four-twenty. Bo wouldn't be home till six, probably. She took paper, pen, and ink and went into the dining room. Somebody to talk to. The best she could do was Kristin, fifteen hundred miles away. Sitting with the pen in her hand she found herself crying again, her eyes running over without effort or strain or sobs, as if she were too tired to cry properly, but had to sit and simply drip from the eyes. And she knew she couldn't write it, even to Kristin.

All she could do was think it, wonder why Chet had thrown up the whole works, even the trip with the ball team, even the chance he had been dreaming about for two or three years. Why he should be so humiliated and shamed that he would run off that way, take Laura with him, be so sullen and unapproachable when the police finally brought them back . . .

But she knew, really. He wouldn't have anything to do with anything his father had ever touched. He had meant that runaway as a final pulling-up of all the roots—he had meant never to come back. He had it in his mind that he couldn't ever face anybody he knew, now. If he appeared at the ball park with the team he was afraid the people in the stands who knew him would say, "There's Chet Mason. His old man got pinched for bootlegging a while back. He's got a nerve, showing his face around."

But to get married! she said. At seventeen! To run across the state line into Wyoming and lie about his age four years, and with only a few dollars in his pockets. To hate his father so bad he would do anything like that, give up his whole ambition, just to get away . . .

Oh Lord, she said, and leaned her head on her hand. The whole business was mixed up and confused, but the confusion couldn't eliminate the certainty of what had happened. It couldn't make her forget the fury Laura's father had been in, the way he gobbled and strangled over the telephone when the runaway had first been discovered, and the way Bo had shouted back at him. He would blame Chet himself, and be hard as nails with him, but he wouldn't let Laura's father blame him.

And all that argument, and Chet so sullen that he wouldn't speak, and Laura shut up in her house and kept even from telephoning. She tried to think of what she might have said to Kristin if she had written, how she would have told about all that, even the buggy whip that Mr. Betterton had used on Laura, and how she had had to be peace-maker, calm Bo down, finally go down herself in a taxi and insist that Laura be allowed to come up and talk with her privately. She would have said how she had urged them both to submit to annulment, save trouble by letting the proceedings go through. They couldn't fight it anyway. All they could do would be to make themselves and everybody else unhappier than they were. It was best to pretend that they hadn't been for two days man and wife. They could go back to work and save their money and get married again after a few years, and it would be better.

Talking like that, all the time with Chet's sullen face before her, and Laura twisting her hands, crying, so frightened of her father that she wailed, and said she had to get away, she couldn't go back, why couldn't people have left them alone? But it was Chet she worried about. He was too grim and silent, he too obviously hated Bo, and even if this was smoothed over she knew there would be other things, that Chet wouldn't stay now.

It was Laura, she would have had to say to Kristin, who finally weakened. Chet would have stood up in court and shouted that they had lived together, and that the marriage shouldn't be annulled. It was Laura who listened when she told them how hard life could be without enough money, how a few years spent saving now might make all the difference later. It was Laura who accepted the promise of help later, and agreed to let their fathers cancel the marriage. And it was Laura who convinced Chet.

Not, Elsa said bitterly, his mother. His mother couldn't convince him of anything. Only his girl could, and she only because she was so scared, poor thing.

And what Chet had said when he finally agreed: "I'm doing this for you, Mom, not for him, and I'm never going to live at home again." She hadn't had the heart to tell Bo that. It would have made him boiling mad, but it would have hurt him too. And she hadn't pointed out to Bo (and this she couldn't have said to Kristin at all) that it was the whiskey business that was the cause of the whole trouble. She knew what his answer would have been: What could he do? He had to make a living somehow, didn't he? How was he going to make up the loss brought on by this last raid? Christ Almighty, did she think he *liked* having the law in his hair all the time? Let him get a little ahead, and he'd quit, sure, but how could he quit now? And could he help it if the prohi making the raid was a hysterical damn fool and pinched the kid? Did she think *he* liked it?

Elsa pushed away the pen and ink and stood up. There wasn't any of it you could tell Kristin. It was nothing that could be told. All you could do was shut your mouth and make the best of it. But the mere thought of making the best of it, reconciling yourself to the thought that your son went white with hatred when his father talked to him, that he had blown all his chances and might never pick them up again, that his sullenness might drive him to any sort of foolish and reckless act, made her bite her lips. Like the last two nights Chet had been home. Drunk both nights, she knew. But what could she say? What could she do? What argument could she have used to move him, brace him up, give him the feeling that his whole life wasn't ruined? He was so sure it was. First, his mind seemed to say, Bo had spoiled his life at home for him, and now he had spoiled the only other life that had been open. All right, with both spoiled he would go to hell as fast as possible. It was silly, it was childish, but it was unstoppable, unless Chet came to himself, got a decent job up in Idaho where he'd gone, got on his feet again and hooked up with another ball team, something to give him confidence in himself and the world again . . . This trouble was only a moment, if he looked at it straight. There was his whole life ahead of him.

She thought of what Bruce had said one day at Brighton. He had amazed her then, as he sometimes did, with the things that went on in his mind. People, he had said, were always being looked at as points, and they ought to be looked at as lines. There weren't any points, it was false to assume that a person ever *was* anything. He was always becoming something, always changing, always continuous and moving, like the wiggly line on a machine used to measure earthquake shocks. He was always what he was in the beginning, but never quite exactly what he was; he moved along a line dictated by his heritage and his environment, but he was subject to every sort of variation within the narrow limits of his capabilities.

It was too complicated an idea for her, but it seemed to her now that if she could bring herself to look at Chet as a line and not as a point she might even be able to laugh. If she could only look back and fix her mind on escapades of his childhood. He was always getting into scrapes, having the neighbors over for drinks during the flu epidemic in Whitemud, stealing that gun from Tex Davis' shack and thinking how big and tough he was with a man-sized forty-four, getting into trouble years ago back at that home in Seattle, when she had had to take the boys out and go home to Indian Falls . . .

She shut her mind on that too. There was danger in looking at people as lines. The past spread backward and you saw things in perspective that you hadn't seen then, and that made the future ominous, more ominous than if you just looked at the point, at the moment. There might be truth in what Bruce said, but there was not much comfort.

Chet came home, but not because he wanted to. A week after he and Van went up into Idaho they got drunk in Idaho Falls and were thrown in the bullpen for the night. When they were released next day and asked to get out of town they decided to hit for Ashton, up in the high timber country, to see if anything was stirring in the sawmills or placer mines. Ten miles out of Idaho Falls they hit a pile of gravel and rolled over. Van, wedged behind the wheel, had three broken ribs, a broken collar bone, and a badly skinned face. Chet, thrown clear, broke his right arm in two places. A passing motorist took them back to Idaho Falls, where they spent all their remaining money for doctor bills. As soon as Van was able to travel, they came back to Salt Lake on the train, their fare paid by Van's mother.

For almost two weeks Chet stayed sullenly at home, hardly going out of the house except to the drugstore for newspapers and magazines. All morning he sat with the paper, all afternoon with a magazine, his feet propped on a chair and his sling adjusted across his stomach. Even to his mother he said nothing about his marriage or what had come after it, nothing about how the accident had happened, nothing about what he was going to do when his arm knitted. He did not, so far as any of them saw, have any communication with Laura. Nobody ever saw him use the telephone or write any letters.

At the end of two weeks, when his arm was out of the cast, he asked his mother for a little money. She had none at hand except a few dollars left from the household allowance, but she gave him that without asking questions. He counted it. Eleven dollars.

"Can you get me a little more?" he said. "Ten dollars or so?"

"Are you going away again, Chet?"

He nodded. "For good," he said.

"Where?"

"I don't know."

"Will you write? Promise."

"I'll write," he said. "Don't think I'm blaming you, Mom. You've been swell. I'll write to you."

That night she asked Bo for twenty dollars. He looked up in surprise, because she rarely asked him for money beyond her allowance. But he didn't ask what she wanted it for. Without a word he dug it out of his wallet and she slipped it under the base of the lamp by Chet's bed.

The next morning, after Bo had gone downtown, Chet came into the kitchen with his suitcase packed. She wanted to hold him, hang onto him, beg him not to go, to stay and get a job in town and forget all that had happened, but his face was so somberly still that she didn't. She was as helpless to keep him with her now as she had been to prevent the whole debacle that had driven him into himself.

"Goodbye, Chet," she said, and felt his arms tighten around her. There was that comfort at least; he loved her, nothing that had happened had alienated him from her. "You've got so little money," she said. "Why don't you wait and I'll get some more."

"I wouldn't want more," Chet said. "I'll take enough of his money to get me out of town, and that's all."

"You're bitter," she said, searching his eyes. "Don't hold things against your dad. He feels bad that things worked out the way they did. And if you get in any trouble, or even if you don't, write to him. He'd be pleased to help you, Chet. Do you know that?"

"I guess he won't have the chance," Chet said. "I'm not going to get into any trouble."

"But you'll write . . . him too."

He squeezed her hands, the grip of his left hand hard, that of his right weaker, feeble from the recent injury. "Take care of yourself," he said. "I'll let you know where I land."

And there he went, Elsa thought, there he went, this time for good.

Three months later, from Rapid City, South Dakota, she got a postcard. Chet and Laura were married again.

VIII

From his window on the third story Bruce could look out over a flat acreage of lights climbing upward to the signboards and the tall mills along the Mississippi. The river itself was a sunken black channel with firefly lights moving mysteriously along its bottom, and against the glow of the St. Paul side he saw the superstructure of the bridge he crossed every morning on his way to class.

He had picked the highest room he could find, because he hated the flat country. The sky came down too close all around, like a smothering tent, and an eye that wanted to look out was constantly interrupted by buildings, trees, the swell of low hills. Even outside the city, where he had gone hopefully on walks, he had found no place high enough to give him a view, no place flat enough to let him see more than a quarter of a mile. The upper-floor room helped some. It gave him a chance at night to pretend that the lights he looked down on were much farther away than they really were, and to cultivate his nostalgia for the high benches around Salt Lake with the forty-mile valley wide open below him, the state road a string of distended yellow lights on down toward the Jordan narrows, the slag dumps at Magna and West Jordan belching gobbets of fire on the black slope of the Oquirrhs.

He was homesick and almost terrifyingly alone. He ought to go out to a movie, or get busy on torts. There were plenty of things to do if he could bring his mind to them, but instead he went and sat on the window sill, opened the sash to let in a blast of cold January air, and sat looking out.

Bruce Mason, he said. Bruce Mason, first year law. There was something almost cosmically ironical about his choice of profession. He remembered what Bill Levine, a friend of his father's, had said when he heard it. That big gross animal with the shrunken legs, sitting in his wheel chair all day with a sanctimonious look on his face, a look that said, "See, I'm a cripple, I have to sell taffy and nuts on the street for a living. A nickel for a bag of nuts will help keep life in a body that the world has miserably misused!" And under cover of the taffy and nuts he would arrange you a woman, sell you a stolen car, get you a bottle or a case, give you a card to the hop joints in Plum Alley, play procurer and pimp with his patient, resigned smile that covered a lewdness as deep and stinking as the pit.

"There's nothing like a lawyer in the family," he had said. "Eh Harry?"

Bruce shut the window and stood up. And what, he said, would you do if you became a public prosecutor and found yourself prosecuting your old man? Would you send him to McNeil Island for two years for conspiracy to evade the prohibition law? That would make a nice little problem in family loyalty and public duty. Would you sprinkle dust on Polynices' head, or leave him for the wolves?

If I only understood better, he said. If I really knew what I think, what I am, what he is and mother is and Chet is, how everything got off on the wrong foot. If I knew how and why mother has stood it for over twenty-five years, I might know something.

He got out his mother's last letter, delivered that morning, written three days before. It was a good letter, but it told him nothing of what he wanted to know. Everything that was tangled or thwarted or broken in the family relationships was carefully held back.

If a man could understand himself and his own family, Bruce thought, he'd have a good start toward understanding everything he'd ever need to know. He laid his mother's letter down and sprawled his legs under the desk. The book on torts was at his elbow. He tossed it over on the cot and reached for a notebook.

"This is not a journal," he wrote. "It is not notes for a novel, not a line-a-day record of the trivia my mind dredges up. Call it an attempt to understand."

Understand what? he said. Where do I begin? With myself, my father, his father, his grandfather? When did the germ enter? Where did the evil come in?

"I suppose," he wrote, "that the understanding of any person is an exercise in genealogy. A man is not a static organism to be taken apart and analyzed and classified. A man is movement, motion, a continuum. There is no beginning to him. He runs through his ancestors, and the only beginning is the primal beginning of the single cell in the slime. The proper study of mankind is man, but man is an endless curve on the eternal graph paper, and who can see the whole curve?

"What is my father? What is my mother? What is my brother? What am I? Those sound like fatuous questions, but they occupy our whole lives. Suppose I said my father is a bootlegger who lives in Salt Lake City, is easily irritated, has occasional spells of intense good spirits? Suppose I said he wears a diamond like a walnut in his tie and another as big as a pickled onion on his finger, that he pays a hundred dollars apiece for his suits. Those are observable characteristics. Or suppose I said that all his life he has been haunted by the dream of quick wealth and isn't quite unscrupulous enough to make his dream come true, that he is a gambler who isn't quite gambler enough, who has a streak of penuriousness in him, a kind of dull Dutch caution, so that he gambles with one hand and holds back a stake with the other. He might have made a mint playing the market before the crash; instead he bought gilt-edged stocks outright and made less. Suppose I labelled him: a self-centered and dominating egotist who insists on submission from his family and yet at the same time is completely dependent on his wife, who is in all the enduring ways stronger than he is. Suppose I listed his talents: a violent stubbornness that butts through things and often overcomes them, immense energy (generally in the wrong causes), a native tendency to be generous that is always being overcome by his developing greediness and his parsimonious penny-pinching. Add a vein of something like poetic talent, a feeling for poetry of a certain sort, as witness his incredible performance last summer of quoting, after a lapse of almost thirty years, pages and pages of Burns that he had learned in the Wisconsin woods.

"When I have put that down, I have perhaps sketched a character, I have done the sort of thing a novelist probably does before writing his book. But I have not even scratched the surface of Harry Mason. Everything I have listed is subject to contradiction by other characteristics, open to qualification in degree and kind; everything has a history that goes back and back toward a vanishing point. His history is important. It is important to know that he ran away from home at fourteen, and why; that he worked in the woods and on the railroad; that he was disappointed in his ambition to be a big league ball player. It is valuable to remember that all his ancestors as far back as I know anything about them were pioneers, and that he was born when almost all the opportunities for pioneering were gone. It is necessary to look at his father, about whom I know nothing except that the Andersonville prison spoiled his disposition. Probably it didn't spoil his disposition at all, but only let out something that was already there. It would be as accurate to say that the strain of living outside the law has soured my father's temper. Actually he has always had it. It's like the tar in tar paper. When it's new and fresh the tar is distributed, the paper holds it. Under conditions of sun or rain or exposure the tar begins to lump or ooze out. The process of growing older is perhaps a simple process of breaking down cell walls, releasing things that have for a while been bound up in the firmness of young muscle.

"And how far back beyond one ought to go, and how infinitely much one could fill in to the bare outline of two generations! I can't, obviously, make even a beginning. What bred that evil temper and that egotism and that physical energy and that fine set of senses and that manual dexterity and that devotion to pipedreams into Harry Mason, into his violent old father, into the generations hidden down below the eroded surface of the present?

"To know what Harry Mason is, as of January, 1931, I should have to know every thought, accident, rebuff, humiliation, triumph, emotion, that ever happened to him and all his ancestors, and beyond that I should have to weigh him against a set of standards to which I was willing to subscribe. That would be understanding, but that kind of understanding can only happen instantaneously in the mind of God."

So where do I start? he said. He had been writing furiously for three quarters of an hour, but he hadn't even come to a starting point. Nothing in the whole texture of his life or his family's life was arbitrary, yet he could approach it only by being arbitrary. There were too many things he couldn't know.

All right, he said, I'll start with the things I do know.

"I suppose I have always hated him, probably not always with justice. Most children whose fathers are not completely housebroken must have that same hatred in greater or less degree. Yet if a father is housebroken he is less than God, and open to contempt. It must be a hard thing to be a father. To get away with it, a man should have both strength and patience, and patience my father never had. I know that I hold things against him that were my fault, times when I whined or disobeyed or didn't listen, but still, to have one's nose rubbed in one's own excrement, or have his collarbone broken by his father's knocking him end over end across the woodbox, are humiliations that a child cannot easily forget or forgive. It helps not at all to know that your father is often sorry and ashamed after a blow-up.

"When the child is a cry-baby, as I was, the situation gets worse, because the cry-baby runs to his mother and there arises a combination of mother and child against father. (I wonder what cry-babyishness in a child becomes as the child matures? What is the connection between uncontrolled bawling in a child and uncontrolled rage in a man? It is curious to think that maybe my father as a child was a cry-baby.)

"My hatred of him seems to arise from two things: his violence to me, and his inability or unwillingness to see that he was misusing my mother. It is possible that she has never thought herself misused, though I know she has always hated the liquor business, and has thought that Chet with another kind of start would have done better.

"Add to those reasons my own adolescent snobbishness. I was ashamed of the old man all the time I was in college. I was envious of boys whose fathers were respectable, companionable, understanding, everything that mine was not. I hated the flashiness he put on in his clothes, I hated what I saw as boorishness in his manners. I don't believe we've had a friendly and open conversation since I was twelve, and I know he hasn't kissed me since at least that long ago. I think he has been afraid to.

"It used to drive me crazy, wondering why mother stayed with him. I have asked her a dozen times why she didn't leave him. I'd get a job and support her. She always said that I didn't understand.

Understand what? There's only one thing she could have meant, that she loved him. That, and her belief that loyalty to your own actions is the highest virtue, are the only reasons she would have stayed. She made her bed, and she'll lie in it till she dies in it. That kind of loyalty, without love, would be stupider than I think any action of mother's could be, but even without love, it is more admirable than anything the old man can show. I don't think he has ever faced the consequences of an act; he shuts his eyes and gets mad.

"Chet's the same way, only he never did have a bad temper. It was only when the old man pushed him around that he got hard and mulish. Somehow the tar missed him; and though it seems a mad thing to say, I think he is weaker for not having it. When things go wrong for him he broods. He was that way at Christmas, having trouble with Laura, thinking about how he had to come crawling back last year and ask charity from the family. It's a pity that he couldn't have stayed with baseball, but once he got his back up he wouldn't admit his mistake about Laura. If he had, he wouldn't be out of work now, and he wouldn't have had to take that blow in his pride. I could have cried, almost, at Christmas, the way he's got so gentle with me. He used to be always horsing around and sparring at me and kidding me. Now he's Big Brother, obviously proud of me, taking me on as an equal and in some ways, painfully, as a superior. And there was that graduation present he bought me just after he'd come back, when he didn't have a dime and was still looking for work and was still raw from having to ask the old man to help him out. I know he stole the money for that cigarette lighter from the baby's bank, and that Laura found him out and they had a fight.

"That was a nasty time for him, and I don't imagine it's much better now, driving a taxi. I remember how he was when he came back, after the mine closed down and he lost his job. All day he'd sit in the front room learning to play a Hawaiian guitar, twanging away on 'The Rosary,' a sick tune if there ever was one, sitting there all alone, wrapped in some kind of personal isolation, while the baby cried and Laura scolded and mother tried to keep things smooth . . . There's a defeat in that picture that I hate, because Chet is a good fellow. He'd give you his shirt in zero weather. I guess he missed the old man's selfishness, too—and in a way that too weakens him. I hate to see him whipped before he's twenty-four, hopelessly practising a home course in taxidermy, and fooling with that damned guitar.

"And the dreams, the hopelessly rosy dreams. I remember just after I'd gone back for the holidays, when we were taking a shower together and harmonizing in the bathroom. He thought we could work up some songs, go in for a vaudeville act, try to get on the Pantages circuit. He actually had got himself believing it was possible. It isn't, even though he can sing. I don't know why it's impossible, but I know it, and I knew it then. It all belongs with the taxidermy and the dead magpies in the basement and the glue and paper and feathers, and the interminable damned guitar twanging 'The Rosary.'

"That's a defeat that the old man is at least partly responsible for. Mother's is another.

"Yet it's important to remember that he isn't a monster, as I used to think he was. He doesn't tramp on people out of meanness. They get in his road, that's all, or he's tied to them and drags them along with him. He can even be kind, and I guess that now I think of it I can see why mother loved him once and maybe still does. I saw that when she got sick a year ago.

"When she came out that morning with the queer look on her face and said that she'd found a big lump in her breast, their eyes jumped to meet each other, and it seemed to me that all of a sudden I could see what living together twenty-five years can do to two people. They asked and answered a dozen questions in that one look.

"I remember her operation, too, the way the old man woke me at six in the morning to go to the hospital. He probably hadn't slept much. But he couldn't stand it down there. He held her hand while they gave her the ether—and I suppose I was jealous that she wanted him, not me—but the minute they began getting ready, and Cullen came out of the washroom with his scrubbed hands in the air for a nurse to pull the gloves on, the old man lurched out as white as chalk. Once or twice during the operation I saw his face looking in the operating room door, but it never stayed more than a second or two, and when Cullen came back with the slides and said it was malignant, that it meant radical surgery, we had to hunt for two or three minutes to find the old man. He was sitting out on the fire escape, gray clear to the lips. He just nodded when Cullen told him, and he never made a move to come in again. If he had he probably would have fainted, because it was like a butcher's block.

"Afterwards he visited her twice a day, brought her candy, filled her room with flowers. He even tried to talk to me about her and get me to say she would probably be all right now, wouldn't she? There wasn't anything left for cancer to grow in, was there? I'm afraid I didn't give him much help. I didn't think then, and I don't now, that she has more than a fifty-fifty chance of its not coming back. I suppose I acted cold, but it was only because I was talking to him. I agonized over it enough, because I love my mother, and respect her, more than anyone I have ever met, and that's not anything a psychologist can grin about. Why shouldn't I? There's a positive flame in her, a curious little bright flame that never goes down.

"But the old man was good to her then. He wouldn't have talked her into going to visit Kristin if he had been thinking only of himself. Maybe he thought that she might not live long, that he owed her a visit home. He suggested that she go through Hardanger and see the people they'd known when they first married, and just before she left, when Chet and Laura and the baby came in from the mine, he agreed without a whimper to take them in. Give him credit: he's kept them ever since, even if he has grumbled.

"She enjoyed that trip. Nobody in Hardanger recognized her at first, and she had fun being mysterious and letting recognition dawn on them. They gave her the keys to the town, apparently. That must be a curious feeling, to go back after twenty-five years and see all your friends grown gray and fat and bald, and count the stones in the graveyard, and know that you've grown older along with everything else. Anyway she enjoyed it, and she came back in better health.

"Maybe she'll get by. Maybe there's a chance that after I finish here I can get her to break loose from that life. She deserves some friends, she deserves a rest. She's had too long a vacation from any sort of normal woman's life.

"It's an almost marvellous fact that a dozen years of living among bootleggers and pimps and bellhops and all the little scummy riffraff on the edge of the criminal class hasn't touched her—simply hasn't touched her. Neither has the constant sacrifice she has had to make of her own wishes and her own life. It's almost comical to see how completely those small-time thugs respect her. She has been the repository of the confessions and woes of half a dozen kept women, she's been within smelling distance of a dozen stinking episodes, she has had for companions altogether too many foul-mouthed, unscrupulous, lying, cheating, vicious people, but all they have succeeded in doing is to make her kindly-wise. For all her yielding and her self-sacrificing, there is something in her that doesn't give when it's pushed at. She only gives up her wishes, never herself."

Bruce stretched his cramped fingers and looked up. This could go on all night and he would be no closer to what he was after. Probably when he read over what he had written he wouldn't even agree with half of it. He picked up his mother's letter again. No mention of how the double-family arrangement was going now, nothing about how the old man was behaving. Chet had finally agreed to go back to the business school, which he had started once and then dropped. His father was looking at a little sporting goods shop down on Second South, with the idea that he might buy it and set Chet up as manager. They hadn't said anything to Chet yet, and it was still only an idea, but she hoped it would come about. Chet was sick now, in bed. A week ago they had driven up to watch the ski jumping at Ecker Hill, and Chet had helped push some people out of the snow, and had got overheated and caught cold. He was running a little fever, and if he didn't get over it by tomorrow she was going to send him down to the hospital. The baby was fine, it was wonderful to have a child around the house again.

Without moving from the desk, Bruce scribbled off a letter. He had been hitting the books pretty solidly since he came back. Examinations came up next week, but he wasn't worrying too much. Maybe he'd go over to see Kristin one of these days. She was one of the great cookie-makers, and whenever he got tired of cafeteria food he liked to go over and have an orgy at her house. Also her kids were nice kids and George was a good quiet sensible sort of guy. A little home atmosphere was good after a few weeks of grinding. Too bad Chet was sick. "Give him an enema," he said, "from me."

Feet clumped on the hall linoleum and knuckles rapped at his door.

"Come in," Bruce said.

It was Brucker, the fellow from the floor below, a graduate student in economics. "Just got sick of sitting on my tail," he said, peering in. "You busy?"

"No. Come on in."

His visitor flopped on the cot. "If I ever again hear the words Malthus, Mill, Pareto, or Marx," he said, "I'll puke."

"That's something I've been meaning to ask you," Bruce said. "Who is this guy Marx?"

Brucker stared at him. "You go to hell."

"Come on, tell me about him. What'd he write?"

"I'll strangle you," the economist said. "I'm in no mood to be toyed with."

Bruce laughed. "By the end of next week there won't be a sane man in the house."

"There isn't one now," Brucker said. "Boyer is down in his room lying on the bed playing with his toes, cackling like a madman. Nicholson has clutched his books unto his breast and rushed into the night toward the library so as to avoid a fine. Hadley has chucked the whole works and gone hunting a woman. How do you manage to stay up in this attic dungeon and crack the books?"

"One way is to send your only good pants to the cleaner's so you can't go out. Or maybe you have two pairs of pants."

"Three," Brucker said. "All of them so thin on the backside you can read a newspaper through them. That's why I'm studying economics."

"Come on out and let the wind blow through them," Bruce said. "I've got to mail a letter."

They went down the two flights of stairs and Bruce opened the door. Brucker sniffed. "What's the smell?" he said suspiciously.

"I don't smell anything."

"By God, I do believe it's fresh air," the economist said.

As they walked to the corner, their collars up against the still cold, a messenger boy on a bicycle passed them. Under the arclight his face looked blue. He had a muffler wrapped around his ears and his cap crammed down over it. "Brrr!" Brucker said. "I'll never again send a telegram in the winter time. It's cruelty to animals."

They sprinted from the corner back to the house, yelling, racing each other in an unpremeditated burst of energy up the stairs. At the top they met the messenger, his nose red and leaking. "Mason live up here?" he said.

"Yeah," Bruce said, surprised. "Here."

He watched the boy take the yellow envelope out of his hat. The single hall bulb threw his shadow hulking down the wall of the stairway. "Got a telegram with a money order attached," he said. "You sign right here."

"A money order?" Bruce said. He looked at Brucker and frowned. The shadow of the runty messenger heaved on the wall as the boy extended the book. Bruce looked at it without reaching out. The certainty was like ice in his throat. He looked again at Brucker. His voice came out of his tight throat in a dry, difficult whisper.

"My brother's dead!" he said.

2

He had been playing with Chet and a bunch of other kids in the loft of Chance's barn, back in Whitemud, and Chet had slid down the hay on top of him and they had had a fight. Chet had thumped him unmercifully, got him down and tried to make him holler enough, but he wouldn't holler enough, even when Chet bent his arm back in a hammerlock and he felt his shoulder heaving out of joint. "I'll give you an enema!" he kept screaming. "God damn you, just wait, I'll give you an enema!"

"Friend or enema?" Chet said. He put his grinning face down close to Bruce's and twisted his arm harder. "Come on, friend or enema?"

"Enema!" Bruce screamed. "Do you hear me, enema!"

Chet's face began to fade, the grin dwindled and sobered until the face hanging above him was serious and frowning, thinning away, going . . .

"Chet," his mother's voice said, and without surprise Bruce saw that she was there and that the kids had gone. "Chet, I wish you'd try not to scowl so. You look as if you didn't have a friend in the world."

"I'll give him an enema!" Bruce screamed. He opened his eyes and saw the row of green chair backs, the blue night lights, the sprawling figures of sleepers, the pale gleam of bunched pillows half falling off the arms into the aisle. Outside there was a thin and watery light, not yet strong enough to be called daylight, but not quite darkness. His mouth was bitter with the taste of coal smoke, and his throat was sore.

In the curious unreality of the chair car, less real than the dream he had just awakened from, he straightened himself, lifted his aching shoulder from its cramped position. Half stupefied, he rose and rocked back between the sleepers to the men's room, rinsed his mouth, washed his face and hands, looked at himself in the mirror. His face was pale and floating, his tie twisted, and for a long time he stood stupidly wondering where he'd got the overcoat. It wasn't his. He didn't own one. He had got around to combing his hair before the realization came to him, not suddenly, but as a dull transition from not-knowing to knowing. Brucker's coat. He remembered Brucker, solicitous, almost anguished, and himself wandering down the hall, shaking off Brucker's hands, standing with his back to the top of the stairs while the messenger boy's scared face went on down and the fact of death lay in the hall like a heavy foul smell. Then Brucker putting him on the twelve-fifteen later, pressing his overcoat on him, shaking his hand hard, wringing it, his face stiff with sympathy. A good guy, a good friend.

He moved a spittoon with his foot so that he could sit down on the leather bench by the window. The pane was so streaked that he could barely see out. What he could see looked like Nebraska. Farms, windmills, occasional trees, fields and fences, a strip of ghostly highway and a car on it, its lights still on. He put his hand in his overcoat pocket, felt the paper, drew it out yellow and crumpled, read it again.

"Chester passed away this morning wiring you train fare love. Harry Mason."

Harry Mason, Bruce thought. Not "Dad." Not "Father." Harry Mason. As if he didn't dare use any familiar word, or were so confused he didn't know quite what he was doing. Or as if the loss of his one son had made him realize what a bottomless gulf lay between himself and the other. A stiff and formal telegram. Chester passed away this morning . . .

Oh Jesus, Bruce said, poor mother!

Tears squeezed between his lids, and at the sound of a step in the aisle he rose quickly and washed his face again. The brakeman looked through the curtain, nodded, and went on. Bruce went back to his seat and lay down, his eyes close to the smeared window, staring out across the flat land. It couldn't be Nebraska. It had to be Minnesota or Iowa. They weren't due in Omaha till sometime around six. Then a thousand miles of Nebraska and Wyoming and Utah. He'd get into Salt Lake at the worst possible time, two or three in the morning.

Chet is dead, he said. Your brother has died suddenly and you are on your way back to his funeral. Your father has sent you a telegram and a money order. You change at Omaha to the Union Pacific and you will arrive very early in the morning in Salt Lake. You will see your mother with the knife in her. You will see Chet's wife, whom you do not much like, parading her grief, and his little girl bewildered and whimpering. You will also see your father, whom you hate, and how will he be taking it? He always liked Chet better than you, even though he treated him harder.

And Chet, he said, is dead. His life is finished at twenty-three, before it had a chance to begin. Never, he said. Not ever. He was, and now is not.

Suddenly he was flooded by memories of terrifying clarity, he and Chet trapping muskrats together on the river in Canada, playing soldier down in the burnouts on the homestead, singing together in school cantatas, getting into fights over the Erector set, swimming in the bare-naked hole down by where Doctor O'Malley's tent used to be pitched, playing map games on the long ride down from the Canadian border to Utah. The smell of gasoline from the auxiliary can in the hot grove near Casper, the mourning doves that cooed all that morning from the cottonwoods, and the ledge up behind, where they killed the rattlesnake. The pride he had felt, the tremendous exuberant exultation, when Chet caught the pass in the last quarter to beat Provo, and himself running out on the field hysterical with "school spirit," pushing through players slimed with black mud from head to foot, only their eyes unmuddied, to grab Chet's hand and pound him on the back, and the way Chet had grinned almost in embarrassment behind his mask of mud, still holding the ball in his big muddy hands . . .

It had never seemed that he and Chet had much in common, that they had ever run together much. Chet had been above and beyond him, with the big gang. But there were thousands of ties, millions, so many that he was amazed and saddened. They were brothers, something he had never really considered before.

Had been, he said. Had been brothers. That was all gone. Everything that had force to make them brothers was already done. If he wanted to find a brother now he had to find him in the past, in recollections that he hadn't even known were there.

He bit his lips together and bent his forehead against the cold windowpane. But he did not cry much. His eyes were dry when they ran through the shacktowns and suburbs of Council Bluffs and across the river and into Omaha.

For two hundred miles across Nebraska he thought of nothing except how clean the Union Pacific kept its trains. At Kearney he bought a newspaper and read it through painstakingly, knowing what he was looking for and completely aware that it was not there.

People died everywhere, all the time. Why should anyone in Omaha take note that Chet Mason had died suddenly in Salt Lake City? Who was Chet Mason that anyone should mark his death? Yet the strange lethargy that held him, the torpor waiting on complete realization, did not believe that slip of yellow paper in his overcoat pocket, and the absence of any notice in the paper was almost comforting. He knew he would not believe Chet was dead until he had more proof than the telegram.

At North Platte he bought another paper. At Cheyenne he bought another. From Cheyenne clear on across the plateau to Rock Springs he sat in the club car playing poker with three drummers, and won eighty cents. When they hiked the ante he left the game and went back to his seat to try to sleep. Out past the panes of double glass the moon silvered the empty waste of the Wyoming Plateau, and the telegraph poles were like the ticking second-hand of a watch, the muted racket of the wheels the grinding of a remorseless mechanism carrying him closer and closer to the time when he had to wake up.

When the train swung out of the canyon in a long curve and backed into the yards at Ogden he roused himself and got off for a cup of coffee. Forty miles to go. In the station washroom he washed and combed his hair, and at the newsstand he bought a Salt Lake paper.

He didn't look into it until the train started again. Then he went back to the men's room and sat down. He found it immediately, a little three-inch story on the local page, and the fact that Chet was not stuck away in a column of nameless and unimportant deaths brought him an instant of fierce pride. "Former High School Athlete Dies," it said. So Chet was not entirely unknown. Some of the people reading that three-inch notice would recall games he had starred in, plays he had made spectacularly.

Why try to fool yourself? he said. Why pretend that Chet was anything, amounted to anything? Why back up your grief by making believe Chet mattered to anyone outside his family? He mattered to you, isn't that enough? Does he have to be important to other people before you'll think him worth a tear?

But those three inches of type helped, nevertheless. He was more calm when he stepped off the train than he had been all day, and when he saw his mother, alone, coming toward him with her face twisting toward tears, he did not break down. He spread his arms and she came into them.

"Ah, Bruce," she said.

He held her tightly, looking over her head at the people moving toward the exits. "Mom," he said.

She was back out of his arms, shaking tears from her eyes, trying to smile. "You've got an overcoat," she said. "I imagined you coming through in this cold weather without either hat or coat."

"I borrowed it," he said. "Where's Pa?"

His mother looked at him. "He . . . couldn't come." Bruce put his arm around her and led her toward the exit. "Let's not talk," he said. "Let's not try to explain anything."

"I came down in a taxi," she said. "Your dad is terribly broken up. He's like a madman. Just walks and walks. He hasn't slept at all."

She took a handkerchief out of her purse and fumbled with it while he called a cab. In the car she held his hand hard without saying anything. Bruce stared stonily at the back of the driver's neck.

At home Bo Mason met them at the door, shook Bruce's hand, stared into his face a moment, and swung around to disappear into his bedroom. He did not come out again, but later, as he lay sleeplessly staring upward in the bed that he and Chet had shared during the Christmas vacation less than a month ago, Bruce heard a sudden cry from the room down the hall, a smothered scream and the thud of feet heavy on the floor, and his mother's voice saying, "Bo, Bo, please! Bo, you mustn't! Get back into bed, please." After that there was a sound that made Bruce grit his teeth in the dark, the sound of his father sobbing, a muffled, uncontrolled weeping, a little shameful and completely shattering.

When Bruce got up his father had already gone. "He had to get out," his mother said. "He can't stand to be still a minute."

She waited on Bruce at breakfast, even tried to butter his toast. She was pale but perfectly composed. On an impulse, while he was eating, he reached out and covered her hand with his. "Mom," he said, and his smile was so great a strain that it hurt. "You're taking it like a Trojan."

"What else can you do?" she said.

"Would it help to tell me about it?"

"If you like," she said, her eyes steady and clear. "I guess there are . . . two or three things I ought to tell you."

"Where are Laura and the baby?"

"That's part of it," she said. "Laura left him, you know. She took the baby and left to live with her family just a few days after you went back."

"But you said in your letters . . ."

"I didn't want to bother you with it," she said. "I thought it might straighten out."

"They were fighting pretty much at Christmas," Bruce said. "Did she . . . when he got sick . . . ?"

"When he got bad. It went so fast. He was only in the hospital two days. Afterwards she went all to pieces. She's in bed now."

"It's a little late, isn't it?" he said. "She might have shown a little of that when it would do some good."

Her eyes were steady and very blue. "You're thinking about your dad too."

"Maybe I am. Maybe I'm thinking about myself. Everybody but you."

"Don't," she said. He watched her, thinking that there was a dignity, a nobility almost, in the clean bony curve of her temple, the way her hair went back from her forehead, the way her mouth could be firm without being hard or bitter. "Please don't even hint anything like that to your dad," she said. "That's what makes him crazy, almost. He blames himself for everything." She shook her head. "I don't know," she said. "It's everybody's fault. Chet's too. We tried to do something for him, tried to get him to go to business school. He started for a while, you know, and then he quit. I found out after three weeks that he'd never been near the place after the first few days, and had got his tuition money back."

"What was he doing?"

"It's such an unhappy, tangled mess," she said, and shook her head again. "Chet was having trouble with Laura, and she kept throwing it up to him that she was working and all he could do was drive a taxi, and I think . . ." She laughed a little as if in pain. "I've never talked to you like this. I think she wouldn't let him come to bed with her. For a long time. You know how Chet was. He got sullen and swore he'd find somebody else, and they had a fight."

Very carefully Bruce said, "Was he running around with another woman, then?"

"You mean about the tuition money."

"Yes."

"He didn't have any other woman," she said. "He just . . ." Her face flushed, and she bit her lips. "That taxi job was no good," she said. "It threw him in with a lot of no-good people."

There were tears in her eyes. "He never did get a decent break," Bruce said.

"Oh, let's be honest," she said, almost violently. "Chet was a good boy, he always was, but he was impulsive, and I'm afraid he was a little weak. He made a lot of mistakes, but you couldn't blame him for them because he *was* such a nice boy really. He just . . . I guess Chet didn't have much backbone." She stared at him, her eyes bright with the tears that swam in them. "It hurts me to say it, and I don't say it to blame him," she said. "He *was* decent, and generous, wasn't he? But he didn't have much backbone. He got hurt too easily."

"It might take a lot of backbone to live with Laura," Bruce said.

"Oh, let's not blame her either," she said. "Chet had bad luck. If he'd been stronger he could have come out of it, but it whipped him." She turned her face half away and sat with her hand pressed against her mouth.

Bruce stood up and went around the table to put his hand on her shoulder. "It sounds like sentimental hypocrisy," he said slowly, "but maybe Chet's better off. Maybe he couldn't ever have got back."

"You know what he said to me just before he died?" she said. "I talked to him just an hour or two before, when he came out of the coma. He knew then that he was going to die, and I think he was almost glad. It was as if just then he was more peaceful than he'd been any time in years. Just as I was leaving he took hold of my hand and said, 'I'm leaving you the dirty work, Mom. I'm sorry.' That was the last thing he ever . . ."

Bruce's jaws were locked, but he couldn't break down. The old man was already doing too much of that, throwing more strain on her. Chet, sick and lost, had already done too much of that. He stood with his face stiff and dry as paper, with his hand on her shoulder.

"Bruce," she said, "do you believe in a Heaven, a hereafter? That we might see Chet again?"

For a long minute he did not reply. When he did he almost whispered, he was afraid of taking something away from her. "No," he said.

"I guess I don't either," she said. "Ever since he died I've been wondering if I still believed that, but I really don't. It's too much to wish for. It would be too good. I guess I've about come to believing that anything we wish for too much is bound never to happen. Probably it's better that way."

"What can I do?" Bruce asked later. "Are there any arrangements I can take care of?"

"Everything's done."

"Would you like to go down with me, to see him?"

"No," she said. "I've said goodbye. I'd rather you saw him alone."

"I don't like to leave you."

"You go," she said. "I'll be all right. I'll be getting lunch."

"Why don't we go out to eat?"

"It's better when I have something to do," she said.

He took a streetcar to the funeral parlor, spoke Chet's name to the girl in the office, and was directed to the third room on the right. His feet dragged in the deep carpet. Panic mounted in him as he passed the first door, the second. Quick glances, as if he shouldn't look in at all, showed him empty rooms like sitting rooms. The third door was also open. He came up to it slowly, stopped outside, and looked in.

He had had no previous acquaintance with death, and he did not know how it can make an outsider of a living person. From the moment he looked in the door he was ill at ease, an intruder, and the emotion that made him move on tiptoe was not so much grief or fear as embarrassment. Chet lay fully dressed, ready for burial, on the wheeled table under the windows. There were three or four baskets of flowers in the room, and the quiet was so deep that his own breathing bothered him.

For a long time he stood beside Chet simply looking. This was the end of it, then. This was the way you said goodbye, when he was already beyond all goodbyes, beyond hearing you when you said you wished you'd been a better brother, had understood better, had given him a hand when you could. Now that it was too late you wished you could tell him how you'd felt about that cigarette lighter at graduation, when you knew really, without his ever saying so, that he was desperate and sick and lonely, down to his last dime and quarreling with his wife and ashamed of having come crawling back. You wished you believed that he could understand you now as you stood thinking it, how you had really felt that gift, how you had known he was reaching out for you, trying to indicate a love that neither you nor he could ever indicate, and how you were really his friend and brother, you'd stick to him as he was asking you to. This was the way it was, all of it too late. There was that in death which made the living humble and ashamed.

He reached out and touched one of the stiff inhuman hands. "So long, boy," he said softly, and backed out. He was so shaken that he had to go into one of the empty rooms and stand looking out into the dirty snow for a long time before he dared go out through the hushed office and into the street.

The funeral was set for two-thirty. At twelve-thirty Bruce and his mother sat down to lunch alone. "It's probably no use waiting for Pa," she said. "He couldn't eat anyhow."

In the middle of the meal he came in, his eyes bloodshot, his face sallow and sagging, his hands curiously fumbling and helpless. He sat down and began eating as if he tasted nothing.

"Anybody call?" he said.

"Harry Birdsall," Elsa said. "And Mrs. Webb, a woman I met up at Brighton that summer. I haven't heard from her since. It was nice of her to call now."

"None of Chet's friends?"

"No," she said. "Now Bo, don't . . ."

He was already standing, half shouting. "What's the matter with them? Don't they *care?*"

"They probably don't even know," she said. "Please, Bo."

"Why don't they know?" he shouted. "It's been in the papers, hasn't it? The funeral's been listed in the papers. There won't be ten people there."

"They'd all come if they knew," she said. "Chet had lost touch, that's all, he'd been away so long."

He sat down again, heavily, the outburst dying in a kind of groan. He stared down at the dishes on the table, picked up his fork, laid it down again. His eyes came up to Elsa's with a glazed, terrified glare.

"He didn't have a friend in the world," he said.

"Please!" she said again, and put her hand on his. She shot a look at Bruce that asked him to say something, start some conversation, and Bruce grabbed at the first lie he could think of.

"I saw Ham Roberts downtown this morning," he said. "He didn't know, but he's coming. He was pretty badly shocked to hear . . ."

His father's dull voice cut in on him. "I went down to the mortuary," he said. "There were no more flowers there than there were yesterday. Three or four little handfuls."

His face twisted, he stood up again holding the napkin in shaking hands. "I'm going back down now," he said. "If there aren't any more flowers there now I'm going to buy three hundred dollars' worth!"

He had lurched into the hall and got his hat and coat and gone before either of them could speak. The outside door slammed. Bruce looked at his mother. She had her hand over her face.

3

Salt Lake City
Feb. 14, 1931

Dear Bruce,

I suppose that by now you must be taking the examinations you missed by coming home. I hope everything goes well—I know it will. It has been very quiet and lonely here since you left. Neither of us has much heart to do anything. Your dad is better, but he still wakes me sometimes sweating and screaming. He blames himself so much. He's wanted for a long time to do something for Chet and get him back on his feet, but he never did know what it should be, until the sporting goods store came up. He wanted that for Chet, because he thought even an inside job, if it was handling guns and sporting equipment, would suit him. I think it would have, myself. There are so many things we would do, and so many we wouldn't, if we could do it over.

We're leaving Salt Lake for a while to go to Los Angeles. I think it is a good idea, your dad is so miserable here, and everything reminds us both too much of what has happened. We have enough money put away so that we can afford a vacation. Pa is blessing his stars he bought his stocks outright instead of on margin. Everybody we know is losing money hand over fist, and getting sold out. We've lost some, but not everything by any means. I wish . . . but I guess you know what I wish without my telling you.

I'm sending a sweater and some cigarettes for your birthday. We'll go within a week, I think. As soon as we get settled anywhere I'll send you a postcard.

Be careful of yourself, Bruce, and don't work too hard. I know what you're likely to do when there's nobody there to boss you around.

It's just possible that when you come back we may be living permanently in Los Angeles. Your dad talks that way sometimes. He has visions of an orange ranch, but probably those are like the other visions. I guess I must be getting cynical about visions. Still, it would be pleasant to have a home in an orange grove, wouldn't it? I'll keep my fingers crossed.

All my love,
Mother

Los Angeles, March 12, 1931

Dear Bruce,

Well, put the vision of the orange grove away with the others. That would have been too tame for Pa anyhow. He's got a new bug now. In the last couple of weeks he's been feeling much better, and just sitting around has made him nervous. But one thing seems to be pretty well settled. He's going to get out of the liquor business. I suppose I should be glad, and of course I am, that he's pulling out, but what he's probably going into now doesn't make me exactly happy. He's been having conferences for a week with a couple of men from Reno, one of them a Frenchman named Laurent and the other a Basque whose name I can't even pronounce, much less spell. They've got a big deal brewing to open a gambling place in Reno.

Honestly, Bruce, when he comes to me with his plans I don't know what to say. He wants to be encouraged, but how can I encourage him to open a gambling house? I guess I hurt his feelings. I said it looked to me like jumping out of the frying pan into the fire. Then he got mad and said I'd been after him long enough to quit the whiskey business, I ought to be tickled to death.

Maybe I want too much, I don't know. Everything that attracts him seems to be on the wrong side of the law. Of course gambling is legal in Nevada, but there are so many other things that go along with gambling that even though we don't have that fear hanging over our heads all the time we may have something just as bad. Still, it may be some improvement. The trouble is, he'd have to put into it most of what we've saved in the last ten years, and your dad isn't as good a plunger as he used to be. He gets thinking about what might happen if things went wrong, and he goes half crazy worrying. But I think he's about ready to plunge, so I suppose I'd better start getting reconciled to gambling. It isn't a business to be very proud of, but at least its legal, and Pa thinks it will make us a lot of money. If it will, he'll be happy, and that's something. But sometimes I wish we lived on a salary of a hundred dollars a month and never had any hope of more. We might be a whole lot more comfortable in our minds.

So now when he comes around and asks me for the thousand dollars' worth of Utah Power and Light preferred stock he gave me for Christmas two years ago I guess I won't make much of a fuss. He's already been hinting that he'll need them. He can have them, for all of me. I never did think of them as mine, and he never did think he was really giving them to me. The only thing I wanted them for was for you or Chet, and if you get to the point where you need them I'll get them back. Just to tease him, I'm going to make him sign a note for them, or cut me into the profits of the gambling house, or something. Do it all up with legal red tape. I must be getting mean in my old age.

You've been good about writing. And we're both anxious for the time when school is out, so we can get acquainted with our family lawyer.

All love,
Mother

Reno, April 8, 1931

Dear Bruce,

Pretty soon you won't be able to keep track of us at all, we move around so fast. We came on up here to look over the proposition your dad's got on the fire. It was really a nice trip, and I wished all the time that you could have been along. We drove up the coast as far as Monterey, and then over to Merced and up to Yosemite just for the fun of it, to see the gorge in the snow. We stayed all night at the Ahwahnee Hotel (ten dollars apiece per day. I never felt so extravagant!). The snow was going in the canyon, but the cliffs were marvellous and the waterfalls looked as if they burst right out of a glacier. From Yosemite we went back to Merced and then up to Sacramento and the Emigrant Pass and on to Tahoe. There was a lot of snow there, higher than the car in the pass, but the sun was as warm as late spring, and it was lovely. We stopped in another fancy hotel there, where most of the people came down to dinner in tuxedos and evening gowns. I tried to get Pa to stop somewhere else, but when he gets a streak like that there's no holding him, so we dressed up as well as we could and played millionaire. I swear that if your dad had had a tuxedo he would have worn it all the time we were there, breakfast and all. Yesterday afternoon we came down here to Reno and this morning your dad is out looking things over. He's all excited about the deal now. So many divorcees are around, most of them with too much money to spend and too much time to kill, so that the night clubs and gambling houses run twenty-four hours a day. But it's a big gamble. Each of the three will have to put up between fifteen and twenty thousand, cash, and that's a lot of money for us. It will mean selling most of our stock when it's low. Even if we make money, I doubt if this gambling is going to do your dad any good. He thinks it would be pretty dandy to roll in money and hobnob with movie stars and prize fighters, but he wouldn't be comfortable in that kind of company, and I think he knows it at bottom. It's a funny thing, but I keep remembering how contented and good-natured he was all the time he was building that house on the homestead. He went around whistling, and he could get absorbed in his job for hours. Ever since we started making money more than five dollars at a time he acts as if somebody were behind him all the time. But how can you tell him that you think he'd have been three times as happy if he'd stayed a carpenter? And what good would it do now?

He's having fun laying plans, anyway. We'll live in this tourist cottage for a while, but when things get moving he'll buy a lot up on Tahoe or Donner Lake and build us a summer house where I'll stay all the time and he'll come up when he's off shift. It's only a couple of hours up there from here. When he's resting from looking at catalogues of roulette wheels and chuck-a-luck cages and wheels of fortune and crap tables, he's already started looking at motor boat catalogues. The summer home of the well-known millionaire sportsman Harry Mason is already taking shape.

Oh Lord! I guess my main impulse is to laugh. But I'd be glad of a place on Tahoe, so I can't laugh too loud. I don't think I'd do very well as the Madame of a gambling joint.

Sometimes the way we live reminds me of Bill Glassner. Remember him? He used to come around the house a good deal four or five years ago. His whole stock of conversation was "Never a dull moment, eh Bo?" When he got drunk he used to imagine that he was somebody named Scissor-Bill who had pushed Buffalo Bill Cody in the Platte. Never a dull moment, no fooling.

Anyway, if we do build a place on Tahoe, you might have a nice summer. I don't know why you couldn't ask a friend or two from Salt Lake to come down. That might be one blessing of being out from under the law. We could have friends again.

Now I sound like your dad, laying little plots and plans. But maybe this will turn out. It's funny what a few weeks free from pressure will do. I'm ashamed sometimes at how good I feel, when I think of Chet. Laura, I hear, has bought a car with Chet's little insurance money, and has a job as a stenographer. I don't know why she shouldn't buy a car, but it made your dad mad. He thought she owed that to little Anne. But I don't know. Hard as it is to get used to the idea that Chet is dead, I can't help thinking that we owe the living more than we do the dead. I must always have thought that. When my mother died I could have died too, because I loved her more than anyone, but there were Erling and Kristin and Dad and even me, and we were all alive and needed to live. Laura is still young, and has her own way to make now, and she ought to be the best judge of how to do it. Chet is at peace finally. I try to keep remembering that. Pa and I don't talk about it much anymore. He's afraid, somehow.

Here comes Pa now. I suppose we're going out and dine in style at some night club. I'd rather get groceries and cook meals here, but he has to throw his money around for a little while longer. By the time the place opens he'll have a fit of stinginess and I'll probably be taking in washing. Never a dull moment.

All my love,
Mother

4

When Bruce drove west in June, after the frenzy of examinations and the rush to clear out his room, settle his bills, pack the Ford, have a last round of beers with the Law Commons boys, he drove directly from rainy spring into deep summer, from prison into freedom. That day was the first bright warm day in two weeks, and the year was over, he was loose. He watched the sun drink steam from the cornfields, heard the meadowlarks along the fences, the blackbirds in the spring sloughs. Even the smell of hot oil from the motor could not entirely blot out the lush smell of growth.

It was the end of his first year away from home, and he was going back. Ahead of him was the long road, the continental sprawling hugeness of America, the fields and farmhouses, the towns. Northfield, Faribault, Owatonna, Albert Lea, and then west on Highway 16— Blue Earth, Jackson, Luverne, and the junction of Big Sioux and Missouri. Then Sioux City, Yankton, Bridgewater, Mitchell, Chamberlain, Rapid City, the Badlands and the Black Hills breaking the monotonous loveliness of the Dakota plain. Then the ranges and the echoing names: Spearfish, Deadwood, Sundance, the Wyoming that was Ucross and Sheridan and Buffalo and Greybull and Cody, the Yellowstone of dudes and sagebrushers, the Idaho that was the Mormon towns along the Snake: St. Anthony, Rexburg, Sugar City, Blackfoot, Pocatello, and the Utah of Cache Valley and Sardine Canyon and the barricade of the Wasatch guarding the dead salt flats and the lake.

The names flowed in his head like a song, like the words of an old man telling a story, and his mind looked ahead over the long road, the great rivers and the interminable plains, over the Black Hills and the lovely loom of the Big Horns and the Absaroka Range white against the west from Cody.

It was a grand country, a country to lift the blood, and he was going home across its wind-kissed miles with the sun on him and the cornfields steaming under the first summer heat and the first bugs immolating themselves against his windshield.

But going home where? he said. Where do I belong in this? Going home to Reno? I've never been in Reno more than six hours at a time in my life. Going home to Tahoe, to a summer cottage that I haven't ever seen, that isn't even quite completed yet? Or going home to Salt Lake, only to go right on through across the Salt Desert and the little brown dancing hills, through Battle Mountain and Wells and Winnemucca and the dusty towns of the Great Basin that are only specks on a map, that have no hold on me? Where do I belong in this country? Where is home?

Maybe it's Minnesota, because my mother came from here. Certainly I picked Minnesota as a school to go away to, partly because it seemed that I knew it some, having a grandfather in Indian Falls and an aunt and uncle and cousins in Minneapolis, and second and third cousins, and great-aunts and great-uncles, in a dozen towns where Norwegian is still spoken as much as English. Does that make Minnesota home? Maybe I'm going away from home, not toward it.

Or maybe I've never been home. Maybe I'd recognize the country along the Rock River where the old man came from, maybe I'd feel it the minute I saw it. Or maybe I belong back in some Pennsylvania valley, where the roots first went down in this country, where the first great or great-great grandfather broke loose from his Amish fireside and started moving rootless around the continent.

He bounced into the streets of Faribault talking to himself. On a corner he saw a young man squiring two dressed-up girls—altogether too dressed up for this hour of the morning—across the intersection. The earnestness of the young man's attempt to be scrupulously impartial, to offer an arm to each, to keep his head turning on a metronome swing from one to the other, made Bruce laugh.

"There were two pretty maidens from Faribault," he said, and nursed the rhymes along as he edged the Ford through the morning traffic and out into the highway again.

> *There were two pretty maidens from Faribault*
> *Who agreed they would willingly share a beau.*
> *But one beau to a pair*
> *Was no better than fair.*
> *It was worse than just fair, it was taribault.*

Nuts, he said. You ought to go into the Christmas card business. But thereafter he made up limericks for every town he passed through, intoxicating himself on names.

> *A maiden from Alibert Lea*
> *Thought her knee had been bit by a flea.*
> *She lifted her skirt*
> *To see what had hurt,*
> *But it wasn't a flea, it was me.*

It was me, he said, just a boll weevil lookin' for a home. Do I belong in Minnesota? Do I belong in Albert Lea where Kristin went to school? Do I belong in Minneapolis where I go to school and have relations? If I did I wouldn't be so glad to get out of here.

Or is it North Dakota? he said. That's where I was born. Grand Forks, North Dakota, behind the bar in a cheap hotel. I ought to go back some day and put up a fence around that old joint and charge admission to see the birthplace of the great man. What would Jesus Christ have amounted to if he'd been born in a commercial hotel in Grand Forks, North Dakota, instead of in a barn in Bethlehem? Suppose his earliest visitors had been barflies with whiskey breaths instead of sheep and kine with big wondering eyes and breaths of milk and hay? Suppose the Gifts had been brought by drummers instead of wise men?

In a minute he was back on limericks again.

> *A Jesus from Grand Forks, No. Dak.*
> *Went hunting his home with a Kodak.*
> *There were plenty of mansions*
> *And suburban expansions,*
> *But no home, either No. Dak. or So. Dak.*

Well, where is home? he said. It isn't where your family comes from, and it isn't where you were born, unless you have been lucky enough to live in one place all your life. Home is where you hang your hat. (He had never owned a hat.) Or home is where you spent your childhood, the good years when waking every morning was an excitement, when the round of the day could always produce something to fill your mind, tear your emotions, excite your wonder or awe or delight. Is home that, or is it the place where the people you love live, or the place where you have buried your dead, or the place where you want to be buried yourself? Or is it the place where you come in your last desperation to shoot yourself, choosing the garage or the barn or the woodshed in order not to mess up the house, but coming back anyway to the last sanctuary where you can kill yourself in peace?

Still feeling good, bubbling with the sun and wind and the freedom of movement, the smell of the burning oil in the motor like a promise of progress to his nostrils, he let himself envy the people who had all those things under one roof. To belong to a clan, to a tight group of people allied by blood and loyalties and the mutual ownership of closeted skeletons. To see the family vices and virtues in a dozen avatars instead of in two or three. To know always, whether you were in Little Rock or Menton, that there was one place to which you belonged and to which you would return. To have that rush of sentimental loyalty at the sound of a name, to love and know a single place, from the newest baby-squall on the street to the blunt cuneiform of the burial ground . . .

Those were the things that not only his family, but thousands of Americans had missed. The whole nation had been footloose too

long, Heaven had been just over the next range for too many generations. Why remain in one dull plot of earth when Heaven was reach-
able, was touchable, was just over there? The whole race was like
the fir tree in the fairy-tale which wanted to be cut down and dressed
up with lights and bangles and colored paper, and see the world and
be a Christmas tree.

Well, he said, thinking of the closed banks, the crashed market that
had ruined thousands and cut his father's savings in half, the bread-
lines in the cities, the political jawing and the passing of the buck.
Well, we've been a Christmas tree, and now we're in the back yard
and how do we like it?

How did a tree sink roots when it was being dragged behind a
tractor? Or was an American expected to be like a banyan tree or a
mangrove, sticking roots down everywhere, dropping off rooting ap-
pendages with lavish fecundity? Could you be an American, or were
you obliged to be a Yankee, a hill-billy, a Chicagoan, a Californian?
Or all of them in succession?

I wish, he said, that I were going home to a place where all the
associations of twenty-two years were collected together. I wish I could
go out in the back yard and see the mounded ruins of caves I dug
when I was eight. I wish the basement was full of my worn-out ball
gloves and tennis rackets. I wish there was a family album with pictures of us all at every possible age and in every possible activity.
I wish I knew the smell of the ground around that summer cottage
on Tahoe, and had a picture in my mind of the doorway my mother
will come through to meet me when I drive up, and the bedroom I'll
unload my suitcases and books and typewriter in. I wish the wrens
were building under the porch eaves, and that I had known those
same wrens for ten years.

Was he going home, or just to another place? It wasn't clear. Yet
he felt good, settling his bare arm gingerly on the hot door and opening his mouth to sing. He had a notion where home would turn out
to be, for himself as for his father—over the next range, on the Big
Rock Candy Mountain, that place of impossible loveliness that had
pulled the whole nation westward, the place where the fat land
sweated up wealth and the heavens dropped lemonade . . .

> On the Big Rock Candy Mountain
> Where the cops have wooden legs,
> And the handouts grow on bushes,

And the hens lay soft-boiled eggs,
Where the bulldogs all have rubber teeth
And the cinder dicks are blind—
I'm a-gonna go
Where there ain't no snow,
Where the rain don't fall
And the wind don't blow
On the Big Rock Candy Mountain.

Ah yes, he said. Where the bluebird sings to the lemonade springs and the little streams of alcohol come trickling down the rocks. The hobo Heaven, the paradise of the full belly and the lazy backside. That was where his family had been headed for all his life. His father had never gone off the bum. That Bo Mason who had gone bumming in his youth out from Rock River, seeing the big towns and resting his bones in knowledge boxes and jungling up by some stream where the catfish bit on anything from a kernel of corn to a piece of red flannel, was simply an earlier version of the Bo Mason who now fished for big money in a Reno gambling joint and rested his weekend bones among the millionaires on Lake Tahoe.

So when, he said, do we get enough sense to quit looking for something for nothing?

He looked up the straight road running clean and white westward between elms and wild plum thickets, cleaving the wide pastures and fields. The sky to the west was a clear blue, not as dark as it would be beyond the Missouri, and paling to a milky haze at the horizon, but clean and pure and empty, as if there were nothing beyond, or everything. If he hadn't known that beyond the rise limiting his view there was western Minnesota and then Dakota and Wyoming and Idaho and Oregon, if he had been moving through waist-high grass with nothing in his mind but the dream and the itch to see the unknown world, he could easily enough have been a chaser of rainbows. It was easy to see why men had moved westward as inevitably as the roulette-ball of a sun rolled that way. What if the ball settled in the black, on the odd, on number 64? There were so many chances, such lovely possibilities. And if you missed on the first spin you could double and try again, and keep on doubling till you hit it. You could break the bank, you could bust the sure thing, you could, alone and unarmed, take destiny by the throat.

Oh yes, he said. If you don't recognize limits. But that's all over now. That went out with the horse car.

Oh lovely America, he said, you pulled the old trick on us again. You looked like the Queen of Faery, and your hair smelled of wind and grass and space, and your eyes were wild. Oh Circe, mother of all psycho-analysts, you can shut the gates of the sty now. We are all fighting for the trough, and the healing fiction is fading like a dream. Oh Morgain, bane of all good knights, click the iron in the stone, for we know now that what we took for fairy was really witch, and it is time we planned our dungeon days while making friends with the rats and spiders. Oh Belle Dame sans Merci, do you enjoy our starved lips in the gloam?

The music from behind the moon was silent, the lemonade springs were dry, along with half the banks in America. The little streams of alcohol that used to come trickling down the rocks were piped now into the houses of the great, and the handout bushes didn't bear any more and the hens had the pip and the bulldogs had developed teeth and the cinder dicks had x-ray eyes and the climate had changed. So what did you do, if you didn't want to get caught as Bo Mason had been caught, pumped full of the dream and the expectation and the feeling that the world owed you something for nothing, and then thrown into a world where expectations didn't pay off?

He sang again,

> *You're in the army now*
> *You're not behind the plow*
> *You'll never get rich,*
> *So marry the witch,*
> *You're in the army now.*

Oh beautiful, he said, for spacious skies, for amber waves of grain, for purple mountain majesties, and penury, and pain.

Don't you think, he said, that this has gone about far enough? Who are you to philosophize about the problems of a nation? For all the part you or your family have taken in this nation's affairs, you might as well have been living like Troglodytes in a cave. Who are you to mouth phrases, when you don't even belong to the club?

All right, he said, I'll shut up. But I'd still like to join the club, in spite of the Ford Motor Company and the Standard Oil of Indiana and the murder of Sacco and Vanzetti and the emptiness of Main Street. I don't want to bet my wad. I just want to ante.

Oh let us sing, he said, of Lydia Pinkham . . .

Nuts to Lydia Pinkham. Let us sing. Oh what? Of man's first disobedience, and the fruit of that forbidden tree whose mortal taste? No. Arms and the man, who first, pursued by Fate, and haughty Juno's unrelenting hate? Arma virumque canuts. Let us sing of purple mountain majesties. That's what we're always been best at, the land.

The roadside cabins with Simmons beds, Flush toilets, Private showers,

The barns and cribs and coops and sheds, the houses buried deep in flowers,

The towns whose names are Burg and Ville, whose maximum speed is Twenty Mi.

Whose signs point in to the business block to lure the tourists who might shoot by.

"We love our children. Please drive slow." We're also proud of our hybrid corn.

"Registered Rest Rooms. Road maps free. Snappy Service—Just toot your horn."

Ma's Home Cooking and Herb's Good Eats, Rotary every Thursday noon,

Lions Friday. Then straggling streets, the foot on the throttle, the outskirts soon

And the corn again, and the straight flat road, and the roadside split with the wedge of speed,

And the wind of a hurrying car ahead blowing the flit green tumbleweed.

The kids by the roadside who yell and wave. Texaco. Conoco. Burma-Shave:

> *Blighted romance*
> *Stated fully.*
> *She got mad when*
> *He got woolly.*

I'll take it, he said. I love it, whatever good that does. Even if I don't know where home is, I know when I *feel* at home.

At the next service station where he stopped he felt it even stronger, the feeling of belonging, of being in a well-worn and familiar groove. He felt it in the alacrity with which the attendant shined up his windshield and wiped off his headlights and even took a dab at the license plates, in the way he moved and looked, in the quality of his voice and grin. Anything beyond the Missouri was close to home, at least. He was a westerner, whatever that was. The moment he crossed the Big Sioux and got into the brown country where the raw earth showed, the minute the grass got sparser and air dryer and the service stations less grandiose and the towns rattier, the moment he saw his first lonesome shack on the baking flats with a tipsy windmill creaking away at the reluctant underground water, he knew approximately where he belonged. He belonged where the overalls saw the washtub less often, where the corduroy bagged more sloppily at the knees, where the ground was bare and sometimes raw and the sand-devils whirled across the landscape and the barns were innocent of any paint except that advertising Dr. Peirce's Golden Medical Discovery. The feeling came on him like sun after an overcast day, and in pure contentment he limbered his knees and slouched deeper against the Ford's lefthand door.

At sunset he was still wheeling across the plains toward Chamberlain, the sun fiery through the dust and the wide wings of the west going red to saffron to green as he watched, and the horizon ahead of him vast and empty and beckoning like an open gate. At ten o'clock he was still driving, and at twelve. As long as the road ran west he didn't want to stop, because that was where he was going, west beyond the Dakotas toward home.

5

The summer cottage nestled back in a bay in the tall cedars and pines on the east slope of the Big Rock Candy Mountain. The water in front, beyond the strip of gravelly beach, was in the mornings clear emerald, and sometimes at moonset clear gold. Strung out along the shores were the summer homes of the wealthy and comfortable, and of the not-so-wealthy and not-so-comfortable who wished to appear so. A few miles up the road toward the summit was the monument to the Donner Party, symbol of all the agony in the service of dubious cases, archetype of the American saga of rainbow-chasing, dream and denouement immortalized in cobblerock and granite, its pioneer Woman and unconsciously ironic portrait of endurance and grief.

In the cottage, still not finished, its bedrooms only partly partitioned off, its windows still stopped with bent nails, its yard littered with a half-raked-up mess of shavings, nail kegs, ends of two-by-fours, and chips, Bruce and his mother lived for a while a summer idyll.

His mother was proud of the cottage. "Pa built most of it himself," she said. "He had some carpenters put up the studding and the frame, but he sheathed the whole thing, and shingled the roof, and framed the windows and doors, and even made all the inside doors and cupboards, in his spare time. He's been working like a horse every minute—too much, but I think he liked it. Didn't you, Papa?"

"There's still plenty to do," his father said. "You can take off your shirt any time and fall to. Soon as we finish up the inside here we can start landscaping."

He was heavier than when Bruce had last seen him. His cheeks sagged a little, his mouth was rarely without a cigar in it, his columnar neck had softened and whitened, and he had obviously been cultivating a hearty laugh. His plans for the cottage were grandiose. What they had here was just a beginning, turn out to be the servants' wing when they got steaming along. This big room here, with the fireplace, would stay the main living room, but sooner or later they'd build a wing straight off the back, and another wing off that to make a sort of enclosed court—pave it with flagstones for outdoor dining, looking out on the lake. The kitchen and storeroom and laundry room could be built off the other way, where the view was blocked by the woods. Then they'd have some guy come up and plow the yard up and dump on loam, and sow a lawn, and shine the whole grounds up, put in plenty of shrubs and flowers, maybe a little stone terrace. Make it the snappiest place on the lake.

"What do you want to do, make a mansion out of it?" Bruce said. "What's the matter with pine needles for a yard?"

"Hell with that," his father said. "This isn't just any old shanty in the woods. This is a house. Once we get the driveway scraped off and gravelled we can live up here most of the winter, put in a wood-burning furnace. If it gets too cold we can run over to the coast for a couple of months of the year."

"Well," Bruce said. "Give me my orders. I haven't done anything with my hands for so long I've about forgotten how."

Thereafter the two of them worked every morning, nailing in window stops, fitting shutters to the outside frames, lining the interior with wallboard. Bruce protested at the wallboard. "What can you do with it after it's in?" he said. "You can only paint it, and then it'll look like a cheap imitation of a town house. Why not leave the studs showing? It looks more like what it is, then."

"You don't know the seat of your pants from ten cents a week," his father said amiably. "How can you make a room look like anything as long as it's unfinished? You want this place to look like the homestead?"

"That's all right up in the woods."

"Not for me," his father said. "You can build yourself a ratty little shack somewhere if you want. I'm making this one snappy."

"Why not make it really finished, then? Plaster it, put on mouldings, cover the floors, lay in parquetry, go in for indirect lighting and picture windows."

His father made a sound of disgust. He wanted a snappy place, not a shack. But he wasn't going to blow his whole roll on it, either. He'd use his own labor and wallboard instead of lath and plaster, and he would get, Bruce assured him, exactly what he wanted —a compromise, a half-baked thing.

Elsa stayed out of it. She told Bruce that she was saying nothing whatever about how the house should be made unless Bo asked her. He was having so much fun puttering that she'd rather let him jazz the whole place up than protest. He loved building things, it took his mind off Chet and business. Not that he had many business worries. The gambling house was coining money, even with expenses over twenty thousand a month. "He's in the money," she said. "That's where he's always wanted to be. Let him play with it any way he wants. It isn't worth an argument. The lake is so lovely no kind of house can spoil it."

"It's just silly, that's all," Bruce said. "Wallboard isn't necessary at all, but he spends a couple hundred dollars for it that he might have put into something good. Then he has to buy panel strips to cover the cracks. Then he has to buy paint. He just builds up a lot of unnecessary expense. First thing you know he'll be putting in crystal chandeliers."

His mother smiled. "I wouldn't be surprised. What harm does it do?"

Bruce shrugged and let it go. But he couldn't keep from arguing again when his father came out from town with a five-gallon pail of brown paint. "Good Lord," he said, "what do you want to paint it for? Those shakes will weather the loveliest soft gray in about two years."

But within an hour he was swinging a paint brush, and he swung it rebelliously for the next week, putting two coats of oak-leaf brown over the shakes that he would much rather not have touched. He was maliciously pleased at how bad it looked, but his father found nothing wrong with it. He came out, looked it over with approbation, and produced a pail of white for the trim. "How's your painting arm?" he said.

Bruce shrugged. "Now that the place is ruined this far, we might as well finish it."

His father shot him a quick, suspicious glare. "Oh, ruined!" he said. "You got a lot of funny ideas in college. Don't colleges believe in paint?"

"Not in the wrong places. But I'll paint it. It needs it now, as far as that goes." He ducked out of the argument, because every word he said betrayed to the old man the chasm that separated them. It wasn't worth it. He kept his mouth shut when it came time to mix saffron and green shingle stain for the roof. He didn't even open it to squawk at the line of round niggerhead stones that his father one Sunday laid neatly along the edge of the drive, and he was not at all surprised when his father came out the next morning with a paint bucket and painted them all white.

"Give him another week and he'll be putting blue spots on them," he told his mother. "The more he works on this place the more it looks like Camp Cozy."

"He's a good carpenter," his mother said, as if that settled something.

"Sure he's a good carpenter. He's a heck of a good carpenter. He's a cabinet maker. But why doesn't he stick to carpentry or cabinet making, and let somebody whose taste isn't all in his mouth design things? Why does he have to add all these nightmares?"

"He said the stones would outline the drive so people coming in wouldn't run off."

"Who's coming in?" he said. "Once a week, maybe, somebody from Reno. Every other day a delivery truck. What if they did run off? They've got reverse gears on their cars."

She laughed at him. "You're butting your head against a wall," she said. "He'll do it the way he wants, no matter what you or anybody else says."

"And we get blamed for his taste. People drive by and look at the place and hold their noses and say, 'Holy cats, look at the monstrosity.'"

"Do you care?" she said curiously. "Even if it were as bad as you say, which it isn't, would you care? Does it matter that much to you what people think?"

"I don't know. It just makes me mad. The way he has of putting his fingerprints on everything. This place ought to be yours, and look it, not his."

"Ah Bruce," she said. "You're hard on your father."

The expression he saw in her face surprised him. "I'm sorry," he said. "I'm an intolerant lout. Let's go for a swim."

It wasn't worth an argument. His mother was right. And with the old man gone from noon until almost midnight they had the place to themselves. They could swim, fish, putt around the lake in the motor boat. The boat had a mast step in it, and in a few afternoons Bruce cobbled a mast out of a cedar pole, got an old sail from a camper down the lake, and improvised a rig. He was no sailor, but it was fun to come ghosting into the bays over the water that shifted cobalt to emerald, and to hear the silence along the forested shore. A motor was all right, it was a lazy man's way to go boating or fishing. He supposed it matched his old man, somehow. But a sail, even a clumsy and inefficient one, was better. A canoe was better. Even a rowboat was better. The more labor-saving the machinery the less the pleasure. But not for Bo Mason. He believed in modern improvements. Anything that wasn't the latest was an old granny system. He had even come to the point now where an unpaved road was a personal insult, and a detour a deliberate conspiracy to spoil his day. Considering the roads he had driven on in his time, that was quite a step.

His father's was a curious state of mind, Bruce reflected. He and his mother would probably have been content to sit on the pine needles and watch the lake. They would never have finished the cottage inside, or painted it outside, or lined up the driveway, or projected any landscaping. They liked the present, they preferred the static, but for the old man today was only a time in which to get steamed up about tomorrow. The world went forward as a wheel turns, and if you didn't keep up with it you were an old fogy. Your bank account got bigger, your needs became more and more elaborate, your appetites required stronger and stronger stimulation, your ideas of what was your just due became more grandiose. Even the gastro-intestinal tract, he said. Even the amount of laxatives you take to keep your bowels open. Last year one Feenamint, this year two Ex-Laxes, next year three Seidlitz powders. By God, it was laughable. Oh for the to-morrow when you have graduated to Pluto Water. Oh for the day of the daily enema.

Yet he enjoyed those weeks. He liked working with tools, he liked fishing, swimming, sailing. He liked the days when they all went down to Reno. He had fun playing nickels on the chuck-a-luck cage, me-thodically playing the odd and doubling when he lost. He took pleas-ure in the two or three dollars he won every time he went in, and he even got a certain rueful enjoyment out of the cleaning the game took him for when it finally took him.

He played the slot machines and had beers at the bar and watched the crowds mill through the place, jamming up by the crap tables and the Wheel of Fortune and the roulette wheels, thinning out toward the back where the intent games of poker and blackjack and panguingui went on, thinning out still more at the very back, where deadpan Chinamen and professional gamblers sat endlessly playing faro.

He met dozens of gamblers, shills, bouncers. Prize fighters and movie stars and tourists and shrill women surged through the place night and day. When one of the janitors of the club died of a heart attack in the little back room among his brooms and brushes, his father offered him the job, twelve dollars a day for pushing a broom eight hours among the multitudinous feet. He might have taken that job if his mother had not asked him to pass it up.

It took only a few visits to the club to understand his father's excite-ment about the place. There was excitement merely in the stacks of silver dollars on the tables, in the flat chants of the dealers, in the screeches of touring school teachers when they hit the jackpot on a slot machine or won two dollars at craps. There was excitement in the three or four "floor managers," his father among them, who went constantly through the crowd keeping an eye out for pickpockets or slot machine sluggers. The afternoon when a much-advertised fugitive from justice passed a stolen traveler's check at the cashier's window and was picked up at the door by a pair of bouncers, relieved of his shoulder gun, and led off to jail, was a fine and thrilling afternoon.

There was something not so thrilling about what was done with the men who were occasionally caught cheating or slugging a machine. Bruce had seen them two or three times being led quietly downstairs by a pair of husky bouncers, and he had seen the bouncers come back after about fifteen minutes and quietly mingle with the crowd again. None of the tinhorns ever came up. When he asked his father what went on down there his father said the bouncers beat hell out of them and tossed them out into Douglas Alley by a back door.

He could see how the big money, the quick money, the easy money, could take hold on his father. He did not know how deeply it had taken hold until one afternoon when a photographer and a reporter from a magazine came to shoot and investigate the place. Bruce saw his father shouldering through the crowd with his glad-hand smile, his hearty laugh, escorting the photographer around. He saw him laughing with self-conscious playfulness when the photographer stood him up at the edge of the crowd and took a shot of him, summer jacket, stickpin, smile and all. When the article appeared only a couple of weeks later Bo Mason loomed over the crowd, his chin up, his smile gleaming, his hand up in a gesture of greeting or fellowship. The Big Shot. The instant he saw it Bruce was reminded of the night he and Chet graduated from high school and Chet came up to get his football sweater. The same look, the same inability to keep the gratified and self-gratulatory smile off the mouth, the same playing for the gallery. He hated that picture and the things it reminded him of. He didn't want to think of Chet that way.

In July Bruce's mother reminded him that if he wanted to have friends come and stay a while she would be glad to have them, so he wrote to Joe Mulder in Salt Lake, and later in the month Joe and his sister came down. Bruce half expected to have his father object to putting them up. It had happened before. What was the idea of asking everybody in the world to come see you, eat up twenty dollars' worth of food, burn up a lot of gas, cost you a lot of money and waste your time? Let them stay at a hotel if they wanted to stop over. But this time his father even seemed to want them. Perhaps being free of the fear of the law let him loosen up; perhaps he merely was proud of himself and his place and wanted to show off. Anyway, to Bruce's half-cynical surprise, he put himself out. He was jovial at table, he took the visitors for boat rides, he personally escorted them through the club and showed them how to shoot craps, he made booming wisecracks to the dealer so that people looked over at him, and Bruce saw them whisper to each other. Must be the boss. Look at him toss out the bucks, there! Big shot, obviously.

Joe and his sister were delighted. They whirled through Reno like a pair of sand devils. They loved the gambling, they were tickled by the way you could go up to any cop and ask where the nearest speakeasy was and have him direct you. There was no city or state liquor law, and the city cops didn't have any percentage in enforcing federal laws. They loved the mineral springs where Bo took them all swimming, they were full of admiration for how rich Bo Mason was, and they laughed themselves helpless at his wisecracks. Even Bruce, grudgingly, admitted that he was really funny when he got wound up. The night after the swimming Bo was still expansive. He took them out to Steamboat Springs, set them up to dinner, flirted with Helen Mulder and kidded her pink, crooked a lordly finger at the soulful-eyed Mexican with the guitar who was singing sweet sad sentimental songs to the diners, and had him over to sing Helen's favorites. For every song he tossed the Mexican a silver dollar, and for an hour afterward, after he had gone to sing hopefully at other tables, the Mexican kept looking back at the Mason table, showing his teeth and eyes, flirting at a distance with the girl there, hoping that the big man with the diamond would crook his finger again. That was quite an evening. Bo stooped to dance—a thing he had not done in twenty-five years—and he cut his shift at the club.

For a good many weeks there was nothing wrong with that summer. The jazzy excitement of Reno could be sluffed off in the lake's quiet, the hangover of too many cigarettes and too late hours could be dissipated simply by lying under the pines and watching the shifting color of the lake that Mark Twain called the most beautiful in the world. There were books to read and good long hours of puttering with tools, the hands busy and the mind quiet.

The club was still doing well, though the fantastic take of the early summer had fallen off. The prize fight crowd which had come in to watch the Baer-Uzcudun fight, and the Basque sheepherders who had come in in droves to bet money on their woodchopping countryman against the Livermore butcher boy, had flocked out again. Rings still went into the Truckee regularly, and the court house pillars still acquired new smears of lipstick from the grateful mouths of pilgrims, and the kids who planted dimestore rings in the river and then fished them out again to sell to gullible tourists still did a fair business. The town was good, but not as good as it had been. Business at the club fell off just enough to make Bo sit down occasionally to his figuring, to make him curse the neon company that charged twelve hundred dollars for a sign, to make him chew his lips over the two men who came in one afternoon with plenty of money in their pockets and played dimes on the chuck-a-luck cage. In one afternoon they took four hundred dollars out of the game with their little penny-ante bets, and it made Bo mad. There were several things like that. The faro game had a streak of losing, until Bo had half a mind to take faro out of the club entirely. There wasn't enough percentage in favor of the house. A smart gambler could win at it, and most of the people who played it were professionals as slick as the dealers. Yet in the long run you couldn't afford to close out the monte games and lose those professionals.

Increasingly Bo left the finishing of the cottage to Bruce, and even when he did work on the place he was likely to be jerky and irritable, to burst into an inordinate flood of swearing if he made a mistake or couldn't get a joint to fit or hurt his hands. He complained of headaches and sleeplessness.

"Why don't you just rest when you come up here?" Elsa said. "You're down there too much, and then you come up here and work instead of resting. Just sit around and take it easy, or go fishing."

"Yeah," he said. "I'd better do that. No use getting myself run down."

But he couldn't sit still. The first morning he tried it he read the paper for an hour and sat for a half hour more on the porch. By ten thirty he was out in the yard making a bench out of two short lengths of log and a wide slab of pine. It would, he said, make a nice place for anyone to sit down under the trees if they wanted to lazy around in the yard.

Every night the faro game was in the red when checks were counted after the midnight change of shifts. After a week, following a talk with Laurent, Bo fired one of the dealers, a little cold-eyed man who had been a boxer, and hired a dealer newly arrived from one of the gambling boats outside the twelve-mile limit off Long Beach. O'Brien, the dismissed dealer, was sore. He called Bo names and got abusive and violent, until Bo had him thrown out of the place by a couple of shills.

"The God damned guy," he said later up at the lake. "He's been losing at that table ever since he went in there. We pay those cookies twenty bucks a day. That ought to be plenty to make them want to work for the house. What does he want, for Christ sake? I wouldn't be surprised if he'd been chiseling all the time."

"Well, he's fired," Elsa said. "I wouldn't worry about him."

"I'm not worrying about him. The hell with him. I'm worrying about that monte game. We're making money on everything else. If we made money on that we'd be in clover. It takes the profits from two crap tables to pay for that damn thing."

"Doesn't it work in streaks?" she said. "Won't it start winning again sometime?"

"That's what I'm talking about!" he said. "Sure it will. It's got to. But this streak has gone on for three weeks. Can't you understand what I'm telling you?"

"You needn't get mad at me," she said. "I'm not making it lose. I should think if you're going to be a gambler you'd have to make up your mind to take what the luck brings."

In his glare there was something like pity for anyone who could make a remark like that.

The next afternoon Bruce was sitting in a bathing suit on the gunwale of the boat, repairing the cobbled rigging, when his mother came down to the shore. "Can you drive me into town this afternoon?" she said. "I hate to take you away from the lake on such a nice day, but I've got to go in."

"Sure," he said. "Need some groceries?"

He was bending down twisting a wire tight with pliers, and when she didn't answer he looked up. Her face wore a deprecatory grimace, and her eyes were puckered at the corners.

"I've got to see the doctor," she said.

He laid down the pliers. "What for?"

"I'm sorry," she said, and he saw that she was embarrassed. "I didn't tell you. The lumps have been coming back, and I'm taking x-ray treatments. I'd have gone in with Pa, only he went early, and I'd have had to wait till midnight to get back."

"You needn't worry about that," he said. "I'm not doing anything."

He turned to pull the boat further up on the sand. When he stood up and turned she was still standing there, looking at him.

"You should have told me," he said. "How long have you been taking treatments?"

"Since about April." Her eyes puckered still more, and she put her arm around him as they walked up the cottage. "I hate to be a worry and a bother and an expense," she said.

"Nuts to that. Do the treatments work?"

"They take the lumps away, all right, but others keep coming, up in my armpit. They're all just in the skin. I go in once a month. I hate it. They cost like anything."

"Forget what they cost. Don't they give you bad effects?"

"They knock me out a little sometimes." She laughed. "I fainted once. Scared your dad half to death."

"I should think." He opened the screen door for her and shook his fist under her nose. "From now on," he said, "don't you hide things like that from me. You need me to keep you looking after yourself."

She paused on the steps, her blue, clear eyes searching his. Then she patted his hand lightly. "Don't you start worrying," she said. "It's just little nodules under the skin."

But when she went into her bedroom to dress before going into town he sat on the couch and stared into the black empty fireplace and felt the heavy beating of his own pulse. In the one minute when he looked into her eyes by the door he had seen that she knew she was going to die.

6

Three people were in the doctor's office. There would be at least a half hour to wait. "There isn't any use of your waiting around," Elsa said. "I can sit here and read a magazine and you can come back in an hour or so."

"Well," he said, "I've got a few things to buy." He looked at her uncertainly, thinking that there wasn't much chance to talk to the doctor about her as long as she was here. He could go over to the club and see what the old man knew. "I'll just be a little while," he said.

At the club the crowd was even thicker than usual. He pushed his way through it to the cashier's window, leaned on the ledge to look around. His father was not in sight. The cashier, a young Basque who played football for St. Mary's, raised his eyebrows and lifted his head in recognition.

"My dad around anywhere?" Bruce said.

"I thought he went home," the cashier said. He shook his head slightly, as if to say, half-smiling, "Too bad!"

"What for?"

The cashier fished for a cigarette. "You didn't see it, then."

"See what?"

"Come on in," the cashier said. He clicked the lock and pushed the door open. Puzzled, Bruce went in and shut the door after him. "What happened?"

"I thought probably you'd seen it," the cashier said. "Little mixup. O'Brien came around with a gun and a pair of brass knucks."

"The faro dealer?"

"Was. Your dad canned him, that's what he was mad about. He got a few drinks in him and came over to clean up."

"What'd he do?"

The cashier seemed embarrassed. "Knocked the old man down," he said. "Right over in front of the slot machines. Old man wasn't expecting anything. They were just standing there arguing a little when O'Brien let one fly." He looked at Bruce sidelong. "Give them an even break, your old man'd bust him in two," he said. "He wasn't expecting anything."

"Don't apologize," Bruce said. "A guy half his size knocked him down."

"Knocked him kicking," the cashier agreed. "Hung a shiner on him big as a plate. Course he's younger than the old man, and in better shape. Couple shills grabbed O'Brien and took him down cellar, but Pete's a pretty good friend of O'Brien's. I imagine they just opened the door and turned him loose in the Alley."

"Yeah," Bruce said. He looked out through the grilled window at the milling people, men with straw hats on the backs of their heads, coats over their arms; dealers in long eyeshades bending, reaching, leaning back to let their mouths go loose on the interminable chants. Right over in front of the slot machines, right in the middle of the crowd, with a couple of hundred people around, the Big Shot had been knocked silly by a little bantam who came to his shoulder. It was funny. It made him want to laugh right out loud.

But he didn't laugh right out loud. He was ashamed and furious, and he hated the apologetic cashier who really wanted to laugh, who was outside it and could laugh, but who didn't quite dare laugh in the face of the boss's son.

"You think he went back up to the lake?"

"I don't know," the cashier said. "He left here with a towel over his eye. I supposed he was going to a doc. If I had that eye I sure wouldn't be around at work for a day or two."

"I suppose I'd better get on back and see how he's doing," Bruce said. He nodded to the cashier and let himself out.

In the hot bright street the traffic was thick. Cars coated with dust from the desert nosed into the curb to let out women in bloomers and wrinkled blouses and men in creased plus-fours. But the traffic and the blare of horns and the heat and the hot tourists and the light blazing up from the sidewalk were out beyond Bruce, beyond arm's length, and between them and his eyes was the image he had had ever since he stepped out of the office, the image of his father, summer jacket, stickpin, heavy dark face, Big Shot air, going down kicking under O'Brien's fist, and the surprised look on his face, the purpling skin, the expression of heavy struggling impotence and rage and consternation. It was not a pretty image; it made him crawl. In spite of the heat, he walked very fast back to the doctor's office.

His mother was not in the waiting room. He peeked through the door and saw her sitting in a muslin gown, one shoulder bare, with her breast pressed against a little window in the wall. She turned her head at his step, and smiled at him, making a little face.

"How's it going?" he said.

"All right. I'll be through in about ten minutes."

"I'll wait outside here."

Lips smiling, eyes puckered, she made her deprecatory face again. "I'm a nuisance."

"You're terrible," he said. "I don't see how I stand you."

He went out and sat down, tried to read a magazine, put it down to stare at the white wall. His father's humiliation was as raw in his mind as if he himself had been knocked down. He found himself hating O'Brien. A damned little hard-eyed chiseler, a borderline gangster, a brainless tough guy. Yet the old man had probably earned what he got. He couldn't fire anybody without insulting him. He'd sit at home and worry about the monte game and work himself into a fury, and probably snoop around when O'Brien was on shift, and make his suspicions perfectly plain, and then finally he would take out all his dissatisfaction on O'Brien, make him the goat. You could hardly blame the dealer for getting sore.

So maybe this is better than bootlegging, he said. So this is legal and no cops knock on your door late at night. But you play around with the same cheap people, the same flashly men with big rolls, the same cheap squaws. You get yourself into a situation where somebody swings on you or takes a shot at you in the alley, and when you get up off the floor with your eye pickled and the crowd gaping at you you haven't even got a sense of outraged virtue to lean on. All you've got is the officious sympathy of flunkeys who will dust off your clothes and get a towel for your eye and laugh after you're gone, and you know they're laughing because anybody likes to see a big shot taken for a ride.

He got up from the chair and looked in the door again. His mother sat patiently, her forehead against the wall, her mutilated breast exposed to the healing eye of the window.

God damn, he said miserably.

On the way to the lake she lay back in the seat with her eyes closed, her face paper-white and pinheads of perspiration on her upper lip. The smell of ozone clung in her hair. Bruce drove fast, looking at her now and again, afraid that she had fainted, but when he said, "You feel all right, Mom?" she opened her eyes and smiled and said, "Sure, I'm all right. I just feel a little weak is all."

"You go to bed when we get back, and stay there."

Her only reply was a mild, withdrawn smile, as if the effort of moving her lips were almost too great, and in a kind of terror he started up the long, swinging grade. The smell of ozone that clung to her was like the odor of disease, and looking at her he felt that with that mild smile on her face and her eyes closed she was contemplating the battleground of her own body, warring cells going crazy, multiplying, proliferating, spreading and crowding out the healthy cells, leaving her less and less of herself. A body completely replaced itself in seven years, but that was done to pattern, according to a plan. This was something else, an insane crowding of formless hostility, a barbarian invasion, blotting out the order and the form and the identity, transforming it into a shapeless thing that was not his mother at all, but an unidentified colony of cells, functionless and organless and hopeless. For one blasted moment he stared at her in panic, almost expecting her to bulge and puff and swell, lose her features, change into a grotesque horror before his eyes.

She sat with closed eyes, her lips together, breathing quickly but softly through her nose. The crowsfeet of laughter were not gone even in repose from the corners of her eyes.

The new LaSalle was in the garage when they pulled up under the pines. The good mountain smell came down across the cove, and the lake wrinkled under the wind. Stepping down to help his mother from the car, Bruce set his foot on one of the white stones with which his father had lined the drive, and he swore under his breath. "Feel all right, or do you want to rest a minute?" he said.

"I'm all right." She stepped out and stood straight. "It never lasts very long." She looked along the curve of bright lake shore where the slant sun glittered off the water and glanced on the red-brown trunks of the trees flanking the house. "It would be pretty hard not to feel all right up here," she said. "It was hot in town, that was all."

"Bed for you anyway," he said, and steered her up the steps. He was hoping that the old man would be off in bed or somewhere. But the first thing he saw as they stepped into the living room was his father, sitting in the big chair by the window, a white pad over one eye and his other eye glaring at them, bloodshot and furious. He said nothing when they came in, but jerked in his chair.

"Bo!" Elsa said. She broke from Bruce's hand and crossed the room, laid a hand on Bo's head above the bandage. He flinched irritably away. "What happened?" she said.

"Isn't it clear enough what happened?" he said. "I got a black eye."

"Oh." She stood for a moment, steadying herself by a chair back. "Have you been to a doctor? Have you had it fixed?"

"Did you think I patched this thing on myself?"

"Come on," Bruce said, and took her arm again. "You're feeling pretty rocky yourself. You go and lie down."

But she held back. "Bo," she said. "Who?"

He jerked around in the chair again and his one visible eye glared out the window. His teeth were bitten together, almost chattering. Here we go, Bruce thought almost wearily. He's been humiliated and now he's mad, and he'll take it out on anybody within reach. He pulled at his mother's arm.

"You're supposed to lie down."

"But your dad is hurt," she said. "Let me be a minute."

"Go and lie down!" Bruce said, suddenly furious. His mother looked at him, glanced at Bo, frowned as if a pain had hit her, and went silently into the bedroom. Bruce, turning from watching her go, found his father's bloodshot eye fixed hard on him.

"What in Christ's biting you?" his father said.

"She's sick," Bruce said. "She just had a treatment and I thought she was going to faint all the way home. She's in no shape to doctor anybody, or even talk to anybody."

His father glared a moment longer, then turned away with a grunt.

"If there's anything you need done to your eye," Bruce said, "I'll do it."

His father didn't bother to answer.

For almost a week the old man sat around the cottage reading the papers, figuring, sprawling back in the chair while Elsa fixed poultices for the injured eye. By the third day the soreness was gone, but the flesh from his cheekbone to his nose was swollen and purple, with a streak of dull yellow along the upper eyelid. Every time he looked in a mirror he swore, and when he got up on the fourth morning and found that the other eye had developed sympathetic purple and yellow streaks he was untouchable for hours. He got the idea that sunlight was good for it, and sat in the yard with his face tilted back, but if a delivery truck came into the drive, or walkers passed along the lake front, he turned his head away, or raised a newspaper in front of his face, or went inside.

Bruce was cynically amused. "He looks like one of those obscene colored baboons," he said. "A sensitive baboon who can't stand his own looks."

"That's not a very nice thing to say."

Bruce shrugged.

"You don't feel a bit sorry for him, do you?" she said.

"I guess not."

She shook her head, and her voice was almost pleading. "There's nothing shameful about being knocked down by a person half your age."

"And half your size," he said.

"O'Brien used to be a prize fighter," she said, "and your dad is pretty close to sixty years old, did you realize that?"

"I can't help it," Bruce said. "If he's sixty he ought to be the sort of person of sixty that you just don't hit in the eye."

She shook her head, her mouth sad. "You're hard. I guess I don't understand how you can be that hard."

He knew he ought to stop. He was hurting her, and he didn't want to. But he kept on anyway. "Maybe I'm getting even," he said. "Maybe I remember once when he broke my collarbone knocking me over the woodbox, and once when he rubbed my nose in my own mess."

She was looking at him startled, close to tears. "I knew you remembered that," she said. "You never forget anything, do you? You never make allowances for hot temper or anything."

"Forget it," Bruce said. "I don't really hold that against him. I just get sick and tired of all his airs and his self pity."

"Sometime you'll learn," she said. She turned away and began pushing the carpet sweeper over the rug, talking straight ahead of her, not at him. "Some day you'll learn that you can't have people exactly the way you want them and that a little understanding is all you need to make most people seem halfway decent. What you don't understand is that your dad is ashamed to death."

"What you don't understand," Bruce said, "is that I'm ashamed too."

She turned and their eyes met for a moment. "Yes," she said finally. "Of course. So am I. But I'm more sad than ashamed. I know your father better than you do, and I know that just one thing, one little disgrace like that, is about all that's needed now to make an old man of him. He isn't young any more. Everything goes down from here. I don't think it ever occurred to him before that he wasn't just as young and just as strong as he ever was."

"What that means," Bruce said, "is that he'll come to you all the more to be babied."

He knew he ought to be slapped, but his mother merely looked at him with her eyes clouded. Then she turned again and took up the handle of the cleaner. "I babied you too," she said. "I couldn't have lived with you if I hadn't."

On Sunday a long convertible pulled up in the drive and the Frenchman, Laurent, slid his fat stomach from behind the wheel. Bruce, down on the shore sawing up driftwood, saw him waddle up on the porch and go in, and he deliberately stayed away until Laurent was gone. Then he took the bucksaw up to the garage, got a bottle of beef from the icebox, and came through the living room to the front porch with it. His mother and father were talking in the living room. "Yes," his father said, "but they've got to honor their notes. If they don't, we can collect from whoever signs them. That part of it's all right."

"Wouldn't they think there was something wrong if you both . . ."

"We've got the books. We can prove it to them, can't we? We've been making money."

"I should be getting dinner," she said, as Bruce went through the front door. "You hungry, Bruce?"

"Not so hungry I can't wait a while. I'll wait out here."

From the porch he watched the lake between sips of beer. A speedboat cut across the cove leaving an emerald and white wake, and after three or four minutes the waves began to slap on the beach. It was a good place, a quiet place, a lovely place—but he was already getting a little restless. Doing nothing all summer was a little wearing. He should have got a job. Still, it was the middle of August now. In another month he'd be threading the Ford into the sun's eye across the desert.

So you're capable of staying in one place two months and a half before you get jumpy, he said. You're the guy who was looking for a home. He shifted himself comfortably and let it go. The hell with a home. You had to get out and do something, not just vegetate and sail and saw wood.

His parents were still talking inside; it was an hour before his mother called him to dinner. The old man, sitting at the dining room table, had a pencil and paper and was figuring. He figured until he had to move to make way for a plate.

"No," he said. "I'd be a sucker to get out just when things are rolling smooth.

"What's up?" Bruce said. "Are we planning to move?"

"Laurent's got an offer for his third interest," his mother said. "Some gamblers from Denver want to buy in."

"Doesn't he want to sell?"

"He isn't sure. Pa got talking with him and figured that he might sell if Laurent didn't want to."

"I thought the place was making money."

His father's face across the table was heavy and thoughtful. The discolored flesh around his eye made him look as if he were wearing a mask. "I don't know," he said. "I'm damned if I do. It's made money so far, but there's no telling what it'll do in winter. It's bound to fall off."

"What would you do if you sold?"

"How do I know?" his father said irritably. "I could find something, I guess."

Out of the corner of his eye Bruce caught his mother's glance, and bent to his food. Her look and the expression on the old man's face were equally clear. The club was getting him down. He'd been scared of it from the beginning, it was too big a gamble, he wasn't up to gathering the gold off the Big Rock Candy Mountain once he got there. It weighed him down, it worried him, the excitement it gave him was tinged with fear. He was riding a tiger, and he knew he wasn't the man to do it. It was a sure thing the old man wanted, not a gamble.

But that, Bruce said to himself, wasn't the biggest reason why the old man was toying with this chance to get out while he was still ahead. As much as anything else, it was that eye, the humiliation of going back after ten days of hiding and having the dealers and shills and steady customers look at him sideways. It was the fear he had of coming back a soiled big shot.

Like Chet, Bruce said. Just exactly like Chet. He'd blow this money-making club in a minute to save his pride, only he'd never admit why he was doing it. After working up—or down—to something like this all his life he'd sell out just because a little tinhorn hit him in the eye.

"How much has the place made in the last six months?" he said.

"It's only been running four," his father said. "I don't know exactly. We put in fifteen thousand apiece. These Denver guys are offering eighteen for a third interest. It's worth more than that. I expect I'm ahead about eight thousand in four months, if I could sell my third for twenty thousand."

"Rate of twenty-five thousand a year for each of you," Bruce said. "You can't gripe at that, except when you come to pay your income tax."

His father laughed. "Income tax!" he said.

"Have you ever paid an income tax?"

"No," his father said, "and I don't intend to."

"Some day they'll haul you off to the pen for three years."

"They've got to catch me first," his father said.

Bruce buttered his roll and laid his knife down. "I'll bet there isn't a family like ours in the United States," he said. "You've never paid an income tax. Did either of you ever vote?"

"I never did," his mother said. "Isn't that awful? I never knew enough about it to make the effort."

"I guess I voted once," Bo said. "Back in Dakota. How long ago? Twenty-five years? Nearer thirty, I guess."

"Ever serve on a jury?"

"No."

"There we are," Bruce said. "Two of us have never voted, and the other one voted once, thirty years ago. We never lived in any house in the United States for more than a year at a time. Since I was born we've lived in two nations, ten states, fifty different houses. Sooner or later we're going to have to take out naturalization papers."

"And now we might move right out of here," his mother said, "just about the time we get the cottage finished up. Wouldn't that be typical? Let's not sell this place, Bo, even if you do sell out of the club."

"This is headquarters," Bo said. "I've paid taxes on this already. That ought to make us permanent residents."

"Do you think you will sell out of the club?" Bruce said.

"If I got a good enough offer I might. I've got a feeling this whole racket is going to be a flash in the pan."

Bruce laughed. "Here we go round the prickly pear," he said.

"What?"

"Nothing."

His mother rose to clear the table for dessert, and he saw her wince. "What's the matter?" he said.

"Oh, my darned hip!"

"What's the matter with your hip?"

"I don't know. Rheumatiz, I guess. I must be getting old."

She made her special face and limped like an old crone into the kitchen. Across the table Bruce's eyes met his father's, and he saw the question there that he knew must be in his own. And the fear.

Thereafter he had two things to watch, one working in his father and one in his mother. His father's problem he did not worry about. It made no great difference to him whether the old man sold the club or not, except as it might affect his mother. But his mother's condition was another thing. Once he had noticed that she was hiding a pain, he couldn't seem to look up without catching her wincing or favoring one side—the same right side always. Her appetite was like a bird's, and she got out of breath easily.

"Maybe it's the altitude," he said. "Maybe this is too high for you."

"Oh, it isn't anything. I'm getting old and rickety, that's all."

But he watched her, and he saw that now in the afternoon she lay down for a rest, something she had never done as far back as he could remember. And when the old man powdered up his discolored cheek and went into town he heard her ask him to bring out some sleeping pills. The fear that made him sensitive to her least gesture of weariness or pain made him pretend with her. He kidded her about her rheumatiz, told her that all she needed was a little exercise, like a nice dip in the lake. When she took him up he was horrified and wouldn't let her. The lake was getting too cold. Finally he compromised on a mild walk, but when they came back she was out of breath, weak, her mouth set in a hard line. They had walked less than a mile.

"Your hip?" he said.

"I guess I'm not much good any more."

"You're going in and see the doctor."

"Oh, fiddlesticks," she said. "It's nothing but a little stitch. Probably I've got an abscessed tooth or something."

"It wouldn't do any harm to find out."

"All right," she said. "If it will make you feel better I'll go, next time I go in."

She lay down and rested for an hour while he sat in the sun and whittled aimlessly. At five-thirty his father came back. "Well," Bruce said. "Sell the gold mine?"

His father hesitated on the step as if debating whether to sit down and talk or go inside. "I can make a deal, I think, if I want to. Where's your mother?"

"Lying down."

"Sick?" His father's face turned sideways to look at him with a fixed, almost vacant expression.

"Her hip's hurting her."

The old man chewed his lip and took off his hat. His hair, Bruce noticed, was getting thin, and he was almost white above the ears. "What the devil you suppose that is?" he said. "It just seemed to come on all of a sudden."

"I know what I'm scared it is," Bruce said.

His father's eyes wandered away. He tapped his hat against his trouser leg. His lips moved slightly, and he blinked his eyes.

"I'm taking her in to the doctor tomorrow," Bruce said. "There just isn't any point in not finding out."

"Yeah," his father said. He flapped the hat against his leg. "Yeah. Well. . . ." He went up the steps and into the house. Bruce followed him, almost as if he were guarding his mother, keeping people who were worrying about selling gambling houses from bothering her with their problems.

She was still, apparently, lying down. They went together down the little hall between the partitions and looked in the door of her bedroom. She lay face downward on the bed, and as they looked they could see her body writhe.

"Mom!" Bruce said. He jumped to the bed and knelt, his arm over her shoulder. "Mom, for God's sake!"

Her shoulder stiffened. For a moment she kept her face in the pillow. Then she turned it and smiled, and he saw that her cheeks were wet. "I'm a baby," she said.

Bruce looked at his father, irresolute at the foot of the bed. The old man wet his lips and came closer. "Maybe," he said, "maybe you ought to take a couple aspirin."

She smiled again, and as she shifted on the bed the smile froze whitely against her teeth. "I've taken . . . six," she said.

"Damn it," Bruce said wildly. "Why didn't you call me?"

"I couldn't seem to . . . make much noise."

Without saying goodbye or where he was going, Bruce went out of the bedroom, walking fast, running as he hit the back steps. The Ford was blocked into the garage by the LaSalle, so he took the LaSalle. As he roared out the drive he saw his father run to the front door to look after him. At the paved highway he didn't even bother to wonder which way he was going to turn. He just turned. There were cottages, stores, little centers for groceries and boats and fishing tackle, in both directions on that side. He let the LaSalle out, and was startled at how fast it leaped under him, how smoothly it ran, with hardly a sound except an eager low humming. His foot was almost to the floor when he saw the first store, and he rode the brakes through the loose gravel of the turn-out. A man came running out of the service station with a pail in his hand, as if he were going to a fire.

Bruce leaned out the window and shouted. "Know of a doctor close around here?"

"Might try the C.C.C. Camp," the man said. "Know where it is?"

"No."

"Go right on. Exactly seven tenths of a mile, I measured it. There's a sign . . ."

He took his foot off the running board and Bruce slammed the car into second. The gravel spattered. Bruce's hand went onto the horn and stayed there as he swung around a party of girls parked at the roadside with a flat tire. They started to flag him down, and stood with upraised arms and opened mouths as he roared by. At exactly seven tenths of a mile a road wriggled off into the timber, and he tramped on the brakes and careened in. Back in the timber a half mile he came to four long low barracks, one of them with a flagpole in front. A man in army uniform was sitting at a desk inside.

"Is there a doctor here?"

"Not right now," the officer said. "He went into Carson this afternoon. Ought to be back by now."

"Damn!" Bruce said. He was panting as if he had run all the way from the cottage. "You haven't got any morphine or anything here, have you?"

"The doctor'd have to give you that," the officer said. He rose from behind the desk. "What's the matter?"

"My mother's in a hell of a pain," Bruce said. He looked at the officer and saw that the officer thought he was out of his head. It wasn't worth explaining. "Could you ask the doctor to come over when he gets back, if he comes in the next hour?"

The officer nodded, then lifted his hand and made a motion of shooting a revolver at the door. "Here he is now," he said.

Bruce was at the car door before it could open. "Can you come over and look at my mother?" he said. "She's had cancer—carcinoma—had an operation for it. Now she's got awful pains in her hip. I don't know what they are. She's been taking x-ray treatments . . ."

"Wait a minute," the doctor said. He was in army uniform like the man in the headquarters building. "I'll get my bag."

He stepped out and walked with what seemed callous slowness into the building. In five minutes he came out, closing his black bag. "You lead," he said. "I'll follow along."

"I can take you and bring you back."

"No thanks. I'll drive my own."

To the officer, standing before the building, he said, "Tell that lousy cook to keep my dinner warm, Harry."

She was still in pain when they got back. Bo Mason sat at the head of the bed holding her hand, looking helpless and clumsy. He got up when the doctor came in, and stumbled against the chair. The doctor set his bag where Bo had been.

"Hello," he said to the woman on the bed. "Having a little pain, eh?"

To Bruce he said, "Can you put a tablespoon in a pan of water and boil it a couple minutes?"

Bruce went out, and his father followed him. "Where'd you find him?" he said.

"C.C.C. Camp."

"Couldn't you get anybody better than that? He's probably some horse doctor."

"I don't give a damn," Bruce said. "He can give her a shot of something. I was just looking for somebody quick, and he was the quickest." He filled a pan with water and threw a spoon into it. Leaving it on the burner, he went back into the bedroom. The doctor had his mother bare to the waist and was pressing with his finger tips under her arm, feeling down the scarred side, over the bulge of her hip bone. Bruce turned away. But when the doctor had covered her again, without comment, and gone into the kitchen to sterilize a needle, and came back with a hypodermic full of brownish liquid, he watched, because that was what he had got the doctor for. The needle stabbed in, a slight bump of liquid swelled under the skin.

"That will fix you for a while," the doctor said. "You'll sleep a good while, probably. Then you'd better go in and see somebody in town."

She nodded. "If she wakes up," the doctor said to Bruce, "give her some orange juice or broth or milk, anything. If she doesn't wake up for a long time don't worry."

He pulled the quilt across her. "I wouldn't even bother to undress," he said. "You're getting sleepy already."

"I can feel it in my tongue."

"You'll feel it all over in a minute," he said. He went out and held the door open for Bruce and his father, shut it quietly.

"How long since her operation?"

"A year and a half," Bruce said.

"Umm."

"What is it?" Bo Mason said. "What could be giving her pains like that way down in her hip? She's awful hard to hurt. I never saw her cry for pain in my life before. . . ."

His voice was almost babbling. The skin of his face was slack. The doctor shrugged and shook his head.

"You'd better get her in to a specialist," he said. "I wouldn't want to say, but my guess would be that it's a secondary growth. When that stuff gets so far along it breaks off and the bloodstream carries it around. You say she's been short of breath?"

"For the last month or so," Bruce said.

"Sounds like lungs too. Probably she'll have to be tapped."

"Has she got a chance?" Bo said.

The doctor looked at him a moment. "I doubt it," he said.

She slept until past noon the next day, and when she finally awoke, fuzzy-tongued and drowsy-eyed, she had apparently been dreaming. Her mouth was drooping and sad. That evening she asked Bo if they could go back to Salt Lake.

"Salt Lake?" he said. "What for?"

"I want to," she said.

"I don't know why you'd want to go back to that smoky hole for the winter when we could go to L.A. or somewhere."

"Bo," she said. "Couldn't we? Even if you don't sell your share in the club, couldn't we?" She took his hand and held it, watching his face. "That's where Chet is," she said, and Bruce saw that it shamed her to have to tell him. She was going to die and they all knew it. The next morning, his face gray and haggard, Bo went down and without a word to anyone closed the deal for his share of the club.

Bruce closed up the cottage by himself, refusing to let his mother get up. His father had gone down to the coast, vaguely on business, and would meet them in Salt Lake. It was clear enough what he was going for. With the club sold, the notes of the Denver gamblers laid away to mature, the move back to Salt Lake coming up, his mind frayed and undone, he turned naturally and immediately back to whiskey. It would give him something to do, it would bring in a little cash.

"By hell, it would make me laugh if it didn't make me want to kill him," Bruce said to his mother. "What if we get raided in Salt Lake? That would be a fine help to getting you well, wouldn't it? Why couldn't he wait till you got back on your feet, at least?"

"He'd just sit around and stew himself to death if he didn't have something to keep him busy," she said. "I don't care. He's better off doing something, even that."

She was thinner, a week had made her thinner, and her cheeks looked sunken, but her eyes were still a sudden and incredible blue, unmisted by sickness. "You're not going to be too comfortable going across in the Ford, either," he said. "He might have thought of that."

She shook her head and smiled. "Don't worry about me. You help us get moved and then you go back to school and be the head of the class."

"Head of the class," Bruce said. "I've been head of the class quite a lot, haven't I?"

"You have," she said, and the pride in her voice made him crawl. "You've got a good head. You can be an important man if you try, Bruce."

"Will you promise to come and live at the White House?" he said. With a fury that was close to tears he went back to his half-finished packing. There were only two possibilities that he would go back to school this fall. One was that she would die before school opened. The other was that he would deliberately leave her to die with only the old man for company. He would have cut his throat before he would have agreed to either.

They were packed for two days, waiting, before they had word from Bo. He wired from Salt Lake that he had taken an apartment and that they should come on. In the afternoon a truck came and got their freight. The next morning at six, with the woods all around them showing the first fall color and the lake a sheet of pure emerald and the eastern sky so pure and blue it hurt the eyes, they started down the Big Rock Candy Mountain for home, for Salt Lake City, for the spot where the dead was buried and the living would die, and there was for Bruce none of the exhilaration that had blown him westward in June, though he was now more truly than then going home.

IX

All through September she lay dying in the dark little apartment, in the bedroom through whose open windows in the morning Bruce could smell the bitter tang of the winter pall of smoke, coming down now, settling in the evenings and lasting until the valley breeze cleared it out about noon. Through those windows, when he came in at six or seven o'clock to find his mother wide awake, awake for no one knew how many hours, maybe all night, he could see the thin morning sun touching the back lawn of the apartment house opposite, and the yellowing leaves of the hickories along the sidewalk, like sunlight cut into long ovals.

But no sun touched the bedroom. It was gloomy even at mid-day, and more than once Bruce felt like kicking the windows out of their frames, tearing down the curtains, pushing the wall out to let one sweep of sun and light cleanse the room. The very air in the place was the color of patience and pain. The old man might at least, he thought, have found her a pleasant room to die in.

He told her so, obliquely. "A pleasant room to be sick in," he put it, but she smiled at him from the bed, trying to braid her long hair with fingers that tired after a few motions. "It's a nice enough room," she said. "It could be more cheerful, but then your dad never did have much of an eye for what made a house pleasant."

"No," Bruce said. "Here, let me do that."

He took the rope of hair from her and braided it, found a rubber band for the end of each braid, and lifted her while he smoothed out sheets and pillow. "Now what for breakfast?" he said. "How about some ham and eggs this morning?"

Her smile was like the smile of a very old, very wise, very gentle grandmother. "Maybe some orange juice," she said.

"Nothing else?"

"I'm not hungry, really."

Seeing how thin she had grown, he said miserably, "You need to eat to get your strength back," and he saw in her eyes, the bright, incredibly blue eyes, unmarked and clear, that she was smiling inside herself at the idea of getting her strength back. If she pretended not to know that she was going to die, she did it to spare him, not herself.

"No milk?" he said. "Some milk toast, maybe?"

"No thanks. Just some orange juice. Don't go to any trouble."

"I'll bring you in an orange and you can peel it yourself," he said. He took the tray from the bed table and went into the kitchen. Orange juice, when she had hardly eaten anything for ten days! He squeezed a big glass of orange juice, poured a glass of milk just in case it might tempt her, opened the icebox door and got out some grape juice for the same reason, scooped a dish of bright jello. The icebox was full of invalid's dishes that he had made and never got her to eat. He ought to give it up, he thought, lifting the tray. He ought to quit urging her to eat, let the weariness take her, shorten it for her. But how could he? She didn't want it that way. She wouldn't deliberately shorten her agony one second.

Play it out till the whistle blows, he said bitterly, and hardened his mouth at that football-field stupidity that was here somehow present in his mother and that he could neither fight against nor condemn. Sixty to nothing against you and the other team with a first down on your five yard line, but play it out, break your neck on that last tackle in the end zone. That was the way she had done it all her life, and there was no changing her.

His father was in the sickroom when he came back, standing near the door looking big and uneasy and out of place, his lips forming the platitudes that were all he could ever say to her now. How you feeling this morning? Having any pains? And, stooping to look out the window. Nice day again outside.

He moved aside when Bruce came with the tray. His eyes were bloodshot and wandering. "There you are," Bruce said. "Let's see you clean that tray."

She laughed. "My goodness, I can't eat all that."

Bo Mason wagged his head, and Bruce hated him for his fumbling bulk, his stupid, vague embarrassment. "You want to eat," he said, and catching Bruce's eye he almost flushed.

At least he feels it, Bruce said. At least he feels frozen out. Nobody wants him around, and he knows it. And by God he's earned it.

"Well," the old man said, and looked out the window again. "Going to be a nice day." He moved toward the door. "Anything you want from town?"

"Are you going down already?" she said. "You haven't had breakfast yet."

"I can get something downtown."

"There's plenty of stuff here," Bruce said. "I'll fix something in a minute."

Nothing to do, he thought. No place to go. But he has to rush out of here before breakfast, just so he can hang around cigar stores and hotel lobbies all day.

He watched his mother sip her orange juice. "Come on," he said, "let's get out of here and let Mom eat in peace." He went into the kitchen and started breakfast. He was just putting the toast in the toaster when he heard his mother in the bedroom, and ran in. Leaning back against the pillow wiping her lips, she gave him a weak, apologetic smile. "I'm sorry," she said. "I couldn't keep it down."

"Feel all right now?"

She nodded, and he took the pail into the bathroom. Not even her orange juice this morning. Worse and worse.

"Pa," he said when he came back. "I think we ought to get a nurse for Mom, till she gets back on her feet."

"You're better than any nurse," his mother said. "Unless you get tired of taking care of me." She wiped her lips, puckered her eyes at him. "You're stuck in this apartment too much," she said. "But I don't need a nurse. I guess I can still do a few things for myself."

"And tire yourself all out," Bruce said. "I don't know how to take care of you right."

"You take care of me beautifully," she said. "A nurse would be expensive, too."

"Only six dollars a day."

"Six dollars a day!" his father said. He seemed suddenly angry, the indecision and helplessness dissolved in violence. "My God, doesn't that show you? The minute anybody gets sick there's ten million vultures waiting to pounce. What makes a nurse worth six dollars a day?"

"See?" Elsa said. "It's out of the question. Now why don't both of you go out and get some fresh air? You don't want to stick around with me all day."

"Yeah?" Bruce said. "What if you got a pain?"

"I guess I could stand it. Maybe you could pull the telephone close, and if I need anything I could call Mrs. Welch."

"What does she know about giving hypos?" He looked at his father, and it was with difficulty that he kept his voice down. "If you were sick yourself you'd think a nurse was worth six dollars a day," he said.

His father threw up his hands and walked to the door. "Fifteen dollars a shot for x-rays," he said. "The doctor coming here three or four times a week at five bucks a throw. Medicine to buy. Syringes to buy. God Almighty, we're not made of money. We have to eat, too, you know. I'll play nurse myself, if we need a nurse."

"You'd be a lot of good," Bruce said between his teeth.

"Please!" Elsa said. "I don't need a nurse, Bruce. Really. We're getting along just fine."

The old man came over to the bed, stooped to kiss her. His face was sober and tired and his eyes redder than ever. "Don't think I don't want you to have the best care," he said. "It's just so damned quiet now, all out-go and no income. How'd it be if I got some good woman who could cook and clean and do things for you?"

"No," she said. "I'm an awful expense. I'm sorry."

He stared at her with whipped, bewildered eyes, rolled his shoulders, winced, "I've got a damn boil coming on my back," he said. "Every time I move it half kills me."

"Oh dear!" she said. Her instant sympathy, the spectacle of her lying there in the bed she would die in, crucified by unbearable pain every few hours, and wasting sympathy on a great booby's boil made Bruce so furious he couldn't stay in the room. When his mother called him to fetch iodine and a bandage he brought them sullenly, looking sideways at his father's milk-white body stripped to the waist, the angry red swelling between his shoulder blades, and his mother propped on one weak arm, all her attention and strength focussed on painting and dressing the boil. He couldn't stand it. He escaped again.

Boils, he said. Wouldn't it be just like him to have boils, the dirtiest, messiest kind of affliction he could get, and then come running to let his half-dead wife waste her strength babying him! Oh my God, he said, if he was only the one on that bed, and she the one on her feet!

And he knew that that too was wrong. It would have been obscene to see him have to bear the things she bore.

When his father came out, shouldering himself gingerly into his coat, Bruce went out into the hall with him and confronted him there. "Mom just simply has to have a nurse," he said. "I can't do the things to make her comfortable that a nurse could."

His father sighed. "If you can tell me how we can afford six dollars more a day . . ."

"Go in debt!" Bruce said. "She's dying in there, can't you get that through your head?"

His father's eyes were glassy. He looked dazed, as if he had not slept for a long time. The outburst of irritability a few minutes ago had gone completely. "None of it can save her," he said. "That's just it. Do you think if she had a chance I wouldn't do everything, spend every cent we've got?"

"All right," Bruce said. "She's dying, so let's let her die. I'll cut out the orange juice. That'll save fifty cents a day."

For an instant, watching his father's hand clench, he thought they were going to have a fight there in the hall. He stood up to it, so furious himself that his stomach was a sick fluttering. Then the dark face of the old man twitched, his hands loosened, and without a word he turned and went out.

"You mustn't be too hard on your dad," his mother said later. "He never was any good in sickness, his own or anybody else's."

"No," Bruce said. "Witness his boils."

"Boils are painful," she said. "There's hardly anything worse than a boil."

"You're having a little pain yourself," he said. "Why should you have to tend that big baby? What does he do for you when a pain hits you, except stand around looking helpless?"

"He wants to help," she said. "He just can't stand to see anybody in pain, that's all. It drives him frantic. I remember when I scalded my arm, he was ten times more scared than I was. He almost cried."

"If he wants to help so bad," Bruce said, "why won't he let me get a nurse? If he's so broke he can't afford a nurse for a couple weeks he ought to apply for charity." He went to the window and tried to make the shade roll higher, to let in a little more light.

"Broke!" he said. "He's rolling in money. Twenty or thirty thousand dollars, and he can't even . . . !" He turned on her. "You're going to have a nurse, whether he'll pay for her or not."

"Bruce," she said strongly, "I won't let you spend your money for a nurse. It's silly. I don't need one."

He made a bitter mouth at her. "Do you think you wouldn't have one now if I had any money? I haven't got ten dollars to my name."

He went out to wash the dishes and clean up the house, and when he came back she was in pain. She didn't want a hypo. It wasn't bad yet. But he gave her one anyway. "The object of a hypo," he said, "is to keep you from having any pain at all."

"You'll make a dope-head of me."

"I guess we can take that chance."

A few minutes after the hypo she dropped off into a heavy sleep, and when she awoke, an hour or so after noon, he got her to drink a little grape juice. She wasn't hungry enough to take more.

For a while he read to her. He had filled a shelf with books from the library, but they were law books, history, things she wouldn't have liked or understood. So he started again on *South Wind,* which he had half finished, and she lay quietly like a dutiful child being read to. When he came to Miss Wilberforce his mother giggled.

He lowered the book to his lap. "Like it?" he said, pleased.

"It's good," she said. "That Miss Wilberforce reminds me of Edna Harkness. You remember Edna."

"Sure. I didn't know she was a drunkard, though."

"Edna was lonesome," she said. "She used to sit alone drinking until she couldn't stand it, and then she'd come over to our house to cry. She tried to commit suicide there once."

"What for?"

"She was in love with somebody—not Slip, he was just a piece of saddle-leather as far as she was concerned—but another man, a Catholic. He wouldn't marry her unless she turned Catholic, and if she turned Catholic then she couldn't get a divorce from Slip. She used to take off her clothes too, sometimes."

"In Whitemud?"

"It sounds funny, doesn't it? Three or four times. She kept saying she wasn't ashamed of her shape. She was so dreadfully afraid of getting old and homely." Smiling, she shook her head. "Poor Edna."

Seeing the life he had known as a small boy now strangely re-focussed through his mother's eyes, remembering Edna Harkness as a somewhat sallow and sagging woman married to a Texas cow-puncher, Bruce felt for a moment the strangeness of that past, those almost-twenty-three years that were behind him now, irrecoverable, but more real than many things that happened in the present. Edna Harkness, with troubles that were silly and self-begotten, coming to his mother for sympathy and consolation. They had always come that way, every lost sheep they had ever known had fed on her.

While he groped back in that past, watching his mother's face, he saw the sweat pop in tiny beads on her forehead and lip as if it were something squeezed through porous cloth, and saw her lips even in the midst of a wry smile for poor Edna go white and stiff. The blue eyes looked straight upward. Bruce dropped the book and stood up.

"Pain?"

She nodded, still in the throes. Her legs moved slightly under the spread.

"How long?"

"It's been coming on for a little while."

"Why in God's name didn't you tell me?" he said.

"I didn't want to interrupt. I thought it might go away." She grunted, a startled sound as if someone had knocked the wind out of her, and rolled half on her side.

Full of anger and panic that came over him when he saw her stricken with the pain, he ran into the kitchen, flipped on a burner on the stove, dissolved a codine tablet in a half teaspoon of water and held it over the blaze. In a moment the water sizzled around the edges, the tablet dissolved brownly, the mixture bubbled. Then fit the syringe together, draw the cooled mixture into it, press out the air bubbles carefully, and hurry back to the bedroom, for your mother is in agony and this little weapon will straighten her cramped body, put her to sleep for a while, stall off the pain until next time, until this evening maybe.

The first paroxysm had passed, and she lay on her back again. "Arm or leg?" he said.

"Make it . . . leg," she said and stiffened. He tore back the covers, found an unpunctured spot above her knee, a clear patch on the blue-punctured skin, swabbed with the wad of alcohol-soaked cotton, laid the needle against her skin, slanting, and jabbed. The codine made a tiny bluish bump under the skin, and the needle-hole wept one colorless tear as he swabbed again and covered her.

"Feeling better?"

"In a minute." Her smile was so strained that he bent over her. "Why don't you cry?" he said. "It'd be easier."

She let out a shuddering breath, as if exhaling the pain with the air. "I guess I've forgotten how," she said, quite seriously. "I try sometimes. I can't."

For a few moments he stood over her watching. The tightness went gradually out of her face, the forehead smoothed out. "Want to take a little sleep?" he said.

She nodded, and he opened the window, pulled the shades down, straightened the sheet under her chin, kissed her, and went out. In the other room he tried to read, but he couldn't concentrate. Once, reading through a discussion of riparian rights, his eyes distinctly saw, in print, the words: "Codine at nine o'clock. Codine again at two. Only five hours between pains now." Tiptoeing to the half-open door, he saw that his mother was asleep. On an impulse he slipped into the hall and up to the apartment of Mrs. Welch, the only person they knew in the building.

"I wonder if you could do me a favor?" he said. "Are you going to be busy for the next hour or two?"

"No," she said. "What is it?" She was a fat, comfortable woman, too sympathetic and too-continuously ready to weep, but she would do.

"Could you sit with mother? She's asleep, and ought to sleep a couple of hours. I have to go uptown for a few minutes."

"Why sure," she said. She gathered up her magazine and came along, and Bruce put on his coat and went out into the air.

Dr. Cullen sat at his desk twirling a swab stick between his palms. "Anything wrong at home?"

"There's nothing much very right."

"Mother worse?"

"Oh, I don't know!" Bruce said. "About the same, I guess. Maybe she's worse. The codine doesn't seem to have the effect it used to. She had to have a hypo at nine and another one at two."

"Yes," the doctor said. "We have to expect that." He scribbled a prescription on the pad and tore it off, holding the sheet by the corners and blowing on it gently so that it rotated. His face was smooth and impassive, and his voice was the careful, flat, guarded voice Bruce remembered from the operating room.

"How is she eating?"

"Not at all. She can't even keep fruit juice down now."

"Um," Cullen said. He blew the prescription sheet. "If you want to," he said, "we can feed her by bowel. It would mean prolonging her life a week, two weeks."

"Would it make her any stronger?" Bruce said. "Would it help her stay stronger right to the end, even if she has to be full of dope, so she won't just dwindle away . . . ?"

He felt his face twisting, and forced himself to look straight at the doctor. "It's that dwindling that's hard to watch," he said. "She gets smaller and thinner every day."

"Bowel feeding would help that," Cullen said. "You couldn't do it very well, though."

"That's what I came to see you about," Bruce said. It was difficult to talk. The office was too padded, too quiet, the doctor's voice too carefully controlled. He knew Cullen liked and admired his mother, and that made it harder to talk to him. "I spoke to the old man this morning about a nurse," he said. "He says it's too expensive." With fascinated helplessness he heard himself shouting. "I can't stand to sit around there and watch her die *cheaply!*" he said. "She's got to have a nurse. I'll mortgage any money I ever make . . ."

"No," Cullen said. "I wouldn't want to see you do that." He looked out the window, and Bruce dabbed furiously at his wet eyes. Crying, sitting here bawling like a baby . . .

"I know a woman," the doctor said, turning. "I'll send her over tonight. And don't worry about the bill. I'll have Miss Ostler pay it and then add it to my bill. Your father can think I'm a hold-up man."

"Thanks," Bruce said. He took out his handkerchief and blew his nose. "I'm sorry I blew up. I just get so . . ."

Cullen rose and laid the prescription in Bruce's hand. "What are you going to do," he said. "Afterwards?"

"I don't know. Go back to school, I suppose, if I can find any way to work it out."

"Coming back here to practice after you get your degree?"

"I hadn't thought much about it."

"Don't," the doctor said.

"What?" Bruce said.

"I'm a busy-body," Cullen said. "I'm giving you advice. I've known your family for a good many years, and I can't help knowing a few things. Give yourself a chance. Get away from all that history."

"I suppose that's right," Bruce said.

"I might as well say my piece out," Cullen said. "Stop me if you want." He paused, and Bruce made a little motion with his hand. "Your mother is an exceptional woman," Cullen said. "I don't imagine she ever had any opportunities at all, but she's arrived at something without them. She's wise and brave and decent. But she's going to die, and there's nothing we can do for her except make her comfortable. When she does, clear out, and if there ever comes a time when your father wants to use you, live on you, get anything from you, keep out of it. He could spoil your life."

He laid his hand on Bruce's shoulder. "I'll drop by in the morning," he said as he went.

Bruce stayed in the room for five minutes with his back to the hallway, looking out the windows into the paved court. Even though you knew it, even though you were watching it every day, it came hard to hear the doctor say she would die. He remembered looking at the pictures of her lungs with the roentgenologist, the scientific finger pointing out the blurred and darkened places in the web of ribs and organs that was his mother. "She's doomed," the x-ray man said that day, and his big voice, too big for so small a man, boomed in the hollow office. He could hear it now.

The nurse and another patient came in. "Oh, I'm sorry," she said. "I thought Dr. Cullen had finished with you."

"He has," Bruce said. He brushed by her and went out.

The coming of Miss Hammond, the nurse, changed the quality of living in the apartment; it gave to his mother's dying a dignity it had not had before, a professional neatness, an air of propriety and authority. Miss Hammond was a neat and efficient and tireless young woman. She took complete charge of the place, cooked the meals, made the beds, fed and bathed and changed her patient. She even, when Bo Mason came in the next morning to have Elsa dress his boil, took charge of that too, in spite of his grumbling and distrust.

From the moment she came in the door Bruce knew he had an ally. Her first look around, with its covert criticism of the respectable gloom of the rooms, and the immediacy with which his mother liked her, cheered him up. And when his father had gone out, he saw her fussing with the blinds in the bedroom, trying to coax them up, as he had, to let a little light and sun in.

"It's no use," he said. "The place is like a dungeon. There's no help for it."

She smiled a little as she looked at him, her lips curving slowly, a pleasant, cheerful face. "Some flowers might help," she said.

Bruce looked from her to his mother and back. "My God," he said. She had lain in the gloom for three weeks, and he had never once thought to bring her flowers.

"Bruce has been stuck inside with me so much," his mother said. "He's hardly had a chance to poke his nose outside."

"Don't alibi me," he said. "I ought to be kicked." He looked at Miss Hammond and laughed. "I'll be back in an hour or two," he said.

In ten minutes he was on his way up Mill Creek Canyon. He had little money to buy flowers, and it would take twenty dollars' worth to brighten up that bedroom. But there were other things. Ahead of him the steep scarp of the Wasatch rose like a mighty wall, and on all the slopes, in every erosion gully, the oak-brush lay like a tufted, green-bronze blanket. He could see the tufts, tender and soft as wool, clear on down past Olympus and Twin Peaks, on down to the long ramp of Long Peak, running down to the point at the Jordan Narrows. In one gash down the side of Long Peak, ten miles away, lay a tongue of brilliant scarlet.

Ahead of him the sharp V of the canyon mouth opened, and in it, only an occasional tree at first, but higher up more and more, the ripe maples bloomed, fiery as poinsettias. He parked the car in a side road on the flat above the Boy Scout camp, and started up the rocky slope.

High up, his arms full of branches of sumac and maple and yellow aspen, he sat down and smoked a cigarette. West of him the view opened, framed in the V of the canyon—the broad valley still green with truck gardens and alfalfa, the petit point of orchards, the broad yellow-and-white band of the salt marshes, and beyond that band the cobalt line of the lake, the tawny Oquirrhs on the south end feathered with smoke from the smelters. At the right, just visible, was the end of Antelope Island, yellow-gold in the blue and white distance, and far beyond that, almost lost in the haze, the tracery of the barren ranges on the far side, almost seventy miles away.

He picked a leaf from the sheaf of branches beside him and chewed the bitter stem, his eyes on that view. He had seen it dozens of times, from the top of Olympus, from the saddle of Twin, from the westward rim of the Wasatch at a dozen different points, but looking at it now he narrowed his eyes and thought, as a man stopped by a noise in the heavy dusk of the woods might stop and peer in search of what had startled him. There was something lost and long forgotten stirring in the undergrowth of his memory. Something far back, as far back as Saskatchewan. That sweep of flat land below the abrupt thrust of the mountains, the notched door through which he saw it . . .

Then he had it. The Bearpaws, the picnic they had taken from the homestead when he was very young, the afternoon on the wooden shelf beside the spring, with the whole Montana plain under them. His mother had carried armfuls of leaves back with her from that picnic, in love with their cool feel and the memories they stirred in her of Minnesota. Maple leaves, pointed like a spread hand. And he himself, then as now, had been smothered by a memory, had been groping all afternoon to remember something from still another time in the mountains when he was very young indeed, barely out of infancy. This haunting sense of familiarity, this dream within a dream . . .

For a moment his brain whirled. Memory was a trap, a pit, a labyrinth. It tricked you into looking backward, and you saw yourself in another avatar, smaller and more narrow-visioned but richer in the life of the senses, and in that incarnation too you were looking back. You met yourself in your past, and the recognition was a strong quick shock, like a dive into cold water.

If you could pass that door, if you could look back through many funneling memories instead of one or two, you might be able to escape the incommunicable identity in which you lay hidden. You might remember your mother's memories, or your father's, contain within yourself the entire experience of your family, going back and back in time, a succession of diminishing images like the images in double mirrors, go back and beyond in time as the ranges went back and beyond in distance past the cobalt line of the lake.

He was not Bruce Mason, but a girl of eighteen named Elsa Norgaard, and he was sick in his mind to escape from the prison that home had become. And he was a boy named Harry Mason, running away from home at fourteen, the world wide ahead of him and at his back a house full of hatred and bad treatment.

He opened his eyes wide and breathed his lungs full and shook his head to clear it. He felt drunk, dizzy, but he thought he knew something that he hadn't known before. That was the way it went. The dog-wolf killed its young, the young wolves turned on the strength which begot them. You hate your father and I'll hate mine, in a circling, spiralling continuity up from the time-hazed past. You honor your mother, I'll honor mine. The varieties of family experience, he said, and thought of Proust, the sick man, crawling backward among the obscenities of recollection, and of Samuel Butler, so cursed in his heritage that he would never marry and have children to dominate and tyrannize over.

Sick and cursed, he said. As sick as Proust and as cursed as Butler. But he didn't exactly understand what he meant by it, and his mind shied away, wary after that tottering moment when memory had opened under him like a gulf and the solidities of the known world, the comfortable assumptions of his own identity, had slipped out of reach and left him poised on the brink of the unknowable.

Carefully, his mind as cautious and deliberate as his feet, he started climbing down the rocky slope with the bundle of brilliant leaves in his arm.

2

October first was his mother's birthday. On that morning, because he had time now to go and come as he wanted, he went downtown and with part of his few dollars bought her a quilted satin bed jacket. She had visitors sometimes. She ought at least to look nice, as if she were being taken care of.

When he gave it to her she looked as if she were going to cry. She fumbled with the wrapping, and when she had it open her fingers lay on the satin quietly. "Bruce, you shouldn't have," she said. "I won't . . ."

"Hush," he said. "You needed it. And I couldn't let your birthday go by. There's something important about birthdays."

"I guess I haven't forgotten how to cry after all," she said, and squeezed his hand.

At eleven she had a bad pain, and the hypo, morphine now instead of codine, put her almost immediately to sleep. Miss Hammond went out for a walk and Bruce read. When she came back she said immediately, "I've got a suggestion, if you won't think I'm butting in."

"No. What?"

"I was just talking to the landlord. There's an apartment vacant on the other side, much lighter than this, with plenty of sun."

"Is it clean? Ready to move into?"

"It's just been all cleaned and redecorated."

"I'll go see about it," he said. "Will you help? If it's all right, could we do it alone?" He paused, looking at the bedroom door. "How about moving her?"

"If you carried her. It would be much pleasanter on the other side."

In ten minutes he was back. The new apartment was five dollars a month more, but he would let the old man worry about that. "Come on," he said. "Let's get this done before she even wakes up."

At five his father wandered in, stood in the door of the stripped apartment staring. "What's going on?" he said.

Coming out of the kitchen with the last bags of condiments, odds and ends, spices, groceries, Bruce said, "We're moving downstairs and across the hall." He half expected his father to be enraged at the way all initiative had been taken from him, all decision in his own house, but the old man simply moved aside as he came through the door, stood a little stooping with the pain of his boil, his face slack and tired.

"Sunnier down there?" he said.

"A lot." Bruce stopped with his arms full, willing for just that minute to let him back into her family. "Did you remember Mom's birthday?"

"Birthday? Is it her birthday?"

"Today," Bruce said.

"I forgot, I guess," his father said.

"You could do something nice for her."

The quick, suspicious look stopped him. His father, for all his fumbling helplessness now, was no fool. He knew he was an outsider, but he wouldn't be pushed around and told what to do. Bruce started to go on, but his father stopped him. "What?" he said.

"It'd be nice if she had some flowers when she moved in. I'd have got some, only I didn't have any money."

His father's answer was so prompt and hearty that it surprised him. "I'll get some," he said. "You got all the stuff down?"

"We'll be through in about fifteen minutes."

As if his tiredness had left him suddenly, the old man went down the steps and outside. When he came back he had his arms full of flowers, a great sheaf of gladioli, a bundle of bronze and yellow chrysanthemums, a potted geranium and a big potted fern. He gave them up gingerly to Miss Hammond, walked all through the apartment looking it over, stepped into the sleeping porch, glassed on three sides, with venetian blinds for privacy, where the sick woman would be put.

"It's better, don't you think?" Bruce said.

"Yes," the old man said. "Is your mother asleep?"

"She was a few minutes ago. The hypo before lunch laid her out."

"Yuh," his father said. His eyes were vague, wandering, looking anywhere but at Bruce, and his cheeks were thinner than Bruce ever remembered them. He looked sick himself. "Have you noticed about her lately?" he said. "That dope is getting her. She's so far off all the time, as if she didn't know where she was."

"I haven't noticed it."

"No?" His father jingled change in his pocket. "Well . . ." He turned toward the door. "We might as well bring her down."

She was awake, but still dreamy and thick-tongued. Her face and throat were wet with perspiration, and the pillow case under her head was soaked. As they entered, all three at once, she turned her head to smile, a smile in which sweetness and wry apology were mixed. She held one braid in her hand, back on the pillow.

Bo approached tiptoeing, and the way he moved made Bruce mad. Why did he have to act as if she lay there with candles at head and feet and the death-house hush already in the room? He stooped to kiss her, and she made a face. "I'm ashamed," she said. "I sweat so, and my hair gets so sour. I couldn't have a shampoo could I, Miss Hammond?"

"I'm afraid not," the nurse said. "I'll get a towel and dry it for you."

"I'll get you some perfume tomorrow," Bo said. "Make you smell like a flower garden." He picked up the quilted jacket that lay on the foot of the bed. "Where'd this come from?"

"Bruce gave it to me. Isn't it lovely?"

"Yuh." His eyes wandered. Stymied again, Bruce thought. Too slow to think of her birthday himself, but resentful of having anyone else do it. "You're having quite a birthday," he said. "Moving, and everything."

"Moving?"

"Didn't you know?"

"No. Moving where?"

The vague and wandering look on his face gave way to a look sly and sidelong. His eyes caught Bruce's. At least I'm in on this, they said. Here's one thing you haven't shut me out of. "We've got a little surprise for you," he said, and the "we" was a clear insistence on his right to have a place in his own family. But the sick woman's eyes, Bruce noticed, turned away from him, turned to Bruce himself, for an explanation, and that was triumph of a sort.

Miss Hammond came in with a bath towel, unbraided the damp hair, helped the sick woman to sit up, and began drying her hair, rubbing handfuls of it between folds of the towel until it stood out all around her head. It was like a light in the room, like the brilliant leaves, curling and dry now, that were still banked in a vase between the windows. Miss Hammond began smoothing the hair down with a brush, but when she took hold of it to rebraid it Bo Mason said, quite unexpectedly, "Leave it down a while. Let her look pretty for her birthday."

"Pretty!" she said drowsily. "I'll bet I look pretty!"

"You do," Bruce said, and now he was trying just as his father had to intrude on something that was between the other two. Her prettiness had been the old man's, not his. All his own memories of her were worn like an old tintype, the shadow of pain and resignation lying behind the calm face so that many times he had had the impression that his mother's face was sad, though there was nothing tangible to base that impression on. Her mouth did not droop, her eyes had light crowsfeet of laughter at the corners, there were no bitter lines. "You do look pretty," he said in a kind of desperation, hating his father for seeing and saying it first. "You've got a glow on you."

"It's her hair," Miss Hammond said. "She's got lovely hair."

"It's because everybody is so nice to me," Elsa said. "If you baby me I might cry."

Miss Hammond held the jacket for her to slip her arms into, tied the foolish pom-pom strings at the waist. *"Doesn't* she look pretty!" she said. Elsa made another face, the color higher in her cheeks, as if they had caught a reflection from the gorgeous hair.

"Well," Bo said. "Ready to move?"

"Where are we going?" She looked at Miss Hammond with crinkling eyes. "All my life he's been moving me around," she said.

"I can't even get sick and stay quietly in bed. He has to move me within a month."

"You'll like this move," Bo said. Again Bruce felt a twinge of irritation at the way the old man butted in and took credit for something he would never have thought of for himself. Then he remembered that he hadn't thought of it either. Miss Hammond had thought of it. He lifted the dried leaves from the vase and stuck them crackling into the waste basket.

"Bruce!" his mother said. "My nice leaves!"

"They're all dead. There's something better where you're going." His eyes held his father's in ironic renunciation of his part in the birthday change. Let him have it. He couldn't hold it anyway. And at least he was being pleasant, he had had the inspiration or the good luck to call his wife pretty, and bring a bloom on her. Let him have it, as long as she was pleased.

"How are we going to do this?" she said. "Is it far?"

"Just a step," Bo said. "I'll carry you."

"Carry me! I can walk."

"In a pig's eye," he said. "Here."

He bent over, and as the coat tightened across his broad back he stopped as if paralyzed. A grunt of pain escaped him, and her eyes jumped to his face in alarm. "What is it?"

"My God damned boil!" he said between his teeth. He straightened up carefully, moving his shoulders as if to tempt the pain into revealing its location. Bruce stepped forward.

"You'd better not," he said. "I'll carry her."

But his father blocked his way. "I'll take her," he said. "Keep your shirt on."

He bent again, slowly. "Bo," Elsa said, "do you think you'd better? There's no need to hurt yourself."

"I'll carry you!" he said harshly. "Take hold of my neck."

She put her arms around his neck. "I'm pretty heavy," she said anxiously. Bruce, watching, saw his father set his teeth and lift, saw the pain hit him and his mouth tighten. And he saw something else. The sick woman's body came up lightly, easily, and the old man staggered a little as a man expecting another step in the dark staggers when his foot finds none. Bruce knew. He had lifted her in bed. She had wasted away to nothing. But he saw in the instant of his father's lifting that the old man hadn't known, that he was surprised and shocked.

His right arm was under her knees, and her white face trailed out from the nightdress. Her arms were around his neck, her hair falling down the back of his coat.

"Okay," the old man said grimly. "Here we go." He shot one look at Bruce, a look with pain and triumph and horror in it, and stepped out through the door, swinging her feet carefully to avoid bumping them. Miss Hammond darted ahead to make the bed ready. Bruce followed behind.

"Hurting you?" Bo said.

"No," she said. "How about you?"

He stepped carefully down the stairs. Over his shoulder Elsa's face twitched with something that might have been pain, and Bruce smiled at her with stiff lips. "Just like a bride over the threshold," he said. That was what he had been planning to say as he himself carried her into the new apartment. He hated the sight of his father's broad back with her hair shawled across it.

In the new living room she exclaimed aloud. The sun, just setting, came full through the west window, flushing the perfect gladioli against the curtains. "Oh," she said. "The sunny side!"

Steadily, without pausing, Bo carried her into the glassed porch, and Bruce saw her hand come down to brush the petals of the geranium as she was carried by it. Carefully Bo laid her on the bed, and Miss Hammond drew the sheet up around her waist, leaving her shoulders propped high.

"There!" Bo said. "How do you like it?"

Her eyes went over the neat room, the geranium and the green delicacy of ferns against the venetian blinds. Her fingers touched the crisp sheet at her waist, and the cry that was wrenched from her was like an accusation.

"I told you I'd cry!" she said, and put her hands over her face.

3

That night Bruce sat reading a dull and blundering volume of history while his mother and father talked in the glassed porch. He heard their voices, and even more clearly the pauses in their talk. Miss Hammond sat under the other lamp stitching at one of her patient's nightgowns. Once she glanced up and said, "What are you studying so hard?"

"History."

"What for? Going back to school?"

"Sometime, maybe." He saw her lower her head again, embarrassed at having come too close to the thing they all avoided.

His eyes were on the white jamb of the door through which the voices of his father and mother came low and intimate. What could they find to talk about so long?

In a few minutes his father came to the door of the sickroom. "I guess she wants to get to sleep," he said to Miss Hammond.

The nurse went in, came out after awhile and nodded to Bruce, and he went in and took his mother's hand. "Well," he said. She squeezed his hand and shook it lightly. Her hair was braided again for the night, and the shaded bedlamp threw shadows on her face so that it looked pinched and starved. "It's been a lovely day," she said.

"I'm glad. You look better than you have for quite a while."

"I feel better," she said. "You must be tired from moving." She lay for a while looking quietly past and beyond, at the wall or at nothing. "Where's everyone going to sleep down here?" she said. "You've given me the nicest place, and Pa says there's only one other bedroom."

"He'll be in that. I'll sleep in the murphy bed in the living room, and Miss Hammond's got a cot set up in the dining room."

"She can't be comfortable on a cot. Isn't there anything . . . ?"

"I tried to make her take the murphy. She won't."

Her hand held his, patted it, as if unwilling to give it up. "Well, goodnight, then," she said.

"Goodnight." He stooped to kiss her. Trust the old man to sit and talk and tire her out completely. She hardly had strength to turn over in bed. The old brainless fumbling . . .

"Sleep tight," he said, and left her.

Miss Hammond closed the door all but a crack, so that the light would not bother her, and then the three sat in the living room, the old man with his hands on his knees, vacant and unoccupied, his body slumped in the chair. He looked old and dissipated and sick, his face dark, with black bags under his eyes. Bruce watched him covertly, saw him put up a hand to rub his face, heard the rasp of bristles under the big square hand.

He looked like a man with a foot in the grave
And scarcely the strength of a louse . . .

The lines jumped to his mind, and with them the memory, clear and sharp, of the family around the stove in the little parlor in Whitemud, his mother darning, he and Chet hugging their knees on the floor to hear their father read Robert W. Service. Liking it, he said. Lapping it up, fascinated and impressed, loving him then, briefly, absorbing images and inflections and words that would never leave the mind, that would always be a part of his memory of the time when they had lived in one house for five years. It was incredible that at times, in his childhood, he had watched the dark face of his father with love and admiration and trust . . .

> *His eyes went rubbering round the room*
> *And he seemed in a sort of daze . . .*

"She's gone," his father said. Bruce lowered his book and looked up. His father's face was ghastly, and his mouth worked. "You can see it just to look at her," he said. "She's so quiet, she's got no interest in anything."

Bruce said nothing, and Miss Hammond, after one quick look, dropped her head over her mending. "All but her eyes," the old man said. With a puzzled face he looked directly at Bruce for the first time. "You'd never know it by her eyes," he said. "They're just as bright and clear . . . You'd never know she'd been sick a day."

He rubbed his palm across his face again. "What're you reading?"

Bruce held up the book.

"Studying, uh? Yeah." The momentary interest flickered out. "It's the dope," he said. "She's hopped up all the time. She can hardly make herself listen to what you're saying."

"Maybe she didn't want to," Bruce said. "She's weak. She hasn't got the strength to talk much."

His father stood up. His trousers were bagged and wrinkled, and there were cigar ashes on his sleeve. He started to say something, closed his mouth, shot a look of quick hard suspicion at Bruce, and wandered over to the dining room table, through the sliding doors. He swung around.

"How long?" he said.

Bruce shook his head. "I asked Cullen. He can't tell. He says if she didn't have a heart like a horse she'd be gone now."

The old man moistened his lips. "Yuh," he said vaguely. He stayed with his finger tips touching the table, turned again. "Do you think

I . . ." He stopped, took his fingers off the wood, and went through the hall to his own bedroom, shutting the door behind him.

Bruce drew a deep breath, looked once at Miss Hammond's troubled face, and opened the book again.

He awoke late. Miss Hammond had his place set at the breakfast table, but the other dishes were all washed and put away. His father was not around.

"My dad gone uptown already?" he said as he came in from the bathroom.

"He's gone away," Miss Hammond said. She went to the cupboard and got an envelope. "He left this, and said he'd be gone three or four days."

"Well what in hell!" Bruce said. He opened the envelope. The were some bills in it. Forty dollars. "Did he say where he was going?"

"No. I gathered it was business. He had to go, he said."

"Yeah!" Bruce said, starting for the bedroom. "Is mother awake?"

"Yes. She seems to know all about it."

At the door of the porch Bruce checked himself. He couldn't rush in there in a fury and demand an explanation. For a moment he stood gnawing his lip, and glancing back at Miss Hammond he saw with absolute clearness the nurse's complex of bewilderment and sympathy and desire to stay back out of family troubles. But even while he was looking at her he forgot her. So the old man had skipped. He put his teeth together and went into the porch.

"Hi," he said. Her smiling face turned toward him, but in the first glance he knew that something had happened to her. She was worse. There was no brightness in her. He came up and laid his hand on her forehead, cool and moist as putty. "How is it this morning?" he said. "I was a pig. I slept till eight thirty."

"Good," she said, as if her mouth were almost too tired to form the word. Her smile was only a crinkling of the lines around her eyes.

"Miss Hammond says Pa's gone," he said, watching her, seeing in her face how close the end was now, how she seemed to grope in a mist, make an effort to look out from somewhere, like a person looking backward from the moving observation car of a train. The wrinkles deepened around her eyes, that was all.

"He's been shut up too long," she said.

"I don't see . . ." he began, but she stopped him.

"Don't blame him," she said. "He just . . . wasn't made for it."

"He must have had an excuse," he said. "He's always got an excuse."

His mother smiled. "He went for a load. He had to be doing something."

"Did he tell you first?"

"He told me last night. Patton's got some stuff waiting for him in Los Angeles. He'll be back in a few days."

He said nothing more, but he saw in her face everything he needed to know. She wouldn't last those three days, and the old man had known it. She had said her goodbyes and sent him out knowing she wouldn't live till his return, and she lay there now ready at any time, living only by physiological habit. That was the change he had seen when he came in. There had been an air of resistance in her before. Something (the old man's cowardice?) had broken the brightness and will in her.

"Shall I read to you?" he said.

"Yes. Would you?"

Even while he read with an automatic voice, using only the top of his mind, the floor of his mind was uneasy with rage and contempt and wonder. To pull out, to run, to leave her when he knew she was dying, to go after a load of whiskey, worry himself into a fifteen hundred mile trip on the pretense that he was getting low on money, couldn't afford to stay off the job any longer . . . At his wife's funeral he would probably take orders for cases of Scotch. Oh the God damned contemptible selfish cowardly heartless old bastard!

"Yes?" his mother said. He looked up, confused, and realized that he had stopped reading.

"Sorry," he said, and picked up the story where he thought he must have broken off.

Now for two days he watched and waited with sick and hopeless certainty, his mother farther and farther away, withdrawing deeper into herself and the numbing morphine.

It was obscene and unjust the way she had to die. Loving her as he did, he was offended a dozen times a day by the sour smell of her sweat in the sickroom and the horror of the noises she made in breathing. It outraged him that she could not die sweetly and quietly, with her family around her, wrapped in love and the sense of a life that had fruited and borne. Instead, she lay most of the time like a stranger, her hair soaked and her skin clammy, running down like an old cheap clock, with her husband gone and one son miserably dead and the other unable to reach her.

In the times when she roused from her doped coma, Bruce sat with her, sometimes reading, though he was sure she didn't listen except to the sound of his voice. But she was altogether better awake than asleep. Her breathing was easier, and far away as she was, her words had sometimes a strange oracular wisdom, a tolerance untouched by personal feeling, as if she had withdrawn far enough not to be moved any more, far enough to see her life as a wry comedy, the world as a goldfish tank in which fishes of all sizes and shapes and colors went after food, made love, nosed with incomprehensible and unimportant compulsions up and down, up and down, against the glass walls, or lay suspended among the water plants, insulated from watchers by the different element they lived in.

"Did you know," she said to Bruce on the second afternoon, "that your dad is keeping another woman?"

"No," he said slowly. "I did not!"

She smiled. "For quite a while now," she said, and made her little face, the lines deepening around her eyes. "He had her in Reno. Now he's got her here."

"How do you know?"

"I can smell her," she said. She shook her head at him slightly. "I shouldn't have told you. You'll take it hard."

The biting edges of his teeth were set precisely together. He felt the little trench along the edge of the incisors, and his mind said, accurately and scientifically, Faulty occlusion. But through his teeth he said aloud, "Why shouldn't I take it hard? Why shouldn't you?"

"I don't," she said. "I don't seem to care. I can't blame him. I haven't been any good as a wife for a long time."

That intimacy outraged him, as he had been outraged during adolescence to see them kissing. He sat very still and said nothing.

"Bruce," she said, and took hold of his fingers. "Don't blame him too much. There's something in him that has to have a woman to lean on. He's leaned on me all his life, but he can't now."

"When you get sick," he said. "When you can't take care of his boils and wipe his nose and listen to his troubles, he abandons you and finds some slut . . ."

"No," she said. She smiled at him wearily, wiser than he would ever be, not bothered either by her husband's weakness or her son's hatred, not part of it any more, withdrawing, smiling remotely on the pillow with her braids down across her shoulders. "Don't," she said.

"Oh my God!" He stood up, blinded by the pressure that in a moment would be tears. Abruptly he left her, motioned at Miss Hammond as he went through the living room with averted face, and shut himself in the bathroom.

During that day workmen had installed a neon sign on the front of the apartment house across the street, and with the apartment darkened the bluish echo of its light lay on the walls. Miss Hammond was lying down, and Bruce stretched out on the murphy bed, forcing his mind away from the snoring breath in the sickroom, forcing himself to think of anything, everything, that there was life in—the sensuous shape and texture of the world, the nights and days and hours and moments when the burden was removed and a man was himself and himself only, wrapped in his own bright identity beyond which there was nothing. He thumbed them over like pictures from an old album, discarding these because there was a shadow on them, laying others aside to be looked at more carefully. His mind adjusted itself, re-focussed, as the eyes adjust to the parallax of a stereopticon lens, and in the timelessness of memory the pictures sprang into three dimensions, permanent and ineradicable, the things that had life in them instead of death.

The sky was a wonder to him then, the immense blackness and the lustrous stars, on a night when his parents took him out to a neighbor's after dark, put him to sleep in a strange bedroom, and out of his sleep pulled him lost and groping and clinging to slumber, to load him into the buggy. There, cradled in his mother's lap, he opened his eyes fully and saw the wonder, the black roof with the glory streaming through its rents, and the miracle of a night sky would always be with him; there would never be another night of his life when the sight of the stars would not have in it some of that first awe and wonder, when his jaded perception would not borrow freshness from that original bright image in the eyes of a star-gazing child.

That was one. That was one of many. They were not all visual images, he discovered, sorting them out. There were smells and sounds and old tunes sung over and over until they gathered to themselves all the associations of the places and times in which they had been sung.

His mother's snoring breath went up catchily, grating in the sick lungs to its tremulous climax, paused, came out in the windy sigh. Bruce shut his mind on it, turned away, fled, just as he had lain still and pretended to sleep as a child, when the windstorms blew the slatted curtains and tubs and buckets began tumbling in the homestead yard: he had lain snug and warm, hearing the padding of feet and his father's grumbling, and he had known he should get up to help, but the sheets were warm, the bed was comfortable, sleep lay just around the corner where he had left it . . .

There was the smell of hot chokecherry patches, hillsides hot under the sun, and spice and bark and leaf mold and the fruity odor of the berries, and the puckery alum tang of a ripe cluster stripped into the mouth, the feel of the pits against the palate—the free and wild and windy feeling of late summer on the bench hills, and the odor of the berry patch through it like a theme. It was an odor that he had never quite found again, though dozens of times, in the canyons, on sunny streets under the lines of Lombardy poplars, in warehouses, in stores, he had stopped, sniffing, his nose assailed by a tantalizing fragrance that was almost it but not quite. That smell, or its ghost, could bring him out of reverie or talk or concentration deep as a well, and leave him for a moment free from time, eager and alive and excited, in search of an odor that was more than a memory, that was a permanent reality.

And the songs:

The Bugle Song on the bank of the coulee among the early summer blossoming of primrose and cactus and buttercup, with the ghostly mountains far down across the heat-scorched plain; the song that had always meant, and meant now, all romantic yearning, all nostalgia for the never-never and the wonderful; that still, in spite of all he had learned since, could have an instant effect on him, choke him up, clog his tear ducts, make him, driving alone on an open road singing to himself, wipe his hand across his eyes and laugh with self-conscious shame.

A childhood-hunter, a searcher for old forgotten far-off things and battles long ago, a maunderer. He knew it. Yet the words of life were in those songs and those smells and the green dreams of childhood; in his life there had been the death of too many things.

He shifted in the bed, realizing that not anything he had been thinking of had cut off the sound of his mother's breathing. Oh Christ, he said. I wish . . .

He sat up. The light had gone on in the bedroom, and the breathing was broken. In three steps he was through the door, the fear like a hand clenched in his shirt. His mother lay moving her head weakly from side to side, her forehead puckered, her face and neck wet.

"Will you turn . . . on the light?" she said.

He stared at her. She was looking straight up into the brightness of the lamp.

"Sure," he said, from a dry mouth. "I should have put a string on that switch." He rattled the metal pull of the lamp. "Better?"

She did not answer directly, but moved her hand toward the water glass. The bewildered look was fading from her face. He helped her take a sip of water, wiped her face with a towel, turned her pillow. When Miss Hammond appeared in the doorway he told her to go and lie down again. He would sit up a while. It was still early.

His mother lay back, the light stark on her sunken cheeks and wet skin. "It was so dark," she said fuzzily. "I thought everyone . . . had gone."

"Try to go back to sleep," he said. "I'll sit here with you a while."

Her fingers found his and clung, and with her hand alternately clenching and relaxing on his she appeared to doze. The agonized fight for breath went on. After a few minutes he pulled off the light. The neon blue fluttered for a moment through the venetian blinds, steadied to a pale laddered glimmer. The tires of passing cars whispered and hissed in the rainy street.

This is it, Bruce said, sitting still, sitting quietly, unwilling to shift his cramped body for fear of disturbing her. Any breath may be her last one.

He bent his head on his hand and let himself slump, tired, ready to fall asleep but fighting sleep and hating his tiredness because they were treachery, because she was dying now, tonight. At any minute the worn heart might go, the breathing shiver to a stop.

He listened to the breaths, up and up and up, painfully, and the wheezy escape of the hard-won air. Miss Hammond came out on tiptoe and laid a sweater across his shoulders, and he pulled it around him, aware that it was chilly. The traffic was less on the street, but the neon light drifted in steadily, like vague blue smoke, a slight tremor in the shadowy room. He heard the courthouse clock strike eleven, then twelve. The breathing faltered, strengthened, slowed, went on.

The vitality, he said, is lowest during the early morning hours.

If she lived past three, she might last another day, stubbornly clinging to the life she had already given up. He found himself hoping
that she would die, now, and the imminence of the thing he had
been watching and fearing for weeks made him move cautiously,
straighten his slumped and aching back, thrust one chilled hand into
his pocket.

His mother moved. Her fingers tightened, and her voice, flat and
muffled, said, "You're a good boy, Bruce."

He sat thinking of that, thinking of the times for years back when
he had been selfish or thoughtless, of the girls he had chased and
dated four or five nights a week, never remembering that his mother
might be alone, that the old man went off to prowl with his friends
or deliver whiskey, leaving her in an empty house. He remembered
the few times he had taken her anywhere, to movies, for drives in the
canyons, to dinner, and those times seemed so pitifully few and
mean that he writhed. You're a good boy, Bruce.

Yes, he said, twenty years too late, and overpaid in advance, fifty
times in advance, and now paid with gratitude on her death bed.

Oh Jesus, he said, let her die.

The clock, heavy and solemn over the sleeping city, gathered itself
and struck once. The sound aroused the sick woman. She struggled up
on one elbow, her hand hard on Bruce's fingers. Her head turned
to the right, then to the left.

"Which . . . way?" she said.

"It's all right, Mom," he said, and pushed her gently back, pulling
the covers to her chin. She lay still, immediately back in the drugged
coma, and he sat on in the straight chair, listening to her fighting,
impossible breath, holding his own breath when the snore labored
to its peak, relaxing again when it was released, counting her breaths,
almost, because at any point in the difficult scale her heart might
quit like a tired horse in the harness.

The vitality is lowest during the early morning hours. One fifteen,
or thereabouts, and the minutes crawling, and his mother retreating
breath by breath. Which . . . way?

His nodding head jerked up. The *ah-ah-ah-ah-ah*—had stopped.
snagged, at the top of the scale. The long pause between inhalation
and exhalation was slow, was too long. He yanked on the light.

"Miss Hammond!"

She came instantly, it seemed, was shoving him away from the bedside. In the shouting silence he saw her seize his mother's shoulders,

put a finger in her mouth, jerk it out again to grab a spoon from the table and with the handle pry against his mother's tongue, pulling it back out of her throat. The legs under the covers moved slightly, the clogged breath gave easily, in three little sighs, and he was staring into the sick face of Miss Hammond, the spoon in her hand free now, and his mother's eyes closing, very slowly.

He saw the tears come into Miss Hammond's eyes as she groped without looking to lay the spoon on the table. The covers were disarranged over his mother's body, and the nightgown was pulled aside. He saw her breast, the unmutilated one, like a lumpy mummified thing, the nipple retracted, pulled in as if by a terrific suction, and the skin blue-black and withered over her whole side.

"Oh my God," Miss Hammond was saying, "Oh my God."

He turned, blind and terrified, and fled.

4

When he came in again, the light was on in both front room and porch. Miss Hammond looked up quickly. He could not meet her eyes for more than an instant, because behind her was the lighted porch, and his mind went around that door and stopped at the foot of the bed.

Instead of going in, he went to the telephone and called long distance, waiting with the blank wall before his eyes and the receiver against his ear, fixing his mind on the efficient buzzings, the unknown voices speaking crisply, the long regular unmusical ringing on the other end. Death travelled fast. In three minutes he could spread death. He waited, the receiver humming at his head.

What would the old man say? Would he pretend grief, he with his cowardice and his kept slut? Maybe she was with him. That would make it just dandy. She could ride back with him, consoling him all the . . .

"Hello," he said, breaking in on the voice at the other end. It was a man's voice, probably Patton's. "Hello," he said. "This is Bruce Mason. Is my father there?"

"Yeah," the voice said surlily, and then quickly, as if remembering, "Yeah, sure. Hold it just a minute."

He waited again. Through the open line he could hear steps coming. He looked straight at the yellow wall, his tongue like an unbendable rod in his mouth. "Hello?" his father's quick voice said. "Hello, Bruce? What is it? Is . . . ?" There was a rattling noise, and then his father's voice again, quick and anxious. "Hello? Dropped the damn phone. What's the matter?"

"She's dead," Bruce said. "Two hours ago. I thought you'd want to know."

There was no answer for so long that he dropped his lips to the mouthpiece to say "Hello, hello," but as he did so he heard the sigh of his father's breath, distorted and rasping over the wire, and then his voice, quiet, almost a whisper. "Yeah. I'll be right home."

"All right," Bruce said. "I'll make the arrangements."

There was another pause, only a kind of panting coming through the receiver. "Was it bad?" his father said. "Did she . . . was she in pain?"

Bruce raised his head. On impulse, out of pure contempt, he lied. "No," he said. "She just went to sleep."

The nurse moved aside, and he stepped past her into the porch. His mother lay with the sheet up to her chin. Her hands, folded on her stomach, made a little draped mound under the sheet. Her hair had been dried and re-braided, and her face was wiped clean of any expression, even the lines rubbed away as an artist might erase lines from a sketch. It was a younger face that lay there, a face completely calm, a prettier face actually than he had known. But it was not his mother. His mother had been wiped away with the lines that living had left on her. She was the shading, not the face itself. In this wax image there was none of her patience, none of her understanding and sympathy, none of her kindness, none of her dignity. This corpse was a thing you could bury without regret, put into the ground beside your brother's body; and the other things, the qualities that had been mystically your mother, you buried within yourself, you became a grave for her as you were a grave for Chet, and you carried your dead unquietly within you.

On the evening of the next day he sat reading in the deserted apartment. He had gone grimly through his duties, half grateful for something to do, half appreciating why the race made a ritual of death. He had bought a casket, feeling that if he left that to his father his father would throw away hundreds of dollars in a useless sacrifice to his own shame and fear. He had talked to Cullen, signed the death certificate, gone to the cemetery and seen the sexton about the grave lot next to Chet's. After dinner he had said goodbye to Miss Hammond.

Tomorrow, probably around noon, his father should be back. The funeral was set for three. If the old man was late that was his bad luck. He could be shown where she was buried, that would be all he deserved.

He looked at the clock on the end table by the sofa. Ten fifteen. He might go to bed, but he knew he couldn't sleep, even though he was exhausted. He moved the light closer and opened the book again.

At eleven thirty he stopped reading to listen. Someone was fumbling at the door. He stood up just as his father opened the door and came in, and in the silent apartment, with the fact of death between them, they confronted each other.

His father's face was like a dirty dough mask. The unhealthy bags under his eyes had swollen and darkened, his cheeks sagged, his eyes were furtive and haunted. For a moment he stood with his hand on the knob, moistening his lips with his tongue.

"You got back quick," Bruce said.

"I . . ." The old man closed the door and took a step or two into the room. His eyes darted past Bruce toward the door of the porch. Without the door to hang to he staggered a little, and put his hand down on the arm of the sofa, lowering himself into it heavily. "I . . . got lost," he said. His lips moved in the parody of a smile, and his eyes went secretly past Bruce toward the porch door again.

"You couldn't have stayed lost very long. I wasn't expecting you till tomorrow."

"I don't know what was the matter," his father said, rubbing his hand back and forth on the arm of the couch. "I was dazed, I guess. I've been over that road a hundred times." He shook his head. "I left right after you called."

Bruce watched him, wondering if he were quite right in the head. He must have driven like a madman.

"Down around Yermo somewhere," his father said. "I got out on some God-forsaken road with sand to the running boards. Just ran around in circles in the desert. Didn't know where I was. Dazed, I guess." He took out his watch, looked at it, turned it over in his hand two or three times, put it back in his pocket. His eyes came up to Bruce fleetingly, wavered away again.

"I'll get you something to eat," Bruce said. He wondered how long they would play this game of steering away from mentioning her death. The old man came back from a trip and they passed banalities back and forth and had a snack to eat. In the kitchen he almost smiled. The old man was out again, like a bum who has been thrown out of jail and stands with the bars in his hands, wishing he was back in the warmth and light getting three meals a day.

"What . . . time did she pass away?" his father said behind him.

Even that, Bruce thought. Even "pass away." But there was such a strained harsh quality in the old man's voice that he turned around. The watch was in his father's hand again.

"A little after one," Bruce said. "About one fifteen." He saw the spasm cross the dark heavy face, the harsh lines contracting as if at a sudden pain.

"That was twelve fifteen in L.A.," the old man said. He turned the watch over slowly in his hand, looked at the face. He looked back at Bruce, swaying a little, breathing rapidly through his half-open mouth. "Look," he said, and passed over the watch with its dangling chain.

The watch said fourteen minutes past twelve.

"I was in bed," the old man said, and his tongue came out to touch his upper lip. "I heard it stop. I thought it needed winding, but it didn't. It wouldn't start again."

The blank terror in his eyes made Bruce look away, down at the watch. He shook it, held it to his ear.

"That won't do any good," his father said. "I tried everything."

His face contorted again, twisted, softened. He sat down on a kitchen chair and put his face in his hands, and his body shook. After a minute, unwillingly, not knowing exactly why he did it, Bruce laid a hand on the wide, shaking shoulder.

"It's no good now," he said. "We just have to stand it."

That was all he could think of to say. He did not believe in his father's grief. It was not grief, but self-pity and superstitious fear. With his hand on the heavy shoulder, troubled and embarrassed, he kept thinking, "You might have given her a little of this while she was alive."

5

Bo Mason could not stand to stay in the place Elsa had died in. The door of the porch seemed to bother him. His eyes were always wandering to it with the vague, groping, puzzled expression that was now very frequent on his face. Every night he had nightmares, and on the fourth night they moved across the street.

Bruce, shrugging, carried their little household accumulation across. This move was all of a piece with the rest. The old man couldn't bear to think of her dead, pitied himself for being left, couldn't bring himself to mention her except in roundabout euphemisms like "passing away," and now couldn't stand to be near the room she had died in. It made little difference to Bruce. In January, if he got back the scholarship he had written about, he would be pulling out for school again, and he would not be coming back.

He felt so little established in that barren apartment that he didn't even unpack his suitcases completely, but left them propped open on chairs in the bedroom. And this was what it finally came to. For thirty years his mother had tried to break the old man to family life, had wanted to make something rooted and continuous that would bridge the dissonant generations, and in the end, with her death, it came down to an apartment in which he and his father, the survivors, lived together in perpetual armed suspicion, with half-packed suitcases in the bedroom ready for instant flight.

He got a few jobs through friends at the university, typing theses and reading papers, and the money from those jobs he hoarded like a miser. There would be little enough to live on once he broke away, and he would ask nothing from the old man. Meantime, if he was keeping the house, he was entitled to anything he could save out of the expense money. He pinched nickels and dimes like a housewife hoarding for Christmas, spent little and went out little. In the time he had free from his jobs he sat in the apartment and read, read with lunch, read with dinner, read in bed, woke to read with breakfast. His friends he never called, even Joe Mulder; they would have tried to take him out and cheer him up. When he saw his father watching him, he made no sign, buried himself in a book, until the old man put on his new black hat and went out. For whole days, sometimes, there were not twenty words between them.

October slipped into the shortening, smoky days of November, and the color faded from the scarp of the Wasatch. In the afternoons the sun hung like a monstrous orange over the Oquirrhs, and the night air was bitter with smoke. On one such night Bo Mason tried to blunder through the barrier of suspicion that lay between him and his son.

He had come home for dinner, which was unusual, and after dinner, instead of going out again, he sat in the living room looking at a magazine. Every few minutes he looked over as if inviting conversation, but Bruce kept still. Finally his father said, slapping the magazine down on his lap, "By God, I don't see what a man can do."

"What's the trouble?" Bruce said.

"Everything's the trouble," the old man said. "Nobody's got a dime, there's no business, the place is dead as a doornail. There isn't a damn thing stirring, not a thing."

"Haven't you got enough from the sale in Reno to hold you till things pick up?"

"That wouldn't last," the old man said. "I've only got six thousand out of that so far. The rest is tied up in notes. And with nothing coming in you can't live on the interest on a few thousand."

Bruce shrugged.

"I've been talking with some guys down at the Newhouse," his father said. "They've got a proposition they want me to come in on."

Something stirred in Bruce like a quick wind moving the leaves and then dying again. The old man was repeating the performance he had gone through with his wife every time a new bug hit him, asking advice, coming around and hinting and opening it up little by little. Only it wasn't advice he wanted. It was justification, encouragement.

"What sort of proposition?" Bruce said.

For a moment his father's eyes were quick and clear, the vague look gone from them. "A mine," he said. "Looks like a pretty good thing."

"A lot of mines look like pretty good things," Bruce said. "Only when you take a good look you find that the good things have been blown into them with a shotgun."

"All right," his father said. "You know it all."

"I don't know anything about it," Bruce said. He felt himself flushing, and for a moment their dislike was hard and ugly, in the open. "I'd just be suspicious of any mining deal, on principle. The Utah Copper and the International and the Apex and all the other big mines have got every prospect in the state tagged, just waiting till it will pay them to open them up."

"This mine," his father said, "isn't even in Utah. It's in Nevada. And it's got gold enough in it to be damn well worth looking at."

"Then look at it," Bruce said. "I wasn't trying to knock it. I'm just suspicious of any kind of scheme that's going to make you rich overnight."

"Uh," his father said. The groping look had come back and two little dewlaps of skin sagged below his jaw. He fumbled in his inside coat pocket and brought out a bundle of papers. "This is a fairly low-grade lead," he said. "It'd take money to develop it, need a stamp mill and one thing and another. But it's a big lead, a vein twenty feet wide. We can get this fellow's claim and options on four claims joining it."

"Have you had an assay?"

"Four ounces of gold to the ton," the old man said. "Some silver, some lead."

"How do you know the samples came out of that hole?"

"Paul Dubois has been down looking it over. He knows a sound mine when he sees one."

"What do they want of you?"

"Want me to come in for a third. We could put up three or four thousand apiece, enough for some development. Then we incorporate and capitalize for a hundred thousand or so, sell enough stock to put in the mill. Once it gets producing we can either work it ourselves or sell out for a fat price to some big outfit."

"Make a million dollars," Bruce said. He laughed. "I'd sure want to take a good geologist down with me before I dove in a hole like that. And I'd want to know about water, and transportation, and a lot of other things."

"There isn't time for much of that," his father said. "Hartford Consolidated is snooping around. They had a prospector out there last month. And there's a tunnel going in on the other side of the hill, about three miles off. If we want to get the jump, we've got to move fast."

When Bruce sat looking at him silently, the old man's brows drew down and his face darkened. "I suppose you'd say it was dangerous."

"When somebody wants you to jump quick," Bruce said, "there's a good chance there's something fishy. But it's your funeral. Have you got the three or four thousand?"

"I'm not so hard up I couldn't raise three thousand," his father said. "I could sell some stock. The damn stuff's never going to come up again anyway. I've still got some Firestone and some U. S. Steel."

"Suit yourself," Bruce said. "I'm no gambler, and I don't know beans about mines."

The old man put the papers back into his pocket. Bruce had never made a move to look at them. "Well, we'll see," his father said. He was wearing the black tie he had bought for the funeral, and there was a stain on it. Picking up his hat, he started for the door. "I may be out pretty late," he said.

The door closed, and Bruce sat thinking. If the old man started playing the wildcat mines he'd be cleaned in a year. He was not a good gambler. He was careful and suspicious to a point, and then he opened up like a grain chute in an elevator. Anybody who got past his first caution could pump him like a well.

And I don't give a damn if they do, he said. Remembering the miserly unwillingness of his father to get a nurse, he tightened his lips across his teeth. Not so hard up he couldn't raise three thousand. And now mourning! he said. Now it's a black felt hat and a black tie, and an armband probably, if he could get anybody to sew one on him.

Oh yes, he said, sitting furiously with his hands tight on the book. You can't come home and accuse me of anything. I wear black to commemorate my bereavement! I have put the cross above my door and tossed the salt over my left shoulder and spun three times round and said the words. My dead can't touch me. I have fulfilled the forms, buried the body deep in the ground, spread flowers on the earth, paid the sexton for perpetual care of the grave lot. And I have bought a new black hat and a black tie.

I hope, he said to the barren walls of the apartment, they roll him for everything he's got and leave him stranded in the gutter without carfare to the poorhouse.

In the last week of November, when the leaves were pulpy in the gutters and piled high on the curbings waiting for the trash trucks, Bruce borrowed a shotgun and went duck shooting up on Bear River Bay with a carful of friends. For just that one day, in spite of cold and chilblains and a raw, wet wind, he felt liberated and happy. It was so much positive joy to crouch uncomfortably in the blind waiting for the swift flights to come over, listening to the sodden boom of an automatic up the marshes; so much fun to leap upright in the tules and slap the padded butt to his shoulder, follow the speeding ducks with the muzzle, lead them a little, let go and be thumped by the recoil. It was so much fun to see a racing long-necked duck fold suddenly and fall like a stone that he wondered at himself. Why should it be fun to kill ducks? What possible joy was it to spread death, when you had yourself lived with death too much, and hated the very word? But he could not deny that it gave him a hot bright pleasure.

Maybe it was just the fun of knowing you were a fairly decent shot. The ducks were scared, and flew fast. Not everybody could hit a target the size of a saucepan, moving sixty miles an hour.

And that was something he had learned from his old man. At least in the business of killing his instruction had been good. But even that reflection couldn't spoil the fun of being outdoors, getting the wind on him, seeing the brown tules emerge from the mist and the gray channels of water open up as the light grew.

He thought of Chet, lost and miserable, the heart taken out of him, his health shot, trying to learn taxidermy in the last months of his life, going out in his off hours to the salt marshes and shooting small birds, fussing with them on the bench in the basement, working in patient protective abstraction with wadding and glue and pins, the mailorder taxidermy book open beside the crows and magpies and snipe he had brought home. Chet had always loved to hunt. For an instant, in the cold circle of tules under the sky like cold lead, he felt naked and alone and scared, and he would have given anything to have Chet there with him, just for an hour, just to say hello, just to lend him the gun for a shot or two.

Chet had been too soft, not soft like his mother, but weak. His mother, soft and gentle as she was, had beaten the old man in a way. It was he who ran at the last minute. Because she knew how to renounce without giving up herself, she could win just by being herself in spite of everything. Chet couldn't. There was enough of the old man in him to spoil him, enough of his mother to soften him, not enough of either to save him.

What about you? he said. What have you got? But he knew without asking. He had got enough of the old man's hardness to armor him. He was as hard as his father—harder. The old man could still bluster, but he wasn't what he used to be. He was whipped, and he knew it. His wife had whipped him, without ever meaning to and without

realizing it, and his one remaining son was going to whip him
further.

It was a curious thing that once he got away from Salt Lake for
a day he could see how in a way his mother's life, which had shut
her off from everything she wanted to have, had forced her to become what she wanted to be. The older she grew the richer she became in herself, and the older and more affluent the old man became,
the more he deteriorated. He lost friends where she gained them, he
weakened as she grew stronger, he lowered himself year by year . . .

Going home after dark that night, his chilled feet aching with a
hard constricting pain, he leaned back in the seat contentedly,
thinking of that day, only a month or so away now, when he could
pull out for good. The thirty-four dollars he had put away would
get him there. Once there, he could make out somehow. There was
always some way you could make it, something you could do to live
if you wanted to live. You could wash dishes, scrub floors, fire fur-
naces, wait table, do something. You could renounce everything but
the essentials, and the essentials included only a minimum to eat and
wear.

He was asleep when they reached Salt Lake, and awoke only when
the car pulled up in front of a drugstore on Third South and State
while Joe went in for some cigarettes. Bruce stretched, yawned, moved
the pile of ducks a little with his aching feet. He looked out at the
crowds coming from the movies, swarming into the drug for a snack.
The clock on the Sears Roebuck store said ten fifteen. He yawned
again.

He shut his mouth so sharply against the yawn that it hurt his
jaw. His father was coming down State Street, strolling, and with him
was a woman holding the leash on an ugly Boston bull. The pup's
wide chest was clothed in a red and blue sweater, and his legs
strained as he surged against the thong.

So that, Bruce thought, is what he's been keeping. He watched
her. Youngish—early thirties, probably. Hennaed. Small, well-made,
mounted on heels four inches high, her legs and ankles the kind of
legs and ankles he had seen on dozens of women of her kind, small-
boned and rounded, the calf muscles bunching a little as she walked.
That was what the old man picked when he wanted a woman. With
a quarter of a century of a good woman behind him, he could
pick up a sleazy little chippy like that. He watched her pull to-

gether the collar of her black fur coat, laughing a little as the dog pulled her off balance. Then he slouched down in the seat for fear his father would glance sideways and recognize him in the parked car.

That night he fell into bed after a hot bath, too tired for anger and weary of anger anyway, sick for the time when he could leave. There was his own life to live, and none of it lay here any more.

In the morning he looked into the other bedroom. Either his father had not come home, or was already gone. The kitchen table was still cluttered with dirty dishes, a piece of kippered salmon had been left out of the refrigerator and was curling on a plate, a half bottle of milk stood out. Sourly he washed up before getting his own breakfast, and after breakfast he started sweeping up the other rooms. On the end table in the living room he found the letter left out for him. It was from Minnesota, and it said that no scholarships were available at the mid-year. If he chose to come on, some work could perhaps be found for him, and in view of his record of the past year Doctor Aswell had offered to take him on as an assistant. That would pay two hundred dollars for the semester. Other things would perhaps turn up if he were on the ground.

He rattled the letter and read it again, lifted his head to look out into the bare branches of the hickories. It was not as good as he had hoped for, but it was good enough. In a pinch he could almost live on two hundred for the semester.

Hi de ho! he said. He was loose, he was free. He might even leave a little early and stay with Kristin for a few days before school opened. In a month, at most, he could shed the whole dead weight of the past and start over.

He felt too good to read. His fingers itching to pack, he estimated the cleaning bill he would have to run up in order to leave with his clothes in shape, calculated the date he would have to send the laundry so as to get it back the day before he left. And in the middle of those calculations he thought of his mother's clothes. He hadn't had the heart to go through them and sort them out, lay aside a pile for the Salvation Army, give her better things to her friends. It was stupid to keep them in the closet till the moths destroyed them. That was the sort of sentimental, useless gesture his father might make.

He went to the hall closet and opened the door, but the instant emanation, the something of his mother that emerged, made him pause. He put out his hand and touched a house dress, neatly starched and pressed, left that to finger the silk of what had once been her best dress. She was in these clothes, somehow. She was in them as she had not been in the body the undertakers wheeled out that night. These were things her taste had selected. Her spirit as well as her body had worn them, and they had in them something of her plainness, something of her simple dignity. It was hard to destroy this too, to give away every fragrant remnant of what she had been.

But there was her fur coat, there were two or three good dresses, some shoes, a good many things that some of her friends would appreciate and use. It was only decent to divide her among people who had liked and respected her. The coat, for instance, could be sent to Laura, who had moved to California.

He rattled the hangers down the rod, frowned, slipped them back one by one, looking. Then he lifted the clothes back to see the hooks on the wall. The fur coat was not there, though he had put it there himself only a couple of weeks ago.

For a second he stood furious and incredulous. He yanked the hangers sideways, thumbing through them with shaking hands. The best dress was gone, the black velvet. Two pairs of the best shoes were gone. There was no sign of the quilted bed jacket he had given her on her birthday. And that slut on the corner last night had been wearing a black fur coat, seal with a squirrel collar, and it was only the best things, the new things, that were missing.

The closet swam in a red mist. He was shaking so hard that he had to feel his way out, and when he found a chair and sat down on it he hung onto it with both hands. The red mist lay over the whole room; his sight was bloody with it. In that moment, if his father had been in the room, he would have tried to kill him, and he knew it. Even if he wasn't in the room . . .

He jumped up and rummaged through his father's dresser, found the .38 that the old man carried on trips, broke the cylinder and found it loaded in five chambers, the hammer down carefully on the empty sixth. It was a heavy, solid satisfaction to his palm, it was iron and it was murderous.

Putting on his coat, he slipped the gun into the side pocket and went out, and all the way down the hall and stairs and into the hazy brightness of the morning street he moved with his jaw locked like a trap and a singular quietness in his muscles, as if he waited for something. The red smear of mist was still before his eyes.

He started walking up West Temple toward town, heading for the New Grand Hotel where his father sometimes hung out. His hand was in his coat pocket, holding the sag of the gun.

After all these years, he said. After twenty years of hating him!

He noticed that the morning was fine. The smoky air lay over him soft as feathers, the sunlight was diffused and mellow. Trucks were working down the street picking up heaps of leaves still sodden from the rains. His eyes were very sharp: things fixed themselves on his senses. He had a curious feeling that his mind was a steel plate, a mirror, which reflected impressions without absorbing them.

Quick tears stung his eyes as suddenly as if he had had acid flung in his face, and he bent his head, still walking, still with his fingers curled under the weight of the .38.

Ahead of him was the hotel, and he closed his fingers hard around the gun. Now! his mind said. If he's there . . . His body was curiously light, a steel framework, as if he were not solid, as if he were invisible, and he did not hear his own steps on the tile floor as he crossed the lobby to the desk.

"I'm looking for my father," he said to the clerk. "Harry Mason."

"Yeah," the clerk said. He stood up and looked up and down the lobby. "He was in here a while ago. Seems to me I saw him just a few minutes back."

He beckoned a bellhop. "Seen Harry Mason around?"

"Not for a while," the bellhop said. "He was sittin' over by the windows for a while, talkin' to a woman, and then a couple guys come in. I guess they all went out together."

"Thanks," Bruce said. "I'll look somewhere else."

He went across the open lobby again, and as he turned sideways to avoid a man coming in the door he saw the clerk and bellhop watching him. He took his hand out of his pocket, put it back again because the gun showed through the cloth.

On the street he hesitated, his mind carefully numb to everything except the simple question of where his father might be. As if he were bearing a message, as if he had no personal interest in his father but had to find him for someone else, he went up a block and pushed open the door of the cigar store. Two men were leaning against the counter, but his father was not there. He looked toward the back room, but the door was half closed and he could see nothing. The man behind the counter recognized him and spoke. "Looking for your dad?"

"Yeah."

"I think he's gone out of town. He was in this morning, said something about going to Nevada to look at a mine."

"Oh," Bruce said. An instant sickness, a feeling as if he might faint, made him put his hand on the counter. "Well, thanks," he said, and turned away.

"Anything wrong?" the clerk said.

"No."

So it would have to wait. On the sidewalk again, breathing deeply, he felt his body come back to him, heavily, a tired weight of flesh. He took his sweating hand off the gun and rubbed it on his coat, and without much thought of why he went, he turned back toward home.

In the apartment he sat down and looked fixedly at the half-filled bookcase. Somebody would have to take those books back to the library. He imagined the landlord coming in sourly, looking around the place, wondering what to do first in this apartment, what to do with the property of the dead man and his jailed son, picking up a book and seeing the library stamp on it, laying out a stack to send back, looking into the closets, shaking his head at the burdens people laid on him . . .

This is the end of that, Bruce said. They will hang a considerable amount of reading when they hang me. He took the gun out and laid it on the table. Beyond him the open closet door yawned, and with petulant haste he got up to slam it shut.

For some time he sat looking at the gun, the blued steel, the brown wooden butt gracefully and powerfully arched. I thank you, he said, for teaching me to shoot. But he felt the closet door behind him, and he broke a cigarette taking it from the pack. Everything material that was left of his mother was in the closet, and he heard it talking to him.

I held no grudge, it said. Why should you? Your father was lonely, lonelier even than you, probably, because he's old and you're young. He had to have a woman to lean on and to reassure him that he was a man, and strong. And the clothes were no good to me, they might as well have been given to someone.

"But my God!" he said aloud. "To that slut!"

You don't know, the closet behind him said. You never met her. Maybe she's good for him, better than I was.

He picked up the gun and went into his bedroom. His suitcases sat open on their chairs. There was all that, the whole life he had planned for himself, the studies he wanted to finish, the career he wanted. Did you blow things like that, blow your mother's faith and pride in you, blow every chance you had to live down your old man's life and make something useful of yourself, just for the pleasure of ridding the earth of him?

He went into his father's room, slowly, and put the gun back in the drawer. He knew he couldn't do it now. He had known it, actually, from the time of that momentary sickness in the cigar store. If he could have done it in a rage it would be done now, but the minute he started thinking about it it was impossible. Back in his own room again he began frantically throwing clothes into the suitcases, dirty ones and clean ones together, shirts and socks and handkerchiefs and pajamas jammed in with shoes and laundry, cramming them in as if he had only minutes to catch a train. He was still cleaning the dresser drawers when he heard the front door open.

In the flash of returning rage he wished for the gun. He saw his father in the red haze, framed by the door, and he saw himself shooting him down, felt the hard jumping kick of the gun in his wrist, saw the heavy black-hatted figure stagger and slump, one hand hanging to the jamb . . .

He turned and went on with his packing, and from the living room heard his father's voice. "How was the hunting?"

"Fair," he said without turning. "I got seven."

"Ha," his father said. "A duck feed. I haven't had a duck feed for two-three years."

"I gave three to the fellow I borrowed the gun from," Bruce said, "and two to the boy who loaned me the boots. There's two in the icebox."

"You can't have a duck feed on two ducks," his father said. "What did you give them all away for?"

"To pay my debts," Bruce said. The old man came into the bedroom behind him.

"Packing up?" he said. "Where you going?"

"I'm pulling out for Minneapolis," Bruce said, turning. His father was staring at him with quick, prying eyes, the little dewlaps of skin below his jowls giving him a pugnacious, bulldog look.

"I thought school didn't start till the middle of January or so."

"It doesn't. I'll go visit Kristin."

"You make up your mind pretty sudden, don't you?"

"I got a letter," Bruce said. "They'll give me a little job. There's nothing to stick around here for."

Standing with one hand on the lid of the suitcase, he set himself. In a minute he wouldn't be able to do this patter-chorus any longer, and then they would be out in the open. There was a light trembling in his legs, and his face was stiff.

"No," his father said after a pause. "I guess not." He wandered to the dresser, fingered the corner of a pile of handkerchiefs. He turned around. "Need any money?"

Bruce's lips flattened against his teeth. "Not from you," he said.

Now they were looking at each other as they had wanted to look for twenty years without either of them daring. The trembling came up inside him, came up and outward, and he clenched his hands to keep them steady. He saw the dark face before him go darker.

"What the hell is eating you?" his father said. "Nobody's been holding you here."

"Nobody could," Bruce said.

He saw the symptoms of his father's quick and growing anger, the old old symptoms, remembered from his cradle, it seemed to him, the way his head wagged back and forth, the way his teeth came together, the way he snorted through his nose and his eyes got hard and boring.

"I'll tell you what's eating me," he said, and it was as if he were sitting on his voice, holding it down. "It's the same thing that's been eating me ever since I was old enough to walk. You've never been a decent father to me . . ."

"What?" the old man said. "What are you talking about?" He was in a shaking rage, but Bruce's voice, coming like a sharp thin blade, cut him off, stabbed him with the accumulated grievances of his whole life.

"You never were a decent father to Chet," he said. "You broke him before he ever had a chance to get started. You never were a decent husband to mother . . ."

Both his father's hands were over his head. "Shut up!" he shouted.

His whole head shook, and his hands came down in a pounding gesture. "Shut up! What in Christ's name are you saying?"

The abrupt, wide-shouldered lurch with which he swung away said that he was not going to stand and listen to any more damned nonsense, but in an instant he had pivoted as if in a dance step and come back. His voice was a harsh rattle. "How haven't I been a decent father? How did I break Chet?"

"You cowed us both from the time we were out of diapers," Bruce said, the shaking like an ecstasy inside him. "You bullied and stormed and never tried to understand that you were dealing with children. You kept on running whiskey when you knew all of us hated it and suffered for it. You made Chet ashamed in front of his friends, and you chased him into finding friends he didn't need to be ashamed in front of. You led mother a dog's life all the time she was married to you."

The rage had disappeared from his father's face, and he looked tired, weak, flabby. "You too, I suppose," he said.

"I went through college being ashamed of you," Bruce said. "Lying about you on questionnaires and registration forms. Father's profession—rancher, cattle buyer, veterinary! Other people could respect their fathers. I couldn't. All I could do was . . ."

His father's voice was so like a groan that he stopped, out of breath and panting. The old man's face twisted, the loose flesh puckered in a wild grimace. "Oh Jesus God," he said, "I had to make a living, didn't I? I had to support you, didn't I? You lived on me all the time you were having such troubles being ashamed of me, didn't you?"

"I paid my own tuition and most of my expenses for four years," Bruce said. "I worked from the summer when I was thirteen. Remember? When I worked at the news company and didn't even know that checks should be cashed, and kept them every week in a cigar box till the manager told me to cash them so he could keep his books straight? And why do you suppose I worked? I worked so I could get free from you at the earliest possible minute. Even at thirteen. If it hadn't been for mother I'd have been free of you five or six years ago."

The rage tried to come back into his father's face, but he saw that it wasn't real rage; it was an attempt, lost from the beginning, to generate a passion and bully him down, and Bruce closed his mouth over the cold words. It was as if he stepped back, watching the old man's contorted features trying to be the old fighting domineering face, and failing.

The old man acted as if he were strangling. He swung around again, swung back. His face was black with dark blood, and a distended vein beat in his temple. In two steps he came close to Bruce and seized his arm.

"Bruce," he said, "I hope you make a success. I hope you make a lot of money and get everything you want." His hand was shaking Bruce's arm, and his breath, tainted with stale tobacco (the old, stale father-smell, remembered and constantly renewed down the years), beat against Bruce's face. "I hope you have all the luck in the world," he said, and shook his arm, dropped it. "But I never want to see you again!"

He turned away, for good this time, but not before Bruce saw the tears in his eyes. As he went out the door, walking fast and cramming the black hat on his head, his shoulders were almost as wide as the opening, but they looked bleak and strengthless and strangely forlorn.

It was not until the fast hard steps had diminished and gone down the hall that Bruce felt his own face wet. There was a hard agony in his throat and chest, and when he turned again to his packing he did it wearily, without enthusiasm, and in his mind was a dull wonder that the break with the father he hated could make him almost as miserable as the death of the mother he had loved.

Late in the afternoon he took his suitcases to the Ford, came back for the books that would have to be returned to the library on the way, and closed the door of the apartment, leaving his key on the table inside. There was his whole life ahead, but he went toward it without eagerness, went almost unwillingly, with a miserable sense that now he was completely alone.

X

"I was just standin' there, see?" the desk clerk said. "Right in front of Joe Vincent's. This big Duke guy was chewin' a toothpick out in front, talkin' to Imy Winckelman—you know, the lightweight. Then these four soldiers come by. By God, that Duke must hate soldiers like poison. First thing I know I see Duke saunter up behind and kick one of the soldiers' ankles together so he almost falls down, and when he staggers, Imy is right there to be bumped into, and Imy shoves the soldier, and first thing any of the soldiers know they're gettin' the hell beat out of them. I saw Duke slough one and give him the boots, and Imy was standin' in the doorway sluggin' with two others, and the fourth one jumps on Duke's back and starts battin' his ears off. Duke must of shook him twenty feet, right on his head. By the time you could spit twice there was nothin' but old Army store duds around."

The telephone rang, and he picked it up wearily. "Winston Hotel. Yeah, he's right here." He held the phone dangling. "You, Harry." He waved the phone at the booth to the right of the desk and Bo went in and pulled the door shut. Probably Dubois. It was about time.

"Hello," he said.

Dubois' voice crackled in the earpiece. "Talk a little slower," Bo said.

"I say I just got back," Dubois said. "Thought I'd call you up and put you wise."

"Well, how is it? How're things going down there?"

"They're making progress," Dubois said. "It's a tough place to get going. They practically have to pack things in and out on their backs."

"I know all that," Bo said. "What I want to know is when do they start taking out ore?"

The voice crackled and fizzed. Bo's left arm was growing numb again, propped on the shelf. He changed hands in the tight booth and put the receiver to his right ear. "Talk a little slower," he said.

". . . about three weeks," Dubois said. "But there's one thing down there I don't quite like the looks of."

"Oh Christ," Bo said. "What is it this time?"

"You know those options we hold?"

"I ought to."

"Well, they aren't enough."

"What do you mean, they aren't enough?"

"Janson's got us surrounded, did you know that?"

"How can he have us surrounded when we own that whole strip?"

"Not on the west," Dubois said. "And that's where the payoff is going to be. Creer's got his tunnel in three hundred feet now, and if you ask me, he's got something. And where'd we be if he struck it and bought up those options of Janson's? We ought to get Janson out of there before somebody gives him the idea he's got something valuable."

Bo stared at the corrugated metal wall of the booth, its green paint flaking off and its surface scratched with addresses, names, numbers, doodle-marks. "How much dough would that mean?"

"I smelled around," Dubois said. "I'd be willing to bet we could pick up the whole block for two thousand."

"Yeah," Bo said. "Where would we get the two thousand?"

"Hell, we can raise that," Dubois said. "Three ways, that's only seven hundred apiece. The way I figure it, it's a good gamble."

"Maybe it's a good gamble," Bo said, "but I tell you, Paul, I'm all tied up."

Dubois was laughing at the other end. "Hock your overcoat," he said. "We just can't afford to pass it up, the way I figure it. If Creer or one of the big outfits picks them off they'll buy us out at their price, you watch. Or freeze us out."

Bo moistened his lips and shook his left arm hard. "Have they moved any ore at all?"

"Getting a shipment out in a week or two. They've been in the vein for three or four days, and it looks good."

"A week or two," Bo said. "Tomorrow. Next month. By Jesus I wish something would ever happen today, instead of next week. Where are you now?"

"Over at the Newhouse."

"Going to be there a while?"

"Yeah."

"I'll be over," Bo said, and hung up.

"I'd hate to tangle with him," the clerk was saying. "He's a tough monkey."

Old Fat Hodgkiss, one of the permanent roomers, was rubbing his bald head. "I wish he'd come around in front of here and pick on somebody," he said. "I could use a little excitement." He yawned his chins tight, relaxed them again. Mrs. Winter, the "widow" on the second floor, passed through the lobby and gave them all a bright smile. Getting skinnier every day, Bo thought. A bird could perch on her hipbones.

"Going over town?" Bo said.

"Yes."

"Guess I'll give you a break and walk along," he said. To Dobson, the clerk, he said, "If Mrs. Nesbitt comes in, you haven't seen me."

The clerk raised a weary hand. "What makes you think she'd be looking for you?" he said. Fat Hodgkiss laughed.

The afternoon street was bright after the lobby. Mrs. Winter pegged along beside Bo, swinging her handbag. "What's the matter?" she said. "You and Elaine still on the outs?"

"Don't talk about that squaw," he said. He was feeling, clear down his left side and into his leg, the barely-perceptible numb tug, the feeling as if he had been lying down and had put half his nerves to sleep. But no prickling, no itch of returning sensation when he walked or when he shook the fingers of his left hand. He was remembering what Elaine had said to him the last time he mentioned it: "For the love of Mike, quit belly-aching. What you need to do is go out and do something. You're just rotting on your own bones."

"How you feeling?" he said to Mrs. Winter. "Any better?"

"I always feel better in the spring," she said. "I cough myself purple all winter, and then in the spring I'm better."

"It's a hell of a town," Bo said. "Deader than a dead fish."

"How's your mine going?"

"How'd you know I had a mine?"

"You told me."

"Did I? I'm just on my way over to see my partner about it now."

"Something stirring?"

"Maybe."

"Oh, I hope so," Mrs. Winter said. "Waiting is the worst job there is." She looked at him under her mascaraed lashes. "Especially when you're having trouble with your lady friend."

"I said to skip her!"

Mrs. Winter paid no attention. "Maybe she's tired of waiting too. Some women are like that. She'll be all right when you get your break and the mine comes in."

"Maybe she'll be all right," Bo said. "But she won't be in on the mine."

Mrs. Winter swung her handbag. In the bright sun the lines showed through the paint on her face. "This is where I go in," she said, stopping by an entrance. She lifted her peaked face and breathed deeply. "Smell that air!" she said. "Spring's wonderful. Everything turns out right in the spring. First thing you know you'll be right back on top of the world."

"How much you charge for a course in cheering-up?" Bo said, kidding her.

For just a moment her eyes were blank and cold as stone, and he found himself thinking that she looked a little like Emmy Schmaltz in the funny paper. Then she waved her handbag at him playfully. "It's just my nature," she said. "I'm just a ray of sunshine."

Dubois was shaving when Bo knocked and came in. He twisted around and waved the razor at a chair and tilted his head back to get at his throat, shooting his underlip out and squinting his eyes.

"What's all this new come-on for more dough?" Bo said.

"Be with you in a minute," Dubois said. "Look in the bag there, there's a map."

Bo opened the gladstone on the bed, lifted up shirts and socks, found a folded paper. He spread it out. There were angling plats laid out with names printed on them: Siskiyou, Magpie, Bozo, Alma, Pieut, Rosebud, Independent. Across the top of the map was a long arrow, and under it a double-lined box. "Being a sketch map of the

Loafer Hills or Hobo District (unsurveyed) lying to the northwest of Winnemucca, Nevada. This is not a transit map, nor official as being absolutely accurate in all details, but believed to be approximately representative of the district. Black stars indicate approximately points where ore has been discovered to date."

In the rectangle marked Della Mine, checked with red pencil, there were two black stars, and further to the right, at a large square marked Galway Gulch Town Sight, a red arrow led off the map to the margin, which read, "Call on Mr. Janson, he will show you correct location."

"What's there new about this?" Bo said.

Dubois washed the razor and dabbed his throat with a towel. "See all those blanks around the Della, up toward the ridge? Those are the ones Janson holds options on. He's a long ways away, clear over in the Big Fortune, there, but he's right next door to Creer, see? And Creer's tunnel is going to turn something up. If we get to Janson before he catches on to what Creer's got, we ought to be able to buy him out cheap. He's got options on half of Nevada."

"You're sure you didn't give him the idea you wanted them bad."

"Do I look silly? I never cracked my mouth to Janson." He slapped the towel over the rack. "How I figure it, after looking the place over again, is that the vein comes right down here through Creer's property, and maybe across the corner of the Big Fortune, and then right through the hill." His finger made a wiggly line across the plats. "That means that probably all but the top one of those optioned properties is good, see? We ought to get that block of stuff for at least a half mile west."

"Wills' doodlebug said the lead bent off north from the Della."

Dubois smiled. "You know that doodlebug. I saw him demonstrate it once out on Exchange Street and it made a noise like a jackpot right in front of the Copper Bank."

"Well, he wasn't so far wrong," Bo said, and laughed. He watched Dubois slip a tie into his collar. "How soon would we have to pick up this stuff?"

"I'd say quick," Dubois said. "The minute we start hauling ore out of there, and Creer hits anything, Janson'll be wise. We ought to get down there before the first of the month."

Bo looked out the window at the flag flying from the postoffice building. "By God I don't see where I can raise seven hundred right away," he said. The fury that lay always just under the surface, the balked, frustrated sense of waiting forever for something to happen, the hatred he had for the hard times, the clothes getting shabby, the way he had to cross the street when he saw O'Brien coming, because he owed O'Brien a ninety dollar hotel bill from last year, lashed him to his feet. "Four thousand bucks I've poured into that God damned hole!" he said. "Next week it'll get moving, next month it'll make us rich. Only first we have to dig up another seven hundred apiece. I can't raise it. I'm broke."

Dubois stood pursing his lips and frowning. "You got to expect things like that in the mining game. It's a slow racket, till you hit it right. Considering what that seven hundred may mean to you this time next year, it doesn't amount to a hill of beans."

It was just possible, Bo thought, that Dubois was bleeding him and keeping him stringing along. His hands tightened, and he felt the numbness under the left thumb. But Dubois was in it as deep as anybody. He straightened his fingers again, feeling shaky. "I don't know," he said, and sat down on the bed, pushing the gladstone bag aside. "If something doesn't break pretty soon I don't know what I'll do."

"Try a loan," Dubois said. "Ninety days ought to clear it. How about one of the boys over on the exchange?"

"They wouldn't lend me a dime."

He saw Dubois looking at him queerly. "You really hard up?" Dubois said. "You really scratching bottom?"

"I've been scratching the bottom for three months," Bo said. "Nothing coming in, everything going out. Whiskey business is gone. I used to be able to depend on that to pull me out of a hole." He hesitated, realizing that he sounded too broke. "Oh, I've got it. I've got collateral from here to Winnemucca. It's the cash that crowds me. Nick Williams owes me four thousand—notes due two months ago. But Nick sells out of Reno and ties himself all up in a gambling boat off Long Beach, and I have to wait till he gets wheeling again."

He glanced at Dubois' face to see how he was taking it. "What makes me the maddest is that God damn Patton in L.A.," he said. "Did I tell you what that son of a bitch did?"

"No."

"We used to do a lot of business together," Bo said. "Plenty of times I've trusted him for three or four thousand. He kept on running a little booze, beating the liquor taxes. There was money in it, if he was careful. A year ago I sent him down a certified check for twenty-five hundred, to get me some stuff off the boat. I was sick, had a kind of stroke or something. Left me all numb down this side. So I sent him the money and was going after the stuff as soon as I felt a little better. Next I hear they've picked up his speedboat, and the grand jury indicts him on a conspiracy charge, and there goes my twenty-five hundred. Patton skips his bond and hits for the Philippines. Not a God damned word out of him since."

"Tough," Dubois said.

"I hope it's tough," Bo said. "Now you want seven hundred."

"It isn't me that wants it," Dubois said. "I just think we'd be damn fools to let that possibility slide."

Bo rose. His legs were tired, and he was filled with abrupt rage at the thought that he didn't even have a car any more, and would have to walk all the way back up to First South. "Well," he said, "I don't know. I don't know whether I can raise it or not."

"If you can't," Dubois said, "why I suppose Clarence and I might scratch it up. I'd rather see us all even, though."

"I'll go take a gander around," Bo said.

"I'm going back down in about a week. Want to go along?"

"Yeah," Bo said. "I would."

"Okay. I'll let you know."

Back in his room, Bo lifted the blind a little, dug in the desk drawer for the bundle of papers, and hunched down to go through them all carefully. Nick Williams' notes—due not two months ago, but a year and a half ago. If he wasn't so washed out he'd go down to the coast and take that four thousand out of that tinhorn's hide. He'd been over a year paying the other fifteen thousand, dribbling it out five hundred at a time so that you could never do anything with it, you never felt that you'd got your money. And then welch on the last four thousand, sell out and beat it. Four thousand. That would put him on his feet again if he could get it.

Carefully he laid the papers to one side and wrote a letter to Nick putting it up to him strong. But he knew when he sealed the envelope that there wasn't much chance. The fellow who had signed Williams' notes, the vice-president of a Las Vegas bank, had blown his brains out six months ago down in Needles. One chance in a thousand that Williams would honor his obligations, and how could you sue a guy living twelve miles off shore beyond the law?

He laid the letter on the bed and went back to the papers. Cards, addresses scrawled on envelopes, some of which he no longer remembered the significance of; slips for safety deposit boxes he no longer had; receipts for payments in a building and loan association he had been cleaned out of in 1931; a deposit book on a defunct bank. He threw them all in the waste basket, went on. A Nevada fishing license, two years old. A tax receipt for the cottage on Tahoe.

Picking it up in the fingers of his awkward left hand, he looked at it. He had almost forgotten he owned that place. Two thousand he must have sunk into that, and there was the boat, the motor, his shotgun and deer gun, equipment like stoves and refrigerators and furniture, a lot of it almost new.

Holding the slippery paper down hard, he scratched a note to a real estate shark in Reno. He would sell the whole place, just as it stood, two-car garage, boat, motor, guns, furniture, for . . . He stopped, thinking. How much? Nobody would want to put two thousand into a summer cottage in times like these. Fifteen hundred? He wrote in the figures, putting a long firm bar on the five. Fifteen hundred cash. It was worth a damn sight more. He'd paid a hundred and twenty-five for the boat alone, and that much more for the motor.

"What I want," he wrote, "is quick action. At the price I'm asking, you ought to be able to move it in a week. I'm clearing out everything I've got a finger in in Nevada, and I'm willing to take a loss."

Still holding the opened pen, he pawed through the rest of the papers. Junk. His certificate of stock—only a notarized paper signed by both Wills and Dubois—showing that he had four thousand dollars, a third interest, in the Della Mine in the Loafer Hills district in Nevada. The insurance policy, only five hundred dollars, and he wouldn't have got that, with his blood pressure where it was, if it hadn't been for Hammond. The deed to the cemetery lot, and the receipt for the payment for perpetual care. Those he put together and put back into the desk.

Two possibilities, Williams and the Tahoe place, and only the Tahoe place worth much even as a possibility. If they both came through he'd be set. He should have been riding Nick's tail every week for the last year and a half. But he just hadn't felt well enough. He shook his fingers, trying to get a tingle. No dice.

If neither of them came through, he was in the hole. His diamonds had gone a year ago, when he was raising money to send to Patton.

His watch? He took it out and looked at it. Fifteen dollars maybe, at a hock shop. He looked around the room. Suitcases? Maybe fifteen more. Overcoat? He might get five. He had paid ninety six months ago. He took his check book out of his coat and looked at the last stub. A hundred and three dollars left. He might as well close that out. There was no use paying a damned bank a dollar a month on an account like that.

Anger made him rock in the chair. Twelve hundred shot when the bank blew. The damned bankers sitting behind their mahogany taking your money and losing it for you. But he figured that dead account anyway. Eventually, when the Bank Examiner and the rest of them got through and got theirs, he might get another twenty or thirty percent of that. Forty or fifty altogether.

Forty or fifty? he said. I ought to get a hundred percent plus interest for all the time they've had it!

But maybe a couple of hundred more from the bank sometime. Next week. Next month. Next year.

Damn it to hell, he said. By rights he had six thousand dollars, over eight thousand counting what Patton skipped with. Only he didn't have it, any of it. And what if nothing paid off? Where was he going to raise seven hundred?

Maybe he ought to try selling out of the Della. It was a comer, it looked good. Somebody might take his four thousand interest off his hands clean.

And then what? Sit around on his can and eat up the four thousand and then what?

You didn't have a chance, not a show. You were sixty-one years old, sick, broke. Everybody you trusted snaked on you, beat it for the Philippines or the twelve-mile limit with your money. The woman you kept in style for two solid years turned iceberg as soon as the money got tight, cold-shouldered you in the lobby, wasn't in when you came around, even had the God damned gall to stay on in the same hotel and act like you were somebody she'd met once but didn't quite like.

By Jesus, it was . . . ! Some day, he thought with his eyes narrowing, he'd kill that bitch. Nice as pie as long as he had the dough, and as soon as he slipped a little she was out hustling some other sugar daddy.

The bitch, the dirty blood-sucking gold-digging squaw. Some day he would kill her, so help him.

But he couldn't hang onto the rage. It seeped out of him, leaked away, left him sitting slumped and tired, thinking: Sixty-one years old, and sick and broke and alone. Who gives a damn about you now? They were all your friends when you had it. Now where are they? There isn't a soul cares whether you live or die.

Bruce, maybe? he said. Bruce had written a couple of times in the year and a half since he left. Maybe he'd got over the way he felt after Sis. . . . He tightened his muscles, staring hard at the wall, feeling the tears come hot and acid into his eyes. He put his forehead down on his arm and ground his teeth.

After a minute he raised his head again, thinking of Bruce in Minnesota. He worked after classes and then worked all summer. He might have something, he might be willing to help his old dad when he got in a hole. *He* had sent money back to Rock River, hadn't he, long after he'd run away from there. And they'd never done a damn thing for him, not a tenth as much as he'd done for Bruce. He took out another sheet of paper and unscrewed the pen.

But he found himself writing almost with his breath held back, almost pleadingly, and he hadn't even the will to tear the letter up and throw it away. He had told Bruce he never wanted to see him again, and he didn't, the ungrateful whelp. But he was writing, and he kept on writing, and as he wrote the vision of the Della grew brighter. If they could just get that into production, capitalize and get a smooth organization going. It was a sure thing, a dead immortal cinch, a gold lead as good as anything ever dug up in Nevada. But it took money to get it started, for the mill and everything. He had four thousand in it, and when it got going he'd get it back twenty times. But meantime the whole thing might fizzle for the lack of a few hundred dollars. If Bruce wanted to come in, he'd cut him in share and share alike for whatever he put up. It wasn't too far-fetched to say that a few hundred now might put him on Easy Street the rest of his life, and he'd be helping his dad at the same time. The main thing was to get that mine going, so he could get back on his feet. He wasn't feeling too good, that stroke or whatever it was had left his left side numb. He might not live very long, and that was another reason why Bruce ought to get in on this while he could. He'd get the whole third share anyway, in the course of a few years.

Writing that made him feel better, more optimistic. And he felt better toward Bruce. He was a good enough kid. Bright as a whip.

It was Elsa's death that had put him off that way, made him bitter. He was doing all right now, going to be a good lawyer sometime.

Ought to send him something, he thought. Some little present, just to show him that his old man still wished him well. He dug the loose change from his pocket, counted the two dollars and forty-five cents in his palm, thought of the hundred and three dollars in the bank, looked in his wallet and found two fives and a two. Maybe he'd better take it easy. He had to eat, himself.

Then he noticed the pen on the desk. It was a good pen, cost seven fifty when he bought it. He took it up and wrote at the bottom of the letter, "I'm sending you a little present, something you may be able to use in school." He carried the pen to the wash bowl, squirted the ink in a blue stream against the porcelain, drew the bulb full of water two or three times, wiped it off carefully with toilet paper. It looked practically new. He shined the point clean and rummaged in the closet till he found a shoe box from which he cut strips to make a little carton. When he went down to the desk after stamps he felt better than he had for quite a while, and he straightened his tie at the mirror by the desk before he left the hotel.

Looking pretty seedy, he thought. Coat all out of press, pants baggy. You got down and forgot to watch your appearance. You'd never get back on your feet looking like a tramp. People had to be able to look at you and see that you were a responsible looking guy. Dubois, with his little thin look, asking if you were really scraping bottom. You couldn't take chances on things like that. They hurt your reputation.

In a tavern just off State Street he had a quick beer, standing straight in front of the bar and looking at himself in the mirror. From the tavern he went straight to the shine parlor of Joe Ciardi, his old whiskey outlet.

"Look," he said, almost before Joe could say hello. "I need a press job. Got a closet I can sit in?"

"Sure thing," Joe said. "Got a date?"

"I've been so damn busy I haven't had time to wipe my nose," Bo said. "Just looked in a mirror and saw I looked like a bum."

He sat down with a magazine in the curtained closet. After a minute he pulled off his shoes and opened the curtain and beckoned to the colored shine and slid the shoes across the tiles to him. Sitting in his shirt tails, he remembered that he still wore his hat, and took it off. Pretty sloppy. He opened the curtain again and whistled at Joe and sailed the hat toward him. "Might as well shoot the works," he said.

Joe, smoothing the trousers on the goose, caught the hat and hooked it over a blocking form. He took the wallet from the hip pocket of the pants and cleaned the side pockets of change. "This for me?" he said.

"Some of it's for you if you ever get done," Bo said.

"What the hell," Joe said. "I got to use the goose, not magic. I think you got a date."

"I got half a dozen dates. Get busy and don't talk so much."

He was impatient waiting, but he didn't feel as tired as he had that morning. When he stood in front tying his tie he found himself whistling. There was a spot on the tie, and he fixed it so the vest covered it. The newly-creased trousers were warm on his legs, the coat fitted smoothly across his shoulders again. He looked in the mirror steadily while the shine gave him an unnecessary brush-off, and he tipped the shine a dime.

Then he cut diagonally across the street to the building which housed Miller and Weinstein, Tailors.

Louis Miller, sidling, peering near-sightedly, came around the immaculate counter in front of the dressing rooms. Bo gauged exactly the cordiality of his greeting. It was all right. Miller would sell him anything in the store. He ought to. He'd got cash on the nose for enough clothes in the last ten years.

"Ah," Louis said. "Mr. Mason. What can I do for you?"

"Like to look at some of your rolls of burlap," Bo said.

"Yes!" Louis Miller said. "Any special color?"

"I don't know. Gray. Blue."

Miller put his hand up to the door of one glass-fronted case. "You don't want just anything," he said.

"Did you ever know me to want just anything?" Bo said. "I want a *suit*."

The fawning agreement of Miller's smile warned him clear down. "Now right back here," Louis said, "I have something I think you like."

When he left at five-thirty, Bo had ordered a ninety-dollar suit, had stood while Louis gave him the old line during the measurements. You are a wise man to have suits tailored to measure. You are a hard man to fit. So big up here.

And he carried with him to the sidewalk six of Louis' best ties, telling Louis offhand to put them with the bill. He had felt of his bare head and asked Louis if he had any hats. Louis did not. Bo toyed with the idea of going somewhere else and getting one, but gave it up because he didn't have a charge account at any haberdasher's and would have to pay cash. The hat could wait till Joe polished up the old one.

It was only when he started walking that he remembered he didn't have anyone to see or anywhere to go except the hotel.

In the lobby of the Winston, after dinner, he sat smoking a cigar, the first one he had bought for two weeks. His legs were crossed, one glittering shoe swinging slightly. The cigar was sweet and fragrant in his mouth after the sour pipe he had been smoking.

"You look all spiffed up," the clerk said. "Isn't that a new tie?"

"That's a new three-dollar tie."

"Must have cleaned up."

Bo winked. "Killed a Swede," he said, and lay back on the back of his neck. By now all three of those letters were on the way. One of them was sure to turn up something. A man didn't have anybody but himself to blame if he let a little hard luck get him down. Keep up the appearance, that was the thing. The world looked like a different place with your shoes shined and your pants pressed.

The scratching of the dog's claws made him turn his face toward the door. The bulldog came in, tugging at the leash, his wide chest pushing close to the floor, and then she came, letting the door go behind her and tinkling a little laugh as the dog pulled her off balance. Bo saw her face freeze slightly as she saw him. He remained where he was, sprawling in the chair.

"Hi, Good-looking," he said.

He noticed that she stopped the dog all right when she wanted to. That was another of her God damned poses, that little game of being dragged along helplessly behind the pup, and laughing, and getting herself noticed. Now she hauled the pup short with a curt jerk of the leash and stood looking Bo over.

"Well, if it isn't Baby Harry, named after his father's chest," she said. "I thought you'd left town."

Bo motioned to the next chair. "Sit down."

"What for?"

"Not for anything. Can't you sit down and pass the time of day?"

She glanced from him to the clerk, and he could see her wondering what was up. They hadn't been on speaking terms for ten days, ever since she threw that cheap-john stuff at him and he cussed her out. "I'm a pretty busy woman," she said.

"Yeah," Bo said. "So I've heard."

As if a hinge had given away, she sat down suddenly on the arm of the other chair. Her eyes were hard. "What do you mean by that?"

"You've been too busy to talk to me," Bo said, and shrugged.

"Who *could* talk to you?" she said. "The minute anybody opens their mouth you jump right down their throat about something. I don't have to take that kind of treatment."

"No," Bo said. "I guess not."

She was giving him the once-over, obviously wondering why he had asked her to sit down and talk. Let her wonder. He didn't know himself, exactly. While he was looking up at her from under his eyebrows, she put out her finger and touched the new tie. "Mmm," she said. "New tie."

"Check."

"Handsome."

"Glad you like it."

She looked around the lobby, humming a little song. The bulldog sniffed at Bo's glittering shoes, and she jerked the leash. "So you're not really mad at me," she said.

"No," he said, watching her. "No, I'm not mad at you."

She slid off the arm of the chair onto the cushion, bent to unsnap the dog's leash. "Heard anything from Dubois?"

"I saw him this morning."

"You look as if something nice had happened," she said.

"Something nice has."

"Oh, I'm so glad!" she said. (He saw her fix her face for that one.) "What?"

Now she was wondering just how nice she ought to be, estimating the value of what had happened, trying to guess whether he was worth making a play for and taking back on. The bitch. But she was good looking, you couldn't deny it. The meat was put on her bones just right.

"Oh, come on," she said, and leaned a little forward. "You know I'd be glad to hear anything nice that had happened to you."

Whatever game it was he had been playing—and he didn't know himself why he was sitting here gassing with her—was swallowed in the enormous angry contempt he felt. "Especially if you thought I'd made some dough," he said.

She was no longer leaning forward. "Now don't start that again!" she said.

"It's true, isn't it?"

"No, it's not true," she said. "You think you put me up so damned handsome, and I ought to stick around while you let loose of nickels one by one! You talk about all the money you spent on me. All the money you ever spent on me you could put you know where, and it wouldn't clog you either."

There was nothing in the whole lobby but her spiteful face. He wanted to reach out and slap it bloody. The blood came heavy and slow into his own face, a smothering weight of it. "You thought when you came in here I'd made a killing, didn't you?" he said. "So you thought maybe you'd snuggle up and play sisters again. Well, you can go to hell. Maybe I've made a killing and maybe I haven't . . ."

She stood up. "I don't give a damn whether you have or not," she said. "You could be rolling in gold and you'll still be nothing but a filthy old goat to me!"

"If I was rolling in gold . . ." he said, but she cut him off, whip-lashed him.

"You could go roll in the manure for all I care. It wouldn't make you smell any different!"

She started for the stairs, turned with set face to whistle up the dog, and disappeared. Bo worked his hands. He was standing, ready to leap after her, knock her down, kick her apart, beat her damned good-looking weasel face in. He breathed loudly, heard himself gasping for air, and sat down again.

The clerk was looking at his nails behind the desk. In the doorway off to the side Mrs. Winter stood as if not quite sure she should come in at all. She must have come in the back way while they were shouting at each other. Furiously fumbling for a match to re-light his cigar, he ignored her, but she came over and sat down anyway.

"Oh dear!" she said.

He grunted.

"I don't see why she has to be that way," Mrs. Winter said. When he didn't anwer she turned the handbag over in her lap and picked with her painted nails at the patterned alligator leather. "Don't be downhearted about her," she said. "It'll all come around."

"If you think I'm downhearted about her," he said through his teeth, "take another think!"

She smiled and patted his knee. "That's the way. Don't let her bother you. Just between you and me . . ." She leaned her skinny face toward him.

"Just between you and me what?"

"Just between you and me," Mrs. Winter said, "she's a bitch."

He grunted again. The anger had ebbed away, leaving the old dead weariness. Mrs. Winter smiled at him coaxingly. "You need a drink," she said. "Come on up to my room and I'll buy you one."

"Oh, I guess not, thanks."

"Come on. You'll feel better after a shot."

He let her lead him up to her room on the second floor. He had not been in her room before. It was fussed up, he noticed. Curtains on the windows with tie-backs on them, woman's junk around. Mrs. Winter got a bottle out of the bureau drawer and rinsed out the two bathroom glasses. She poured two stiff slugs and passed him one.

"Success," she said. "Everything you ever wanted."

"Mud in your eye," he said automatically, and tossed it off. It went down smoothly, warmly, and he raised his eyes from the glass to see Mrs. Winter's birdlike face smiling a birdlike smile at him.

"Feel better?" she said.

"Yeah," he said. "Good Scotch."

"Have another." She poured him one, and they sat on the edge of the bed and drank. This old crane of a Winter, he was thinking, was all right, even if she could hide behind a toothpick. By the third drink he was telling her about the Della, Patton, Nick Williams, the closed bank and the bankrupt building and loan association, the notes and the debts and the possibilities.

"It's hard," she said. "Once you've been up it's harder to climb back after a streak of bad luck. You're all alone, too, aren't you?"

"All alone," he said. "Got one boy left. He's studying law in Minneapolis." He felt for his wallet. "Want to see his picture?"

He showed her the frayed newspaper photograph of Bruce with a golf bag over his arm, taken one day three or four years ago when he had been the medalist in a golf tournament.

"He looks like you," Mrs. Winter said.

"He's a bright kid," Bo said, folding the picture back. "I haven't seen him for a couple years, almost. Away at school." The weariness had left him, but he felt sad. Everybody gone. Sis dead, Chet dead.

"I had another boy," he said. "Good ball player. He'd have made the big leagues with any kind of breaks. Died of pneumonia a little over three years ago."

"And your wife too," Mrs. Winter said. "I know how it is. My husband died four years ago last April. I've just never seemed to belong anywhere since."

Bo heaved himself off the creaking bed. "I better run along," he said. "Thanks for the drinks."

But Mrs. Winter was in front of him, her peaked face working. "Don't go," she said. "Please don't go!"

"Why not?"

She twisted her twiggy fingers together. Her rings hung loosely, upside down, above the bony knuckles. "I don't know," she said. "I just . . . I don't know."

"Lonesome?"

She nodded. "I guess. Lonesome as hell. I been through the mill. I just sort of feel like you've been too, you know how it is."

"Baby," Bo said softly, "I'm not worth the try. I'm broke. I'm an old man, and I'm sick, and I'm broke. You'd be wasting your time. I couldn't give you a thing."

"I don't want anything," she said. "It's just tonight. I feel as if everybody'd gone away and left me. I wish you'd stay."

For some reason he kissed her, and felt her bony body crowd him, shivering. A sound that he meant for a laugh half strangled him. Not a soul in the whole damned town who wanted you except an old consumptive whore, and the hell of it was you liked it. "Look," he said. "Think I'm a piker all you want. But I'm so strapped I couldn't even afford two dollars. What little I've got I've got to keep to eat on till something breaks."

"I don't care about the two dollars," she said.

He thought briefly of Elaine up on the fourth floor, bedded down in her silk pajamas reading a magazine in bed, soft and warm and ten years younger than this poor old skin, and the thing that rose in him was quick and light as a bubble and bitter as a curse.

"Okay," he said.

She was surprisingly passionate. Her thin arms were like a vise, her fingers like birds' claws. For a while, for ten minutes, he was powerful, he felt his own weight and the undiminished strength of his body, but afterward he lay spent and breathing hard beside her, and when he got up quietly and got into his clothes and went down the night-lighted hall to his own room he was old and tired, and the numbness was back in his side and arm.

2

The sky that morning was like blue water with a white surf of clouds rolling eastward under a high wind, though no wind blew down on the city and the campus trees stirred only to the shrill of the seventeen-year locusts. Standing in the long line of gowned figures, waiting for the officials and the president and the visiting dignitaries to head the procession, Bruce sweated under the black serge and the heavy square of the mortar board. He opened the gown to let in some air, and as he did so his hand came close to the inner pocket of his coat, where the letters were. He reached in to feel them.

There was no use to worry himself about what the last letter said and the others hinted. All those letters meant was that the old man wanted to squeeze some money out of him.

Yes? he said. Then why did you telephone Joe Mulder in Salt Lake to go and see him, and tell Joe to lend him some money if he needed it, and send the bill to you?

Because you were worried, he said. Sure you were worried. You are now. But you don't believe it, anyway. If he's down and out, you'll give him what you can, but you're not going to give him money just to throw down a worthless mine shaft.

How much had he sent, anyway, since the first letter came in April? More than he could afford to send, anyway. You're a sucker, he said. You let yourself be gouged because you have a sneaking feeling of guilt, God knows why. And you don't even quite believe Joe when he writes that the old man is all right, a little worn looking, but all right. But of course he's all right. You'd have heard if he wasn't.

And that damned stock. That was what really bothered him. Either that was a very shrewd way of pumping him for money, or it meant something. Why should the old man send on a paper indicating that he had put forty-seven hundred dollars into that mine, with the note: "Hang onto this stock, Bruce. Some day it will make you a lot of money. It's all I've got left to give you. Good luck and don't worry about me. I'm at the end of my rope, that's all."

He looked up as the gowned line stirred and murmured. The president came down the steps of Northrop. At least this silly rigmarole was beginning. It irritated him to have to stand in a hot gown for two or three hours while they went through a lot of medieval mummery. He ought to be doing something, either getting on down and starting work in George Nelson's office, or hitting for Salt Lake to see what he could do there.

No sir, he said. I won't go running out there on a wild goose chase. If he needs money to live he knows he can get it from Joe. If he's sick, Joe will see that he gets into a home or a hospital. There's nothing else I can do. I'm a fool to take that much trouble.

It was the eighth of June. His father's last letter had been written on the first. If he had made up his mind before he wrote that letter, why hadn't anything happened by now? It wasn't going to happen, that was why. Joe would telegraph or call if anything did, and Joe had sent no word except the airmail letter dated the fourth. The whole thing was a squeeze play. Talk about losing your pride! The Big Shot stooping to use a trick like that worthless stock!

He tried to be angry, but all he could feel was a baffled sense of frustration, of pain and regret and loss. To get mad was to kick the old man when he was down, and whether he meant that last letter or not, he was down.

The procession began to shuffle forward. He shuffled with it, still thinking, still bothered, and he forgot to hook up the throat of his gown until the officious man ahead of him turned around and motioned. Ah yes, the forms, he said, and walked shufflingly, tipping his head back to watch the clouds wheel over before the unheard, unfelt upper-air wind.

He saw the young woman a long way away, coming up along the procession as if looking for someone, moving against the stream and searching the faces under the flat black caps. He almost chuckled, thinking what a job it would be to locate any one particular face in that half mile of people all dressed alike. She came on, peering, not waiting for the line to come past her, but walking fast herself, and when she got nearer he saw that it was Mary Trask, the secretary of the Law School, and then he knew that she was looking for him.

He stepped out of line, aware that heads turned to watch him, and with a frozen quiet that was like walking in sleep he went to meet her. She was agitated, half out of breath.

"Oh, I was afraid I wouldn't catch you till you got in," she said. "Can you come?"

"Telephone?" Bruce said.

"Yes. They tried at your room and the landlady told them you were at the exercises so they called the school." They were already walking fast away from the line, across the clipped and manicured carpet of lawn under the still trees, with the locusts' noise loud as a wind in the branches but not a leaf stirring. Mary glanced up at his face. "I'm afraid it's something bad," she said. "I wouldn't have come, only they said it was a matter of life and death."

Bruce said nothing. He was locked tight, everything inside him put away and the doors slammed shut.

Except for a couple of stenographers the office was empty. Mary let him in behind the hinged door and picked up the telephone. He saw her turn aside to avoid meeting his eyes, and there was relief in her voice when she got the operator. "This is the Law School," she said. "Mr. Mason is here now."

Silently she handed the instrument to Bruce, and he stood listening to the far-off buzz, the half-heard monosyllables of the operator, the click of connections. In a minute now death would walk its slack wire from Salt Lake City to Minneapolis, that buzzing and those monosyllables and the mechanical clicks would jell down into their real meaning, and Joe's voice would be saying . . .

"Hello!" he said.

"One moment please."

It seemed to him that half his life had been spent going through this monotonous ritual of death. Long distance calls, telegraph messages, a flying trip to Salt Lake. He was like a vaudeville performer caught in an act he loathed but forced to go on through endless repetitions, starting at the same stale cues, going into his dance at the same habitual moments.

"Hello," Joe's voice said. "Hello?"

Bruce stiffened. "Hello," he said. "Hello, Joe. What is it? Has he . . . ?"

"It's hell," Joe said. "You all right?"

"I'm all right."

"He's dead," Joe said. "Shot himself this morning in the hotel lobby."

There was no shock in the words. Bruce was braced so hard that nothing could have moved him then. "Yeah," he said.

"It's worse than you think," Joe said. "He shot a woman too."

"Oh Jesus," Bruce said. "Dead?"

"Yes. I didn't get her name. Maybe you'd know who she was. One of our workmen lives in that hotel. He heard about it just a minute after it happened, and I went right over. There wasn't much I could do, so I started calling you."

"Yeah," Bruce said. "Yeah, thanks, Joe. Can you do me a favor?"

"Anything."

"Have him taken up to the mortuary."

"I already did. The one where Chet and your mother were."

"Good," Bruce said. He started to ask what about the police, saw Mary Trask's pained face as she listened, and said only, "I'll be there tomorrow night. Have to drive. I haven't got the money for a plane or train. Take me about thirty-six hours."

"Hell," Joe said. "Hold it two hours and I'll wire you some money. You can't drive right through."

"I'd better drive," Bruce said. "Look for me sometime before midnight tomorrow."

He hung up. The two stenographers were sitting behind their typewriters, watching and listening, Mary Trask was looking as if she might cry. The noise of the locusts rasped through the opened windows. "I'm sorry," Mary said. "Is there anything . . . ?"

"Yes," Bruce said. "If you would." He stripped off the gown and mortar board and laid on a desk. "Could you return these for me? They're paid for. Somebody comes around to collect them, I think."

"Of course," she said. "I'll fix it about the graduation. The dean will be back after the exercises, and I'll see about a degree *in absentia*."

"That's good of you," he said. "Thanks very much."

"And you're going to drive straight through to Salt Lake?"

He nodded.

"I couldn't help hearing," she said, confused. "I could lend you some money."

"No thanks, I'd rather drive." He was already through the gate into the outer office.

"Who?" Mary said, following him. "Who was it?"

"My father," Bruce said. "He's dead."

He went outside. The last ragged end of the procession was disappearing into the building. He stood a moment on the edge of the grass to look in his wallet. Ten dollars, and his last check from the school wouldn't be out for three or four days. He'd have to get some from George Nelson. This part too was familiar—the things to do, the mechanical completion of necessary details. Get the money—fifty ought to do it for the time being. Get a tank of gas. Stop by his room for some clothes? No. He would get along with what he was wearing, buy a shirt or two when he got there. Even while he planned the campaign he was hitting for the car, parked off at the edge of the campus, and within ten minutes he was in his uncle's office explaining, his voice cold, his insides still frozen hard against any feeling whatever.

His uncle asked few questions. He wrote a check and cashed it from the safe, made a note of two or three things that Bruce wanted him to do, shook his hand, told him not to worry about the job. He could come back and go to work any time he got through out there. He stood in the doorway hanging onto Bruce's hand, his earnest, good-natured face puckered.

"I haven't seen your father since about 1912," he said. "More than twenty years. I liked him then. I'm sorry."

"Thanks," Bruce said. "He was down and out. Maybe it's better the way it is." He broke his hand away. "Thanks for everything. I've got to run. I ought to be back in a week or so."

He couldn't stand and listen to George talk about twenty years ago and what the old man had been like then. He had heard it before, from both him and Kristin—the grudging, half-willing admiration they had had for him in spite of their disapproval. There were other compulsions on him. Within an hour of the time Joe Mulder called, while the graduates were still listening to the Commencement Address, he was pushing the Ford down through the traffic toward Northfield, seeing his own frozen face in the windshield and thinking of nothing except drive, cut around that truck, unreel the miles, hit the trunk line west and push it. A body did not keep forever. He was going home to bury the last of his family, straighten out the last tangles that the old man in his desperation had wound himself up in. Straighten out the police, straighten out the funeral arrangements, get the sexton to dig a third grave beside the others in the half-rod of ground known as lot 6, block 37. He was going home again, the next to last time, and there was no doubt where his home was, because part of him was already buried in those two graves and in two days another part—admit it—would be buried in the third.

Now the old familiar catalogue of cities, towns, villages, the old perennial bee-line pilgrimage across the great valley hammocked between Appalachians and Rockies, the familiar feel of the throttle's round button under his sole and the green June tumbleweed blowing flat on each side under the speed-whipped wind.

But no quiet in the mind this time, no limericks, no idle speculation to pass the miles, no fine free feeling of space and air. Only the disbelief, like the disbelief he had had going back for Chet's funeral, only the endless prodding and the endless repudiation and the everlasting no. He had not believed in that first death because there had been practically no warning, because he had never met death close, because he had a boy's feeling that nothing of his could die. Now he refused to believe in his father's death because of the manner of it.

How? he said, in God's name how? In one of those rages that sent him berserk? Then why the letters with their increasing hopelessness, why the pitiful sheet of paper showing that he had poured his last forty-seven hundred dollars into a worthless hole in the ground, and his hopes and his life with them?

But plan it? Make up his mind to shoot that woman and then himself? Do it coldly and deliberately? Bo Mason, who believed in tomorrow as he believed in himself, deliberately scheme to commit murder and suicide on a tomorrow? That called for a cold-bloodedness, a calculation, he had never possessed.

Revenge? Self-pity? Despair?

If he could once convince himself about how it had happened, he could believe it. He knew it was true, he was on his way to bury his father, but he still couldn't believe that last violence. Somehow he had always thought that violence stopped short of finalities for the old man. It had always been at least part show, for an effect, to compel obedience or bully someone down. There was no point in bullying if you were going to die immediately. There was a desperation in this last act that would probably never be quite credible.

The afternoon waned ahead of him down the long straight road, moving faster than he moved, flattening, sinking, going dusky. Sky and earth were a bowl over a disc, then two planes, the upper lighter than the lower, between which he moved. He turned on his lights and unwrapped the sandwich he had bought the last time he stopped for gas.

This too was familiar, the feel of the car's motion, oil-smell and night-smell, the sweet muffled roar of the motor, the phantasmagoria of half-seen shadows, trees, buildings, outside the running headlights.

It was old and familiar and even comfortable, and all he had to do was to keep the hard hot accelerator button under his foot, keep the white center line of the highway just off his left front wheel. The dawn too would be familiar, the slow lightening of the sky until the two planes became again disc and bowl: the windless pale light just barely not darkness, the horses standing in the pastures, the cars cutting along the road with lights still on, the clatter and smoke of the Los Angeles Limited coming behind him, catching him, passing him, the shades down on the dark pullmans, the observation car with windows palely alight, an early-rising passenger on the rear platform watching the vanishing point of steel.

It was all familiar. It seemed to him, yawning, scratchy-eyed, that there was the whole rhythm of his life in it, that all through his remembered life the days had gone under him like miles, that he and his whole family had always been moving on toward something that was hidden beyond where the road bent between the hills. As he shifted to ease his aching back he thought of the old man, always chasing something down a long road, always moving on from something to something else. At the very end, before that fatal morning, he must have looked down his road and seen nothing, no Big Rock Candy Mountain, no lemonade springs, no cigarette trees, no little streams of alcohol, no handout bushes. Nothing. The end, the empty end, nothing to move toward because nothing was there.

He began to see, dimly, why his father had shot himself, and half to believe that he had.

"You can't go down there now," Joe said. "You haven't had any sleep in two days. Let it wait till morning."

"I'd better go," Bruce said. "I don't think I could sleep anyway till I did." He looked at the clock in the kitchen, and yawned so wide he couldn't see the hands. Joe, watching him from across the table, pulled the corners of his mouth down.

"I feel all right," Bruce said. "I'd better get it over." It was only nine-forty. A bath had helped, the clean shirt and underclothes and socks borrowed from Joe had helped. He could stay awake another hour or two. And until he got down to that hotel and got a few things straight he wasn't going to be comfortable.

Beside him on the porcelain top of the kitchen table was yesterday's paper, the front page, with a two-column story and a picture of Elaine Nesbitt holding the leash on a straining bulldog. "S.L. MINING MAN KILLS WOMAN, SELF," the headline said. He read the story through again, trying to get that "how" straight in his mind, but what the newspaper said didn't help much. Harry Mason, local mining man, had met Elaine Nesbitt in the lobby of the Winston Hotel at nine in the morning. They had quarreled some time previously over mining interests in which both were interested, according to James Dobson, the hotel clerk. They quarreled again in the lobby, and Mrs. Nesbitt, pretty auburn-haired widow, struck Mason with her handbag and ran out toward the side entrance. Mason jerked a gun from his coat pocket and followed. Dobson, trying to grapple with him, was thrown against the desk. He heard the outside door slam, then two shots. When he got to the door Mason was slumped against the radiator with a bullet through his head. He was still breathing, but died within ten minutes. There was a bullet hole through the door, and outside Mrs. Nesbitt lay face down, shot through the heart.

So it was rage, blind berserk fury.

But he read on, and it wasn't so clear. According to Desk Sergeant Walter Hill, Mason had come in three days previously to get a permit to carry a gun. He had mining interests in Nevada, and was accustomed to carry considerable sums on his person. In granting the permit, the sergeant had asked him if he had any criminal record, a routine question, and Mason had said jokingly "Not yet." At the time he had seemed calm.

"I've just got to go down there," Bruce said. "It shouldn't take more than an hour or two."

"Want me to go along?" Joe said.

"You're already mixed up in this enough."

"That's all right," Joe said. "I'd be glad to come along, if you want."

Bruce shook his head, tore the story out of the newspaper and folded it into his pocket.

He remembered the hotel, a dark little semi-respectable place on First South. The lighted shelf above the entrance looked dingy, and the door opened hard. There was no one in the lobby except the clerk behind the desk. Bruce's eyes darted past the desk, spotted the hall leading to the side entrance, and the radiator's dull gilt gleaming in the desk light. He locked his insides as if he were trying not to vomit.

"I'm Bruce Mason," he said to the clerk. "I just got in."

The clerk had a cast in one eye. The other one jumped, startled, in his pale face. He came out from behind the desk, hurrying. "Oh yeh," he said. "I'll get Dobson. He was on when . . . Just wait here a minute."

He ran up the stairs two at a time, and Bruce stood still by the desk. In this dingy little lobby, yesterday morning, the thing had been done. He moved toward the side entrance. The carpet down the little hall had been taken up, and he saw the unpainted boards and the splintered tack holes. Against this radiator, within reach of his hand, his father had stood, in what desperate frenzy, and spattered his brains against this wall. He shut his jaw and turned away, and as he turned he saw the bullet-hole in the panel of the door.

Steps were coming, and he went back to the desk. A short man with a bald spot came down and shook his hand. "I been expecting you," he said. "Your dad left some papers and things. Want to look at them now?"

"I might as well."

The little man looked at him sidelong. "It's a hell of a thing," he said. "You seen the papers? You know how it happened?"

"Let it go," Bruce said. "I've seen the paper." For all his need to settle the tiniest detail, the facial expression even, of that last furious minute of his father's life, he did not want to talk to the clerk. It had to come without any coloring. But the lobby had told him nothing. The radiator was a radiator, nothing more, and even the stains of his father's blood on it, if there had been any, would not have made this thing any more believable.

"I never had any idea he was feeling that way," Dobson said as they went upstairs. "Oh, I knew he was having a little trouble about money, and he'd had a spat or two with Elaine, but Jesus . . ." He turned down the hall, unlocked the door of a room. "The cops told me to keep it locked," he said, "but you can go in."

Bruce stood half in the door. "Would you mind?" he said. "Could I look things over alone?"

"Sure." Dobson hesitated. "I don't want to push, or anything, but Harry owed me twenty dollars. If he had any insurance or anything I wonder . . ."

"I'll fix it up," Bruce said. "Did he owe anything else, do you know?"

"I know he owed something to O'Brien, from the Cantwell Hotel. O'Brien came around here trying to collect once or twice. I think he owes some rent here, too."

"Well, I'll go through things and see what's here," Bruce said.

"And he owed for a suit of clothes," Dobson said. "He wasn't hardly cold before that Jew Miller was calling up wanting to know where he was going to get his money."

"Where is the suit?"

"He was wearing it."

"All right," Bruce said. He closed the door and looked around. The bed was made, the closet door open. Inside the closet there was a suit and a pair of black shoes and a bundle of neckties, several of which had apparently never been worn. On the dresser, under a silver shaving mug, was a large envelope addressed to Bruce Mason.

Then he had known he was going to do it. It hadn't been done in a rage. The letters and the worthless stock certificate were not blackmail or begging. As he sat down on the bed with the heavy envelope in his hand he felt as if he were going to be sick.

The envelope contained an insurance policy for five hundred dollars and a receipt book showing that his father had made monthly payments, the last one on June first. Clipped together there were five pawn tickets with pencilled scribblings on the backs. The tickets said overcoat, suitcase, watch, suitcase, suitcase. There was a map with red markings in the corner, showing the location of the Della Mine. There were the three letters that Bruce had written during the last two months, in answer to his father's. His own handwriting looked incongruous and strange to him now, seen as his father had seen it.

And what about the letters? he said. Nothing in them but little bread-and-butter checks and a lot of smug free advice. Take a brace, keep your chin up, you're not licked yet, why not get a job at something, any kind of job, till you get a stake again, instead of waiting and depending on this mine? He held the three letters in his hand hating himself.

The last thing he looked at was a certificate of ownership for the cemetery lot, together with a sexton's receipt and another receipt showing that perpetual care had been bought and paid for.

He sat on the bed weighing the papers in his hands. No note. The letter written on June first was the last. He had known that long before that there wasn't anything left.

The shaving mug on the dresser caught his eye, and he reached to lift it down. The metal was tarnished, one side was dented, the inscription on the side was worn almost away, but he held it up to the light and read it:

Champion of North Dakota
Singles Traps
Harry Mason, 1905

That was the final sum, the final outcome, of the skill and talents and strength his father had started with. One dented silver mug, almost thirty years old. One pair of worn shoes, one worn suit, a dozen spotted neckties, a third interest in a worthless mine, a cemetery lot with perpetual care. A few pawn tickets, a few debts, a few papers, an insurance policy to bury him and a cemetery lot to bury him in, that last small resource hoarded jealously even while the larger and hopeful resources were squandered.

Quietly he set the mug down, folded pawn tickets and papers into the envelope, and stood up, thinking of the radiator downstairs, the little hall with the carpet taken up, the door with the bullet hole. His father had wasted himself in a thousand ways, but he had never been an incompetent. Even in that last despair, that last shattered minute when rage led him to include the woman in his plan of death, he had done a workmanlike job. He killed the woman with one shot through the door, and he killed himself cleanly with another. There were so many things the old man could do a good job on. He had had a knack for versifying and story-telling, he was a dead shot with any kind of gun, he could take an automobile apart and put it back together in the dark, he was a carpenter, a cabinet-maker, he was strong as a bull, stubborn as a mule, single-minded as a monk. And all of that wasted in the wrong causes, all of that coming to its climax with a neat and workmanlike job of murder and suicide.

There was a light knock on the door, and he swung around, stuffing the papers into his coat as if he had stolen them. A tall and very thin woman stood there, looking at him with a soft, almost dewy expression in her eyes. Her mouth twitched. "You're his son," she said.

"I heard you were here," she said. "I had to come and see you. I'm Mrs. Winter, I live just down the hall."

"I see," he said, wondering what she had to do with it, where she came in. Another of his father's women?

"You look like your picture," Mrs. Winter said. "He showed it to me once."

"You mean he had a picture of me?"

"In his wallet."

That shamed him too. The man he had hated all his life carried a picture around in his wallet, showed it to people, perhaps with pride. Everything in this bare, cheap little room shamed him.

"Did you see much of him . . . before?" he said.

She had started to cry, without noise. "He was just desperate," she said. "He told me a month ago he was going to do it, and he was so violent and hard you couldn't come near him. He told me a couple of weeks ago he was going to do it the next day."

"What stopped him then?" Bruce said. His imagination was on ahead of her, seeing the despair and hopelessness and desperation coming face to face with the final violence, and shying away, weakening.

"I don't know," she said. "I did what I could. I got a friend of mine with a car and we all went out to the lake and drove around all afternoon, and I talked to him. I told him he'd get back on his feet, but he just looked out the window and gritted his teeth. I kept him up as late as I could that night, but when he left I was scared to death. Then I saw him the next morning, and I was so relieved!"

"Yes," Bruce said.

"I thought he was all over it," Mrs. Winter said. "The last three or four days before it happened he was just as sweet, just as gentle and smiling, you'd have thought all his troubles had been settled. And all the time he had that gun he'd got the permit for."

"I guess," Bruce said, "that nobody could have done anything to stop him. You were good to try."

"I liked him," Mrs. Winter said. "He was honest."

Honest? Bruce said. Honest? Well, maybe, with everyone but himself. He could cheat himself, and fool himself, and justify himself, every time. But those last few days? he said. Those three or four days when he went around quiet and smiling and gentle, with the pawn-shop gun in his pocket? He was honest with himself then, for perhaps the first and last time. Everything was over for him then. Even the last act, then, must have seemed unimportant.

He put out his hand to Mrs. Winter. "Thank you for being his friend," he said. "I guess he didn't have many, at the last."

"Everybody turns against you when you're down," she said. "I know." With her face bent she went with short quick steps down the hall and turned in a door.

And there was one version. Harry Mason, that old lush who hung around the Winston lobby and sponged meals and five-dollar loans from anybody he could collar, that old broken-down Big Shot who still dreamed of fantastic wealth out of a Nevada gold mine, was to one woman at least an honest man, a kind man, a misunderstood man, an unhappy man.

Oh most certainly an unhappy man, he said, and stood in the open door of his father's room with the tears hot and sudden in his eyes, thinking of that picture in the wallet and of those three or four days when he was kind and gentle and smiling, with a gun in his pocket.

At eleven thirty he fell into bed at Joe's and lay sleepless for hours, his eyes burning up into the darkness and his hands and feet feeling immense, swollen, elephantine from the quarts of coffee he had drunk on the road. He threshed it all through and cried hard racking sobs into the dark, and when he finally fell asleep he slept until noon.

Then there was the undertaker to see, and the discovery, this third time he had used him, that the undertaker was an old whiskey customer of his father's. He laid out the things taken from Bo Mason's clothes—a wallet with five dollars in it, a handful of change, an address book, some keys, a couple of pencils—and talked sadly and thoughtfully, drumming with his finger tips on the desk. He had seen Harry around occasionally. No idea he was hard up or in trouble. It was a terrible and mysterious thing. Couldn't have been money only, because Harry had plenty of friends who would have been glad to see him through a bad spot. He'd have given him a loan himself, if he'd known. He was full of friendship and sympathy and careful avoidances, he made no effort to sell Bruce an expensive casket, he loaned him a car to run errands in. Bruce wanted to despise him for his profession and his careful talk, but he couldn't despise him. He was too genuinely helpful.

While he was talking in the office a woman came into the hushed parlor, and through the door, in a tearful whisper, asked if she could see Mr. Mason, asking as if she expected not to be allowed to. She looked at Bruce once, then ignored him, but as she was starting down the hall she turned to look again, stared steadily with an anguished pucker between her eyes. Her face was vaguely familiar.

"Aren't you," she said, coming back a few steps. "You aren't . . . Bruce?"

"Yes."

In an instant she was in his arms, hanging onto him, sobbing, her ravaged and repaired face close to his, crying out that it was terrible, oh my God it was terrible, why did he do it, why did he ever get mixed up with that woman, oh my God she couldn't believe it. She would have come to him, she would have left her family and everything else, and had told him so, but not while Elsa was alive, she wouldn't have hurt Elsa for anything in the world, but she could have kept him from that woman, and my God, Bruce, she wished she had, she wished she had.

Leaning back a little, Bruce said yes, and no, and yes. She mustn't take it so hard, there was nothing anyone could do now, nobody was to blame.

She clung to him for a little while, got control of her babbling and her tears, wiped her eyes, blew her nose, looked at him yearningly, and finally went down the hall, and he never did find out who she was or where he had known her or what connection there had ever been between her and his father.

Next there was the insurance man, Hammond. He too shook Bruce's hand, asked him about his studies, wanted to know where he was going to hang up his shingle. He too kept his face closed and his mouth discreet, looked up the policy and found that sixty dollars had been borrowed on it. That would have to be deducted from the claim.

"I got Harry this policy after he got sick a couple years ago," he said. "Pretty hard to get it through the office. He wasn't well, he wasn't well at all. Had some kind of stroke, blood pressure way up."

He filled in blanks and asked questions, shook his head as he waited for the ink to dry. Words of condolence, of sympathy, were on the tip of his tongue, and Bruce knew it. The man might even be grieved at Bo Mason's death. But it was not a death you could talk about. All Hammond could say was "Yes sir, I've known Harry for almost fifteen years." That seemed to express what it was possible to express under the circumstances. He repeated it when he shook Bruce's hand in farewell and assured him that the policy would come right through, two weeks or so at the most. A graying and not-too-prosperous business man, he stood shaking Bruce's hand thoughtfully, saying Yes sir, he'd known Harry for fifteen years.

Not, Bruce thought angrily on his way out, "Yes sir, Harry was a swell guy, one of the best, his death is a loss." Not that. Not even

"Yes sir, Harry and I have been friends for fifteen years." It took courage to say to the son of a murderer and suicide that you liked him, that he was your friend. It took courage even to talk about the manner of his death. The best you could say was . . .

Damn them, he said, if they can't say anything good about him why don't they keep their mouths shut?

The minister who said the few ritual words in the funeral parlor was obviously embarrassed. He clearly found it difficult to say much over the body of one who had lived and died by violence, and though he was bound to ask God's grace on this poor sinner, he did it only with half a heart, and spent most of his ten minutes on the afflictions that are visited upon mankind, the trials that come in life, the unhappiness that burdens us from the cradle to the grave. Man is born to sorrow as the sparks fly upward. This little family, for instance, had been grievously stricken. Within three years the mother, the son, and now the father had been struck down. He prayed that God's mercy would be with them all, and with the young man who survived.

As he halted on, avoiding direct reference to Bo Mason, making solemn generalities in the solemn padded parlor, talking about a man he had not known, and lamenting for a family he had never heard of until today, Bruce could feel him all the way wanting to make the body of this Bo Mason the subject of a sermon on the wages of sin, holding back because the offices he was conducting prohibited any ill-speaking of the dead; and so, morally indignant and yet unable to speak his mind, limping through his solemn and meaningless ten minutes. As he talked, Bruce's mind worked in ironic counterpoint:

This man whom today we consign to the grave, this Harry Mason, was a man whom I and many others have condemned. We have sat in judgment on him, and we have found him guilty of violence, brutality, wilfulness. He was frequently inconsiderate of others, he was obtuse about other people's wishes. He was a man who never knew himself, who was never satisfied, who was born disliking the present and believing in the future. He was not, by any orthodox standard, a good husband or a good father. He chafed against domestic restraints, ruled by violence instead of love, forced his wife and children to live a life they despised and hated. He broke the law, he blasphemed, he served Mammon, he was completely incapable of anything remotely resembling social responsibility, and with dedicated selfishness he went after the Big Money. He wore out his wife and broke her heart, he destroyed one son and turned the other against him. At the end he degenerated into a broken old man, sponging a bare living and sustaining himself on a last gilded and impossible dream; and when he could no longer bear the indignities which the world heaped upon him, and when the dream broke like a bubble, he sought some way, out of an obscure and passionate compulsion to exonerate himself, to lay the blame onto another, the woman who had been his mistress. He shot her and then turned the gun upon himself, thus ending his life appropriately and fittingly, in violence. God may have mercy on this Harry Mason, but he may also wreak justice. God's will be done.

Yet this Harry Mason, violent and brutal and unthinking, this law-breaker and blasphemer, kept for over a quarter of a century the love of as good a woman as ever walked, my mother, and when he appeared to abandon her just before her death, he did so because the prospect of her death was intolerable to him, because in spite of his bullying and self-willed spirit he loved and cherished her, and he knew that the best of himself would die when she died.

This same father who broke the spirit and spoiled the chances of his older son took a very great pride in that son's exploits, had dreams for him as golden as his dreams for himself, shook with night-mares for months after that son died. This same father who turned his second son into an animate cold hatred carried a photograph of that son in his wallet to the morning of his death. This same selfish fortune-hunter was so little cold and calculating that in his last years he was a sucker for the really calculating, the women and promoters who drained off his money and left him sick and broke in a second-rate hotel. This Harry Mason, this anti-social monster, could be nobly generous on occasion, could be affectionate, could weep like a child.

It is of that child that we should be talking and thinking while we sit here in judgment over the body of Harry Mason, that child with a quick mind and talented hands, a child off on the wrong foot and unable to see that he was wrong, a child with tremendous self-reliance and tremendous energy and a tremendous drive toward the things that seemed to him good. If he went wrong, he was mistaken, not vicious; or if vicious, his viciousness was merely the product of the balking of his will. And let us remember that at the end he did not run or try to hide from himself, he saw himself for a little while honestly, and only the last minute of rage which led him to kill the woman too prevented his death from being a thing almost humble. As it was, he saw near at hand two people who had wronged and betrayed and disgraced him, and as his last act he killed them both.

Harry Mason was a child and a man. Whatever he did, any time, he was a completely masculine being, and almost always he was a child, even in his rages. In an earlier time, under other circumstances, he might have become something the nation would have elected to honor, but he would have been no different. He would always have been an undeveloped human being, an immature social animal, and the further the nation goes the less room there is for that kind of man. Harry Mason lived with the woman who was my mother, and whom I honor for her kindness and gentleness and courage and wisdom. But I tell you at his funeral, and in spite of the hatred I have had for him for many years, that he was more talented and more versatile and more energetic than she. Refine her qualities and you would get saintliness, but never greatness. His qualities were the raw material for a notable man. Though I have hated him, and though I neither honor nor respect him now, I can not deny him that.

Into the grave. Into lot 6, block 37, beside Elsa Mason and Chester Mason, and let the bodies of the united family unite more intimately in the deep earth than they ever did in life. There is the makings of a man in that family, and more of it than I ever thought will have to come out of the tissues of my father.

The preacher stopped. Bruce had not heard him for several minutes. Now he saw him fold his hands and bend his head. From the pews behind, where a sprinkling of acquaintances, nondescript pall-bearers recruited from his father's old intimates, banker and broker and bootlegger and pimp, sat and listened to the preacher's words, there came a light sniffle. The attendants came to the edge of the curtains and stood ready. The minister finished his short prayer, the chapel organ began to cough and mourn. Dry-eyed, Bruce stood up and stepped three steps forward to where the coffin lay open. He had not yet brought himself to look at his father's body.

The heavy square hands were crossed on the neatly-pressed coat-front. The thinning hair was brushed back, and the right temple, where the bullet had entered, was so smoothly patched with wax that only a knowing eye could have detected it. The mouth was gentle, almost humorously curved; the jaw was blunt and strong. Whatever violence had been in the face had been erased.

But what he noticed most strongly, before the attendants stepped forward and lowered the lid of the casket, was the enormous, powerful arch of his father's chest, and the width of the shoulders in the satin-lined box.

As he followed the handful of people out through the entrance into the sun of the court, he could feel no grief for his father, nor for his mother and brother whose graves were grassy beside the new raw hole at the cemetery. He could think only of the brightness of the sun, an excessive sparkling brightness, as if there were some meaning in it, or a blessing, and he saw the sweep of the spring-green slopes up to the worn peaks above Dry Canyon. His past was upon him, the feeling he had had two or three times that he bore his whole family's history in his own mind, and he remembered the time when he had gone with his mother and father on a picnic to the Bearpaw Mountains, the wonder and delight of his childhood, and the shadow behind it of the things that his mind had caught from infancy, from other times, from some dim remoteness that gave up its meaning slowly and incompletely. He remembered the great snake his father had killed by the roadside, and the gopher that had come slimy and stretched from the snake's mouth, and the feeling he had had then was like the feeling he had now: it was a good thing to have been along and seen, a thing to be remembered and told about, a thing that he and his father shared.

Perhaps that was what it meant, all of it. It was good to have been along and to have shared it. There were things he had learned that could not be taken away from him. Perhaps it took several generations to make a man, perhaps it took several combinations and re-creations of his mother's gentleness and resilience, his father's enormous energy and appetite for the new, a subtle blending of masculine and feminine, selfish and selfless, stubborn and yielding, before a proper man could be fashioned.

He was the only one left to fulfill that contract and try to justify the labor and the harshness and the mistakes of his parents' lives, and that responsibility was so clearly his, was so great an obligation, that it made unimportant and unreal the sight of the motley collection of pall-bearers staggering under the weight of his father's body, and the back door of the hearse closing quietly upon the casket and the flowers.